THE FALL OF
DRAGONS

Also by Miles Cameron from Gollancz:

The Traitor Son Cycle:
The Red Knight
The Fell Sword
The Dread Wyrm
A Plague of Swords

Writing as Christian Cameron for Orion:

The Chivalry Series
The Ill-Made Knight
The Long Sword

The Tyrant Series
Tyrant
Tyrant: Storm of Arrows
Tyrant: Funeral Games
Tyrant: King of the Bosporus
Tyrant: Destroyer of Cities
Tyrant: Force of Kings

The Long War Series
Killer of Men
Marathon
Poseidon's Spear
The Great King
Salamis
Rage of Ares

Tom Swan and the Head of St George Parts One—Six
Tom Swan and the Siege of Belgrade Parts One—Seven
Tom Swan and the Last Spartans Parts One—Five

Other Novels
Washington and Caesar

THE FALL OF DRAGONS

MILES CAMERON

This edition first published in Great Britain in 2018 by Gollancz

First published in Great Britain in 2017 by Gollancz
an imprint of the Orion Publishing Group Ltd
Carmelite House, 50 Victoria Embankment
London EC4Y 0DZ

An Hachette UK Company

1 3 5 7 9 10 8 6 4 2

Copyright © Miles Cameron, 2017
Maps copyright © Steven Sandford, 2017

A CIP catalogue record for this book is
available from the British Library.

ISBN 978 1 473 20890 2

Printed in Great Britain by
CPI Group (UK) Ltd, Croydon, CR0 4YY

www.traitorson.com
www.gollancz.co.uk

This book, and indeed the whole series, is dedicated to Joe Harley (Elves/Irks), Robert Sulentic and Jim Dundorf (the Empire), Rob Gallasch and Delos Wheeler and Stephen Callahan (Etrusca/City States), Greg Hauser (the Steppes/Horseclans), Jevon Garrett (Galle/Gargencel), as well as Chris Schulitz, Mark Stone, Doug Snyder, David Stier, Regina Harley, Frank Gilson, and all the other players in the endless RPG and war games campaign we all called "Alba." In fact, this book is also dedicated to the men and women of the SGA, the GLA, and the Drama House, who played games for days, or taught all of us nerdy gamers how amazing role-playing could be with trained actors, or how much fun it was to game with people who'd never tried a game, and how easily we could let pretend take over our lives if we were not careful. It was thirty years ago that I folded away the maps. I miss you all. And to Celia Friedman—that's C. S. Friedman, if you read fantasy—who taught me to be a GM.

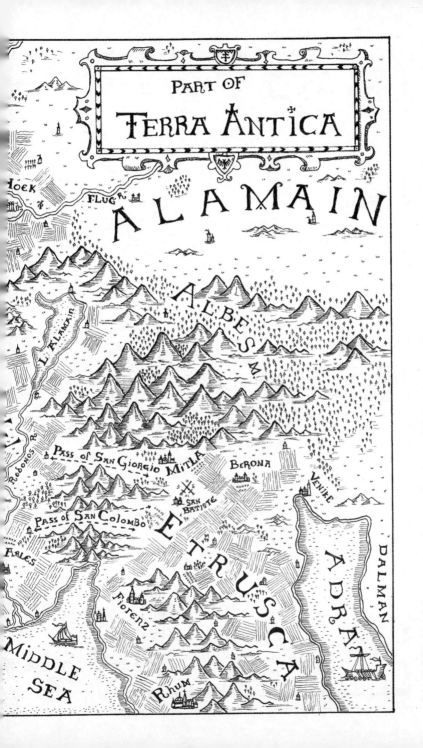

THE ROADS ✦ VALLEY BETWEEN
LISSEN CARRCK ✦ ABINKIRK

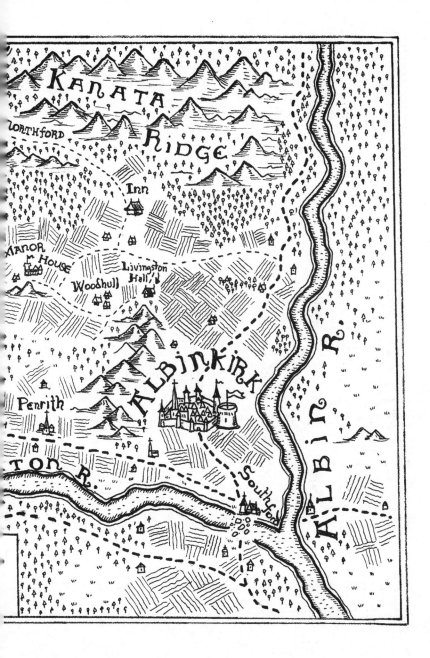

THE FALL OF DRAGONS

Prologue

Alba

The Vale of Dykesdale—Bill Redmede

The sun was setting in a sky of gold, and the bronze light suffused everything, gilding the endless forest, bronzing the stones left by ancient glaciers, and burning on the spear-tips of the retreating Army of the Alliance. The golden light set fire to the bright hair of the oldest irks and kindled the fur of the Golden Bears. It smoothed faces deeply creased by terror and fatigue.

Bill Redmede looked down the long column of weary men and a few women and then looked at the strange golden sky.

"Rain?" he asked John Clothyard, who was now, to all intents, his lieutenant. Nat Tyler had left him; killed the king, or so some men said. Ricar Fitzalan had gone east to serve with Aneas Muriens as battle comrades or lovers or both. The Jarsay-born Fitzalan had been a fine leader and the best second a commander could ask for, and Redmede missed him. He missed Tyler, too. Instead he had Grey Cat, who tended to wander off into the woods, and Clothyard, who was solid and dull.

Clothyard was a broad man of middle height, and his looks weren't helped by a four-day growth of beard.

"Rain," he responded.

Redmede was so far past exhaustion that he didn't have to think much about his actions. He put a hand on the bow slung over his shoulder in a linen bag and trotted back along his Jacks. "Rain!" he yelled. "Put your bowstrings in your shirts."

"Who the fuck are you? My father?" muttered one Jack. In a single summer of constant fighting, the Jacks had dispensed with camaraderie and turned instead to discipline. Some resented it.

"I never wanted to be a goddamned forester," said another voice. This was directed at the grim reality that royal foresters, the king's law in the woods, were the traditional enemies of the Jacks, broken men and outlaws, and now they marched together, the last Jack only two paces in front of the first forester. Not one forester or Jack was so dense as to miss the grim irony that in the eyes of the world's powers, they were exactly the same: superb woodsmen and rangers. Ser Gavin, the army's nominal commander, had put the two bands together with some hundreds of irk knights mounted on forest elk and irk ponies, an armoured cavalry that could glide through heavy woods with the agility of wild deer. Together, they were a match for almost any forest foe.

"Keep your bowstrings dry," Redmede repeated as he trotted down the column. Not everyone was surly; Stern Rachel gave him half a grin, but she was mad as a felter and loved war; Garth No Toes hummed to himself as he flourished a little beeswaxed bag.

Most of these men and women had survived the rout after Lissen Carak; had fought at Gilson's Hole; had marched west again to face Ash and his million monsters. They knew how to survive a little rain.

He told them anyway. Tired people make mistakes.

He forced himself up the rise he'd just descended, looking for the blank exhaustion that was like a sickness; looking for signs of people who hadn't drunk enough water. His thighs burned, but it was these displays of routine prowess that marked him out, and he knew it.

He reached the top just as Long Peter and Gwillam Stare came over the crest, glanced back into the hell of Ash's army, and shook their heads.

"We fightin' agin?" Stare asked.

Redmede shrugged.

"Only have nine shafts," Stare said.

Long Peter didn't speak much at the best of times. He kept walking.

"I hear you," Redmede said.

"Meaning we might fight," Stare asked.

"Meaning I don't know a goddamned thing," Redmede said.

He could see his brother trudging up the hill. The same irony that made the two bodies of men and their decades of enmity irrelevant in the current crisis was sharpened by the two Redmede brothers: Bill, the leader of a rebellion against royal authority, and Harald, his older brother, who had risen to command the foresters. That maturity had brought each to a better understanding of the other's position might have been the reason that the two bodies could cooperate at all.

"Harald?" Bill said.

"Bill." Harald nodded. Both Redmedes were tall and ruddy-haired and rough-hewed; where Bill wore the stained, loose off-white wool cote of the Jacks, his brother wore a sharply tailored jupon in the forester's forest green, although he carried his hat in one hand like a beggar. He stopped at the crest, and his weary men shuffled past; Bill was starting to know their names, and John Hand, tall and strong as an old oak, sporting a knightly beard and mustache, was Harald Redmede's best officer. He grunted a greeting and kept going, glancing back at the rising tide of bogglins behind them as almost every man and woman did on reaching the crest.

"I heard a rumour we won a big fight in Etrusca," Harald said. "Heard it this morning from Ser Gregario."

"I heard that there's a thousand dead of the plague in Harndon," Bill said.

"Aye, or three times that." Harald Redmede leaned on his bow staff. The first drops of rain fell from the golden sky.

"We winning or losing?" Bill asked his brother.

"Losing," Harald said. He held his hat—full of berries—out to his brother, who took a handful and ate them, seeds and all; black raspberries, fresh picked.

Bill nodded. "Well, that makes me feel better," he said.

Both of them looked down the ridge they'd just abandoned without a fight to the enemy, who were already crowding the ground below them; a flood of bogglins, so many that the ground seemed to move with chitonous lava.

The irk knights were the last in the column. Even their magnificent animals seemed dejected; stags with racks of antlers that were themselves weapons walked with their heads down, and their riders walked beside them.

"We're fucking doomed," Harald muttered. "Sweet Jesu, I'll end up being taken for a Jack if I keep on like this."

Bill Redmede shrugged. "I trust Tapio," he said. "He'll see us right." He didn't say, *The happiest hours of my life were spent in N'gara and I'll fight for it.* N'gara was just a few leagues away, and Ash's entire autumn campaign seemed bent on taking it.

Harald smiled without mirth. "My brother the fuckin' Jack believes an elf will save us, and I think that the queen's commander is a lack-wit. Well played, my brother. We can change off; I'll take the Jacks, you take the foresters."

Bill shrugged. "You always was contrary, Harald." He looked at the looming sky. Thoughtfully he said, "We need shafts."

"As do we. Best hope the mighty Ser Gavin knows it, too." Harald shook his head. "If'n we stand and talk any longer, we'll be eaten alive by bugs."

The two men turned, and began to trot along to catch their people, who were retreating into the strange, wet, golden evening.

The Vale of Dykesdale—Ser Gavin Muriens

Ser Gavin Muriens sat heavily on his destrier, feet out of his stirrups to ease his back, great helm and gauntlets on his squire's saddle-bow, idly picking something wet and grisly out of the spike of his little axe.

He was looking out over the valley that the irks called Dykesdale, watching his vanguard (in this case acting as his rear guard) toil down the far ridge like a line of ants slipping along to a food source.

At his feet, the Vale of Dykesdale stretched for some miles below a long ridge whose top was dominated by old maple and beech trees in the full colour of late summer growth. Many of them had lost their tops, as if a winter ice-storm had swept along the ridge, and there were gaps where men and irks had hewed away patches of wood.

Below, in Dykesdale itself, a crisscross of streams and beaver dams funneled all approaches to the ridge into two main routes: the Dyke, an ancient dam built by long-vanished Giant Beavers, and the Causeway, a stone and earth tribute to the Empress Livia's failed attempt to wrest N'gara from the irks fifteen hundred years before.

Ser Gavin had chosen it as the ideal battlefield, with Tapio, the Faery Knight, and Mogon, Duchess of the West, and Kerak, her mage, after the two defeats farther west. They had stood here, on the same bare, round crest that the Outwallers called "The Serpent's Rest," and looked out over the magnificent country.

"It's like an impregnable fortress, built by nature," Gavin had said.

Tapio smiled so that his fangs showed. "It isss an impregnable fortress, oh man. But it wasss built by my kind, to defeat all comersss."

And Mogon had lowered her great crested head. "Armies founder here, as the wardens know all too well. But our enemy comes in numbers that this place has never withstood."

"Aye." Tapio nodded.

Lord Kerak smiled. "You see only defeat. But we have discussed this, Lords of the East. We have slowed him, and made him show us his real warriors, his broken wardens, his hastenoch, his trolls. All I ask is that we make him use his power. Harmodius and Morgon and I have...a surprise."

"Will it work?" Ser Gavin asked.

"That depends on the depth of his arrogance and some fortune," the scholar-daemon said. His heavily inlaid beak opened to reveal the purple-pink tongue within—the Warden's equivalent of a smile.

Gavin was still coming to grips with the idea that the battlefield had been built. "It is all apurpose?" he asked, somewhat awed.

"Every tree, every branch," Tapio said. "We didn't build the ssstone caussseway." His fangs showed. "We jussst left it asss a monument to the ssstupidity of men."

Tonight, with the sun setting in a ball of fire beyond Ash's legions, Tapio's confidence seemed empty vanity. So did Kerak's.

"We can't fight many more times, and lose, without the whole will of this army snapping," he said. "We need a win, even if it is fleeting."

Kerak shook his head. "In this war there will be no victory, short of a miracle. Tomorrow, if we make a stand here, I will invite the opportunity for a miracle, but that is all I promise."

Why did I want this job? Gavin said, but only inside his head. He'd already learned the key role of a commander in an alliance is to show relentless good humour and confidence.

So instead of speaking, he looked back west into the setting sun. The light was turning bronze from gold, but the strange metallic quality of the light was unchanged.

As far as Gavin could see, a carpet of moving creatures covered the earth, so that instead of grass, shrubs, and marsh, he could see only a vast blanket of enemies stretching to the horizon.

At his elbow, Tamsin's voice was soft. "He has emptied every nest along the banks of the West River. Every bogglin. He has stolen the wills of millions of beings and he will use them as fodder for his vanity. Oh, how I hate him."

"Tomorrow, I will use that vanity against him," Kerak said.

"From your beak to God's ear," Ser Gregario said with his usual humour. "Let's sleep. Unless you think they will come at us in the darkness."

Tapio was still watching the endless carpet of foes. "If we lose here, we lose N'gara," he said.

Tamsin kissed him. "Yes," she agreed. "I am ready to lose it. Are you, my love?"

Tapio looked at Gavin. "We are all sssupposed to trussst your brother. Perhapsss I do. But even sssuppose that in the end, we triumph. Will there be anything left of my world?"

Very softly, Tamsin said, "No, my love."

They all looked at her, for she was renowned as an astrologer and prophetess.

She shrugged. "When the gates open, the world changes. It has always been so. I need no wizardry to predict this."

Gavin shook his head. "Let's get some sleep," he said. Far off to his right, the last of the column of rangers arrived at the foot of the great ridge to find rough shelters built of bark, and hot food. And bundles of arrows. There was fodder for man and beast, and fresh water. Everything that the hand of man and irk could do had been done.

"Tomorrow," Tapio said. "I can feel it. I think we can stop him. My people have never been beaten here."

Kerak bowed. "Tomorrow," he said.

Mogon laughed. "In my youth, when this tree was young, I tried to make it up this ridge against you, Prince of irks, and my nest died like bogglins," she said. "It is really quite pleasant to be on this side. Tomorrow we will win."

Gavin nodded. "Tomorrow," he said.

The sun rose somewhere, but over Dykesdale there was first fog, and then light rain, and the light grew very gradually.

Not a man or irk or bear or warden had slept damp, though, and every one had a hot breakfast. When Gavin had eaten his share of oatmeal porridge and bacon, he mounted a riding horse and rode the length of the ridge with Tapio and Ser Gregario. The highest summit, on the far right, was held by Mogon's main battle; Exrech's veteran bogglins, and Mogon's hardened Saurian warriors, demons all, their inlaid beaks and engorged red-crests shining like myths come to life in the grey light of morning. In reserve, two hundred of the magnificent bears of the Adnacrags, the Long Dam Clan inured to war and many of their cousins and outbreeds, their golden fur darkened with damp. Many of them were sporting the heavy maille that the Harndon armourers had made for them over the summer, and almost every bear was wielding a heavy poleaxe as big as a barge pole in their paw-hands. A handful of Outwaller warriors stood with the bears; most of their kin were off in the east or fighting in the north against Orley, and the Sossag, once the mightiest of the Outwaller clans, were now protecting Mogon's heartland from giant Rukh and yet more bogglins coming along the Inner Sea from the west.

In the center were the feudal hosts of Brogat and the northern Albin. There was Edward Daispainsay, Lord of Bain, commanding the dismounted knights in the center of the line although his wounds from Gilson's Hole were not yet fully healed, and Lord Gregario with the mounted knights in reserve. The feudal levies were well armed with spears and armour; they had withstood days of attacks by bogglins without much loss, and they were more confident than most militia. They were beginning to be soldiers.

Tapio commanded the left of the line. There, the ridge was lowest and most vulnerable, and there were the Jacks and rangers; there also were the irk knights, and every irk regardless of gender who could be spared from N'gara. There, too, was Ser Ricar Fitzroy, with the knights of the northern Albin and Albinkirk, as well as fifty or so knights-errant from Jarsay, the Grand Seigneur Estaban du Born with another two hundred belted knights of Occitan, and there stood 1Exrech, his chitonous white armour spotless, at the head of his phalanx of spear-armed bogglins; they held the lowest ground, almost two thousand strong.

All told, they had almost eighteen thousand to face Ash's million or so creatures. Or odds of roughly fifty to one. Gavin told his allies and his own more human officers that they were fighting for ancient N'gara, to show the irks that men and women could be trusted. But in his heart, Gavin was fighting because his brother had laid out a strategy and expected him to implement it, part of a plan so vast that Gavin could not imagine it would succeed. And yet, despite everything, he trusted his brother.

Gavin trotted his riding horse back up the central ride, the Serpent's Hill, and dismounted. His page took his riding horse while his squire brought up his charger. A young man he'd never seen before handed him a cup of hippocras and he drank it while he considered the odds. They had to fight; that much had been made clear by his brother Gabriel all spring and summer. Every fight would bleed Ash, and only by fighting for every member of the alliance; the irks, the Jacks, the people of Alba and Morea; only by showing all of them that they could be defended would the alliance be preserved. This was not a war that could be won in an afternoon; Gilson's Hole proved that. It was a war that might continue for generations.

In Gavin's ear, Lord Kerak said, "Ready."

While Gavin had reviewed his dispositions, the battle had begun. The tide of bogglins had rolled across the swamps and the dyke and causeway; had come forward like a seeping tide and splashed against the carefully sited earthen walls, the coppiced trees and "natural" stone features of the Dykesdale ridge.

The tide came in for an hour. Gavin watched, issuing no orders. There was nothing he could do but watch, but he stood as Ser Edward launched a counterattack that cleared the lower line of the center when the Brogat levies wavered. Tens of thousands of bogglins were used as filler by the creatures behind them, trampled to death and then walked over in the swamps.

The fog began to burn off. Off to the north, some low-level workings began to flay the waves of bogglins.

They broke. The tide flowed back; the waves receded into the swamps and ten thousand more bogglins drowned.

Gavin considered a second cup of hippocras and wondered what the hell his brother was doing, wherever he was.

Kerak spoke again from the *aether*. "Now he sets his will on the bogglins. Now they come again."

This time the bogglins raced in, heedless of losses or terrain. They skittered over the carpet of their own dead and straight onto the spear points of the Brogat Levy. Below Gavin's position, men and irks were dying again. His exhausted troops, manning the barriers and thickets, lofted clouds of arrows and stood their ground with sword and axe in hand. A hundred bogglins had fallen for every man; in some parts of the line, a thousand bogglins had fallen for every irk. But the second attack was pressed with more enthusiasm, and the drowned bodies in the swamp were now so thick that the next wave could cross dry-shod.

Off to the right, Mogon's wardens and Golden Bears had lost less than a hand of their creatures, but even there every bear's fur was matted and the wardens' crests already deflated with fatigue. Along the first defence line on the ridge, the stacks of dead bogglins were already so high that the line had to be abandoned.

Out in the marshes, the dead were so thick that the course of the stream had been altered.

The Army of the Alliance was unrolling every scroll on war, and playing them out—ambushes, incendiaries, raids, dashing charges, destructive volleys.

Gavin looked out over the infinite fabric of his foes, and tried to wall off the rising tide of despair.

"Millions," he said aloud. "But we are slaying mere thousands."

Tapio smiled grimly, showing his fangs. "Millionsss are made of thousssandsss," he said. "Hisss lossses are ssstaggering."

Gavin shook his head. The tide had risen high; the sea of bogglins had swamped the first line entirely and were now facing the second, two hundred paces higher on the hillside. The sound was loud and constant; screams, war-cries, the despair of men wounded and eaten by bogglins, the equal despair of a bogglin whose carapace was penetrated; a week to die or a month, the creature was nonetheless already dead.

And then, like the changing of the light or the dissipating of the morning mist, the great assault failed. It did not fail suddenly; but inch by inch, bogglin by bogglin. Ash could take their minds and conquer their wills, but there came a point when flesh and blood conquered sorcery. Even bogglins had a scent sign for self-preservation.

The sky was turning blue overhead, and smell of bogglin blood was everywhere.

And so the tide went out for a second time.

"Blessed Saint Michael," Gavin said. Across a nine-mile-wide battle-field, his people had held.

Far away to the west, almost lost in the mist, something rose into the air.

"Here he comesss," Tapio said. "Pray to your godsss, or whatever else ssseemsss besssst to you, friendsss." But Tapio was grinning. "We have hurt him."

In all the other days of combat, Ash had never shown himself; not since Gilson's Hole had his red-black form risen over a battlefield. His minions, most of them bogglins armed only with their natural claws, had flung themselves forward under compulsion, and Ash had not shown himself, nor, until two days before, had he committed a single wight, troll, or great hastenoch from the deep swamps of the north, not a single wyvern or irk.

These creatures were somewhere far off to the west; so far that no amount of sorcery or scouting could locate them. *They were in reserve.*

The black speck grew.

Gavin sighed. The real battle was about to begin. And his army was already so far beyond fatigue that the moment the tide of bogglins receded, the knights of the Brogat fell to their knees like monks wit-nessing a miracle.

The Vale of Dykesdale—Ash

Ash surveyed his foes with an impatience and annoyance that had become his constant state since being "embodied" in this, his cho-sen avatar. Annoyance, and fatigue. He had forgotten fatigue in the *aethereal*.

"Stupid children," he said aloud.

He'd flung his almost limitless supply of animated chiton at their battle line in hopes that someone among his "foes" was bright enough to get the message and surrender, or skitter off into the woods. Time was growing short; the stars were moving, and his timetable was actu-ally endangered. His "allies" in the sea required an enormous invest-ment in will and time and immaterial power; but he needed them in place to wall off his competitors in Antica Terra.

That left him alone in Nova Terra; alone except for one rival of his own race and a host of smaller foes. Since none of these foes could possibly know what the game was, and how great the prize, except just possibly the old irk Tapio, he was annoyed that they even played at resisting him.

It is Lot, he told himself. *Lot is using them as I use the bogglins, and to the same end. Stupid boy. He is far too late entering the game, and all his allies are too self-willed and too independent. But I still need to finish him, and quickly.*

Ash had long since decided to have no allies at all—only slaves. It saved time and explanations. Even Thorn...

For a moment, the mighty Ash allowed himself to miss Thorn. But Thorn had not been loyal; Thorn had wanted too much of his own power. Like Orley.

Ash pondered the problems of metaphysical logistics; he had in his own right an enormous reservoir of power; his connection to the *immaterium* was nearly perfect, although never as perfect as it had been before he had made himself *corporeal.* And he had a strong connection to Thorn's fortress at Lake-on-the-Mountain. Beneath it was one of the purest fountains of *ops* anywhere in the real, an out-welling that amounted to a tear in reality's fabric; a tear someone had made in a war ten thousand years ago. He sucked at it like a baby on a teat, and used it to power the binding of millions of wills. Those bindings required two things he now had in short supply—his own will, and his *time.*

He hated time. He wasn't used to it; it wasn't "natural." But he understood it well enough, and it ticked away with the movement of the stars only he could see, and pressed against him like an infinitely powerful phalanx of foes, and the onward press of time forced his talons.

And his tiny, contemptible foes had *hurt* him. He bore wounds on his immortal hide; signs of failure, signs that wrenched at his vanity as much as they caused physical pain. Pain. Another aspect of the material that he had forgotten.

Yet there was power—power to work his will—not through shallow intermediaries and foolish acolytes, but directly, as it had been in the beginning. He rose slowly over the battlefield on the cool autumn air and prepared a mighty working; something beyond the comprehension of most of the mortals below him. Not just a blow in the physical, but a message.

Surrender. Despair. Leave and let me have my way.

As a creature to whom the *aethereal* was a natural state, he merely willed and his will made manifest, and the world was affected.

But his thoughts, especially those of Lot, moved him and he twinned his consciousness so that a second Ash could, with only a slight diminution of his main effort, begin casting a delicate web, a tracery of *aethereal* strands to locate Lot wherever he moved in the real. And such was the dichotomy of Ash's innermost mind that he didn't admit to himself that he'd learned the technique from combatting the human mage, Harmodius. Even as he was aware that his failed assault on Desiderata had armed his enemies against him, and that he had, himself, betrayed Thorn, and not the other way around. A mighty mind has many holes and many traps and many concealments.

And self-knowledge had never been Ash's strongest trait.

Instead, Ash balanced his expenditure on his Eeeague allies, strengthened the bonds that held the Orley and his creatures to his will, caressed the winds of scent and power that made a million bogglins his slaves, and relished the unfolding of a human betrayal he had motivated in the south, where, despite his own contempt for all men, Ash sought to destroy the magister Harmodius before he could reunite with his other allies. Because Harmodius was a *foe*. As was the human Morgon; so much potential there, but duped into the pit of Antica Terra. Let the mighty Morgon face Ash's foes. That was a delicious victory. Perhaps he would defeat the elusive *shadow*; Ash allowed himself to laugh aloud. Or *shadow* would defeat him. Or *rebel*.

Shadow, rebel, will, Lot. Ash had played them all; all the rivals who mattered. Of them, he only feared the *will*.

Ash thought all these things and a hundred more while simultaneously plotting and commanding both his physical and his sorcerous assaults on the immediate battlefield. The bogglins flowed forward to their necessary deaths and his real troops, the troops he would need for the true contest when the gates aligned, came from their staging areas and began to move to the battlefield. With a beautiful economy that won Ash a bit of grudging self-admiration, he used the energy of the deaths of his first bogglins to power the Wyrm's way working that moved a whole century of black-stone cave trolls straight into the center of the enemy, wreaking havoc. He'd never shown this tactic before;

the result was immediate and spectacular, as a generation of Brogat knights were winnowed like ripe wheat.

But they died where they stood, and a dozen of his precious tolls became splintered rock.

What annoyed Ash most was this constant waste of resources. His were enormous but limited; his time was running like blood from a gaping wound, and his awareness of time was like pain; so very different from the way time molded itself when he had been outside it. He had things to do, and fighting bloody Tapio for this useless ridge was annoying. *Annoying* was the perfect word.

It was time to use his powers, because he was in a hurry and his beautiful trolls were dying.

Gavin watched the gradual defeat of his center with weary fear. In his ears, the two available great sorcerers and dozens of Morean and Irkish and Alban mages conversed rapidly, and he ignored them, watching instead as Ser Edward Daispainsay pounded a troll to the ground with a set of flawless strokes of his great hammer and then led another countercharge; farther north along the ridge, Ser Gregario, Lord Weyland, charged into the flank of the trolls with the mounted chivalry of the Albin, and the trolls were annihilated. But the damage was done; the whole second line would be lost, because subtle tactics were of no use against a million bogglins.

"Christ, he almost broke us in one assault!" Gavin said. "Where did the trolls come from?"

At his side, Tapio shrugged. "He hasss begun to ussse hisss actual army," he said. "He moved the trollsss by sssorcssery." He sounded smug. "Thisss tellsss me he mussst hurry," Tapio added.

Gavin took a deep breath and wished his brother were there. "I hope you are right."

"Here he comes," Kerak said in his ear.

"He's casting," said Master Nikos, the former master grammarian of the university. He sounded satisfied.

"Now we will see something," Kerak said.

Miles away and high above the battlefield, Ash detected the emanations of a dozen casters in the *aethereal*. Even as he knit his heavy magic, a massive working even for him, he lashed out against all twelve in a single pulse like a leven bolt the colour of dried blood that left patterns in the cloudless sky.

Tamsin hummed to herself as the brown bolts rolled across the sky. Her emanations were all constructs; in fact, they were reflector-beacons for actual casters located elsewhere. Before the lightning, almost as fast as thought, burst in pinpoint explosions of wood splinters and sulphur and raw *ops*, Tamsin had tracked each of them back to their point of origin and passed that vector to Kerak, who wove a diagram and passed it back—all in *aethereal time*.

As the sound of the explosions rolled along Dykesdale, Lord Kerak and the choir of mages of the allied army *cast*.

Even as they cast, Ash recognized both their method of observation and their method of detection and reacted, shed any working that he no longer needed and protected himself so that their mighty attack detonated in empty air.

But he clung to his enormous working, reaching far out into the *aether* itself for the ancient stones that rode there, moving along the star paths beyond the ken of any alive in the world of Alba. In the nigh infinite lore stored in his huge brain, Ash knew that the hollow rocks had been made by the *Rhank* aeons before, in an attempt to evade the gates and attack through the *aethereal* into reality. Perhaps fifty thousand years ago.

He took eight of them and started them on their way.

Kerak left the choir. *There it was.* Exactly as Harmodius had predicted; when pushed, Ash was going for the largest, heaviest, most spectacular magik. And fortunately, Thorn had used this one repeatedly, although its power and details were beyond any mortal caster.

Casting was beyond them. Interfering was not.

Kerak entered *his memory cave, and was bathed in the warmth of a queen-mother's love in his memory, and standing there, strong, secure, amid his own kind, he pulled from their nest a selection of memory larvae and swallowed them; and then plucked a single great albino bat that hung from the roof. This he patted, murmuring endearments, and then, tying symbolism to intent, he threw the little mammal, favoured pet of his kind, into the* aethereal, *and it flew.*

Under the cover of a phalanx of attacks and a barrage of aggressive workings, Kerak's subtle working of will climbed away into the *aether*, following the broad path of *potentia* left by Ash's massive spell, homing in on the heavy scent of power.

Kerak watched it climb away and then went back to the choir.

"Done?" Nikos asked.

"Away," Kerak said.

In the *aethereal*, the bat rose, faster than a real bat, and its white shape smoothed out as it rose; from bat to owl, and from owl to arrow. And once it was an arrow, it flew like an arrow, but the head was heavy with design and art and the tail powered itself with constant emissions into the real.

It was Kerak's most extensive adventure into the world of the human *ars magika* as discovered by young Mortirmir and Master Nikos and the university, and it was the most complex single working any mortal, human, irk, or Saurian had attempted since the empire fell. But the Saurian mind excelled at holding layered, complex images, and this one was so complex that it seemed possible it would simply fail because he'd dropped a stitch.

"Break," he whispered into the Green Earl's ear. "This is the time."

"Break," Gavin ordered. He'd prepared all his commanders for this; the moment would come when they would run. They all knew.

His trumpeter blew a single, long call, and as one, thousands of men, irks, bears, wardens, and bogglins turned and began to run back over the ridge. The knights of Brogat took losses breaking contact; in the center, brave pages pushed forward with their master's horses so that the knights could mount and run, and some of them died. All across the ridge, the Allies turned tail, and slipped east, over the ridge, abandoning the best defensive position in all of Nova Terra.

For almost a minute in the real, sparks and bolts crisscrossed the air over the battlefield. A Morean mage died with his blood boiling in his desiccated veins, and Lord Kerak's second apprentice, Mehghaigh the Black, exploded like a tree struck by lightning, leaving Kwoqwethogan, Mogon's sorcerous brother, to hold the choir together. It was the heaviest load of *ops* he had ever carried.

He held.

Well to the east, the choir of Lissen Carak sang, and the *potentia* they purified passed west into the hands of Lord Kerak, whose golden and green shields rose over the ridge and held, and held, and held.

Ash flew closer; his response time decreased, and the rate of his attacks rose, so that a series of red, green, and brown lines seemed to connect him to the glowing dome over the ridge. His talents showed him the rout of the enemy army, but despite his near infinite *puissance*, each time he reached into the *aethereal* to divide and conquer the choir of magisters opposing him, he took wounds. He could reach deep into the maw of the *aethereal* and find an Alban mage by the fire of his soul, and he could strike, but even for his ferocious intellect and mighty will, such a focus left him blind to the assaults of the myriad casters opposing him. He was balked like a cat who has caught a mouse and cannot kill it. Or to be more accurate, a cat who has found a tribe of mice and cannot kill them all.

The irony was not lost on him. His adversaries were using the same tactic on him in the *aethereal* that his legions of bogglins were practicing in the real, and for a moment he faltered, appalled at the sheer number and diversity of the hermetical talents displayed against him. Four of them were of considerable power and not to be ignored; but the vast choir of their supporters tore at Ash's certainty of victory.

Uncertainty fueled his rage, and rage remained Ash's favourite reaction. Fire flew. His talons glowed, he breathed death, and his assault rose to a climax against the choir's wards.

Of course, that was a distraction anyway. The real weapons were on the way. Ash loved the levels of his deception and he exhaled death with satisfaction.

Far out where the edge of the real touched the first terrifying wisps of the *aethereal* eight great rocks, or castles, or ships, remnants of a war fought so long before that only two of the races that had fought the war survived to tell the tales, tipped past the point where they might have slipped back into the ebbs and tides of the *aethereal* where they were at home and began their long, spinning fall into the real. Long, and not long; as the rocks (if rocks they truly were) teetered on the edge of the real, stars were born and died, and eventualities became impossibilities, and the infinite struggled with the finite.

All overcome by the will of Ash.

And the stones became manifest, and began to fall. Sometimes this could happen naturally; it was where star iron came from, as any smith or magister knew. But there was nothing natural about Ash's calling. Eight great bodies from beyond the edge of reality began to fall to earth, carefully aimed by Ash's malevolence.

Yet in the long but finite instant in which they tipped into reality, Kerak's working opened and burst into *effect* from the body of an arrow of thought to a *becoming* like the wings of a flock of very complicated butterflies; from an arrow, his working became a shield, or rather, a set of shields each fluttering subtly at the very edge of the real.

Each of the falling meteors struck one of the butterfly wings, and was altered very, very subtly.

And then they fell like Lucifer's angels. As they fell through the outer reaches of the real, they gathered contrails that appeared to the mortals below like pointing fingers.

Ash turned away from a new wound that burned deep in his right side. He was only a mile from the enemy ridge, and now his workings were bubbling along Kerak's glowing shields. He was burning through the shields but they were still holding; indeed, Ash's last emanation of blue fiery rage had immolated a dozen ancient bears and as many wardens, a terrible blow to the Allies. Flint, oldest of bears, died there, and the eldest of his clan with him.

And still the choir's layered shields held. Royal foresters lay dead in charred heaps; the northern Brogat would have a thousand new widows; and yet Ash could not pull down the shields.

None of it mattered, because his very presence was a deception.

Ash turned and raised his long head on his sinuous neck to see the glory of his skill. One part of his intellect had counted down to the moment where his meteors would impact; he glanced round to see a distant contrail as a volley of sorcerous attacks forced his focus onto survival; he slew the least of the hermeticists attacking him and turned to see eight lines in the sky.

Something was wrong.

He didn't even have time to think.

The concussions were titanic. Each meteor struck the earth like a great fist from the heavens, and each, perfectly aimed, burning from

17

a thousand miles of friction, fell along the Vale of Dykesdale and not onto the Dykesdale Ridge as Ash had planned.

Something had altered their paths; some by a few hundred meters, and two of them by *miles*.

One missed him by the length of one leathery wing, and suddenly Ash was fighting for his life; the near miss created a hurricane of air-currents that tore at his left wing, and then the explosions...

Ash spent all of his hoarded *potentia* to ride the cyclone winds and not have his vast wings ripped from his suddenly frail body, and even as the titanic blows struck across the sky, he was rolled, and the unhealed wound dealt him by an unsealie weapon months before burst asunder and his hot ichor flowed.

But Ash's roar of anger was lost in the chaos of a false dawn.

He reached into the *aethereal* and drew power from the north.

Six meteors struck in a line along the marshes. Every tree on the nine-mile ridge was blown flat; a million years of tree life exterminated in an instant, and the heat of the impact started fires that would burn for days.

Half a million boggles died in a single beat of their collective hearts. Off to the west, Kerak's redirected meteors missed the very heart of Ash's real army and still annihilated hundreds of wyverns and trolls, started forest fires, and turned a whole broad lake to a rising column of steam visible from Harndon. A river's course was forever altered; the crust of the earth was ruptured along the floor of Dykesdale. Red lava flowed, and the bodies of the dead became ash, literal ash, rising into the heavens to choke the sun.

But despite Kerak's best efforts, none of the meteors struck the dragon.

The two he had directed at Ash's reserves struck together, so close that they, too, blew a hole in the hard outer shell of the world, and a fiery chaos erupted. A mountain was born from the fire.

Every man or irk who had lingered on the western face of the ridge; trapped in combat, or too brave or foolish to run, or willing to sell their lives as rear guards to save their friends; all died. There fell Ser Edward, holding back the trolls so that his knights could escape, with all his squires, and there fell a dozen wardens, old souls who had roamed the north woods, covering Mogon's escape.

And the survivors on the reverse slope might, at least in the first moments, have preferred death. The sky went dark; the sun was shadowed, and the air was full of smoke; even the wardens lost their hearing from the cataclysmic concussions, and most men could not hear well for days. Every horse bolted, despite careful precautions. And then the sky began to fall; first dust, and branches of trees, and splinters, and then rocks, and then more dust, and some bits of bogglins. Men were killed right through their armour; a falling rock could kill an armoured horse and his rider in one blow.

Tamsin, who had lived a thousand summers and seen many things, had never imagined the aftermath of the strikes, and she watched in utter horror as the malevolent rain flayed the Allies. She and Kerak raised shields to ward their people in the real—

And then Ash struck.

The choir was in chaos, and unprepared, and for eternal moments Tamsin and Lord Kerak tried to hold their adversary by themselves.

Far away in Lissen Carak, the choir raised its voices all together; Miriam's high alto and Amicia's low alto and over them all, a young novice's magnificent soprano raising their praise of God to heaven. Amicia spread her arms, and the glow of golden light that suffused her began to intensify.

The choir's power grew. The power passed west to Kerak and to Tamsin.

Ash could no long ignore the immanence of Amicia. It was a crisis for which he was prepared, and yet unprepared.

"Damn," muttered Lord Kerak, and he was hit as Ash's power began to leak through his mind, unable to hold the power of the choir and the power of Ash in his head. In no time he was dying, but the Army of the Alliance lived, and Ash turned, rushing east to try to prevent a disaster to all his plans, and he cursed, his curses palpable, abandoned any immediate hope of destroying the Allies, and cast from the *ops* he sucked from the fountain at Lake-on-the-Mountain and he took the wyrm's way to Lissen Carak in a single mighty effort of will.

Tamsin herself left her fortress and stepped through reality to save Kerak. She reached as far down Kerak's lifeline as she could, trying to save the ancient Warden sorcerer, greatest of his kind and perhaps as great as Harmodius himself.

Kerak's physical body lay in a crumbled heap in the midst of the

Whale's Jaw, a huge rock outcropping on the reverse slope of the ridge where two ley lines converged, hiding him in the *aethereal*. Tamsin stepped through reality even as she reached far into the *aethereal*, but Kerak was far beyond her, his fading self already almost gone even from the farthest halls and tunnels of his great and Wyrm hole–like memory palace.

"Oh, Kerak," Tamsin said, or something equally foolish. Tamsin and Kerak had been allies and foes many times in many contests; now, at what she knew to be the end of her age, she would have traded every knight and archer and every irk in the Army of the Alliance for Lord Kerak, her peer and friend.

She knelt in the darkening cave of his memory palace, and bowed her head. And ash and grit fell on her from the lowering sky.

Far to the east, in the darkening sky over the great abbey, Ash poured fire onto the battlements to no effect. He cursed, and raved; a thunderstorm, feeding on his excess and rich in volcanic ash, burst over the high castle. He was unwise in his expenditures, and his will lost adherence, and still he could not penetrate the choir's canopy of resistance.

And then, to his embodied senses, chaos came. The roof of the abbey's central church did and did not open; and the simultaneity of the two realities, invisible to mere mortal observers, terrified Ash. And from the paradox arose Amicia crowned in golden glory, and against her will of shining adamant gold Ash did not try his own, but turned, too late to stop what he could see, and he fled into the near *aethereal*. He could only see her as a new and potent adversary, but perhaps not yet a contestant. Not yet. Not this epoch, not this aeon.

Nonetheless, in her moment of apotheosis, he fled before her.

Pass me by, he said quietly. *Another day I will eat you.*

Light gathered in the shadowed remnant of Kerak's palace.

Tamsin knew it was time to leave, but the sudden accession of light gave her hope.

And then, above her, an immortal appeared, holding Kerak as if the great Saurian were a toy. Tamsin raised her eyes to see that it was no angel, but Amicia, like a living statue of solid, glowing gold, and her eyes were too bright for even Tamsin to meet.

"Now, Faery Queen, fear no evil," she said. "This one goeth to my house,

which indeed has more rooms than any mortal could imagine. But listen! I speak with the last breath of my living. The undead dragon Rhun is falling to his last death; Gabriel is victorious in the Antica Terra. All the world is balanced on the razor's edge."

"Counsel me!" Tamsin begged.

"Save Lissen Carak," Amicia said. Then she blinked. "Or not."

Then she smiled the warm, rich smile that Tamsin remembered from the Inn of Dorling.

And she and the glowing form of Kerak vanished into the darkness.

Tamsin tore herself from her friend's silent palace, taking with her a web of workings she didn't understand, and—

Found herself standing amid the great stones of the Whale's Jaw. Kerak's body was *gone*.

Tamsin fell to her knees.

A mile to the east, in a sheltering stand of ancient beeches, Tapio and Ser Gavin were gathering the army. Mogon knew of Kerak's death and of Flint's; the loss of two powers of the Wild was a heavy blow, and for Gavin, the loss of the Lord of Bain and his retinue was as bad. A terrible wind gusted from the west with a smell of burning and corruption, brimstone and heavy treacle. The sky was dark, the sun aglow like a distant fire on a dark night.

"We can't make another stand," Gavin said. His archers looked haunted in the queer brown light; they flinched every time something fell through the treetops. The N'gara Jacks looked as if they had been beaten with sticks; the royal foresters were slumped with their packs on, as if they had been struck by lightning.

In fact, they *had* been struck; they had watched fifty old comrades immolate and scream to their horrible deaths.

Tapio sighed and looked west. The sky was blood orange at the base of the horizon, and the air was stifling and close, like an old house with the windows closed. There was hot ash falling from the sky.

"If we have lossst my lady Tamsssin, we are indeed doomed," Tapio said.

"Tamsin is right here," she said, kissing her love. She appeared as a beautiful mortal woman, in a red *houplande* with a gold belt of heavy plaques.

Men looked up.

"Lord Kerak is dead," he said. "I saw his soul in the arms of Sister Amicia."

No one spoke.

Tamsin bowed her head, and then raised it. Her fanged mouth opened and she sang like a minstrel, "The impossible is now everyday. I have called down fire from the sky, and I have seen an angel of the Lord, and she was the embodiment of a nursing sister named Amicia, and she took Kerak away to heaven. Or so it appeared to me. Is she the Lady Tar? Your confusing Virgin? Or now a God unto her own right?" Tamsin shrugged. "We live in a great tale. Let me say only what I saw. She told me that Gabriel has triumphed in the East; that the dragon Rhun is destroyed. And that we must protect Lissen Carak."

Tapio looked hard at the magister. "A glowing angel of *their* god told you this, my love?" He was curious. Cynical, perhaps. "Lissen Carak? Not N'gara?"

"She said, 'Save Lissen Carak...or not.'"

Tapio laughed without bitterness. "No ambiguity there, my love."

Tamsin looked at the ground in weariness. "I would trust her," she said simply.

Ser Gavin looked over the army, such as it was. "It is two hundred hard leagues to Lissen Carak," he said. "Fifteen days. Without rest."

Ser Gregario had come up, eyes red. "It'll take us that long to unfuck all this," he said. "And none of these lads and lasses will be any good in a fight for a long time."

Tapio looked at the human, and looked, too, at Bill Redmede, who looked sixty years old and not thirty. Redmede nodded. He was having trouble hearing what the others were saying.

"If we retreat, N'gara will fall," he said.

"Can't you...hide it?" Gavin asked.

"No," Tapio said. "Not from Asssh. Not anymore."

"Three times we have stood, and three times been defeated," Gavin said.

"This was no defeat," Tamsin said. "Hear what I sing. We have dealt Ash a blow that may prove mortal."

Tapio shook his head. "Even ssshorn of hisss insssane horde of bogglinsss, he is puisssant beyond our besssst effortsss," Tapio said. "And now you have taught him to take our sssorcccerersss ssseriousssly." He

22

turned and looked at Gavin and his dark eyes glinted. "I would hold my N'gara. I would hold it and send you all to your devil."

Tamsin shuddered in the strange light. "No," she said.

"No, my love?" Tapio shook his head. "Together we could stop Asssh. Or at leassst hold N'gara."

"No," she said. "It is a fine dream, but when we entered this war, we risked all we have. Now the bet comes due."

Tapio grunted. "We are losssing. Perhapsss we have already lossst."

"Yes," admitted Tamsin. "And we lost Amicia and Kerak in one day. We will never be a choir like this again." She sighed. "Unless Harmodius and Desiderata come."

"Next time Ash will come with caution and sssubtlety," Tapio said. "And you will die, Tamsssin."

Men shuffled and one spat. Ser Gregario fiddled with his sword, and Ser Gavin wished he were good at speeches.

Bill Redmede spoke cautiously. "What does it mean that Ser Gabriel is victorious?" he asked so quietly that other men, deafened by the concussions of the falling rocks, made him repeat himself, and he flushed.

"So the Red Knight won?" he barked more loudly. "What does that mean?"

"It means he's drinking good red wine in Etrusca while we face fucking Ash," muttered Ser Gregario.

"It meansss he hasss traded my N'gara for Arlesss," snapped Tapio.

Tamsin nodded. "Yes. If we wish to save Lissen Carak, we must leave N'gara."

"The gates align, or open, or what have you, in twenty-three days," Gavin said. "Whatever happens..." Gavin closed his eyes, and opened them again. "We're on our own."

Tamsin raised her hands despite her weariness. "Listen; our workings, and Ash's, have turned Dykesdale into a carbonized desert with a pool of molten rock at the bottom. We have a day; perhaps two. We can break off, move east, and... begin laying traps and ambushes. Every day."

Tapio looked away.

Bill Redmede looked at his brother. "Twenty days?" he asked.

Harald Redmede was captain of the royal foresters, the hardest man in the woods, some said. "You only die once," he said, and spat. It wasn't contempt; his mouth was full of wood ash.

"And then we try and hold Lissen Carak," Gavin said, thinking it over. "Sweet Christ. With the twelve thousand we have left? Mayhap?"

"Yer brother held it wi' five hunerd," Redmede the elder said.

"The king came and rescued us," Gavin said.

Tamsin nodded. "We will have to pray for Harmodius and Desiderata this time." She paused, opened her mouth to speak, and then said nothing. She looked at Tapio.

Gavin looked back to the east. "The Prince of Occitan and the Count of the Borders are raising the royal army in the east," he said. "We are not alone."

"You are asssking me to give all I have," Tapio said. "To sssave the world of men."

Gavin drew himself up. He was still the Green Earl; he was far from beaten. "I have lost Ticondonaga," he said. "When we are victorious, I will rebuild it. I pledge the Kingdom of Alba to rebuilding N'gara."

Tapio nodded slowly. Then he raised his arms as if invoking the aid of heaven.

"It isss done," he said.

Tamsin vanished.

"Tamsssin hasss taken our people and run," Tapio said. "Now let usss take the time we have won, and not sssquander it."

Gavin nodded. "Break and run," he said.

Weary men and women clambered to their feet, and hauled their mates up; men donned packs. Bess was with the matrons; Bill Redmede missed her, but he got his pack on his shoulder. Bill wondered if it was symbolic that the Jack's white wool cotes had grown to a colour more like summer green, and the crisp dark green cotes of the royal foresters had bleached in the sun to a colour lighter than the leaves of a summer oak, so that the two were nearly indistinguishable in the shade of the old beech trees.

"I'm tired of getting beat," Redmede said to his brother. He was too loud; no one could hear well, and the dark sky frightened everyone.

Ser Gavin heard him, and he looked down and his smile was tired and grim. "Fight, get beat, rise up, and fight again," he said. "That's our job."

Some men laughed, and some muttered darkly, but authority called; sergeants and vintners ordered men into lines or columns, and despite everything, a rear guard of Jacks and foresters and Irkish knights was formed and, as if daring fate, went back up the ridge above them.

Gavin found his heart rising. "Damn," he said. "Damn me. We aren't beat yet."

Tapio nodded. "Indeed," he said. "We mortals are not ssshort of courage. Perhapss it isss becaussse we die so fassst anyway."

Behind a screen of rangers, the Army of the Alliance of Men and the Wild formed into columns and tramped off into the last light along the very same trail that Bill Redmede's shattered Jacks had traversed in the other direction just a year before.

Grey Cat, the wiliest of his hunters, grinned. "Just eight days to the Cohocton Country," he said.

Redmede took a long pull at his nearly empty canteen and spat. "I'm too fuckin' old for this," he said.

Gavin had a notion, as a squire brought him a horse, and he played with his stirrup leathers while he refined it.

"Where is Lady Tamsin?" he asked Tapio.

"Clossse," Tapio replied. "She isss doing what can be done for N'gara."

"I need her," Gavin said.

Almost instantly, the Lady of Faeries appeared.

"If we could hide," Gavin said to the Lady of Illusions, "we might avoid some fights we would surely lose."

She nodded. "This is both subtle and good," she said. "And we can use this ugly darkness against our enemy."

Then Tamsin and Tapio stood together for so long that the last tail of the army passed them, marching east into the twilight, lit by mage lights and will-o'-wisps. They stood like statues, and then, together, they faded into a more-than-twilight obscurity and were gone, not suddenly but very slowly, like the colour bleaching from wool in a tub of laundry.

When Syr Ydrik and his hunters rode by on their tall war elk, they saw nothing of the magister or the irk queen, and a dozen veteran rangers passed east and could find no trace of the army they had so lately left.

Gavin kept the column moving all through the night, through exhaustion and near mutiny, to fresh water and another strong camp. He dismounted, took a message from the latest imperial messenger bird, wrote out a long response about the battle just fought, and directed the Abbess Miriam to take command of the peasants of the North Albin and begin digging trenches. And as he rode east, he looked at the stars, and wondered if the same stars were rising over his brother and the company.

He scratched the scales that now covered most of the left side of his body, and wished the Red Knight would appear. Or send a messenger bird, or something.

"Where the hell are you?" he asked the eldritch sky.

Part I
Maneuvers and Evasions

Chapter One

Harndon—Queen Desiderata of Alba

The same sky, still unstained by the line of new volcanoes belching ash in the north, hung over Harndon. The queen had come home to her capital, flushed with victory and new motherhood, cradling her son, Constantine, in her arms, to the thin cheers of her hungry and plague-infected people.

Harndon looked like a woman beaten by a drunken spouse; signs hung awry, there were burns and smoke damage everywhere, and no one smiled, or sang. The city seemed empty of children, and too quiet. The center of the city, the "palace" as it was known, rich stone houses packed close in around the Episcopal Palace, was a gutted ruin. A spring and summer of civil unrest and war had decimated the city's nobles and left its mark on merchant and guildsmen alike.

And where the Knights of Saint Thomas had reopened their hospital, there was a line of anxious women, all with silent children. The only sound was coughing. There was a fashion growing for women to carry black linen handkerchiefs, to hide signs of the plague; men and women were wearing hoods, and some wore linen over their faces, too.

Grand Prior John Wishart left the queen to a palace full of spiders and roaches and mice. The former Archbishop of Lorica had hated cats, and ordered them exterminated, so there were suddenly rats in the grain supply. And the first detachment of nuns and brother knights looked exhausted; they had dark circles under their eyes and many were utterly drained of *potentia*. Prior Wishart dismounted with sixty Knights of the Order at his back and another fifteen nuns from the northern priories, and before the evening bells rang for vespers, they were grinding Umroth bone to powder and working *ops* in the infirmary.

Harmodius, the greatest magus in the kingdom, was with them. He had spent his power like a wastrel son on the ride south from the Inn of Dorling, working cures every day, casting wide into the countryside and returning empty in the evening from visiting plague-stricken hamlets and solitary farms, sometimes alone, sometimes with a priest and a pair of nuns with powers of their own, or merely with the human power of their devotion.

Ser Gerald Random, the kingdom's richest merchant and the acting Chancellor of the Kingdom and Mayor of Harndon, had seized every ounce of Umroth ivory in the city, and sent it to a pair of veteran practitioners—just emerged from the archbishop's prison cells—to be tested. As soon as the ivory was judged and valued, it was ground to powder by apothecaries and sent to the grand priory in the ancient temple. There, workmen struggled through the night to fit panes of horn to mend the great windows smashed by Gallish brigands and the Harndon mob, too; the sound of breaking glass had proven equally beautiful to both sides. Even as they blocked the draughts, novices and squires mixed philtres while the mages and the brother knights with power to heal worked on the growing crowds of plague victims; and too many people who were merely afraid.

And there, while attending to a woman so afflicted that her life hung by a golden thread, Prior Wishart heard the news from one of the Order's initiate squires; Eufemmie Muiscant had just come from the castle with more Umroth ivory, and she had seen the imperial messenger bird and heard the queen's comments.

Wishart tried to keep his focus as he wrestled with the notion that the nun with whom he'd debated the perils of love just months before had had a public apotheosis in the midst of her convent.

The Prior of Harndon, second officer of the Order in Alba, Ser Balin

Broadarrow, looked up from his own patient in the next bed when young Eufemmie was done telling her news.

"Squire, be so good as to fetch clean linens for this bed," Ser Balin asked courteously. As soon as the young woman was gone, he shook his head at Ser John. "Sister Amicia is a saint? In my lifetime?" The Prior of Harndon was a round-faced, portly man; a life of arms and abstention did not seem to affect either his girth or his good cheer. "God works in mysterious ways."

Wishart bore down, concentrating on his working; cleaning the afflicted woman's blood in a laborious sweep that was far more like the drudgery of a long patrol in the Wild than like a reckless cavalry charge of power. The cure took time, power, concentration, and patience, and any missed animiculae resulted in the caster having to work the patient all over again; it had happened too often, and every failure wasted the precious resources of *ops* and ivory.

But there was a specific feeling in the patient and in the *aethereal* when the *corpus* was clear of infection, and *Wishart could feel the denouement coming. He honed his concentration the way he would have done in prayer, walling off thoughts of Amicia's elevation, of her powers and their loss. His thought became a torch, burning away the poison in the woman's blood, and then the moment of triumph was reached, and she sighed, and he sat back, his attention relaxing gradually until he could* release his focus. Almost no time had passed in the real; he glanced at Ser Balin and replayed the brother knight's words inside his head.

He smiled. "I'm really not surprised," he said.

Balin put a hand on his own patient, testing her for a recurring fever. "But... in our lifetimes! Someone we know!" He laughed aloud. "What a wonderful thing!" He winked at his commander. "Perhaps I'll address a prayer to her now."

"Balin," Wishart said.

"Is it true?" asked Sister Mary. She burst in, arms full of creamy white linen sheets, and she didn't even curtsy.

But Balin grinned. Sister Mary was one of his favourites; she had been with Amicia until Easter, and was developing into a fine young doctor. And had just tested for enough latent power to be trained further. "Yes," he said without preamble.

Wishart shook his head. "Friends," he began, and then he heard the cheering.

He had been about to caution them to keep the news to themselves, but throughout the priory, men and women were cheering.

Sister Mary dropped down on her knees and began to pray.

Harndon—Master Pye

Master Pye had returned immediately with his apprentices; the smoke of their forges had appeared within days of the fight at Gilson's Hole, and now they were casting metal. He felt the lack of Duke and Edmund, away with the emperor and the army, but he had absorbed all the staff of six master bell-casters and they were fine young men and women, and with a dozen of his older younglings, he was hard at work. He had Master Landry, the best bell-maker in all Alba, at his side, to supervise the casting.

In the next yard, sixty out-of-work millers learned how to use spoke shaves while a dozen carpenters under a journeyman knocked up shave-benches from planks and firewood.

"Ye want *six hundred wheels*?" the wheelwright master, Master Pearl, complained. "Blessed Saint Thomas! Is this on top o' yesterday's order?"

Mistress Anne Bateman, now Lady Anne, and Becca Almspend, soon to be Lady Lachlan, stood in the muddy yard, their overgowns filthy to the ankle, each carrying wax tablets covered in dense columns of markings. "Yes, master," Lady Anne said. "Six hundred more wheels."

"I dinna ha'e the wood," he protested.

"Buy it," Almspend snapped. "We are paying."

"Blessed Trinity. Lady, there's no more good board lumber to be had..." He shook his head.

"If I find you the lumber...?" Lady Anne said.

"Then I need some loons to work it!" the northerner shouted. "By the cross o' Christ, madam!"

"Find them," Almspend said. "Stop all work on any other project."

"I ha'e that already!" he protested.

"In the city. The queen orders it. No wheel is to be built for any reason, nay, not even for the queen's carriage or a baby's pram, until these wheels are completed and these wagons built."

The wheelwright looked at them for a moment. Then he crossed his arms.

"Fine," he spat.

"Master." Lady Anne put a hand on his arm. "We are in a fight to the finish, and just now, that fight is as likely to be won by wheelwrights as by swordsmen and magisters."

He thought about that a moment, and a smile lit his face. "Well, that's bra'ly put," he admitted. "I'll do wha' I can." He paused. "Jesus." He bowed his head at the name, piety, and blasphemy mixed in a single gesture. "Wha' in the de'il's name is Pye doin'? Consortin' wi' daemons? That's the stink o' hell!"

Indeed, the sulphur reek rolled across the wheelwright's yard like a cloud of poison.

"He's making the cargo," Almspend said. "You make the wheels. Oh, and all of your apprentices are seconded to the royal army. As of now."

"By all that's holy!" the master complained. "But..."

"War," said Lady Anne. "Send your people in groups of ten to the Order of Saint Thomas for inoculation against the plague." She handed him a pass bearing the royal seal.

"What's next?" she asked Becca Almspend.

"Paper-makers," Becca responded, looking at her tablet. "Master Elena Diodora. Or should I say, Mistress."

The two left the yard and trudged north along the street.

Harndon—Lessa

Lessa moved quickly through the darkening streets. Above her head, a great, dark column like distant smoke climbed out of the north and west, a reaching hand of darkness that scared her more than the scarred killer she'd chosen to follow. She had her reasons, just as no doubt he had his own.

She was dressed like a beggar or a prostitute, in ragged wool kirtle several sizes too large and a shapeless overdress whose lower hem was almost black with old mud. She was barefoot, and the filthy streets oozed a cold mud that stank like nothing she'd ever encountered before she'd undertaken this adventure.

She didn't like the looming darkness in the north, and she didn't like that men watched her as if she was prey. She was careful, moving from cover to cover, aware that Tyler should have sent Tom or Sam on this mission except that they were both as stupid as the oxen they'd followed all their lives.

Yet for all her care, she didn't see the man until he stepped out from a narrow alley. His open palm slammed into her shoulder and with the same arm he spilled her into the muddy street.

He put a booted foot on her stomach. "Whose little whore are you?" he asked. "Mine now, sweetie. Someone's a fool for letting you walk alone where big bad men like me can find you."

He was tall, strongly built, with a handsome face and a sword at his hip and fine gold earrings. He might have been a courtier in foppish Galle clothes, but everything about him shouted *pimp*. The clothes were too tight, the shoes too worn.

He leaned down. "Oh, sweeting, fear not. We will be *such friends*." His smile was as false as the jewel in his dagger hilt.

Lessa glanced at the mouth of the alley to make sure he didn't have a bravo at his back and then plunged a little dagger into the back of his calf. He shrieked and fell; she rolled over, fouling her whole gown, and ran.

Her limbs felt weak and she hated her weakness; her hands trembled even as she ran, and she had to lean against a building and master herself, so great was her fear and revulsion. But there was no pursuit and in a minute she had her head together. Then she went more carefully, passing along the north of Cheapside and glancing briefly at the crowds outside the grand priory. The word was that the knights were curing the plague. Tyler said the knights were their enemies as much as the king and queen, and Lessa wasn't sure she agreed.

But she passed them, passed the ruins of the Episcopal Palace, and went up the hill past the burned stone shells of a dozen rich houses that now protruded like rotten, crumbling teeth in a fresh corpse's mouth. She climbed the mound that led to the oldest part of the castle, almost directly above the temple, and there were a dozen inns nestled under, and in some cases, resting against the walls of the great fortress; the Inns of Court, where young men and a few women went to learn the law and the ways of courts, the rules of courtesy and knighthood and government, at least in better times. Since the troubles and the plague, the inns were all but deserted, which Lessa knew was bad for her little mission. She looked terribly out of place in her stinking muddy overgown.

But her bad fortune was balanced by good; the old soldier at the door of the Queen's Arms Tavern knew that he had an empty tap room behind him and he wasn't going to turn away a customer, even if it was some drabble tail puke from Cheapside. He reached out to give her a casual squeeze and only withheld his hand at the smell of her muddy gown.

Lessa promised herself that when the *Day* came, he'd be dead. Then she slipped past him into the common room, where fewer than a dozen men sat at the ancient tables, drinking the inn's excellent beer.

And her good fortune continued, for there, at the farthest table, was a man in a green hat with a yellow feather. She swayed her hips and arched her back and moved across to him with a confidence that she didn't feel; that she almost never felt, in fact, except when she had a bow in her hand.

He was older than she had expected; forty or fifty, with grey in his beard and hair. He looked as hard as iron; as hard as Tyler. For all that, his nails were clean and his sword was good.

"Do you like to hunt the deer, then?" she said as she went up to him.

"Only in the season of the year," he answered. Correctly.

Her knees were weak with relief. She vowed inwardly that she would never do this again.

"Christ, you stink," he said.

She stood frozen. She didn't know what whores did; did she sit down?

He glanced up. "Don't sit. We're not friends." He gave her a very small smile, as if to soften the words. "Beer?" he asked.

"Yes," she said. "I was attacked," she said softly.

He shrugged, as if people were attacked every day, which might have been his notion of the world. He waggled a finger and a tall, heavyset man appeared with the bushiest eyebrows Lessa had ever seen.

"A pint of bitter for the whore," her mission said. "And someplace I can get my business done."

"Not in my place," the keeper said, shaking his head. "We're a royal inn."

The man at the table leaned back and showed a golden leopard in his hand.

"Perhaps you'd like a room?" the keeper suggested wearily.

"If I must," the bastard at the table said. "A kitchen bench is more her speed."

"Not in my kitchen," the keeper said. He vanished.

"You have to dress better to come in here," the bastard said. He shook his head. "This is bad enough already."

Lessa shrugged. She was afraid all over again. Because a man with a sword, in a room with a lock, could go very badly for her, and no one was going to come and help her.

At the top of the inn stairs, when he glanced into the room, she paused.

"I'm no whore," she said softly.

He raised an eyebrow. "I know," he said, and went into the room.

She followed, and he closed the door behind her.

"Get rid of that overgown," he ordered her.

She shook her head.

"Mary Magdalene, girl!" he spat. "I won't rape you. My word on it. But you stink like a sheep a week in the grave."

She stripped off the overgown.

He threw it out the window. "I'll give you my cloak," he said. "So, here we are."

"My friend wants to meet your friend," she said.

"My friend is watched night and day," the man said. "And your friend's the most wanted man in the kingdom."

Lessa shrugged. "Our friends want the same thing," she said. Although personally, she didn't think it true. She knew that the *voice*, that shadowy demon thing that talked to Tyler, had ordered him to make this approach. She knew because she listened in the night. They lived with beggars; there was no privacy. She knew why she was here, and she didn't fully agree with it.

The man with the grey beard frowned. "I'm not sure of that at all," he said, as if echoing her thoughts. "My friend is a loyal servant of the queen."

"Really?" Lessa asked with more tartness than she ought to use. "Then why are you meeting me at all?"

The question hung in the air.

There was a knock at the door, and the man rose from the chair, went, and fetched two earthenware cups and a pitcher of ale from the keeper.

"Shall I pour?" he asked with old-fashioned courtesy.

Lessa nodded.

He handed her the bitter and she took a sip, and then more, with gratitude. She felt better immediately.

The man smiled. "That's a proper mug," he said. "Aye, you're a sharp one. I didn't expect a woman, and I didn't expect a whore, and I didn't expect a witty answer like yon. So…mayhap you and your friend know a thing or two. What's the game?"

She looked at him. If he was false, then once she said the words, she was a dead woman. But Tyler was in a hurry, and she had, for her sins, volunteered. It seemed stupid now.

"We kill the queen and her babe," she said. "Towbray becomes king, and we're all pardoned. An' we weren't born yesterday; we get guarantees so that we don't find ourselves dancing in halters at your friend's coronation."

The man flushed. "Treason," he said.

"Your friend's hobby," she mocked.

"Fuck you, witch," he said. But he didn't come at her. She sat, and was afraid, despite her mouth, which usually ran away with her. *And how did he know she had Power?*

"You aren't a whore," he said. "You're not even a peasant."

"Right now I'm a fucking beggar," she said.

"You're the only beggar in Harndon who pronounces all the letters in *fucking*," he said. He took a long pull on his bitter. "Noble?"

"Not your business," she said.

"Actually it is," he said. He leaned back, as if he wanted her to feel unthreatened. "It is because if you are gently born, I'm more likely to trust you, frankly. I don't love Jacks, and neither does my friend."

"We don't love you, either," Lessa said.

"East Brogat?" he asked.

"I'm not a lord. I'm a Jack," she said with pride. "Who I was and what crimes I committed are no man's business, nor woman's."

He met her eyes, and his were steady. "I'd hate to think you were some well-born runaway," he said. "A little adventure, a little fun, and then you run home and sell us all to the hangman." He smiled. "Maybe a boy you want rid of?"

"Fuck. You." She had no trouble meeting his eye.

He shrugged. "Let's do it," he said suddenly. He drained his beer

37

and stood up. "Next time, in the Oar House in East Cheaping by the docks. It's rough; send a man, or dress like a real whore. Wear a scarlet hood and carry a black handkerchief; no one but a madman troubles a chit with the plague."

She wanted to bridle, but his words made sense. "When?" she asked.

He shook his head. "I have no idea," he said. He tugged at his beard. "Day after tomorrow, same time," he said. He opened the door slightly, tugged at his sword and used his left thumb to crack it out of the scabbard, looked both ways in the empty hall. He looked back at her and winked and tossed his cloak on the bed; a fine wool cloak with fur in the hood. "Room's yours for the night," he said. "Though I wouldn't linger," and he was gone out the door and down the steps.

Later, after she'd told everything to Tyler, she lay under the man's cloak in the beggar's hall, the undercroft of the former Guild Hall of the Drapers, burned by the Galles. The upper stories had fallen in, but the basements were mostly intact, and the King of the Beggars and his court had moved in.

Tyler came and sat cross-legged like a tailor by her palette of straw. "One more thing," he said.

She rolled over. Out in the smoky hall, a man was beating another with his fists. Closer in, two women made love in relative silence. "Yes?" she said softly.

He gestured with his thumb. "What'd he look like? Your contact?"

She thought about it. "Middle height, grey beard, sharp nose, beard and mustache like a courtier, sword hands; clean nails, calluses. Clean linen."

"Scars?" Tyler asked.

"On the backs of both hands."

Tyler made a motion with his mouth; she didn't like it, because she associated it with his hiding something. But in this case the old Jack nodded. "Kit Crowbeard," he said. "You did well," he said, the rarest of praise.

"Comrade?" she asked. "Why kill the queen?" She paused. "I mean, I know why. But why for Towbray?"

Tyler leaned close in the whisper-filled darkness. "We will bring it all down," he said softly. "Let it all burn. Then we'll be free."

But you take orders from a demon, Lessa thought. She was still trying to parse it when she fell asleep.

Albinkirk—Mistress Helewise

Mistress Helewise was watching her daughter flirt. Her daughter was standing in their yard, now finally clear of refuse, with swept cobbles and one neat pile of horse dung by the stable door, there apurpose. The well worked and had a pump, and by the pump stood two tall, well-muscled young men, Jamie Le Hoek and Haegert Coucy, squires, and today, reapers. Most of the women had been out in the fields; the wheat was tall and dark autumn gold, the grains full and hard so that the stalks bent a little with the weight; the wheat and the oats were both ready to be harvested, and it was the fullest harvest anyone could remember, if on the fewest farms. Viewed from the roof of Helewise's stone manor house, there were more fields fallow than tilled, stretching away to the walls of Albinkirk; the red and gold of the trees had to replace the glowing gold of crops in too many places. But if the planting had been sparse, the crop was rich beyond imagining, and they were too few to reap it all and get it into the barns and stone silos.

Helewise had used her store of favours to bring a dozen tall young men from Albinkirk. She was a good neighbor; she'd helped with many a birth, with the serving of fine dinners, the presentation of a supper to the great Duchess of Ticondonaga, the laying out of corpses. People liked her, and because of that, the acting Lieutenant of Albinkirk, the recovering Grand Squire, Ser Shawn LeFleur, saw to it that the squires and junior men-at-arms left behind by the alliance when the army marched west were at her service. He'd come himself; his left side swathed in bandages, his face largely covered in an elaborate silken hood he wore buttoned tight to hide the burns. Now he sat behind her in her best settle, his muddy boots on a scrap of burlap; he'd worked the day through despite his fine clothes and the obvious pain of his burns.

"Your hippocras is the best in the county," he said with his usual courtesy.

Her daughter had just hit Jamie Le Hoek in the head with a very accurately thrown wedge of soap. Her *best* soap. Phillippa had worked all day in the fields; her hair was a brown tangle, her forehead shone with sweat, and Helewise was sore afraid that her daughter was the most beautiful woman for a hundred miles. And she had never looked better, despite sweat stains and some honest dirt, or perhaps because of it.

Pippa's friend Rose, who'd lived with them since the first attacks killed Rose's papa, came into the yard, tossed her hair, and crowned her friend with a garland of roses.

"Queen of the field workers, that's me," Pippa said. "Ouch! Thorns!"

Rose vanished behind her hands, laughing, and young Coucy joined her. "Perfect," he said. "A crown of thorns for the prickly Pippa."

"Prickly Pippa picked a peck of perfect pears," Rose said.

Jamie frowned. And said nothing. He usually said very little, which didn't help him press his love. Helewise noticed he'd caught the thrown soap, though.

"Why don't you louts finish up so girls can wash?" Phillippa said. "Otherwise I'll show you prickly."

"You can wash while we're here," Coucy said.

"Not in my lifetime," Phillippa shot back. "The smell alone..."

By the saints, she's good at that, her mother thought. *I wonder where she got it from?*

Other squires and two big men-at-arms came in from the fields; all dirty, and all tired. But the older women were laying food on the tables in the back, where the hawthorns hid the standing stones, and the smell of roast mutton and turnips filled the air. Old Mother Crabbe came by, directing a pair of younger women in carrying a magnificent, steaming pie, and many of the men lost interest in all else and followed the pie.

The squires dried themselves with their shirts and then put them on, lacing their sleeveless doublets carelessly and moving with all the gawky grace of the young. Haegert Coucy made as if to hide in the stable and watch the girls wash; Jamie grabbed him by the ear and twisted, they exchanged uninspired punches, and then they were off into the back.

"Mind you brush your hair," Helewise shouted at her daughter.

Phillippa frowned and didn't deign to answer.

Helewise went back in to her guest.

"You are too courteous for my poor hall," Helewise said. "You and your little army have saved my harvest."

Ser Shawn smiled grimly. "Our real army is fighting for its life in the west," he said bitterly. "The least I can do is see the harvest in."

She was collecting her good pewter and what little silver she had, so that she could make the harvest table a little brighter. She'd worn the mask all day, but now, without having intended it, she turned to Ser Shawn.

"Will it ever end?" she snapped. "The war?"

He made a face. "Yes," he said firmly. It was the best thing about him, she thought; the confidence he had. "Yes. We'll win, and we'll rebuild."

"Your words to God's ear," she said. "Any word from the east?"

"Antica Terra?" Ser Shawn asked. "Or Liviapolis?"

"I'd settle for any news at all," she said. "Beyond the state of the crops and Mag's sick pig."

Ser Shawn smiled.

The bell rang for dinner, and Phillippa, transformed by a bucket of well water and a heavy hairbrush, went past like a lightning bolt, leaving a tale of perfumed soap and—

"Hey!" roared Helewise. She looked at Ser Shawn. "What was my daughter wearing?" she asked, her question purely rhetorical. Phillippa had somehow managed, in five minutes, to change into a skin-tight dark red kirtle with no shift underneath, so that her sides showed between the lacings, although by the bizarre logic of the young, she still had her reaping hook hanging from her belt like a badge of honour.

"I didn't notice," Ser Shawn said, although he was turning a healthy shade of pink.

"Damn it," Helewise said, knowing that her daughter was out in the back already, secure that her mother would not make a scene in front of guests. "I will not have Haegert Coucy as a son-in-law," she spat.

"I'll speak to him," Shawn said, getting slowly to his feet.

But the harvest feast was a great success. They were short on men, and there was no Etruscan wine to be had at any price in Albinkirk; Ser Shawn brought one good bottle and she shared it with Mother Crabbe and Ser Shawn; sugar was dear, and saffron and pepper almost unattainable because the seas were closed and the shipping all taken for the war. But there was a bumper crop of honey; the turnips were of legendary size, and the salmon that Jamie Le Hoek had pulled from Ser John Crayford's favourite pool brought tears to Lady Helewise's eyes; that man and his fishing rod...

They drank beer instead of wine and were little worse for it, and Helewise had to admit that Haegert Coucy was a very funny young man. She laughed at his antics, and then listened to Jamie play an old romance of courtly love, and a nasty Hillman ballad of war and treachery, and then he played a new love song from Harndon, or so he said. Only Helewise thought he'd written it himself and aimed it at her daughter, but Pippa was playing hide-and-seek like a much younger girl, darting in and out of the trestles with Rose and Carli, the daughter of the next farm toward Albinkirk. The three of them ran, and screamed, and laughed, all of them wearing sharp reaping sickles curved like the rising orange moon, and Helewise was afraid people would be injured, and she called to her daughter. But Phillippa ran on, as if her mother didn't exist, as if Jamie was not singing with shining eyes and holding his audience, too; he had a beautiful voice and his playing was far better than most people in Albinkirk ever heard, outside of a few wandering nuns and friars.

Then he was done, and Haegert was back, throwing purses in the air and juggling them like a mountebank. He pretended to steal Mother Crabbe's bonnet and then produced it, crumpled and soiled, from under his arm; even as she shrieked in protest, he restored the undamaged original to her head—backward.

Helewise enjoyed herself so much that she missed the moment when her daughter threw a single glance at Jamie and stepped out of the lamplight and into the darkness beyond the hedgerow.

She slipped down the path, damp at any time of year. She wondered at her own boldness, and at her choice; until moments ago, she'd have said that of the two older boys, Haegert was by far the more attractive with his court clothes and fine manners and his easy laugh. And Jamie was an old hat; he was around often, helped her mother, and had been Ser John's squire.

She'd never heard him sing like that before, though.

She'd never thought him *intelligent* until that moment. She'd been running by—fully aware of the song, thank you very much, and she'd glanced at him, and he'd...winked. A different wink entirely.

Would he have the sense to follow her into the dark? She'd played this game once or twice in Lorica and learned not to trust boys; and to be cautious. And not to count on them being any too smart, either.

She heard him coming. She saw him silhouetted against the table lights and she knew his size and his gait instantly, and she drifted back past the hedge to the standing stones.

"Pippa?" he called very softly.

She laughed and went deeper into the stones.

He followed, but he was quick, too. He caught her about the waist...

His hands were good, firm and warm and clean, and she kissed him before he'd even thought to kiss her. And he didn't move his hands to grab her breasts, like boys in Lorica; he just kissed her.

He had definitely kissed someone before.

He stumbled, off balance with the kiss, and laughed. Then he turned her slightly, and rested her back against one of the standing stones. She put both arms up over his head and pulled him down, and then she felt something like a worm wriggling against her back.

So great was her revulsion that she pushed his not inconsiderable size away and leapt clear.

"Yech!" she said.

Jamie looked as if she'd stabbed him with a sword. "Oh, Pippa," he said. "I'm so sorry."

"There's worms on the stone," she said. Even as she said the words, she looked, and then the hair on her head tried to stand up straight.

The surface of the stone seemed to be writhing as if it was alive. There was almost no moon; the terrible smoke and soot rising in the west made the full moon into a dull orange ball like nothing anyone had ever seen, and by that strange light, the stones all seemed to move.

"Christ protect us," she said.

"Archangel Michael," Jamie said. He stepped between her and the stone and drew the short rondel dagger at his waist with practiced ease.

"Tight against my back," he said.

She crushed herself against him.

He began to back up. One of his arms moved.

"Back up now," he said. "Oh my God," he moaned.

Pippa had a number of sins, but cowardice was not among them. She turned and put her back against his. She was tempted to call out; to scream. But all the stones had writhing shapes on them in the dull orange darkness, and she was damned if she, Pippa de Roen, would summon good people to their deaths.

"I'm the eyes in the back of your head, Jamie," she said with her mother's crisis voice exactly.

"With you," he said, and when she stepped, he backed. Their spines touched, and sometimes their hips, and one more time, at the edge of the stone circle, by the outlier they called "The Forlorn Lover," he moved away—a sudden lunge, and she was alone.

She looked back, and he was grappling something with both hands.

"Run!" he shouted. One of the worms was going for his face; he grappled it, but seemed off balance...

Pippa turned on her heel and whipped the sickle off her purse hook. Her arm was strong and her aim true despite the bad light, and she cut the writhing thing just under Jamie's hands and her knife went through it as if it had been smoke, and Jamie stumbled. She caught his shoulders and pulled him back and they both fell in the soft turf, and the worms, barely visible in the ashy air, still stretched obscenely toward them.

Pippa got her bare feet back and rolled.

Jamie gave a great spasm and got his feet under him, caught her, and leapt.

"Holy Saint Michael and all the saints," Jamie said in awe. "What the *fuck* was that?"

Pippa hit him. "I've never heard you swear before."

Then, hand in hand, they ran the long way, around the standing stones, to warn the others.

Chapter Two

Arles—The Red Knight

Gabriel awoke. Blanche was lying on his arm and his hermetical hand, and her hair seemed to glitter gold in the darkness. Gabriel smiled, and lay content for a moment gazing at her. He could hear Anne Woodstock moving, and he realized with a nearly hermetical impulse that he was in the castle of Arles.

In almost the same tendril of time he saw with revulsion that it was not Blanche's hair that was glittering with gold in the darkness. Or rather, it was her hair, catching the light from his nonhermetical hand, which was glowing very faintly with gold.

Gabriel Muriens, the Red Knight, Duke of Thrake, Emperor of Man, cursed.

Blanche stirred. She turned her face to him, and snuggled gently but insistently against his side.

Arles.

The dragon Rhun was...*dead* seemed the wrong word.

Destroyed?

Arles was liberated, and on the plains under the high town, thirty thousand former bondspeople, the not-dead, now living, wandered at the point of starvation. Thousands of men and beasts had already died. More would die.

Gabriel lay and looked at Blanche by the light cast by his own skin, and just for a moment, the words formed in his mind.

Fuck you, God.

He smiled.

Or, be it according to thy will, he mused. Annoying as that might seem.

Blanche awoke. She looked at him, leaned to kiss him, flinched, and gasped.

"Oh, by the Blessed Virgin! You are glowing!" She sat up.

Gabriel was still gazing at her. He managed a smile.

"What happened?" Blanche asked very quietly. When you are empress, everything you do must be quiet; servants and friends and allies and enemies are always at your elbow; conversation, lovemaking, defecation, all very, very quiet.

Gabriel sighed. "An angel visited me and said, 'Ave, Gabriel,' and…"

She hit him.

He held out his right hand, his sword hand, in the darkness, and the glow was barely perceptible. "Really," he said. "I have no idea."

"I don't see you as a saint," she said.

"No one sees me as a saint. It's a secret role and I relish it." He had begun to stroke her shoulders and back.

"Ssssh!" Blanche said a moment later. "Everyone is getting up!" she giggled. "Damn. I walked into that."

There was some rustling.

Anne Woodstock closed the door to the bedroom, as if by accident, and went back to laying out clothes. Cheeks burning.

Toby came in with a steaming mug of hippocras.

Anne glanced at him and turned away.

Toby shrugged and walked to the door. "They up?" he asked.

"I don't think…" Anne said.

Toby smiled. "Ahh," he said. He put the cup down on a tile and went to the fireplace, a fine hearth with a separate chimney, as was all the fashion in the Antica Terra. He mulled a cup of cider poured from a fine creamy ceramic flagon.

"Cider?" he asked his page.

She blushed.

"Anne," he began, and then smiled. "Cup of cider?"

"Yes," she said. "He's to be shaved today."

Toby nodded.

"Only I can't find anything. His razors are with the army baggage." She started at a sort of sighing sound from the next room. And blushed again.

Toby nodded. "Probably my fault. I'll ask the staff."

"He'll want to shave as soon as he..." At a loss for words, the page shrugged and looked away.

"Gets up?" Toby asked. He laughed.

Master Julius, now the emperor's private secretary and no longer merely the notary to a company of mercenaries, laughed aloud from the next room.

Toby finished fussing. "Ser Michael's here. Does Robin have razors?"

Anne glanced at him. "Didn't ask."

"I'll ask him." Toby started for the door and there was the notary, pen in hand.

"Ser Pavalo is here to see the emperor as soon as he receives," he called softly. "And Ser Alison." He pointed at the door to the scriptorum. "Lord Pavalo appears to have ridden all night."

Toby handed Anne a cup of steaming cider and walked out through the solar, where Master Julius settled back down. He and two clerks were already writing, by candlelight, and a third man was cutting hides of vellum into strips.

Toby stepped out into the narrow and labyrinthine halls of the mighty fortress of Arles. The emperor was in the northeast tower. Toby had no time to search the towers for Ser Michael. He had to go down to the hall before he found one of Duchess Clarissa's officers.

He bowed.

The officer made a full reverence. The men who had saved Arles from the Odine were being treated to a level of worship and courtesy that they all enjoyed very much.

"My lord," Toby said, pleased and embarrassed. He bowed deeply again. "I am the emperor's body-squire. We've left all the emperor's shaving gear in camp. I need to find Michael; that is, Ser Michael..."

The marshal sported a beard and mustache that were the envy of many younger men, despite the iron grey colour. He rubbed his grizzled cheeks absently. "I am Pierre La Porte, the marshal of this fortress. I will find you something, monsieur," he said.

And he was as good as his word.

Toby climbed back to the tower, where he found Anne pressing a shirt of fine lawn, her iron as deft as her sword.

"Don't do that yerself," Toby said. "Get the new kid to do it. The Hillman."

"He's too useless to iron," she said.

She had two more irons heating on the fire and the great man's linen and hose laid over a towel rack. She was wearing her arming coat and hose, but had an apron wrapped around her hips and a linen towel on her head.

She had no idea how much Toby loved her. Which, Toby felt, was probably better for everyone.

He smiled, she raised her cider, and before he could take up some task, there was a knock at the outer door and a page in the duchess's livery handed over a pair of razors with Umroth ivory handles and a leather box of shaving equipage.

Toby thanked the page, who blushed like Anne. "You saved us all," he said. "Can I see the emperor? Just...see him?"

"Well," Toby said, "not me personally. But thanks. And no. Sorry. You can't see the emperor." He tried to close the door. "Cully? Guard the door, for a friend?"

The master archer was up and dressed, neat and professional in his scarlet padded coat and matching scarlet hose, a heavy gold earring in his ear. He had on a heavy arming sword with a hilt in the Venike fashion. He looked far more like a noble knight than like an archer, until you looked into his eyes.

"Will the...emperor...take us with him? To fight the Necromancer?" the page asked.

Toby relented at the hero-worship and, feeling older than dirt, asked, "How old are you?"

"Thirteen," said the wide-eyed page.

Cully smiled to Toby and used his hip to slam the door on the page. "I'll hold the door," he said.

"He's awake," Anne called from the solar. "Or what have you," she added. Her sarcasm was in Sauce's intonation, mostly because Anne Woodstock was sixteen and she all but worshipped the older woman and imitated almost everything she did. Or said.

They both grinned, and then Toby picked up the still-warm hippocras and pushed through the door into the bedroom with his hip against the heavy oak door.

"Good morning, Majesty," he said without a trace of irony.

Gabriel stretched, found that his leather case with his linens was nowhere to hand, and casually stripped a silk veil off the bed-rail and passed it into the closed bed. "No towels for the emperor," he said with mock severity.

Blanche stretched, took the veil, and snarled.

"That's my *silk veil*," she said. "I asked for a *towel*."

"Good morning, Majesty," Toby said, pushing through the door. "Hippocras is warm. Cider for Her Majesty is on the way."

"Toby, we need a towel." Gabriel shrugged.

Toby nodded. "Majesty, we need Master Nicodemus." Master Nicodemus was Gabriel's Morean steward, and he was with the army.

Gabriel nodded. "Right, and I didn't list him. My apologies, Toby, you must be buried."

Toby met his master's eye. "Yes," he said.

Gabriel bowed slightly. "Noted. Towel."

Toby vanished.

"Damn," Blanche said from the bed. "I forgot Nicodemus, too, when I read your list."

Gabriel stood naked at the window, looking out over the sun-drenched fields and the thousands of near-starving wretches who had been rudely seized back from the Necromancer and inconveniently continued to need food. "Everything...every damned thing is going to depend on systems. I need people to wait on me efficiently so I can help make good decisions and make them stick. Toby needs to be knighted."

"Kronmir," Blanche said.

Gabriel went over, opened the bed, and leaned down to kiss her. "You are not just a pretty face."

Toby leaned in and tossed a beautifully embroidered linen towel to the empress. He vanished.

"Absolutely, Toby must be knighted." She laughed. "When?"

"This morning, after I bathe. No joke. The gates open, or whatever you want to call it, in twenty-five days. We don't have time for ceremony." He sighed.

"People like ceremony," she said. She wondered if making love when you knew you were pregnant was a sin.

It didn't seem like much of a sin compared to the world she lived in. He paused and looked at her.

"Penny for your thoughts, miss?" he asked.

"What will the world be like, when this is over?" she asked.

The door opened again, and Anne Woodstock and Cully, the emperor's personal archer, entered with a huge, steaming wooden tub of water.

"Majesty," Anne said with a bow.

"Good morning, Anne." Blanche put on her public face, which was already different from "Blanche, trustworthy maid of the queen" or "Blanche, mistress of laundry." She *almost* never allowed herself any display but humour and helpfulness.

"Shave when you are washed, my lord." Anne directed this to the emperor.

The new rules—unofficial but widely understood—were that the emperor did not want to be "majestied" more than once a day by any-one unless in formal situations, which would be defined later. "My lord" was less formal than "Majesty" and many of the company still called him "Ser Gabriel" or just "Cap'n" to the delight of some and astonishment of others.

"Excellent," Gabriel said. He sank into the tub, which forced him into an odd, knees-up position. Anne poured water over his head, and he sputtered, and Blanche laughed.

"We have your bath coming up the stairs," Anne said to her naked empress. "Majesty," she added. Anne had known Blanche when she was the queen's laundress.

"I could just use his, if he didn't get it all on the floor," Blanche said. Anne clucked.

She handed the water-ewer to Cully, who poured the hot water ruth-lessly over his emperor despite faint protests and some screams.

"Majesty," he said in a tone that suggested something other than reverence.

Anne moved back to the solar and began to lay out razors, soap, a towel...

The empress's water arrived. The emperor emerged from his bath clean and as red as his epithet and put on a clean shirt and braes without any help. They were short on servants, and he was not to be waited on by any but members of his military household.

Kronmir had made that rule. Kronmir, who was that moment out in the scriptorium, copying maps of northern Etrusca for his staff. Who had, just yesterday, caught a patriarchal assassin, a young woman from Mitla who had come with a "diplomatic" party who were currently all under arrest. Kronmir…

The emperor walked out into the solar. Anne snapped, "His Majesty," and the roomful of secretaries, servants, and seamstresses all rose and bowed deeply.

The emperor looked at Anne for a moment, as if he suspected he was being mocked.

"Castle people," she said quietly.

He sat, and she wrapped a hot towel around his face. She was just seventeen years old; in fact, the day before had been her birth day, or so he thought. *Blanche would know.*

"The blessings of your birth day," he said.

Anne grinned. "Thanks, er, my lord."

"We were busy," he said.

"So we were," she agreed. "My lord." Two years before, she had been a well-born farm girl in the Brogat. Now she was laying a razor to the throat of the Emperor of Man, in a castle in the Arelat. She tried not to think about it too much.

She began to lather him.

He ignored her, as was his right. "Toby?" he asked.

"Duchess Clarissa when you are dressed. Ser Pavalo and Ser Alison are waiting outside and taking breakfast. There are no new messenger birds. The army has passed the morning signal."

They had a simple smoke signal. All it conveyed was "We're alright," but both Arles and the army passed it with variations three times a day. With the enemy known as the Necromancer still at large and other enemies, palpable or secret, all around them, signals had become vital.

"Pavalo?" Gabriel asked. "He must have ridden hard. Bring him. Bring Sauce, too."

"Sir," Toby said with a slight bow.

Gabriel couldn't turn his head. Anne had begun to shave him, and the razor was outlining his mustaches. Scrape, scrape. The particular feel of the sharp blade on his skin.

"Majesty!" Ser Pavalo said.

Ten feet away, Gabriel could smell the horse on the man.

"Long ride?" he asked.

"Nothing compared to yours!" Ser Pavalo Payam, known to most of the company as Payamides because they found his names difficult, was tall, heavily muscled, and black. As Anne lifted the razor, Gabriel turned his head to smile at the man who'd saved both his and Blanche's life (twice) and Amicia's.

Payam smiled back. He was dressed in emerald silk minutely embroidered, and even covered in dust, he looked magnificent.

"I'm guessing this isn't a social visit," Gabriel said.

Sauce appeared in his peripheral vision and blew a kiss.

"We're moving north and we need to make a general...plan of attack," Payam said. Toby brought him a chair and he sat, carefully keeping his robes out of the water coming under the bedroom door. "How is Lady Blanche?"

"Wet," Gabriel said. "Your timing is, as ever, impeccable, as there's too much to discuss by bird. After breakfast, a brief council. You, too, Sauce. You will be taking the army."

Sauce choked.

Gabriel smiled inwardly. "You and the Duchess of Venike."

"Ooh," Sauce said. "Good. I like her." She paused. "Why me?"

"I have Tom and Michael on other missions. You've never held the command and now's the moment. Have fun. Don't break the army."

She sighed audibly.

"Messenger bird," said Toby.

Toby was leaning out the solar door. Gabriel could hear Kronmir on the other side. And another voice, quickly hushed.

"What was that?" he asked, and Anne pulled the razor off his carotid artery when it moved.

Payam was unrolling a chart. Sauce was already looking at it, her dagger holding a corner. Jock MacGilly, the Hillman who'd just joined the *casa* on Bad Tom's recommendation, was trying to pretend that he was not ironing a woman's shift, a job he clearly felt beneath him. Morgon Mortirmir pushed into the solar, carving an apple with a silver knife.

"...but the duchess!" said a shrill voice and then there was a little silence.

Toby reappeared. "My lord, the Duchess of Arles has sent you a basket of fruit." He rolled his eyes.

Gabriel nodded. "Kronmir?" he asked, without moving his face.

"My lord, your brother the earl has fought a third action near N'gara. He has retreated, and N'gara is abandoned to the enemy. The Lords Kerak and Flint were killed. Harmodius..."

At the pause, almost every breath in the room was held.

"Is still in Harndon fighting the plague...Tamsin and Kerak launched a successful attack on the...dragon. Your brother is now retreating through the western lands toward the Cohocton and believes that he will make Lissen Carak in fifteen or twenty days."

The razor had begun to work its way to his temples.

Gabriel tried not to nod. "Ouch," he said softly. "What bird?"

"E.21," Kronmir said. "He's been especially good, and fast at the long hauls."

Gabriel smiled very slightly.

The solar door opened and Blanche, dressed in a very plain overgown, no shift, and wet hair, came in.

"Empress," Anne said sharply.

Gabriel heard them all bow, or curtsy. It was a distinctive rustling noise, a silence, a thump as knees went to stone.

"I don't seem to have a clean shift," Blanche said cheerfully.

Jock MacGilly gulped audibly. "Which..." he began.

Toby stepped past the big Hillman. "It'll be ready directly, my lady," he said.

Blanche stepped up next to the nervous boy. "Is that my shift?" she asked.

MacGilly almost expired. He turned bright red.

"Your iron isn't hot enough," Blanche said. "Here, look. See, Anne's put all the irons...nicely done. Take a little water..." She flicked her damp fingers and the droplets sizzled against the mirror-bright surface of the iron. "Perfect."

"I told him," Anne said cuttingly.

"Ironing isn't easy," the empress said. "Not like fighting military campaigns or learning to joust. Laundry takes patience and concentration." She smiled, and MacGilly became redder.

She waited.

Ser Paval came and kissed her hand. Sauce gave her a hug. Blanche rolled her eyes.

"I can do this faster myself," she said in the voice she'd have used to a laundry maid.

Sauce laughed aloud. "Aye, welcome to command," she said. "Just when you get good at something, you get promoted, and suddenly you have to give orders to some lout to do something ye can do better yersel."

Blanche laughed, and then like an adder striking, her hand reached out and plucked the iron from the Hillman's hand. "I hope you are good at fighting," she said.

"I am that!" MacGilly said.

"Because you need a lot of help with ironing," she said. "I may be empress, but at the moment I have two shifts, and this is one of them, and if you burn it, I'll burn you."

She hip-checked the big man, took his place, and deftly finished the neckline of her shift.

Cully put an assortment of fruit in a solid gold bowl on the sideboard.

"Duchess of Venike is requesting admission," he said in a growl.

"Christ," Ser Michael said, yawning as he came through the solar door. "Let's go back to the army. It's too cramped here." He swayed to miss the reinforcement of Anne's shaving water, fresh from the hearth, and seized the emperor's hippocras and drained it.

"Bastard," muttered Gabriel.

"Only a rumour," Ser Michael said. "My mother was in fact a saint." He finished the hippocras with relish. Then he relented and handed his cup to Robin, his squire.

At the word *saint*, Blanche flushed and Gabriel looked at his right hand. But the sun was well up, the light good, and there was nothing to see.

"Isn't drinking my morning cup some form of *lese majestie*?" Gabriel asked plaintively.

"The Duchess of Venike," Anne said as she began the left side of his face.

The duchess sketched a brief curtsy in response to the volley of bows and gazed adoringly at Blanche, who was finishing her shift with one eyebrow raised and had, when she raised her arm, a good handspan of attractive flesh showing.

"I think you might start a new fashion," the Duchess of Venike said.

Blanche smiled. "Pregnancy?" she asked.

"That's not a fashion, it's a curse," Kaitlin, Michael's lady, pushed into the crowded room. "Blanche, do you have a clean shift?"

"I do now," Blanche said. "And you can't have it."

The duchess held up a pair of scrolls rolled in green leather. "I finished it," she said. "Who is next?"

Gabriel looked up. "Sauce. That is, Ser Alison. When she's done, Ser Pavalo."

Pavalo looked up. "What is it?" he asked.

"The Empress Livia's codex on war and the gates," Gabriel said. "I found it in Liviapolis."

"We should have copies…" Pavalo said.

"No copies," Michael said. "No copies ever. Until we pull this off, no one can be allowed to know what we plan. This room is the sole place where it is safe to discuss these things; everyone is checked."

Kronmir nodded. "Repeatedly," he said.

Toby went through the door, determined to find linens for the ladies of the *casa* if he had to strip them off the Duchess of Arles and her ladies.

Robin, always his best comrade, pulled his arm. "I know just the man," he said. "Come."

The two walked down a short staircase that Toby had missed, and Robin hailed a squire, a well-dressed young man of his own age, in Gallish.

The man bowed. He turned to Toby and said in fair Alban, "I'm the marshal's squire, de Coustille." The marshal's squire was tall and so thin that he appeared ill; Toby realized that almost four months of siege had not been kind to even the rich and powerful here, and the bowl of fruit really was a noble gift.

"Toby," Toby said, holding out his hand.

"Ah, Jean," said the other. "We use surnames." He nodded to Robin. "As I told Lord Robin, my lady sent us to help you." He indicated half a dozen men and two women, all well dressed, although every one of them was somewhat too thin for their clothes.

"God bless you," Toby said with real feeling. "Can your lady produce some clean, ironed shifts for ladies?" He paused.

Jean grinned. He looked at the older woman, an aged crone of perhaps twenty-six. "Meliagraund?" he asked.

She frowned fiercely. "I'll see it done. Give me a strong back and ten minutes, my lords."

Jean bowed. "Done. Our duchess said you would need us."

Toby nodded. "While I have your ear, my lord, the emperor desires a meeting—a council. At the duchess's pleasure..."

Jean de Coustille smiled. "A quarter hour?" he asked.

"Great hall?" asked Toby, as if they were conspirators.

Jean swept an only slightly ironic bow and pointed; two of the young men ran off.

Toby ducked back through the door and up the steps.

"I found them last night," Robin said apologetically. "I meant to tell you and then I went to sleep."

Toby shrugged. He was thinking that four months of siege had made the Arlatians a strong team; all the bureaucracy and falsity was stripped away. They could move quickly.

Back in the main solar, the Red Knight was out of the chair and toweling his face; the Hillman, MacGilly, had the emperor's clean hose over one arm and his doublet over another. Cully had his boots and a sword belt, but he set them on a stool when Toby motioned him to the door. The Duchess of Venike was sitting on the fireside stool, crouched forward over the chart with Ser Pavalo, Kronmir, and Sauce. Anne was very carefully oiling the razors she had used.

"Toby," Gabriel said over the chart. "Great hall if we may use it, the duchess herself if she is willing, fifteen minutes."

"Done," said Toby with infinite satisfaction.

He watched Ser Gabriel's face register this.

"Attend me yourself," Gabriel said. "Sauce? Duchess? Kronmir and Paval; Michael. Blanche?"

"Military?" Blanche asked.

"Yes," he answered.

Blanche leaned out of the bedroom. "May I decline?" she asked.

"I don't have Sukey and I don't have Nicodemus," Gabriel said.

"Damn. I'll come," Blanche said. "Where's Sukey?"

"Saving the world," the emperor snapped. "Like everyone else."

Kaitlin took Anne's arm and looked at Gabriel.

"Yes," Gabriel said, freeing his best page to help his wife dress.

Cully came through the solar door with an incongruous armload of women's linens. Lady Meliagraund was framed briefly in the doorway, a look of unfeigned pleasure on her face.

Kaitlin shrieked, took the whole pile, and dove through the bedroom door.

Cully looked smug. He and Sauce shared a look, and both laughed.

The Duchess of Venike looked back and forth. "What is so funny?" she asked.

Sauce shrugged. "When I was a whore, Cully was our bouncer. He used to hate bringing us our laundry, right, Cully?"

Gabriel smiled and put an arm into a tightly cut sleeve.

Silence fell; absolute silence.

The Duchess of Venike leaned back and roared. She slapped her booted thigh. "Well," she said. "It's good to know we all had busy lives before we met."

"Isn't it?" asked Sauce with a wicked grin.

The duchess shrugged. "I was going to be a whore, but I killed someone."

"I did the same in reverse," Sauce said. "I was a whore, and *then* I killed someone."

Pavalo Payam was blushing through his beard.

Toby stepped in and began lacing the emperor's skin-tight silk doublet.

Gabriel was leaning slightly over the chart on the table. "We need to find Du Corse," he said.

Kronmir nodded. "If he is still in the game—" he said.

"Exactly!" Gabriel replied. "I suppose you'd tell me if you'd located the Necromancer," he said.

Kronmir shot him a look.

Toby began to lace a sleeve.

Cully picked up a boot and rubbed his elbow across the leather and made a face.

"MacGilly, we'll want small beer, this bowl of fruit, and perhaps some bread while we take counsel," Gabriel said.

The Hillman stood, apparently appalled that the emperor had spoken to him by name.

Michael took a piece of Mortimir's apple, cut it in half, gave half to the Duchess of Venike, and went over to help Toby. "You getting shafted here?" Michael asked. He was the former squire.

"Mightily," Gabriel said.

Michael nodded. "I'll help and so will Kaitlin."

"Almost there," said Toby. He took the overdoublet with hanging sleeves and held it up while the emperor laced his own braes to his doublet. There are things a man has to do for himself.

"I'd take a bite of apple," Gabriel said.

Mortimir cut him a slice, took out the seeds, and put it directly into Gabriel's mouth as his hands were otherwise occupied.

"I think I have found the Necromancer," the mage said, as if it was a matter of little consequence.

Every head turned.

Mortimir was a tall, gawky, difficult seventeen-year-old prodigy. He shrugged. "I knew he wouldn't cast. So I looked for someone not casting."

"How?" Gabriel asked.

"Must I?" Mortimir asked. "I feel like a performing seal."

"Humour me," Gabriel said.

The mage shrugged. "He is as mighty a practitioner as Harmodius or I. Mightier. When he casts, he no doubt uses the natural waves of *ops* that flow over the world and through the earth. Yes?"

Gabriel nodded.

"But *the guilty flee where no man pursueth*," Mortimir said. "He must be aware of his use of the waves of *ops* both here and in the *aethereal*. So all I had to do was look for places that were *too* still. Normal places have a steady ebb and flow of *ops*. Like a breeze. I found a place where there's no movement of *ops* at all, in the real or in the *aethereal*."

"Because?" Gabriel asked.

Mortimir sighed in exasperation and even rolled his eyes. "Because he's dampening the flow to hide himself!" he said, as if this explained everything.

Gabriel nodded. "So...you...found him."

Mortimir made a moue. "To be accurate, I found a place where these conditions pertain. I'd have to go there to flush him into the open. And he might eat me if I did. We took him by surprise, night before last. We won't surprise him again."

"May I ask you to speculate how he evaded us in the first place?" Gabriel asked.

Michael was settling his former master's collar. "Is he still a threat, shorn of all his not-dead?"

Mortirmir shrugged. "I have no idea. I'm going to guess that he wasn't here with his not-dead; he was on his way to face us in the real. Over by the mountains. But honestly? I have no idea."

Gabriel nodded. "We have no idea about most things, Michael. Until two days ago, he was one of the major players in the Game of Gates. I think we need to finish him."

Payam nodded from the chart. "Exactly what I came here to say. And to be honest, lord, to my master and *my* people, the destruction of the Necromancer was always the first priority."

"Whereas to my husband and my people," the Duchess of Venike said from the other side of the map, "it is the new Patriarch of Rhum who is the threat."

"And that, my friends, is why we are meeting in five minutes in the great hall," Gabriel said. He was fully dressed: red silk hose, red silk doublet, red silk overdoublet with the imperial eagle embroidered in red silk thread. Toby put his golden plaque belt around his hips and Cully put a dagger on one side and an arming sword on the other, but Gabriel shook off the arming sword.

"War sword," he said.

Cully fetched it and buckled it on while Gabriel drank down a full cup of hippocras.

Blanche emerged from the bedroom in a gold silk overgown over a skin-tight midnight blue kirtle with gold trim that matched her hair. She, too, wore a knight's belt of gold plaques. She had a white silk veil on her hair and a very simple circlet, also of gold, and Michael got the Red Knight's hat, or rather, the emperor's, a red wool bycocket with the Red Knight's pentagram and a gold circlet and a purple-crimson ostrich plume that stood up two feet over his head.

Toby handed him white leather gloves, which he put on.

Blanche curtsied to him, and he bowed to her, and together they swept through the solar, through the outer study, where Master Julius and his two secretaries rose and bowed before going back to an endless series of orders and passports. Gabriel paused and leaned very close to Master Julius's ear and whispered.

The former notary glowed with pleasure. "An hour," he said. "Two if you want the message to your brother to go out on schedule."

"Do that. I can give you … four hours," the emperor said, calculating quickly. "Toby, I will *not* need you to attend me. Stay here and take a breath." He smiled, and Toby smiled back.

The emperor took his wife's hand and slipped through the door, followed in order of precedence by the duchess, Ser Michael, Pavalo, Sauce, and Kronmir, and then Kaitlin, now dressed in linens and still lacing her kirtle, and MacGilly, who, for his sins, had all the *dirty* linens to take to the laundry.

Anne went to the sideboard, picked up her cold cider, and drank it off.

Toby was staring into space.

"We lived," Anne said. The solar was empty but for the two of them.

Toby sighed. "I should be attending him," he said.

"Let him stew a minute," she said, and poured him some hot cider.

Toby sat where the emperor had sat to be shaved, crossed his legs, and drank his cider. He ate a piece of fruit.

Then he froze. "Damn MacGilly!"

He said, leapt up, took the bowl of fruit, and headed for the great hall.

Anne was left alone. She sighed for another missed opportunity, and started cleaning the room.

The Adnacrags

Nita Qwan sat comfortably, his back against a tall spruce, and smoked, and missed his wife. He passed the pipe, which had a bitter tang, to young Ser Aneas. Nita Qwan had had a day in which to get to know the youngest Muriens, and the man reminded him powerfully of someone, but Nita Qwan couldn't quite put the arrow in the target.

It didn't matter.

Aneas was using his small baton to build an image of the Adnacrags and the plains beyond, where the mountains sloped down into the basin of the Inland Seas and their two great outflow rivers. To the east, the river flowed north and east out of the Inland Seas and into the ocean. To the west, the great Meridi, or central river, flowed almost due south into the unknown, watering lands no man had ever seen, even Outwallers; where the great hives of bogglins and the deep swamps full of hastenoch and the hills were the exclusive preserve of the trolls. Or so it was said by the irks.

Aneas's model didn't include any of that. He limited himself to the edge of the Adnacrags, and the plains that ran down to the River, from the Cranberry Lake, which Outwallers called Wgotche, and into which the Woodhull flowed from the south. The Cranberry flowed south in a larger river, the Cranberry or Wgotche, which flowed into the river from the south, to the rocks and islets that filled the end of the Inland Sea, the Mille Isles opposite Napana, which lay in ruins.

"Thorn was learning strategy," Aneas said. He pointed at the dot that marked the former Outwaller town of Napana. "By destroying Napana, he divided us from the Outwallers. Your people from my people."

Nita Qwan glanced at his mentor, the old hunter Ta-se-ho. "Many among my people would be deeply happy to be separated from yours, Lord of Ticondonaga." He shrugged. "I mean no quarrel. But you are lords of the wall, and we are the peoples who live outside the wall."

"Allies," Aneas said.

Nita Qwan nodded. "But not subjects."

Aneas looked affronted. Ta-se-ho passed the pipe and shook his head. "Nita Qwan says what the matrons have charged him to say. And the destruction of Napana is worse than you say; in the first rustle of spring, our people fled west to Mogon. The Squash Country is empty."

Aneas was looking at his map. "Imagine that Orley is somewhere here," he said, pointing to the banks of the Great River between Cranberry River and the Rocks. "He must be. And trying to move his new army and his old adherents across the sweet water into the Squash Country."

Ta-se-ho nodded.

Nita Qwan nodded.

Looks-at-Clouds, the changeling shaman, squatted bonelessly. Behind her, the camp was coming down. Where, just days before, Aneas had a hand of rangers on what seemed a hopeless pursuit, now he had hundreds; all woodsmen; Jacks and foresters and some long hunters; irks, some bogglins, and a powerful band of Sossag warriors, the victors of two great battles in the Wild. And Slythenhag and her brood, a hand of wyverns; and young Lilly, a two-year-old Golden Bear, with two males, Darkroot and Berrydrunk. By the standards of war in the Adnacrags it was a mighty host, and the tireless wyverns brought supplies while the Outwallers built canoes, fragile bark craft to pass the Cranberry River.

"At the inn, I heard tell of Galles on the Great River," Ta-se-ho said, and Nita Qwan nodded.

Aneas shook his head. "We can't face Orley *and* Gallish knights," he said.

Nita Qwan, who had sat at the great council, rocked forward. "They may not be enemies," he said. "There are new councils. The King of Galle is dead. The Sieur Du Corse is an ally, not an enemy, or so we were told at the inn." He shrugged, because the affairs of Antica Terra were as unreal to him as legends of the past. Except that legends of the past were rising every day to face him.

"And Gavin is already fighting in the south," Aneas said. "Gabriel is in the Antica Terra. We are the sideshow of a sideshow."

Looks-at-Clouds glanced at him. "An arrow will kill you just as dead," s/he said.

He smiled. "Good point," he admitted.

Gas-a-ho had sat silently, staring into the smoke of the dying fire for many minutes, but now he spoke. "We are not forgotten," he said. "Listen. Plague, fire, and war. The alliance is together not for glory but to maintain the gates. Master Smythe fears that there is a gate in the north; we at the council dreamed together, and solved nothing."

Looks-at-Clouds glanced at her fellow shaman. "Lake-on-the-Mountain?" s/he asked.

Everyone at the fire knew the place, although more recently, men had called it "Thorn's Island." A place of immense power, at the meeting of two of the greatest channels of *ops*, a sacred place to the Outwallers and irks alike.

Skas-a-gao shrugged. Ta-se-ho handed him the pipe. He drew deeply. "I was there as a boy, when I chose the way of the seer," he said. "I feel that I would have known if there was a gate. But perhaps not."

"So we must win the race to Lake-on-the-Mountain," Aneas said.

Ta-se-ho raised an eyebrow.

Aneas nodded. "Yes, yes," he said. "We must win the race while remaining aware that mayhap that is not the goal at all." He looked around at them. "But it will be a bold stroke, and mayhap it will be like one of those strokes in a sword fight that steals time from the enemy. Make Orley dance to our tune."

Looks-at-Clouds wore an odd expression. "Even if the enemy has other plans," s/he said, "the seizure of Lake-on-the-Mountain would rally the Outwallers and provide us with a base and access to power."

"Beware so much power," Skas-a-gao said.

Looks-at-Clouds shrugged. "Always our people are wary, like small animals in the woods where every rock hides a wolf. I wish to be a wolf."

Skas-a-gao winced. "That is not the way of the shaman," he said.

"Maybe it is time to change," Looks-at-Clouds said. "I am a changeling. I bring change. The wise adapt."

Aneas cleared his throat. "Friends," he said cautiously.

Nita Qwan rallied to him immediately. "Beware the quarrels of shamans," he said lightly. "Usually caused by a shortage of pipe weed."

"How long until the canoes are complete?" Aneas asked.

"Tomorrow, midday, if the sun is hot," Ta-se-ho said.

"And we have more supplies coming today," Gas-a-ho said.

Looks-at-Clouds nodded to Aneas. "Will you send Irene home?" s/he asked.

Aneas shook his head. "I have not decided."

Looks-at-Clouds nodded. "Keep her, is my rede. She wishes to be a hero. She belongs here, with us, who are heroes."

Aneas smiled. His smile widened to a grin. "Sometimes you say the best things," he whispered.

"Yes," s/he said. "I bring change. I revel in it. And sometimes, it is necessary. We may all die in horror. But if we triumph, I see her as... something wonderful."

"The thing in her head..." Aneas raised an eyebrow.

Looks-at-Clouds made a face; almost the face of an adolescent girl. "I look at it every day. I almost have the secret of its unmaking. Give me time."

"You are in love with her," Aneas snapped.

"We share that, do we not?" Looks-at-Clouds snapped back.

Gas-a-ho laughed. "Perhaps I will cut her in half for you," he said.

Both of them looked at the shaman, who shrugged.

Ta-se-ho banged the pipe out against his moccasined heel. He was smiling, but he added no words.

"Let's get to work," said Aneas.

Two hours later, there was an enormous disturbance on the flow of *ops*. Looks-at-Clouds, Aneas, and Gas-a-ho all detected it; so did their two university-trained mages, young Moreans who never stopped slapping at the endless midges and mosquitoes. The magisters all came together at the council fire. The various Jacks, rangers, foresters and Outwallers stopped working on boats and sprang to arms. As the camp was well sited, on a long peninsula running far out into Cranberry Lake, the only approaches were across open water and along the base of the peninsula, which was less than ten horses wide at its narrowest. The Outwallers had built a brush wall; the rangers had added a breastwork of downed trees.

Beyond the rough walls had been a mighty stand of old birch trees—white birches in the prime of life. Ta-se-ho had offered tobacco to their spirits and chose fifteen of them to become boats, and the rest left standing, but the result, which Aneas had intended, of a day's work there was to create a wide swathe of open ground beyond the narrowing of the isthmus. Three hundred men and irks with axes and saws could clear ground faster than beavers, and the peninsula was, by the standard of wilderness war, impregnable.

Now the rampart was manned, the two rocky beaches covered, and the skies watched. Slythenhag leapt into the air with her brood, and they wheeled away north and south, watching.

Slythenhag gave a great, long call of warning.

Aneas shook his head. He was standing, bow in hand, by the council fire. His small baton was in his hand. "It's like watching a volcano," he said. "And yet, everything slides off it."

Looks-at-Clouds was raising shields. "It is the enemy," she said, and for the first time, he heard a crack in the changeling's voice. S/he was afraid.

Aneas continued to search in the *aethereal. He went into his memory forest, where a huge maple tree dominated a little meadow of pine needles and sparse grass. A pool lay in the shade, with a burbling spring. He often stood on the rock at the head of the pool to cast, but today he watched the pool.*

Irene came out of the woods with a light axe in her hands. She was covered in sweat, had twigs in her hair, and wore a short, heavy blade at her belt. Ricar Lantorn was just behind her, and Heron, the Huran war leader, his woods shirt dark with sweat.

She smiled at both of them.

Aneas was far away, watching his pool in the *aether* but that smile snapped him back.

Looks-at-Clouds shook hir head. "Don't go into the *aethereal*. It is huge. And hunting us."

Aneas looked at Irene.

She shrugged. "Nita Qwan ordered us back here."

Lantorn was looking out across Cranberry Lake, like fifty other woods' warriors.

"Nothin' out there," he said.

Heron was silent, but his nose wrinkled, and he took an arrow from his quiver.

"Except me," said Master Smythe. He walked out of the same woods that Irene had appeared from, and bowed his superhuman bow. "I am sorry, but I have to move very carefully these days. Ash is hunting me, and I am vulnerable out here."

Skas-a-gao embraced the tall "man." "We are honoured to have you at our fire," he said.

Master Smythe grinned wryly. "Slythenhag isn't so sure, but she'll come around."

"How did you come here?" Aneas asked. He was somewhat awed and, like a young man, trying to hide it.

"The usual way. I flew. In the real." Master Smythe smiled. "You look more like your brother Gabriel every day. What an extraordinary family you all are. Despite everything. He smiled. "Or is it because of everything that you are so extraordinary?"

He looked around, and his gaze fell on Irene. "Ah," he said. "Greetings, Princess of Empire."

"You are the dragon," she said.

"More precisely, I am *a* dragon," he said. "Calling me 'the' dragon would be like my calling you 'the patricide.'"

Irene flushed. Her hand went to the heavy sword in her belt.

"You know," the dragon said companionably, "I counseled your removal. Permanently. Gabriel chose another way. And I find his way better. This gives me great hope. In fact, in a backwards way, Irene, you represent the greatest hope of the alliance."

Irene's flush mounted. "Why?" she asked. She hated to be baited.

Master Smythe shrugged. "I am a dragon; I am thousands of years old, deep in cunning, matchless in guile. The organism of my brain weighs more than two human beings. And yet, Gabriel was right, and I was wrong. Think on it, friends. Our enemy ought to be unassailable in his *puissance*. Why is it that any of us can outthink him?"

Silence.

Master Smythe shrugged. "Well, I don't know, either, and it is more entertaining to ponder than moral relativism. In the more immediate reality of the now, I have brought you a truly stupendous cargo of supplies, and I wish to add that I believe this marks the very first time that one of my race has condescended to serve as a beast of burden."

Looks-at-Clouds smiled. "Do you always speak this way?" s/he asked in High Archaic.

The man's overly smooth brow furrowed. "Is there another way to speak?" he asked.

Aneas felt a pang of jealousy. Looks-at-Clouds regarded the dragon with something like awe.

He returned hir regard. "You are a remarkable being," he said.

"Yes," Looks-at-Clouds returned. "As are you."

Aneas cleared his throat.

Master Smythe had the good grace to look faintly embarrassed. "What a delightful triangle you three make," he said. "It is like fate. I will not interfere, but..."

And then the sky split open.

For a moment, an eternal moment, there was a tear in the fabric of the heavens. Aneas saw stars, and a deeper black than any night; there was a dazzle before his eyes as if he'd stared into the sun.

A dragon emerged from the rift. It was longer than a ship, bigger than a castle. Its emergence from the blackness defied perceptions of reality. Men screamed, or hid their faces.

"Damn," said Master Smythe.

Looks-at-Clouds cast, cast, and cast. Aneas, in excellent training after two weeks of near constant combat, matched the changling working for working.

Master Smythe vanished.

Ash dove.

Heron loosed the arrow off his bow, and a thicket of bolts and arrows rose to meet the dragon.

Contemptuously, he breathed, and his breath eliminated every shaft aimed at him. They simply *were not*.

The dragon cast, or worked—the action, in the *aethereal*, was too reflexive to merit the term *working*—and Looks-at-Clouds's glowing green prism was extinguished. S/he fell to the ground, but Skas-a-gao stood over hir and raised a working of a type Aneas had never seen, a shield, or a net, that appeared as the shadows of leaves cast by the sun. It was fractal, fabulously complex, it had a logic of its own, and the dragon's second assault entered it...

...and could not leave. Inside his own fortress, Skas-a-gao feverishly raised the golden wall of indomitable will that Desiderata had taught them all at the Inn of Dorling, and from its foundations he elaborated his forest trap of light and darkness, and it held.

Aneas was still working. He observed, but not in any detail. And he loosed a dozen illusions; himself, Irene, Looks-at-Clouds. They began to turn and run, spreading out; he continued to work. Deep in the forest of his palace, he placed pebbles on other pebbles, altered a tiny watercourse, summoned a fish from the mere.

Ash. It is Ash.

He laced his illusions with the flavour of his hatred for Kevin Orley.

He put a complex shield of his own devising over the simulacrum of Irene.

He was peripherally aware that all of them were only alive because Ash was searching frantically for Lot. Who was Master Smythe.

Another gout of dragon breath smashed against their shields. Men died. Irks died. Bogglins died.

Another forest of shafts rose into the heavens and were banished.

Ash reached out, and cast a simple scent. In a single heartbeat, most of the bogglins fell subject to his will. Ash relished their betrayal and sent them against their friends.

Ricar Lantorn drew his heavy bow. It was not his; it had been Wilful Murder's bow and he had not yet shot it. It was the heaviest bow he'd ever pulled.

Mark my words.

Lantorn got the nock of the heavy arrow to the very out-curl of his lip and loosed, almost straight up, with a grunt of real pain. His arrow was out of time with the last two volleys. It escaped the dragon's massive counterspell and slipped past his breath and struck in the enormous beast's side, smaller than a blackfly bite on a man.

But it was the first damage they'd done to the behemoth.

Ash turned.

Aneas's working came to its completion. It bore every mark of a son of Gause: labyrinthine, deep and a little musty and very dark. And it carried everything he had. And it was a titanic risk; he left himself neither defence nor reserve.

Amid the lean-tos and wigwams of their encampment, dozens of hornets and wasps were seized in mid-career. Most were chasing the innumerable flies and eating them, but suddenly their wills were suborned, and they chose a higher prey. Mighty predators of the insect world, they knew no fear, and they rose into the air, searching their new prey, drawn by his signature across the sky.

Looks-at-Clouds raised hir head, snapped the fingers on a hand, and cast. A simple bolt of lightning followed the turning dragon, and struck home. Ash turned again, trading altitude for speed in his anger.

A second dragon appeared in the sky.

Ash became aware of the second dragon rising to meet him from the south and he turned *again*.

The wyverns began to gather to the north.

Ash breathed, and the other dragon breathed, and where their breath met, a three-dimensional curtain of brilliant light framed them.

Unafraid, the white-faced hornets rose into the sky; a dozen died at the interface of the two contenders' clouds of power, another dozen were lost in a cyclonic vortex when Ash's tail whipped at incredible speed across the sky.

The rest continued.

Aneas reached into the *aethereal* and spoke the key to his working in Archaic. "*He watches even the sparrow's fall.*"

In the real, Ash beat his wings strongly. He was black, but the scales along his neck and belly were gold and seemed to glow; his eyes were a jewel-like green, his tail so long that it appeared to follow him through the sky like a second beast, a serpent, and there was a sting at the end.

Lot, or Master Smythe, was smaller, and his as-yet-unhealed wing was protected in a web of fire and light. He was green, his scales tipped in gold, his snout longer and more sinuous, his tail shorter. He turned inside his larger adversary's turn; Ash was too low and too slow to be evasive, and the very end of Lot's exhalation of fire and *potentia* crossed Ash's spectacular tail and severed it, so that the lashing serpent fell away into the lake; a huge gout of steam rose even as the waters parted, and there was a flash like an explosion. The dragons were so close to the ground that their wingbeats knocked branches out of trees and their breath ignited fires where the mages' shields didn't cover the vegetation.

Ash forced himself up, his titanic wings beating against the thickness of the air. Above him, the open gate into the darkness beyond the *aethereal* towered above everything, and every creature on the battlefield of the real felt a tug of horror, of disbelief, of impossibility, yet where Lot's exhalation crossed the void, it was healed and reality seemed to grow like a scar forming across a wound.

The white-face hornets hit Ash.

But Ash was no novice. The layers of his wards were as deep as the armour of his layers of scales; integral, in fact. The first hornets found nothing to bite; they slid off his impervious shields and their clever, subtle workings were wasted even as Ash was forced to notice the nature of the working cast against him.

Even in a life-or-death struggle with Lot, he took the time in his immeasurable *aethereal* self to master a pair of the hornets and turn them, subtly enhancing, conquering their tiny wills, subverting Aneas's working, sending them back against their caster. He didn't trouble to learn their purpose; he merely turned those he could reach.

In the same moment he located Irene by the egg inside her soul and he passed her by, found another tiny foe and his dried-blood lightning flew, but to his disgust he crushed, not a man, but an illusion of a man.

Ash had become too entangled; Lot sprayed him with *potentia*. He was below, too close, perhaps aware of his vulnerability, perhaps as desperate to close the void as to defeat Ash.

Ash was hurt. But he bided his time, and in the real, one vast taloned foreclaw licked out like a knife the size of a tree, except that like a Fell Sword, Ash's claw existed in both real and *aethereal*. In one blow he severed Lot's wing of fire, and then, closing, almost lovingly, his other foreclaw ripped Lot's other wing from his vast body and the broken green dragon fell away between his claws, and Ash laughed despite the black smoke rising from his underside where Lot's breath had carved along the same scar that Tom Lachlan had made and Ricar Lantorn had struck with an arrow and Kerak had gouged with primal fire.

Lot screamed, in the real and the *aethereal*.

Four white-faced hornets, now the size of falcons, sped down through the hermetical shields of four mages and began to hunt Aneas and Gas-a-ho and Looks-at-Clouds.

The last of Aneas's hornets survived being crushed by Lot's enormity and slipped into the space between the two dragons, tracking its prey, ignored because of proximity to the other dragon, and by luck or fate or *fortuna* struck amid the damage wrought by Lot's breath and bit deeply into the still-bubbling flesh. The bite of the insect was nothing; the channel for Aneas's spell of corruption, as dark as his mother's heart, was perfect, the more so as the insect struck against a wound.

Ash was aware of the burst of *ops*, but such was the background of power that he paid the blow little attention, instead tracking his counterattack to the ground. Ash *loved* the use of an enemy's work against him; he reveled in the sheer superiority of such an attack.

Lot fell into the lake.

Tons of water were thrown into the air.

Men and irks were unable to respond. Most men and women were lying flat in the leaf mold, overwhelmed by the sound, the fire, the gouts of *ops* from rival alternatives of reality, the fires ignited by the heat and whipped to an inferno by the huge wingbeats at low altitude. The mass of water thrown into the air by Lot's fall then collapsed back in turn, falling on the peninsula and the surrounding forest, knocking anyone standing flat or sweeping them against the ground or grinding them against rocks like a sudden spring torrent. Ricar Lantorn lost Wilful Murder's bow, ripped from his hands as a tidal wave swept away the encampment, taking every scrap of canvas and food. Irene found herself locked in Aneas's arms, wedged against the cross of a pair of ancient fallen tree trunks, and Looks-at-Clouds held strong and continued to work, reading Ash's casting even as it emerged from him and working a counter almost instantly in the *aethereal*, an act as subtle and difficult as reacting instantly to a sneering jibe in a crowded room.

Cleverly, elegantly, s/he used hir own powers, and even as the waters hammered them and swept by, the reaching cloud of the changeling's will gathered the surviving houseflies that had troubled the camp and drew them in a frothing sphere across the path of the giant hornets who turned, wings beating frantically, engorged heads bobbing, as nature fought subversion in their uncomplicated nerves.

One turned away and followed the flies. The others slowed, lost their focus, and then rediscovered their prey and attacked.

One dove for the three lying in the cross of downed trees.

Aneas had no time to think. He pulled the pipe axe from his belt, rose from his knees to a standing posture, and threw.

Ash's wings beat.

Time seemed to slow to a crawl.

Looks-at-Clouds's fingers made a web of light—a dreamcatcher of cobwebs stolen from the sun.

The throwing axe struck the insect. The shaft struck first, a glancing blow, but the impact cracked the thing's head and moved it off its course, and it struck a tree and fell to the ground, made a terrible noise as its wings beat furiously against the mud...

Ash began to feel the effect of Aneas's spell. Every *iota* of the great monster's concentration was shattered as the whole of his great, multi-faceted mind attempted to comprehend the damage he'd taken. And like any massive predator experiencing peril, he fled.

The rent in reality had never left the sky, but Lot's workings had caused it to begin to close, or heal. Now, with two enormous wingbeats, Ash cast himself back through it into the looming outer darkness.

There was a scream, or a roar; a sound so immense it was pain, making and unmaking, and despite it, Looks-at-Clouds stood and raised both hands, the labyrinthine complexity of the dreamcatcher pattern increasing with every heartbeat, and a mighty heart of light pulsing between the patterns.

Ash's truncated tail passed through the gaping hole in reality, and Looks-at-Clouds was clearly struggling to master something incredibly powerful. Even as Ricar Lantorn cut at the downed hornet with his cutlass; even as Irene, freed from Aneas's weight, struck the monstrous insect with the axe still in her hand; and even as Gas-a-ho effortlessly blew the third hornet into a messy rain of syrup, Aneas *reached through the* aethereal *to Looks-at-Clouds. He could feel the shaman struggling*

71

under the weight of the potentia; *he guessed that s/he was trying to close the gate behind Ash lest he return.*

Looks-at-Clouds's casting palace was unlike any he'd ever seen: fluid, organic, like an animal seen from inside instead of outside. Nor did s/he stand or sit, an avatar of self; it was as if he was directly inside the changeling's mind and s/he had no avatar. But even in the aethereal *there was no time to savour this, or be appalled or frightened. He followed the direction of the changeling's thought to the surface of a pool of… intention, and rose through it, the metaphor flowing into the reality.*

Looks-at-Clouds was indeed struggling to close the gaping tear in the sky.

Something was helping, but despite it all, s/he was inarticulate. The ops *required a trigger and an expression of will.*

Almost unbidden, the thought formed in Aneas's mind, and his palace expressed it, and Looks-at-Clouds's eyes snapped open, and in hir flawless High Archaic s/he said:

"En arche en ho LOGOS."

And the sky was healed. The rift was *not*. Irene's axe pulped the hornet's head.

Silence fell.

The sheer shock of the combat lasted some minutes, and yet, for whatever reason, Aneas's mind was clear enough, and he retrieved his fallen throwing axe even as Ricar Lantorn retrieved Wilful Murder's red-painted bow floating in the wrack of the dragon's fall. Men began to move; some unaffected, others unable to speak. A woman cried; another woman saw a man drowning, unconscious in the water, and saved him.

Bogglins who had, moments before, turned on their companions now dropped their weapons, sickened. Some were slaughtered. Some fled into the forest.

It was chaos, and Aneas rode above it. He was trying to imagine what the death of Master Smythe would mean; he was trying to see through the thicket of problems besetting him to imagine his next step.

Nita Qwan and Gas-a-ho were already on their feet. Ta-se-ho was slower, sitting holding his head.

All over the peninsula, people discovered that others were injured, or dead.

Aneas put his wet horn to his lips and blew. The first sounding might have been the call of a sick moose, but the second roared, and heads turned.

"Look sharp," he said. "Change bowstrings! Prepare for an attack." He roared these words so loudly that his throat hurt, but people moved. They were so shocked that none argued. Aneas ran from point to point. He rescued a knot of bogglins, but had them disarmed; he found the old bogglin, Krek.

"They are young," Krek said. "They cannot...understand. That the scent is not...legal." He rustled his wing-cases and his four mandibles clashed. A pair of royal foresters watched him, arrows on bows.

"Watch them. Slay *none*," Aneas snapped at the foresters, and ran on. He didn't see anything that could attack them, but he was painfully aware of how vulnerable they were.

In the next ten minutes, he learned that his camp was gone, irretrievably; the canvas washed into the lake in a tangle of rope; most of the dried food already ruined. Almost a hundred of his woodsmen were dead; some, their bodies flung grotesquely into trees to die impaled on branches stripped bare by the conflict, some drowned, some burned or simply missing, gone forever when the hermetical defences burned through.

"Why hasn't Orley attacked?" he asked Irene.

She was playing with a light crossbow, trying to see if that heavy string was wet through or still capable of dealing death. She met his eye. "He can't," she said. "If he could, he'd kill us all this instant. So, he can't."

"No boats," Ta-se-ho said with a nod.

Looks-at-Clouds shook hir head. "That was..." s/he breathed. The changeling's features had always been mobile, but now a series of expressions ran across hir face like an actor demonstrating emotion. "The enemy acted in the *aethereal* instantly. They *live* in the *aethereal*. The...dragons."

Gas-a-ho's forehead furrowed.

Dmitri, the taller of the Moreans, shook his head. He was maintaining a shield over them. "I do not understand," he said slowly.

Looks-at-Clouds glanced at him. "There was no plan. Our enemy is a great predator. His prey moved from cover, and he struck." S/he lowered hir head. "And triumphed." S/he shook hir head. "But he never enlisted Orley."

"But he will now," Aneas said.

"Damn," Lantorn said. "Of course he will."

Aneas could see it all. He'd never had such a feeling of absolute certainty before. He could see his plan, his enemy's intentions, his own response. He wondered if this was a product of shock; he wondered if this was how his brother felt and acted.

"Is Master Smythe dead?" he asked.

No one would meet his eye.

"Damn," he said. "Very well. Ta-se-ho, the canoes are the highest priority."

"We have no food," Irene said with devastating practicality.

"We will salvage some food. Dried peas become peas, in water. We think Orley is a day away, perhaps two? Will he turn and come back at us again, when we beat him the last time?"

"Yes," Lantorn said.

The other warriors agreed.

Aneas almost smiled. It was...like the moment in a fencing match when you *know* that your feint has succeeded. He should have been depressed, perhaps mourning the fallen dragon, but Master Smythe had been a name to him, and he saw a way to lead Orley to defeat, and it was all he could do not to grin.

"We are naked to the enemy if he returns," Looks-at-Clouds said.

"No matter what we do," Aneas agreed. "Perhaps we could hold him for a minute. Gas-a-ho, you have a working..."

Gas-a-ho was handling a charm around his neck. "Yes," he agreed. "Yes. Maybe longer. Maybe a really long time."

"Boats," Aneas said.

Ta-se-ho looked out over the bay of flotsam behind them. He shrugged. "Birchbark floats," he said. "Water does it no harm. Tomorrow, at nightfall."

Aneas nodded. "We need to salvage what we can, to bury the dead, to tell people we are not beaten."

Irene smiled. "We are not beaten?" she asked. "I like that. We are not beaten." Her eyes wandered over the wreckage and the dead, and Aneas wondered if he was being mocked.

Ta-se-ho smiled at her. "What makes men so dangerous is that we are too stupid to know when we are beaten."

Irene's look was as feral as a wolf's. "I know," she said.

Harndon

Harmodius was washing, a routine matter made complicated and even dangerous by circumstance, standing up to his hips in cold water with a borrowed bar of soap. Around him were seventy other naked and near naked men; some wearing their linens and washing them as well. Many had only just been delivered from the plague. Harndon was only just recovering. There were still women coughing, and men, and lines at the hospitals that ran down the Cheapside hill. But there were no longer so many that they needed a corps of crossbowmen to keep them from violence; the nuns of the Order of Saint Thomas were not threatened, and only the shortage of Umroth ivory prevented the outright defeat of the disease.

Harmodius felt the blow in the *aethereal* and he instantly raised a working and looked very carefully about him, passively, a little like a veteran warrior peering around his shield.

But the ripples were very far away in the real. In the *aethereal, the shades of green and gold had a darkened cast to them, and there was something…*

…Harmodius would have ducked, if hiding was really possible in the aethereal, *or flinching. He did so symbolically, hoping his outward sign would drive reality.*

There was something like a detonation and he was cast back into the real.

He stood, naked, in the Albin River, in the shadow of First Bridge by Harndon, and wished for a place to hide. But when the feeling passed, Harmodius dressed on the riverbank, visited his patients, and went to the castle.

Desiderata had spent less than a week in her capital. Already she was exhausted; already she remembered the heady days of tournament and battlefield as a time of joy. Since her hurried return downriver, she had held more than a dozen council meetings, and she had spent more time watching scribes write and seal parchments than she had spent with her child, who had vanished into the care of wet nurses she scarcely knew. Her foe, the archbishop, had done much to destroy the palace staff; she interviewed every servant and officer herself, with either Ser Gerald Random or Ser Ranald by her side.

The rooms were full of her husband, the king; the corridors reeked of her imprisonment, and the foundations of the castle tasted of Ash.

She found that she did not love Harndon, whose cheerful bustle and magnificent shipping had so pleased her when she first arrived as the beloved bride of the king.

Ricar Fitzroy, acting as the steward of her household, was with her almost every waking moment.

"It will pass," he said yet again.

She raised both eyebrows. "So you tell me." She gave a small shrug. "You were my first friend here, and I want you to be correct. And yet, right now, I hate this place."

Fitzroy tried not to gaze too long at her more-than-mortal beauty. So he looked out the window. They were in the throne room; in the brief interval between a formal meeting of the Small Council and an informal review with various guild heads of the commercial state of the city.

Fitzroy's eye went to a faded posy of wildflowers, hung by a ribbon.

He didn't move his eyes in time, and she saw it. "And it hasn't even been cleaned yet," she said.

"The staff are doing their best," Fitzroy said. "The guard are pitching in; Master Pye has sent some trustworthy people. My Queen, you must relax."

Desiderata smiled at him from her throne, but her eye caught on the brown stain at her feet, and she flinched. "He died here," she said, a hand at her throat. Then, rising, "I want to see my son."

"Madame, the guilds." Fitzroy wore armour all the time.

"If they kill my son, we are undone," Desiderata said. Then she sagged. "By our Lady, what a harridan I am becoming. Never mind, my dear knight."

A page came in, and handed Ser Ricard a note. Rebecca Almspend came in with a bowl of fruit, mostly new apples, and placed it on a waiting sideboard. "I miss Blanche," she said. "I suspect we never noticed how much work she was doing."

Desiderata smiled at the name. "And now she is empress," the queen said with quiet satisfaction. "She will keep him steady and true; the kingdom will have a stout friend there."

"My Queen, the Magister Harmodius requests audience." Fitzroy was already up, despite the weight of his harness, and moving.

"Immediately!" She clapped her hands. Lady Mary, once known as "Hard Heart," appeared and curtsied, and then went out and returned with the magister on her arm.

Harmodius went down on one knee. "My lady, the fighting in the north is..." He paused. "I feel I am needed there."

"You have word?" the queen asked.

Lady Mary put a hand to her mouth. After all, she was affianced to Ser Gavin Muriens, who was in command of the alliance in the north.

Harmodius shook his head. "No, my Queen. I merely feel the concussions in the *aethereal*."

"As do I," the queen admitted. "We are wasted here."

Harmodius saw it in a glance: the tawdry hall, the tapping foot, the pen knife and the litter of a dozen cut quills and some spilled sealing wax. He bowed again. "Lady Queen, I must disagree. Three thousand of your subjects would be dead today, or more, if you and I had not returned."

The queen put her chin in her hand, a most un-Desiderata-like pose. "I feel that I should leave Ser Gerald to rule as king, and perhaps take my place as Abbess at Lissen Carak," she said. "He makes every decision well; I wish to be at the battlefront."

"But your child?" asked Lady Mary softly.

"Already has nurses, and a tutor!" the queen spat. "A tutor! When the only thing he practices is sucking at my nipples!"

A few of her ladies gave little shrieks, but the queen's sense of humour was well established.

The queen smiled at Harmodius. "Magister, I do not mean to be difficult."

"Madam, you are the soul of courtesy," the magister said. "But I feel that the plague is passing; fifty pounds of Umroth ivory and we would be able to defeat it utterly. And the north..."

"We should go back north," the queen agreed.

"Your Grace," growled Ser Ricard.

"My guard are the best knights in Alba," the queen said. "My kingdom and my world are at risk. Why am I here?"

"Because we must to hold Harndon above all places," Ser Gerald said. "I am sorry to be the endless source of boredom and anxiety, Your Grace, but if Harndon falls, everything falls. The Red Knight..."

"Is the Red Knight your king?" Desiderata snapped.

"My Queen, that is unfair," Random snapped back.

"He wrote our orders, and we must obey him?" Desiderata asked.

Random glanced down. And then met her eyes. "Yes," he said.

"I am wasted here," Desiderata said. She sighed. "He takes too much upon himself, your Red Knight. Emperor or no emperor."

"Perhaps, Your Grace. And yet, my sense is that we have not yet been tested here." Random shrugged. "Harndon is not yet restored to its power, Your Grace."

Becca Almspend stood up beside Random. "I must agree, Your Grace," she said with a bob of a curtsy. "Harndon must be held, and I agree that we have not yet been attacked. We are weak; our strength is a tithe of what it would have been a year ago. Look at the creatures you have discovered working in the palace."

Desiderata sat back. She frowned, and then, in a moment, her face changed. She smiled, and a shaft of autumn sun fell across her and she seemed to light the room, and the warm honey brown of her hair was like a pool of gold, lit by the star that was the emerald in her plain coronet, and the light of her face poured on them.

"So be it," she said. "But if outward piety leads to inward sanctity, I will have the same in my hall." She summoned power, and in a single wave of her *puissance* banished roaches and rats, and the tawdry decorations of a lost Holy Week vanished in little puffs of incense-scented smoke.

"I should have done *that* when first I arrived," she said.

Harmodius bowed again. "Your Grace remains mistress in her own house," he said. "I still feel I am needed in the north."

"Go. Go well, my dear. Send us word. At a word from you, I will come with my little army and all my talents." She smiled and held out her hand, and he kissed it. "But first, let me offer counsel and receive it, too."

Harmodius bowed.

As he leaned close, she said, low and urgent, "He will try to kill you when you are alone, and outside our defences."

Harmodius looked up into the warmth of her eyes. "Madam, the dragons have begun to fall. I have wiles enough to save my hide, and if I have not"—he smiled grimly—"perhaps it is time to have it over."

"Master Smythe was ever our friend," she said.

"No," Harmodius said. "Just a foe in a friend's guise. But if I make my guess, all the disguises will come off now."

She turned pale.

"And you wish my counsel, ma'am?" he asked.

"Lady Jane," Desiderata spat. "My husband's paramour. Is pregnant."

Harmodius shrugged.

Desiderata narrowed her eyes. "I cured him of his sister's curse so that he could..." She paused.

Harmodius nodded. "It is nothing to you, my lady. Give her gifts and send her home to her family and offer to have her son or daughter at court when of age."

Desiderata looked at him. "Just that?"

Harmodius looked over at Random, who looked away, and at Rebecca Almspend, soon to be Rebecca Lachlan, who raised an eyebrow as if to say, *She's all yours.*

Harmodius knelt and put his hands between hers, like any man swearing his allegiance. "Most High Lady," he said in Archaic. "You feel that she attacked you. But this is a child or a very young woman, who only did as any young person is inclined. Let her go; give her reason to thank you for it." He lowered his voice so that she heard him only in the *aethereal.*

You are no common woman. Revenge is for the weak. This is unlike you.

And she cried out, *I am alone! And what if they raise this bastard against my Constantine?*

Harmodius shrugged. *Take the advice of an old fool. She is no threat. Make her your friend, and her son your son's friend.*

In the real, she leaned forward. "You were ever the best of counselors," she said, and kissed his brow.

Harmodius came down from the old corner tower that lurked over the moat, leaning slightly as if it was ready to fall. He came down the long widening steps in the turret, and in the courtyard, a pair of grooms held a superb riding horse, a magnificent bay already saddled and bridled, with a pair of leather satchels tied behind.

He had a strong feeling of *déjà vu*; a sense that he was not acting entirely on his own volition; a surprisingly strong memory of walking down these same stairs and out this same door to what seemed like the same horse. Had that been two years ago, or twenty? And since he had subsumed Richard Plangere, he had all the dead man's memories; a dozen other days of going out from this very gate to ride.

He paused to ponder whether, if he had all the man's memories, the man was actually dead. What life and death actually meant.

Very little.

Perhaps the religious had it right, after all.

Life and death. Gold and green. Names men gave to things they didn't really understand.

He needed to spend the time to unpack Plangere. The memories hung there, the side product of his *sublimation*. Or perhaps the memories were the point and the accession of power was the side product.

Harmodius considered these things while a groom put a mounting block in front of him and while the magister bowed, thanked the men, and mounted. He had a six-day ride in front of him; time to work through many things he had ignored.

He paused, still inside the incredibly puissant wards of the walls of the castle, and raised his own defences. In the fastness of his mind, he checked the construction and colour of every great golden stone in his mind-shield; a talent he'd practiced every day with the queen, whose mind was indeed impregnable. But over that he layered screens that would deceive and a series of illusions and even a pair of surprises for an attacker, Harmodius's first serious dabbling in the *ars magika* that the university was suddenly peddling.

It is like a rebirth, Harmodius thought. *A renaissance of hermeticism in my lifetime, coincidentally timed when we, the mortals, most need it.*

Then he checked the sword at his side and the buckler at his saddle bow. Because one indisputable difference from his last riding forth from this gate was that he was in a different body, a younger, stronger body that craved sex and exercise.

Bold enough, he thought, *but not bold enough to tell the queen that I need to leave before I throw myself on her.* He smiled at himself, and the force of his lust, and her kiss burning on his brow, and shook his head, because his head was old enough to mock the pretensions of his young body, and also to be amused at its ability to overpower the wise old head.

He thought of a love-spell of his youth. *My pleasure is my power to please my love. My power is my pleasure in my power.*

"Idiot," he said fondly. And put his heels to his mount's well-trained flanks.

He rode down the castle mount and into the East Cheaping, past the ruins of the Episcopal Palace and the neighborhoods devastated by fire. Because of his work with the poor, especially on healing the plague, men and women knew him, and so, unlike his solitary riding forth two years before, he rode slowly, his way clogged by many friends.

Because of this, and by coincidence, he was crossing the open market before First Bridge when the first of the antlered men sprinted into the market.

There were perhaps two thousand men and women in the market, and a hundred farmers had wagons or carts; sometimes merely a boy with a sack of onions or a young girl with ten round cabbages on her head. There were no merchants in the river; every hulk that could shoulder the seas had been pressed for military service.

He felt the darkness, and the antlered men found him utterly prepared.

They knew him, as well. Two of them sprinted straight at him.

He was confident enough in his layers of defences, active and passive, to spend a timeless interval *looking* at them.

And he saw.

He breathed, and in breathing he summoned power, and there he was *in his palace, and he made himself ten magisters; and each Harmodius went to a different task and target. Two made bottles of hermetical power, drawing* ops *from his breathing and spinning off the containers like magikal glass-blowers, and a third took the constructs in hermetical claws and arranged them; three more did exactly the same task, arranging* ops *and making it to be fire. Because all things are fire and from fire cometh all things, Harmodius thought in the sanctity of his mind, and watched his ten twinned selves process a flow of* ops *that even a year before he could not have found, much less made real.*

A ruddy, stag-headed man, his oversized genitals and massive pectoral muscles a caricature of power, pushed past a farmer's wife and she drew breath to scream.

There were seventeen of them.

Harmodius raised his right hand, although the gesture was scarcely necessary anymore, and he felt the power run down his arm, although this, too, was really a symbol. His eyes widened a fraction and he cast...no words, no rising tide of song, no passion. The power passed through him and out, and every one of the seventeen stag men was encapsulated in a hermetical bottle, and in each one, a fireball as hot as the surface of white-hot steel fresh from the blast furnace flared and burned for as long as each had fuel—a fraction of a second.

Air flew into vacuum, as any alchemist knew, and seventeen thunderclaps sounded as one, the sound ringing from the front of the cathedral and pulsing off the walls of the castle above them to frighten thousands of gulls and ravens into sudden flight.

Harmodius stood alone on the wide plane of the aethereal, *searching. Ash? he called.*

But no one answered.

He was ready to fight, even alone, and as he searched the aethereal *landscape of the city, which was nothing like the real because it had gradients, hills and valleys and cesspools that had nothing to do with physical geography and everything to do with realities like pain and love and lust and death...*

"Shit," Harmodius said out loud. Elsewhere in the city there were people screaming.

He could see them. He reached through the aethereal, *reckless now, burning them where he found them, but some had already set themselves off to burst like summer puffballs, and the spores of the new contagion hung in the air.*

He turned his horse and rode back to the gates, to find Ranald Lachlan. And the queen.

The Vale of Dykesdale—Ser Gavin Muriens

Nikos, master grammarian of the Imperial University, had become, *ipso facto*, the magister maximus of the army. Wearing his academic robe over a coat of maille made him look not dangerous, but curiously harmless. Only an eating knife and a pen case dangled from his belt. He stood squinting into the unnatural darkness. Beyond him, men were cutting trees at noon by candlelight, and at his back, the retreating army had to be guided with torches as if they were moving at night. The smell of burning rock filled the air.

Master Nikos fiddled with the heavy wooden-rimmed spectacles on his nose. He had Gavin's squire holding a book, and he wrote a note in neat Gothic letters with hermetical black ink before he looked up like a puzzled owl in his heavy-lensed, ivory-framed glasses. He shook his head and glanced at the Faery Knight. "I don't know what the hell happened," he said.

Tapio frowned. "Nor I, magisssster. But I will guesss that one of them fell. And I sssee that one was our ally. Sssadly."

The magister licked his lips as if he could taste the *aethereal*. He glanced at Tamsin, who appeared, as ever, as fresh as the break of a new dawn.

"To my mind, none of their kind are allies," he said after a moment.

Gavin Muriens stared west over his latest ambush site. "I hope you are wrong. I liked him, and he's an ally." He glared at the grammarian. "I know allies I have trusted less."

"Harmodius does not trust them, and he is magister maximus," Master Nikos said. "I met the Wyrm at Dorling. That one is a master at pretending to be a man, and yet he is no man. Charming, devious, and manipulative. As good a candidate for Satan as the one we face now. My order..."

Tapio sighed. "Here they come," he said, pointing at a veritable wave-front of hastenochs flowing along the meadows that led to the stream crossing. "Let us fight the monster of today."

The grammarian bent his head in agreement, entering his palace. "Apologies," he muttered absently.

Gavin watched the first heavy arrows fall on the antlered creatures. "We're starting to lose more than we win," he said. "I know this feeling from other fights. You don't lose in one blow. You take a hit here and a blow there, you get rocked, your balance slips, you don't have a great grasp on your weapon, and then suddenly you are lying on your back."

"We are far from beaten," the grammarian said. "*He* is absent from the battlefield today."

Gavin set his face. "I wish I was sure of that. Or that you are wrong, and we didn't just lose our dragon."

Out in the reeds at the edge of the river, the hastenoch struck the buried stakes set in the mud, and died, impaled, and the creatures behind the wave front pressed the leaders into the traps. It was Harald Redmede's idea; the royal foresters were the masters of traps.

Master Nikos took off his spectacles, wiped them, and closed his grimoire with a snap. He pointed out over the massacre. "We are not losing," he said.

Gavin Muriens fingered his axe. "It is the second day of our retreat from N'gara," he said. "Every day we use another trick; we're teaching them to make war. We will run out of tricks before they run out of bodies. And they have no shortage of bodies."

"Perhaps it is time to take some risks, then," the Morean grand mage said. He tasted the *aethereal* once more and frowned as if he misliked something he found. But then, more suddenly than most human mages, Master Nikos gathered potential into *ops*, spread his fingers, and unleashed a carefully crafted *word*, a spell that unleashed small spheres of compressed workings, each a ball of lightning. He studded them across the back of the traps, and for an instant, every man and woman on the little ridge could see the *words* like glowing marbles across the stream.

Tapio glared at him. "That isss a mad risssk. You could draw our enemy to usss!"

Master Nikos watched a thousand creatures reduced to ash in a single heartbeat—one of the most devastating workings he had ever thrown—and smiled. His smile made Gavin flinch.

"Ash is not the only power of this world," the grammarian said. "And we will not triumph through caution. Today, our enemy is... indisposed." His old eyes glinted. "Or so I wager."

"How do you know?" Gavin asked.

"Master Smythe, I must suppose, has handed him a little defeat in the north. I can see it. And he is overspent, and now I will cash his bills." Magister Nikos was academic and superior; but the power was rolling through him.

"What does that *mean*?" Gavin asked.

"I just spelled his name in letters of fire and he didn't respond," Master Nikos said.

He cast again. Ash's vanguard continued to die.

The old grammarian laughed. "By God," he said. "I have always wanted to do this."

He raised his arms and poured destruction on his foes.

He only lasted a few minutes, but in those minutes, a generation of cave trolls was annihilated, and no being came to shield them. The hastenochs were roasted alive; the wardens raised their shields and survived, most of them, but the larger creatures were destroyed. Wyverns fell, wings afire, and a rolling wave of white fire flowed over the bogglins, and Ash did not manifest.

For the first time in weeks, the Army of the Alliance held a position for an entire day. And then, wily in victory, Gavin left his fires burning and slipped away into the cover of night, and Tamsin sang her songs of deception, and the alliance vanished into the great North Woods and left Ash with piles of his own dead and his own rage.

Arles—The Red Knight

The griffon's wings reached out as if to grab the air, and the golden feathers rippled as if each pinion had a mind of its own; the saddle pressed into Gabriel's gut, and then they were down, the lion's legs racing along the ground, the dust rising around them.

Gabriel was almost used to it. Almost. Almost, he could look forward to flying, and not feel the pit of his gut flinching, the way he had once felt about hermetical classes with his mother.

Love you, the great monster said.

In answer, as he kicked his legs out in his dismount, he put his arms around the feathered neck and squeezed, and the griffon gave a sign of contentment not unlike a purr.

Ariosto had recovered quickly from the fight with Rhun and the ensuing raid on the Necromancer's not-dead. But he ate too much, and with half the population of Arles teetering on the edge of starvation, the griffon's appetite was dangerous.

And Gabriel needed to talk to Tom Lachlan. The hourglass was running, every hour counted, and Gabriel had to do this in person.

Gabriel was greeted with cheers, which, despite war, fame, exhaustion, and the exhilaration of flying, he still found delightful. He was met by Bent and by Long Paw, who was officer of the day. Corner, the baillie of the Venikan marines, came, bowed, and received a scrap of parchment with the duchess's private seal.

"How's Tom?" the Red Knight asked Long Paw.

"Very much hisself," Long Paw said. "Your majesty."

Gabriel smiled. "Are we ready to move?"

"It's like that, is it?" Long Paw asked. They were passing practice butts, already erected and in use. Twenty archers were shooting and another fifty were waiting and Gabriel had a moment's *crise de coeur* as he realized how few of them he actually knew, considering that every one of them wore the red surcoat.

He nodded to No Head, who stood with a bogglin. Both had bows strung, arrows on string, ready to loose at distant butts.

Gabriel paused. "You must be the only bogglin in the whole of the Antica Terra," he said.

Long Paw put a hand on the thing's wing cases. "Urk of Mogon. He tied with Cully in the long bowls at the Dragon's Deed."

Gabriel, who, despite being emperor, was not immune to guard-room gossip, took the creature's hand. "I've heard about it from Cully," he said. "So they recruited you?"

The four mandibles cracked open, but almost no sound emerged.

"He's quite shy," Long Paw said. Or Ser Roberto Caffelo, as men sometimes called him.

"And this is Heron," No Head said.

Gabriel had to think for a moment. It annoyed him that there were men in his company whom he'd never met. That men might die in his service and be unknown to him. That was not what he had wanted at all when he started this.

"I...am...honoured..." Urk said.

"We're lucky to have you," Gabriel said. "Do we have armour to fit?"

Long Paw nodded as if he'd hit exactly the right question.

No Head grinned. "Sukcy has two girls and Gropf sewing and has had since Venike. He's goin' to have the nicest arming cote in the company."

"Fer a bug with six arms, that is," Tippit said. "How do ye, Cap'n?"

Gabriel grinned. He couldn't help it. This was the life he craved. His family, of his own making. "The better for seeing you, Tippit," he said. "Heron? Outwaller?"

"Huran," the young man said proudly. He had a company surcoat over a good padded arming coat, but instead of hose he had deerskin leggings and a breechclout, and he had a small axe in his belt instead of a knife or sword.

Gabriel nodded. "How are you fixed for tobacco?" he asked.

The Huran shrugged. "I have none," he admitted.

"I might be able to fix that," the Emperor of Man said. This was how he commanded—by knowing them all, by being part of their lives. Not by being bowed to. It was good to remember.

Heron grinned and slapped his back. "That is good!" he said with enthusiasm.

Archers turned away to smile. Outwallers had very few outward signs of respect; they believed in an equality that the ancients would have envied.

Gabriel laughed, put a hand on the Huran's shoulder, and was introduced to other newcomers: Iris, a tall irk with bright yellow hair, and her war brothers, Elaran and Sidenhir. He watched them shoot, and smiled at their overly perfect High Archaic.

"They fart flowers," No Head said. "Or leastways, Iris does."

Long Paw nodded in agreement. "Good archers, though," he said.

Gabriel looked back at the three irks. "How are the Venikan marines about the irks?" he asked.

"Fine," Long Paw said, suggesting that the issue was complicated and a good captain would not ask again.

Gabriel knew all about questions not to ask. He followed Long Paw through the rest of the archers, to the barricades at the main gate of the camp, where fifty men-at-arms in full harness were standing or sitting. A single pair were sparring, carefully, with sharp swords. Their slightly old-fashioned armour, fine maille and not much plate, marked them as Occitans. Again, Gabriel didn't know them.

Tom Lachlan, known to most of the world as Bad Tom, stood at the barricades in full harness. He'd got a new harness in Venike; it was a magnificent blue-black, with latten trim burnished to a bright gold. The words *Lachlan for Aa* were engraved over and over all the way around the latten edging, along with a particularly complex charm that Gabriel could see in the *aethereal*.

"Very nice," Gabriel said.

"It is, at that," Tom agreed as if they'd been talking all morning.

"This is the quarter guard?" Gabriel asked.

"Aye. The archers shoot and the knights ken their swords and spears," Tom said. He smiled. "An' we practice that little trick ye insisted on. The one fer stormin' a bridge."

Gabriel nodded. "A bridge?"

Lachlan shook his head. "Ye really love yer secrets, but I ken a bridge crossing when I see one. A mickle great bridge wi' a road atop her, twenty feet wide wall to wall. Eh? Am I right?"

Gabriel smiled back. "Ahh. That bridge." He refused to be drawn. "Ready to move?" he asked.

"Aye," Tom answered and then suddenly leaned forward and shouted, "Is that a lilly wand? Are ye a knight?" at the two combatants.

One of the Occitans struck the other a very hard blow. The other covered, and sparks flew.

"I don't really need to lose any more men-at-arms," Gabriel said.

Tom shrugged. "Ye want killers, ye must make 'em train. Training costs in time, kit, and blood. When's the last time ye swung a sword?"

"I fought in a tournament two weeks ago. I fought you in my shirt a few days before that. I poked at Michael yesterday." Gabriel was watching the Occitans again. Both were fighting better—half-swording very close—and suddenly they were grappling.

"Ye should exchange a few blows wi' Long Paw," Tom said. "He fair skewered me last night."

Long Paw looked pleased with himself.

"I'm here on business," Gabriel said. "I'm taking you with me."

"Who's taking command?" Tom said.

"Sauce," Gabriel said.

There was a moment of silence.

Tom shrugged. "Right then," he said.

Gabriel wanted to hug him.

Instead, he turned to Long Paw. "Care for a few blows?" he said. "I only have my flying kit."

Long Paw nodded, leaped over the barrier with a fair display of agility for a man over fifty, and picked up a light bassinet with a very elegant, high back point and a spiky-beaked faceplate. He was wearing maille over an arming coat and an expensive, velvet-covered brigantine.

"Did everyone buy new armour in Venike?" the captain asked.

"Close enow," Tom said. "You did. Or leastways, whur the solid gold stuff come from? Eh?" He looked out at the next combatants: Ser Danved and a knight Gabriel didn't know in a very fine harness.

"Is that Lord Wimarc?" Gabriel asked.

"'Tis. Danved is going to make his noble arse sweat." Bad Tom turned. "Why? Why are ye pullin' me?"

Gabriel had been carrying his flying helmet, and now he put it on his head and snapped the hinged cheeks down over his neck. "For a fight," he said.

"Oh aye then," Tom said, smiling. "I thought I'd cocked up."

Long Paw was flexing a gauntlet. His squire, a handsome boy-man of fourteen or fifteen with bright gold hair and a new coat of maille, came over.

"I don't know anyone," Gabriel complained.

"Yon's Hamish Comyne. One o' the lads who joined us out of the Brogat. He's got Hillman blood in him; he'll grow." Tom pointed out at the two Occitans. "Ser Oliver and Ser Matteos." He watched the two currently in the lists exchange blows and then stagger apart. "Stop being sae polite, Wimarc! Gi' him a blow!"

But Danved was utterly the slim aristocrat's master, and in another moment, Wimarc was on his back in the grass, with Danved's poleaxe at his throat.

"That's enow! Out o' the lists!" he called. And then, to Gabriel. "Why Sauce? She's ne'er had a big command."

"That's why," the captain said. "Listen, Tom. I have maybe twenty of you I trust. Who know the whole plan. When I go down... if I go down... it's on you all. Sauce has to be able to command an army."

There was a pause. "Aye," Tom said. "She's going to fight the Patriarch?"

"Yes," Gabriel said.

"Damn it all," Tom said. "I wanted that fight."

"You come with me and Morgon to get the Necromancer," Gabriel said.

A slow smile spread over Tom's face. "Oh," he said. "That's grand. When?"

"As soon as Long Paw and I cross blades," Gabriel said. "I can't let the Necromancer combine with the Patriarch and the Duke of Mitla." He leaned very close. "There's a theory that there's another one. Another... foe."

"Christ on the cross. Tar's tits." Tom's slightly mad eyes met his friend's. "Another power?"

"Yes," Gabriel said.

"Ye can't let 'em combine." Tom whistled. "And we have twenty days?"

"Or less," Gabriel agreed. "Du Corse is marching east from Lucrece. Mortirmir has the Necromancer to within a dozen leagues. Payam rode back this morning; I hope he'll be going north from the coast. We're going to race west."

"Wi' what troops?" Tom asked.

"The Guild Levy and the imperial household and all the garrison of Arles," Gabriel said. "The duchess and Sauce get all the company and the Venikans and the Beronese."

Tom was pulling his beard. "It's not much," he said. "We didn'a ha'e much to start, and now we'll have less."

Gabriel shrugged. "We're really just along to be bodyguards for Mortirmir," he said. He put a hand to his visor. "Although I'd like Ash to notice all the shipping I'm moving to western Galle, and how we're all marching in that direction. I need him focused on my attempt to return by sea."

Tom grunted. "Last I heard he didn't see you?"

"Not me, personally. But all of us, and Mortirmir especially, must burn like the sun in the sense of potential enmity." He shrugged. "I hope so anyway," he said, and pulled his visor down and walked out onto the springy turf.

Long Paw followed him out, wearing a different pair of gauntlets. He flexed his fingers several times and then nodded to indicate all was well. He knelt, and Gabriel saluted him, and Gabriel was painfully aware that a thousand men and women were watching him.

So he was cautious.

He and Long Paw circled for a long time.

Then Long Paw came closer with a slow circling step.

Gabriel tossed a cut at Long Paw's hands.

Long Paw covered and stepped in, his sword perfectly skidding down the length of Gabriel's as Gabriel stepped back, attempting to leave the bind.

Long Paw was so-called for a reason. It wasn't just the immense length of his arms but the speed with which he moved, his legs as well as his hands, all catlike. Despite Gabriel's retreat, he closed the distance, and his sword point missed his captain's armoured neck by the breadth of only three fingers as he won the bind and came on. Gabriel felt his hands rotate; he was in the weaker position, and to his immense consternation, Long Paw reached *between* his hands and plucked his sword away, disarming him.

He stood for a moment, blinking in an agony of outraged pride.

Long Paw handed him back his sword with a bow.

Gabriel *hated* to be mocked. He'd had a bellyful as a child.

"You alright?" Long Paw asked, his concern genuine.

Gabriel blinked away an irrational answer. "That was beautiful," he admitted. "I just wish the victim had been someone else."

Men were shouting; Oak Pew was applauding.

Both men made their reverences and saluted. Gabriel was now more cautious. He circled, he declined various provocations, and he tended to withdraw every time Long Paw advanced.

"Don't be such a priss!" bellowed Tom.

Gabriel had forgotten how annoying it was to be surrounded by the judgments of men.

But when Long Paw attacked, a simple fendente, he covered and stepped forward strongly into the cover. He went for his dagger immediately, even as Long Paw's left hand went for his sword and he let it go and tapped the lanky man on the helmet with the butt of his heavy dirk.

Long Paw laughed. "Ouch," he said. "Well struck, Cap'n."

Gabriel sheathed his dagger, his hands shaking, and stepped back to salute again.

Long Paw scared him in a different way to Bad Tom. Tom could hurt him, but Long Paw could *defeat him*. Gabriel lost a beat in the circling as he understood some implications of this.

A matter of mind-set.

Something that applied to the contest with Ash, too.

He went over to the attack, throwing combinations: one-two, one-two.

Long Paw parried, but didn't attempt a difficult counter-time attack; Long Paw prided himself on a clean kill, and never, ever allowed himself to be "doubled" in the company sparring.

Doubling being when both companions struck each other in the same tempo. Both dead, with real blades.

So he parried and retreated, parried and retreated.

Parried and parried and stepped off-line, waiting for Gabriel's flurry to exhaust itself.

Gabriel, on the other hand, was well fed, newly married, and had just been cured of a disease that was eating his lungs. He'd seldom felt so fit.

He threw a triple: three blows. He cut a diagonal from his own left to right, descending: a *reverso*. Then he cut from his forehand: right to left, flat, eye-level. *Mezzano*.

Long Paw parried hard, and the edges of the two sharp swords cut into each other.

Gabriel was grinning in his helmet. He let go his left hand from the hilt and pivoted the blade on Long Paw's blade...

Reached to take it at the half-blade on the other side...

And watched in appalled wonder as Long Paw reached between his hands and caught *his own blade* at the half, the point at Gabriel's throat, a perfect counter-time.

"Shit," Gabriel said.

"I've waited my whole life to do that to someone," Long Paw gloated. "By the Blessed Virgin!"

He let out a loud whoop.

Cheers rang out.

Gabriel wilted, but no one seemed to be mocking him, and he got his visor open. Young Hamish was gazing at Long Paw with something like adoration. Veteran swordsmen came and pounded his back; the company was the kind of place where the counter to the *punta falsa* was known, discussed, and practiced the way priests examined the Trinity.

But never performed.

Gabriel shook his head and his eye was caught by a man sitting, filing nicks out of the edge of his sword.

It was Philip de Beause.

No one seemed to want to talk to a defeated emperor, so he walked across the turf to de Beause.

The jouster rose and bowed. "Majesty," he said.

"Philip," the emperor managed. He couldn't stop himself. "You *died.*"

De Beause shrugged. "Oh aye. I did." He looked away. "And not for the first time, my lord."

Gabriel turned to find Tom Lachlan at his shoulder. "He doesn'ae like to talk about it," Tom said.

Gabriel nodded. But de Beause shrugged. "I had an amulet," he said. "An old thing. It broke, the last time. I suppose the next time I eat a lance, I'm done for."

"Like the rest of us," Gabriel said.

Tom nodded.

De Beause said, "I thought I was brave." He sighed. "Now I find I'm afraid of death."

"Join the club," Gabriel said.

Tom frowned. "What ha'e ye." He looked at Gabriel. "You fear death?"

"All the time," Gabriel said. "Death, decay, humiliation, torture, agony, failure, success...you name it, I fear it."

Tom grunted. "I misdoubt ye."

Gabriel nodded, and smiled at de Beause. "Since you are alive, I need the household with me. Atcourt's near run off his feet."

"I need a new archer," de Beause said. But he rose. "But I'm still game."

"Take the bogglin," Tom said.

De Beause smiled. "I will, at that," he said. "I like the little bug. Do you mind having him in the *casa*?"

Gabriel shook his head. "I can thole him," he said in Hillman cant.

His attempt at Hillman was lost on Tom. "Good," the big man said. "I don't suppose we'll all fit on yer flyin' beastie?"

"No. Get the company ready to move, and send the imperials along the road with the food shipment." He waved at the Scholae. "I'm leaving Comnena and Michael with Blanche to garrison Arles. And run things."

"Aye. Because?" Tom asked.

"Because Michael is my replacement as captain and Comnena is my replacement as emperor," Gabriel said.

"Aye," Tom said. "Ye should crown young George."

Gabriel smiled. "I forget how close you Hillmen are to the empire," he said. "I should."

Tom grinned. "I ha'e a tanist. And I don' ha'e the weight o' the world on my back. Just some coos."

Gabriel laughed. He really laughed, better than he had in days.

"Food?" Tom said.

"There's a four-hundred-wagon train coming up the pass right now," Gabriel said. "Didn't you wonder where Sukey was, Tom?"

"She tol' me not to ask," Tom said with a secret smile. "We still on our dates for...you know. The gates?"

"As far as I know," Gabriel said. "I didn't expect to have refugees to feed. At least, not so many. Otherwise, all is well. I mean, except that Ash keeps winning and the Necromancer is out there and Harmodius thought a month ago that there was a third player, whose hand has not yet been seen. And the plague is undefeated. And anything else we've forgotten. Aside from all that, everything is fine."

Tom laughed. "Well, I'd love to chat," he said. "But I have a mort o' work to do."

Gabriel walked back to where Ariosto was polishing off the juicy hindquarters of what had once been a hefty bullock. No one followed him; the company remained the family it had always been, and he didn't need courtiers here.

But there were two boys watching Ariosto. One offered to catch the griffon's reins.

Gabriel smiled. "Don't even think it," he said.

The boys ran off and left him alone. Blessedly alone.

"You do kill them before you eat them?" he asked.

Ariosto purred. *Always.*

Gabriel nodded. He leaned on his mount's saddle and watched the camp. The landing ground was also the parade ground; he was at the head of the camp. He saw a tall, lanky woman kissing No Head where she thought no one could see them. He saw two archers in a fight, both men throwing heavy, angry blows. They didn't seem serious. Oak Pew was talking to Heron. There were people walking to the latrines, people washing clothes, people eating, people shooting bows or swinging swords. Two farriers worked on horseshoes.

And yet, even as he watched, things began to change. A whistle trilled; in the center of camp, near the command tents, a whole lance's worth of wedge tents came down, *one, two, three.* The pavilion of the Primus Pilus rocked back and forth, and then suddenly it was being stripped, the outer walls removed.

A trumpet sounded. They had a new trumpeter—from Harndon. Gabriel had never met the lad, and he had an irrational temptation to go and introduce himself.

The new trumpeter was damned good. His call, "Break Camp," rang across the grass, and tents came down. Some of the veterans had seen the emperor arrive and drawn the correct conclusion.

Harald Derkensun, wearing a long red tunic and not much else, ran to the head of a street of linen tents and blew a golden whistle. Big men boiled out of the tents.

Gabriel watched it all with a sense of heartbreak, of loss. His eyes filled with tears.

I will never have this again, he thought. *I will have love and lordship. But not this.*

Why so sad, boss? Ariosto asked. Gabriel had forgotten that the big beast could read his emotions, if not his thoughts.

I love these people, Gabriel said. He hadn't ever really allowed himself the thought.

Of course you do, boss! Ariosto beamed approval.

Gabriel laughed. His eyes were hurting, and he wiped his cheeks and felt a fool.

They launched without fanfare, and as Ariosto patiently climbed, Gabriel looked down at a long line of wagons that had come through the pass just to the south. A single heavy wagon had lost a wheel and the whole train was stopped, high up, but there was a knot of men around the wagon.

He couldn't see over the pass into Etrusca, but he knew that a hundred and fifty leagues to the south, the new Patriarch of Rhum, Lucius di Bicci, was marching north as fast as he could. Trying to join with the army of the Duke of Mitla, currently huddled behind four long leagues of earthwork entrenchments and bastions at the head of a long valley by Lake Darda. Their combined force would have twenty thousand men.

The duchess and Sauce together might have eight thousand.

But behind him, on the plains of Galle, the ancient sorcerer whom men called the Necromancer was trapped, or at least, he was on parchment. No one knew exactly what he could do on a battlefield. Convert an army of men to not-dead?

Even while flying, Gabriel shook his head.

He didn't know, and he was about to find out.

Under Ariosto's magnificent wings, Count Zac saluted with a golden mace and rode north toward Arles. His cavalrymen were the very tip of a long lance of men who were forming in a camp that had almost ceased to be, stripped to the ground in an hour. The fires were out, the last horse shod. Gabriel touched Ariosto's side and his mount began a lazy turn north. Just over the next ridge there was dust—Sauce and her staff, coming to take command.

Just off to his right, the Company Saint Catherine was unfurled. Men were ready to march.

The dice were flung.

Gabriel had time to organize a little food; to change from flying clothes to his red jupon and silk hose. Then, with Blanche on his arm, he returned to the great hall, and bowed deeply to Lady Clarissa, who was, if anything, even younger than the emperor, her brown hair and clear skin somehow magnified by short rations. She was as thin as any of her people, and her brown wool gown was almost as simple as that of her maids, except that it was covered with embroidery in brown silk thread; like Blanche, she wore a knight's belt of plaques to show her authority, but unlike Blanche, from her belt hung a sword.

Blanche leaned over. "I want a sword, too," she said. "And lessons in how to use it."

Gabriel made a note on his wax tablets. And showed it to Michael, who had the grace not to laugh.

Clarissa smiled when she saw Gabriel and even more for Blanche and Kaitlin. She waved for them to join her on the dais of the hall, where heavy chairs had been set for all of them, including Ser Michael.

Below the dais, Jules Kronmir, in green, moved small wooden blocks on a large map of Arles and Galle even as a pair of monks worked on the map itself from another table, adding details and cursing when they rubbed wet ink with their elbows.

"It's done," Gabriel said. "Tom's on his way here with the household and the Harndoner guilds. Sauce and the duchess will have the rest. Master Kronmir, I understand that you wish to accompany Sauce? If so, you have about an hour to prepare."

Kronmir nodded. "I can be little help against the Necromancer," he admitted. "I am increasingly concerned about reports from Etrusca. Have you read the material in the yellow tab?"

Kronmir had organized all the imperial correspondence by colour code. Yellow was the most secret, for the simple reason that Kronmir thought most people would expect red to be the most secret.

Gabriel nodded. But he said, "A synopsis, please?"

Kronmir shrugged and beckoned to Mortirmir, who looked naughty and produced a field of shimmering, sparkling black.

"I thought we didn't use black?" Gabriel asked.

"We didn't," Mortirmir said with adolescent insolence. "Look where that got us. I'm practicing."

Kronmir, despite a shimmering *aethereal* field of forbidden sorcery that blocked every spectrum, leaned close and whispered.

"We are all agreed that Master Smythe has not been particularly forthcoming about our adversaries. Yes?" the master spy asked.

Gabriel did not enjoy being patronized any more than anyone else, but he waved the man on.

"We are under the impression that the Necromancer was *the* adversary in Antica Terra. But information is coming to light to challenge that. One possibility is that the Necromancer represents... rebel odine, rebelling against the *will*, by which we mean the 'main' Odine..."

Gabriel leaned forward. "Is that even possible?" he asked.

Kronmir glanced at the surrounding black bubble. "Magister Mortirmir says it is possible," he said.

Gabriel sat back and swallowed a curse.

Kronmir shook his head. "I think there's another player," he said. "I no longer think that the Patriarch of Rhum is a tool of the Necromancer. I have a little information on Lucius di Bicci now; may I summarize?"

"Be my guest," Gabriel said.

"Bicci was a professional soldier. He was in orders as an *archimandrite* and he may have been a monk. Some years ago, he went east to find Holy Ierusalem. When he returned, he was a changed man—religious, charismatic. And he had arcane powers."

"Possessed?" Gabriel asked.

Kronmir shook his head. "Hermetical powers are so much rarer here than in Alba, my lord. Magister Petrarcha; Al Rashidi; the famed Yahadut astrologer, Bin Maymum; a dozen in a generation, with ten times our population. And nothing like our hedge witches."

"Or our Mag," Gabriel said with a grim smile.

Kronmir bowed his head in assent.

"So?" Gabriel asked. "The point?"

"Your Grace, the point is that we might have three or thirty adversaries here. The Necromancer made the *first* move for the gate. I wonder if he was the best player? Or merely the least subtle?" Kronmir narrowed his eyes. "Or the most desperate?"

"He's not done yet," Gabriel said.

"Admitted. But if the Necromancer represents a rebel faction in the Odine complex-mind..."

"What does that mean, Jules?" Gabriel asked.

"That every worm is part of a greater... assembly."

Gabriel sat back. "Clearly..." he said. "A single *will*."

"Except that Mortirmir has this theory of *rebel* wills," Kronmir said.

"And perhaps it needs to be said that the evidence of the past...is very strong that the Necromancer is the one who looked for...evidence. About the workings of the gates, their locations, their interrelations, if I may coin a phrase."

Gabriel digested this in silence.

"If all these monstrous powers were mere states playing the game of kings, I would guess, based on the evidence I see, that the Necromancer was never a lone player. He had an ally with whom he intended to work. Always. May I speculate?"

"What else do I pay you for?" Gabriel asked.

"I lack the mind of a Power, but something tells me that the Necromancer was and perhaps still is working toward either escape from here or reconciliation with the *will*. Perhaps both."

"Even God has rebel angels," Gabriel said. He shook his head. "So the Patriarch is the puppet of the *will*?"

Kronmir spread his hands on the table in the weird, shimmering light-dark of the shield. "Maybe. I want to go south with Ser Alison and make contact with...my network. I need more information."

"What do you fear?" Gabriel asked.

"I fear a terrible surprise on the day the gates open," the spy said. "I fear that we are dupes playing, not for ourselves, but for some other power."

Gabriel scratched at his beard. "I fear to lose you. After myself, you may be the next most important man in the empire."

Kronmir flinched. "Sire!" he said.

Gabriel shrugged. "Knowledge is power, Jules. And you hold all the threads of knowledge in your hands."

Kronmir nodded. "Your wife...is adept. The messenger birds all know her. Ser Michael is very competent; if he were not a great lord, I would employ him to gather intelligence, and to read it."

"You know, Jules," Gabriel said, "There is something terrifying about having you, a man who tried to kill me several times, telling me that my wife and my best friend are...competent."

"They are," Kronmir reassured him.

Gabriel laughed. He laughed, and laughed, and laughed.

Eventually, his sides aching, he paused, wiped the tears from his eyes, and blinked at his chief intelligencer. "Very well. You can accompany Sauce; I want regular reports."

"Yes, Your Grace."

"But first," Gabriel said, and he smiled. He tapped a wand *and in the* aethereal*, in his palace, he waved at Mortirmir, who snapped his* aethereal *fingers.*

The shimmering black shield fell.

Everyone in the hall was looking at them. You cannot raise a shimmering black globe in a crowded room without drawing attention.

Francis Atcourt entered, in armour, at the head of a file of knights and squires. They moved to stand like an aisle of steel in front of Gabriel's chair. Toby brought a low wooden stool with an elaborate stool whose cushion was embroidered in the ancient arms of Arles.

Blanche reached up and unpinned the simple gold circlet she was wearing. Gabriel nodded to the Archbishop of Arles, who was in on the plot.

"Lady Clarissa de Sartres, please approach the imperial throne, such as it is," Gabriel said.

There was a steady buzz of talk, occasioned by the shimmering black globe; now the hall was silent.

Lady Clarissa, acting Duchess of Arles, rose, walked down the aisle of knights, and knelt on the cushion.

"By the ancient power of my office, I restore the crown of Arles, falsely seized by Galle, to you in token of which I give this circlet," he said. He rose, bowed deeply to the archbishop, and handed the man the circlet.

The archbishop nodded in return, took the circlet, and placed it on Clarissa's head with a prayer.

Gabriel bowed. Clarissa rose.

Gabriel nodded. "In the fullness of time, if we triumph, you can have a coronation: anointment, a heavy cloak, choirs, sycophants, everything." He smiled. "But the office is done. You are Queen of Arles."

Clarissa bowed her head. "My father would have given his life for this," she said quietly.

Gabriel nodded. "I know," he said. "And it may be that you are also Queen of Galle. Honestly, no person alive can tell that right now. I would that we leave the Sieur Du Corse to act as constable and regent until such a time as we can determine what is best."

Clarissa nodded. "You don't plan to marry me off to one of your knights?" she asked.

Blanche winced.

Gabriel smiled. "You beat the Necromancer," he said. "You held your castle against all comers. I don't think you need a man to make you stronger."

"Today will live on in history," Clarissa said.

Gabriel held out his hand, and she found her chair had been moved next to his, and Blanche's. She sat.

"Master Kronmir," Gabriel said.

Kronmir looked up from writing. "My lord?"

"Come here," Gabriel said.

Kronmir passed between the household knights and knelt.

Francis Atcourt produced a pair of golden spurs.

Gabriel drew his long war sword. "By token of this blow, I make you knight," Gabriel said. "Despite your methods, you have prevented two assassinations, countless attempts on other lives, and your work has repeatedly placed us and our empire at an advantage over our foes. Your courage would be a legend among my knights if only they were allowed to know what you do."

Kronmir maintained his face, but he was in shock. He did his best to accept the buffet.

Toby put the belt on Kronmir while Atcourt adjusted his spurs.

"Other assassins will be jealous," Gabriel said very quietly.

Michael leaned over to Kaitlin and said very softly, "Prevented two, made two of his own; that just makes him even."

Kaitlin giggled.

Kronmir flushed. He rose, saluted with his sword, and went back to his charts, the gold belt glowing on his hips.

"Toby," Gabriel said.

His squire froze in the act of pouring wine.

"Approach."

Toby's heart beat very fast.

It was hard not to hope. Especially when he could see that Queen Clarissa was smiling; that Francis Atcourt had another pair of spurs in his hand; that Blanche was beaming at him.

"Kneel," the emperor said.

Toby could never remember the rest.

Fifteen minutes later, he was back in the solar, packing the emperor's traveling kit.

Anne Woodstock was hiding behind the door. "Which, I'm chang-ing!" she spat.

"He's leaving!" Toby answered her. He took one razor from the bundle that the Marshal had loaned them, and put it in the big leather saddle trunk. *Razor, towel, soap; small pot, clean shirt, clean braes, spare points…*

"By Saint Katherine," Anne went on. "Am I riding, too? I was just changing into girl's clothes."

"Change back," Toby said heartlessly. "We're riding in an hour." He smiled. "Or stay here and serve Lady Blanche and Master Nicodemus."

"No thanks," she said.

"Want a clean shirt?" he asked, looking into his master's armour basket to check on his maille.

"Yes," Anne said.

Toby took one from his own pack and threw it over the door. "I won't peek," he said. He went on packing, his back to the door.

In a minute, she emerged in doublet and hose. "The clean shirt is everything," Anne said. "I owe you—Sweet Christ, what's that on your hips, you lout?"

Toby grinned. "A knight's belt, sweeting," he said with a bow.

She whistled. "He knighted you?" she said.

"You're the squire now," Toby said. "So you're lucky I'm doing your work for you."

Anne gave him a cautious hug.

"Your turn will come," Toby said, trying not to relish a chaste hug too much.

Anne nodded, also trying not to relish the hug. She had the briefest notion of putting her lips on his, and dismissed it in despair.

Gabriel sat with Master Julius, and the orders rolled from his mouth through their pens and onto parchment. The stacks of orders sat in piles of scrolls like the skulls left by some conqueror.

Blanche sat in the corner with a six-fold wax tablet, prompting Gabriel.

"Venike rangers," she said.

"Damn," he said, and dictated an order—really a polite suggestion that the Venikans use their ranger corps or anyone else they could find to collect wandering farm animals taken by the Darkness and get them fed and watered.

"An incredibly difficult and inglorious job," he said when he had finished dictating.

"Shall I put that in?" Master Julius asked.

Gabriel sighed. "But the world will not, I hope, end in twenty-two days," he said. "So there must be food. In fact, we'll need to ship food to Alba just to keep the Brogat fed. If the new Queen of Arles can save enough of our former not-dead, they can bring in the harvest and ship it."

"So right now you're stripping northern Etrusca to feed Arles," his wife said.

"Exactly," he answered. "If we fail, none of this matters. But we may as well plan to succeed."

"Because you like to win," she said seriously.

"Because we all like to win," he said. "Especially when the alternative is personal extinction. Eh? Now, wagons. I need them all."

"You are a fearsome tyrant," Blanche said.

"In this moment, what is needed is a tyrant," Gabriel said. "Can someone take a note for Captain Parmenio? Venike? And a copy to the Doge? We'll need every ship they can muster, and some covering warships, to move food. Parmenio will know the odds, and he probably knows more about fighting sea monsters now than anyone else."

"Giselle will not appreciate being bypassed," Blanche said.

"I will make sure I mention it to Giselle before I ride," the emperor said.

The orders rolled on.

In late afternoon, the imperial household arrived. Master Nicodemus threw himself into the work of the imperial chamber; he relished it. Toby and Anne handed it over with relief and satisfaction.

Count Zac, golden mace in hand, directed the distribution of a hundred wagons' worth of flour and dried peas. The other wagons were laagered and the whole surviving Milice of Arles marched out, spear in hand, and mounted guard over the largest food supply in the duchy. News of the emperor's elevation of their duchess to be a queen was electrifying. The men of Arles stood taller.

The Huscarls of the guard rode east into the setting sun, leaving just six of their number to guard the emperor. The rest never halted, and neither did the Harndoner guildsmen and women on their Venikan ronceys, nor the fifty wagons of supplies that were moving east with the army. By nightfall they were ten leagues to the east, almost as far as the site of the disastrous battle between the Duke of Arles and the Necromancer in the spring.

The rear guard, Syr George Comnena and his Scholae in their scarlet and maille, arrived last. Pages were waiting to take their horses; Comnena knelt to his emperor.

Gabriel sat in the hall with Blanche and Michael and Kaitlin. Francis Atcourt stood guard; Adrian Goldsmith, now Atcourt's squire, wore full harness but sat sketching.

The Bishop of Arles bowed to Gabriel and indicated a cushion.

The emperor rose and returned the bow. "George Comnena," he said softly, "I am about to have you crowned Caesar."

Comnena muttered a piece of blasphemy that would have shocked his wife or his sister.

"There isn't another time," Gabriel said. "I could die tomorrow. Understand?"

"Yes," George Comnena answered. "My great-uncle was emperor," he said. It made no real sense; it was the comment that floated into his head.

"Exactly," Gabriel said.

Just at dark, Tom Lachlan and all of the remaining knights of the *casa* rode into the citadel of Arles and were given rooms.

Gabriel met Tom in the hall, cloaked in artificial anonymity to save time. "Straight to bed, gentles," he said. "We ride at dawn."

"I thought we was riding all night," Tom said. "And that's a party or I'm a blind leper."

Gabriel shrugged. "I'm running behind. We just crowned George as Caesar. Emperor-heir-apparent."

Tom laughed. "I'll just toast the wee man before I totter off to my mattress, then," Tom said. "Or ye could get yer wee arse mounted and we'd be away."

"I'd rather leave in the morning, and I'm the emperor," Gabriel said. He was very slightly drunk.

"You just want Blanche another time," Tom said. "Who's to blame ye?"

But regardless of any further endearments, the sun had not risen when he was fully dressed and mostly armed.

He kissed his wife. "I'll be back. Two weeks, I hope."

She sighed. "I'm really about to be empress," she said. "By myself."

"You have George and Clarissa and Michael and Kaitlin and Nicodemus," he said. "And Master Julius. But yes, my love."

"A year ago I was a laundress," she said. "In point of fact, as you like to say, I was a laundress four months ago." They had reached the point in their relationship where each had adopted a legion of the other's speaking ticks; *point of fact* was one of them.

He kissed her again. "That was then. This is now," he said, and dry-eyed, went out.

Jock MacGilly was ironing. Badly. Blanche was tempted, but she did not fall. Instead, despite the hour, she passed into the scriptorium, went into the aviary and checked and fed all the messengers herself, then sat down with the night's dispatches and began to read.

Down in the courtyard, Gabriel stood, now fully armoured, as Anne brought Ataelus, his tall black warhorse, to the mounting stool. Michael held the reins.

"I can't believe you are leaving me," he said.

"You are the Megas Dukas now," Gabriel said. "Your time as an apprentice is over. You and Blanche are the helm."

"Why don't you take the helm and I'll go hunt the Necromancer?" Michael asked.

"Because I am probably the third or fourth best human mage in the circle of the world, and this is an exercise in magistery," Gabriel said. He got a leg over his gigantic horse, who grunted.

"Then why is Tom going?" Michael said. He knew he sounded like he was whining. He *was* whining.

"Because he's the best killer I've ever met." Gabriel moved his hips back and forth, establishing his seat. "And since you and Tom are equally unhappy, I must have done something right."

"Tom's just mad you chose Sauce," Michael said.

"Advise Blanche," Gabriel said, taking a white staff of command from Toby. Ser Tobias. "Pray for victory. Make sure—"

"That you get a digest of incoming messages. I know!" Michael patted Gabriel's armoured knee.

Both men smiled.

Across the yard, Tom Lachlan vaulted onto the back of his eighteen-hand-high warhorse in his full blue-black armour. Men cheered.

Bad Tom snapped an order, and the *casa*, Gabriel's personal retinue of knights and archers, fell in, a neat column of twos, every man leading a spare horse. The *casa* had once been four lances; now it was twenty: twenty belted knights, twenty armoured squires, twenty of the most expert archers, twenty veteran pages, all of whom wore turbaned bassinets and maille shirts and carried light crossbows. Adrian Goldsmith, the artist and Atcourt's squire, carried the banner of three lacs d'amours on a field all sable. It rippled and snapped in the dawn breeze. Anne Woodstock waited by Ser Gabriel with the *casa*'s new trumpeter, an Etruscan: Alessio Monteverdi. He was tall, gangly, and ludicrously well read; Gabriel barely knew him, as he'd been recruited by Sauce in Berona. Behind him was the new page, an Islander, Jon Gang; short-legged and cheerful, he had signed on to the company after the coronation and had served two other knights and was ready to be a squire. He wore the scarlet jupon as if unaccustomed to so much finery, and alone of all the men and women in the yard, he wore his black bycocket backward on his head.

The *casa* filed out of the gates. Down on the plain below, Count Zac had his Vardariotes formed in a column of fours—almost three hundred easterners.

"Michael," Gabriel said. He reached into his breastplate and handed a roll of parchment to his former squire. "A letter for Blanche in the event of my death," he said. He took a chain from around his neck. "And the key."

It didn't look like much.

"If we fall, you take Sauce and go. Leave Clarissa to hold here; this place has sorcerous protections as good or better than those at Lissen Carak. Understand me? This isn't just an order; it is the only hope we'll have."

"I understand. What if you and Sauce both fail?" he asked.

"You really want to know?" Gabriel asked.

"Yes," Michael answered.

"Then you have a choice. Stay here until everything else falls, or go and die at Lissen Carak. Hope for a miracle. Ash can be a fool; Gavin and the alliance may have a fighting chance even without us." Gabriel shrugged. "There may be miracles in store. But to me, nothing has changed, and we need to win and win and win to even get a place at the table. Oh, and read everything in the yellow tab. Every word."

Michael nodded. "Yellow tab?" he asked. "Yellow tab..."

"Until now you didn't know there was a yellow tab," Gabriel said. "Read it."

Michael nodded. "I will. You go win."

Gabriel smiled. "Generally, we do," he agreed. "That's why I'm so popular."

He smiled.

Michael turned his head and saw Morgon Mortirmir in a passionate embrace with his young wife.

It went on and on.

People began to laugh.

Mortirmir surfaced. And spluttered. He turned bright red, and a little flame licked at the ends of his fingers.

Tancreda smiled beatifically.

"Let's ride," Gabriel said. But as the words left his mouth, Kronmir appeared at the top of the great hall steps, and Blanche was behind him. The iron-clad *clip-clop* of the heavy horses going out under the portcullis sounded like the footsteps of some approaching doom.

Kronmir came out to the emperor's horse and handed him a flimsy straight from a messenger bird. Gabriel read it while Blanche came down the steps. She climbed the mounting block and waited.

Master Smythe dead.

Gabriel found that he had tears in his eyes. He looked down at Blanche. She looked up at him.

"Go quickly, and win," she said. "Oh, Gabriel!"

Oh, Gabriel. Someday, perhaps tomorrow, I will receive a bird, and it will be you who is dead, and you will expect us to march on.

And we will, by God.

She kissed him.

"And I almost forgot," she said, and gave him a sleeve of sheer silk, cunningly removed from a sheer wedding-night shift and embroidered with his motto.

As soon as he saw it, he knew where it had come from, and he smiled. He extended his left hand, and she pulled the loose sleeve over his golden armour and tied it by points to his red surcoat. It matched perfectly; she was a seamstress, after all.

He kissed her again. "You are my heart," he said.

He raised his white wand and pointed it at the gate. "March," he said. He waved to her, and she waved once, and then he was gone.

At noon he changed from Ataelus to Ariosto, and he rode above the plains of Arles. He could already see the high ridge where the King of Galle had failed to make his last stand; he could see the Royal Army of Galle's last camp, the defensive lines full of weeds but stark and clear. Most of the Gallish army had died; the Odine hadn't needed them. But it was still possible that one of the naked, starving survivors of the not-dead was the King of Galle. Michael had his orders.

It was odd to do his own scouting, but he had the magical mount and the skills to defend himself, and he located the Huscarls and the Harndoners, jogging along at a fast trot, commanded by Harald Derkensun. He descended in a lazy spiral and waved, and they cheered, and he flew on, chose them a campsite, and landed to tell Derkensun. It was very late when the first of Count Zac's outriders approached, but the fires were lit and the food was cooked, the wagons laagered. The weather was cool and dry, and not a tent had been pitched. They had no tents; not even a pavilion for the emperor.

Nor did they dig in.

Gabriel slept between Anne and Jon Gang, and awoke in the darkness to find frost on his blanket. It was coming to autumn in Arles. He rose and stretched, told Anne he was not going to shave, and began to arm with Gang.

The man was incredibly competent, but then, he'd been chosen to serve the emperor. Anne appeared with hot cider. The sun was rising as they set off into it.

"Twenty-one days," Mortirmir said as they crested their first ridge of the day.

They rode together for a while. Behind them, Ariosto gave a bark of annoyance and then a short scream; he was hungry.

"Do you ever think about how powerful we are?" Mortirmir asked, apropos of nothing.

"All the time," Gabriel said.

"Really?" Mortirmir said, in his most annoying, I'm-so-much-smarter-than-you voice.

"Well, I am emperor, and while an emperor can be powerless, the current situation has given me almost unlimited—"

Mortirmir waved a hand to interrupt. "Oh, temporal power," he said, as if the ability to command nations and armies were a thing of no consequence. "I mean magery. Real power."

Gabriel managed half a smile. "I have been known to give it a thought," he said.

"Lot is dead," Morgon said.

"*I* told *you* that," Gabriel managed. Mortirmir was never easy to talk to.

"You and I are inarguably the most puissant mages alive. Well, and Harmodius." Mortirmir spoke of the royal mage as if he were an afterthought.

"You think you are more puissant than Harmodius?" Gabriel asked.

Mortirmir frowned at his emperor. "By an order of magnitude," he said. "Have you tested your powers since we flayed the souls off the Necromancer?" He laughed. "I am like a god. I can be anywhere, do anything. I assume you are the same."

Gabriel hid a smile. "There are limitations," he said.

"Really?" Mortirmir said. "Beyond our own ideas of ethics? Really?" He smiled. "I begin to think there are no limitations to mastery, Gabriel. I think that you reach a point at which the horizon is infinite, and there is nothing but will. A place at which we...I...you... become the only defining points in reality."

"I have had those thoughts since I was thirteen," Gabriel said. "It's a fine point of view if you want to justify doing something really excessive."

Mortirmir slumped. "You mean this is not original?" he asked.

Gabriel thought a moment. "No. It's just more terrifying from the most puissant mage in the world than it is from most seventeen-year-olds."

There was a loud snort from behind them, and Bad Tom loomed over them; even on horseback he was bigger than life.

"Any loon can take what he wants," Tom said. "But then he has to hold it. An' he has to watch his back. Take a man's woman; take his land; kill his mother. Aye. See what crop you reap."

"I'm not talking about *force of arms*," Mortirmir said dismissively. "I'm talking about altering reality."

"I'd hate to think you were takin' me for a fool, Ser Morgon. Because mayhap I ain't one, for all my Hillman way of speakin'. And force of arms alters reality. Ask any dead man." Bad Tom raised both eyebrows.

Mortirmir narrowed his eyes. "Are *you* threatening *me*?"

Tom grinned. "Never, lad. Because the difference between us is that if I want you dead, I won't mention it. I'll just make you dead."

"Gentlemen," Gabriel said brightly.

Mortirmir wasn't offended. "I wonder," he said. "Could you kill me?" He raised a hand. "Not a challenge!" he said, and smiled. "Very well. Force of arms alters reality as well. I accept it."

"So what Tom is saying is that your philosophic revelation is pretty much the reason that chivalry exists," Gabriel said. "Because every thug with a sword has the ability to alter reality to his own will."

"Fascinating," Mortirmir said. He thought for as long as it took them to ride down the eastern face of the ridge, while scouts reported and they watered their horses at a river and waited their turns to cross at the ford. Adrian Goldsmith was drawing the watering spot in charcoal, and Gabriel went and watched him sketch the look of intense concentration on Mortirmir's face.

Gabriel smiled. "When this is over, you can put a whole series of mosaics into the imperial palace," he said.

Goldsmith chewed on his charcoal, with the result of making him look like a monster. "I'm thinking fresco," he said. "I've seen quite a lot of it in Etrusca. More subtle. And cheaper."

Gabriel nodded. "Well, if we win all this, we will be poor."

Goldsmith frowned. "Not too poor for art, I hope," he said. "Majesty," he added as an afterthought.

Gabriel walked back to where Mortirmir was standing with his reins in his hand. Mortirmir glanced at a bird, then at a rock by his feet, and finally at Ser Gabriel. He made a face. Then he nodded. "It's good that I'm a knight, then," he said finally.

Tom Lachlan nodded. "Aye, lad. Good for everyone. Even you."

Gabriel tried not to laugh.

Mortirmir raised an eyebrow at the emperor. "Is that why you made Kronmir a knight? To put chains on him?"

Gabriel gave the mage a twisted smile.

That afternoon, he got a messenger bird direct from the Sieur Du Corse. They were fewer than two hundred leagues apart, and Du Corse had just had a brush with the not-dead.

"Get me Ariosto," he said to Anne.

He launched into the autumn afternoon air. It felt summery until he was half a league above the plains. Below him, his column was trotting; Bad Tom had them moving at alternating walks and trots. Gabriel could see for miles, and he rolled to the left and right, climbed farther into the cool air, and looked to the east and south, hoping to see the rising dust of Pavalo's cavalry. The men of Dar as Salaam had fought the Necromancer for generations; they were the most eager to see him finished, and yet he'd heard nothing. Gabriel had begun to fear that Pavalo had not made it back to his column.

It was late afternoon when he found the men of Dar. They were far to the east of where he'd hoped to find them, and locating them in the great circle of the world was far more difficult than he'd expected.

He landed, to the intense consternation of a number of the Royal Mamluks, and their horses. But once some reassurances had been made, Ser Pavalo cantered up on a magnificent bay. He looked old.

"I have had no sleep for three days," he said. "I just caught them myself."

He and Gabriel drew pictures in the dirt of Galle for a quarter of an hour.

"They turned east to get clear of the Darkness," Pavalo said. "The people are gone and all the animals. If we can get into inhabited lands, there will be food."

Gabriel hoped they were right. "But now you are to the east of the Necromancer's last position. Which is a guess anyway."

"We are very fast," Pavalo said. "And as long as there is grass for our horses, we can move. Some sheep would make us all very happy, though. Grass is only good for horses; men need meat."

He looked at Gabriel's rough map in the dirt. "Still three days away."

They both shook their heads. "Three days," Gabriel said. "And fight him, win, and get back."

The next day there were twenty days left until the gates were open, or so Gabriel had to believe. He rose and mounted his griffon immediately. He had a brief conversation with Mortirmir and launched, leaving his column to continue racing east and north. They were entering the central hills of Galle and there were deep woods along the crest of every ridge.

They would slow down the column. The imperial force was fast, but it was not faster than rumour and smoke.

And there was nothing to be done about it. Gabriel spiraled up into the morning, caught the sun peeking over the eastern hills, and then rose still farther.

He used Mortirmir's technique, and located a dozen places of apparent hermetical calm in the first minutes. And hour later he tried again, labeling them in the *aethereal*. His faith in Mortirmir's method dwindled, and in the end, he stopped circling and had Ariosto fly north and east to Du Corse. It took him almost three hours to reach the Gallish army.

Du Corse was moving south and west, with a long line of pages moving ahead of his force. Gabriel circled for a while, and finally landed.

Du Corse came to meet him with a dozen men of his retinue. They knelt. Gabriel was still not used to men kneeling, and he smiled.

"What do you have for magisters?" he asked, by way of a greeting.

Du Corse shook his head. "I freed two men who'd been arrested by the church in Lucrece as witches." He shrugged. "I have the creature who served the Bishop of Lorica. That is, the former bishop."

"Tell me about the not-dead," Gabriel said. "I need to be back in the air in an hour."

"It was not even a fight, my liege," Du Corse said, as if Gabriel really was his liege. "We stumbled across a... nest... of the things. We slaughtered them."

"Damn," Gabriel said. "I wanted you to be in contact with the Necromancer. That sounds..." He shook his head. "No idea. I hate being in a hurry. Is the ground clear behind you?"

"All the way to the coast," Du Corse said with satisfaction. "The feudal levies are combing the countryside, but I think we're safe." He grinned his ferocious grin. He reminded Gabriel a little of Tom Lachlan. "In as much as anything is safe. How far is your army?"

"Three days' march," Gabriel said. "The army of Dar is here, at Cattilon. We're here, at La Forêt d'Aix."

Du Corse whistled. "And we hope the Necromancer is between our claws."

"And we hope that our other enemy is watching us gather shipping at Lucrece," Gabriel said. "You did order that?"

Du Corse gave a wry grin. "Every ship in Havre, and every ship I could beg or borrow from the Conte de Hoek. Who is miraculously unaffected by *anything*. He says that the Nordikaans are pressed hard from the east; a veritable horde from the Wild."

"I wish the Count of Hoek the best, as long as he doesn't make any further attempt to undermine Alba's coinage." Gabriel was staring at the map.

"I suggested such a thing, by messenger," Du Corse said.

"In other news, I have appointed you constable and regent of Galle," Gabriel said. He had a scroll to that effect, and he retrieved it. It was odd, functioning without servants, but Ariosto put him in the unique position of traveling alone.

"And Clarissa is Queen of Arles," Du Corse said thoughtfully.

"Yes," Gabriel said.

"So you have restored the Kingdom of Arles in the stroke of a pen," Du Corse said.

"Yes," the emperor said. Their eyes met and locked, and the two men stared at each other for enough time that Du Corse's squires grew uncomfortable.

Du Corse pursed his lips. "I would like to have been...consulted," he said, as graciously as he could manage.

Gabriel thought of saying what was on his mind, but he recognized that Du Corse had not, in fact, spoken what was on his own. So he nodded. "There was no time or place," he said. Quietly, "Let me add, as one villain to another, that we have not found the King of Galle, and if we do, he will not survive our finding him."

"Will he not?" Du Corse asked. "Ahh." He nodded. "And I am appointed regent by the emperor." He looked over the high plains of Galle. Ripe wheat ran in an endless sea of gold to the horizon, broken only by hedgerows of summer green.

Gabriel nodded. "Yes."

"No lawyer in Lucrece would accept the right of the emperor to rule over Galle," Du Corse said, his voice low.

"You mean, while they look under their beds for the not-dead?" Gabriel asked. He shook his head. "That's last year's news, my lord."

Du Corse took in a deep breath. "Majesty—and by God, Gabriel Muriens, I admit your majesty...if we *win*, if we hold the line..." He shook his head. "Then what?"

"You are King of Galle," Gabriel said.

Du Corse's eyes narrowed. "*I know that*," he said. "I mean...you've broken the old order. Not just here. Everywhere."

"I know that," Gabriel said with the smug satisfaction that made him so easy to hate.

Du Corse flushed. "Will you rule us all? The once and eternal king and magister?" He looked away. "I'd hate that."

Gabriel flirted with various half-truths. Then he shook his head. "No. I mean, mayhap, if I survive, there will be some *fiats* from the throne. We need a set of concords. We know so much now; we need an agreement of all the races as to the defence of...everything. We need to build a structure of governance that will survive a thousand years and produce the soldiers and magisters to hold the gates without...becoming barbarians."

"By Saint Michael the Commander of Paradise," Du Corse said. "You are an idealist."

"I am," Gabriel said.

Du Corse nodded. "I'm in," he said. "But then, you knew that."

Gabriel chose not to answer. He needed Du Corse chained to him by chains of steel, but then, that was true of all the men and women he had to trust, and if Ash suborned just one...

He spent an hour he didn't have instructing three very untrained Gallish mages, if mages they could even be called. None of them wanted to allow him access to their rudimentary memory palaces; in each case, Gabriel performed the kind of reconstructive work that Harmodius had invented when dealing with Mortirmir. He left them with simple structures that were solid, and he left them with the ability to build a competent shield. A golden shield. And he lectured a small legion of priests who were less than enthusiastic.

"Don't try to face the Necromancer with an army," he told Du Corse. "These three can buy you minutes. That's all."

Du Corse cursed. "Can you give me a magister?" He laughed nastily. "I told the king we needed mages." He looked back. "I'm going to have trouble with the church. The rumour is that you are about to fight the Patriarch of Rhum."

"I'm not going to face him in person. But he'll cease to trouble us, one way or another. He's in league with the Necromancer." Gabriel considered what he knew from Kronmir and frowned. "Or at least, with someone."

Du Corse pulled on his pointed beard. "Now, how do I know that?" he asked.

Gabriel thought of a number of responses. He shook his head. "You don't. But I do. I'm sorry, messieurs, but we are at the point here where every throw of the dice must be as close to rigged as I can make it, and my empire is really a house of cards balanced by your trust in me, and nothing else."

Du Corse smiled. It was a nasty smile. "I know," he said.

His smile was feral, and yet, in response, Gabriel had to grin back.

"How does it come, Majesty, that with the fate of the world in the balance, the hands shaping the defence of humanity are such rogues?" He smiled. "I include myself."

Gabriel was able to shine his genuine smile. "Think of what we're doing," he said. "We're lying to the most dangerous immortal being we know of, unless God is real. Honest men would not do."

Du Corse and he clasped arms. "I may still need magisters," Du Corse said.

"If worst comes to worst, it will be me, in person," Gabriel said.

He leaped into Ariosto's saddle. His mount had eaten three sheep, and looked a little cross-eyed. He thought about Du Corse.

Despite Du Corse being his first great opponent, a ruthless adversary in a dangerous game, Gabriel trusted him.

The more so as he had the right bribe in hand. Carrot and stick.

Is this what it is like to be a dragon? he asked himself as he started back.

Distances in the air were deceptive; only today, after days of flying, did he realize that he could reach Arles if he wanted, and curl in Blanche's protective arms, and...

That way madness lay. He watched the hills rise before him, and then—

There was a sharp tug at his reality, as if someone grabbed his life in the aethereal *and gave it a shake.*

In no real time at all he was in his palace. He pulled the shield off Prudentia's arm; the one he kept ready, and he deployed it—

Slam.

The entire shield crumpled in a single blow. But Gabriel was not new to combat in the aethereal. *The overflow of power from the attack roiled into a second layer, which absorbed it and used it creatively in a series of, not shields, but baffles, so that the second and third attacks were channeled into the* real *as heat and light.*

Ariosto was up on one wingtip, and a new sun burned a bowshot below them, but none of the energy touched them.

Dive.

On it, boss.

In his palace, he deployed the most powerful shield-working he had to hand and he began another, using Prudentia to run the working while he funneled her power, changing raw ops *to* potentia *at a speed that most practioners would envy.*

There was no fourth blow.

He had time to look; there was no hermetical source anywhere near him.

The world of the aethereal *was and was not like the world of the real. It was very empty at high altitude; the plane of action had no other players and almost no gradient of power. All that was located elsewhere in more than three dimensions, but as the ground rushed at him in the real, so that gradient of probabilities approached from all directions and dropped toward a singularity.*

He had no time to ponder the philosophy of it. He deployed Mortirmir's search working; the one that looked for signs of nothing, generated by purpose.

This time, the result was unambiguous, or rather, the probability was startlingly high.

So his attacker had launched attacks like an assassin and then vanished under a curtain of very subtle manipulations.

Or so it appeared.

In the real, Gabriel hauled on Ariosto's reins, both really and metaphorically, and the great avian's wings cupped air and they slowed their descent very suddenly. They were perhaps half a league above the forests of the Massif. Gabriel leaned out over his saddle and cast a very unsubtle bolt of golden lightning.

Once, when Gabriel was very young, he had been hiding from his brothers, who were, as usual, tormenting him. Or perhaps he had tormented them. It didn't matter; he ran into the stables to hide, and he ran into the cellars where the winter grain was stored for the destriers, and there, when he kicked a bag in his rush to hide, a veritable carpet of mice flowed out; hundreds of them, perhaps thousands. He had stood in shock, unable to move; the carpet flowed away into the darkness and away from the shaft of sunlight coming down the stair shaft.

His lighting bolt struck something, and it exploded outward like the tide of mice. It was organic, it was malevolent, and it had a *passive shield*, which Gabriel has assumed, until that moment, was impossible.

And then he was blinded by the thing's response.

Chapter Three

The San Colombo Pass—Ser Alison

Hundreds of leagues to the south and west, the combined strength of Venike, Berona, and the company descended the San Colombo Pass and wound its way back into Etrusca.

Sauce and the duchess had discovered that they had a great deal in common, and there was a good deal of laughter as their armies drove south.

Kronmir envied them. The duchess paid him little attention, and as both of them were well versed in the tactics of scouting and exploration, they had little need for the Thrakian, who rode with ill-concealed temper.

It wasn't just being ignored. Knighthood lay on Kronmir's shoulders like a burden, an unasked-for reward that threatened his equilibrium.

I am a spy, not a man of honour. If I have honour, it is my secret. And when I order a man's death by stealth, is that knightly?

Who does he mock? Me, or chivalry?

Why can Giselle not notice me, if only for a moment? To be polite?

Why am I behaving like a child?

It was a little more than a hundred imperial leagues from Arles to Mitla, leaving aside the towering mountains and the winding San Colombo Pass through them. Six days' march for a determined army.

They came down the San Colombo on the second day like a torrent from the mountains, and Kronmir was delighted in a dour way when Daniel Favour, acting as commander of the green banda, invited the Thrakian to join him in leading the push into the forests of the Mitlan highlands. Kronmir was unemployed until he could find Brown; he'd already sent a message summoning Lucca, who had to be healed enough to function. Or so Kronmir had to hope.

The green banda moved fast, even by Kronmir's professional standards, and every man and woman of the company's scout had a bag of flour and a slab of bacon at their saddlebows.

They reached the endless waves of ridges that Kronmir remembered so well from his first visit by nonnes. The land was still; birds sang, but no large animals moved, and no church bells sounded.

"This land is still in Darkness," Kronmir said.

Favour changed horses. "We need to go further," he said. "Nightfall in seven hours, give or take."

The whole banda split into groups of five; hands, the company scouts called them. Two hands rode south, toward the sea.

"Genua is at war with Venike," Favour said.

"Agreed." Kronmir nodded. "Sooner or later they will take the field against us, without a single Odine being involved." He was nonetheless impressed to see that a junior officer in the company could make a political decision. The scouts would watch the Genuans; and capture a few if it came to that. Or kill them.

"What do I do?" Favour asked him.

He shrugged. "It is really Ser Alison's decision. But we watch everyone, Daniel. I have spies in taverns in Arles. I have spies in Venike. We should be watching Genua."

The rest of the banda rode north and east, spreading out as they went. An hour after they crested the first ridge, Kronmir and Favour were almost alone; a tall Hillman named Gilchrist moved with them carrying a heavy oliphant, or ivory horn, in his hand. From time to time, horn calls echoed along the ridges.

Kronmir enjoyed the ride, and the speed, and being away from the duchess. He had no role to play, except that he'd covered the terrain before, and twice he was able to guide them.

At midafternoon, a low horn called three times, paused, and called again.

Favour smiled. "That's good to hear," he said. "Long Paw has found the Venikans."

Kronmir was startled at how young they all were; Favour was twenty-one, if even that old. But two years of uninterrupted war had made them masters, and they covered the terrain without breaking a skyline or crossing a valley except by stealth.

They rode along the highest ridge through oak trees so old that there was no undergrowth, and emerged into a clearing with the ruins of an ancient temple amid a grove of apple trees.

Standing in the ruins were a trio of rangers, all wearing dark green and carrying the crossbows preferred by all the Venikans. Kronmir dismounted and tied his horse to a sapling. He took Favour's as well; the younger man was in command.

Favour looked puzzled to hand his horse to anyone. "I'm not much of an officer," he commented wryly.

Suddenly Kronmir was in demand. He spoke Etruscan fluently; Favour's Low Archaic was not up to detailed planning. Kronmir listened to the Venikan officer, Lorenzo. Long Paw, the eldest, stood patiently in shadow, saying nothing. Kronmir knew that Long Paw spoke Etruscan and several dialects, and assumed that the man was employing an excellent caution.

"He says that the Mitlans are snug behind their entrenchments waiting for the Patriarch. The Patriarch is close; perhaps two days south," Kronmir said.

Favour nodded. "Do you know where the Patriarch's troops are? And how fast they are moving?"

Lorenzo nodded. He spoke rapidly, drawing on a wax tablet.

"I think I got all that," Favour said with a smile.

Kronmir translated anyway. "He says that the Patriarch is north of Firensi, and that he is making less than twenty leagues a day; he has infantry and baggage. He says that he saw them himself yesterday."

Lorenzo said in Etruscan, "I do not think that the Patriarch or the Duke of Mitla know exactly where the other is."

Kronmir translated.

Favour chewed the end of his mustache.

Kronmir glanced at him. "Ser Alison should know this immediately. I'll go."

"Do it," Favour said, nodding. "Tell her I'm going to assume we'll attack the Patriarch. I'll push south; start beating up their scouts, if they have any. I'll leave Captain Lorenzo to watch the Mitlans."

Kronmir nodded. "I have it."

"What do you think?" Favour asked.

"I think that surprise is Ser Alison's greatest ally. Don't be seen, would be my advice." Kronmir hated giving advice, but in this, his views were simple.

Favour was confident enough not to bridle. He thought about it a moment. "Alright. It'll be dark before I could make contact anyway. Get her to tell you what her plan is. And you can guide the column to here. Ask Captain Lorenzo how far to the Patriarch's outposts from this ridge?"

Kronmir asked.

"If he marched fifteen leagues today, he's forty leagues away right now. Mayhap as little as thirty. There is a...hmm...hand of the Venikan rangers watching; he'll have a report eventually." Kronmir shrugged. "Do you need me here to translate?"

"Yes," Favour said. "But I imagine Ser Alison needs you, too. We'll muddle through." He glanced at Long Paw, his mentor. The older man smiled.

"I can manage a little Etruscan," Long Paw ventured.

Kronmir took his mare, originally provided by the Duchess of Venike in what seemed like another time and another world, and a spare horse given him by the Hillman, Gilchrist, and he was away. It was a little like fleeing the not-dead dragon; if he allowed himself nostalgia, he could imagine the duchess riding beside him.

He did not allow himself nostalgia.

He covered three ridges in less than two hours, and found the company's pioneers just planting the little banners that marked a camp. They waved him to the rear, and less than a league on he found the two commanders with Conte Simone of Berona on a little knoll above a stream, watching the army march by.

He dismounted and bowed.

Ser Alison waved him forward. "From Favour?" she asked.

"Yes, my captain," he said.

She grinned. "You and I may yet be friends. Say your piece."

"My ladies, before terce we made contact with the duchess's rangers.

They report that the Patriarch is less than fifty leagues hence; south, toward Firensi. The Duke of Mitla is behind his entrenchments and under observation."

All three of the commanders dismounted. He extracted his wax tablets from his saddle pouch and drew a map.

"Ser Daniel will push forward but will *not* make contact until ordered. With the Patriarch. Captain Lorenzo will continue to observe the Duke of Mitla." Kronmir bowed.

"Eh?" Ser Alison raised an eyebrow.

"My lady, we assumed you would go for the Patriarch before he can join the duke." He looked at her, and then at the duchess, who winked, warming his heart absurdly.

"You guessed right, for all you are is a hired killer, *Ser.*" She looked at him as if he were a particularly loathsome insect. Then she grinned. "Best news I've heard in a week. You willing to ride all the way back?"

"I am, but Ser Daniel thought you'd want me as a guide."

"I have the duchess as a guide." She looked at him as if buying a horse.

The duchess smiled at him. "As we were together the last time we passed these ridges," she said.

Kronmir bowed. "I can reach him before the last light if I ride now."

"Tell Ser Daniel I am behind you. We will not halt or camp if we can reach the old imperial road before dark." She looked at Giselle, who nodded.

"We can," she said.

Ser Alison nodded. "Then tell him to cover the crossroads..." She looked at Kronmir's wax map and then snapped her fingers and her squire unrolled a chart on parchment. "San Bastide is the third town on the pilgrim itinerary," she said, looking at a scroll. "Between Fortalice and Mitla."

"That's San Bastide," the duchess said. She reached over Ser Alison's shoulder and pointed with her dagger. "Where the Via Etrusca turns to come here. And the Berona road crosses the river."

The two women smiled at each other.

"Perfect," they said in unison.

Ser Alison turned to Kronmir. "Ride back to Daniel and tell him the battlefield is at San Bastide. You know it?"

"No," Kronmir said. "But I will, and I see where it must be."

Giselle glanced at him.

"Where we crossed the river, and took our doses," she said. "You'll know it."

Kronmir nodded.

Giselle vouchsafed a smile. "Where's your friend?"

Kronmir actually had to think. "Ah," he said with a bow. "I would hope he is on his way to us by now. He was paying a visit to . . . Mitla."

The duchess laughed. "Of course he was. Well, that would simplify matters, would it not? You know that the Duke of Mitla has a brother . . ."

"Who hates him . . ." Kronmir said.

Giselle laughed. "Perfect," she said. "He was really a fine neighbour until last year. Now he rapes choir boys and burns people for entertainment."

"So I understand," Kronmir said.

Sauce watched the two of them with ill-concealed impatience. "Are you two done?" she said. "You taking my orders forward, or not?"

"I am," Kronmir said.

"You have it all?" Ser Alison asked. She really didn't like him, he could tell. Many employers did not.

"San Batiste is the battlefield. Move forward, no contact." He nodded.

"I didn't say no contact," she snapped. "But you are right; I want surprise. He's got to cross the river?"

"Yes," Giselle said.

"It really is perfect. Let's get him. Just before dark tomorrow." She snapped her fingers to avert ill-luck. "Dammmmn this is fun."

Kronmir bowed and went for his horse. He defied himself and glanced at the duchess, but Giselle was talking to the captain of the marines.

He changed horses, left his second riding horse in the hands of Ser Milus's squire, and rode off with his best horse on a lead.

His horse was fresh, and he felt well enough. It was curiously relaxing to have no responsibility beyond that of courier; he had time to think. He thought about how much Ser Alison disliked him, and he had to assume it was her extreme loyalty to the emperor, whom he had, it was true, attempted to kill on several occasions.

He hadn't thought about Brown in a week; now he was seized with worry. Brown was as close to a friend as he counted; Kronmir had sent him to Mitla without a qualm.

Examining Giselle, he had to assume that, now that she no longer needed him, his friendship was inconvenient. The thought depressed him, but there it was. Or perhaps her new friendship with Ser Alison precluded him. He knew the duchess's tastes; he didn't imagine, as some men did, that he'd change them.

He avoided examining himself. It was as if the knight's belt had unleashed a torrent of emotions, each more irrational than the last.

And why am I not standing at the side of the empress? he wondered. *She needs my guidance, and she likes me. Why did I choose to go with Ser Alison?*

And then he thought, *Of course, she must resent me; she must see me as the emperor's eye on her.*

Of course.

He sighed.

He spent a good deal of the ride examining the problem of the *secret rivals* as he called it in the code inside his own head. He had access to details and nuances that he merely summarized for the emperor.

There was a fairly reliable report, for example, that people who touched the Patriarch were burned, and that the robes he wore were woven almost entirely from metallic wire and some Ifriqu'an substance that would not burn. There were tidbits; he'd read a dozen reports on the Ifriqu'an fabric, trying to find a commonality.

The commonality had been reported four days ago, when Brown reported that the Duke of Mitla burned people he touched, and wore clothes woven for him in Ifriqu'a, and had done so for over a year.

And Kronmir had begun to piece together a theory about the Odine that held water, but for which there was little evidence. That the Necromancer was the "Rebel Odine."

Old rebels. Rebels from the last opening of the gates, when the dragons were triumphant. The rebel Odine must have been allies of the dragons. The *will* was imprisoned; might still be imprisoned, capable of acting only through intermediaries. Until it was released. Thus, it would have only allies, not not-dead. Perhaps the Patriarch and the Duke of Mitla.

Kronmir tasted his theory, testing it the way a man might suck at a bad tooth. He was almost certain that he had detected a real flaw in the way that Odine matured; that as they took other creatures into their thoughts, the thoughts themselves matured. Perhaps the Odine functioned like democracies, and in time, the *will* ceased to be a unified entity and began to divide and divide again...

Perhaps not.

How many of them will appear on the day the gates open, Kronmir wondered.

The sun was no longer visible and he had pulled his hood out of his pack when he found the ruined temple. There were two Venike rangers there; they passed him forward to a long ridge overlooking the Mitla road, where he found a hand of the green banda eating a hasty supper.

They sent him south; one offered to guide him, and he declined. He crossed two ridges as darkness fell, and he cursed when his horse almost fell in a deep hole. He was tired, both of his mounts were done, and the woods and hills of northern Etrusca were vast.

The moon rose, and Kronmir dismounted, had a mouthful of wine, and *listened*. It didn't help. He rode south again, and tried angling east.

The moonlight increased. He was about five leagues east of the ruined temple; he knew the imperial road was in the shadowed valley at his feet. He just couldn't find the green banda. He felt foolish for declining a guide.

There was nothing else for it. He would have to ride all the way back to the post, and ask for a guide. The message had to be delivered.

He considered riding openly along the road. On the face of it, it appeared reckless, but he had to assume that Favour would scoop up any courier or rider on the road, and his main fear was being shot down in the moonlight instead of taken.

But this part of his night, at least, went well. Before midnight, two green-clad men appeared out of the darkness; Wha'hae recognized him.

"How in *fuck* are you comin' fra' the *south*?" the man asked.

"I don't know myself," Kronmir admitted.

But five minutes later, by lantern light and a small mage light, Kronmir was showing Favour where San Batiste was.

"The boys and girls will be tired," Favour said. "She'll want to make camp right here; on this ridge, or behind it." He nodded, his face monstrous in the lantern light. "Want to scout the battlefield or set the camp?" he asked Kronmir.

Kronmir had been tired, but the younger man's enthusiasm was infectious. "Battlefield, if you don't mind."

"Off you go. Take this lot; Wha'hae may smell like a farmyard, but he's a good scout."

Kronmir found himself in command of a dozen scouts without a scrap of uniform among them. In fact, except for some weapons, every one of them might pass for a pilgrim or a minor merchant. They all spoke Etruscan except Wha'hae, who barely spoke at all.

They grumbled, but they mounted, and they rode down the last ridge, well strung out, and then they were in a river valley, which Kronmir knew more by sound than by sight. It was very dark; the moon was too new to provide much beyond a pale and confusing glow. Off to the north there was another long ridge; to the south stretched the beginning of the richest agricultural plain in the old world.

The comet was clear in the sky above, burning white, a pointing finger that seemed aimed at the bridge. As the comet rose off the horizon, it provided more light than the moon.

"We'll want people on that ridge," Kronmir said. "In case..."

Wha'hae grinned in the comet light. "In case it all goes to shite?" he asked softly. "Aye. The ridge; Enri, you take Cranmer and Cromwell and More; ride the ridge end to end, flash me, and then get some sleep."

The four men grunted and rode off.

"I want to see the bridge," Kronmir said. "I'm going to guess there's a ford."

Indeed the river, whose name he didn't even know, wandered along the flat valley bottom and seemed shallow in the moonlight. But from the height of the high-arched imperial bridge, it looked considerably wider.

Kronmir was looking south, at the plains, which shone in the comet light, because they were covered in golden wheat or the stubble thereof.

He and Wha'hae rode west, looking at the river, and found a broad cattle track that led into the black water.

"How'd you come to being a scout?" Kronmir asked.

"Better than stealing coos," Wha'hae said. He shrugged. "Looks deep."

"Nothing ventured, nothing gained," Kronmir said and rode his borrowed horse into the water. It came up chest high to the horse, just to the tops of Kronmir's boots; the bed was sand and gravel under his horse's hooves. Downstream, toward Genua, there was more gravel; a long gravel island gleamed in the dying light.

Dying. Because clouds were coming in. First long streamers of cloud, and then suddenly the moon was gone, and most of the stars; the big bear lingered, the eye burning through the thin cloud for a long minute before vanishing. But when his horse was clear of the water, the whole sky was obscured, and it was darker.

Off to the north, a flicker of flame winked on the ridge, surprisingly high up.

"Now put it out, you fools," grumbled Wha'hae, but the fire lasted only for as long as a pious woman would say an "Ave" and it was gone.

"Rain," Kronmir said. He pulled out his riding hood again and buttoned it with the hood down. He put his hat back on. "It looks to me as if the whole river is fordable from here west."

"We can't guess that," Wha'hae said.

Kronmir liked the man's intensity. And his professionalism. "Aye," he said, unconsciously imitating the Hillman's delivery.

So they rode west again. Sure enough, the river broadened in sandy soil. Big rocks stuck up out of the black water, but it was shallow; a quarter of a league west of the cattle ford, they crossed to the south bank without the water passing their fetlocks.

"Why is there a cattle ford at all?" Kronmir asked.

Wha'hae grunted and his horse let go a long fart.

"You hungry?" Wha'hae asked. "How'd ye come to be a killer, then?"

Kronmir met his eye. "I did it often enough, and it became a habit," he said.

Kronmir smelled the garlic sausage before it was in his hands, and he wolfed it down.

They rode back along the north bank, and there they had to pick their way across a rocky streambed. Both men had to dismount.

"That's why the cattle ford is where it is," Wha'hae said. "No drover wants the like o' yon. Bad on the coos."

"Just so," Kronmir agreed. He ate the rest of his sausage.

"Let's go look at the Patriarch's camp," Kronmir said.

"Fuck, I knew you'd say that," Wha'hae muttered. "You an' Favour are kin, I reckon?"

They rode east into the night. Wha'hae sent men away; a messenger to Ser Alison, half a hand to move parallel to them in the darkness.

Twice they stopped to get their bearings, but the light of the comet and the moon served to guide them, and before the moon set, they could see watch fires and campfires.

"Fewkin' long way to march to get to San Batiste," Wha'hae said. "We may not fight at all tomorrow." Then he looked back at the wooded ridge on which the fire had long since been extinguished. "And not so far, neither," he admitted.

Kronmir was trying to get an idea of the terrain in the darkness when he saw a movement off to the south.

"Run," he said.

Wha'hae's head snapped around, and he, too, saw the glint of comet light on armour.

He gave an owl cry, and he was away, galloping furiously on his small horse into the darkness. His two men turned with him, and Kronmir turned his horse and realized, his heart sinking, that they were on fresh horses and he was not.

His horse was done; had come eight leagues or more without rest.

Kronmir went for the woods to the north.

He looked back, and saw that all of the enemy light horse were following him. He was glad for Wha'hae, but very sorry for himself.

An amateur's error. I am a fool, and I will die very hard.

He sighed.

He rode on, but already his poor mare was flagging, and he wished he was on the horse Giselle had given him. Gilchrist's spare horse was a third-class nag with no heart, and Kronmir knew he was doomed.

He considered suicide.

It wasn't in him. It was too bad, really; what would follow when they caught him would be horrible. Unless he could hide his identity, which was possible, but his sword was fine and he had his knight's belt on his hips. He undid the latch on the buckle and dropped it in the brush through which his tired horse was cantering heavily.

He began to rid himself of everything he could think of, but they were closing in on him, only a few dozen yards away, and the brilliant moonlight and comet light were too much; he saw a rider pull up when he dropped his purse, and he cursed.

He saw another way.

He wheeled his horse to face them.

She fell.

Kronmir kicked his feet out of the stirrups and got clear. It wasn't his finest dismount, but he was on his feet in seconds, and the first of his pursuers died when he turned to ride Kronmir down and got Kronmir's sword through his groin and out his back. Kronmir got the reins of the dead man's horse and swung into the blood-soaked saddle, took a blow on his back that was turned by the maille under his hood, and he was off, riding west now.

Men came up on either side.

It had been worth a try.

Kronmir turned and cut at the closest, but the man on his right raised a latchet, a small, self-cocking crossbow, and shot his horse. The bolt went into Kronmir's horse's rump; Kronmir's sword deceived his left-hand opponent and cut straight into his skull above his nose, and for the second time in two minutes, Kronmir was leaping from a foundering horse.

His knee struck a rock in the darkness.

In that moment of pain, he knew he was done.

But he couldn't stop trying, even though his left leg was useless, the pain awful. He fell. He drew his dagger; considered suicide again. Thought of the little ballestrina and the poison, which were, thanks to God, back in his bags at Arles.

He thought of Giselle.

He used the same rock that had apparently shattered his knee to get a purchase, and he rose unsteadily on a rising tide of pain. A rider came out of the darkness. He was moving slowly; he knew Kronmir was down.

Kronmir put his rondel dagger into the man's horse. It was a stupid thing to do, but the man was not in the right position for Kronmir to kill *him* and something in his head wasn't working well. The horse kicked him.

And died.

He assumed his pelvis was broken by the kick, but he crawled to the rider and put his dagger in the man's neck.

If I kill enough of them, they will not take me prisoner, he thought.

Or perhaps it was just self-rage at all the mistakes he'd made.

He lay in the dark, wet ground, listening to them search. The pain came in waves. He had thoughts, and once, he put the tip of his own rondel dagger to his own throat.

But it was his way to struggle, and never surrender.

Which was another stupid mistake, of course.

They got him in a wave of pain. One kicked him in the head, and another stood on his dagger hand.

Captured.

Between Arles and San Batiste—Ser Jules Kronmir

Kronmir awoke to find himself in a fine room, a timbered hall with tapestries, not that he had any eye for them. He was lying on a table, about waist high, and his hands were chained over his head. The pain was immense, and his left leg simply would not move.

A man came into his line of sight, blocking out tapestries of unicorns.

"The blessings of all the saints on you," he said. He had a tonsure, like a monk, but he wore armour. He put his hands on Kronmir's head and his fingers made the sign of the cross. "What is your name, my son?"

Don't talk. Say nothing. Once you start, you never stop.

"Is he too badly injured to be questioned?" asked a voice over his shoulder. A sibilant voice. Flat.

The priest jabbed a finger into Kronmir's shattered pelvis.

Kronmir screamed.

"No," said the priest. The man giggled nervously.

Amateur, Kronmir thought through the pain.

Kronmir was gone briefly, and then he was awake again. Cold water was being poured on him.

"You know," the priest said kindly, "nothing will save you. This is all a question of how you die. You are a professional, aren't you?" he asked kindly.

Say nothing.

Someone he couldn't see pulled at something that moved his arms and feet. The pain was terrible.

I'm hurt internally. With a little luck, I'll be dead. Soon.

"You have a wax tablet with some words on it. Can you explain them? Who is Alison? Why no contact? Is that no contact with Alison? Come, sir. You are a knight. Do not die unshriven and go to hell. Tell me what I need to know and I will shrive you, and Carlos here will send you on your way." The priest was friendly. "Or we can gradually pull you apart."

Kronmir knew how it all worked.

"Cut off some fingers, Carlos," the priest said. "I'm in a hurry."

Kronmir could watch.

Three fingers from his right hand went, one by one.

He screamed for each one. Never again to hold a sword, or a pen. Of course, that was faulty thinking, as he was not getting away. *Never again* now applied to everything.

Actually, none of it hurt as much as his hip, when he writhed at the pain from the fingers.

"He is someone very important," the priest said to someone else. "He has been trained to resist. This is an extraordinary discovery."

"Is this their Red Knight come in person?" the sibilant voice said. "That would be excellent. But it is not he. He is in the north, fighting the *rebel*."

"God's will," said a third voice.

"I need this to move faster," said the sibilant voice. "I have no time for this. Cut his manhood."

"Holiness, I have found. . . ." said his torturer.

"Speak," said the voice.

"Once you cut the manhood, they surrender to death, not to you." The priest-torturer shrugged. Kronmir could see him. He was young; the same age as Favour.

Kronmir wished he had magical powers of communication. Brown might avenge him. He certainly wanted to be avenged. He had no Christian forgiveness in him. He hoped that Brown would, someday, track them all down.

"Have him raped, then," said the voice. "I am told this works."

"His pelvis is broken," said the priest. "He could die."

"Sssssssss!" the voice said. "Break him! The sun rises in an hour! I have no time for this."

Kronmir was just congratulating himself that they needed to hurry, and then Carlos rolled him on his back.

There was a jolt of incredible pain.

Kronmir took refuge in unconsciousness.

It didn't last long enough, and then he awake again.

He knew immediately that he had been gelded; the whole of his manhood cut away. He could feel the wound.

He felt curiously detached now. The priest knew something about torture; Kronmir agreed with him. He had crossed over. The man's giggles were not nerves, but a tick. He was skilled, and his principal was not letting him do his job.

There was light coming in the windows. He turned his head to it.

"Fine," said yet another voice. "Send for the archpriest. We will use the worms."

Kronmir lay, mutilated, alone, and terrified. He knew better than most what the worms were.

He lay and prayed fruitlessly for death.

The mutilation of his body had been seamlessly healed; not the pain, or the brokenness. Someone had used the sorcerer's art to stanch the blood. Not the pain. Not the mutilation.

Not even the fever he already felt. Or the feeling of defilement.

Kronmir's only armour was that he had always expected to end this way, and he had imagined it many times. It was not too horrible to be real; it merely was. He was dead; he needed to be dead, before they broke him. That was now the contest. And the worms...

But the light was growing. He was in a strange place, where time had little meaning, and the pain was something for which he had practiced. He had been tortured twice before. Once by experts, and once by amateurs. Of course, there had been limits on them, both times, and people coming to save him.

Not this time.

The light was growing. Even pain, terror, and death could not hide the sound of an army breaking camp, and every moment he did not break was a tiny moment of victory. He screamed and whimpered, but in the fortress of his thoughts, even if that fortress was breached and considering surrender, he could acknowledge that he'd done pretty well with this part.

"Now, you have been very brave," said the voice. "You know you are going to die."

It was all Kronmir could do not to agree, and thus, speak.

"The Patriarch wants me to feed you to these worms. Do you know what they are? They go in through your eyes and eat your soul. Your soul is destroyed. No heaven, no hell. They master your will and you *never were.*"

Weak theology, Kronmir thought, and was delighted he could think such a thought.

"And once they eat into you, we'll have your whole life at our disposal in a few hours," the man said.

Kronmir heard himself whimper.

I will break in a few seconds, he promised himself. *Just not yet.*

Not yet.

Not yet.

"Open your eyes, or I will pull the lever again," the voice said.

Eventually, there was an eternity of pain, and then Kronmir's eyes were opened physically. He felt the invisible Carlos put thumbs on his eyelids. The big man put pins through Kronmir's eyelids into his forehead, pinning his eyes open. Tears and blood cascaded down, blinding him.

He writhed again, in fear and loathing of the end he faced, and his hip exploded in pain.

He vomited.

They cleaned the vomit off his lips and face.

And he saw the worms. The tears were slowing, and his eyes focused, without his volition, and they were *there*.

There were the long, sinuous grey worms, writhing in a man's armoured hand. A hydra of six; their mouths were purple, their tiny teeth just visible to the human eye.

Kronmir screamed. He could not help himself.

"Who is Alison?" the voice asked.

Kronmir was at his limit. Somewhere, in the part of his head that could still think, he knew that every man has a limit for torture; he was far past his. He'd really done very well, and they'd killed him and ruined his body anyway. It didn't matter. Or it did.

But the mouth he needed to talk with was screaming, and he couldn't master it.

The voice said, "And who is Giselle?"

Giselle.

Giselle.

Giselle.

132

The name went through him like magic. For an instant, he was himself; he had command of his mind.

He thought of Giselle, fighting the *will*.

He thought of Giselle. He loved, and he would not betray. His resistance rose and his surrender fell away.

And he said *nothing*.

"I'm afraid this is your very last chance. No repentance, no afterlife, no hope." The priest's hand moved a fraction, and the heads of the worms all but brushed his eyes, pinned open now.

I was destined for hell anyway. Perhaps extinction is what I deserve. But I will not betray. I will defeat you.

"You fool! The worms will have it all from you anyway. Your entire life. Speak, or be damned!" the priest growled, frustrated.

"Just do it," said the sibilant voice.

And as Kronmir screamed out what little life was left to him, the worms ate his eyes and started into his brain.

The San Colombo Pass—Ser Alison

Sauce stood at a small camp table while Daniel Favour sketched a chart on a large sheet of cheap paper from Venike.

"Isn't paper wonderful?" the duchess asked.

Sauce shook her head. "Really?" she asked. "I'd rather have Mortirmir to make me a piece of sorcery. With the terrain. And colour."

Behind her, in the darkness of the early hours of morning, her army snored, sound asleep except for a handful of sentries.

A messenger arrived, and then another. The duchess read the messages and passed them to Sauce, and she drank *quaveh* and looked over her chart.

"The river is rising," the duchess said.

"Better and better," Sauce said.

She began to dictate orders to her two scribes and No Head, whose literacy had now reached churchly proportions.

"What do you want?" she asked Giselle.

"I'll take the attack on his baggage." Giselle was cleaning dirt from under her nails with the tip of her eating knife. "It is the kind of war I know best. And mostly my own soldiers."

Sauce nodded. "Whole point of the battle," she said. "Time?" she asked No Head.

He raised an eyebrow and looked outside. "Half past three."

"Officers," she snapped.

"You are enjoying this too much," No Head said.

"Fuck yes," Sauce said.

It took almost half an hour for the captains and senior corporals to come in; many attended by squires or pages still arming them. She had all the red banda and all the white, with Ser Milus commanding the red and Ser George Brewes taking Ser Michael's place.

She had only three battle mages, the best of whom was Mortirmir's wife, Tancreda, university trained and strangely ruthless; and in addition to the three, she had Magister Petrarcha, whose skills in combat were untested, although Mortirmir and Gabriel both seemed to think he was a peer.

Conte Simone had six hundred excellent knights; she doubted that her opponents could match the quality of her heavy cavalry.

But then, she didn't plan to use her heavy cavalry unless things went wrong.

Which, her experience told her, they always did.

"What's the first thing you do in a sword fight, gentlemen?" she asked, looking around. She and Giselle, Duchess of Venike, were the only two women present; odd, as they were in command. Sauce was smiling, trying to will one of the old salts to answer her. She needed them to participate; to participate was to accept her authority. She didn't expect to be challenged, but she wanted enthusiasm, dammit.

Ser Milus grinned. "Defend myself," he said.

Dammit, Bad Tom would know the answer.

Corner, the captain of marines, made a very Etruscan face.

"I hope he's an idiot," he said.

Sauce gave the Venikan her full, broad smile. "And then?"

"And then, if he's a fool, I kill him without risk." He nodded.

"And if he's no fool?" she prompted him.

Corner raised an eyebrow. "Then I work harder perhaps."

Sauce nodded emphatically and turned her broad smile on the candlelit tent. "Exactly. First try the easy way. Without risk. If that doesn't work, then we all have to work hard. Here's my plan."

She laid it out, with schemes and a timetable.

Milus nodded. "Pretty simple, lass," he said.

"Didn't Ser Jehan always say to keep it simple?" she asked. She looked at Conte Simone.

The great count was frowning. "We will never fight," he said.

"You can have my part," said George Brewes.

"You will if something goes to shit," Sauce said. "And to be fair, in war, something always goes to shit."

The Count of Berona shook his head. "I do not generally wait to charge. I like to settle the battle myself."

Sauce thought again of Bad Tom. "I know someone who would suit you very well," she said. She laughed. "Listen, my lord. If you have to charge, you will settle the battle yourself; this, I promise you. There is no dishonour in being in reserve; I will, in fact, be beside you."

For a moment, she wondered if he would say that she'd been a whore and knew nothing of honour.

It hung there a moment, and then the older man tilted his head like a hungry hawk. Half a smile lit his lower face. "Ah," he said. "As long as I have the pleasure of your company, Ser Alison," and he snapped his fingers. "That for the enemy."

"You are the very soul of courtesy," Sauce said with a curtsy. In armour. Then she turned back.

"Remember what Gabriel says. We have to win every time. Play this careful; like a sword fight. Try easy, then try blunt, then try subtle. We can't afford losses and we don't have any time. So just get it *done*." She looked around. "Listen for the signals. Follow orders. But you are all good captains; you know your business. If you have the moment to, then get it done. Understood?"

They all smiled.

In seconds, the pavilion was empty. To the east, a smear of orange had been spread across the base of the sky.

"You are a strange woman," Giselle said.

"This from you, darlin'?" Sauce asked.

"You have just told them they may use their own initiative, something my husband at his strongest would not have done." Giselle was eating berries. She looked as if she had a mouthful of blood.

"They are all masters in their own house," Sauce said. "Why should I put reins on them?"

Giselle toasted her with *quaveh*. "You are as remarkable as Blanche, or Sukey. Or Tom or Kronmir. Where did your emperor find you all?"

Sauce smirked. "Whorehouses mostly," she said. "Well, Blanche was a laundress. Kronmir...is no man's friend, nor woman's."

"I must disagree, although we are sisters in most things," Giselle said. "He saved me. He had other options, and he chose to save me." She sat languidly for a bit, and then rose. "I should arm."

"If'n he saved you, then it suited another agenda," Sauce said. "He's not a man. He's an automaton. After we win, I'll put him down, just to make sure he doesn't work for someone else."

"I wouldn't like that," Giselle said softly.

The two women looked at each other.

"You fancy him?" Sauce asked.

"I do not *fancy* men," Giselle said. "But I can be loyal to one who was loyal to me."

Sauce thought about that a moment and kissed her friend's cheek. "Mayhap I'll come to see what you see, then," she said, and went out and started giving orders.

Giselle stretched, and called for her squire.

San Batiste—The Patriarch of Rhum

An hour after first light, the Patriarch's scouts entered the town of San Batiste and found it empty. They weren't particularly thorough, but they checked cellars and pillaged the church like normal soldiers, and then pushed on.

A handful crossed the bridge, saw the enemy vanguard waiting for them, and retired, chased by inaccurate crossbow bolts. Messengers tore back along the road and found the Patriarch under his canopy of embroidered cloth of gold.

He issued orders.

The Patriarchal army had more than twelve thousand men, mostly trained militia from the powerful towns around Rhum, and the great city itself; some thousands of armoured spearmen from the Rhumanol, and three thousand knights and squires from the south of Etrusca, mostly sell-swords, and some mounted crossbowmen as well, prosperous merchants' sons and a handful of adventurers. He also had a small band of foreign mercenaries from Dar as Salaam—exiles from the Sultan, and fallen Mamluks.

He tended to listen to their advice; they knew more about his enemies than anyone he'd ever spoken to, and they knew a good deal about war as well.

The Patriarch snapped his fingers and pointed at Ali-Mohamed el Rafik. The exile was never going home; he'd killed the sultan's son. And he looked the part of the dangerous infidel: dark skin, and a scar across the bridge of his nose that made him look more like an imp of Satan than was quite right.

"Holiness," he said when he came even with the Patriarch's red shoe.

"This enemy army is waiting on our road north. At the bridge at San Batiste." The Patriarch pointed north. "Go and look at them and come back and advise me."

"This is the only crossing for ten miles, north or south," said one of the endless priests who surrounded the Patriarch.

"What did the prisoner say?" Ali asked. He knew a high-ranking prisoner had been taken.

"Nothing yet," muttered the Patriarch.

"Impressive," said Ali. His mustaches moved into his imitation of a smile. "I will return," he snapped, and whirled his horse and rode away in a little whirlpool of dust. He enjoyed showing his superior horsemanship.

The morning passed while he rode forward and reconnoitered the edge of the river. He noted the shingle of gravel and the cattle crossing, but there were fewer than two hundred enemy soldiers in sight.

He galloped back to his master.

"I think perhaps you are being bluffed," he said.

The Patriarch was no novice to war. "You think this is some rear guard, and my enemy has gone to face the Duke of Mitla?" he asked.

"That is one explanation," Ali said. "There are many. If I had a hundred Mamluks, I would ride across the bridge and see what could be seen by the ridge." He shrugged. "There is nothing in the plain. The enemy captain either is bluffing, or is a fool. We can cross the bridge either way. And once across, we cannot easily be stopped from joining the Duke at Mitla." He shrugged. "Or the enemy captain is using the plain to trap us against the river, in which case he is absolutely confident that his army is superior to ours."

"The enemy commander is a woman," the Patriarch said.

"Holiness," the man called the archpriest said. "Surely, if she is a woman, we can assume she is a fool. Women know nothing of war. And we caught her spy, did we not? So she will not know the terrain."

Ali-Mohamed raised an eyebrow. "Women can be devious," he said quietly.

The Patriarch looked around, but none of his other captains or advisors was bold enough to speak, perhaps because of his policy of punishing those who failed. He sat above them, in a palanquin entirely of metal, and he seemed to emanate heat like a furnace. People said no horse would bear him.

"I have won ten battles and never met a woman who could lead an army. Let us cross the river. At worst, we will have more men and more knights, and we will simply break out." His voice was low and sibilant, and his delivery flat and unemotional.

Everyone nodded.

Except Ali-Mohamed, who began to look at the girth on his horse.

"Let us march." The Patriarch turned to one of the younger priests. "What of the prisoner?"

"He is infected. It will be another two hours before he can be questioned." The priest shrugged.

The Patriarch shrugged. "If there *is* no enemy force, kill him and harvest the worms," he said. "Really. I do not desire the *will* to know more than we know ourselves. In two hours, we'll have this over with. So much for torture."

"Yes, Holiness," the priest replied.

Half an hour later, the Patriarch's advance guard crossed the bridge. There was very little resistance; a few dozen peasants with crossbows, all Brescians and Beronese, pelted his vanguard and slipped away into the woods on the slope above.

They killed two men. Their lack of success cheered the whole Patriarchal army; the rain was sapping their will to fight, and they were a patchwork of loyalties at the best of times, to the Patriarch's intense irritation.

The rest of the Patriarch's army began the laborious process of crossing. Soon enough, the scouts explained the cattle ford, and the army crossed twice as fast. Ali and the Patriarch's constable, both mortal men, breathed easier when the cavalry was across, and a battle line formed.

High on the slope where the green banda had built its signal fire, Sauce looked down through an opening in the forest canopy at her opponents on the plains below. She knew from Wha'hae that Kronmir had been taken. She cared little for the man, but was painfully aware that he'd known most of what she planned.

And what Gabriel had planned.

And that Giselle valued him.

In retrospect, sending him scouting sounded like the stupidest thing she'd ever done.

But if there was one thing at which Sauce excelled, it was dealing with problems as they unfolded, and not thinking about things that didn't need to be thought on. She had sold her body for money; and then put that away. She examined Jules Kronmir as a problem, and then she put him away. She had to win the battle. Then she'd deal with the next thing.

"Sound the signal," she said.

Horns rang off the hillsides and echoed along the beautiful valley floor.

Ali-Mohamed el Rafik shook his head. "Why not just stop us at the river?" he asked the djinns of the air. "We're across now."

Down on the lower slopes of the wooded ridge, steel was glinting in the trees.

The two battle lines were slightly misaligned. More than slightly; almost half of the Patriarchal army faced an empty wooded slope, and to Ali's left almost a third of the enemy army hung off his flank.

He winced. He tied back the heavy silk of his khaftan to leave his bow and sword arms free, and while he did that, he watched the hillsides and thought dark thoughts.

Eventually, when he was sure that his employer was not working some dark magic, he pushed himself into the group of priests, so close to the Patriarch that Ali-Mohamed could feel the unnatural heat coming off the man. If he was a man. He pointed.

"Holiness, we will need to crush these before that cavalry crushes us," he said, pointing at the woods almost directly to their front.

The Patriarch sat above him in a great palanquin of gold, held aloft by twenty men already given to the worms. They wore plate armour and yet would walk all day.

Most of them were the Patriarch's former political enemies.

"Now I sense a trap," the Patriarch said. "Those woods could be full of men."

Ali shrugged, as if to say that anything was possible.

"Speak," the Patriarch said.

"Holiness, what you say is possible. But standing still is never a good thing in war." Ali shrugged again. "It is too late to go back across the river."

A few hundred men on horseback emerged opposite their center. They took a little time to form up; they had become entangled in the deep woods. But when they were formed, their order was superb.

There were perhaps a thousand of them, Ali thought. They rode forward as if they were alone on the field.

"Banner?" the Patriarch asked.

"Saint Katherine," said a priest. "The foreign sell-swords."

The Patriarch's sibilance increased. "We were assured they were in the north? Chasing the *rebel*?"

None of the priests spoke. Some looked uncomfortable. Ali-Mohamed had spent enough time with them to know that the Patriarch's tone and even his language had changed very rapidly in the last few weeks; that he said things that were openly blasphemous; that the priests were upset. And that the Patriarch often spoke of the *will* and the *rebel* in ways that defied theology.

"What are they doing?" the Patriarch asked.

The soldiers under the banner of Saint Katherine advanced alone. They came forward almost half a mile onto the plain, their brilliant red surcoats and polished armour flaunting their presence. Every eye was on them.

Two hundred paces from the front of the Patriarch's army, they halted.

The Patriarch raised a screen of hermetical defence. It was done quite casually. Uniquely, in Ali-Mohamed's experience of sorcery, the Patriarch's signature colour was scarlet.

"God's blessing be upon us," he said. The red dome towered over the field.

Quite close, the enemy mercenaries dismounted.

A *woman*, her feminine form clear in a kirtle and overgown, stepped out of the ranks of the dismounting men and raised her hands as if invoking God.

San Batiste—Smoke

Six hundred veteran Alban archers reached for arrows.

"Nock," shouted Smoke. His voice carried on the light breeze.

"Ready," said Mistress Tancreda, her voice thin and quavering with nerves.

"Mark," Smoke called.

Tancreda released her working, and opened a two-hundred-yard hole in the Patriarch's shield, about seventy feet in the air where it was weak. It worked just as it ought to have worked, and she was surprised and almost lost her concentration.

"LOOSE!" shouted Smoke.

Six hundred heavy arrows rose into the air at a steep angle, passed through the enemy shield, and dropped into the empty air behind, and then into flesh.

Of six hundred arrows loosed, perhaps a tenth struck flesh. But others struck armour and shattered, sending needle splinters in all directions, and the loss of forty men, with as many more wounded, in a single stroke, had its effect.

So did the effortless penetration of the Patriarch's glowing red shield.

The army had to endure three more volleys before the Patriarch mastered the difficulty of making all the parts of his sphere of equal strength; it was really much harder to stop arrows in the real than assaults in the *aethereal*. Men and horses were dead; a dozen priests who had been near the Patriarch were lying full length in the grass, their magnificent copes stained in their blood, and the Patriarch himself was nearly incandescent with fury. His skin seemed to glow; the smell of burning meat pervaded the air.

"Withdraw," Ali said. "Holiness, it is you who were correct. It *is* a trap." He meant that he'd been correct himself; life as an exile had taught him to pretend that his employers were always right.

The Patriarch had been forced to change the shape and size of his scarlet shield to make it more robust. Now it covered only the center.

Crossbow bolts began to flay his left. They were coming from the Beronese peasants who'd run before. They were back, in a clump of brush almost two hundred paces from the left of the Patriarch's army. And suddenly their shooting was much more accurate.

The Patriarch rose on his throne and threw gouts of raw red *potentia* into the leftmost ridge. Two of his emanations started forest fires.

The rest skidded along a low shield and vanished.

His fury was such that he continued a little longer, loosing two more, and heads craned to follow the roaring fireballs as they crossed the sky.

A dozen of the Venikan marines died where they lay, silent, in their ranks, far from the sea and their usual enemies, their bodies burned by the Patriarch's fury when it splashed through Magister Petrarcha's shield, and the old man had tears rolling down his cheeks.

"I didn't know," he said. "He is like nothing I have ever endured. Red? I know nothing of this."

"Now's not the time," the duchess said, putting an arm through his to steady him.

"I will try attenuation," Petrarcha said. "I will change his colour."

The next pair of fireballs were defeated.

"He is puissant," Petrarcha muttered. "But untrained. Or rather, not trained as we are trained. He's like a...dragon."

Giselle was watching the far hillside. Now that she knew that the old magister was up to the task, her next worry was timing.

The center of the enemy sparkled again as a hundred pinpoints of fire rose from the Patriarch's shield.

Petrarcha snuffed them out.

The center of the enemy army began to bulge.

"He's charging the company," Giselle said with satisfaction.

"Mount!" bellowed Smoke. The pages came forward, and the horses were to hand, and even as the spears of the enemy militia wavered and came on, the company archers rode to the rear.

They rode two hundred yards.

And dismounted.

And of course, by then, the militia were out from under the blood red shield.

The Duchess of Venike turned to her cavalry: the green banda, the best of the company's pages, and a hundred professional light horse who were her husband's bodyguard in happier times.

"Let's go," she said.

At her feet, Corner stood up. He waved his sword at his men. "Did you want to live forever?" he asked. "Let's go."

With a cheer, six hundred Venikans rose to their feet and left their dead to be buried later. They flowed through the wood edge, and out onto the open ground. They were already behind the enemy flank, because of their position.

Corner had his orders, and he knew his part. And he added to them, embroidering quickly. He had been told to engage, but this was sweeter than engagement, and the bastard Patriarch had killed his men, and now Corner would avenge them. His marines were with him; they knew that they were about to deliver a hammer stroke. They strode across the plowed fields as if they were giants of legend, not mere men.

He formed his men up, and then started forward at the leftmost flank of the enemy army, at a trot. It wasn't lightning fast.

Not to him.

To Sauce and to the Patriarch, it was like a bolt of lighting.

The Venikan marines did not stop at the range of their magnificent crossbows.

Or at half the range.

They trotted forward, three hundred paces wide and two men deep, until their own right was against the river. Another three marines were dead by then; a handful of crossbowmen in the enemy army had begun loosing at a hundred paces. Most had missed the narrow line. Some bolts struck home, and the line closed up.

The enemy line flinched back, trying to find a formation that could resist the Venikans and their rapid advance.

Corner smiled.

His men continued forward, crossbows cocked, thumbs holding their bolts in the grooves.

The enemy line flinched again. They weren't professionals but butchers and papermakers and perfumers and silversmiths.

At twenty paces, Corner shouted, "Halt."

Somewhere, a voice was demanding that the mercenary knights charge.

Behind Corner, farther west, Duchess Giselle led her light cavalry across the gravel flats and over the second ford; almost a thousand horse.

"Make ready," Corner said. His part was already done, really. The movement of the enemy's cavalry to crush him had been shadowed by the Conte Simone. It wasn't exactly what Ser Alison had planned, but it was close enough, and Conte Simone liked a good charge. In his rapid advance, Corner had turned a third of the enemy army and opened a hole in their line.

"Present," Corner said. Six hundred crossbows went to six hundred shoulders; massive crossbows that could throw a bolt two hundred paces or penetrate a small boat. Or armour.

The militia facing him wore breastplates and had magnificent painted pavises, and they knew what was coming.

Men began to flinch, and men broke from the back of the formation and began to run.

"Loose," Corner said.

Six hundred bolts struck home.

None missed.

A hole seventy paces wide appeared in the enemy spear wall. There were screams.

"Charge," Corner called, and blew his sea whistle.

His marines dropped their heavy crossbows, drew their swords, and trotted forward, strapping on their bucklers as they went.

Ali-Mohamed saw the enemy light horse go for the baggage. He pursed his lips.

"Holiness?" he said. "We must leave right now."

The Patriarch was watching his militia in the center fail to catch the company.

He heard the screams and turned to see the collapse of the militia on his left. Who had moved, and thus opened a gaping hole...

Into which a wedge of knights was trotting as if they didn't have a care in the world.

Ali-Mohamed began to shake his head, because it was as he had predicted. Their left would now collapse; the mercenary knights, if they had any collective brains, would not even try to match the chivalry of the infamous Conte Simone of Berona, whose silk banner was now covering the enemy flank. And the knights in a wedge…could ride straight to the Patriarch without any interference.

"I am not beaten," the Patriarch said. He drew himself up. He raised a hand and loosed a scarlet beam of coherent light at the wedge of knights, and Conte-Simone's banner bearer immolated. The next two men in the wedge died; their armour *burned* and the edges welded together, the soft tissues cooked away inside.

Ali-Mohamed grabbed one red-silk-clad foot. It burned him; he jerked his hands away in shock.

He did not, personally, want to die, but he almost never abandoned an employer. "You are beaten, and worse, Holiness. Now it is only a matter of…"

The Patriarch was shifting his shields to cover his militia.

Three enemy casters all worked together, and there was an *emanation*.

A levin bolt struck the Patriarch's shield, and a second passed under the moving shield to detonate in the grass under the hooves of the knights of the Rhumanol, spooking horses and maiming them.

The third working struck by the Patriarchal banner. The Patriarch and all his palanquin carriers were struck to earth as if by a fist, and many did not rise. Ali-Mohamed's charger was killed and he was down; it took him a long minute to pull his way clear of the dying animal.

He cut its throat. He had loved that horse; more than he did people.

But he'd been paid and well paid to help the Patriarch. Who was on his feet, and casting. There was blood everywhere; the enemy manifestation had been puissant and dozens of messengers and officers were dead. Ali-Mohamed gave the army perhaps fifteen minutes before it broke up; when he saw Conte Simone's magnificent armour deep in the mercenary knights, he revised that. Shocked by the hermetical attacks and their horses terrified, they'd been caught almost at a stand. The Rhumanol knights were already running. Conte Simone's banner was back, held aloft by another knight, advancing at a trot, the wedge of his knights cutting like a knife, and the lance in the conte's hand was bloody and unbroken.

Ali-Mohamed cursed.

He spent another long minute catching a horse.

Then he rode back to the Patriarch, who was rebuilding his shields. By then, Lucius was deep in conflict with four mages. He was not winning.

The Venikan marines had cut their way onto the bridge and now stood astride it, closing off any hope of retreat by the main army, while the smoke rising from the Patriarch's baggage told him that they had lost even if they could fight their way out. They now had no food.

A whole, untouched enemy battle line emerged from the woods to Ali's front.

"Now, Holiness. We must run right *now*."

The Patriarch rose on his toes, and then continued to rise until he was several feet in the air. He cast another beam of scarlet; the whole ridge was on fire above them.

Ali-Mohamed rode for the cattle ford. He looked back, and the Patriarch was following him, like a tethered kite.

The Duchess of Venike sat her horse in the middle of the rout of the Patriarch's baggage. Her cavalry had their orders, and the baggage was set alight, the wagons broken or overturned, the patient oxen and terrified horses slaughtered.

The frightened acolytes and fearful whores of both sexes were driven off and ignored.

Daniel Favour took the green banda south along the road, making sure there were no reinforcements coming to save the day for the Patriarch. They spread out as they went.

The duchess was unmoved by the screams of the horses or of the women caught by her cavalry. She moved out of the smoke when it got in her eyes, and looked back north, where the serious butchery had begun. The Patriarch's army had collapsed, and now they were going to drown. The river had risen.

The Duchess of Venike looked at the wreckage of the Patriarch's army and began to consider a new future for the whole Etruscan peninsula. Her dream of unification was punctuated by sounds of desperation and despair, and she didn't hear them.

She did hear the hoofbeats of the horse coming through the mess, and she turned to see Petite Moulin, one of the company pages, emerging from the smoke of the burning baggage. She looked around, spotted the duchess, and came straight to her, reining her light warhorse so hard that the animal skidded.

"My lady," she said with a crisp salute. "Corp'ral Favour says he's taken a messenger; that Ser Jules was captured last night, and that he's being—"

"Take me," Giselle said, her face harder, if anything, than it had been a moment before.

The priest they'd taken had made no pretence at resisting; Wha'hae had broken his arm and twisted it a few times, the man had soiled himself, and now he sang like a bird.

Giselle ignored him. She spotted immediately that Wha'hae wouldn't meet her eye.

"Well?" she asked Favour.

"Ser Jules was taken last night," he began.

"And no one told me?" Giselle said patiently.

"Sauce said not to," Favour said. He shrugged. "Sorry, Duchess."

Giselle pursed her lips.

"This bastard says they've tortured him for eight hours. It's bad." He met her eye. Even with her anger burning on her, she admired that he could meet her eye.

"I know what eight hours means," Giselle said, weeping inside.

"Couple hours ago they fed him worms. Odine," Long Paw said. "Way I see it, we have to find him and put him down before the Odine can read his memories." He never took his eyes off her. "Sorry, lady. But that's how I see it and I'll need all the light horse to do it. And I'd want the same if it was me."

"Yes," she said tersely. Her gut writhed as if the worms had her. "As would I," she said softly.

He saluted. "On me!" he roared.

Men began to fall in, cantering up over the fields. "You—" Long Paw began.

"I'm coming," she said. She raised a hand to forestall him. "I'm the Duchess of Venike. I know what torture is. This is *my* command. Let's get this done."

Long Paw and Favour bowed in their saddles.

Alfred Gowp raised the little-used green banner. The horns sounded, and all across the south bank, men in green and brown raised their heads and then went for the flag.

The little headquarters group grew, and burgeoned. Word spread.

They were the men and women who went out and sometimes got caught. They knew what Kronmir faced. Men crossed themselves, or spat.

Loosened their weapons.

Petite Moulin licked a long dagger. "Let's fuck them up," she said in her Galle-accented Alban.

They rode in no particular order, and they killed every fugitive they passed, deviating only to overrun farmhouses. Their methods were ungentle, and a line of burning barns and small holdings marked their progress.

"The body you have provided is not acceptable," the monster said.

The priest stood as far away from the prisoner and his *possessor* as he could.

"I require access to his memories," the priest said.

"The body you have provided is ruined. Why are you so foolish? I need a better body than this. This one is broken and cannot even walk, much less fight or procreate." The voice was mellifluous, like a choir, as if different men sang a harmony out of Jules Kronmir's former throat.

"His memories..."

"Are very difficult to find. Because he has been abused. You make me bathe in filth for a meal not worth eating. Truly, mortal, you tempt me to..." The voice slowed. "There are horses coming in great numbers."

The priest raised his cross between himself and the thing on the table. "If I promise you a better body later..." he began. Then he got a hold of his loathing and began the spell, the exorcism, or so he hoped, that would allow him to make a safe bargain with the *possessor*. The Patriarch promised them that these methods were sanctioned, but lately the priest had begun to have doubts.

The *possessor's* voice cut across his prayer like a song in a crowded tavern. "Your promises are all lies, mortal. Tell your fiery master that if the *will* is treated like this again, it will focus on him. Tell him that."

A door opened above them in the house, and there was shouting in a language that the priest didn't know. He turned, motioning to the two men-at-arms who attended him, and they drew their swords.

The door to the underhall opened, and a tall blond woman came through. She had a crossbow, and she shot one of his men-at-arms from so close that the bolt went through his front plate, his back plate, and into the doorjamb behind him.

Behind her, a man in green emerged even as the woman produced a sword. She made the man-at-arms parry, a strong cut, and the second green-clad man shot him under her arm. Carefully. In the abdomen.

Another man, older, pushed past the dying men-at-arms even as Carlos ran at him with a heavy sword. The older man drew across his body, passing back; his arming sword seemed to flicker in the air, and Carlos fell to his knees, both of his hands severed.

The woman continued walking down the hall. She looked at the thing on the table once.

The priest fumbled for his sword.

"Who are you?" he asked.

"A fury," she said.

Favour put a hand on her shoulder. "We need to... kill him. Kronmir. I'm sorry, lady. But he knows... everything. If the worms get it..."

Giselle seemed to surface through the thoughts on her face. The priest was still very much alive. "Yes," she said thickly.

"Axe, Wha'hae," Favour said.

Long Paw was standing over the man he'd behanded.

"Wait," Giselle said. "I must try something." She still had the priest at sword's point.

"Somewhat that's worth the fate of the fuckin' world?" Favour asked.

She looked at him.

"Try it. I need an axe anyway." They all knew how hard it was to "kill" the not-dead. And what lay inside them.

She let go her long sword with her left hand and wrapped an arm around the priest like a lover forcing a kiss, and then jacked him by his shoulder joint, hard. She dislocated his shoulder, at least. Then she took the middle of her blade in her left hand so that it forced his bent head farther down, locking his head against her steel.

He screamed.

"This is so fitting," she said quietly. "Though I have no idea if it will work."

She forced the priest, step by step, across the floor to where the broken shards of Kronmir lay in a terrible caricature of crucifixion on the torture table. "You were talking to this creature?" she asked the priest.

"I was ordered. Oh, by the Blessed Virgin, I was only—"

"So they talk," Giselle said. "To you."

"Please please please please...It is angry, it doesn't want that body..."

"This body is ruined," Kronmir said in the flat voice of the not-dead.

Giselle knew exactly what was speaking. She could feel it in her head, and see it in his eyes. His right eye; the left still showed the wound where...it...had entered.

She shifted her weight slightly. "Why don't I give you this one instead?" she said.

"That is acceptable," Kronmir said.

Then she forced herself to do it. She fought her terror of the Odine, and her revulsion at what Kronmir had been made. She forced the priest's face down and down against the priest's incredible, desperate strength with the inexorable arm lock and the keen edge of her sword. Down and down, inch by inch, until the priest's face almost touched Kronmir's like a pair of lovers. And the worms slithered out of Kronmir's eye. She fought her revulsion while the worms emerged in bloody sinuous horror and took the screaming priest. His struggles stopped slowly.

Wha'hae, entering with an axe, turned away in revulsion.

"Acceptable," said the priest, who suddenly stopped screaming. The voice was flat. "Much better. Only the shoulder is damaged. I will begin repairs."

Giselle swept his legs before he could effect full control, and with two blows of her pommel broke his knees.

The not-dead did not cry out. But its arms lashed at her, and she kicked one, stepped past.

"This is not useful," the voice said. "We are in pain. Stop this."

"Take it," she said. "Put it in a net, and take it to Sauce."

"This is inefficient," protested the priest's body.

"Aye, lady," said a very impressed Daniel Favour. "And Kronmir?"

"Leave me," she said. It was kind enough, for an inhuman voice, and

Favour wanted out of that room; he was a tough man, but this was too much for him.

"I'll guard her," Long Paw said. He nodded. The torturer was bleeding out on the floor.

Wha'hae broke the rest of the thing's limbs with the haft of the axe. Then they bundled it into a hunting net. "About six hours before the worms have enough strength to attack a horse," Hobb said to two other men, but they were all careful anyway, and as soon as they found a dozen of Conte Simone's knights, with armour and visors, they handed the thing over with deep gratitude. Everyone feared the Odine. Like the plague.

But in the underhall, Giselle sat by the broken remnant of her friend. She talked to him for a while, and he didn't respond. She never remembered what she said. Perhaps she spoke of her helpless passion for the empress, or about her first kitten, or her life in the woods. But at some point his right eye moved, and one of his hands spasmed.

Outside, on the road, the Patriarch's fugitives were mostly allowed to run, but some were slaughtered, and she cared not. She sang some songs.

She hated herself, because she was so revolted by what had been done to him that she couldn't touch him. But she was brave, and she overcame it. She took his hand. The one with three fingers cut away. The one that seemed to twitch.

She held it as she would have held a woman's, and she was silent a moment.

His right eye fluttered open. Blinked. And a little life came into it.

"You," he croaked, his voice as ruined as his body. The remains of Jules Kronmir took a deep breath and released it. "Dream. Bad dream."

She couldn't think what to say, except to pray to God for mercy.

"Report," Kronmir said.

Something like a shock went through her. She kissed his hands.

"Will," he said. "Not... Will."

She shook her head.

He made a face, whimpered, and a little blood came out of his mouth. His good eye closed. Behind her, a door opened and closed, and she didn't turn.

"Necromancer," Kronmir said with enormous effort, pronouncing every syllable. "Necro...man...cer...is...rebel...."

She listened.

"Odine. Will is..."

Father Davide, the company padre, was kneeling by her. His lips moved, and she could hear his words as he sang, *In nomine Patris...*

Kronmir's attention went briefly to the cross in front of his face. "Damned," he said clearly.

"N-n-no m-man is d-damned except..." Father Davide concentrated. "B-b-by his own will," he said softly. "Evil is a choice."

Kronmir's lips twitched, and he made a horrible sound. Then his right eye snapped open. It met Giselle's.

"Love you," he said. Then he gave a shudder, and he screamed. Giselle pushed the priest away and leaned down to Kronmir.

"Will not Necromancer," he said clearly.

"You did not tell the Necromancer?" she asked.

"I think he is saying that the *will* is *not* the Necromancer," Father Davide said without a stutter.

Kronmir's one eye looked at the priest and blinked.

"I *know*," Kronmir said. "Ahh," he said. He seemed to smile.

Even as Father Davide held the cross in front of his eyes, Giselle lost her ability to leave Kronmir to suffer. She leaned down and kissed his lips, and then she passed her knife across his throat, and then she wept.

And Father Davide sat with her, his arm around her shoulders, as if they were old friends. Or perhaps for a moment, they were.

"Duchess is in a state," Favour reported.

"Don't blame her. No one trouble her." Sauce shrugged at the loss of Kronmir, and a little at the strange intersections of men and women. "The Patriarch?"

"We missed him," Favour said. He shrugged. "Sorry. We all went for Kronmir."

"Right answer," Sauce said. She was in her harness, and she hadn't struck a blow, and thousands of men were dead. It all felt a little odd.

She'd won, though. A great victory; a master-stroke, even though it wasn't her original plan. Conte Simone had done the right thing, emerging from concealment to cover the marines. Corner had done the right thing; Milus had done the right thing. Petrarcha and Tancreda had held the enemy sorcery.

Did that make it their victory? Or hers?

Prepared as she was for men to claim all the credit, that hadn't happened, and her people all glowed when they saluted her, so she assumed she'd done well.

"Pity we missed him," she said. "Will his army rally?"

"His army is dead," Favour said. The man was virtually brown with the blood of others. The light horse had been savage.

Ser Milus nodded agreement and handed her a cup of red wine. "Some o' the boys liked Kronmir," he said. "Lot of dead after they knew what'd been done." He shrugged at the inferred atrocity. "Cap'n ain't around to hold anyone's hand..."

Sauce was distantly aware that Gabriel might have acted to prevent a massacre, but Sauce was made differently and was fully aware that the Patriarch's army, massacred, was a problem solved for the next few months at least.

Sauce shrugged. "I'd like the Patriarch's head on a spike," she said. "But I don't always get what I want, so let's talk Mitla."

The silk door of the pavilion rustled, and the duchess entered. Her face was composed. Her eyes were red, but not exceptionally so.

Everyone rose to their feet and she smiled. It was a very brittle smile.

"Mitla," said the duchess. "We have eighteen days."

"We need at least thirteen to march back over the pass," Sauce smiled at the other woman. Their eyes met.

"I'd like someone to track down the Patriarch of Rhum," the duchess said. "I feel like we should tidy up as we go." Her voice was light. "I am in a position to pay well."

Favour nodded. "I'd be happy to get him," he said. "So would Ser Robert."

Everyone looked blank.

"Long Paw."

Sauce shook her head very much the way Gabriel might have. "I'd like to get him, but there are bigger things at stake. Mitla's behind nine miles of forts and trenches; any idea how to get him?"

Conte Simone bowed to her. "My lady, I assumed you had a plan." He smiled. "So far, you always do."

Sauce liked Conte Simone; for all his male vanity he was a bonny fighter. "I fight one fight at a time," she said. "And I always drop the easy punter first."

Everyone nodded.

"Punter?" Simone asked.

"Customer?" Sauce said. "Or, er... adversary?"

Giselle barked a laugh. She took a deep breath. "Mitla," she said. "While we move food. We don't need to beat him. If we hold the river line and keep open the road to Arelat, then we need do nothing more." She looked at a set of wax tablets from her purse. "Captain Corner says that we should have our first convoy through here in two days. Let's make Mitla dance to our tune."

Sauce was looking at a map. She realized with a start that it was one of a sheaf of maps Kronmir had drawn himself. She also realized that Giselle knew who had drawn it.

She's a tough girl, Sauce thought. She tapped her gapped teeth with a brass-bound pencil.

"I wanted him beat," she admitted to her captains. "But fuck it. That's just my pride. Duchess is right. Let's start moving food. Milus, you dig in here." She pointed at a town called Fornello. "Make it sturdy. You're the covering force. Simone, you are with me, in reserve."

"I very much enjoyed this 'reserve,'" he said. "Good fighting."

"I was hopin' that this time it'd be a little more restful," she said.

"I am hoping to see you favour us by breaking a lance on an enemy," he said.

She licked her lips. "You callin' me out?" she asked.

He looked startled. "No," he said. "I assumed, as you are a knight, that you are... sad?... that you were not fighting."

"Christ, are you sure you ain't related to Tom Lachlan?" she said. "But aye. I like a scrap. No doubt we'll find one. An' since we're coverin' the road and not pushin' north, Daniel, why don't you take some of the lads an' lasses and fetch us the Patriarch?"

"If the Patriarch is... roughly handled..." Simone said carefully. He fingered his elegant beard. There was blood under his nails. "It could... have consequences."

"I would like to go with the party to catch him," the duchess said.

Sauce looked at her and shrugged. "On your head be it," she said. "I need you here. Or I'd rather you were here. Kronmir should never have been where he could be caught, and that was my fault. Now I'm not *happy* to let you go, but you're the duchess and I can't stop you." She turned to Simone. "I was no great friend to Kronmir but he was one of mine. The Patriarch..." She smiled in a way that made her ugly.

She thought of a man who had done her a wrong, long ago. And Cully's hands on hers, and the blood. "I cover my debts. So does the duchess. The Patriarch will pay..." She gave a small shrug.

Daniel Favour nodded.

"They say you'll go to hell if you kill the Patriarch," the duchess said, as if contemplating the words.

"Oh," Sauce said with a shrug. "I doubt God's that stupid."

"'Vengeance is m-m-mine,' s-s-saith the Lord," quoted Father Davide. "B-b-but I agree that G-G-God is in f-fact not a f-fool." The thin man wore only a robe and sandals and would not wear even a dagger. He was very different from Father Arnauld, and yet many already accepted him despite his stutter.

"I will share my vengeance with him," said the duchess.

Sauce smiled. She rose. They all rose. She was human enough to savour her moment; triumph and power over others, love and respect.

A life she'd never even imagined having. She thought of them: the tormentors, the evil ones. The right bastards and the casual bastards, and how she had once felt. She looked at Giselle, and had a glimmer of what was in her head.

She smiled at Giselle. "Fuck it then. Go get him," she said. "But I need you here, and it seems to me, sister, that you don't actually need to get him in person."

As they filed out of her pavilion, Father Davide remained. "Rev-v-venge is ugly," he said.

Sauce shrugged. "We're not choir boys, Padre," she said.

He shook his head. "C-c-choir b-boys are not c-c-choir boys, C-C-Captain."

"Listen, Padre. You will have my confession, and you know what we are doing." Sauce shrugged. "It may be vengeance for some, it definitely is for Giselle. For me, it is strictly business. When they scrag the Patriarch, that's one job done." She looked away, poured them both wine, sat back. "You'd try this line on Gabriel?"

"Every t-t-time," Father Davide said.

She nodded, looking out the open side of pavilion at the quiet bustle of a camp at night.

"People did bad things to me once," Sauce said after a long pull at her wine. "Cully helped me fuck them up." She nodded.

"And that made it better?" Father Davide asked without a stutter. "Or is that just a s-s-story you t-t-tell yourself?"

"Isn't religion a story we tell ourselves?" Sauce asked. "C'mon, Padre. It's all a story. Yes, it made me feel better, and no, none of those bastards will ever have a chance to fuck with another girl, nor boy. Eh?"

Father Davide drank his wine.

Sauce looked at him. "How're we going to win this without leaving a trail of blood?" she asked.

"I have no idea," Father Davide said, with a trace of bitterness Sauce had not heard before. "Sometimes I f-f-feel like the f-fucking court jester." He took a deep breath, finished his wine, and rose to his feet. "But actions have c-c-c-consequences, my lady, and the k-killing of innocents..."

"The Patriarch?" she asked.

"Granted," he said. "The m-men standing by the P-P..." He paused and looked away. "Patriarch? The foot soldiers from Firensi?"

She nodded.

"Honestly, my lady, I wasn't here to d-d-debate the m-morality of our m-methods," the priest said. "The d-d-duchess is n-not herself, but K-K-Kronmir said something as he d-died. He s-s-said," and Father Davide paused again.

Sauce had time to wonder to whom priests turned when they were out of faith. Father Davide looked bad.

"He said," Father Davide's eyes locked with hers, "That the *w-will* is not the Necromancer."

Sauce thought of her interview with the worm that had been in Kronmir. "Ahh," she said. "I interrogated Kronmir's worm."

"You know I'm going to tell you that even the Odine are part of God's creation," Father Davide said in one go.

"Of course. From the same time he made mosquitoes and cockroaches, no doubt." Sauce gave the priest a look, as if to say that her faith gave him a certain license, but he was nearing its limits.

He bowed. "I m-merely relate what K-K-Kronmir s-said. He d-died...with incredible c-courage."

Sauce had trouble reading the priest in the candlelight. "And he would know, I guess," she said. "Blessed Saint Michael."

She called to her new page. "Alissa! I need to change the message."

She then dictated it all: Kronmir's death, his last words, and the curiously naive ragings of her captive Odine.

Who had complained bitterly of the perfidy of something it called *the Fire*.

Chapter Four

Arles—The Red Knight, over central Galle

Gabriel's layered shields were up now, and mostly held the incredible flash of *ops*, but despite losses, he loosed back, throwing preset counters down his opponent's line of thought in the *aethereal* while *Prudentia spun and spun his memory palace, catching, amplifying, shielding…*

Another godlike fist of power struck his shields, and his shields held again.

He had time to think about what Mortirmir had said about the accession of powers. He had already turned to flee; his reactions in the *aethereal* were defensive…

But he was untouched.

He leaned, and Ariosto turned.

There, below him, was a forest, and in the forest there were Titans. Hundreds of them, their size a little distorting until he saw one by a tree.

Umroth.

A whole herd.

Connections were made; more, when he saw the herd draw power in a great indrawn *aethereal* effect like a breath taken; every one of the four hundred or more not-dead beasts…

A *distributed* intelligence.

Odine. Rebel Odine, if Kronmir was correct.

He knew the working that Mortimir had used to free the not-dead at Arles, but he didn't have it cast, ready at hand, hanging on Prudentia's arm or around her neck. It was something that would take time and patience to work, and right then he had neither.

And he was taking an utterly unnecessary risk.

Inside his helmet, his lips twitched involuntarily, and Ariosto screamed, pivoted, and struck like the great predator he was. His wings overshadowed one of the Umroth, and the thing, thirty hands high, forty feet long, with four legs like pillars and huge tusks that curved like Mamluks' scimitars.

The huge thing reared on its hind legs, reaching for the heavens.

Gabriel's *ghiavarina* shot lightning, which careened off the thing's black hermetical shield—the only *passive* shield he'd ever seen. He coveted it; a shield that was always on . . .

Ariosto screamed. His talons slammed into the shield.

Leaning out, Gabriel's weapon sliced through the black shield, and the combined assault of talon and weapon defeated it; it vanished, Ariosto's talons raked the thing's head, and Gabriel pulsed three bolts into the stinking carcass of the ancient, not-dead hulk, the third a different hue from the first two, and they were past, rising away as two more of the monsters charged them from the deep, dark spruce forest.

A ripple passed over the herd, almost as if their colour was changing. The one Gabriel had hit exploded.

"Home," the Red Knight said.

Behind him, a shapeless black arm reached out of the herd. It grew until it was hundreds of feet high, and then it reached into the east, as if blindly groping for Ariosto.

Gabriel blew it a kiss, and raced farther east into the rain clouds.

Mitla—The Duke of Mitla

Three hundred leagues to the east, the Duke of Mitla drank two cups of wine, spilling some in his haste to get it down. He had to put aside his burning impatience at the tardiness of his allies; he was angry, and his anger frightened his guards and servants. Then he shed his armour. No squire helped him, and as the armour fell to the floor and met the spilled wine, it *hissed* with heat.

Dressed in Ifriquy'an *aesbaestos*, he went out into the public square under heavy guard to give alms to the poor on his way to mass. His chamberlain handed him a heavy purse of chain maille, and he went along a line of poor men, putting a solid gold coin in each hand. The coins were hot.

"Pray for me," he said as he came to each man.

They fawned on him, but they had learned better than to touch him. They took their coins from a slight distance. Which he enjoyed. He hated it when the poor were not appropriately thankful for his largesse, and he basked in their proper admiration.

"Pray for me," he said, putting a gold coin in a woman's hand.

"Your bravos killed my man," she said. If the touch of his fingers burned her, she gave no sign.

He paused. And glared. "Take the coin from her," he said to his chamberlain.

The woman must have known she would forfeit the coin by making any protest, but she struggled and a pair of soldiers beat her with their scabbarded swords. The gathered crowd watched, silent, as the thugs beat the woman, who was old enough to be anyone's mother. It wasn't a severe beating; no bones were broken. It was merely humiliating.

Infuriatingly, the woman smiled throughout her beating.

"You'll see," she said through her split lips.

"See what, Mother?" asked one of the soldiers. "You don't have anything I want to see." He smacked her again for emphasis and then tugged at his hose to smooth them while his partner rotated his head, reseating his chain maille collar.

The duke moved on, putting coins into hands of fawning men, now well ahead of his escort.

"You missed one," whispered his chamberlain.

The Duke of Mitla was at the part he always dreaded—the lepers. He tried not to touch them at all, and indeed, he feared them.

But in his hurry to get it done, he'd skipped a man, a sort of huddle of rags with a round, nondescript face.

He held out the coin and the man seized his hand, a shocking invasion of his space. And used it to pull himself to his feet.

"Pray for me," spat the duke in revulsion. The man *was* a leper. And he had touched the duke. The duke turned away and hurried through the others, avoiding contact as much as he could.

His right hand began to hurt. The duke had a good understanding of the darkness of his own head; he knew that he was manufacturing pain because he feared the leper. He resisted his own urge to look at his hand; he told himself the throbbing was in his mind. But the last of the lepers actually flinched when handed the coin; the horrible man had no lips and no nose, and yet he had the effrontery to pull away from the duke's coin.

One of the soldiers at the duke's side gave a low hiss.

The duke's hand was *black*, and the black was spreading rapidly up the veins of his arm and under his shirt cuff. The leper shrunk away.

The duke gave a choked scream.

His chamberlain grabbed his shoulders. "Your Grace! We must cut it!"

The duke spun away. "Out of my way!" he bellowed. The pain was incredible. He couldn't think. Fire played around his lips; his soldiers flinched.

One of the soldiers cut down the nearest leper, and people in the square began to scream.

The whole skin of the Duke of Mitla seemed to split apart and the duke's head opened as if cut with a battle-axe.

The man who had been the nondescript bundle of rags grabbed the beaten woman by the hand and hauled her along as if she were a child. The soldiers were killing indiscriminately, but everyone was trying to escape the creature that seemed to be clawing its way out of the duke's body. Whatever it was, it was turning black. It moved with incredible speed, but it bludgeoned into the wall of the cathedral garden as if blinded, and cannoned into a trio of screaming women.

They were ten paces away, and the nondescript man went into an open house door on the square and out the kitchens into a small garden, where the gate was open. He dragged the woman behind him. His right hand had a burn mark across the palm, and so did hers.

They went through the gate into an alley.

Up the alley to the back of the cathedral.

The bundle of rags shed his rags and his face makeup and became a notary in fine, but difficult to describe, brown and grey wool.

"Sorry they beat you," he said in unaccented Etruscan.

"Worth it," the woman spat through her split lip. "Why is he so hot?"

"No idea," said the man. "I still don't know what just happened."

They walked through the back of the crowd in the cathedral; the same crowd whose front had just watched the duke contract some dread disease. They crossed the nave and left by the side chapel door, which was open, and crossed the street into the poorer neighborhoods behind the church school. They walked fast, but that was normal for well-dressed people in this area, and as soon as they entered the stews, they were clear of the press of people flocking to see what had happened. The duke was a very unpopular man, and the series of open doors and gates they'd just passed mapped his unpopularity across the city.

The middle-aged couple walked out the back of the stews and along a line of traveler's taverns by the city's Berona gate. There were soldiers there, but there were soldiers everywhere, and the couple went into the second-to-last inn, and emerged with the lady's face clean, at least; she looked as if she'd been beaten, but that was not so uncommon. Both of them riding good horses. Excellent horses, in fact—Ifriquy'ans.

They rode to the gate with a baggage donkey behind them. By then, there was a rumour that the duke was dead and a demon had emerged from his body and now it was dead, too, and the soldiers were on edge, debating closing the gate.

The couple were patient and meek, a merchant and his wife going to Firensi on business.

"There's a war in the way, you fool," growled one of the soldiers.

The merchant bowed. "I have a pass from the duke," he said. "And one from the Count of Berona."

The gate captain assessed the cost of two such passes and the magnificent riding horses and became more respectful.

"We should close the gate," demanded his sergeant.

The gate captain nodded. "No one's ordered it," he said, pocketing the golden coin he'd just found stuck to the merchant's pass with a bit of beeswax. "Let 'em through!"

The merchant and his wife rode slowly out of the city, their horses ambling, and could be seen for half an hour as they made a quarter circuit of the city walls at a glacial pace before turning into the countryside.

A mile south of the city, they turned sharply off the road, onto a farm track that led into a farm yard where two infidels were holding horses.

M'bub Ali emerged from the barn. "Well?" he asked.

Brown shrugged. "A fucking disgrace."

"Did you get him?" Ali asked.

Brown shook his head. "No idea. The poison didn't kill him outright; never seen anything like it."

The woman, Donna Beatrice, raised her face. "I saw," she said. "There was a daemon from hell inside the duke. He ripped the duke open and came out into the light of the sun, which shriveled him black."

Brown turned and looked at her. "A word of advice, goodwife. Go far away—Venike, or Rhum. Never mention this again, even to yourself. One of these lads will see you have a change of clothes and a bag of gold."

"Killed my husband," the woman said. "Killed my son. I'd have done it for free." Her head was high, her eyes shining. "I don't care if they catch me." But then she seemed to shrink. "I don't even know what to do now."

M'bub Ali gave her a slow smile. "No husband, no brother, no sister, no child?" he asked.

She shook her head.

M'bub Ali raised an eyebrow. "You might as well come with us," he said.

Brown, who mostly disliked people, sighed. "We're not recruiting," he said.

Arles—The Red Knight

"Sauce beat the Patriarch. Kronmir's dead," said Bad Tom.

Gabriel got his helmet off. "You bedside manner's still a little rough."

"Aye, I liked him." Tom shrugged. "Loons get kilt. Live by the sword, die by the sword. Aye?"

"Och, aye," Gabriel said. He was reading the thin parchment in

Tom's fist that had been brought by the messenger, and anger and depression settled on him. He told himself it was a reaction to the fight.

"Jesus," Gabriel said. "Oh God."

Tom Lachlan smiled a hard smile. "Ye ken it was a *man* who did that to him, aye? Nae monster. Nae dragon. Nae worm. Only fuckin' men."

Gabriel blinked. He was in the place he went, where all he could see was all the people he'd killed. "Yes, Tom. I take your meaning."

"Sauce talked to the worm. It never got into Kronmir's head."

Gabriel let go a breath.

"That close," Lachlan said, and suddenly his arms were around Gabriel. "Fuck it, Gabriel. We almost lost it all, and Kronmir, that slippery bastard, held 'em. In his wee head. 'Til he *died*." Bad Tom was looking out at the falling darkness. "Mayhap the bravest fuckin' thing I've ever heard."

"Aye, Tom."

Tom Lachlan shook his head. "Didn't even like the loon," he admitted.

Gabriel took a deep breath. "I did," he said. "Get me Mortirmir, please."

Mortirmir found Gabriel watching Ariosto eat.

"You found him," Mortirmir said with satisfaction. "I have him to the inch."

"Yes," Gabriel said. "He's distributed in a whole herd of Umroth." He described the passive shield.

Mortirmir raised both eyebrows.

"I'll save the time of saying that's impossible," he said. "It's fascinating."

Gabriel had out a map. One of Kronmir's maps.

"He's dead," Mortirmir said.

"I know," Gabriel nodded.

Mortirmir shook his head. "Tancreda was instrumental in winning the battle," he said. "I wonder what I'd do if they did to Tancreda what they did to Ser Jules." He frowned.

Gabriel winced. "I also agree with you that we have increased in power. I assume that distributed intelligence is the Necromancer. He couldn't get through my shields."

Mortirmir nodded. "I can find the Patriarch," he said. "Any idea what the Patriarch actually *is*?"

"We need to finish the Necromancer," Gabriel said. "And we have some evidence that the Patriarch isn't the tool of the Necromancer, but serves *another* will. Or is a new player."

"I *want* to find the Patriarch," Mortirmir said. He glanced at Gabriel. "Ahh. Yes. A third player. Master Smythe never even hinted at such a thing. Kronmir did."

Gabriel took a deep breath. "I know. Necromancer first." He looked at Mortirmir. "Kronmir was afraid we're being played."

Mortirmir shrugged. "Very well. When?"

"Day after tomorrow," Gabriel said. "Then we'll find the Patriarch."

Mortirmir nodded. "Shorn of his army, I suppose he's nobody."

Gabriel smiled. "And if Giselle finds him first, he'll be very thoroughly nobody," he said. "But I worry that we have a third player and we know so little."

Mortirmir pulled at his mustache. "We could have ten more players," he said. "If they are dragons, they can take men's shapes. If they are Odine, they can control men. How would we know?" He looked at Gabriel and frowned. "We could even have players who *are* men. And women. Anything we have learned may be known by others. Dame Julia's prognostications are not exactly a secret."

"Christ," Gabriel muttered.

Mortirmir waved a hand in adolescent dismissiveness. "Never mind. Let's just kill the ones we can find. Life is complicated enough already." He raised an eyebrow. "Speaking of which, I've unpacked most of Magister Rashidi's workings."

"And?" Gabriel knew that he had *not* unpacked his set of tiles. And he needed to.

"I know how to make a Fell Sword." Morgon smiled.

"Harmodius..."

"He knows how and chooses not to share." Mortirmir shrugged.

Gabriel was staring east.

"Gabriel," Mortirmir said with a familiarity no one else used anymore except Sauce and Bad Tom. "You don't think it's all about Ash? It won't *end*. That was Master Smythe's great point, and he made it well. Even if we win here, there will be another and another and another. To the last syllable of recorded time."

"Thanks for that cheerful thought. You are right. Let's just squash the ones we can see." Gabriel sighed. "Jehan once asked me if I could fight all the time, every day. And today I find the answer to be: no. I'm *tired*."

Morgon looked raised an eyebrow. "My point about the Fell Swords..." he said.

"Yes?" Gabriel asked, mystified. Perhaps even annoyed, because Mortirmir, once launched on a topic, was as tough as one of his own shields to dislodge.

"I could make them." Mortirmir smiled.

"Really?" Gabriel asked.

"It is really just an exercise in linking points in the real to points in the *aethereal*. Mortirmir *entered Gabriel's memory palace and showed him.*

"That's incredibly power intensive," Gabriel said. The process took his breath away; it was, to a startling degree, beautiful.

"I could do a few a day, when I was safe and didn't need the ops.*" Mortirmir raised his eyebrows.*

"A few a day?" Gabriel said. "It would take me all day to make one."

"Do not," Mortirmir said. "I feel in you that same transcendence we saw in Sister Amicia..."

"Yes, I know. Thanks so very much."

"You are welcome, of course. You should restrict your casting to the bare essentials. Yes, I think I could manage three to five a day at first; more later." Mortirmir's velvet-clad avatar gestured grandly.

"Arm the casa?*" Gabriel smiled.*

"Yes. Although I will note that there is a direct relation between the mass of the matter and the difficulty of the transference. So that a long sword is a masterwork; an arrowhead is a mere bagatelle." Mortirmir pursed his lips. "Do I mean bagatelle?" He frowned. "I have been circuitous, I find. Listen, then...I want to say that we will be fighting increasingly...hermetical opponents."

"I certainly hope so," Gabriel said.

"Well, a little interface between the hermetical and the real would spare us some effort."

166

"That's one way of putting it." Gabriel stretched.

"You are truly growing tired of war?" Morgon asked.

"Never mind," Gabriel said. "It was years ago." He paused, and a look of confusion passed over his face, and he grimaced. "Like, two years ago," he admitted.

Adrian Goldsmith stood a few yards away, sketching them.

They marched before dawn, following Count Zac's guides through the woods, heading north and west. The easterner had a new weapon, which he demonstrated for Gabriel and Bad Tom; a tube which fit to his bow, so that he could shoot very short, heavy darts from his powerful horn bow.

"So?" asked Tom.

"Watch," Zakje said. He put the half-tube against the lacquered bow and used it to draw a slim arrow with a long steel head. He loosed it through the moonlight at a small ash, and the arrow *went through the tree*.

"It turns your bow into a crossbow," Bad Tom said.

"It will help us kill the big monsters," Zakje said. "And knights, too," he added with a wicked grin at Tom Lachlan.

Forest of Northern Arles—Cully

The stars were bright and seemed very close, and the comet was so brilliant that its light created shadows that crossed the shadows cast by the equally brilliant moon. The trees seemed almost infinite, their branches silver in the starlight, rolling away to east and west in a mysterious majesty of leaf and branch.

Urk of Mogon looked into the vastness and nodded at Cully, breaking open his mandibles. "Want to walk away," he said. "Want to walk into cool dark and green and never come out."

Cully frowned. "All I see is standing firewood."

Urk looked at him, his all-too-human eyes registering revulsion. "Here is beauty," he said.

Cully put an arm around the thing's wing cases. It had taken an act of will once, to embrace the bug, but that was weeks and many shared dangers ago. "If'n you say so, mate," he said. "In the dark, I see danger, spiders, wet, cold, and hunger." He shrugged apologetically. "No pay, no wine, no women, and no fuckin' song."

Urk smiled, his four jaws yawning in a particularly loathsome way. "You make war," he said. "And this war is nothing but cold, damp, and danger."

"True for you, mate," Cully muttered. "But there's pay."

"And?" the bug asked.

"Oh aye, yer fewkin' point is made." Cully looked out into the dark and threatening woods, trying to see a shred of beauty.

Adrian Goldsmith watched the captain, which was to say the emperor, mount his griffon. He sketched rapidly in the book he now carried all the time. Ariosto stretched, a particular motion he made before his wings began their beat, and in that moment he was perfectly caught by the rising sun; the fractal complexity of his feathered wings, before he blazed into a single glory of ruddy gold; the scarlet of his saddle and reins and holding strap, the brilliant scarlet and steel of his rider.

The captain launched into the morning air, and Tom Lachlan was suddenly everywhere, bellowing orders, and Edmund went down the guild line, stopped to look at Duke, and the two mocked each other for a moment, as usual.

Adrian Goldsmith felt a pang of homesickness. He was, after all, guild born and bred.

Lachlan was right behind Edmund, and he stopped to talk to two apprentices from the Cutlers' Guild. He leaned forward a little, his darkly burnished armour somehow one with the last of the night, the gold edges glowing with the rising sun. Adrian switched targets, flipped his palette, and began to sketch the Primus Pilus.

Lachlan was hefting one of the heavy bronze tubes on a long spear pole. "Hard to carry?" he asked.

Donald Leary, Cutler's apprentice, was the kind of Harndoner who was not ever abashed. "Heavy as sin, mate," he said as if he and the giant knight were old friends.

"Aye," Lachlan agreed. "An' how many rounds do ye ha'e?"

Leary smiled. "Forty," he said.

Bad Tom looked at the thing, like a mace on a pole. "Sweet Christ," he said. "Well, Gabriel thinks the world o' yon. I ha'e me doubts." He shrugged and looked at the crews of the two long bronze falconets on their wheeled carriages.

Francis Atcourt, who was nominally in charge of the *casa* and liked to divert Tom's attention if he could, spoke up. "We've hauled these blessed things over hill and dale for a year," he agreed. "And never used a one."

Tom nodded at Edmund. "They work?" he asked.

Edmund nodded. "I promise you they do, Ser Knight. Show us a dragon."

Bad Tom Laughed. "Aye, that's the spirit," he said, his tone indicating that he didn't believe the things could harm a house cat. The head of the column was long gone, and Tom realized he was slowing his own march. "Off wi' ye," he said. "Tomorrow we'll see what yer smelly de'il's powder is worth."

Forty leagues later, and again the force made camp with few fires and no tents. Men were hungry; the dash across the Massif had taken a toll in men and horses. The food wagons were mostly empty, and Gabriel ordered them unloaded and sent back. But he ordered a dozen kept, and gave no reason.

"I wish you could ride Ariosto," he said as an aside to Morgon.

"I don't," Morgon admitted. "Sufficient unto the day is the evil thereof. That beast mislikes me."

"Beast my arse," Gabriel said. There was a silence; both men had their own thoughts. Finally Gabriel said, "Sometimes I suspect I am the junior partner."

"I am sure your temporal power more than balances my superiority of hermetical talent," Mortirmir said graciously.

"I meant to Ariosto," Gabriel said.

There was a little more silence.

Gabriel smiled to himself, and was saved from further insulting his most vital asset by the arrival of his officers. Toby hovered, no longer a squire but eager to help Anne; Anne laid out a folding table, and two pages placed the top across the sawhorse-like folding legs. Another of Kronmir's carefully drawn maps was laid down and the curling corners tacked with eating knives.

Kronmir's beautiful calligraphy, each place name carefully labeled, stood as a monument to the man. Gabriel felt a lump in his throat; had more than a passing qualm about the bodies he was leaving behind. He paused.

"I assume we're out of wine?" he asked Anne. She looked startled, and blinked, then waved to one of the pages.

Gabriel sighed. He took a breath, steadied himself, and pointed at the map. "Here's where the Necromancer is. He must know what's coming for him. Today he tried to slip south and ran into Pavalo's pickets, so now he's coming for us. Du Corse is hard on his heels, here." He drew them out. "Pavalo cut up most of his not-dead people and trapped two of the Umroth, the way they do it, in pit traps." He shrugged. "We don't have any soft soil to dig pits in, so we'll need a little luck."

Francis Atcourt handed his emperor a heavy glass flask with a densely woven net covering of linen to protect the precious glass. It sloshed.

Gabriel grinned and took a mouthful. "Ahh," he said.

Morgon Mortirmir leaned over.

Atcourt tapped the map wordlessly and Bad Tom took the wine. "It's more like hunting than like fuckin' war," he said.

"And so, when we move, we move from cover to cover," Gabriel said. "Right here. Mouth of this valley. And we hold there until Pavalo or Du Corse comes."

Mortirmir shrugged. "We can just finish the Necromancer ourselves," he said. "No need for all this elaborate preparation."

"Why don't ye fewkin' go fight the thing in yer hosen and the rest o' we will ha'e a nice day off an' wash our fewkin' clothes?" Tom spat. "Ye talk a mickle stream of shite fer a boy wi' ten hairs on his wee face."

"Tom?" Gabriel said. "He probably can take the Necromancer one to one. I certainly hope he can. The rest of us are here to avert various alternatives. And disasters."

"Thank you," Mortirmir said icily.

"I ha'e said it before and, nae doot, I'll ha'e to say it agin. Ye'r takin' all the joy out o' war." Bad Tom took another swig from the bottle and left the group.

"That oaf thinks we are here to amuse ourselves," Mortirmir said.

Bad Tom reappeared. "Oaf?" he asked. He was smiling ear to ear.

"Tom," Gabriel said.

"Oh aye. I'll beat the fuck oot o' him tomorrow after he cooks the Necromancer," Lachlan said. "I promise ye that, *boy*."

"It's a band of brothers," Gabriel said wearily to Francis Atcourt, who handed him the empty bottle.

Morning dawned and the company was awake, hungry, surly, and moving very fast over the hills. Their riding horses were done in, their bellies were grumbling, and even water was in short supply.

Gabriel was aloft as soon as it was light, feeling his way north and west, flying very low and inhabiting the *aethereal*, leaving Ariosto to handle the real. But the Necromancer was invisible, and Morgon's passive location technique was no help.

And Gabriel felt alone, exposed, and foolish.

When the sky was merely pink, he overflew the Ifriquy'an columns to the west. They were all mounted, moving quickly with a herd of remounts, and a line of dust like surf on a beach marked the front of their skirmish line. He could feel the power of at least four casters, all pupils of the great Al Rashidi, and he was reassured.

He landed. He tried to ignore the signs of looting; the Gallish women in the tents. Galle and Ifriquy'a had known war for centuries. But it still rankled.

A slave led him to a circle of horsemen; Pavalo Payam sat in the middle. Something had changed in him; the slight subservience he had always showed in Alba was gone, as if burnished off as a flaw; now he was a warrior among warriors, the paramount warrior.

He did not bend so much as a muscle of his neck.

"Ser Pavalo," Gabriel said.

"Ser Gabriel. Your beast makes our horses uneasy." Then he allowed his old, easy smile to cross his grave face. "We have him, I think. Salim al-Raisouli brushed his screens less than half an hour ago. He flinched away from us."

Gabriel unrolled one of Kronmir's maps, and the mamluk officer dismounted—grudgingly. Gabriel gathered that most of them viewed war as an exercise in horsemanship, not map reading.

When they were all oriented, Pavalo summoned Salim, and the magister, mounted on a mule, placed coloured symbols of light on the Venike paper of the map.

Gabriel nodded to Pavalo. "I think we've got him. I need to hurry."

Pavalo grinned. "This is a great day. And Du Corse?"

"Close. He has the most men and the worst hermeticals. I don't want him engaged unless we have no choice." Gabriel looked up to see one of the mamluks listening to the translation with what could only be described as a wolfish glee.

"A word with you?" Gabriel asked. He walked out of the circle, until he and Pavalo were as alone as they could be in the midst of an army of ten thousand.

"This is delicate," Gabriel said. "And I have no time. So...please do not consider going for Du Corse when the Necromancer is eliminated." He smiled with what he thought was good courtesy.

Pavalo returned the smile. "I will, in all things, obey the commands of my sultan," he said. "I am not a servant of the emperor."

Gabriel looked back over the column. "You have been to Alba. You heard Al Rashidi. You know what's at stake."

Pavalo nodded. "I do, Gabriel. But sometimes I think it is... naive...of you to imagine that every man you meet can be trusted to keep his eyes on the main goal and not seize some of the prize for himself."

Gabriel nodded, relieved that it was in the open. "Ah, Pavalo, I understand; usually I try to find a way to engage self-interest alongside the greater values." He looked back at the column, letting his eyes rest on a chain of Gallish peasants clearly taken as slaves. "If we fall, he will exterminate us, root and branch," Gabriel said. "There will be no private triumph. And if we triumph," Gabriel said quietly, "do you not think that we will be so puissant that it might be better to be our ally than our rival? Because any power that can break the dragons will be a mighty power for many years."

"This is very like a threat," Pavalo said, stung.

Gabriel shrugged. "Pavalo, I am in a hurry; I am afraid of the Necromancer, I have to ride the air alone, and your mamluks are clearly posturing. And they are taking slaves."

Instead of further bridling, Pavalo stepped closer and put an arm on Gabriel's shoulder. "Ah! That is the sand in the shoe, is it? Yet if I fought them on this, I would have to fight many other battles. My word to them is the same as yours to me. Defeat the Necromancer, and then see what cometh. Yes?"

Alliance was a dangerous process. But he *needed* Pavalo, and the man had been Rashid's paladin. He, of all men, knew what was at stake.

"Yes," he said. But as Ariosto climbed away and the sun peeked over the shoulder of the world, he thought how sad and twisted it was that he found it easier to trust Du Corse, whose ambition he could understand, then Payam, who was a far nobler man, but whose loyalties were almost unfathomable.

Before the red orb of the sun was resting on the eastern horizon, he was standing with Du Corse, twenty leagues to the north.

"No contact at all," Du Corse said.

"Let's keep it that way," Gabriel said, and unleashed a great pulse of *ops* into the real. He did so again from the back of Ariosto as they rose over the Gallish army, cheered by the knights and the foot soldiers, too.

And then Gabriel attempted the experiment that he and Morgon had discussed on the ship, what seemed like months before. For the first time, Gabriel attempted to raise a wave front of emotion, as the great creatures of the Wild did. He found it easy enough to raise fear within *himself, and once raised, to project it, and he was amused to discover that the waves of fear and terror that creatures projected were mere outward signs of their inward emotions. Of course the wardens were afraid of combat; of course the wyverns feared man. Even as he shaped his projection, he understood what Morgon had suggested—that the great powers had developed these emotional fronts as ways of detecting the presence of their ancient enemy. Somehow that was both sobering and profound.*

And there it was. It was so easy that Gabriel might have cursed, if the whole of his attention was not on his projection. But the Necromancer was instantly visible as a vacancy in the emotional world that the aethereal *could be, despite the attempts of humans to render it rational.*

Finding an object or entity in the aethereal *was not always the same as finding them in the real, but in this case, the ranges were short and the resolution surprisingly fine.*

In the real, Gabriel laughed again. And fled, diving to the very height of the treetops to put solid earth between his route and the enemy.

He landed in a beautiful dawn, and Ariosto hopped off to eat sheep.

His force had moved farther than he had thought possible; they were dismounting in a deep valley between two rocky summits. The ground was sandy and full of glacial rock, and despite that, there were ropes already stretched across the valley.

Forty yards away, Cully groaned.

Adrian Goldsmith groaned.

In fact, almost every soldier groaned, because the stretched ropes on neat wooden pegs meant they were to dig. Most men had a pick, and a few had shovels, and most of them were veterans of other engineering feats, but the shallow soil and rock looked particularly threatening.

Bad Tom rode along the rope line, his great warhorse kicking up dust. "However much ye may hate to dig, lads," he roared, "that trench and upcast will seem like yer maether's own hearthside when the Umroth charge ye. Now get it done. And put in yer stakes. Every fewkin' one."

Cully watched Anne and Toby begin to dig, and he took a drink of water from his almost empty canteen and walked back to where the captain and the banner were. Young Mortirmir was casting; he had that look, and he already had shields up. The captain was watching his griffon eat.

The captain was just speaking. "I've never found my cowardice so useful," he was just saying, and Morgon wore a rare smile.

"My lord, I honour you for essaying it, and the result is remarkable." The magister gave a terrible smile. "I cannot wait to try myself," he admitted.

"Sorry to interrupt, Cap'n," Cully said. "You want me wi' ye, or wi' Toby?"

"I'll be in the air soon enough," Gabriel said. "Don't let Toby die. Or Anne."

Cully smiled. "Lads would like it if you'd dig," he said softly.

Gabriel met his eye. His sigh was heavy.

"Fine," he said. "I know you're right. I just don't like it. I'm already tired." He walked forward, still wearing only his arming clothes. Two pages had his flying armour on a ground sheet.

He walked up to the line and wordlessly took a pick from Anne Woodstock. "Go make sure my harness is ready," he said. She wiped sweat off her brow in the chilly autumn air and managed a bow before heading back.

Gabriel began to work the ground with the pick. Anne had found a rock about the size of two men's heads. He worked around it, loosening the soil, and then when the pick used as a crowbar moved the whole thing, he summoned Tom Lachlan, and the two of them lifted the rock and threw it on the upcast.

Cully stepped in with a small shovel and cleared all the loose soil onto the upcast.

"I've got them," Mortirmir said. "Him. Them. Coming this way." He looked down. "I don't suppose I should ask you why you, the Emperor of Man, are wasting your time digging? When you should be preparing your workings?"

Gabriel began to work away at the ground again. The first blow hit yet another rock, the blow almost numbing his hands. "Because I need these men and women, Morgon," he said. "I need them alive. And to survive the next hours, I need them in trenches."

"Yes," Morgon agreed.

"They will dig better if they see me dig," Gabriel said.

"Why?" Morgon asked.

Tom Lachlan slapped Morgon Mortirmir lightly on the head, and Mortirmir flinched. "You ha'e blood an' bone in there, warlock?" he asked. "Or gears?"

"And yet," Gabriel said, loosening his second rock, "He's right. I need to prepare."

Mortirmir looked at the sweating men and women. "If every one of them had a Fell Sword..."

Tom Lachlan paused. "Ye can do that, laddie? I'd stop givin' ye shite if ye did." He grinned.

Then he grunted, dismounted again from his warhorse that was as tall and black as the emperor's Ataelus, and armoured head to foot, took the pick from his captain. He threw one blow, even as the captain muscled his way out of the rapidly forming trench, and his pick-blow split the rock Gabriel had been working at.

He looked up.

"Brawly fechit," Gabriel said.

"Ye sound like a wee fool when you try and sound like a Hillman," Lachlan said with a grin.

"You should hear what you sound like to us," Gabriel said. "Right. I've faced the dirt. Let's face the Necromancer."

*

In the center of the line, a wagon, one of only four left with them, dropped four huge wicker baskets, as tall as a man and as big around as a tree in the Adnacrags. Immediately, every man in the guilds began to fill them with dirt. The dirt came from in front; they were in the middle of the valley, with the deepest soil, and the work went quickly, the more so as every stone they found could also go into the huge baskets.

Horses came up, and the falconets were dropped into position between the baskets. Their crews began to tend to them. The rest of the guildsmen kept digging.

The sun was halfway up into the sky and the more pious had just finished saying their hurried devotions when trumpets sounded. In most places the trench was four feet deep and the upcast at least two feet high. Most of the archers and all the guildsmen had carried long wooden stakes for the last six days; now they planted them as deep as the soil allowed, leaning slightly out, in the top of the upcast, driven in at least three feet. The wicker baskets or *gabions* in the center were full to overflowing, the long bronze falconets gleaming in the morning sun.

Gabriel's hands were shaking.

"You know you are glowing?" Mortirmir asked him. "You are visibly golden."

Gabriel closed his eyes.

"Are you transcendent, then?" Mortirmir asked. "Interesting. Why you and not me?"

"Maturity?" Gabriel asked. He opened his eyes.

Mortirmir raised an eyebrow. "I suppose that I deserved that."

"Can we hide it?" Gabriel asked.

Mortirmir frowned. "Ask me when we're done today," he said. "For all my bluster, I want to keep every iota of *ops*."

"It almost pleases me to hear you speak thus," Gabriel said.

"Here *it* comes," Mortirmir nodded. "It? They?"

Down the valley, a cloud of dust rose.

Trumpets sounded.

Gabriel walked to Ariosto and put a hand on his hide.

Ready?

Sure, boss. A-hunting we will go.

"My lord?" Anne Woodstock was standing at his elbow. "There's a herald."

Gabriel walked back to the line of trenches and watched with Bad Tom and Mortirmir and Francis Atcourt as a man on a skeletal horse came forward.

"Well, well," Mortirmir said.

"Ye'r not goin' to ha'e speech wi' yon?" Bad Tom asked, his irritation increasing his Hillman accent.

Gabriel pursed his lips. "I am minded to speak to it," he said.

"Send me," Mortirmir said.

Gabriel looked at the young magister. "Let me pander to your pride, Morgon Mortirmir. Right now, if one of us is taken by surprise and killed, I'd rather it was me. For the good of all." He waved at Anne, but she'd already brought up Ataelus, who was restive at being left out, as had become usual, and delighted to be ridden.

Tom Lachlan unsheathed his great magical sword, what men called *The Dragon's Blade*, and held it in the air like a man holds a torch. "I'll just ride out wi' thee, eh?"

Gabriel nodded. "Yes," he agreed.

They rode a little outside the new earthworks. The sun was high, and the last damp in the newly dug ground gave a flavor to the air. It was cool and pleasant, and easy to love life.

The herald was a not-dead. He was not carefully dressed; he had a shirt, and braes that were badly soiled, and no shoes. He was tall and very thin, and his eyes didn't move. The horse he rode was as thin as he was himself.

He stopped about two horse lengths from Gabriel and Tom Lachlan. He didn't pull his reins or make a noise; rather, man and horse simply stopped.

"*Greetings,*" sang a choir within the man's throat.

Gabriel took a breath with a little effort. The thing in front of him was terrifying in its similarity to a man, and its alienness. He had never been so close to an animated not-dead, and he found the experience deeply unsettling.

"Do I address the being commonly known as the Necromancer?" Gabriel asked.

"*Yes.*" The voice was not even the half of the effect. "*I was a man once.*" After a pause. "*Or were we? Some of us were.*"

Tom's sword tip twitched like the tale of an agitated cat.

"*You are not dragons?*" the disharmonious voice said.

"No," Gabriel said.

"*Like and not like,*" said the voice. "*We thought dragons.*"

"What is the basis of this parley?" Gabriel asked.

"*I would surrender,*" the thing said. "*If that is even possible.*"

Gabriel's heart beat very hard.

"It's a trick," Tom said, his eyes hard.

"*Listen, oh man. Lord of men and Killer of men. I wish nothing but to leave. I have lost. I know it. I have reached deep into my memories and I remember this thing; that I may be allowed to surrender. Perhaps you will exterminate me. Or perhaps you will let me go. My so-called allies have abandoned me and I have nowhere else to go.*"

"Even if I could imagine a way to keep you a prisoner," Gabriel said, trying to find words to cover his shock, "I have allies who require your . . . end."

"*You have regard for your fellows? Then I have something to offer you. First, if we struggle, I will end many. Perhaps more than you imagine. I have the counter for the dragon's fire.*" The choir was discordant, and the words *dragon's fire* were like the knell of a church bell. "*You will not surprise me today.*"

Bad Tom smiled. "Bring it," he said.

"*Killer of men. You are afraid of nothing. I have lived too long for courage. I have none left, or I would not be attempting surrender.*" The not-dead's head didn't move, nor did its eyes. The whole horse had to move so that he could address Bad Tom.

"What else do you offer?" Gabriel asked. He was unprepared for surrender. He couldn't imagine a path from here so his temptation was to refuse, and get it over with. Couldn't imagine how he could keep an entity as alien and powerful as this to any bargain; couldn't even imagine that such an entity would understand surrender. Wasn't even sure to whom he was talking.

"*This is interesting, and in keeping with my memories of men. You have this much power and you are merely men? We/I were once men/man. Some of us.*" It paused. "*We had no idea humans could be so puissant.*"

The silence was ruthless.

Gabriel could smell the Umroth in the woods beyond the little plain of dirt and scrub, and his nose wrinkled.

"*You hold the gates?*" it asked.

"Let's say I do," Gabriel said, even as Tom's sword point twitched again.

"*Some part of me has been on the other side,*" it said. "*We could be your guide. You intend to conquer? Perhaps we could be your 'ally.' And we know many things.*" There was a pause. "*You are merely men and women, and you are to be the victors? Have you killed all the dragons? How do you escape slavery?*"

The sentences were patched together. Gabriel had to wait and read them back. The delivery was both flat and discordant, the emphasis inhuman.

Gabriel took another breath. It was curiously hard to breathe, and he glad for the comfort of Ataelus, who was solid between his legs; alive, willing, able. "I could make no agreement without my allies," Gabriel said. He was tempted to babble; to explain that when they arrived, the being had no chance at all.

Why? he asked.

He went into his palace and looked at the mirror. And saw the encroaching envelopment as a cloak of mist, a mantle of smoke.

"*Pru?*" he asked.

Her white marble face looked in the mirror. "Coercion," she said. "A masterwork."

In a moment of insight, Gabriel saw that the Necromancer, who had once been a mighty magister, had at his command not just the unearthly powers of the Odine, but human hermetical magistery as well.

"*You cannot merely accept my surrender?*" it asked.

"Serpent!" Tom Lachlan said. "Don't trust it."

Unerring, like a bolt of lightning, the dragon's blade shot out and swept through the space between them.

In the aethereal, *the wisps of coercive fog vanished like morning mist in August sun.*

The horse and rider flinched. *That is a very powerful weapon*, the voice said. *I thought I knew where all of them were. Wait! Who made that? Come, who is your master?*

Gabriel looked at Tom, and then at the herald, even as he backed

Ataelus. He rose in his stirrups, looking at the forest below, where the Umroth were waiting. "I cannot see any way that I could secure your surrender and then trust you, or work with you," Gabriel said. "I cannot imagine how I could chain you and not fear you too much to leave you…alive." He sighed. "Or whatever you are."

"*We feared this.*" The herald's horse moved, backing a few steps; not like a real horse, but without a weight change. "*Action is consequence. But man, I am Patchwork. I am not like the shadow fire, not like Ash, and the will is my inveterate foe. You have brought low my tame dragon and subsumed my puppets. I could bend my back. To live.*"

"You just tried to steal my mind," Gabriel said tersely.

"*We are not one! We are many, and there is disharmony.*"

He's casting again, said Morgon Mortirmir, who appeared suddenly inside *Gabriel's memory palace.*

Gabriel raised a shield.

The necromancer's chorus unleashed a wind; on it were studded the sorcerous roots of the Odine's control, but vastly enhanced by the ars magika. *It was a vast, potent working, harnessing gold and green and darkest black with an intricacy that rivaled Rashidi's magnificent working.*

Gabriel was staggered. But the remnants of his wave front of fear seemed to split the working like an ancient rock splits a river, for a while. Gabriel had plenty of fear; he focused it.

The terrible working, demanding submission, flowed over Gabriel's shields and then struck Morgon's just behind him in the aethereal.

The spell pooled like water meeting a dam, but whether it was a fragile dam of twigs or a mighty dam of stone remained metaphorically unsure, and the dark waters rose. And flowed over it like water over a rock. And Gabriel's fear was not enough to stem the rising flood around him. He was, alone, the target…

In a moment of panic that almost cost him his concentration, he realized that he was not alone; that Tom Lachlan was beside him. In the aethereal, *Tom's armour shone like the sun, and Master Petrarcha's sigils burned like white-hot metal.*

Gabriel wagered his life and Tom's on a hunch, and in the real he put his spurs into Ataelus's sides. His right hand went to his long sword hilt; Ataelus crashed into the herald's horse, and even as the horse began to fall, Gabriel's sword rose from the scabbard, missing Ataelus's left ear by the width of a hair, sweeping over the warhorse's head in a flat cut that caught the not-dead herald where his jaw met his neck and cut diagonally through the falling man's skull, exiting through his left eye and left temple.

The titanic *compulsion* ceased as if a door had been closed.

"Sweet fewkin' Christ," Bad Tom spat.

Mortirmir didn't pause to assess. He countercast, the huge working they'd used together just days before, and the tiny lines of light leapt away from his fingertips like thousands of illuminated bees.

They were swallowed by the darkness to the north.

"Damn," Morgon said. "That should not have happened."

"Run," Gabriel said to Bad Tom, and together they turned their horses as a veritable tide of wild animals came up the valley, thousands, tens of thousands of deer, wolves, dogs, sheep, oxen...some cadaverous, some newly taken, all in a mindless stampede.

All along the line, men and women nocked their bows.

"Not-dead animals," Gabriel shouted.

But Bad Tom had chosen his ground well, and the tide of creatures had two hundred paces of open scrub and arid dirt to cover before they could reach the ditch.

The first falconet rolled forward, its muzzle just two feet above the dirt, well dug in.

It fired over their heads.

A cloud of scrap metal flayed the center of the charging mass.

The second falconet rolled into place between its gabions and also fired, its muzzle rocking back like a barking dog.

The charge of the not-dead animals came on in almost complete silence, broken only by the sound of Cully's orders to the archers of the *casa*; Count Zac's orders to his Vardariotes; Edmund Chevins's orders to his guildsmen.

The guildsmen stepped up onto the back of the upcast dirt, leveled their tubes between the tall stakes...

"Fire," Edmund said.

Two hundred hand gonnes went off in a long ripple; no two went off exactly together.

"Loose," Cully called in his singsong command voice. The heavy arrows leapt off heavier bows, and smashed into the not-dead, falling at a steep angle like a wicked sleet.

Harald Derkensun raised his axe.

The falconets fired again. Their crews had practiced for months; they were more afraid of censure than of not-dead. Where their loads struck, the not-dead went down as if a scythe had cut through them.

Any mortal charge would have faltered. This one had huge tears in it, like an old rug pulled between angry children, and yet the not-dead came on, and any one of them knocked down by round shot or scrap metal that was not destroyed would rise and run, or hobble. Creatures missing two legs would drag themselves forward.

The not-dead came on. And there were still thousands of them.

Men in the line began to consider options. Running was not really one of them, but the archers knew that the time for archery was ending. One more arrow? Two?

The guildsmen stepped up to the wall again. The wave front was less than a hundred paces away. Every man was deeply afraid.

"Present!" Edmund Chevins called. Every tube came smartly down from vertical to horizontal. Men and women squinted down their short bronze tubes, slow match burning in their hands.

"Fire!" Edmund roared. He pushed the match into the touch hole of his own piece and felt the welcome tug of the recoil, and then he reversed it, up and over his shoulder. The stave that held the hand gonne was stout oak with a steel tip; the gonne itself made a lethal mace.

The cloud of sulphur smoke lingered like a collection of old farts and rotten eggs.

Something rippled past them from *behind*, a liquid vortex of colour that passed them at ankle height and made the hissing of a vast tribe of serpents or the fall of heavy rain as it passed. It went through the stakes, out into the smoke. Whatever it was, it seemed to sever the not-dead at their ankles, leaving them writhing in horrible deformity on the ground. The grim working passed over some, and seemed to lose coherence in the mass, but it was terrible in effect.

A stag, its antlers broken, leapt the low wall. It struck clumsily against the angled stake to Edmund's left and turned on him, and Edmund swung his massive bronze pole-mace with all his strength and fear.

The creature was struck, and struck again; its backbone and pelvis broken, and it fell and writhed until Duke severed its head. The worm erupted and Duke cut it on the back stroke.

Nothing else came out of the smoke.

"Load," Edmund said. He was amazed at the sound of his voice. He sounded so sure of himself.

A dog came out of the smoke, already short a leg, hobbling. It was struck down, its skull pulped. No worms emerged.

The smoke began to clear. A wind came up, blowing from behind them, and tore the smoke away in gouts, and *there* were the ancient not-dead mastodons towering over them, or so it seemed, although in fact they were two hundred paces away at the most distant red flags planted only that morning by the guild and the master archers.

A wave of hopelessness, of sheer, unwavering despair, the end of all joy, the extinguishing of the fires of intention, swept over the casa. *But no one ran.*

No one believed that there was anywhere to run.

It was the end of the world. The end of plans, the end of victory, the end of saving the world.

Edmund's heart skipped a beat. Or perhaps it beat too fast for him to comprehend. They were an embodiment of terror, and they came on, hundreds of them. They stretched across the field, as far as his eye could see, and the stench was terrible.

Sorcery played in the air in front of him; a rolling barrage of fireballs struck a black shield like a translucent storm front and either vanished or burst without apparent effect.

"Sweet Christ," Duke, former apprentice and now veteran, said.

The hand gonners froze.

Smoke's voice rose over the evil silence. "And *that's* just another crowd of fewkin' monsters," he said.

Mark my words, said a voice.

Duke found his hands moving of their own accord even as his mind failed to really accept or comprehend all the horror he was seeing.

A dark sleet and a horrible lavender mist rose from the phalanx of mammoths and came back. Duke was praying; Tom dropped his round lead ball into the sand and had to find it. Sam got his load down and his face was white.

"Load!" Edmund roared. "There's nothing out there we can't crush with alchemy and muscle and craft. Five! Four!"

Most of the gonnes were upright, their poles set in the sand, the sign a man or woman was loaded. A few were still struggling. Tom had his ball on the soft leather patch and was pressing it in with his thumb, his eyes on the terrible line of monsters.

Off to his right, a falconet fired. It was a gonner's triumph; the round iron ball struck an Umroth full on. There was a flair of violet lightning, and the thing *unmade*.

The guild cheered. It was thin, and unplanned, but the strike heartened them tremendously.

"Three!" Edmund roared. "Two! Make ready!"

The second falconet spat. Its ball missed.

"Present!"

Two hundred gonnes went from vertical to horizontal. Abby Crom, all five foot ten of her, put her cheek down on the shaft of her weapon and put the muzzle ring just under the center of a monster's forehead, just as if she were practicing in the fields of Berona. Then she put her tongue between her teeth and raised the muzzle the width of two fingers for the range.

"Fire!" Edmund called.

This time, he made the word into one sound, and all the gonnes crashed out together. The smoke billowed.

A hermetical breeze came up from behind them and swept the smoke away, and there were two of the monsters *unmaking* in a brilliant display of blacklit fireworks.

Gabriel was almost out of ops, and all he'd done was defend himself. Morgon had landed one major blow; a rippling plane of dissolution that had broken the back of the assault of the animals.

The line of Umroth came out of the woods when Gabriel threw a simple wind working to give his people a line of sight.

And then he threw a leg over Ariosto's back. The griffon launched them in two strides.

A levin bolt rose out of the Umroth; he deflected it easily enough, and it was followed immediately by a hundred levin bolts. They came from a broad field and cleverly eliminated his favourite tactic learned from Harmodius: the use of small, light shields far distant to block emanations at the caster's end of the *aethereal*. The wide volley forced Gabriel to expend energy at a prodigious rate.

A second volley rose from the Umroth even as they rolled forward against his line. But in the real, the falconets and the guildsmen were hurting them, and Gabriel had enough *entanglement* with his enemy to understand that every Umroth down was a little of its *self* lost.

But the travel time in the air was very short—less than a hundred paces separated them now—and Gabriel was committed. He moved all his shields to the front, and charged. In the real. He didn't have the *ops* to make a long fight in the *aethereal* and he sensed that Morgon couldn't hold for long enough to convert *potentia*.

The second volley from the Umroth was like a blizzard of black light on his visor and then he was through, still alive, and he bore the full brunt of all the coercion that the Necromancer could summon.

His plans were in shreds, his people defeated. Bad Tom died, pointlessly, of plague; Sauce crucified by triumphant monsters, Michael eaten alive, Blanche was torn asunder, Kaitlin's baby ripped from her womb, Petrarcha, his old grey hair brown with his blood, thrown from a cliff to ravening hordes as tides of monsters rippled over the world in the utter defeat of the last attempt of the alliance...

...and Ariosto came through the Umroth's wave front of fear and resistance, his wings beating at the ragged holes he tore in their hermetical shields. Talon and blade slashed at the hermetical reality; and Gabriel remembered the power of his metal hand and, dropping his reins and trusting his mount, rained white fire into the Umroth from above. Ariosto's talons ripped the stinking, rotting hide from the back of one as the light from a second's fiery death backlit its end, and a third towered over all, trying for mount and rider with its saber tusks and finding only sky.

Down he stabbed, down and down, his mount steady between his knees as if Ariosto trod on earth and not on air, moving with his every twist, rising when the tusks came up. The two of them were deep in the herd, under their shields; and there was a line of fallen Umroth behind them. A golden light seemed to suffuse them both.

Their adversary stopped trying to face Mortirmir in the *aethereal* and threw everything at the man on the griffon. It went for the other threat. The one in the real. The one that could fly.

It was *afraid*.

The left-hand falconet fired.

The ball struck an Umroth in the middle of its skull. Black ichor sprayed, and the massive thing slumped like an ox struck by a butcher's mallet. The bronze machine rolled back, belching smoke, and the sponge went in; the ballet of loading began, uninterrupted by the tusks of impending doom.

"One more!" Duke yelled. "One more and run!"

The rammers spun their implements; the round shot went down the long bronze throat.

"Jesus Christ Almighty. Jesus Christ Almighty. Jesus Christ Almighty," muttered one of the loaders over and over.

Twenty strong men rolled the two machines back up. The Umroth were forty paces away; close enough to see the damage a thousand years had wrought; close enough to see the gleam of the hermetical bones and smell the unsealie stench of corruption.

They weren't fast.

They bristled with arrows that didn't seem to harm them.

"Fire!" called Edmund, and his hand gonners vanished in another ripple of fire and smoke.

The left-hand falconet had its target; the porte-fire came down and the piece leapt back with a sharp crack.

The right-hand piece was covered in powder smoke.

The gonner stood his ground and waited, duty at war with terror. And a sinuous and ancient trunk took him and tore him, screaming, to shreds. But another journeyman picked up the fallen porte-fire and slapped it on the touch hole, scattering the powder in the quill, but after a delay that cost the brave journeyman his life, too, the falconet barked, and the ball smacked home in the same heartbeat, its impact inaudible in the roar and the screams.

Forty paces behind the gonnes, Bad Tom stood in his stirrups.

"Steady!" he roared.

All along the front of the valley, the monsters were against the trench and the stockade; all along the wall, brave men and women slammed heavy axes and long swords and spears into the towering, stinking things, and died. Or stood their ground. The monsters had real trouble with the trench and more with the stakes. The bravest of the archers emulated the Nordikaans, and went in under the things, cutting their legs.

Edmund's guildsmen held their last volley until the monsters were at the very lip of the trench, and fired.

The creatures bunched up at the center, and went in over the dead gonners, right at the banner and Morgon Mortirmir. They were silent. Their stench panicked horses and rendered men uneasy.

The household knights were mounted on the best destriers in the whole of the Antica Terra, and none of *them* wanted to face the stinking monsters.

Morgon Mortirmir, ten paces to Bad Tom's left under the household banner, spared a single instant of concentration from the labyrinth he was balancing to toss a *calm* on the horses. Then the monsters burst through, and Mortirmir had no working to strike them with. He was fighting on another plane, and he watched his doom approach.

"Ready!" Tom bellowed.

Forty knights held their lances upright in one hand, like jousters ready for the lists.

Tom used his knees and his left hand to keep his horse in check. The black behemoth between his knees had no more fear than the man on its back.

The Umroth were clear of the gonnes. To their left and right, they were still having trouble with the stakes and the ditch. They were stalled, as if something had sapped *their* will, but in the center they came on and still Tom held his counterstroke. Francis Atcourt's charger pranced forward, out of the line, and Tom turned his head. "Wait for it!" he called.

Atcourt reined in hard, his lance tip bobbing, his face white with fear under the visor of his heavy helm.

The smoke around the gonne position was clearing. There were a dozen of the great hulks down, and the ones behind shambled over them.

And then they gathered speed, a rumbling charge, and the earth shook, the dust rose, and the horrid stench of corruption filled the air...

"Aim fer the head!" Tom called.

Four of the monsters came through the dust and smoke, their eyes burning black in their black and glistening heads. Then, in a leap as fast as a lion's, they were all headed for Mortirmir and the *casa* banner.

Bad Tom felt he could almost *see* the *will* come upon them.

"Charge! Lachlan for Aa!" Bad Tom exploded forward like any

skilled jouster, and his destrier crossed the ground like black lightning. Tom's lance swept down, steadied with his weight change as he leaned forward, and struck the lead not-dead beast dead center of its skull as the solid lance exploded, the pressure of the strength of man and horse too much for twelve feet of oak, but the steel point, a hand-span long and widening from a needle tip to a breadth of four fingers, cracked open the ancient skull even as man and horse crossed to the target's right and danced off beneath the tusks. The great beast plunged forward, fell to its knees, and then the whole edifice of bones began to unknit.

Tom leaned as far as armour and saddle allowed him to the right, plucking his war hammer from his saddle bow without conscious thought as Francis Atcourt followed him. Tom's destrier jumped the left-hand carcass, armour, man, and all, and they brushed past the wheel of the left-hand gonne...

Atcourt's lance tracked the second Umroth; his horse stumbled, or shied in terror, but Atcourt's jousting skill was beyond terror; his point dipped, came up, and went in an empty eye socket; the shaft levering front and rear of the skull for a moment; the bone and the lance shattered together; and Atcourt's terrified horse ran full tilt into the behemoth, even as its unmaking came upon it. Falling bone struck Atcourt a massive blow, but he kept his seat and was suddenly through and into the choking, stinking dust beyond the gonnes.

Phillip de Beause flinched at the thought of death and then leaned forward the fraction that told his destrier to *go* and he passed the first two beasts unopposed and followed Lachlan through the dust, his lance still held high. He saw Lachlan smash another beast with his hammer and ride on, and in a flick of his arm and hand, his lance came down, stooping like a falcon to strike the thing. His lance shivered; the skull cracked, but his horse was brought up at a stand, and one of the great ivory tusks slammed into his horse's breast and threw them down.

De Beause went down hard, falling on his side, but his armour and its padding held and his horse, terrified but still game, rolled away without crushing him. Another not-dead mastodon impaled the horse on its tusk; there was an explosion of deadly amber light and the horse rained blood and gristle across the field, but de Beause was up again, on foot in a horde of giants, and there was no place for the terror he felt. His sword was gone, and he plucked out his dagger from habit, ran under the next creature and stabbed up into its dangling rotting guts with no effect, gagged on the stench, and struck again.

And then he was struck down. Something was broken in his chest, and a worm head was coming for him.

Tom Lachlan appeared in the dust and threw blows with his war hammer so fast that de Beause couldn't count them, and then Lachlan's mount stood up on its hind feet and its steel-clad forefeet struck like a boxer's fists. De Beause watched in distant admiration; the pain from his broken body left him above the fray, an observer, as Tom's superb warhorse pivoted on its back feet, standing like an angry cat, to slam one more blow into the Umroth's head as Tom rolled his hammer through a long arc and leaned between the tusks so that his blow had all the weight of his arm and the gliding step of his heavy mount as well.

This blow smashed through the heavy bone. And even as the thing shifted weight, trying to put a foot down on de Beause, it *unmade*. The pain increased, and de Beause went away.

And then he was back, buried in a fortune of Umroth ivory.

And alive.

The Umroth's worms came for him a few terrified heartbeats later. They were old, and huge, like malevolent pythons, but their very size saved him for a moment. They battered against his armour, their snake-sized jaws trying to get through his steel visor.

Every man and woman of the company had been exhaustively briefed on the worms, but de Beause, wounded and pinned to the ground, could do nothing but lie still and scream while the things sought unguarded flesh and battered at his armour.

But Ser Berengar and Ser Angelo, their own lances shivered, saw the worms and came to his aid, dismounting with poleaxes in a melee of mammoths and warhorses.

Philip de Beause saw a worm turned to an *aethereal* mist before his very visor.

Ser Angelo started heaving Umroth bones off de Beause while Ser Berengar covered him, and de Beause began to breathe again.

"Buried in Umroth ivory," Ser Danved shouted down from atop his warhorse. "What a way to go!"

De Beause managed to get his visor open before he vomited.

Ser Danved laughed. "Lucky you have friends," he said, and rode back into the melee.

Gabriel had gone forward to buy Mortirmir time to cast, but at some point he realized that he had passed from deception to main attack; he'd lost count of the great beasts he'd sent to dissolution, or that Ariosto had; the griffon's talons had a strength as great as any monster in the wild, and Gabriel had a shard of memory of an ancient mastodon, its backbone severed, falling away beneath them.

And then, in one instant in the *aethereal, the conglomerate being known as the Necromancer gave a cry of despair and pain and loss, agony, sorrow, even regret.*

And Mortirmir's voice slapped through the fog of possibility, *ops, potentia*, and violence.

Got him.

In the real, every remaining Umroth unmade and the huge worms that knitted the beasts together began to writhe, screaming in thin voices until a horde of terrified men and women pounded them to mush and mist.

The dust swirled. Wounded men continued to scream.

Gabriel rose above the battlefield, watching under his mount's flashing wings. In three places, the titans had penetrated his wall; the Nordikaans had *let* them cross, and four of the beasts were there, battered to undeath by the axes of the northerners. They'd made it into the gonnes and killed a dozen men and women. And they'd passed the line of stakes where the Vardariotes had stood, but the Vardariotes had never planned to stand their ground; they simply mounted and rode back, flaying the great beasts from a few horse lengths away.

They still had a butcher's bill.

So did the *casa*, and the guildsmen.

And there stood Morgon Mortirmir, beneath the banner. The nearest Umroth had fallen so that its long, curved tusks almost seemed to touch him. The light hadn't changed; the whole fight had lasted mere minutes.

Gabriel looked down with a sinking heart.

I hate killing stuff I can't eat, Ariosto said.

"It had no hope," Mortirmir said. "It never thought it would win."

"Morgon," Gabriel said gently. "I'm not really of a mind to have this discussion just now."

"And yet," Mortirmir said. "It defeated my working. That was bad." He shrugged. "I found the way it linked together and I broke that link."

Gabriel took a breath. And then another. And then, almost against his will, he looked at the young magister. "What link?" he asked.

"The Odine aren't one creature," Morgon began.

"I know," Gabriel said, a little more testily than he had intended.

Gabriel glanced at Tom Lachlan, who was himself watching archers stack the precious Umroth ivory while fully armoured men-at-arms saw to the burning of the worm-infested mounds of bone.

Morgon shrugged. "Of course, my lord. It is only that . . . the passive shield. Nothing went through. And he was striking me over and over; not very hard, but very expertly."

"Yes," Gabriel agreed. "So that every response had to be—"

"Calculated," Morgon agreed. Then he looked at the tall Hillman in the blue-black armour. "Thomas Lachlan, I am sorry. But for your *puissance*, I would be dead."

"Aye, laddy! And where were yer precious warlockeries?" Bad Tom was very much himself.

"I spent too much on the . . . the dragon working. As our adversary called it." Mortirmir suddenly looked seventeen and deflated. "I cocked up. And then I had to scrabble to stay alive in the *aethereal*. Until Gabriel charged, it focused almost everything on me." Mortirmir looked at Gabriel. "You chose to attack in the real. Why?"

Gabriel was watching a burial party while Anne disarmed him. He intended on going to stand and watch his men buried. He shrugged. "I can usually get things in the Wild to focus on me," he said. His voice was distant.

"All the more reason to build Fell Swords," Mortirmir said. "The real . . . is where the sorcerous pay no attention."

Gabriel paused. He was being disarmed of all his harness, but he put out a hand to stop his page and he looked at Mortirmir. "That may be the most profound thing you've ever said."

"I doubt it," Mortirmir said. "First, I said—"

"Not now, Mortirmir," Gabriel said.

Anne got the maille off him, and he sighed. "Do you think it really wanted to surrender?" Gabriel asked.

Mortirmir looked at him. A rare look passed over his face; a raw emotion. Regret. "Yes," Mortirmir said. "Part of it anyway." He paused, and looked under his eyebrows at Gabriel; a rare look of self-awareness from the mage. "When I cut the links between its entities, it was arguing among itself. And then I took down its...connections. And then it...tried to kill itself."

Tom Lachlan shrugged. "Better this way," he said. "Better that it is dead. Ye'r too soft, Emperor-man."

"Better with sixty dead?" Gabriel asked. "I haven't even looked yet. Who did I lose? Cully? Francis? Maybe just Gropf?"

"Listen, lad," Bad Tom said. "Shed no tears for the old monster. Think o' what Pavalo will say. Think o' all the lads an' lasses in Dar. Free to farm. Think o' watchin' the whole fuckin' herd day an' night. Knowin' that in a dozen worms, they'd start the whole fewkin' thing again." He looked at Gabriel.

"Wyverns stopped fighting," Gabriel said through his fatigue and depression. "And wardens. Demons. Whatever. They *made peace*. They even fight alongside us." He shook off Anne's hand. "I need to see our people buried," he said. And turned to stalk off.

"Sixty dead?" Bad Tom insisted. "Sixty, and we scragged the fewkin' Necromancer." He looked out over the stinking corpses. "Wyverns don't ha'e empires, don't lay waste to civilizations. We scragged the Necromancer. We win. It lost. The end."

Gabriel turned back, and his jaw set a moment. "Tom," he said, "Has it occurred to you that we're taking losses in every one of these fights? We lead from in front, and we die. Kerak and Kronmir and Master Smythe and Wilful Murder and John Crayford and, in the end, you and me. You get that? They were alive. Now they are dead."

Bad Tom shrugged. "No, laddie. They will live forever in song. An' so will we. An' when ye go down, I'll be there wi' ye, and that's why what we have to do here an' now is drink the fewkin' wine and sing the songs and e'en, God save us, smell flowers. An' pretty girls. Life is too short to waste on yon; they're dead, all praise to 'em, and we're alive. Amen."

"I wish I found it so simple," Gabriel said.

"Simple, you lout? You sound like bloody Mortirmir here. Nothin' simple about yon, laddie. I kilt fifty loons before I kenned it. They're dead and I'm not." Tom pushed him gently with one ham-size hand. "I ha'e always gi'in ye the best advice, have I not?"

That made Gabriel smile. "That you have," he said. "Except . . . never mind."

"Aye. So take this as read. Mourn the dead when you've the luxury of time. Until then, the only rule is that you are alive and they're dead." Tom raised an eyebrow. "Eh? Don't mourn inside, whatever you do outside. Wastes your strength."

"Tom Lachlan, the philosopher of war," Gabriel said.

"Ach, aye," Tom said with a grin. "Like enow'."

Gabriel turned back to Mortirmir. "What happened at the very end? The . . . Necromancer . . . went out like a light."

Morgon's eyes sparkled. "I subsumed it," he said, unable to hide a gleam of triumph.

Chapter Five

The San Colombo Pass and central Etrusca—Long Paw

Long Paw had just returned from a long patrol south, trying to net the Patriarch or any of his officers; a waste of time. They'd questioned terrified peasants and ridden hard on exhausted horses and they hadn't seen or heard a thing. The Duchess of Venike had just unleashed the whole of the Venike ranger company into the hilly country above Firensi, where the Patriarch was rumoured to be hiding among his own people.

Long Paw put a hand on his back, which hurt, and stumbled a little because his legs hurt, too.

Petite Moulin shot him her open-faced smile. "You are hurt?"

"I'm old," Long Paw muttered.

There was a stir toward the eastern edge of the fortified camp. The peasants were still burying the dead after the "Battle of San Batiste" (after stripping them of every possible valuable thing). Some of them raised their heads; a small horde of children ran toward the shouting.

"The Berona road," Petite Moulin said in her Gallish accent.

"The convoy!" Long Paw said. Fatigue and incidental pain fell away, and he and Petite Moulin ran down their company street of tents to see the huge military wagons roll past the outposts and through the great wooden gate that had already been erected in case of a serious assault from Mitla.

Hundreds of wagons stretched away out of sight over the ridge. In fact, Long Paw wasn't sure he'd ever seen so many wagons in his entire life. They had wheels as tall as a man, and each wagon was drawn by six horses in a complex hitch that wasn't familiar to Long Paw. The wagons were full almost to bursting, piled high, with their covers laced taut against rain.

The wagoners were greeted with cheers, and they grinned, but the convoy rolled on. Long Paw stopped counting at two hundred wagons; there were still wagons coming over the far distant ridge.

"I'm lookin' fer Corp'ral Favour," said an urchin in strongly accented Alban. Long Paw didn't know him, but there were suddenly hundreds of them; all Etrusca seemed to have dumped their unwanted children on the army.

Petite Moulin shook her head. In Etruscan, she said, "He is still on patrol."

The boy nodded politely. "Then I am to find Ser Roberto Caffelo."

Long Paw nodded. "That's me," he said.

"Donna Sugo wishes for you," the boy said.

Petite Moulin and Long Paw looked at each other. Multilingual gears ground in tired brains. Then they both grinned.

"Sauce," they said together.

Desiderata stood in her chamber, looking at her bed linens and thinking of Blanche. She was hardly a delicate flower; she did not actually need her pillowcases ironed to go to sleep, but Blanche was gone, and Desiderata knew every day how much she had relied on the young woman. And on Diota, executed, her head put on the gate like a traitor.

Desiderata went to the window and looked over the city. Almost at her feet, there were cranes, huge assemblies of wood, driven by enormous wooden wheels, by horses and oxen and even men. Forty cranes towered above the lower town; three on the former Episcopal Palace alone.

"We are rebuilding," she said to the city. "We are not beaten."

She wished that she could see hermetically into the workshops where

Master Pye and all his guild allies were building their secret weapon. She wished that she could understand the progress of the plague. She wished that she could leave the responsibilities of being queen, and go north to save what could be saved, as a potent user of magik.

She wished her husband were alive.

She walked from the window to her son's cradle and she watched him for a long time. He lay sleeping; a small being who was intensely curious, who surprised her every day. She had never expected a baby to have so much personality, but he had; jolly, joyous, inquisitive, eyes so wide he almost expected her son to speak.

She wanted to crush the small form to her breast, but she was an experienced mother by then and she had no intention of waking him. Delightful as he was, his demands were endless.

She sighed. Everyone's demands were endless.

She walked to the door of her solar and there was Ser Ranald, with his axe.

"Your Grace," he said. "She's here."

"No one is to come in," she said. "I mean it, Ranald."

"Yes, Your Grace. May I say..."

"No," the queen snapped. "You may not."

Ranald bowed.

The queen nodded. She walked down the passage, to where her guards had taken Lady Jane.

She opened the oak door. It was a good room, and had once been her husband's library and his private study. The tapestries were gone, but the scrolls and books remained. She thought, briefly, of helping him with his armour in this very room, so long ago that it seemed a different world. She was so lost in the moment; the warmth of his response...

"Your Grace," Lady Jane said. She curtsyed.

She was quite young—perhaps seventeen—and very pregnant. She had long, straight blond hair, and she looked more than a little like Blanche Gold.

Desiderata looked at the woman who had been her husband's mistress and tried to imagine what had happened. She could not, really.

"You sent for me?" Lady Jane asked. She was terrified, but she bore it well enough, although her beautiful skin was splotchy with fear, as if a cat had left footprints on her cheeks.

"I sent for you and you ran," the queen said.

"My father..." the lady began.

The queen shook her head. "Never mind your father," she said, suddenly resolute. "Listen to me, Jane. Did you love him?"

"Oh God," Jane said, and she burst into tears so suddenly that she startled both of them.

Desiderata felt a strange urge to weep with her.

"Tell your father," Desiderata said when the sobs had died back into the woman's fear, "that you and your child will be welcome at my court. Tell him that his grandson will be a Fitzroy; that I will see he is raised with Constantine, and knighted, and treated in every way as the king's son." She went forward and put a kiss on Jane's cheek. "Come," she said. "We have other enemies. Let us be kind to each other. And no one should be punished for love."

Lady Jane, unbelieving, fell into the queen's arms. Then, Desiderata found herself weeping. But when they were both done, the queen felt a weight lift from her, as if, in facing this one task, she had begun well on all of them.

She dried her eyes with a fine lawn handkerchief—pressed, folded, but without the scent of rosewater that Blanche would have added—and then she dried Lady Jane's. She passed the door again, and Ser Ranald stood rigidly on the other side.

"Take Lady Jane wherever she wishes to go," the queen said. "I didn't rip out her throat with my fangs, if that's what you were imagining."

Ranald gave her a wary smile.

"And then bring me my council. I need to plan to take the army north."

"Now ye'r talkin'," Ranald said.

"And bring me Lady Mary in private, please. In my solar." She was thinking clearly, for the first time in a week. Maybe it was just sleep. She could see exactly how she could be in two places at one time.

Sauce was standing with the duchess and two men Long Paw had not seen before: a nondescript man like an Etruscan foot soldier, and a well-dressed man with a horribly maimed face and one eye gone, half his hair lost under a tangle of angry scar tissue.

The scarred man bowed to Long Paw when he was introduced as "Ser Roberto."

"Paw, this is Fernando Lucca. He was Kronmir's..." She looked at the man.

"Friend?" the scarred man asked. "Squire?" He frowned; the expression was normal on one side of his face and vanished into the caricature of ruined flesh on the other side.

Long Paw looked at the second man. "And this?"

The man answered him with a very slight smile. "Most people don't notice me," he said quietly.

"This is Master Brown, who helped save my life once," the duchess said.

Long Paw held out his hand, and the nondescript man took it. Very close, he was easier to describe; his face had a forgettable roundness to it, and his clothes were the frayed-hem wools of the lowest order of agricultural workers. He smelled a little bad.

"Just to catch you up," Sauce said, "they came in on the convoy."

The duchess looked tired, but not distraught. Long Paw doubted she'd ever been distraught in her life.

She smiled at Long Paw as if reading his mind. "I want to get the Patriarch," she said.

Long Paw said nothing.

Brown nodded. "Me, too." He looked at the man who'd been named Lucca, the man with the ruined face. "Lucca and I have some... experience."

"Working together," Lucca said, forming his words carefully.

"The three of you can get the Patriarch," the duchess said. "I'm sure of it. And be light enough on your feet to make it to the rendezvous at Arles."

Lucca shrugged. "Emperor is my employer," he said. "A job is a job. Kronmir was my mentor. I owe him. He comes first."

Brown nodded. "What he said," he muttered.

"As to that," the duchess said, "I am not yet decided whether I will accompany the emperor or remain."

Long Paw frowned. "Sauce, I'm not one to gripe, but..."

Sauce nodded. "I'll see you right. You'll be at Arles in time."

Long Paw tried a different tack. "Who's keeping watch on the Duke o' Mitla, then?" he asked.

Brown managed his half-smile.

198

"Apparently the Duke of Mitla will not be troubling us this autumn," Sauce said. "He was assassinated two days ago. Just about the time the battle was fought."

The silence was palpable.

"His brother has already sent us a pair of heralds and tomorrow I'll ride north to meet an embassy." Sauce shrugged. "An embassy for which I'll need the Duchess of Venike."

The green-clad woman nodded. "Ah, duty," she said. "Will you get him?"

Brown and Lucca bowed.

Long Paw nodded to them. "Am I the guide?" he asked.

Brown sniffed. "Yes," he said.

Lucca nodded. "This could take months. You know that, right? But there's more, Donna. The Venikans have prisoners; they've put them to the question. I didn't know Master Jules was dead; I came to tell him, and you, that there's evidence of a third player. The Patriarch is just an ally." Lucca leaned close. "Or the Patriarch is something very nasty indeed."

Sauce tapped her nose. "We've got our own suspicions. Very well—Long Paw is our go-between. For fifteen days. After that..."

Brown shook his head. "Don't tell us," he said fiercely. "I won't die to protect your secrets."

Sauce nodded. "We can pay you for this," she said. "I'm a professional."

Brown nodded. "I heard. Good on you. But this is on the house." He bowed. Looked at Lucca. "I need access to Master Jules's effects."

Sauce nodded.

"And we need a caster. A good one."

"Of course," Sauce said.

Later that afternoon D.13 landed on Syr Christos's outstretched arm and delivered a message straight from the emperor's own hand. Sauce read it aloud to the company; it praised them for their victory and announced the destruction of the Necromancer.

By midnight, six hundred wagons had passed through the army and headed west to the passes. The company folded its tents in the very early morning and marched in behind them as a strong rear guard, and found supplies left in prepared camps.

Long Paw and Brown and Lucca and M'bub Ali were long gone. In fact, all four were asleep while a middle-aged woman named Beatrice watched their horses in a merchant tavern's barn just north of the Mitla Gate of Firensi.

Beatrice had never even contemplated a life of violence. She'd been a capable farm wife until the duke took her daughter as a concubine. A year later, everyone in her family was dead.

And so was the duke.

She watched the darkness, listened to men snore, and tried to imagine herself as a hard-faced mercenary killer, or one of their sluts.

She said some prayers.

They were terrifying men, every one of them, and she knew they were on their way to kill the Patriarch, and it all horrified her.

She said more prayers, and then she woke one of the infidels to take his watch. The man was now in Etruscan clothing; his swarthy good looks were not very different from the men of Rhum, and he grinned at her in the one candlelight of the barn's lower half.

Brown, who had lain awake watching her, now watched her crawl into her blankets, and then let his eyes close. He didn't trust her; he had enough trouble trusting Lucca.

"People," he said to himself.

Arles—Empress Blanche

Two hundred leagues and a mountain range to the north, the empress rose early and read the night's dispatches with Master Julius. She noted in the messages that the Venikans had drovers gathering cattle in the lands that had formerly been the Darkness and she read with interest about the assassination of the Duke of Mitla, although some reports claimed he'd died of the sudden onset of a disease.

She sipped *quaveh* from a small porcelain cup and wished she still had Jules Kronmir.

"Majesty?" said a Hillman voice. "Miss Kaitlin. An' the Queen o' Arles."

"Thanks, Jock," she said, her eyes still on the reports. "Julius, move the main convoy to the base of the pass. Thanks." The former company notary, now functioning as something like an imperial chancellor, was also the keeper of Kronmir's master map, an enormous and not terribly accurate rendering of the whole of the Nova and Antica Terra in Kronmir's own hand, with hundreds of small pins and flags to indicate... almost everything: herds of bullocks, water sources, the known location of imperial couriers, either birds or people; some untagged pins of which only Kronmir and Syr Alcaeus had known the meanings. But before he'd left, he'd instructed her in its use, and now she used the messages to move the pins, or that's how she saw it. She and Julius, and Michael and Gabriel, and Alcaeus back in Liviapolis, were the only ones fully privy to the meanings of the flags; Kronmir had begged her not to commit any of it to parchment or paper.

Jock knocked on the solar's outer door. Master Julius nodded at her and dropped the curtain over the map, and the empress casually closed the heavy leather folder that held the day's uncoded imperial courier messages. Kaitlin was the closest thing she had to a friend; Clarissa de Chartres was one of her closest allies.

Kronmir had said "no one" and Blanche knew he meant it.

Clarissa entered first with two ladies; one the fierce-faced older woman who'd attended her before, the other young, blond, pretty, and eager; she curtsied so deeply that Blanche was afraid she'd fall on her face.

"The Demoiselle Isabella," Clarissa said.

"The Duke of Mitla is dead," Blanche said.

Clarissa shook her head. "I am *so* envious of your... servants," she said.

Blanche shrugged prettily. "It may have been disease," she said.

"The will of God perhaps?" Clarissa asked. She smiled.

"The will of Gabriel Muriens?" Kaitlin said. "Honestly, I've put up with three years of him and he generally gets his way."

Clarissa looked at her hands in her lap and smiled again.

"You know, you could be a veritable demon from hell and that innocent face would confound us," Blanche said to Clarissa, who raised her eyes and laughed.

"I know," she said. "No one ever imagines I have a bad thought."

Kaitlin shook her head. "Unfair," she said. "I apparently look like I'm nothing but bad thoughts."

"What brings you two at this difficult hour?" Blanche asked.

"The smell of *quaveh*," Kaitlin said. "And pregnancy. And because today we have our sword lesson with Michael and I'm to remind you, Majesty."

"Send me Michael when you have time," Blanche said. She was still getting used to sending for people as opposed to going for them in person, an action that caused chaos among everyone's servants.

"And I brought young Beatrice to...serve you," Clarissa said. "Using men-at-arms as maids may well have its charms, but I thought you might like a girl."

Blanche looked at the enthusiastic young woman who was kneeling before her.

"Really?" she said a little distantly.

"I would be the best serving lady *ever*," the young woman said.

Blanche made a face. In her head she thought, *Young woman, I was myself the best serving woman ever.* "I'm not sure I need a—"

"Blanche," Kaitlin said.

Clarissa de Sartres straightened as if Kaitlin had uttered a blasphemy.

"Blanche, it took me months to get used to it. Just do it. You can't dress by yourself; you just slow everyone down. Really, you need two ladies and a couple of maids." She shrugged.

Blanche looked at Kaitlin.

Clarissa looked out the window.

Kaitlin looked at the Queen of Arles. "We weren't born to this," she said. "I can do laundry better than your laundry maid."

"And I can sew and iron better than your staff," Blanche said.

Clarissa burst out laughing. It was not a ladylike laugh, but a snorting, gurgling laugh.

"I can sew, too," Clarissa said, snorting and wiping away tears of laughter. "I wanted to be a nun," she admitted.

The other two woman looked amazed.

"I was *never* going to be a nun." Kaitlin laughed. "Imagine, a Lantorn nun? I'd ha'e been the laugh of the place."

Blanche looked down at Beatrice. "I suppose I must try you, demoiselle."

The young woman's back straightened. Her smile grew, if anything, broader.

"How are you at hair?" Blanche asked, playing with a strand of her own.

Beatrice giggled.

Blanche turned to Kaitlin. "Let's have the swords. Whenever the Lord Michael is available."

"You outrank him," Kaitlin said. "You could just *order* him to come."

Clarissa made a noise of disgust. "You can't really order anyone ever," she said. "This is the first rule of giving orders, I think."

"What do you mean?" Kaitlin asked.

Clarissa raised a perfectly curved eyebrow. "I mean that when you snap an order at a servant, they resent it; if you request the same in gracious language, they resent it less, but ultimately, they do your bidding of their own free will because you are paying them, not because they love you. And likewise, when you snap an order at a great lord, he, too, resents it; when you ask graciously, he resents it less…."

Blanche laughed. "And when you provide his daughter with a juicy marriage, he remembers why he should obey you?"

Clarissa smiled. All three of them were of an age; all three had seen a great deal of life in a very short time.

"No one was ever particularly nice to me when I was serving," Kaitlin said. And then, a little dreamily, "Well, of course, Michael was."

"And look where that got you," Blanche said, patting her friend's tummy.

"You're a fine one to talk," Kaitlin said.

Clarissa looked out the window.

Blanche inclined her head to the Queen of Arles. "I think we'll come to you for lessons, Your Grace. I have a feeling you've had all the training we lack."

"I wouldn't mind improving my ironing," Clarissa said. "Although my real ambition is to write books."

"Ugh," said Kaitlin in distaste.

"Ooh," said Blanche, pierced with interest. "What kind of books?"

"I never really learned to read," Kaitlin admitted. "Michael taught me, but it's work."

Clarissa smiled shyly. "I write some poetry," she said. "And some glosses on religious works." She got up suddenly.

"Would you like sword lessons, Your Grace?" Blanche asked.

Clarissa stopped. "Yes," she said. "My constable…treats me like a woman." She shrugged.

"Aye," Blanche said. "It's an occupational hazard."

Clarissa suddenly spat, "I find it tiresome."

Kaitlin laughed. "Honey, we *all* find it tiresome." She got up, favoured her back, and then stretched like a long-limbed cat. "Never mind. I'll fetch Michael, and we'll have some fun."

Blanche looked at Master Julius, whose quill was moving very quickly. He met her eye and mouthed two words.

"Lord Michael is drilling the Arelat Levy," Blanche said.

"I should have known that," Clarissa said.

"Me, too," Kaitlin said. "He's my husband."

"Let's say two hours," Blanche said graciously.

Both ladies nodded and left her to her solar with her new "lady." Outside the solar, Clarissa stopped dead in the corridor and barked a short, odd laugh.

Kaitlin paused behind one of Clarissa's ladies. "Your Grace?" she asked.

Clarissa looked back at Kaitlin. "Think of how she dismissed us," the Queen of Arles said. "She is a quick learner."

"There's nothing very difficult about using a sword," Michael said with hearty reassurance. He was already tired, and he wasn't sure that giving sword lessons for ladies was what he ought to be doing.

On the other hand, he was looking forward to seeing his wife for an entire hour.

His wife, Kaitlin, as well as the Queen of Arles, Clarissa; the Empress of Man, Blanche; and her maid Beatrice all stood before him on a heavily flagged courtyard. There were ill-concealed faces at every window.

The four women all held arming swords.

"I know," Blanche said. "I've killed a man and a couple of bogglins." All the women laughed.

Michael smiled. "Right," he said. "And that's the point, really. The part I can't teach you is the real part: getting the job done. Any way you do it, if you live and the other bastard dies, is the best way."

"This is definitely *not* what my constable taught," Clarissa muttered.

"Nonetheless, ladies, there are some ways that are better and some that are worse. Let's just start with how to hold a sword." He proceeded to demonstrate; he showed them how to hold the sword like a hammer, how to hold it like a fishing rod, how to hold it with a thumb on the flat of the blade.

"Now, Your Grace..." he said to Blanche.

Blanche nodded her head graciously. "My lord," she said. "I would like to propose, as I really do wish to learn this, and as it takes so very long to say our titles and so *little* time to say our names, that for the duration of these lessons, we all refer to each other by our baptismal names."

Michael laughed. "You know, Blanche," he said, "in my whole life of training to arms, my master never referred to me as anything but 'you idiot.'"

"I draw the line at 'idiot,'" Blanche said. "I'll accept 'you incompetent ninny.'"

"Duly noted," Michael said. "Now, if you could take the sword in your hand properly and strike the pell?"

The pell in question was a large stake of hardwood planted deeply in the courtyard, with a crisscross of marks showing that Clarissa's men-at-arms, at least those who had survived the siege, practiced regularly.

"Don't you teach us a guard and a cut first?" Clarissa asked.

"No," Michael said. "See if you can find it for yourself."

"Jesus," muttered Kaitlin.

Blanche strolled up to the pole, stopped with the sword behind her, held out like a tail, and then snapped the blade forward in a flat cut at the pole, just above waist height.

The sword cut deeply into the hard wood and a chip the size of a woman's hand shot away. The sword was stuck and Blanche started to lever it out, and Michael put a hand over hers.

"Whoa!" he said, as if she were an awkward horse. "Someone has strong arms. Nice cut, Blanche. I pity the bogglins. But only take the blade out on the same line you put it in. Otherwise you use up a lot of blades." He took his hand away and she worked the blade out gently, and got it free.

Beatrice stepped up. Unlike the other three women, she was dressed in a kirtle and overgown, where they were in men's hose, and in moving, she caught the sword point in her overgown. She shook her head. "Sorry." She made a face. "I'm clumsy," she said.

"I doubt it," Michael said. "Take some cuts."

Beatrice was interested in the idea of having her thumb on the flat of the blade, and she stood there, her tongue between her teeth, playing with the feel of the sword in her hand. "I could cut myself very easily," she said.

"Nothing to worry about," Michael said.

She cut at the post. Her thumb grip kept the point low, and her blow was at waist height—not particularly hard, but neat. Before anyone could say anything, she stepped back and cut again, this time with one foot passing forward, and a small chip flew.

"Very nice," Michael said. "Now try another grip," Michael said.

Beatrice cut a third time, this time laying the naked blade on her shoulder and cutting so close to her own ear that Clarissa winced. But she turned her hand in making the cut and the flat of the sword bounced harmlessly off the pell. Michael turned the sword in her hand so that the edge fell on her shoulder.

"Now I really could cut myself," she said.

Michael shrugged. "Swords are dangerous."

She cut, and her sword made a satisfying *thunk* into the wood. She beamed with pleasure. "Ahh," she said.

Michael smiled. "Next?"

Beatrice looked at the empress, who seemed satisfied. She grinned. "I could do this all day," she said.

Kaitlin nodded. "I want a turn, Beatrice," she said, as if they were on a playground.

She stepped up, took a distance, and cut, her blade rising above her head and cutting *down* into the pell. Like Blanche, she stuck the sword so deeply that she needed help and leverage to remove it.

"Again," Michael said. He used a different tone of voice with Kaitlin. "Someone has cut a lot of firewood."

"My brothers were lazy." She frowned. "And my sisters, too, come to that."

She cut again, this time starting on her shoulder, then passing back and rising to above her rounded waist and cutting flat. She hit just above her former angled cut and a large chip of wood flew away.

Michael shook his head. "Weak women," he said. "Where are they when you need them? The poor post has to last out the week, ladies."

For an hour, he cycled them through, allowing them to cut from any angle, any position.

"Aren't you going to teach us guards?" Blanche asked.

Clarissa smiled. "I think I know a dozen," she said.

"Not for a while," Michael said. "I have two early goals for all of you: to feel comfortable striking, and to feel comfortable drawing, which we'll do tomorrow. I'm a heretic; I find that if people use a sword regularly, they develop their own guards based on their own bodies." He flourished his own sword, drawing it, rolling it over the back of his hand and catching it. "That is all the time we have today."

All four women looked dashed. For Blanche, this meant a return to the stacks of vellum awaiting her; for Kaitlin, the loss of her husband to drilling troops; for the new Queen of Arles, the end of the best hour she'd had in four months.

"I wish this would go on forever," she said. "I want to become a master!"

Michael waved to Robin, his squire. "Robin will be happy to guide you in further cutting," he said. "The empress, that is, Blanche and I have to go through the morning reports."

As if this was an official cue, all of them turned and bowed or curtsied to Blanche, who inclined her head with regal dignity. She didn't even smile.

She only sighed. "Beatrice," she said. "You may have another half-hour if you wish it." She held out her hand, Michael took it, and they went up to the scriptorum together. On the stairs, she said, "That was ... so much fun."

"I'd like all of you to be able to draw and kill anything that threatens you. I can't imagine any of you forced into protracted sword fights, but against an assassin ..." Michael let his words trail off.

Blanche nodded. "Not to mention various bogglins, wardens, and other creatures of the Wild coming through my tent."

Michael shuddered, remembering the fighting at Gilson's Hole, when they had come within a hair's breadth of losing the queen, her son, and Blanche. "By Saint George, I hope not."

Blanche stepped off the steep steps at the top of the tower. "By Saint Mary Magdalene and all the saints, I hope it is as you pray," she said. "But this time, if it happens again, I will be ready, and I will be in maille, at least."

"You are pregnant," Michael said quietly.

"Kaitlin told you?" Blanche asked. "Too early to say for sure. But yes, I would guess as much." She smiled. "In fact, I'm very sure. But nothing that will incommode me in the next, say, thirty days."

"I have trouble imagining anything that would incommode you, Your Grace," Michael said. He grinned.

She grinned back. "Good," she said, and pushed open the door to the solar. Inside stood two androgynous young people in the black-and-white clothing of imperial messengers. There was also a bird on Master Julius's fist and another on a perch. Julius held out a tiny scroll and she seized it, her heart suddenly hammering in her chest.

She didn't breathe a moment as she read...

....and then she flushed. "They have finished the Necromancer," Blanche said aloud, her eyes on the vellum before her. "They will be on the way here. There's orders for food."

Michael was reading another message. "And you know where to find food? Here? In Arles?"

"I do," Blanche said. "There is a convoy coming over the mountains. I intend to send Comnena and the Scholae to bring it in. Just in case."

Michael nodded.

Blanche handed him her message. It was in code, and he sat down, began to figure the day's code, and looked up at her. "You can read the code?" he asked.

"Yes," she said.

"It changes every day!" he protested.

She shrugged. "It is only a little mental book-keeping," she muttered. "Like tracking laundry marks."

He whistled.

Master Julius spoke very quietly, as if they were in church. "She saves us hours sometimes," he said.

Michael nodded. "So that's why he married you," he said. "A genius cryptologist."

Blanche glared at him. "I'm sure that was at the forefront of his mind," she said.

Scrolls were read, passed back and forth, read again. The clerks began to copy them fair in plain text.

"But do you need a guard on the convoy?" Michael asked. "We

seem to be in charge of the whole countryside." He shrugged. "A forty-league ride in either direction is no small thing, Your Grace."

Blanche glanced at Michael. "Julius, clear the room," she said. "Just the three of us, please."

"Ma'am," he said, and shooed the messengers and secretaries out. The messengers took the birds; Blanche patted each of them in turn.

When the room was clear, she walked around it, looked out each of the arrow slits, and then opened the curtains on the master map.

"Michael, Master Julius," she said. "Kronmir had a theory that the Patriarch was not a servant of the Necromancer, but of a third, or is it fourth, power." She looked at Master Julius for confirmation. The notary nodded.

"Yes," he said. Outside the rare occasions on which Master Julius drank too much, he became taciturn and wasted few words.

Michael sat back. "That's an uncomfortable notion," he said.

"Gabriel says there could be fifty powers, or more, and we wouldn't know until they tip their hands," Blanche said, tapping a roll of parchment on the table. "From now until Gabriel returns, we guard everything. Messengers go in pairs, convoys have guards. It seems to me that our most sensitive point right now is food."

Julius was nodding along with his mistress.

She passed Michael a large, folio-sized sheet of paper. On it was a report in a small, expert hand detailing levels of dissent inside Arles, especially about the seizure of food.

"Christ, we spy on the new queen?" he asked.

"Michael," Blanche said, the way a mother might speak to an erring son.

Michael grimaced. "Silly me, of course we do. Blood of God, you mean people are angered when we're feeding those starving wretches out there?" he asked.

Blanche nodded. "There is a good deal of anger in Arles," she said. "Not least of which is about how many or how few of the wretches starving out there in the fields may actually be missing sons and husbands. A very prickly topic. Comnena is trying to process people as fast as he can, but it's not quick." Comnena was, in fact, examining anyone who claimed to be from Arles. Twice now they had found men with living worms. "And the city people treat them like traitors; some of them anyway."

"Merciful saints," muttered Michael, reading the report to the end. "I wondered why someone as important as Comnena was on this."

Blanche nodded. "Two reasons," she said softly. "One, because we cannot afford a new infiltration. The second, because at least one of our two cases seems to be a new worm, not an old worm."

Michael paled. "They're still out there," he said.

Blanche shrugged. "We don't even know where they come from," she admitted. "Or how they get into people in the first place." She shuddered. "I used to dread dying of leprosy; then I dreaded rape. Now all my fears have been replaced by this...infestation." She looked away, took a breath. "Kronmir went south to investigate the Patriarch; now he's dead." She rolled her head, stretching her neck. "I need to do more sword swinging." She smiled. "My point is that we're not safe, Arles is not safe, and we need to remain vigilant right to the end."

Michael nodded. "Right. So we send the Scholae to cover the convoy."

"And anything else you can think of to feed the survivors, get them shelter, and get them processed so we can move them," Blanche said. "We have almost six thousand northern Etruscans ready to go home. More by the end of the week. They need food and a safe road. If we're quick, they can, maybe, help bring in their own harvests on their own farms."

Michael was reading another report, also about dissent, this one from Harndon. "So?" he asked.

"What if Comnena marched them to the convoy, fed them from the beef herd there, and then took them over the mountains to Sauce? While we have a clear chain of logistics and outposts?" She leaned forward.

He shook his head. "I know you feel for them—" he began.

"It's not Christian charity," she snapped. "Or if it is, it's also practical. By Thursday we could have ten thousand of them out of the fields; that's ten thousand mouths we are *not* trying to feed at the end of a two-hundred-league supply line. That's a lighter burden on the Arelat, both here in the city and out in the countryside. Because the food coming over the mountains isn't for starving people, is it, Michael?"

"No," he said. "It's for armies." He looked at the paper with the report on dissent in Arelat, and back at Blanche's eyes. "Gabriel said nothing of this," he said.

"No," she said. "He didn't think of it. I did."

Michael looked out a small window. "I hate making decisions," he admitted. "But yes. If we can get ten thousand mouths back over the mountains to Mitla and Berona, let's do it. They'll have to leave day after tomorrow, though. Sauce will come home in three days, unless there's more action. The big convoy will pass her position...later today? I hope?"

Blanche was already writing orders.

Forty leagues from Arles—The Red Knight

It was twelve days until the gates would open, and Gabriel was suddenly awake, his brain busy. His first thought was that he was just forty leagues from Blanche, and he wondered what she might be doing, and with an awkward grunt, he threw his cloak over his squire and page, who were both sound asleep. He lay for a moment with his back hurting, and he flexed, first his silver hand, which caused him no pain at all, and then his flesh hand, which ached from old injuries and because he'd slept on it. His hips hurt, his shoulders hurt, and he lay thinking about people dying.

Sometime in the night he'd rolled off the pile of cut ferns provided for the emperor's "comfort" and he got slowly to his feet and shook his head, shivering from the cold. He crept away, feeling three times as old as he really was.

But his rising woke Anne, and she leapt into action, fetching a copper pot, boiling water at a campfire, and making a tea from spruce tips as her mother had taught her. She added his usual dollop of honey and put the cup in his hand just as Francis Atcourt limped to the command fire with a black-and-white bird on his arm and a leather folder. Anne knew that this was an important time; she slipped away to see to Ataelus.

Gabriel took the tea, sipped it, and took the scroll from the small tube on the great bird's left leg. The bird grabbed his thumb as if it was a perch and pierced his chamois gloves.

Gabriel rolled his eyes. "Is this the famous E.34?" he asked.

"The very same," Atcourt said with pleasure.

Gabriel patted her plumage and kissed the top of her head. "You probably saved us all, sweeting," he said. E.34 had been the first messenger bird to survive the trip into Arles and out again, bringing them word that the citadel on the mountain was still holding. He held her on one hand while he opened the scroll with the other and he smiled. It was in Blanche's own hand, the ink scarcely dry; she had been awake earlier than he.

> Convoy 4 is in. Sauce is moving north; her cavalry may reach the San Colombo today. Clarissa has the harvest rolling in; we went to the fields ourselves yestereven and I'm tired. E.16 reports a terrible attack on Havre, with heavy losses in shipping; "sea monsters" blamed. I have sent Ser George south with a convoy of Etruscan refugees. All is well here. When will you come?

The word *back* was lined through and made him smile. So did the somewhat scattershot order of the information. On the other hand...

They had eight convoys out there; some entirely of cattle on the hoof. Four was the largest convoy of wagons and its arrival was another tiny victory. Gabriel did some mental arithmetic and realized that Sauce would have the main body back to Arles either eight or nine days before the gates opened—a day behind his own column. Clarissa was concentrating on the Arelat grain harvest; everyone needed that grain.

Ash's surrogates had assaulted the major Gallish seaport, which meant that Ash was expending masses of effort on sea monsters.

As soon as he read Blanche's words, Gabriel saw the implications of repatriating the thousands of northern Etruscan peasants and former soldiers who had been taken by the Necromancer. He all but winced that he *hadn't* thought of sending them back to where they could feed themselves.

He kissed the message.

Then Jon Gang appeared with a stool and pushed it behind his legs until he sat; Monteverdi, his trumpeter, produced hot water. Gang brought another stool for Atcourt, who was over forty and happy to have it.

Before the sun had fully risen, Gabriel was shaved and had his rancid arming clothes back on over a clean shirt, and so did Atcourt and Tom Lachlan. The camp, such as it was, was being packed on a couple of horses. Toby was still coaching Anne, whether she needed it or not, and Gabriel was tempted to intervene, but instead he and Atcourt put on their gloves and traded blows; sharp arming swords against bucklers until their breath steamed in the mountain air. Tom Lachlan took a tour of the flying column's horse lines and then rode up and dismounted, already in full harness; but he picked up a buckler and took a turn.

Father François appeared in his nut-brown habit and bare feet, and said mass for the command staff while Gabriel dispatched three birds and a pair of human messengers, one eye on the celebration of the eucharist, the other on his messenger birds. Du Corse was one ridge to the north with a thousand Gallish knights; Pavalo Payam was two ridges to the south with almost two thousand Royal Mamluks and their servants, all mounted. In the last hours, as reports rolled in, their various armies' roles had transformed from a race to Arles to save the gate, the former mission, to a slow ride across the southern Gallish plains, making use of available forage, fattening his horses for the next fights and resting his men and women. Arles was his depot, and any time he spent there would deplete his reserves.

"We have a week in hand," he said to Tom Lachlan after they had swaggered swords and swashed bucklers.

"Lads and lasses need to take a breath," Tom said. "Where's Sukey?"

Gabriel raised an eyebrow. "At Arles as of last night," he said.

Tom nodded. "Hoot, hoot," he said. "That's a treat." He paused, as if embarrassed; a rare moment for Tom. "Let's say we win," he said after a pause.

Gabriel smiled. "Sure," he said.

Behind him, Anne Woodstock and Monteverdi exchanged looks.

Tom looked at his emperor. "I want somewhat," he said finally.

"What kind of somewhat?" Gabriel asked.

"Earl of Eastwall," Tom Lachlan said. "Or northern Thrake. I'll take either."

"You're the Drover!" Gabriel said.

Tom laughed. "That was Hector's world, not mine. He was a pretty, pretty man, and a maun fighter, but his whole world ran from the Inn to the Hills." Tom looked out over the distant plains of Galle. "I want to wed Sukey," he said.

"Tom Lachlan!" Gabriel said. He reined in his horse in surprise.

"Ach, aye. Don't make it worset for me." Tom grinned.

Gabriel grinned back and realized that somehow, at twenty-three, he'd become one of those middle-aged men who liked to hear that other men were getting married.

"But ye ken, Gabriel—I'm not king o' any man, nor duke nor earl nor baron. Drover is just a job." Tom was actually flushed.

"So's emperor," Gabriel said. "It's like being drover. Ask Blanche. Mostly it's about moving cattle."

"Aye," Tom laughed. "I kenned that when Kronmir made me tell him everything about movin' coos. I was maun feared you'd send me to drove 'em."

"I considered it," Gabriel admitted.

"I like leadin' men. I like fightin' but I could, perhaps, be brought to admit I'm a little weary o' the whole thing." Tom made a face. "Never thought I'd admit to yon," he said. "None o' this is worth a kettle o' beans. Here's my point."

Gabriel raised his hand. "I hear you," he said. "Give me a few days. I think you'd make an excellent Earl of Eastwall, but I'm not at all sure we're going to have a wall when we're done. And I'm not sure Outwallers need feudal lords. I'm not sure *anyone* needs a feudal lord."

"An' that's a load o' bull-whallop, Gabriel. Don't go prat'n to me about the rights o' man. You know as well as I that ye're a bloody-handed tyrant in drivin' this war; nor could she be done any other way. Aye?" Tom shook his head. "Most loons can nae more govern themselves nor they could swim in fire."

Gabriel set his jaw.

Tom laughed. "Ye'r plannin' to turn Jack?" he asked.

Gabriel had to smile. "I want to leave our world with a system to hold the next few times without all this…"

Tom laughed. "Well, for me, I would na' ha'e it any other way. A red sword and a bright sunset, that's me," he quipped, quoting a popular epic poem. He shrugged. "Ye'll gi' me somewhat ta make Sukey a great lady?"

Gabriel wondered if this wasn't Tom putting his own dreams on Sukey's head, but he smiled. "Tom, I'll make you Grand Duke of the Moon if that's what you want."

Lachlan laughed. "Now that's my cap'n," he said.

Gabriel smiled at Tom. "Sukey is already a great lady," he said. "The title won't change her." He raised an eyebrow. "But mayhap it should be a title for each of you? And not just a reward for you."

Tom's beliefs didn't always run to equality of any kind. "Hoot, hoot," he said thoughtfully. "Aye, mayhap. In point o' fact, I can all but hear her shoutin' at me now."

Chapter Six

The Adnacrags—Aneas Muriens

In a summer that had been the hardest of his life, entailing the loss of his ancestral lands, his mother and father's death, constant warfare, wounds, fatigue, and hardship, the day after Ash's attack was the hardest day Aneas had ever known.

There were dead people everywhere, and they had to be buried in the sodden, thin leaf mould and sandy soil, and legions of normal Adnacrag predators and carrion eaters gathered in the evening shadows to feast on the dead; Kevin Orley's legions were not the immediate threat. Wolves and coyotes and ravens, and even raccoons, were.

But beyond the grim work of pulling the dead out of tree roots and high tree branches where lake and fire and sorcery had flung them; beyond the backbreaking labour of digging through the topsoil and lifting the endless small rocks to make graves, there was the work of reclaiming their supplies from wind and water and devastation; a ton of split peas soaking in the clear waters of the lake, acres of wet canvas drowned like linen counterfeit jellyfish on a storm-wracked beach.

And atop it all, there was the threat of attack from Orley; the need to complete the boats that lay, half finished or merely ribbed, floating atop the calm waters of the lake.

Aneas was everywhere, and so was Nita Qwan, and so was Irene.

Looks-at-Clouds lay in a coma, wrapped in blankets, teeth chattering; Skas-a-gao sat by hir, working what healing he could. The changeling's eyes were half open, skin pale as parchment, breathing very shallow.

Aneas was terrified that s/he would die. He had not examined his feelings for the changeling, but faced with hir death, he...

... worked. He stacked damp birch bark sheets, he stripped to his braes and swam into the lake with a tin bucket and rescued peas, and he hauled canvas out of the shallow water below their peninsula, he broke his nails and hardened his already calloused hands digging graves.

At first he just worked, silently, endlessly, banishing the daemons in his head with toil; Richard's death, Irene, Looks-at-Clouds. More work. Death, and corruption; bury it. He sent Ricard Lantorn into the woods with a patrol; sent Tas-a-gao south to look at their back trail, sent the wyverns spiraling west. Gave orders, and didn't think.

He worked.

Evening was falling, the red sun beautiful over the crisp blue lake, and Irene put her arm through his.

He started.

"You need to talk to them," she said. "Now."

His first reaction was anger, and he turned on her, his hand going to his dagger hilt.

"If I needed your advice, *Majesty*, I'd be sure to ask you," he hissed.

Irene had changed in just a couple of weeks. She was dirty; her nails were broken, and she wore a curious mixture of men's and women's attire. Her hair was back in a tight braid like the ones the irks wore. She stood her ground and met his eye. "I'm not attacking you," she said. "If you don't start cheering them up, I suppose I'll have to, but they prefer you, Aneas Muriens."

A dozen angry replies leapt into his brain.

He bit his lip, turned away. Stared over the beautiful lake a moment.

"Very well," he said, his voice cold.

Then he regretted his tone and the language of his body, but when he turned back, she was gone.

Still, he took her words as law. When the grave he was digging was done, and he and Tessen had piled dirt and stones on a dead Jack, he bowed to the irk and wandered, first out to the wall of hordles that guarded the peninsula, where he made sure the guard was changed, and then sat with the new quarter-guard and smoked a pipe. He handed his pipe axe from man to man. He didn't say much; neither did they.

"We need a guard," he said finally. "I know you'd rather be burying the folk who fell. We'll get that done as well."

"Then what, Cap'n?" asked a ranger.

"Then we'll strike at Orley's throat," Aneas said.

There was no cheer; just a growl.

"What of the dragon, then?" asked another.

Aneas looked at his hands in the dying light. "We will get him," he said. "He thinks he is God, and we are nothing." He looked up. "But we are not nothing. We, together, have the power to bring Ash down."

Ricard Lantorn, back from patrol and never one of the most vocal of the rangers, growled. "Give a lot to see that," he said. "Give my right hand," he said.

Other men and women nodded.

Aneas rose early in the morning, his head already working. He was curled next to Black Heron, and he lay a moment, looking up through the spruce branches above his head into the endless vista of the dawn sky, which seemed transparent all the way to the boundaries of the *aethereal*. He ached; he sat up slowly, so as not to disturb the sleeping warrior, and saw Looks-at-Clouds lying on the other side of the Outwaller. S/he opened hir eyes and looked at Aneas.

"Hello," s/he said softly.

Aneas grinned. "Good morning, Changeling."

"Ah," s/he said. "Just so. Changeling."

Aneas went to the fire, where Ta-se-ho was already making tea and laying up kindling he had split with a very small axe.

"Going to be a fine day," Ta-se-ho said. "A little cornmeal?"

Aneas watched Looks-at-Clouds get to hir feet with the odd bonelessness that marked the changeling's physicality. Then s/he walked stiffly after rising; teetering slightly.

"What happened?" Aeanes asked. He smiled gratefully at Ta-se-ho, who put a horn cup of hot tea with wild honey in his hands. The oldest man in the camp, Ta-se-ho was always the first one up; he did everything well, and he seldom complained. And he made fine tea.

Ta-se-ho smiled back. "It must be difficult, giving so many orders," he said. His Outwaller tone held just the hint of a suggestion of censure.

"You think I give too many orders?" Aneas asked, stung.

Ta-se-ho shrugged and went back to building up the fire. Cigne, the Occitan woman, came silently through the camp on her worn moccasins and reported the camp secure and the sentries unmolested. She stared at Looks-at-Clouds and then caught her hand and kissed her.

"Now that's a nice piece of news," Cigne said. "Oh, and Tessen has a doe," she added. "Cynthia and her bring it in." Her Occitan accent was very acute when she was tired or excited, and the woman had been up most of the night.

"Sleep," Aneas said.

She shook her head. "*Non, merci,*" she said. "I want to help with the boats."

"We will move tonight if we have the boats ready," Aneas said softly.

"All the better," Cigne said. "Clouds, *ma cheri*, you walk odd-ly." Cigne laughed and put her arm through the changeling's arm.

"It is rather odd, is it not?" Looks-at-Clouds said. "Curious. Fascinating."

Aneas, greatly daring, kissed the changeling on both cheeks. "It's good have you back," he said.

"Yes," Looks-at-Clouds said. "Yes. Interesting."

Not the reaction he'd expected.

"Guard!" came a call. A horn blew to the south.

Aneas caught his bow from against the tree under which he'd slept and ran for the horn, but he was too late for the action.

"A party," Lewen said. "A dozen warriors, one of the antlered monsters, some bogglins."

An antlered former-man lay at the irk's feet, a single heavy shaft all the way through the thing's head at the height of the brow ridge.

"I followed Tessen and Cynthia," he said with a shrug. "Just to cover them. I found these."

Monts, the royal forester, went past, stopping only to lay a hermetically charged wand on the corpse and then springing to his feet.

"Don't get caught in a counter-ambush," Aneas called. He felt like someone's father, sending them to their first tournament; a foolish reaction, as Monts had probably seen more battle than he had.

*

By the time the sun was high, the last six canoes were coming together as fast as Irene's work party could supply pine roots, which they were tearing from the ground in handfuls. The vessels were twenty-four feet long; their hulls were made from the bark of whole trees; each boat had spruce gunnels, forty or fifty ribs, and stems made from trees that had been warped by wind and weather. Aneas had never even seen one built before, although he'd seen them, full of furs, moving on the Great River in his youth.

Ta-se-ho was an exacting builder, and he'd ordered a whole hull unlaced and redone because he didn't like the wrinkle in the hull. Aneas had the sense to let the older man have his way, and the old man pronounced himself satisfied at noon.

Monts returned without loss, having run down a pair of northern Morean turncoats but no more.

Aneas nodded. "It's not so bad, brothers," he said. "If he has patrols looking for us... then he's not atop us. Double the guards; pack. We're off at last light."

He watched Irene and Looks-at-Clouds gathering more spruce root; saw Quill Garter (his own name for a particularly tall Outwaller woman) gathering the tips of spruce trees in a net bag, watched four bogglins stripping a patch of mushrooms. By midafternoon, most of the rescued canvas was dry; the food, such as it was, was packed; a group of Nita Qwan's Outwallers were weaving baskets to carry food in the boats, and Aneas had seldom felt so useless. He rolled his own blanket roll very tight, and then spent almost an hour of real time casting about in the *aethereal*.

Late in the afternoon, a wyvern returned, looking smug, which in a wyvern was a certain contracting of the skin around the eyes and beak, and brought Aneas word of two Gallish ships in the river, just off the mouth of the Cranberry River.

"Twenty leagues," the young wyvern said, as if extremely proud of this feat of counting in human terms. He said it six times.

Aneas bit his lips to avoid laughing, and then gathered his war council: Black Heron, Lantorn, Looks-at-Clouds, Ta-se-ho, Nita Qwan, Monts, and Deadlock, a relative newcomer, an Albinkirk ranger with years of hunting in the north country. But with fewer than two hundred rangers, the council was scarcely secret or private, and a dozen other men and women squatted or sat.

"We leave in an hour," he said. "The skies are clear, and we can be at the mouth of the Cranberry in the dawn."

"Are we going to board this ship?" Deadlock asked. He was a tall, thin man with dark skin and black eyes—an Adnacrag longhunter.

Looks-at-Clouds leaned forward. "There have been big changes in Galle," s/he said. "Let us be careful."

Aneas looked at hir, puzzled. "Big changes in Galle?" he asked. It was a very odd thing for hir to say.

S/he smiled. "I only repeat what I have heard from Ta-se-ho," s/he said.

Ta-se-ho raised an eyebrow at the shaman, shrugged, and nodded agreement. "The Red Knight told us that the King of Galle had fallen and that things were changing. At the Inn of Dorling," he said.

Irene, unsummoned, spoke up. "If we hit them in the dawn, they will not further divide our councils," she said. "If we stop to parley, and they mean to fight..."

Ta-se-ho grinned at her. "You would make a bad enemy," he said. "But in this, I think you are wrong. It is wrong to attack men you do not know."

"Galles slaughtered our people last spring," Gas-a-ho said.

Ta-se-ho shrugged. "Hurans," he said. "Not *our* people."

Aneas looked around the circle. "I hear what you say. We will be ready to strike them in the dawn," he said. "If I can find a way to talk, perhaps I will. But desperate times call for desperate measures."

"Do they?" Nita Qwan said. "Perhaps desperate times reveal who we really are."

As the shadows of the pines stretched out across the lake, the big canoes slipped into the water and the surviving rangers took the paddles and poles they'd carved themselves and began to move the light craft across the mirror-smooth surface of Cranberry Lake. The paddles dipped, and shone in the sun, sparkling in a near-perfect rhythm, and Cynthia raised her voice and began a tavern song, and every ranger knew it, and their voices rose over the Wild:

> *Come all ye brave heroes*
> *Lend an ear to my song*
> *and I'll sing ye in the praises*
> *of brandy and rum*

There's a clear crystal fountain
Near Alba doth flow
Give me the punch ladle
I'll fathom the bowl…

I'll fathom the bowl
I'll fathom the bowl,
Gi' me the punch ladle
I'll fathom the bowl.

The long canoes slipped along the water and into the deepening darkness.

The first check was the giant beaver dam at the foot of the Cranberry Lake where the Cranberry River flowed out between two great stone headlands linked by a dam fifteen feet high and seventy feet long, broken only in the middle by a flow-way no broader than the bottom of a single canoe.

Each canoe had to be emptied of rangers, sent through the flow-way while two rangers held hand lines, and carefully pulled alongside the dam downstream to be reloaded, but they managed without a single mishap, and before the waxing moon rose over the mountains, they were away on the river, which flowed silently by like a river of ink, so calm that the stars were reflected whenever the water flowed flat and straight.

Aneas had never been this far north, and he depended utterly on Ta-se-ho and Gas-a-ho for scouting. They were well ahead in a small canoe and he worried for them. But the river was broad and easy, moving in languorous curves after the first dam, and for hours they raced along until the moon had climbed behind them and begun to sink again. And then, when the river widened, they came to a rapids, as broad as an inland sea, and Ta-se-ho paddled back to lead them well to the west against the looming bank, and even there, most of the boats had to unload and line along the gravel beach, where many a toe was stubbed on rock in the darkness.

Past the rapids, a deep pool and another dam, this one lower and narrower. This time, they had to unload the more heavily laden boats; after the first, and nearly rolling his own boat, Aneas ordered a dozen men to clear all the brush off the point, and he helped build a brush platform for unloading; it seemed faster to him than waiting as people moved one at a time over the broken ground.

Ta-se-ho listened to his orders with some amusement. After waiting awhile, he looked at the sky and nodded. "I'll go poke ahead," he said, as if embarrassed to hear Aneas. Perhaps he was.

Aneas waved him away, and Irene leaned against him, hacking alder roots with her axe, and he steadied her when she looked as if she'd fall into the water.

She looked up, startled.

And grinned. "You," she said.

He found he was grinning back.

"What's wrong with Clouds?" she asked, suddenly serious. "Not hirself."

"Whoever s/he is when s/he's himself," Aneas quipped.

Irene ripped her Alder victim from the thin soil with a grunt of triumph. "Point taken," she said. "But watch him. Her. There's something..." Irene shrugged. And went forward into the darkness.

The very first hint of pale light in the east, and they still weren't all over the dam; the stars hung above them, and twenty men and women stood and smoked on the cleared spit of land while another twenty moved their canoe, cursing the darkness and everything in it. Beaver dams are not smooth under water, and barefoot men and women in one layer of deerskin moccasins were victim to every sharpened branch and every beaver-gnawed end.

"Aneas!" a voice snapped. It wasn't loud...

Aneas had nodded off. He sat up, looked around.

Ta-se-ho was shouldering through the resting rangers. He paused and took a long pull at another man's pipe and then squatted. "The Galles," he said. "I've seen them. We're very close."

Aneas nodded. "Yes?"

"They're under attack. Right now."

"Orley?" Aneas asked.

Ta-se-ho was handed a lit pipe and he had a pull, drank some water, and sat straighter. The old man was tired. "Must be," he said. "I didn't wait to watch. The banks were crawling with bogglins." He glanced at Krek. "No offence, little brother."

Krek opened all four hinges of its jaw and closed them.

Looks-at-Clouds stepped off hir canoe, which had already loaded. "Listen," s/he said. "You should rescue them."

Aneas nodded. "Perhaps," he said. "Easier said than done."

Looks-at-Clouds raised one slim eyebrow.

A chill went down Aneas's back.

Nonetheless, he put his sudden speculation away to be examined later and looked at Tas-a-go. "Show me the lay of the water, and the land," he said.

Ta-se-ho sketched the way a pair of Gallish round ships lay in the bay formed where the Cranberry River ran down into the Great River. He drew in the moonlit silver sand and blackish mulch of the river-bank, and Aneas's mind ran swifter than the river.

"Why don't they just weigh anchor and float away?" Aneas asked.

Looks-at-Clouds nodded. "Doubtless they are waiting for us," s/he said. "For a rendezvous. Perhaps your brother?" Looks-at-Clouds raised both eyebrows.

Aneas shook his head. "I cannot risk everything on that possibility," he said.

Ta-se-ho shrugged and handed his pipe to Looks-at-Clouds, who took it and blew a beautiful smoke ring into the moonlight. "Orley is right there, his creatures have their backs to us..." He smiled. "Odd time for you to be cautious."

Aneas was watching Looks-at-Clouds. He pursed his lips. And looked at Nita Qwan.

The dark-skinned man shrugged. "We can't slip by. Day is coming."

Irene, unbidden, put in, "Better to ambush them than be ambushed."

Aneas could not pin down why he felt so disoriented, so cautious. "Very well," he said. "What do they have for boats? Orley's people?"

The light was just strong enough for Aneas to see Irene's face as slightly more than a pale blob; he could, if he put his mind to it, count the boats behind him. The moon was growing pale, and the air was like wet hair—lank and uncomfortable. Aneas's boat was the lead boat; dangerous, but he wanted to keep the ability to make decisions at the last moment.

The last two leagues of the Cranberry were a series of long, slow curves, so that the mouth of the river couldn't be seen; the river grew, if anything, broader and flatter, and the high ground on either side that defined the banks consisted of steep, wooded ridges that could be seen to converge somewhere ahead in the darkness.

But for the last two curves, they'd been able to hear the thin wailing or keening of bogglins, and to see the mast tops of the round ships, like giant naked trees towering over the horizon and with the eerie, unseelie play of the northern lights behind them.

The canoes raced along with the current behind them and all the paddlers together.

Aneas stood, rocking the round-bottomed craft, and held out his left arm, and silently, his craft slipped to the left, closer against the bank, and the column followed him. They were moving at the speed of a galloping horse, and as the muddy, alder-thicket banks changed suddenly sandy beach and kelp-covered rock, he saw bogglins milling in the early light, and boats—canoes like his own, and cockle-boats, made of hide stretched tight over frames. There were dozens of boats, or perhaps hundreds.

Then the canoes were turning, turning, as the left bank widened into a beach, and the whole of Cranberry Bay lay open before his eyes in the new dawn. The moon hung just over the masthead of the larger of two heavy round ships, and the water around her was black with small craft and bogglins fighting to get up the sides. To his left, the open beach, and now, to his right, a spit of land even more densely covered; antlers, and a cluster of tall Rukh, as many as six or eight, and back in the marsh a great hastenoch roared a challenge to the sun as the first bright rays pierced the eastern horizon and turned everything from shadowed greys to salmon and rose.

Aneas looked hard at the shore on his right hand, flashed a look back to the left, and made his decision.

"Lay us for the ships," he said to Ta-se-ho, who had the steering paddle.

Men and monsters on the beach to his right were beginning to be aware that the canoes coming past were not their own.

Aneas *went into his palace and unlimbered a series of shields, now his standard response to any combat, layering a general shield of gold with a series of smaller shields in green.*

Then he activated his first working.

Light leapt from each of his ten fingers and arched away into the morning; five embers rose to his left and five to his right. On the spit of sand, a green shield leapt into existence; to his left, three heavy curtains rose, and an umbrella of green so dark it was almost black.

Aneas's workings had specific bounds of grammar, and as they met with the shields, they stopped and slid down, down, like falling sparks against a sheet of metal, until they touched the ground, where they burst, not with light or heat or shards of death, but heavy coils of smoke, dense and grey-green.

Looks-at-Clouds shot him a look in the real, hir emerald eyes wide. S/he smiled, the smile of a cat with one paw on the mouse, and s/he loosed a single pulse of light from one finger of hir own hand, violet-white.

Aneas turned his head and closed one eye as the shaman's deadly casting left a streak through the welling smoke and detonated like a thunderclap on a green shield, tearing a gash longer than a canoe through which s/he placed a second working.

Other casters did as they had been bid, throwing fire in the real. Shields in the real cost much more in *potentia* and *ops* than shields in the *aethereal* and were relatively rare at the opening of engagements; the left bank proved to be fully protected, but the spit of sand was covered only in the *aethereal*, and every bark canoe and hide boat on the sandy beach burst into violent fire that under-lit the sorcerous smoke; the orange light of the sun rising in the west picked out the smoke, played on the rising column of ash in the west, and the whole scene was lurid.

The six long canoes raced on. Black Heron stood, loosed an arrow forward, and knelt to keep the trim of the canoe; stood and loosed again. His arrows arched into the smoke and vanished.

The smoke picked out the play of the *ops* and the river behind them was crisscrossed with green and gold light. Some of it sparkled against the various shields cast by the racing canoes, but many missed, passing astern harmlessly, or detonating against the shields on the other side of the river. Arrows began to rise out of the smoke and fall around them, but unaimed, they were more a threat than a danger.

And then, in the blink of an eye, they were on the boats crowding around the two ships. At point-blank, and with no interference from an enemy sorcerer, Aneas put his hand flat, almost on the mirror-calm water, and loosed a prepared phrase; a dark plane, like brown ink faster than a racing tide, rolled out from his left hand and into the packed cockle-boats. Every boat it struck lost a strip of hide wider than Aneas's hand at the waterline; hundreds of bogglins were simply cut in half, and their hide boats sank instantly, unmade.

Ghause's sorcery was still very potent in Aneas.

With his right, he wrote "Friends!" in Gallish on the smoke behind him, and none too soon, as a bolt from an arbalest missed him by a hand's breadth and popped through the heavy bark of his boat as if the stuff were as thin as a lady's shift. Water began to pour in. There were shouts in Gallish.

The bow ground into the enemy boats that had survived his magic, and most of Nita Qwan's warriors dove over the sides. Black Heron loosed an arrow so close to his target that the arrow went through the bogglin as he tried to come over the gunwale, all the way out through his wing cases and into the bogglin behind, and then Black Heron leapt for the next canoe like a leaping deer.

Aneas had never been so surprised in all his life; in three beats of his heart, he was almost alone in the great canoe. The bogglins turned from climbing the slab-sides of the round ship and came at him, leaping lightly into the rising bow of his canoe. Nita Qwan had not deserted him, and he threw a tomahawk into the first foe, dropped a second over the side with his paddle, and then Aneas was at the Outwaller captain's shoulder, his short spear licking over the Outwaller's shoulder to kill a third, and a fourth.

Nita Qwan turned and dove over the side, leaving Aneas alone except for Ta-se-ho in the rapidly sinking stern. Aneas had thigh-high boots of heavy goatskin and a long shirt of maille, and the bogglins held no fear for him, except that the canoe rocked like a trotting horse's back, and Aneas knew that if he went over, he'd sink like a stone.

But other canoes were coming in to the right and left, wedging his against the cockles and the hull of the great Gallish round ship. His spear licked out and took another bogglin, and then he had to shorten the haft. His feet were wet; the boat was sinking.

He used the haft, used the head to slash, thrust viciously with the butt-spike, trying to reach another boat, but the bogglins were reckless, and then he was in the water and so were the bogglins; he took a blow in the back and almost lost his air. He sank.

Then there were rocks beneath his feet; shallow, but the water was full of bogglins and not all of them were dead. He missed the moment when the Sossag warriors, old hands at water-fighting, rose under the cockle-boats and boarded them from the *other* side, slaughtering the shocked bogglins; he missed the moment when the Galles, realizing that they had allies, began concentrating their crossbows on the flanks of the fight, isolating the bogglins and speeding their collapse. He was in the water with twenty of the vicious creatures and he'd lost his spear and had only his heavy dagger; immediately he had to loose a working he would rather have saved for a deadlier foe, blasting a pair of the creatures off his back and head and losing an ear in the process, ripped from his head by a four-hinged mouth. Blood poured down his face into the water, summoning other predators, but the bay was full of blood, and as the new sun rose in red splendour, Cranberry Bay was a brilliant red, the red of new blood under a vivid orange sky.

A wedge of canoes came out of the smoke from the shore.

Once again, a line of violet fire came from Looks-at-Clouds. Hir strike met a shield and dropped it with a concussion like the falling of an ancient tree; not a single clap, but a long, titanic ripping noise.

"Hastenoch," Ta-se-ho said. The old man was in the water with Aneas; he had a short, curved sword in one hand and his pipe axe in the other and his feet on the shingle of sand beneath them. He had a slash wound on one side of his neck, and even as he spat the warning, Nita Qwan leaned out from a captured canoe's gunwale and hauled the older man straight out of the water.

The massive, four-footed troll's head caught Aneas in the midriff, driving him off his feet and into deeper water; luck and the warning were all that kept the blow from being his death, and even as it was, he felt the ribs go on his left side.

His fear gagged him in the bloody water; the huge thing was almost invisible under the surface, and he couldn't find it, and he was sinking, the weight of the maille too much for him. The blow had knocked him off his sandbar into deeper water.

He opened his eyes under water, fighting panic; there were hundreds of bogglins, their corpses neutrally buoyant just below the surface; and there...

It ignored all the boats and came for him. A long trail of bright blood curled away from it in a spiral of almost aethereal beauty, rising into the orange sun over their heads. Archers were loosing into the thing from above and it was taking hits, making the water leap, but the thing came straight for Aneas.

He set his feet in the deep black mulch of the bottom, so different from the sand he'd just been on, and he raised his own pipe axe under water and loosed his last prepared *ops* and light flared, brighter than the sun, brighter than ten suns. It was the merest cantrip, a flash of light to blind an opponent, but in the murky water it dazzled the monster and it made fair to dazzle its caster, who only had one eye closed by virtue of the pain from his head where his ear had been ripped away.

The troll lost its air in shock; bubbles exploded all around it.

He struck with the pipe axe, a feeble blow to its brow ridge, but it was turning, turning, its sense of direction lost, and Aneas grappled it, wrapping the haft of his pipe axe over its antlered head and round its neck and locking it there with both hands as the now-panicked monster shook itself like a terrier and then leapt for the surface.

They burst into the noise and chaos of the battle and Aneas hauled in a breath and cranked the pipe axe haft against what he hoped was the troll's windpipe.

An arbalest bolt, lucky or aimed with great skill, sank right to the fletchings in the thing's side as it rolled, a hand's breadth from Aneas's hips where he straddled it. It spasmed, its strength godlike, and broke his grip and flung him out of the water, maille and all. He fell back; his head hit something hard...

...he was choking, his lungs full. It was all very slow; he was alone in a great field, running to his mother with a handful of flowers, and then he was sitting on Gabriel's chest while Gavin held him down, rubbing pig shit in his hair; he was kissing Anthony, the stable boy, and then Anthony was dead, killed by his father, who loomed over him, a sword in his hand, and his mother...

...his mother...

A spike of pain, and he was choking, choking, vomiting and choking, and he was *upside down* and all the day's disorientation came together and he was...

...gone.

The Gallish officer looked at Nita Qwan. "He's breathing," the man said. He wore an odd smile, and his Low Archaic had a scholarly quality.

Nita Qwan looked at Aneas Muriens, who hung like a gutted deer, upside down, the wound to his head bleeding freely onto the deck of the great round ship. The ship's physician had ordered the drowned captain seized by the heels and hung that way, and had both kissed him and punched him in the stomach, causing Irene to attack him. But Looks-at-Clouds, in precise High Archaic, restrained Irene and explained her, at the same time, and the Galle had smiled his odd, twisted smile again.

Gas-a-ho watched the operation with a clinical detachment. He was smoking Ta-se-ho's pipe axe, and now he grabbed the swaying head of the upside-down captain, pulled him close, and fastened his mouth over Aneas's mouth and breathed out, filling his lungs with tobacco smoke.

Aneas coughed; hacked again, and gurgled.

"Oh, stop it!" Irene said.

Aneas vomited. It was ugly, and watery, and went on too long; the man coughed and coughed.

The Gallish doctor caught his head and shoulders and two sailors cut him down, and they laid him gently on the deck, well clear of his vomit.

"He's breathing," the doctor said again triumphantly; this time in High Archaic, rare among Galles albeit common enough among Outwallers.

Aneas's eyes flickered open.

An hour later he sat, naked but for a white wool blanket, in the stern cabin of the round ship, as a pair of Gallish sailors unshipped the heavy deadlights that had protected the stern windows in battle, loop-holed like a fortress wall. Beyond the windows, the banks of the Great River slipped by, and astern, almost a dozen long canoes bobbed and skipped like captive dolphins. At his side sat Nita Qwan and Black Heron and John de Monts, the forester, and Irene, all ranged along a beautiful stern bench with a velvet cushion. A magnificent scene of the annunciation of the Virgin was painted on a panel and hung on the starboard wall, and on the port side, a rich tapestry depicting the hunt of a wild boar.

"You were *waiting* for us?" Aneas asked. He still felt terrible; he felt as if he were someone else and not himself; death, or near-death, had added to his disorientation; worst of all, he had lost his contact with the *aethereal. There was nothing there, and like the torn ear, whose bleeding stump he could not stop handling, the lack of contact with the* aethereal *was something he kept probing; stepping into his memory forest, wincing at the alien darkness where his clear pool had been, and drifting back to the real.* He felt *sick,* sick to his very core. He felt as if he were another person. The feeling frightened him, and so did the near worship with which he was greeted on deck when he came to; Gas-a-ho claimed he had killed a troll in the water with only his pipe axe. Aneas had no immediate memory beyond choking; it was as if his former life had been stripped away. He remembered Looks-at-Clouds; he remembered the attack of Ash and the night movement on the Cranberry, but of the fight there he had only flashes.

The Gallish captain was called Charles: Charles de la Marche. He remembered that; the man had been introduced a moment before.

The man was older even than Ta-se-ho—in his late fifties. He had a grey beard and dark hair and he hadn't shaved in a week, but his eyes sparkled. "I had a message from one of your black-and-white birds, ordering me to wait in the mouth of the Seneschal River, or perhaps the Chaudiere or this Wgotche...."

Looks-at-Clouds nodded from across the table. S/he had a pipe, a clay pipe from Galle or Alba, and s/he was blowing smoke rings, but s/he leaned forward sharply. "The Huran name for Cranberry," s/he said.

"I looked into each," De La Marche said. "I didn't linger; the south bank is crawling with the Wild."

Aneas managed to muster enough of his usual humour to crack a smile. "We're crawling with the Wild ourselves," he said.

The Galle leaned back in his broad-footed captain's chair. "My men are not so pleased to have these horrid goblins aboard." He waved at the door to the main deck, where Krek and a dozen bogglins sat in the sunlight digesting an excellent meal of their enemies. "And irks!" he said.

Aneas tugged at his beard.

Irene was also wearing only a white wool blanket. She leaned forward clutching the blanket close. "You just happened to be in the river?" she drawled. "We spent the spring and summer fighting Galles."

The Gallish captain's face froze. "My brother was Oliver de la Marche. Does that mean anything to you?" he asked.

Irene was distracted by Aneas, who was smiling at her. She felt herself blush.

Aneas grinned. "You fell in?" he asked.

Monts laughed. "She jumped in to fetch you, *sir*," he said.

Aneas flushed. And looked at the Galle. "Your brother was Hartmut's captain," he said.

"Hartmut killed my brother," De la Marche said.

Irene sat back. "I see," she said quietly.

"Do you?" De la Marche said, his voice flat, devoid of emotion. "I'm still not sure I understand it all. But I have two hundred sailors and forty men-at-arms of my own, and I collected all the men I found at Kebec. I have a commission signed by the Sieur Du Corse."

"What men at Kebec?" Aneas demanded.

Looks-at-Clouds shook hir head. "The Galles," s/he shrugged. "When Ticondonaga surrendered, your brother sent them north."

Aneas frowned. For a moment he'd been himself, and now he felt as if there were a spear through his head. The pain was staggering.

"War makes for strange bedfellows," Irene muttered.

"And who exactly are you, mam'selle?" asked De la Marche.

"I am Princess Irene of Liviapolis, Porphyrogenetrix, Heir of the Empire," she snapped. And at her voice, no man would have questioned her, despite the pale, round shoulders or the white wool blanket or the sodden, mouse-dun hair.

De la Marche rose and bowed. "It is like having legends spring to life," he said.

Irene favoured him with a regal smile. "I find these adventures wearing," she admitted. "And yet…thrones are not won in throne rooms, nor do faint hearts ever win fair gentlemen." She nodded. "We have been fighting Kevin Orley and his master all summer. Even now, the Army of the Alliance is in the west." She pointed out the foredeck windows, where, behind De la Marche, smoke rose into the heavens; trees were on fire, and birch bark burned. And ahead, out the main hatch toward the deck, Aneas could see the sky—pink and red and deep grey—perpetually lowering like a storm front ready to break, at least for the last few days.

Aneas blinked several times, trying to clear his head. There was too much in it. "How fares Ta-se-ho?" he asked.

232

Nita Qwan shook his head. "The old hunter is dead," he said. "He bled out. We lost him and Red Squirrel and you lost…"

Irene looked up. "Ashford," she said.

"Damn," Aneas said. But he sat up. "Is Ashford and Ta-se-ho a fair exchange for singeing Orley's beard and burning Orley's boats?" He felt the darkness settle on him. "What are we doing?" he asked. He sounded lost.

Irene spoke out, her voice assured. "We are moving upriver, headed west into the Milles Isles."

Looks-at-Clouds nodded. "We must go west. We must snatch Thorn's island before Orley can reach it."

De la Marche nodded at the changeling and then at Aneas. "*Oui, monsieur.* This is what your officers said you would want."

Aneas winced slightly at the mention of *officers* and remembered Ta-se-ho telling him that he gave too many orders. It struck him that the man was dead; and that he had been a remarkable man, and without him, they would have had no boats. Something else was flitting around the edge of his mind, but Aneas wasn't anxious to delve too deep in the soup of his head just then.

Then it struck him, what was wrong inside his head.

He had no access to *ops*. He could see his palace; it was dark, and looked as if it was haunted, but there was no connection.

He was dead to the *aethereal*.

He wanted to speak; to say something dramatic. But time passed, and he was still sitting, saying nothing. He looked, first at Looks-at-Clouds, and then at Irene.

Looks-at-Clouds smiled at him and nodded. "We *must* do this," s/he said.

Irene gave him a queer look; the Gallish captain was more sanguine. "You have a chart for this Inner Sea?" he asked.

Monts laughed hollowly. "Never even been there," he said.

"Ta-se-ho knew the waters well," Nita Qwan said. "I do not. Gas-a-ho perhaps."

"Deadlock," Monts said. "He's been up here. But he's wounded." The forester shrugged and got up carefully to avoid slamming his head into the low beams. "I'll go speak to him."

"You have no pilot?" the Galle asked. "Sweet Holy Trinity. *Ventre*

Saint Gris. Par Dieu. You want me to take my ships into uncharted waters? These are not canoes; my ships have draughts. Rocks will sink us."

Aneas blinked. He looked at Irene, and caught her eye. He was having trouble forming words.

Her pupils widened slightly.

"Yes," Aneas said.

Looks-at-Clouds cut in. "If you can't help us, we'll go on by canoes, as we would have gone if we hadn't . . . found you."

The Gallish captain rose, bowing his head and swinging gracefully to avoid the silver hanging lamp. "I make no promise. Let us see what we see."

The San Colombo Pass—Ser Alison

The great fortified camp was almost empty, and all the infantry had marched north, headed for the San Colombo pass.

Sauce was having too good a time to let it all go. She wanted the captain to see how good she was, and she had been reading all of Blanche's messages. She had an idea; she had a strong rear guard of light horse; she had the company, or at least the whites and the greens. She had a steady flow of scouting reports.

In the first light of dawn, she mounted with the Duchess of Venike and two thousand horse, and the moment there was enough light to see her hand in front of her face, they were moving. Not north, to the safety of the pass and the plains of Arles on the other side of the mountains, but south, to Firensi.

Arles—The Red Knight

The falconet barked, and the heady smell of sulphur billowed over the watchers. A hundred paces away, the four-pound stone ball struck an old oak tree and the tree's base exploded, splinters flying fifty paces.

The second falconet fired, and its ball struck the same target, and the old oak tree, almost severed, fell with a crash.

Pavalo Payam peered through the smoke. "Remarkable," he said.

He twitched his emerald silk khaftan as if trying to keep it out of the smoke.

Bad Tom spat. "Aye, they're monsters and nae mistake."

Gabriel was watching his guests. Du Corse had his fingers deep in his beard. He looked at the emperor, his eyes full of speculation.

"You can crack a castle with ten rounds," Du Corse said quietly. "Nothing can stand against you."

Gabriel nodded. His smile almost split his face. "You should ask Edmund Chevins what they did to the Umroth," he said.

"They're too fewkin' strong; they'll take all the fun oot o' war," Tom said. "An' the smell is like all the de'ils in hell ha'e dusted their breeks."

Payam crossed his arms. "My sultan will require these to be shared," he said. "This cannot be something that you alone have."

Du Corse walked over to the crews and looked down the barrel of the nearest gonne, and watched carefully while the sponger ran his sheepskin-headed stave into a bucket of dirty water and then thrust it down the throat of the smoking piece. When he took it out, it was black, and a shred of glowing ember was stuck to the wet sheepskin, and the sponger plunged it in the bucket and sponged again.

The loader stepped up with a small paper bag and placed it in the muzzle. The rammer rammed it down sharply to where Duke had a placed a sharp spike into the touch hole. "Home," he said. He withdrew the spike and then thrust it down savagely, piercing the powder bag, and then a boy stepped forward with a goose quill and popped it into the touch hole.

"Ready!" Duke said.

"Fire," Edmund Chevins said.

Duke slapped the top of the goose quill with his slow match and the gonne fired with a loud, flat *crack* that echoed across the plain.

Du Corse turned and came back, the smoke billowing around him. "*Bon Dieu*," he growled. "It is the end of war."

"I doubt it," Gabriel said. "But I suspect they'll come as a little surprise to someone." His smile was grim.

"I will want my own," Du Corse said, with a smile at Payam. "If no castle can stand against these, then . . ." The Gallish knight left the rest unspoken.

But his second, d'Aubrichecourt, smiled wickedly. "No baron could ever stand against a king who had these," he said.

Gabriel thought of castles, and of Du Corse. And frowned. "I didn't think of that," he said.

Later, as Ariosto was prepared for riding, he came across Mortirmir sitting cross-legged in the sunshine with a clay pot full of arrowheads before him, and then a line of a dozen blued-steel spearheads, heavy, lugged spearheads, on a blanket. Gabriel watched him for a while, as Anne laid his flying harness out on the ground.

There was no blaze of fire, nor was there a thunderclap. Just, finally, a little shimmer, as if his eyes had refocused. And now every weapon bore a small letter M in Imperial Gothic script under its maker's mark.

"Fell spears," Gabriel said in jest.

"Less metal. Much easier," Mortirmir said. "Tom's idea."

Harndon—Lessa

Lessa moved quickly through the streets. They were relatively empty; people were afraid of the new plague, and the horned men and their sorcerous dances, or so it was said, and now there were royal guardsmen and trained band guilds people everywhere, on alert, in full armour; some street corners and larger market squares had apprentice magisters, or initiates of the Order of Saint Thomas.

She'd tried for two days to find anyone who'd seen these horned men and lived to tell about it; there had been at least three groups, and when they exploded, they showered every observer with a fine black dust that almost invariably brought death. There was a rumour that the queen had a counterspell; Tyler put it about that the queen didn't see any need to share the cure with her subjects.

Despite the empty streets, or perhaps because of them, this time Lessa was better dressed, wearing men's clothes: good hose that showed her legs, light boots like a soldier or a forester, and a loose gown that hid her gender and some other objects as well, under a fine hood that suggested she might be a person of quality, and topped with a fine red bycocket. At her side hung a short arming sword and a purse, and as she passed through Cheapside, men sometimes bowed and often cleared her way.

She was late, and annoyed to be late. The time for her assignation had passed with the chiming of the bells of the cathedral, and she worried that her man would simply walk away. But she'd been delayed by attentive guards and lines of suffering plague victims, and already Harndoners knew that when you saw one of the poor unfortunates, faces riddled with black marks like lettering on a page, you walked well around them, because they could burst and spread the black dust as horribly as the horned men. Or so it was said.

But several streets before the site of the meeting, deep in the tangle of alleys of the Scramble, she saw her mark, Captain Crowbeard, as Tyler had named him. She knew him instantly—his age, his erect back, and slightly bent neck, as if he'd spent his life trying to be slightly shorter than someone else. As she'd raised her status, he'd lowered his, and he wore a coarse wool gown, a matching hood, and loose hose held up by garters and bagged into heavier boots. Despite his low attire, he wore a long sword, but many did in the troubled times.

She thought of hailing him and realized what a foolish notion that was, and instead set herself to follow him. She pressed in closer. He paused to bargain with a pie man who was so thin he looked as if he needed to try some of his own wares. Crowbeard held out a pair of coppers and took a meat pie, and just then she brushed past him, laughing inside, and carried on down the narrow street.

After three strides she glanced back and saw his eyes light on her.

He gave a tenth of a smile and raised his meat pie in mock salute.

A hand reached out and seized his wrist.

The pie man was knocked flat by a thug, and every other man and woman on the street fled like pigeons before hawks, some shrieking, some silent.

The thug who dropped the pie man was big: tall and deep-chested, with a long blond beard.

The man who held her mark's hand, pie and all, was the pimp of their first encounter. He backhanded Crowbeard, who spun away and fell across the pie man, limbs sprawling.

"That's your protector, you bitch?" he asked. "You think I don't know you in men's clothes? I could get your nose slit for wearing men's clothes, sweetie. I might just slit it myself." He came toward her. "Bishop pays a reward for women caught in men's clothes."

She didn't run. Nat Tyler needed the man on the ground and his "lord." And this was what she trained for. The pimp scared her, though.

"You stuck me with a little knife?" he said. "I'll . . ."

She drew. She didn't have time to loosen the sword in the scabbard, and in her moment of fear, she forgot to get her left hand down to hold the throat of the scabbard, and so, for a heart-stopping moment, the scabbard's wood and leather clung to the blade, and they came up together, but the narrow belts that bound the scabbard held, and the blade broke free.

Her draw, clumsy as it was, took the pimp by surprise, still moving forward, confident in the awe and fear he could cause, and the rising point caught him at the corner of his mouth, ripped out a tooth, and went up through his nose and stuck a moment in the ridge of bone in his brow before she passed back and got the blade free.

He grunted, slipped to one knee, and drew a heavy cutlass.

"You fucking bitch," he said, except that a bit of his gum came out and he had to spit blood.

The big thug stepped forward and hefted a big oak club studded with nails.

"Shit," Lessa said aloud. She knew that if she'd had her face opened by a blade, she'd be lying on the ground whimpering, or at least, she assumed she would. Not drawing a weapon and advancing. "Shit," she said again.

She circled a little, keeping the big man behind the wounded one, and the pimp stood, swayed, and cut at her with his cutlass. It was an utterly incompetent blow; in one movement, he told her that he was no real threat, that he was untrained, a mere bravo, and weak from her first blow, and her heart soared. She flicked her little sword at his face; he overparried, and she cut his sword hand off his arm, just as Tyler had taught her, with a back cut from her rising *sottano*, her thumb pressed to the flat of her blade.

"Jesus fuck," the pimp muttered. He fell to both knees in the street. "Fuck!" he shouted. "Fuck!"

The wrist was still held together by a thread of gristle, and he was trying to hold his hand on. Blood fountained. She moved, watching the big man.

He was shaking his head, whistling between his teeth. "Bad business," he said in a deep voice.

"Turn," said Crowbeard, who'd gotten to his feet unnoticed in the last heartbeats.

The big man pivoted, a passable *volte stabile* that said he might be a tougher prospect than the man who'd hired him.

But he already had three feet of steel through his chest, and he died before he fell back off the long blade.

Kit Crowbeard leaned down and pulled the big man's hood off his shoulder and used it to clean his long sword. Then he tossed it to Lessa, who caught it fastidiously and used it to clean the blood off her own much shorter sword as if she killed men every day. She was charged with spirit; she wanted to sing, or shout aloud.

"I never like to stab a man in the back," Crowbeard said conversationally. "I have done it, mind. But I don't like it."

Crowbeard sheathed his sword without looking, drew a small knife out of his big boots, and leaned over the pimp, who was still kneeling, whimpering, as he bled out. Lessa thought he was going to finish the man, but instead the older man cut the pimp's purse free from its strap and opened it, casually leaning against a dirty white house wall.

"Help me," the pimp said.

Crowbeard looked both ways on the street. "Thanks, by the way," he said to Lessa. "Nice cut. Next time, use your hips and the hand will come right off like the head of a flower." He popped open the purse, dumped the coins in the mud, looked inside.

"Help me! Please…" the pimp said. His voice already sounded weaker.

Crowbeard looked at the pimp. And grinned. And then looked back at Lessa. "Shall we?" he asked, pointing toward the inn where they were supposed to meet.

"He'll…" she began.

"He'll bleed out in a few minutes," Crowbeard said with a terrible smile. "And then he'll go to hell. Forever." Crowbeard blew the pimp a kiss. "Come. We have a queen to kill."

The pimp subsided gradually into the bloody mud of the street. The pie man got to his feet and searched the mud for the coins Crowbeard had dumped, and then ran off, leaving his pies; the other pickpockets, whores of both sexes, as well as the relatively honest tradesmen like the paper seller and the paste maker all stepped over the dying man and hurried on their various ways as he mumbled and burbled. Eventually his mouth filled with the slush and liquid manure of the street when an urchin shoved his face in the muck to shut him up.

Only then did he die.

By then, the pie man had found Ranald Lachlan. And Harmodius.

They might have paid him more attention if they hadn't just had a tip about the attack of a trio of horned men in Aldgate Street. They ran, a dozen armoured guards at their backs and the filthy pie man trying to keep up. He caught them up at the ancient gate itself.

Three horned figures stood framed in the arch of the gate. They'd killed the guard, who lay at their feet.

Harmodius worked; the three horned men immolated inside shield bottles of worked *ops* and their spores burned with them.

But Harmodius missed the fourth and fifth, who were in the ramshackle house by the gate. Ranald caught the smaller—a rising cut from his scabbard far better executed than Lessa's—and he used his hips and the horned man's head rolled and bounced in the stone gutter. Spores poured out of the severed neck, a torrent of what should have been blood.

"Don't breathe!" Harmodius roared. He cast; the last horned man *unmade* into a cloud of black spores, and the black cloud and the fire met. The spores burned with a sudden *whoosh* that left a vague smell of cooking mushrooms. A royal guardsman grabbed at his throat, choking; in a moment a black fleck appeared on his face.

The man shivered all over.

Ranald Lachlan stepped close like a lover and dug in his belt pouch, dropping his black-bloody sword in the street. He found the phial he wanted and pushed it between his man's teeth, and the man's rolling eyes focused and he swallowed.

Harmodius grabbed the man by the belt and cast, muttered an invocation that filled the air in letters of fire, and cast again.

He stumbled back, healed. And fainted.

He fell over the corpse of the pie man. The man's face was already turning black. Lachlan caught his man's arms and hauled him off, and Harmodius shielded the pie man's still-warm corpse and burned it to ash, leaving a body-shaped patch of dried mud and ordure, backed hard, where the body had lain.

"What was he saying?" Lachlan said. "Poor bastard."

"Plot to kill the queen," Harmodius said.

"Ten a penny," Lachlan said. "Fuck. Poor bastard." He looked at Harmodius. "I need to wash."

"I need to get out of here," Harmodius said. He'd spent two days fighting the horned men; rushing from point to point, casting, healing, fighting. "This is all—"

"Vital?" Lachlan said bitterly. "I ken ye want to be up north."

Harmodius was looking at the spot where the pie man had lain. "This is all distraction," he said.

The Cohocton—Bill Redmede

They moved quickly on moccasin-clad feet; no one had boots anymore. There was almost no light, but they were getting good at moving in low light and their handful of irks guided them expertly. Behind the Jacks and the foresters there were almost a hundred Alban militiamen, running softly with their crossbows on their shoulders. Ten days of near-constant combat had eroded the differences between veteran and novice. And behind them, a century of Moreans, all mountaineers.

Far to the west, something gave a great roar, and was answered. In the northeast, the light was turning orange over the peaks of the Adnacrags; in the west, the sky was an unnatural colour, at least for the heavens; more like slate than like a storm.

They ran on, lungs heaving.

An irk guide turned suddenly, and waved. Bill Redmede knew the ground immediately: a long marsh formed in the distant past by giant beaver. The giant beaver were long gone, but their smaller cousins had moved in. Even as his Jacks ran up behind him, a legion of autumn frogs leaped into the water, expecting predators; out in the orange-lit flat water to the north, a trout leapt, magnificent in its grace.

Redmede gave no order. He merely held his arms out, hands flat to the earth, and all the rangers spread out on either hand, Jacks to the left, foresters to the right, Albin militia and Moreans in the middle, as they had practiced and executed half a dozen times.

They had moved almost a dozen miles in one night—south of the old road, well south—and circled into the rear of Ash's host.

Across the swamp, there was movement. A horn called, long and musical, and another answered.

Redmede blew a whistle. Off to his right, his brother's whistle answered, and all around him, Alban militia began to span their crossbows. Farther left, Stern Rachel raised a heavy war bow and loosed a ranging arrow, and it flew, up and up, down and down, to strike across the swamp. Just to Redmede's right, a short, squat Morean whirled a sling over his head and a stone flew out over the marshy pond and vanished in the weeds.

The autumn mosquitoes began to play among the waiting rangers. At first they came in ones and twos, and then in hordes. It was mostly a warm autumn, and the insects were fierce, and people began to curse in three languages.

Another roar, this one from the north—a fell beast. Horns, low and malignant, then high and piercing.

The light was growing in the sky.

Bill Redmede crouched, waiting, anxious. Worrying about everything.

A wyvern appeared, flying slowly, circling, off to the west, and then another.

Another pair of wyverns appeared from the east.

Redmede cursed.

Across the swamp, something crashed in the alder brake. Heads came up among the rangers. A militia woman clipped a bolt into her weapon, locking the nock against the heavy string. Her hands were shaking, and so were Redmede's.

A Morean knelt with a crucifix in his hand.

Suddenly, the wyverns converged, three against two, their long, high screams filling the air, their movements almost too fast to track. At the merge there was a melee, lasting less than two heartbeats, and then there were four wyverns, two and two, and the fifth falling, falling, one wing torn away, screaming, fluttering, screaming, and hitting the ground deep in the woods a mile to the north.

An irk knight broke cover, his stag labouring in the mud at the edge of the swamp, and then the noble beast gathered itself and leapt into the deep water, sank, and then emerged, swimming strongly.

Another irk appeared, and then Redmede could see Syr Ydrik, on the far shore, directing his retreat. Sorcery flashed; the irk knight's glowing green castle held, and suddenly the irk captain's great white stag turned and dropped into the water. There were dozens of irk knights in the water now; then there were hundreds, swimming for their lives, their surefooted, broad-hooved mounts keeping them alive.

Close behind them came the hastenoch and a vast tribe of giant Rukh; perhaps as many as fifty. A pair of purple-crested warden shamans directed them, casting and casting, and then the hastenochs broke free of the alder and pelted into the water, followed by the Rukh, who came on slowly, ripping each great foot from the ooze and placing it again.

Redmede's nerves were gone. He stood, looked left and right, and put his whistle to his lips.

No one needed an invitation. All the rangers scrambled to their feet. He took a breath and blew.

Four hundred bows wobbled, pointed almost at the sky. Four hundred backs heaved. Four hundred steel points steadied.

"Loose!" roared the forester master archer, John Hand.

The irks were still swimming; their pursuit was too close for the crossbows to shoot over them, but the Moreans, well spread out, began to cast. Their sling stones were lead and weighed more than a war bow arrow.

Redmede held his hand flat. "Bide!" he called to the militia.

The bows were already coming up again.

"Loose," called Hand.

The arrows made a noise in the silent morning, like the sound of doves rustling and cooing in an old barn. The sling stones hissed.

A Rukh woman, up to her waist in water, stopped walking and put a hand to her eye, where an arrow had sprouted. She plucked at it, and it came out. Half a dozen sling stones hit her all together, and she belly flopped forward into the water, dead.

The arrows fell like steel sleet. The sling stones fell almost as fast.

The irks were still swimming. They were close now, and the archers loosed one more, high, and then fell flat. The tired stags powered up the muddy banks of the swampy pond and carried on through the prone men and women, and never stepped on a one. The last dozen irks were slow; tired, or perhaps wounded, they took too long; Redmede found himself calling out to one slight, fanged irk woman, like a man coaxing the best out of a runner in a race.

The hastenoch were close behind her.

Redmede had an arrow on his bow, and he leaned out—well out—brought the back of his thumb to his mouth, and loosed. His shaft went into the thing's haunches, all the way to the fletching; his second shaft went in within a hand's breadth of the first, and Stern Rachel matched him on the left, and two of the monsters *sank*.

The irk woman's exhausted mount got its forefeet onto the bank, but its eyes were glazing.

Two Albin militiamen jumped forward, reached down, and plucked the armoured irk out of the water even as her brave mount seemed to slump and grow smaller.

"Now, Albinkirk!" Redmede roared. "On your feet!"

The crossbows stood. They made two packed ranks, and their captain called orders, and the steel bows leveled at the hastenoch and the foremost Rukh, just a few yards away.

"Shoot!" called Captain Stark.

The heavy arbalests didn't miss. Their bows were very powerful indeed; the bolts short, squat, and heavy, with broad steel heads like chisels.

The rangers on either flank stood again and began loosing at close range; no more ordered volleys, but every archer loosing as fast as she could nock and draw and find a target.

The Moreans had stopped throwing lead bullets. At this range, every slinger picked up stones the size of a dog's head. A sling stone that heavy, thrown by a Morean mountaineer, could knock a Rukh dead in a single cast, break a hastenoch's leg or hip, shatter the limbs of a stone troll.

For a moment, in the bestial mathematics of war, it was all a perfect balance among the speed of the hastenoch, the fears of the rangers, the resilience of the Rukh, the power of the bows, and the weight of the arrows and bolts and stones.

The Rukh pressed forward; the hastenoch filled the marsh with their cries, tentacles flapping. A Morean magister died in fire, and a levin bolt struck the Albin militiamen, killing a dozen outright.

And then a Rukh fell; a hastenoch flinched; a militiaman from the south Brogat spanned his crossbow a little faster than he might have despite the burns on his hands, got a bolt in the groove, and loosed at a range of ten inches in the very face of a monster's fangs, and his mates, emboldened, held their bank another moment, and another...

...and then the balance was shattered. The fall of the arrows was unrelenting, and there were not enough monsters. Between one beat of a terrified heart and the next, everything changed, and desperate battle gave way to heartless, ruthless massacre. The hastenoch and the Rukh were trapped in the swamp as ducks are trapped by hunters, and they cried and trumpeted and squawked and bled and died. The survivors broke back out of the water to the north, and found the irk knights waiting; they'd ridden at no great speed along the old dam, and now they were like figures of myth, rising in their saddles to throw lances of gold into the tight-packed and despairing creatures.

Syr Ydrik rode down one of the *adversariae*, the great wardens, with his engorged purple crest. Hearing the stag hooves, the shaman whirled and loosed a bolt of *aethereal* fire from the haft of his stone-bladed axe, and Ydrik's lance of gold was shivered and unmade. But the old irk leaned out from his high saddle, already taking the long, slim axe off the cantle, and with his left hand he gathered *potentia*. His axe batted aside his opponent's next working, and his next, as the stag surged under him; the wave front of his fear passed through the warden's and then his savage counter filled the shaman's defences with fire, and his axe crashed down; no random blow counting on strength, it cut a steady line, turning the stone axe by so little that the warden never knew the blow that sent half his skull to the ground ahead of the collapse of his body.

Syr Ydrik pivoted his tired stag and he reared it, and whirled his axe over his head, and the rangers cheered. He subsumed his dead foe, drawing the thing's power to himself.

War in the Wild.

And then they picked up their wounded and ran for the main army, twelve miles away.

They moved quickly and silently in the pouring rain, and the sound of the rain covered them. The rangers were all grey with fatigue; even the dark-skinned men and women looked grey in the early light.

It was their sixth day of the little war; chewing on the enemy's flanks, worrying him like dogs on a boar, trying to distract the flankers, trying to kill the high-value monsters on whom Ash's battle plans must depend. It was a very personal war, less about high strategy and more about training, toughness, dogged determination, stamina, pain tolerance, food, and sleep. About how well a man performed when he couldn't think or see; about how well a woman knew where her dirk was when her mind would no longer obey her; about remembering to keep your bowstring dry when you hadn't eaten in two days or slept in three.

For Harald Redmede, it was about picking battles and battlefields, and never making a mistake. Because one mistake and they'd all be dead; no one had the energy for a heroic last stand. The Redmedes planned the swamp ambush, and the attack at the place they all called Bogglin Gully, and brilliant, one-sided massacre of a whole clan of wardens at Cornfields, when Ash's creatures attempted to collapse the alliance rear guard. One Redmede commanded; the other was already searching for the next battlefield, the next ambush, the next massacre site.

And each day the risks changed, and grew; Gavin Muriens had warned the Redmedes that they were training Ash's army, and it was true; the enemy kept better watch, they covered their flanks, they were far more cautious in pursuit. After Cornfields, the enemy mounted wardens on some hastenoch, whether or not the tentacled trolls were under compulsion, and with this monstrous cavalry, they covered their main body; no match for the irk knights, but capable and able to call on sorcerous support from their shamans.

The day after Cornfields, Ash returned to the skies. He stayed well back from the fighting, but his eldritch powers were far beyond anything the rangers could muster, and his observational skills made ambush even more difficult. There was a rumour that Ash was wounded; that he had a gash that dripped gore, visible a mile away. It was a good rumour, and it gave folk heart; unlike the rumour that there were ten thousand dead of a new plague in Harndon and Liviapolis, where horned men and fungal spores were defeating the best efforts of human magery.

Or so it was said.

The Redmedes gave their people a day of rest; the grammarian spent it laying primed traps with the great Duchess of the West, Mogon. The alliance, despite everything, seemed to have the initiative in the woods; the grammarian used it to hide his devices, and when next Ash's horde surged forward, their movements were constantly punctuated by bursts of fire. By noon, the woods north of the Cohocton were afire for three miles, and the wind blew from the east, and Ash had to come in person and quench the fires before his whole horde disintegrated.

246

That night, Tamsin cloaked the whole alliance army again and it marched all night, twenty-two leagues, all the way to the fords, where, so long ago, Bill Redmede had found enough Outwaller corn to keep his starving rangers alive. Behind them, the sky was black from the volcanoes burning in the west at N'gara, and darker still from the forest fires burning north of the river.

The fords were a set of rapids in the Cohocton, where the Black ran in from the north, and where, just a mile downstream and one great, flame-coloured ridge east, the West Kanata came down from the high Adnacrags. Autumn had touched the woods with fire; the woods were orange and gold and pale green.

Gavin Muriens sat his riding horse at the edge of the Ford, the shallows between the two rapids, and pointed with his little axe at the far side.

Mogon shook her proud head. "If we cross, we concede the north bank to Ash," she said.

"So what?" Gavin said. "Ten leagues east of here there's a village— Redesdale-on-the-wall. After Redesdale there's a road. On a road we can *fly*."

"It's not much of a road," Tapio said. "I looked at it in the spring."

Gavin nodded. "Let's look at this," he said. "We need to beat Ash to Lissen Carak. And hold there until we're relieved; at least until the queen can come for us from Albinkirk." He raised his eyebrows. "The rangers are exhausted; Syr Ydrik looks as if he lost a fight with an octopus, and Bill Redmede looks like old pea soup. We cannot expect them to fight every day. And I need to get a message through to the queen."

Ser Gregario tugged his beard. "My people are better, though," he said. "Four days of hot food and sleep."

"That's my point," Gavin said. "If we pass south of the river, one of two things happen. Either Ash passes us by, in which case it's a straight race to Lissen Carak, and we have all the advantages; think of the fortified bridge on the river, and the magicked gate. Right? Or he *follows* us south of the Cohocton." Gavin waited a moment to let that sink in. "Then we've won. In fact, we've won clean, and even if he kills every one of us, he'll lose ten days doing it and have to march *all the way back here* to cross."

Tapio gave Muriens half a smile. "You alwaysss planned thisss, man?" he asked.

Gavin allowed himself one of his brother's smug looks of triumph. "Yes," he said.

Tapio nodded slowly and looked at Tamsin. "It isss brilliant," he said. "Why has Asssh not consssidered this?"

Gavin looked off to the east. "Maybe he has. Geography is a harsh reality. He needed to defeat us at Cornfields; maybe that's why the wardens took such a foolish risk." He shrugged. "Mayhap Tamsin and Gabriel are taking up all his time." He turned his horse. "Listen, I don't know why he's missed it; but unless he has some terrible trick under his black wings, we can buy our people four days free of death, unless he comes against us directly."

The grammarian nodded. "I can make that cost him," he said. "And I can reach the queen, or perhaps Harmodius, if Ash leaves us space to breathe."

Tamsin showed her fangs.

"Predators like their prey to be much smaller than they are," she said. "Predators do not like to be hurt. He is like a giant cat. He will want us divided, fearful, and weak, before he pounces."

Gavin pointed across the fords. "Whereas if we retreat across Cohocton, we will be well rested and strong," he said.

Tapio allowed himself a smile. "You give me a little hope," he said.

Arles—The Red Knight

Ariosto landed neatly inside the castle courtyard. A dozen very thin men were re-laying flagstone in the yard and as many more were repointing the damaged stonework from the siege, and there was scaffolding running all the way up the great tower that dominated the ancient fortress and the hill on which it stood and the plain of Arles below it.

Gabriel had kept his eyes on the scaffolding during Ariosto's descent. He no longer spent every takeoff and landing in a state of mortal terror, but the spiraling, leaf-fluttering drop into the courtyard had been *especially* insane.

Show off, Gabriel thought.

There she is! Ariosto sent. And sure enough, Blanche emerged from the doorway of the tower in a dark blue gown with ermine at the tips of the sleeves and the collar. She looked at him, and he had eyes for no one else; not Kaitlin coming behind her, not Michael.

He dismounted as gracefully as he could manage, and bowed, and she curtsied, her head held perfectly, a very model of good manners. He made himself walk slowly across the newly laid flags and across a trench; he looked away from her to smile at two workmen who were staring in awe at Ariosto, and then he jumped the trench and he was standing with her.

"My lord," she said with another curtsy.

"My lady," he managed. "My God, how I missed you."

She smiled. "I summoned the council as soon as Ariosto was sighted."

"What if I tell you," he said softly, "that I came only to see *you*?"

Her smile told him a great deal; it flirted with him, it hid from him, and it hung evocatively from the left corner of her mouth. "The saddest thing," she said, "is that even if you mean that, the council will prove more important."

"I doubt it," he said, with some fire.

Far above the plain and the newly flagged yard, the Emperor of Man sat in his sweat-damp flying clothes and drank a cup of Etruscan red wine.

"The gonnes worked," he said to Ser Michael, who had his legs stretched out before him, and a cup of wine, and was rubbing Kaitlin's feet. Kaitlin sat in an ancient oak settee, its wood almost black with age, carved with saints who had once been painted, and her feet were in his lap.

Michael nodded. "I knew they'd work," he said with satisfaction. "I wish I'd been there."

Gabriel scratched his beard. They all made him feel dirty; their clothes were clean, their bodies were clean, and there was food. He hadn't eaten his fill in eight days.

Blanche entered with the Queen of Arles and her ladies, and Gabriel rose, feeling less than elegant, and returned their bows and compliments.

"Comnena is taking our starvlings back to Etrusca," Michael said. "Ser Milus has brought the main army back over the pass. He's a day's march away. Sauce is..."

Behind Blanche's shoulder was a woman Gabriel didn't know, young, blond, and pretty. And behind her...

Gabriel lunged forward. "Sukey!" he said, and rose and gave his company head woman a hug.

Sukey was tall, more handsome than beautiful—tall and strong with jet-black hair that had a shockingly white stripe in it from an old injury. The white patch and the scar by her mouth combined to give her a piratical look.

But in years of marching with her, Gabriel had never seen her look so well rested. Nor so well dressed.

"Careful of my gown," Sukey said with a grin. "It's only a loan."

Blanche kissed her on the cheek. "You loaned me your best once," she said.

Sukey kissed her back with gusto. "It was a good investment, as I hope you'll allow. One look at you an' I knew the cap'n would keep you."

Clarissa de Sartres looked out the window. Her marshal came in, and behind him was a man in a Yahadut scholar's cap and a long gown of spotless black velvet. With him was a very handsome man with a heavy black beard and long Ifriquy'an robes. With him were two *mamluks*.

Blanche indicated the scholar with a graceful wave of her arm. She wore scent, and she had been *practicing* that gesture. "Magisters Qatb al-Din al-Shirazi," she said, "and Yusuf Bin Maymum."

He rose and bowed to them both. The Ifriquy'an was not much older than he was—perhaps thirty—and very young to be titled *magister*. Of course, Morgon Mortirmir was only eighteen...

Michael had carefully rid himself of his wife's feet and was now leaning against the carved stone hood over the great fire hearth. On it, Saint Michael was killing a dragon.

Sukey took a seat at the long table. "I brought them," she said. "From Venike."

"She also brought in Convoy Four," Blanche added.

Gabriel was tempted to roll his eyes. *I know. I'm the captain.*

He looked around—Michael, Clarissa, Blanche, Kaitlin, Sukey, Pierre La Porte, the two scholars, a handful of household servants, the mamluks, and Michael's squire, Lord Robin. He thought, *I trained most of you. Why do you suddenly assume I don't know what's going on?*

Yet at the same time, he acknowledged that they were trying very hard to show him that they knew their jobs; Sukey was proud of having had her first command; Blanche was working to be an empress and not a washerwoman, Clarissa was working at being a queen, and he needed them all. Everyone needed everyone.

"Ser Alison has changed her plans somewhat," Lord Robin said deferentially, and he handed Gabriel a flimsy with a trace of blood on it.

"Bird injured?" Gabriel asked. At some very real level, the fate of the world rode on the wingtips of the imperial messenger service.

"C.2 was attacked by something. He survived to make it here, and he's being healed." Robin glanced at Blanche.

Blanche nodded at the two robed men. "Our guests are astrologers," she said. She was clearly already used to being the head of the meeting. Gabriel chewed on that a moment.

"I have been trying to catch you for weeks," the younger man said.

The Yahadut scratched under his cap. "I, also," he admitted.

Gabriel couldn't help himself; the impulse was too strong. "I was expecting *three* wise men," he said. "But not until after the baby is born."

Kaitlin heaved with laughter, her beautiful complexion temporarily splotched. Most of the others either looked away, or looked at him. Blanche *stared* at him.

"Eh?" the Yahadut asked. He glanced at Kaitlin. "This was meant to be humourous?"

"In a blasphemous kind of way," Gabriel said.

"Don't let him interrupt you," Blanche said. "It's just his way."

Gabriel sat back.

The two scholars looked at each other, and the Yahadut put his hand on his heart and bowed, as if granting his space to the younger.

The younger man stepped forward to the head of the table, and waved his hand. As soon as he gathered power, Gabriel's adamantine shield of gold exploded from the *aethereal*.

Gabriel was already out of his chair, his hand on his sword.

The man froze. "I mean no harm!" he cried in heavily accented Archaic.

Gabriel saw that both Blanche and Clarissa had swords in their hands.

Michael had a small shield of his own; he had clearly been learning. "Magister al-Shirazi," he said, his voice attenuated by the shield. "It is not acceptable to summon power in the presence of the emperor without permission."

The magister released his crafted *ops*. "My apologies, my lord," he said.

Gabriel rose and bowed. "I think we're all a little on edge," he admitted. He put back his shields, pried his hand off the sweat-stained grip of his war sword, and forced himself to smile. "It has been a difficult time," he said with a shrug, and folded himself back into his chair.

Considerably paler, the magister was nonetheless unshaken. "My lord," he began again. "I would like to perform a few small demonstrations…"

"Be my guest," Gabriel said. He smiled in what he hoped was a companionable way while trying to quell his shaking hands.

"Bin Maymum and I are astrologers," he said. "We watch the stars. And both of us have read our Dame Julia." He cast his cantrip, and a screen materialized, a glowing, rich black like his robe, and on it hung the stars, like crystals strewn on cloth. "My lord, when I heard that you were in the Antica Terra, I wanted to meet you; but in Venike I understood that you had a schedule; a timetable." The man touched his nose frequently, an odd tic, and used an eating knife to point at his image of the heavens.

"You are not from Ifriqu'a," Gabriel said, leaning forward.

"No, my lord. I am a gentleman of Gilan; perhaps the farthest eastern kingdom held by humans. We are the border with the Wild, just as we hear you are in Ilba."

"Alba," Gabriel said automatically, and then he thought of Blanche. *How we love to correct each other, we humans*, he thought.

"My king, Rostan Dabbaj, is a great knight and a great warrior." The easterner's hair and his pale good looks were explained; he didn't look like an Ifriqu'an.

The Yahadut scholar frowned. "Surely not the easternmost," he said. "Surely the easternmost is Qu'in."

Al-Shirazi frowned at being interrupted. "It is centuries since we have heard anything from Qu'in," he said.

"Perhaps my people have better communications than yours," Bin Maymum said.

"I am sorry to say I have never even heard of Gilan," Gabriel said, wishing they would get on with it. He cast a withering look at his wife,

252

who returned an arched eyebrow. "But I do have a timetable," he said with a hand gesture that any company officer would have known for "hurry this up."

"Yes," al-Shirazi said. "I heard in Venike, and again from Dama Sukeh, that you think the gates open in...well, now...ten days."

Gabriel nodded. Suddenly he could not breathe.

"My lord," the Yahadut said. "I have come from Iberia, and my people, as a rule, do not meddle in the affairs of princes. And Dame Julia was a woman of extraordinary genius, the very queen of all our philosophy. But you should have asked someone to repeat her observations with modern instruments. Our ability to see into the *Aeternium*, the *aethereal* of the magisters, is incomparably better than it was two hundred years ago. For example..."

Gabriel was on his feet. "Just tell me," he said.

The two magisters looked at each other. "We're not sure," al-Shirazi said. "But it's more like a range of probabilities than a finite reality, which, in a way, is an allegory of the whole of—"

Gabriel slapped his open hand on the table. "Gentlemen," he said firmly.

The Yahadut shrugged like a chef who will not be hurried. "There are aspects of this question not easily adaptable to a military schedule," he said. "What is *being*? How do I make a timetable from an astronomical *metaphor*?"

Gabriel was too tightly wound. He went into his *palace and counted to fifty. He looked at the magnificent tiled wall fountain he'd lifted, metaphorically, from Al Rashidi's dying mind, and he caressed it with his unembodied hand. He needed to unpack it; it hung in blackness in a space behind Harmodius's mirror, and despite the brilliant colours of the tiles, it was as if it was black and white in a universe of colour, because he had not yet accepted it.*

Back in the real, Gabriel managed a sigh. "Gentlemen, I have a busy day. If my schedule is wrong, correct me. But get on with it."

Bin Maymum shrugged again. "We do not wish to be wrong," he said. He shuffled his feet. "Honestly, I hoped that by the time I found you, one of your own magisters would have seen it..."

"Unless we're wrong," al-Shirazi said. "But if we are wrong, we have made the same errors together, thousands of leagues apart."

"Gentlemen!" spat Blanche. She had one of Gabriel's hands in hers.

"Eight days," the Yahadut said.

"The twenty-sixth of September," the Gilan astrologer said. "At five seventeen in the morning, local time, in Arles, according to your cathedral clock, which is a little slow." He looked at the Yahadut. "Except..."

"Except that there is an alternate solution," Bin Maymum said. He shrugged again. "Perhaps the gates do not open for three years. Or one hundred and nineteen."

Gabriel felt as if he'd taken a heavy blow to the head. His knees were weak, and there was a ringing in his ears.

"Sweet saviour," he said. "Jesu Christe."

Blanche looked at him.

He was biting his lip.

"What if the gates don't open?" Michael said.

"Gavin is left to fight Ash alone," Gabriel said.

Chapter Seven

The Adnacrags—Aneas Muriens

Aneas was fussing with the stump of his ear. He was vain; and it hurt more than any wound he'd ever taken, including the three broken ribs that ached like the cold grasp of death every time he took a deep breath or laughed or coughed, and the hole in his head that he couldn't describe even to himself. He was standing in a tiny cabin in the stern that had been cleared for him; perhaps the first mate's cabin. It was dark, lit by a scuttle to the brilliant sun outside, and he had borrowed a small mirror of Venikan silver from the captain, who seemed to be a very wealthy man.

There was a knock at the flimsy partition, and Aneas turned, ducking his head, and tapped his wounded ear hole against the overhead deck beam, and cursed.

The knock came again, more insistent.

Aneas opened the door. Gas-a-ho nodded. "May I come in?" he asked and pushed past.

Aneas frowned, at least in part because he was naked. But he wasn't thinking well.

Gas-a-ho pushed him down on the bed and tilted his head to the light of the scuttle. He cast; there was a fringe of green light at the edge of Aneas's consciousness.

"The wound will not heal faster if you mess with it," the shaman said. "I need you to let me in."

"In?" Aneas asked.

Let me in, the Outwaller shaman said as his fingers touched the wound again.

Aneas's eyes snapped open. He *retreated into his memory forest, and stood a moment under a tall maple he had known all his life, on which hung a myriad of artifacts. In the* aethereal, *he was not naked; he wore deerskin hose and quillwork garters and a long shirt of embroidered linen. Then he extended a hand; the other hand held a small flint knife.*

Gas-a-ho was smaller in the aethereal, and had the head of an owl, which was deeply disconcerting to Aneas.

He looked around, and made a soft sound of approval.

Aneas nodded. "I do not allow many in here," he admitted. He let the flint knife dissipate. "Something is wrong here."

Gas-a-ho opened his beak and made a raucous noise. "Brother," he said. "You took more than a bump on the head. You were dead. Among my people, you would take a new name and perhaps a new wife. You have been to a far country, and we need to know that the man who returned is the same."

Aneas was looking at his tree. It was the same tree, and yet it was not; there were scars in the bark, and a shadow hung in the tops. But worst of all, there were things that should have been hanging on the tree that were gone, and other things were hanging in their stead.

"How can I be a different person?" Aneas asked.

"How can you be the same?" Gas-a-ho asked. "You were dead. I lost you, brother. You weren't alive anymore. Irene fetched back a corpse."

"Irene," Aneas said softly.

"Listen to me," Gas-a-ho said. He was looking carefully at Aneas's tree, at the field of raspberry bramble beyond, at signs of use and signs of casting and remnants of memory, sniffing like a hunting dog. "Do you feel anything ... strange ... from Looks-at-Clouds?"

Aneas thought, and wisps of cloud trailed across the sun of his mind.

He was afraid.

Gas-a-ho shook his head. "I am not the gods, to play with your mind. But something here is very wrong." He reached a human hand into the brambles and pulled out an old deerskin quiver. The thorns caught on it, but the deerskin was tough.

"That was my father's!" Aneas said, and took the quiver. He was sure it had been hanging on the tree, and he found a broken branch close to the ground.

Gas-a-ho was poking in the brambles. "Something is very wrong with Looks-at-Clouds," he said. "Or at least, Irene and I think so." He found an arrow, and then another, and then a third, and Aneas, obediently, slid them into his father's quiver.

Gas-a-ho was deep in the brambles by then.

"That should all be pine needles and rocks," Aneas said. "There are no..."

"There's a trail," Gas-a-ho said.

Aneas followed the shaman. He was aware, at some remove, that what they were doing was very dangerous.

The trail was far longer than it should have been, winding in and out of the brambles and crossing a small rivulet that seemed as brown as old blood. Aneas knew that his whole memory forest was not this big, and he knew, too, that all around them was very dark. He wanted to find his clear spring and his casting stone, and they were hidden.

"I am afraid," Aneas said. "I cannot cast."

The shaman turned. "Yes," he said. "That is natural. But this is the thing for which I trained: to take people on spirit journeys. You were dead. Things have changed in here. You need to find whatever the trail wants you to find."

They walked on, and the darkness pressed in, so that Aneas feared to raise his eyes above the muddy brown trail.

The brambles kept catching on his hands, until both of them were bleeding. The blood fell on the trail. The trail was soaked in blood.

"Spirit journeys are mostly safe for the young and inexperienced," Gas-a-ho said. "The older you are and the more you have seen, the more dangerous these places are."

The shaman paused. "I think this is as far as I go," he said. He smiled, and for a moment, the smile and the man's confidence warmed Aneas.

"Whatever awaits will be horrible," the shaman said. "This isn't some nice name quest where you find a turtle or a hawk. But we need you back; and whatever it is, you can deal with it. That I promise. Remember it's only you. Only you."

The shaman stepped back. The trail had become squelchy underfoot, and the shaman's bare feet were red in the unreal light. They were in a fetid swamp, not a marsh now; and the swamp was a swamp of blood.

Aneas stepped past him, and walked on.

It wasn't far.

He emerged into the clearing, and it was and was not his casting sanctum. The rock was the same; the tree, which seemed miles behind them, was there, although somehow they had come upon the pool from another direction. The tree was full of lichen, and now seemed dead.

The pool couldn't be seen, because it was full of corpses.

In the aethereal, he knew them all. They lay in the real attitudes of the dead; crushed together like baitfish, pale and unlovely. There was Ghause Muriens, his mother; and there was Wart; and there, Ta-se-ho; and there was Ricar Fitzalan and there, de la Motte and there, Anthony the stable boy, his first love; the first death he'd ever caused. And there was Gabriel's tutor, Prudentia; there was a pair of men he'd killed to protect a secret; there was a woman who had loved him, and whom his mother had turned to ash.

Perhaps seeing her made him understand that this was a dream—a construct in his own head—just as Gas-a-ho said.

He took some deep breaths.

Gas-a-ho appeared behind him. "What do you think you should do?" he asked calmly.

Aneas made himself look at the pile of corpses. "Clear the spring, obviously."

Gas-a-ho nodded. "We'll smoke together when you are done," he said. "Irene is with us now, in the real. We cannot help you, but we are here."

"The mind is not so very complicated, is it?" Aneas said bitterly.

Gas-a-ho shrugged. "Clean the spring," he said.

Aneas went along the last of the swampy meadow, feet squelching in the blood. It seemed unfair that there was so much blood, or that it was so fresh, but the symbolism was obvious.

He reached down. Wart, the old Jack, was atop the pile. He got his hands under the man's shoulders. Wart's dead weight was horribly real; his head lolled bonelessly, his teeth clacked as his jaw snapped closed.

Get it done, Aneas thought.

He carried Wart all the way to the darkness. The darkness proved to be a cool dark of overhanging spruce trees; not nearly so terrifying, close up. Aneas laid Wart gently on the pine needles and turned and trudged all the

258

way back to the pile of corpses. The second was Ta-se-ho; the old hunter weighed nothing, although the wound that killed him was a terrible ragged tear and a loop of his intestines came out and caught on the brambles. Aneas put the old man down and pushed the slippery stuff back into the wound, and because this was his mind, he put out his hand and closed the wound. Then he lifted the old hunter and carried him to the woods.

A little golden light fell on a patch of green grass, and there was no sign of Wart. His corpse was gone.

"Two can play at this symbolism game," Aneas said bravely, although tears were rolling down his face, and a strange hope burned in his throat. He laid the Outwaller in the sun, and turned away, afraid even to watch.

His mother was the hardest. He didn't even think that he felt he had killed her; hadn't even registered such a guilt, but while he carried her slight, rotting form, stiff with rigor mortis and with the skin moving disgustingly over the hardened muscles, he thought of Orley; of his hatred for the man. Aneas was too intelligent to fail to understand himself.

He placed Ghause in the widened circle of sunlight, on what had become a mound. When he laid her down, he knelt by her awhile, and then he went back and got Fitzalan.

There was something particularly terrible about handling in death a body you had lusted for in life. Ands something disconcerting and paradoxical about the corpse; it was more decomposed than his mother's. And the head was attached. Some of Richard's rotting skin stuck to his; fluids leached out of his friend. The smell was so bad he choked.

He got Richard to the new meadow. He took time to lay the body out, tried to close his friend's eyes, but that proved a bad idea. His gorge rose.

He turned with a muttered prayer and went back for Anthony.

He looked at Anthony for a while, too, wondering whether he'd loved the boy or simply wanted to strike a blow at his father. Who had certainly struck back. In the extended metaphor of his mind, Anthony looked exactly as he had looked when his father had ordered the boy killed. He was not decomposed at all.

"I knew," Aneas said aloud. "I knew what he'd do."

He went back and got Prudentia, and the others. All in all, there were an uncountable number of trips; some he held only as shadowy forms, others had a firm reality of decay and ordure; this, too, he understood.

The strangest was the slim figure that was clearly his own. Without a *wound, and no sign of rot. He paused for a long time, trying to think if there was another message here, or some new action required, but in the end, he carried his own corpse to the new green mound in the cool green woods.*

And then he was done, his task complete, and he stood in sunlight. The pool was clear; potentia bubbled from the ground under his stone, and the stone was clean except for one deep mark, as if of a footprint.

Gas-a-ho came and stood with him. The tree towered over the pool again; the brambles were gone as if they'd never been. The tree was in bud.

"Nice," the shaman said. "Some people never manage it."

"Are they real?" Aneas asked. "The dead people?"

Gas-a-ho looked at him, and his eyes sparkled. "That's up to you, isn't it?" he asked. "Only you decide if other people are real."

He took a medicine bag from around his neck and hung it on the tree.

Aneas sat by the spring. He dipped his hands in the spring, which was ops and not water, and washed his hands and arms of all the blood and filth. Fully visible across the meadow was a mound; it stood as tall as a man, covered in beautiful green grass, brilliant in the sun.

Gas-a-ho sat cross-legged by him. "It is good that you have placed them where you can see them," he said. "You are a strong person. Can you work the ops again?"

Aneas reached into the pool and took potentia in his hand, and formed it.

"Good," Gas-a-ho said. "But you are changed. You know that?"

"Yes," Aneas said. "I was dead. Who am I now?"

"Who is anyone, ever?" Gas-a-ho said, but it was said with a sort of self-mocking humour.

And then Aneas was sitting in the real. Gas-a-ho had his hand; Irene had an arm around his shoulders. Nita Qwan handed him a lit pipe and he inhaled deeply of the smoke and shuddered.

He handed the pipe to Irene, and she drew deeply at it and passed it to Gas-a-ho.

Aneas took a deep breath.

Irene looked into his eyes, and he looked into hers.

"You saved me," he said.

"We don't have time for your thanks just now," Irene said. "We think Looks-at-Clouds is *possessed*," she said very softly.

Firensi—Tippit

Tippit's horse was probably the best he'd ever had in a lifetime of making war. His horse was so good he enjoyed riding it; he rose in the darkness, already thinking of the joy of a canter. He didn't usually name horses; they tended to die faster than he could be bothered to get to know them, but the horse he'd had from the Venikans was a big gelding from Ifriquy'a, with a small, handsome head and a beautiful temperament, and the gelding loved to run.

Which was good, because in the murky dawn he was galloping along a farm road with a dozen other company archers at his back.

The farm road was in Central Etrusca, almost fifty leagues south of the fields of San Batiste. He and his party had ridden all night; they had Short Tooth from the green banda guiding them.

They saw the mill silhouetted against the dawn before they heard the river or the clack of the waterwheel. Dogs were barking at every farm; the dozen of them had made plenty of noise galloping over the plains of Firensi.

Short Tooth reined in. "That's her, Tip."

Tippit chewed on an end of his mustache while he looked at the big mill in the growing light. "No rest for the wicked," he said, loosening the sword on his hip. "Where's Long Paw?"

Short Tooth shook his head. "Not a fuckin' clue, Tip. He were 'ere yestere'en."

Tippit looked around. He had all veterans; of his cronies, only Smoke was missing, back with the main column. In the distance the mill made an odd sound; *tick-bang. Tick-bang.*

"Ready?" he asked.

"Like old times," Simkin said.

Several of them smiled.

They rode to the very door of the mill unopposed, and dismounted. There was a big stone bridge in easy bowshot, and beyond, her towers gilded by the rising sun, was the magnificent city of Firensi—one of the richest cities in the whole of the world. A huge church was being built; even in the pale light, Tippit could see the unfinished dome.

"No Head should see that," he said.

"Ee will, in two hours, if we do our bit," snapped Simkin.

Flarch was busy looking for something to batter the door. Simkin slipped the latch with his dagger and pushed it open cautiously. A man shouted, a woman called, and the heavy shutter opened over their heads.

"Fuck it," Simkin said, and rolled through the door.

Tippit was right behind him. There was a man in a nightshirt roaring in terrified Etruscan. Tippit used the pommel of his sword to sweep the man off his feet; when the man moved, Tippit kicked him, and Scrant hit him again and the man fell facedown on the brick floor.

The woman was screaming now. Tippit raced up the open wooden stairs. The mill was running; he could hear the sound of the grindstone, and something else. His feet pounded on the steps, and he shouted, "Check the mill floor!"

Simkin kicked another door, and hurt his foot; the doors were heavy oak. Scrant put his left hand on the latch and pulled.

Tippit reached the first floor. There was a short hall; the woman was screaming in the first room, and the door was locked. Tippit put his shoulder against it, and broke the wooden latch.

A middle-aged woman with long hair unbound was screaming out her window. Tippit's Etruscan was virtually nonexistent but *banditti* came through.

He grabbed her shoulders and pulled her back into the room, cutting off her screams for a moment. "Shut up!" he roared in her face.

She collapsed onto a stool, writhed, and came at him with the stool.

He blocked it with his left hand, which hurt, and then threw her to the floor with his right arm across her throat. It was not a gentle throw and she squawked.

He put the point of his sword at her throat to cross the language divide.

She lay still.

Scrant went through the door into the main hall of the mill.

There were quite a few men. And they were big. They weren't particularly well armed, but they looked like smiths—heavy arms, brawny chests. Several held bars of iron, or farm implements.

One had a piece of metal glowing white hot.

Scrant drew his heavy dirk off his hip left handed and threw it. It was a clumsy throw and it hit White Hot flat across his face, but he dropped the glowing metal and then screamed as it struck his foot,

262

and then Simkin and Flarch were there, swords drawn, and the fight went out of the Etruscans. A small boy stood, round eyed.

"I thought mills ground wheat for flour," Flarch said.

"I thought there'd be some'at to eat?" Scrant muttered.

There was a mill wheel; it was grinding away, and a pure white flour was pouring from a wooden funnel into a sack. But the main power of the great wheel went to a trip-hammer; and even though the smiths were all gathered in a corner of the room, the hammer went on tripping; tick *slam*, tick *slam*.

"I'll go fuckin' deaf," shouted Simkin. "Tie 'em up."

Tippit appeared.

"You was supposed to yell 'all secure' when you had the rest o' the building," he said.

Flarch shrugged. "All secure?" he said with his usual smile, and farted.

"Oh Jesus," Simkin said, moving away. "Save it for the fewkin' enemy. Anything worth stealing?"

"I ha'e all they purses," Scrant said.

Tippit fetched the rest of his men from the road outside. He put four on the roof keeping watch, and the rest of them tore the mill apart, opening the feather mattresses, prying up flags, tossing the kitchenware on the flags.

The mill was rich, and they found a small fortune in gold and silver; the woman had jewels; the husband had a superb dagger and a matching scabbard and purse that almost led to blows.

Tippit caught Scrant heading upstairs and he grabbed the smaller man by the collar and pulled him back. "No rape. Sauce'll have yer guts for garters."

"Just gonna ha'e a look at her," Scrant snapped.

"No," Tippit said.

"Who died an' made you God?" Scrant muttered.

"The cap'n," Tippit said.

"TIPPIT!" came the call from the roof.

Tippit, already on the stairs, ran to the woman's window. She was sitting on a chair; he'd tied her hands but he hadn't gagged her. He put his head out and saw the armed men coming across toward the bridge.

"Here we go!" he yelled down the stairs. "Time to earn the loot!" He pushed Scrant ahead of him up the stairs to the roof.

Then he followed. The mill was the size of a small castle; the roof was peaked, but had a walkway all the way around, and a low wall, so that it was easily defensible; not crenellated or pierced, but still a tough nut.

The Firensi militia was still out of range. Tippit looked west along the riverbank, and there were farmsteads and towers burning as far as the eye could see; ten leagues or more, the flames like huge campfires, the columns of smoke rising straight in the still air of dawn.

His people began to emerge onto the roof, pulling their bows out of their bags and dumping livery arrows onto the roof tiles.

The Firensi knight commanding the militiamen had stopped riding and was looking back at the columns of smoke all the way along the riverbank.

Tippit grinned. He nocked an arrow.

They made two attempts on the bridge. The first was a straightforward attempt to force a passage; the archery of a dozen master archers filled the bridge with corpses, and the knight, despite his impressive armour, took an arrow to the inside of his elbow and had to be carried back.

But the Firensi militia were tough bastards, and they came on again, this time with their hardier souls crossing under the arch of the bridge and coming up the bank. But they had forgotten the millrace and they were stuck on a stony island, blocked by the pool and the wheel, and after two men died, the rest slipped back under the arch.

Then a dozen knights and men-at-arms came with a big banner; orders were shouted, and the whole body of militia and knights marched away west on the south bank. Tippit made sure that the riverbanks under the stone arches were clear and then he sent Scrant on horseback. The thin man had been gone only a handful of minutes when the bells of the great city rang in alarm.

And then Sauce was there. She rode right up to the mill doors with only a handful of knights at her back, flung her reins to her squire, and ran, in full harness, all the way from the door to the top floor of the tower. The Duchess of Venike was right behind her.

"You can't take Firensi with two thousand light horse," Giselle panted.

Sauce leaned over the low wall. "How d'ya do, Tippit?" she asked.

"Fair well, my lady," he said. "Apple?" he asked, and tossed her one.

She took a bite.

"Bridge is ours," Tippit said. "No one dead. No one hurt. Well, some o' they. None o' we."

She took another bite. "Can't storm it," she said to Giselle. "But I can scare the fuck out of them, and make 'em pay." Her grin was almost ear to ear. "Lovely job, Tip. Woman downstairs?"

"No one touched her," Tippit said.

Sauce's look was a study; a grim smile. "Good. I'd hate to end the day with a hanging."

"Yes, ma'am." Tippit nodded.

"Good. Mount up and join your lances." She gave orders and a dozen of the company's pages took over the mill. The archers were too important to be left in garrison, even to secure her retreat.

The archers came out of the mill. Tippit took the bag of coin and put it on his pack mule.

Simkin slapped his back. "I cut the boy loose and gave him a knife," he said.

Tippit nodded and vaulted onto his horse. "You're a good man," Tippit said.

Simkin shrugged. "When do we split the loot?"

Tippit spat. "When we're in camp. And rested."

"So, never," muttered Flarch.

Firensi—Ser Alison

Most of Sauce's two thousand horse poured over the bridge, and the city of Firensi panicked. Half of the town's army was caught outside the walls, another thousand guildsmen were dead in the fields of San Batiste, and here was the dreaded enemy at the very gates.

The *very* gates. Sauce led her column across the river and through the richest suburbs she'd ever seen. The enormous city walls rose high above the burgh. She waved the column on with the knurled oak baton that some of her knights had made for her and rode on, and in a quarter of an hour, she was at the barriers of the great gate of San Giovanni. It was closed; one knight waited at the barriers; even the postern was shut and locked.

He bowed.

Conte Simone began to dismount, but Sauce put a steel-clad hand over his reins.

"Mine," she said.

Sauce dismounted and vaulted over the barriers; in normal times, taking the barriers of a town was a great chivalric feat. Her troopers cheered.

Her sabatons clinking, she walked to the great gates. She looked up at the murder holes, wondering if her great gesture would be ruined by boiling oil.

The knight of Firensi bowed. "Is there a weapon you would prefer, sir?" he asked.

Sauce returned his bow. "I am Ser Alison Audley, captain of the grande alliance," she said. "I can send for any weapon you name, or we can fight with swords, right now."

The knight raised his visor. He was tall, slim, handsome, with olive skin and a long, silky mustache. "Donna," he said, "if I defeat you, men will say I beat a woman; if you defeat me, men will say I was a man of no worth."

Sauce shrugged. "Your problem, Ser. I'm in a bit of a hurry. I intend to sack your town."

He bowed again. "You may have it, as far as I am concerned. I am the only one who would come out and face your barbarian hordes. The rest are apparently worthless." He shrugged. "Of course I will fight."

"Good," she said, and drew her sword.

She moved forward, her sword moving steadily back and forth between a high guard and a low as she stepped. The Etruscan knight circled, but she was having none of that. She snapped a blow from her high guard and he covered; his cover told her a great deal.

She fell back a step, back in her high guard, sword held with both hands on the hilt, back over her right shoulder, left leg forward.

Her adversary stepped forward, his blade low.

Sauce changed her grip. It was a sudden, practiced move; her left hand shot forward and took the blade at the middle, and she passed forward, into the tempo of his advance. She raised her own hilt, crossing his blade strongly, and he made the error, as a big, tall man, of trying to outmuscle her at the cross. Her mid-sword grip had all the advantages the art of swordsmanship and the science of leverage could give; she pushed his sword aside and stepped deep with her right foot, inserting it behind his left, which had all his weight on it. Her pommel slammed into his visor, doing no damage but buying her a fraction of his balance, and then the pommel was past his helmet, the whole of her hilt across his armoured throat, and her foot behind his, and in one swing of her hips, she threw him to the ground.

Her people roared.

She put her sword point at his throat. "Listen," she said, popping her visor. "If men give you any shit, send them to me and I'll kill a few."

"Ah, ma donna!" he said. "Beautifully struck."

She liked him, so she let him live. She stepped back so her squires could take him, and then Dick Waster, Ser Milus's squire, handed her the white baton of command and took her helmet.

She took her baton and slammed it into the gates. "Open!" she cried. "Come out and treat with me, or by God, I'll blow these gates to flinders and sack your town." She pointed at Tancreda, who had cloaked herself in smoke and fire.

It seemed insane; the high walls and the sheer size of the city dwarfed her and her horse people, but before the echoes had died away, the postern opened, and a white-faced priest in rich vestments emerged, and a man with a heavy gold chain.

Giselle vaulted the barrier behind her. "I don't believe it," she said, and embraced Sauce. "Watch they don't assassinate you." As if reading her thoughts, a dozen of Sauce's knights came over the barriers; George Brewes first among them, his poleaxe in his hand.

"We have come to—" the priest began.

"Don't make me storm your town," Sauce snapped. She pointed at Tancreda. "One word from me and your walls start falling. I'll tell *you* what the terms are."

The Adnacrags—Aneas Muriens

Looks-at-Clouds was standing on the bow, watching the horizon. The ship was well handled; the sailors knew their business, and despite the density of the rocky, tree-covered islets on either hand, the ship was under sail, moving briskly upstream against the gentle current. Deadlock, the Alban ranger, sat out on the crosstree of the stubby bowsprit, watching the water.

One of the ship's boys came and tugged at hir hand. "Captain wants you," he said in his accented Archaic.

Looks-at-Clouds frowned, annoyed at being interrupted, but then hir face changed and s/he settled on an appearance of amicability, and s/he followed the urchin across the deck, hir mind powerfully elsewhere. S/he opened the door to the captain's gallery and saw Irene sitting alone at the captain's long table, and s/he smiled. S/he had a *tendre* for Irene. And...

S/he was very fast, but the blow caught hir by surprise. S/he started to turn hir head and saw Nita Qwan just as his open hand slammed into hir cheek, turning hir head...

Something horrible happened.

In the real, Aneas took hir, off balance, and threw hir over his outthrust leg and down to the hardwood deck. He pressed a dagger to hir throat.

S/he screamed.

Witchbane, witchbane witchbanewitchbanewitchbanewitchbanewitchbanewitchbane!

"Stay with us," Gas-a-ho said from behind a fractal web of shield shards that spun.

Looks-at-Clouds retched, and bile came from hir mouth.

Aneas shook his head.

Irene leaned forward. "You hurt hir!" she cried. "S/he's bleeding!"

Gas-a-ho's voice was steady. "S/he has a witchbane thorn in hir cheek," he said. "Shaman, we are sorry for this."

Looks-at-Clouds felt *unclean. Violated.*

"*Sorry?*" s/he hissed. "You are *sorry?*"

Nita Qwan kept his hand on hir cheek, and his dagger, too, was at hir throat. "Who are you?" he asked.

The changeling could not turn hir head. "Ahhhgh," s/he spat.

"Who are you?" Aneas asked. His voice was hard.

"I am...ssss...the changeling...Looks...at...Clouds...you bastards..." s/he spat.

Gas-a-ho shook his head. "No," he said. "Tell us who you are, or we kill this body. Looks-at-Clouds, we are sorry. But too much is at stake."

S/he felt the daggers. S/he spoke the language of death.

They told hir that Nita Qwan at least meant hir death. Aneas was less sure.

"Witchbane will not hold me!" s/he muttered.

"All the more reason to end you," Nita Qwan said.

"Surrender and let me in," Aneas said. "Or—"

"You attacked me with witchbane!" the changeling said. "You expect me to trust you?"

"Only if you want to live," Nita Qwan said.

The being surrendered. It was sudden, and there was Aneas, *standing in a vast emptiness. There was no memory palace, no field of flowers, no...*

"Damn you, Muriens," said Master Smythe. "I am only borrowing him. Her."

"Sweet Holy Trinity," Aneas Muriens muttered.

"Listen to me. I cannot allow Ash to know I am alive. I lack the power to... do anything. I have Looks-at-Clouds safe. And if we can take the sorcerer's island, the Lake-on-the-Mountain, I will have the power to restore myself. I beg you, Aneas. I will not—"

"You could have just told us," Aneas said.

Gas-a-ho appeared through his link with Aneas, emerging, owl-headed, from Aneas's forest pool. Then he reached back, and Irene rose from the pool, wearing the rich, gold-encrusted robe of the Empress of Man, and behind her came Nita Qwan, a dark-skinned man in a nut-brown linen shirt and deerskin leggings and a fine red sash. He looked around, stunned.

"This is the... magik place?" he asked.

"And this is the dragon," Aneas said.

"The other dragon," Gas-a-ho said. "Master Smythe."

The slim, black-bearded man bowed. "You are the shaman Gas-a-ho?" he asked. "I believe we have met."

"And this," Aneas said, "is Irene, Princess of Empire. And Nita Qwan, war leader of the Sossag."

"I know Irene," the dragon said. "Why have you brought these people? Who have no powers?"

"To judge you," Gas-a-ho said.

"You will judge me?" Smythe spat.

"Show us Looks-at-Clouds," Aneas said.

"I cannot," Master Smythe said. "If I release her, she will retake this body, and I will be no more."

"I think you are lying," Aneas said. "My brother shared a body with Harmodius. For months."

Master Smythe looked back and forth. In the aethereal, *his frustration was evident. "Listen, you fools!" he began.*

Gas-a-ho laughed. He produced a fine bear pelt from the air, shook it out, and sat on it. "Calling us fools will not help you," he said calmly. "There is no hurry. Convince us. Otherwise, we kill your body."

"And doom the alliance!" Master Smythe spat. "The Odine are rising! Even now I can smell them. Him. It. Even now, Ash is turning his powers on the Army of the Alliance. Everything is in the balance."

Aneas sat beside Gas-a-ho, on the endless, infinite plain. The bear fur was comfortable under him. "Perhaps everything is always in the balance," he said.

Gas-a-ho gave him a nod.

Master Smythe pursed his lips. "Listen," he said.

Gas-a-ho nodded. "We are here to listen. We did not kill you outright. Not least because Irene guessed that it must be you. And not, for example, Kevin Orley."

Smythe took an aethereal *breath.*

"Very well. We near the climax. Ash has the force to take Lissen Carak; whether he can manage it before the gates are ready for him is open to doubt. The Odine are rising; their rise will be swift. The will *is strong. If Ash had not attacked us at Forked Lake, I would have been with the army, facing Ash with the help of all the magisters. Instead I am here. But we can still strike a mighty blow! We can take the island. I can make myself whole and restore this person to the body s/he requires. And then we will be stronger than ever."*

"Why not just tell us?" Irene asked.

"A habit of secrecy," Smythe admitted. "And... you are so vulnerable. If Ash finds the time to come after you again... We are easily distracted; I know how his mind works, because it is a mirror of my own, if older. Every second, he must dismiss thousands of thoughts as wasteful, if only to avoid madness. Ash is not omniscient; he trusts his control of Orley to be sufficient to his purpose. But if there was a hint of my presence here..."

"Because you two are rivals for the gate?" Gas-a-ho asked.

"No. I represent the party of fewer negative outcomes. We want the gates closed; ideally, forever." Master Smythe shrugged.

"You have never said as much before," Aneas said.

Smythe sighed. "I am reduced to a kernel of my true self, and you threaten me with death. Shall I beg? Killing me will doom every human, in fact, every sentient, in this circle of creation."

Gas-a-ho sat back and raised an eyebrow. "Really?" he asked. "Aren't you a little worried that we'll just do it all ourselves, without your party? I was listening to the Red Knight and to Irene, Master Dragon. Harmodius wants you all dead. I could do some of his work right here."

Smythe's eyes narrowed. "*I* made *the* Red Knight," he spat.

Aneas laughed. "I doubt he'd appreciate hearing that," he said. "But Ash made Thorn, and look what happened to him."

Irene leaned forward. "You made Gabriel? Do tell."

Smythe shook his head. "Why won't you trust me?"

Irene looked around. "It is all about trust, isn't it?" she said. "You can't trust us, but you'd like us to trust you. But I see two possible outcomes you have not mentioned. First, if we allow you access to the well of power at Lake-on-the-Mountain, we will have no reins on you at all. You will return to your full powers, and we will be a mere party of rangers. Second, a lifetime in throne rooms has accustomed me to listen to what men do not say. I have listened to you, and I have not yet heard you say that your party intends the destruction of Ash. Do you intend to make him your ally against the Odine?"

Aneas looked at Irene with new respect. Dressed as a great queen, in that hour she seemed one.

Master Smythe turned his head to her, and his unnaturally beautiful face had a wry smile. "If I was Ash," he said, "I would now wish that I'd ordered you killed, instead of merely suggesting it. Very well, Irene. You wish to be treated as my peer? There is no force with which I will not ally to save this world, to save the bears and the forests and the earthworms and the wyverns and even Man and Woman. There, 'tis said. We do not love Man. But we have allied with Man in this war. Is that too honest?"

Irene smiled. "Trust comes from honesty," she said. "I have learned that recently."

"So," Gas-a-ho said. "You wish us to allow you to go forward, wearing Looks-at-Clouds. We trust you to behave well when we storm the island, even though we will be utterly at your mercy."

"Worse than that," Master Smythe said. "The island is defended."

"Why do you refuse to produce Looks-at-Clouds?" Nita Qwan asked.

"Both Irene and Aneas are in love with him/her," Smythe said. "I cannot have a hope of their rational minds overcoming their lust. I know humans all too well."

Irene's voice dripped contempt. "I think that is the most patronizing, most foolish thing I have ever heard a dragon say," she sneered. "You ask us to trust you. You do not trust us, or even think of us as peers. More like pets."

"The witchbane is wearing off," Gas-a-ho said. "We must choose."

Nita Qwan raised a hand. "I have a proposal," he said. "A compromise."

Smythe looked from one to another. "You know that I could just pass through your avatars to attack your minds," he said. "If I take any of you, I am free of the witchbane."

Gas-a-ho shook his head. "You will find that we all came through Aneas, not directly into you," he said. "Aneas's palace is heavily guarded. If you try, I guarantee our verdict. The real trumps the aethereal. You will be dead."

For the first time, Master Smythe's inhuman face registered fear. But he managed a smile. "Well do the dragons fear Man," he said.

"Tell us your proposal," Aneas said to the Sossag leader.

"Let Master Smythe relinquish control to Looks-at-Clouds," he said. "Let us see hir in control of this body. Then, if s/he agrees, we allow him to regain control at the island, or before. But he must let the changeling go, and s/he must be allowed a vote. It is hir body."

"S/he will never agree," Smythe said.

Gas-a-ho nodded. "You will be a great sachem, if only we live long enough to plant corn again," he said to Nita Qwan. "I agree that this is good."

Smythe's face was blank.

Irene waved a hand. "He considers desperation. Master Smythe, I appeal to you as one exile to another. Trust us. Trust Looks-at-Clouds, as you ought to have trusted from the first."

"This from you, patricide?" Smythe said.

Irene nodded. "Yes," she said. "Precisely. This from me. You may be thousands of years old, but I have learned this in the last four weeks. Trust is what makes us great. Not deception."

Smythe's black eyes met hers. "You have grown wise," he said.

And then he was gone.

In his place stood a slim man, or a strong woman, with short white-gold hair and slanted green eyes. S/he blinked, and the plain around them became a forest, deep and green, full of forest smells, and the smell of lavender and spruce over all.

S/he wore a shapeless white shirt and hose, and in hir hand was a red crystal that flashed like the beating of a heart.

S/he looked at Aneas. "How foolish can a mortal be?" s/he said. "I drew him into me. I knew what I was doing. Those who play for power are doomed to be fools perhaps."

"You are unhurt?" Irene asked. The woods were magnificent; the trees ancient and hale. Aneas's distant spring looked pale, its trees insignificant by comparison.

"Only my sense of self, a little," the changeling said. "I think he has hurt my ... feelings. But by all the spirits of wood and water, I have learned ... I have learned!"

S/he bent and kissed them one by one. "Welcome to my woods," s/he said. "I vote that he be allowed to return. When he harms us, it will only be by his indifference."

"Is this prophecy?" Nita Qwan asked.

"Yes," the changeling said.

"And you will allow him to take you anyway?" Gas-a-ho asked.

"Yes," the changeling said.

Aneas nodded. "Really, yours is the only vote that counts," he said.

East of Firensi—Long Paw

Twenty leagues east of Firensi, Long Paw could see the columns of smoke in the dawn.

"War without fire is like sausage without mustard," he said with an easy smile to the Etruscan woman who'd followed Brown.

"That is a horrible thing to say," she snapped. "Those are people's homes."

Long Paw shrugged. "Aye," he said. "*Sì.*"

Brown emerged from the cottage wiping his hands on a woman's apron. "He was here," he said.

M'bub Ali was using an amulet; he held it aloft in the door of the cot and watched the white cabochon jewel. It sparked.

"There is *potentia* here," he said. "I can see it. Ahhh. I can track it."

Brown's lips didn't twitch. "Let's go," he said.

Lucca nodded. He had his mask on, which made him inhuman.

They all mounted.

"You should stay here," Long Paw said to Donna Beatrice. "This will be ugly."

She shrugged. "I am with you now," she said. She had a knife, and she loosened it in its sheath.

Long Paw nodded. "I guess you are," he said. "Stay close to me if it's fighting. Can you fight?"

She thought for a moment and then shrugged. "Probably," she said. "Is it different from killing pigs?"

Then they were all mounted, and moving.

Sauce was just approaching the gates of Firensi below them, and the air smelled of smoke. There were storm clouds rolling in from the south, heavy with rain.

They unrolled hoods and kept riding into the hills. They stopped at one cottage and then the next, using M'bub Ali's amulet.

At the third, a crossbow bolt greeted them, killing a horse. Lucca fired the thatch with a word, and the cottage burned. When the smoke filled the place, a man came out; M'bub Ali shook his head, and the man was shot down by his archers. Then another man screamed and tried to come out the back where the roof had fallen in.

Brown disarmed him and stood on his burned arms for three questions, and then after a nod from M'bub Ali, Brown simply walked away, leaving the man with his burns and a broken arm.

"This morning," Brown said.

"If he has the art, he knows we're here," Lucca said. He had the distant look that casters got when they were preparing.

Brown shrugged. And mounted.

"Stay with me," Long Paw said to Donna Beatrice. She shrugged.

"Do I have a choice?" she asked. There was no bitterness in her tone, just a sort of peasant fatalism.

Long Paw nodded. "*Si*, ma donna. You could just ride away."

She shook her head. "And do what? Whore? Cleaning lady?" She looked at the dark sky to the south. "I'm too old for the first and too bored for the second. Maybe I will be a killer."

San Batiste—The Patriarch of Rhum

Ali-Mohamed was asleep, and the Patriarch woke him with a sibilant hiss.

"The enemy is close," the man said.

Ali-Mohamed was still unsure whether the Patriarch was in fact so deeply locked in terror that he created things of which to be afraid, or whether he actually had arcane knowledge, but his eyes had a terrible green light in them, and Ali-Mohamed had to assume the latter.

"I'll get the horses," the former mamluk said, getting his feet on the floor.

"No," the Patriarch said. "You keep them from following me. I need an hour or so. I should have done this days ago."

Ali-Mohamed was about to protest when a slender talon, like the thorn on a rose, burst from the tip of the Patriarch's reaching finger, and scratched his cheek.

He ceased to have his own volition.

East of Firensi—Long Paw

"Here," M'bub Ali said.

They dismounted. There were a round dozen of them: Long Paw and Lucca, Brown and the woman, M'bub Ali and seven of his horse boys.

"We'll hold the horses," Long Paw said.

Brown nodded.

He was watching the stone cottage high on the hillside above them. It was a little after noon, and thunder rolled in the valley below, and the Council of Firensi had just agreed to give Sauce forty thousand ducats in gold and three hundred heavy wagons of grain to march away.

"We'll wait for the rain," Brown said.

"He's casting," Lucca said. His face went a little slack. "Christ risen, he's a strange one. Never seen..."

There was a burst of colour from the stone cottage.

Lucca's ruddy gold shield sprang up, but the bright red working didn't come near them.

And then the storm front hit.

Thunder rolled again, and lightning flashed. The Etruscan woman went down on her knees in the gravel of the road and began to pray.

The sky was a very odd colour.

The rain came down like a waterfall unleashed. It fell so hard that it drowned sound; it almost covered thought. Brown made a hand motion; he and Lucca moved off along one of the stone walls that defined fields. M'bub Ali gave Long Paw a soaking-wet smile. "You have the best job, I think," he said, and slipped over another wall into the olive grove. One by one, his people followed him.

Long Paw collected the reins of all the horses, and staked them with a pair of picket pins in the rising wind. He was already soaked through; his hands ached, but the loss of their horses here would kill them as thoroughly as arrows or sorceries.

The rain was unnatural. Long Paw got Donna Beatrice under her arm, raised her out of the road, which was now something like a stream, and hauled her to the relative shelter of the wall of the olive grove.

Then he slipped over the wall and opened the gate. Watching back toward the cottage all the time; but there was nothing to be seen but the grey curtain of rain. The valley was gone, the city of Firensi invisible, and even the next mountain was gone.

Long Paw went back out into the road, got the woman, and by gestures, explained what he wanted to do. Then each of them took out one of the picket pins, and with twenty horses between them, all spooked by lightning, they moved the picket and the line into the olive grove. It seemed to take forever, but the woman was good with horses. It gave them something to do, and when the horses were inside the walls, Long Paw closed the gate.

Then the two of them huddled in the corner of the wall—a good shelter, if two walls and no roof make a house. Long Paw went and fetched his heavy riding cloak off his saddle and threw it over the corner, and then they could think; the rain fell outside the little shelter, although the cloak filled with water in very little time and had to be dumped.

"I am so cold," said the woman.

An alarm was hammering in Long Paw's head. He'd done all these things to pass the time. *We've been here an hour*, he thought.

And the light was changing. The storm was passing them, but the light was failing.

"Stay here," he told the woman, and he went out into the rain. He grabbed Lucca's heavy riding cloak off the back of his saddle and put it around Donna Beatrice, and she smiled. Then he hauled himself up onto the wall.

Too old for this crap.
He could see the cottage.
He could see a body outside it.

Brown moved very, very slowly toward the back of the stone cottage. The rain would cover most of his movement, but he was a cautious man who'd lived a long time in a dangerous business, and he had no intention of showing himself. He crawled a long time, and then he waited while Lucca moved.

He was crawling through some sort of gorse: green and brown, unpleasant to the touch, growing over very stony ground. He found a shallow depression, maybe only two or three hand-spans deep, but he clung to it, moving parallel to the house.

There was a bright red flash; he didn't raise his head, but he smelled the burning meat.

He waited.

He heard Lucca move behind him, despite the rain. Eventually the man came up almost level.

Brown made some hand signals.

Lucca nodded.

He was very cold.

Someone loosed an arrow from higher up the hillside.

A pair of arrows flew from inside the cottage. And another from the hillside.

Lucca held a thumb up.

Brown nodded, and they both moved, crawling on their bellies as fast as their elbows and thighs would allow them. Brown raised his head when he made the pigsty, and there, twenty paces away at the other end of the farm wall, was M'bub Ali, and they didn't kill each other.

It was a particularly unpleasant patch of mud on which to lie.

M'bub Ali raised two fingers, pointed at the house, then raised three.

Brown shook his head.

The rain came down harder.

M'bub Ali reached into his pack and produced a black, pitch-encrusted bottle. He held it up.

Brown shook his head, having no idea what it was.

M'bub Ali shrugged. Then he took out a tinder kit, and, in the pouring rain, tried to get a light.

There was another exchange of arrows.

M'bub Ali made a face.

More time passed.

One of the horse boys appeared behind M'bub Ali. In one pass he got the char cloth lit.

Brown's eyes narrowed.

M'bub Ali lit the stub of a candle despite the wind, and then lit a tab on the end of his black bottle. The tab flared.

M'bub Ali leaned and threw the bottle straight through the window of the cottage and took an arrow through his arm in return.

The bottle burst with a whoosh, and all hell broke loose.

A line of red fire emerged from the maelstrom and struck the horse boy with the tinder kit, and he was flayed, his skin burned off his muscle, eyeballs melting. He screamed. But not for long.

Lucca's shields snapped into place.

A red line went through the shields, attenuating as it went, and Lucca was hit. By luck, his leather mask caught most of the leakage, but his shields went down as he lost concentration.

A third red dart struck M'bub Ali's amulet, and it burst. He grunted and drew a long knife.

Brown was already moving for the cottage wall.

A figure of flame came to the door; the mamluk, Ali-Mohamed, all his cotton clothes alight; he didn't scream from the pain, and his lacquered bow loosed an arrow that struck M'bub Ali in the body and stuck in his ribs.

Brown didn't question that the big mamluk was still fighting. He shot with his ballestrino from three strides out, and the burning man was hit and seemed to burst, scattering burning tatters of man everywhere.

Brown dropped his precious weapon in the mud and threw himself against the wall as flames roared out of the door and another figure emerged, also afire. Lucca hit it with something, perhaps hermetically summoned water; M'bub Ali's saber severed a reaching hand in one blow, and Brown was rolling around the corner. Everything in his head was screaming that this was a deception; the flaming men at the back were covering something at the front.

He made it to the corner and threw himself flat in the mud, to look around the corner at ankle height.

There was a corpse in front of the door, lying headless in the rain. The fire was not as strong at the front of the house; Brown rolled back, trying to sort what he had just seen.

The front door was open.

Brown made himself go around the corner. He knew he couldn't delay; he was already afraid for the horses and the woman.

Smoke poured from the low windows. Any moment, the front rooms would ignite.

He kept going.

Something was moving, very rapidly, in the gorse of the hillside. Something that seemed to smoke as it moved, and held a long sword in a clawed hand.

Brown cursed; he'd dropped his only ranged weapon; he had no idea where Lucca was.

He paused and knelt by the corpse.

The body wore a silk robe and there was a heavy gold cross on a solid gold chain twisted around the neck and hanging down the back. There was an incredible amount of blood, as if the man had exploded, and the head...

Brown heard the scream from below on the hillside and paused only to curse.

Lucca staggered around the corner of the cottage.

"No fucking idea," spat Brown. "Someone has to cover the cottage. There could be more."

He turned and ran down the hill.

Long Paw saw the bursts of red light, and then the cottage caught fire; a flash of light in the grey, and then smoke. Smoke out the front door...

Something moved on the hillside. The rain was tapering off; he could see the mountain peak beyond the cottage and the flash of a weapon reflecting light.

The truly abnormal is easy to see. It doesn't match the patterns that people build so carefully in their minds; it is *alien*. The thing he saw was wrong: the size of a small deer or a large dog, dark red or black, moving at speed through the gorse. It was not like anything he'd ever seen.

He dropped back into the olive grove.

"Move away from the wall," he shouted at Donna Beatrice, and when she didn't respond, he caught her wrist and pulled her along until they were in among the horses. Long Paw watched their heads come up.

"That's right, ladies," he said aloud. "Something wicked. Just give it a kick, eh?" He drew his sword and took his buckler off his hip.

"Stay close," he said in his best Etruscan.

The woman whimpered.

"I couldn't agree more," he said quietly.

The horses were spooked, right enough. Every head was up; eyes were rolling, and tails lashing.

Something red-black flashed over the wall.

M'bub Ali's stallion screamed and reared.

And then the thing came *over* the back of the horses. Long Paw had time to be afraid; the face like a suckerfish, the body too thin to be real.

It had talons as long as daggers, wicked as stilettos, and a long, glowing sword in its right hand.

Brown's mare kicked at it; one of M'bub's horses landed a bite and slowed it.

Long Paw's blade dropped under his buckler, and his left foot slid forward.

As it crossed the back of the horses, it went from saddle to saddle, and the horses panicked, and where it stepped on a bare back, the talons ripped flesh from the packhorse, but the stallion and two of the mares stood their ground.

Long Paw watched it for a little more than one beat of his heart. And then it was all training.

It was so fast that Long Paw had to start his rising cut, left to right, while the thing was still coming over the back of the last mare, four paces away.

The red-black thing loosed a scarlet bolt as it leapt. The steel and wood buckler in Long Paw's left hand took the bolt, and became slag, and heat burned Long Paw's hand right through the steel gauntlet under the buckler, burning two fingers off his hand and scorching the rest.

His cut severed a reaching, taloned hand and his point went unerringly into the thing's sucker face even as its sword cut the last four inches off his own . . . a late parry with a magical sword. His blade went right through it—no shock of bone—and the whole weight of the thing slammed him off his feet.

He fell back, and hit his head. He didn't go out, but the burning hot, rubbery weight of it pushed him to action—talons screamed across his thigh, and he felt the poison hit him.

His volition started to leak out of him.

Donna Beatrice slammed her dagger into its whipcord-thin back. She'd killed chickens and she'd killed sheep and her arm was sure; even facing something that defied reason, her hand did its task. She severed its spinal cord. She was screaming like a banshee, but her knife was sure. Its sword clattered to the ground.

Long Paw felt it go, because for almost a full second, it had *been* him. It was a terrible emptying; one moment he burned with power, and the next he was an empty vessel.

Long Paw lay in the mud, staring up at the rain-laden sky.

Donna Beatrice continued to stab the dead thing for quite some time. Her blows landed with meaty sounds. She was still screaming at the top of her lungs.

The horses were racing around the inside of the walls as if the little orchard were a race course.

Long Paw wasn't sure who he was. And then he was a little sure, and then a little more.

Brown vaulted the wall of the enclosure and almost died under the hooves of M'bub Ali's stallion. Brown rolled and then leaped and managed to get clear of a wild-eyed mare.

He looked for a moment at the thing. The Etruscan woman was kneeling by Long Paw, and she was thrusting, dagger reversed in both hands, over and over into the thing's back.

Long Paw's sword was *through its head*.

And as fast as Donna Beatrice stabbed it, the wounds healed. He had thought her maddened, but she was merely panicked, and nonetheless doing what she could; the talons were hacked away.

Brown reached into his shirt, leaned down, and plunged ten inches of witchbane into the creature.

It spasmed.

He left it there.

The wounds stopped closing.

The woman looked at him. She was covered in blood like an actor at the end of a tragedy. She was also burned all over her body, her clothes full of holes as if she'd been attacked by deadly moths.

Brown grabbed the corpse. It was hot to the touch, and it felt *wrong*, and he used his revulsion to hurl it as far as he could. It didn't weigh much.

Long Paw's eyes fluttered open.

Brown's dagger hand was steady and the point of the dagger was at Long Paw's throat.

"Who are you?" he asked.

Long Paw's eyes met his. "What the *fuck* was that?" he asked.

Four hours had passed, and they were in the mill at the side of a river. Long Paw was sensible enough to know it when they got him off his horse; the rain was lighter, but he was cold, soaked through, and none of them looked good. M'bub Ali was badly wounded; one of his horse boys was dead and two more wounded. All of them stank of mud; all were cold and wet.

Sauce was there in person with the duchess. Long Paw smiled at her; he knew her; his head was coming back together, although there were odd flashes in the corner of his eyes and things were not right in his head; Donna Beatrice had him under one shoulder and Lucca under the other.

"Lay him down. There's beds. Magistera Tancreda is here and ready to work. And our doctors. Thank God we had no casualties today." Sauce shook her head. "Paw, you look like shit."

They pushed Long Paw down.

"Talk when you are better," she said. "Who is this?"

"Donna Beatrice," Long Paw said. "Put her on the rolls. She killed the fucking thing."

The Duchess of Venike was right behind his commander, but her eyes went unerringly to Brown. "Did you get him?" she asked.

Brown shook his head. "It's a fairly complex matter," he said. "But the Patriarch is inarguably dead."

Sauce waited until the two company doctors and Tancreda were clearly at work, and then she went up the mill steps with the duchess, Brown, Donna Beatrice, and Daniel Favour.

"Who are they?" she asked from the landing.

Brown followed her finger. "Captain, that's M'bub Ali. He is... hmm. An officer of the Sultan."

The duchess nodded. "Alison, they helped us at Mitla; seems like years ago. They were here to scout the Darkness."

"Spies," Alison said.

"Allies," Giselle said.

"Good allies," Brown muttered. He handed over a long bundle. "Fell Sword. It had it."

Sauce raised an eyebrow. But she shrugged and continued up the steps to the room that had once been occupied by the mill's owners. There her body squire poured wine and Brown slumped into a chair.

"Not used to all these people," he muttered.

Giselle smiled. "But the Patriarch is dead."

Brown told the story, drinking his wine. He told it sparely but professionally, and they asked him questions, and then they asked Donna Beatrice questions, and then they ate a light meal, and by then Long Paw was awake and more himself.

"What was it, Paw?" Sauce asked.

Long Paw shook his head. "Never seen anything like it," he said.

Tancreda had all her patients treated; her healing skills were minimal, but with two doctors to support her, she had stabilized M'bub Ali and saved both of his men, and Long Paw's poison was wearing off of its own accord, hurried along by wine. She joined them on the first floor and sipped some sweet white wine herself. She listened to Long Paw's description and then, with his help, drew a picture of a sucker-faced greyhound with hands instead of paws and long, thorny talons.

"Eeeuuuwww," she said in disgust.

Donna Beatrice shuddered. "I will see it until I die," she said in Etruscan.

Tancreda copied out their description of it, alive, and went downstairs with her wine to the blood-soaked bag that contained the thing's mortal remains.

"Oh, sweet Christ," she muttered. She summoned the others so that they could see that the thing had rotted almost to nothing—foul slime and a heavy hide and some bones, like something a month in the ground.

Brown shrugged. "It was *in* the Patriarch," he said. "When I think about it, I have to wonder if there was one *in* the Duke of Mitla."

"Blessed Virgin," Sauce spat. "Worms and fire dogs."

"Salamanders," Long Paw said. "That's what they are."

Sauce read over Tancreda's coded dispatch. She wrote *Salamander* in her own hand under the sketch. And then, in her own code, she wrote, *I think we've found Kronmir's fourth player.* She looked up, sighed for a lost opportunity, and wrote, *I'll be marching north tomorrow.*

Then she took the sword from the old cloak in which it was wrapped and handed it to Tancreda.

"Oh my God," she said. The sword was fine, but the blade was a rainbow of colours unlike normal steel, and set in it in letters of gold, it said, *Durandala.*

Sauce smiled. "Always wanted a magic sword," she said.

Chapter Eight

Loomsack Mountain—Ser Gavin Muriens

S er Gavin Muriens knew he had very little time to get his army across the Cohocton, and he drove them like a cattle herder in the predawn darkness. But bad luck, or fate, sent a flight of wyverns over before the baggage was fully across; the ford was already muddy, the rain was raising the water level, and nothing was moving until he allowed them to use torches, which were like a beacon for the wyverns. Days of fighting were taking their toll; discipline was not the best, and too many of his best people were already across with the cavalry, whom he had sent first.

He rode back across the ford in the gentle rain, and with Syr Ydrik and his Irkish knights as an escort and Tapio as a companion, he rode west to the top of the round-topped mountain that dominated the ford.

To the west, in the very earliest light of day, he could see for a mile or more, and the road and the whole vale of the Cohocton seemed to be alive.

Gavin shook his head.

"He's coming for us," he said.

Tapio looked. "We will have to fight to cover our retreat." He shrugged. "If you are correct, man, then he knowsss by now."

"We need all of Redmede's people and the Moreans," Gavin said. "They're the back of the column. And get us a caster."

He waved at Giannis Griatzas, now one of his squires. "Get the Redmedes and all their people." He thought a moment. "And the Duchess Mogon, if she will come."

Griatzas bowed and rode off into the rain.

"You will sssacrifice them," Tapio asked.

Gavin tugged the water out of his beard. "Not if I can help it," he said. "Look; with this hill in our hands, we can cover the baggage and all the infantry across the ford. And then we slip away; it won't be easy, but we'll be on the wrong side of the river and he'll be caught."

"Man, if he crosssesss the river, it is we who will be caught." Tapio smiled and his fangs showed. "But neverthelessss. If he followsss, he is sssurely defeated by disstance."

"It will be bad, for the rear guard," Gavin said. He was looking at his own knights.

Loomsack Mountain—Bill Redmede

Duchess Mogon was watching the chaos at the river crossing with increasing annoyance and a good deal of fear when Griatzas found her. But Griatzas was a very mature young man and he knew that he was requesting, not ordering; her beak opened and shut twice with a click, but she didn't bridle or raise her crest.

"Very well," she said. "We will come."

She snapped orders to her household, and almost four hundred wardens rose to their feet. Their plumes were soaked, but the inlay in their beaks and the colour on their hides showed.

She herself sprinted at superhuman speed to where Harold Redmede was getting his people on their feet; sheer exhaustion and long habituation had most of the rangers asleep in the rain.

He flinched a little at her wave front of fear, but then grinned. "You comin' with us, Your Grace?"

She yawned her beak. "If the bogglins get into our retreat at the ford," she said, and left the sentence to hang.

"Let's go, you villains!" Redmede called.

Men cursed; Stern Rachel continued her efforts to light her pipe, ignoring her corporal.

Next to her, Long Peter was fondling his dry bow string. "Fucking rain," he said. "But if'n the demons are wi' us, maybe it's not a one-way trip."

None of the rangers were under any illusions about their chances, covering the retreat of the army.

But they turned away from the chaos at the ford and walked back into the rain, headed west; away from safety, and into the face of the enemy.

Magister Nikos joined them on his mule. He rode along, one knee locked over the cantle of his saddle, a book open on his lap, spectacles perched on his nose. He didn't seem to notice that the rain was gradually working on the ink.

Kwoqwethogan, Mogon's nest brother, was the best mage she had left; he trotted alongside her for half a league as they climbed the mountain and then sprinted ahead, his heavy feet slamming onto the rocky trail and making the earth shake, until he caught up with Master Nikos.

His bronze and gold-inlaid beak was level with the grammarian's head. The Morean closed his book carefully, latched it, and dropped it back into a saddlebag full of books.

"My lady says, our enemy will come. In person." The warden bowed his great head. All the wardens were respectful of the grammarian; although his powers were not the strongest, the fineness of his control was without rival anywhere.

The warden mage spoke. "I am to give you my powers, and those of my sisters, too. We will not cast; we will fuel you."

Master Nikos nodded, as if this was perfectly reasonable. It was; but even Nikos knew it was an outstanding example of cooperation and trust. "I want to take this a step further," he said, and outlined a detailed hermetical proposal.

Kwoqwethogan flinched.

"We will always be linked," Nikos admitted. "I don't see another choice."

The great warden shrugged. "You did this with Lord Kerak," he said.

Nikos nodded. "And a little of me died when he died," he admitted. "And now I have an overwhelming urge to catch and eat beaver."

The *adversarius* mage, once an architect of the alliance with Thorn, chuckled. "Beaver are delicious," he admitted. "And when you swim into one of the giant beaver nests and take their young…"

His crest inflated, and his long, purple tongue licked the heavy teeth in his beak.

Magister Nikos held his breath a moment. "Yeees," he managed. When he and the other magister had exchanged their *aethereal* sigils, he managed to ride on without a shudder.

On the western face of the mountain side, Syr Ydrik and Tapio opened the action by charging the enemy scouts on a wide front, collapsing the bogglins and a handful of enemy wardens on great swamp trolls back against their support. But Ash's column was not an organized body in battalions, or even in the traditional human divisions of vanguard, main body, and rear guard; and despite his control of a major part of their wills, there were still instincts of self preservation at work even in the scent-captive bogglins, and the steady casualties among the leaders of the column had led to a certain caution.

Ydrik and Tapio went forward almost a mile, and withdrew only when they were hard against a shield wall of irks. That was an ugly surprise; Tapio had not imagined that all the irks were under his own banner, but the sight of them in their close array, their bronze mail gleaming in the light rain, oppressed him. He called out to him, and they named him traitor, and Man Friend.

A tall irk in gold maille stepped out of the line, axe in hand. "Come and fight me, Man Friend," he said. "You have betrayed the trust of the Free People."

Tapio reined in. "If Asssh winsss, there will be no Free People."

"If your *men* win, there will be no Free People," rejoined the other. "I am Hukas Helli! We are the Free People!"

Tapio shook his head slowly. "I will not fight you, cousssin. Let usss agree that no irk will fight another irk."

"I will kill you, and I will have your woman for my own," Hukas roared. "I will take your slaves and your castles and I will keep the people free. You have forgotten what it is to be an irk. Dismount, and let me teach you."

"You are a fool, and 'my' woman would devour you," Tapio said. "I leave you to find death without me."

He rode away to the jeers of the enemy irks, which fell on him like blows.

Tapio's charge bought the rear guard an hour; by the time that Ash's horde was fully in motion, the lower slopes were defended; Mogon's wardens held the center, with most of the Long Dam Clan bears standing with her; the Morean mountaineers had a small redoubt of felled trees just above them, and the Albin militia were dropping more trees in a crisscross *abatis* to cover the bears. The irk knights went up the hill into reserve.

A very small creek ran across the western slope of the mountain, which the Outwallers called Loomsack, and ran into the swelling Cohocton. Before the first bogglin reached the creek, Magister Nikos spoke a single word, *fotia*. His controlling structure was perfect, despite the rain, and every tree on the whole front on the far side of the tree and extending west almost a hundred paces burst into flame.

The east wind whipped the flames west.

"And now he comes," Nikos intoned.

In the west, Ash rose into the air. Men with no hermetical skill whatsoever could feel him on the air; his presence was oppressive, like the stench of a corpse. Before he was fully visible in the clouds, he extinguished the fire; in time to save it from imperiling his attack, but not before the fire and the hermetical force behind it had created a cleared zone of almost two hundred paces in depth.

Golden globes of power rose over the mountainside.

Off to the east, Gavin and Tamsin and Ser Gregario rode back and forth, soaked to the skin, forcing men and irks and soaking wet Golden Bears and desperate wagoners across the fords. And as the last wagon came up the south bank, Gavin ordered his ballistas assembled, and then waved at Ser Gregario.

"All the chivalry," he said. "Ready at the water's edge."

Gregario snapped an armoured fist to his visor. "Yes, my lord earl," he said.

Loomsack Mountain—Ash

Ash's troubles only seemed to multiply. Everything annoyed him; he was delighted to have an enemy under his claws. But days of conflict, herding his retreating foes before him, had also taught him a respect for their magisters, and as soon as the golden globes snapped into the real, Ash turned in the air and considered his options.

As always, it was a matter of balancing his flow of *potentia*. Far to the east, his monsters had destroyed the human fleet in Havre; yet his spies told him that far off in the Middle Sea, there were more and more of the great wooden round ships gathering. Ash could not leave hold of his serpents yet, the more so as, when the ancient things took losses, the survivors were even less willing to take risks. Ash had time to wish he had made alliance with the deep *kraken*, who now seemed to have made common cause with Lot instead. And the outright destruction of one of his Antica Terra rivals was a mixed blessing; the *rebel* was *dead*, and what that suggested about the power of these upstart humans only underlined why he had begun by promising their extermination to his fence-sitting relatives. And perhaps most disturbingly, Lot's fall had not broken the alliance of Man and Wild. Ash, who seldom doubted, wondered if Lot was truly dead; his foe was wily and some of his workings seemed to still have teeth.

Worst of all, Ash had begun to wonder if dismissing Mortirmir and the human mages in Antica Terra had been entirely wise.

And the *will* was rising.

It was chaos; it was war. It was like all the other gate openings, and so Ash, like the great predator he was, used his powers sparingly, gnashed his great teeth at being a hampered god, took as few risks as he could, and waited his time. This was not the moment for wild abandon. This was the moment to use weight of numbers and just enough power to win the day.

There followed a rattle of workings and counterworkings; light and darkness, lightning and shield, boilings, wood snaps, metal fatigues, and a titanic struggle over the wind that, to Ash's horror, resulted in a draw and a dozen small whirlwinds moving like crazed tornadoes over the battlefield.

If allegory can be held to describe, then the battle between Ash and Nikos was like an encounter between a bull and a wasp; Ash was infinitely more powerful, but the grammarian's focus of will and structure of linguistic *reality* were so much more precise that, as long as the argument rested on structure, Magister Nikos could keep Ash at bay.

In the real, the sky pulsed with power and flashed, and flashed again. Even in the hell of the N'gara battlefield, the flow of *ops* had not been this heavy; the shields flickered, the colours played; blasts rocked them, or threw dirt and trees into the air; flames rained across the battlefront, and the air pressure changed constantly, causing the eardrums of every sentient creature to rattle.

But the shields held.

For the first time in nine engagements, the bogglins hesitated at the edge of the burned ground and would not cross, and Ash had to expend *will* to push them across. There were many bogglins, and in the hurry of battle, even Ash's great compartmented mind could not pick and choose. The outpouring of his will was immense.

It had a cost.

And then the bogglins died.

But this time, Ash had chosen to use his wits and not a bludgeon, and while his bogglins died, he moved his irks and wardens and trolls to the east; a whole clan of his *Qwethnethogs* swam the Cohocton and started west on the south bank, determined to close the ford. His terrible cavalry of wardens mounted on hastenoch swung north, crossed an undefended beaver meadow, and came into the flank of the mountain defences.

The irk knights met them and stopped them high on the hillside, in a tangle of glacial boulders, and Syr Ydrik was wounded there and Tapio assumed direct command, ordering Syr Srylot and Syr Rinir to envelop the pain-maddened trolls. And the Jacks, waiting in ambush for just such an attack, shot into the flanks of the hastenoch and then charged to complete their destruction. It saved the flank, but distracted Tapio.

Down in the vale of the Cohocton, the first Ser Gavin knew of approaching disaster was that Ser Gregario's knights were all dismounting on the south side. He was just wishing that he had a reserve under his hand when the first stone troll appeared *downstream*.

Gavin saw it all in a single beat of his heart. He didn't need to watch more to know that Gregario was fighting for his life against a rising tide of wardens on the south side. Nor to guess that the trolls were intended to cut his rear guard off from the ford.

"Tamsin!" he roared. He could not wait to see if she would come. He had no reserve but his own household knights, but he led them against the trolls at once. Despite the uneven footing of the rocks around the ford, he got his lance from his squire, got it in the rest, and put it dead center in the stone face of a huge cave troll, and the thing went down even as his lance splintered.

But the trolls outnumbered his knights, and the ford was terrible for horses, although not much better for stone trolls; men and horses went down in the water, and so did monsters; slippery stone feet on slippery rock. But the charge of the knights was blunted, and with every beat of Gavin's heart, there was another horse down.

Just east of the ford, 1Exrech inhaled the scents on the wind and knew his enemy was close.

A thousand hardened bogglin warriors rose. They were tired, but they were the spear bogglins; they were the *alliessss*. Ten days of watching their kindred die had not changed their minds; for bogglins, inhaling the revealed false scent of the enemy revealed his evil even to the simplest bogglin mind.

1Exrech formed his people very close, as was his wont; close so that he could protect them with his sorcery, and close because their wall of spear points made them far more dangerous to man and monster alike.

"Come," he exhaled.

But 1Exrech had another tool, another weapon; subtle and weak. Under his vestigial wingcases, he set himself to exude the true scent of command; of nobility of intent, of nests defended and wrongs set to right.

He loosed a perfume called Justice.

Bill Redmede's Jacks couldn't hold the front and flank at the same time; their charge saved the irk knights, but left the Albin militia naked.

The enemy bogglins were flooding forward, and with them were irks and wardens and thousands of imps, fixing the line of the Allies. They shot and shot; the foresters ran out of arrows and stood with their swords and bucklers against the tide, and then, step by step, they began to retreat up the ridge, bleeding men who, when they fell, were stripped and eaten.

The Morean mountaineers pelted the horde with rocks and then charged through the great wardens with their axes, clearing the front of Mogon's clan and giving them a moment to breathe.

Mogon looked left and right from atop a huge rock, and ordered a retreat. The Long Dam bears, freed of opponents, turned left and slammed into the sharp-toothed imps that were destroying the Albin militia, and for a moment, the line was saved.

But Ash had deep pockets, and the Allies had none. Another wave came forward at Loomsack, and the whole alliance line ran.

Mogon, however, had always intended to survive their retreat. She led her warriors to the left, uphill and then down over the shoulder of Loomsack and down toward the fords. Jacks and militia and bears followed her.

The foresters fought on as the rest of the rear guard passed behind them. They had the best position, chosen by Harald Redmede and resting on the place where the little creek had high banks. Even when they retreated, the foresters had a deep swamp on one side and a boulder field behind them.

Harald Redmede was watching his foresters repel another attack, cutting down the handful of long-toothed imps who managed to scramble up the bank, but he turned and trotted to Mogon as she led her clan past him.

"The whole flank is going," she called.

"Where's my brother?" he asked.

She shook her head.

Harald held the stream bank as long as he could, waiting for his brother. But eventually he had to go, or lose all his people. They filed off along the edge of the deep swampy ground to his left and then turned, breaking contact with a sprint that ate their remaining energy. In a few minutes they had caught up with Mogon's people.

But the head of Mogon's retreat had just discovered that the fords were contested.

Off to the alliance right, Bill Redmede's Jacks had slaughtered the hastenoch cavalry but lost the right flank. Redmede was out of options, and he chose to save the irk knights.

By the time they'd wrecked their immediate opponents, they were high on the flanks of Loomsack. Redmede found himself with Tapio, looking west. From their height, they could not see the fords, but the flow of their enemies around the mountain was obvious. His people were exhausted—if that word still had meaning—and most of them were out of shafts.

The irk knights were also done. Most of them were dismounted; some of the great elk had lain down and would never rise, tired unto death.

Together, Redmede and Tapio moved a little farther east, to a rocky outcrop that allowed them to look down into the chaos of the ford. Even as they watched, the ballistae that Ser Gavin had ordered began to search out the trolls in the water; the wardens on the west bank, easily picked out by their engorged purple crests, were beaten, and the enemy bogglins on the far bank were behaving oddly, milling in confusion just beyond the spearpoints of 1Exrech's phalanx.

But closer in, the tide of Ash's flank attack was endless, and the fords were all but lost.

Master Nikos came up, still mounted on his mule, still looking more like a schoolmaster than a great mage. With him were two Morean magisters and half a dozen wardens who moved as if in a trance, all in step.

Tapio watched their doom in the valley below.

"He has beaten us," Redmede said.

The grammarian frowned as if dealing with a student guilty of plagiarism. "That's too bad," he said. "Because he hasn't beaten me. Or I should say, *us*. And that is a very important thing."

As if to emphasize his words, a torrent of red-brown fire fell on the shield above them and made no impression.

Tapio looked up. "I am tired of rain," he said. "I want to fight in the sun."

Tapio had his own powers; he was the *Faery Knight*. So he reached into the heavens, and he rolled back the clouds as if they were a carpet.

And the sun broke across Loomsack Mountain.

The sun fell on his shoulders and made his armour glow; it fell on the elk, and they raised their heads; it fell on the Jacks and made their cotes seem white again. It fell on Mogon's people and made their red crests burn like fire, and it was so bright that it made the stone trolls, trapped between Mogon and the ballistae, quail, and then ponderously turn and look for easier prey.

It fell on the enemy bogglins across the Cohocton, making their eyes light like jewels; a wight, in white chiton and bearing a pair of heavy swords, seemed to glow like an angel. But she wasn't fighting; she was inhaling, over and over, her four-jawed mouth hinged slightly open. Her horde hesitated.

Under Tapio's eyes, Mogon's column burst across the ford to safety, covered by the constant fire of the great crossbows, and covered by a flood of Tamsin's workings; a mix of illusion and terror and subtle enhancement and a tidal wave of confusing scents thrown into the wave front of the bogglins.

"We will never make it across," Redmede said.

Tapio nodded. "You are a good ally," he said, "and never did I do a better thing than to make you my friend. I sssay we go north, and eassst. One fight, to smash through Asssh's people. They will be thin right there... they all pool together for the fight at the ford."

Redmede followed the gesture the irk made with the haft of his long axe.

"If'n you're wrong..." he said.

"If I am wrong, William Redmede, we will die like heroesss and Tamsssin will mourn for a thousssand yearsss," Tapio said.

"Bess, too." Redmede shrugged. "Not a thousand, though. Maybe five."

Tapio's high voice shrieked with real laughter. "Come, friend," he said. "Let usss sssave what can be sssaved."

Down in the ford, Gavin Muriens was on foot, his horse dead; his squires mostly dead. They had failed to hold the ford against the trolls and Gavin had gone down; had taken too long to rise out of the icy water and found his banner down. He was perhaps ten paces from the north bank, at the very edge of the ford, with his back against a boulder as big as a house.

Gareth, his charger, was dead in the water before him, the rising river washing over his high-backed green saddle. But his axe was still hanging from the cantle, and Gavin leaned forward and fetched it, and the feel of it in his hand reassured him. He still had his shield; he settled it, tugged at straps, and prepared to die.

There were more than a dozen cave trolls in the ford, killing his people; mostly stragglers and camp followers.

Gavin watched while his thoughts came together. He'd been unconscious; had taken a blow to the head.

But on the south bank, he saw the ballista loose a bolt, and saw it strike a cave troll squarely, breaking the thing's outer shell of stone and unmaking it. The ballista told him many things: that the south bank was still secure; that Gregario had won his fight; that the chaos in the fords was not all disaster.

His spine straightened.

Behind him, there were horns. He knew them for Mogon's horns.

The cave trolls had noticed him. Slowly, like ships turning into the wind, two of them came for him, their heads swinging almost in unison, and Gavin wondered if Ash was concentrating on him.

Cavalry axe versus cave troll. First lesson. Don't even try it.

It was only ten paces to the bank, but Gavin wasn't sure of the footing and he wasn't too sure of his legs, either.

But when the first troll came on, he decided he had to make a fight of it and not just wait to be crushed against the rock, tempting as that seemed in his current state.

His intention was to pass forward like lightning, and throw a crushing blow to his adversary's ankle before the second cave troll emerged from behind the first to pulp him.

What really happened was that his first step forward snagged on Gareth's reins, rippling under the water, and he fell face forward in the bloody water. But the water was shallow, and the cave troll's blow went too far and *thudded* into Gareth's corpse, and Gavin slammed his iron-bound shield's point into the arch of the troll's foot, chipping stone and costing the thing its balance on the slippery rocks.

It fell with a choked roar.

Gavin got his left knee up and chopped with his axe, down into a flailing arm. He powered forward onto the thing's chest, and buried his axe in its brow ridge, and the red glare of its eyes went out forever.

A beam of green passed over his head, splitting the great torso of the second troll so that its very mammalian guts slithered into the river.

Duchess Mogon stood on the bank, ten paces away, and the haft of her axe was smoking.

Gavin looked back, but Mogon's people were pouring into the ford and more cave trolls were lumbering out of it.

"Sweet Christ," Gavin managed. He sank to one knee in the cold water.

Ash turned again. The Loomsack was his; he could see his *adverserae* on the crest and a veritable tide of bogglins flowing around the base of the mountain, but somehow he'd lost the ford again.

He could see Mogon in the *aethereal*. Her power was innate; and she had two artifacts of legend, items so old that they were old even to Ash. She had just used one.

She was clearing the ford, allowing thousands of men and bears and wardens to escape his trap.

Ash weighed the odds. His timetable was wrecked, and he had yet to face the *will*, the most dangerous opponent of all. And then the gates would open...

It was time to take some risks.

He tested his powers; sighed inwardly in a sort of conservationist disgust at the sheer waste of power required to control his distant oceanic subjects and the expenditure to keep his bogglins loyal and moving forward. He sensed a countercurrent of mutiny among 53Exrech's bogglins.

He was arranging to spend analytical energy on the root cause of the bogglin mutiny when he felt the distant tug of an alarm. He had dozens of them; he set them to remind him when things needed to be awakened, put to sleep, reenforced, destroyed, created...

This one was shrill, a high, keening wail.

The bogglins were passing out of his control.

A bolt of white fire struck his innermost shield, taxing his energies yet again to the moment of immediate defence. And then, as he continued his turn, Tamsin struck, a web of deceit, a tissue of lies, and for an instant, he feared nothing more than that his infected wound was mortal; he focused his analytical *powers* on a diagnosis before he understood that his will was under attack; rage consumed him, and he raised a mighty foreclaw and red fire fell on Tamsin.

He reached into the vortex of his empowerment and pulled, drawing realized *ops* from the vast reservoir in the north.

Then he completed his turn, and Loomsack Mountain passed under his left wing, and he stooped on the ford. The scream of his challenge blasted across the real and the *aethereal* alike.

In the same predawn light that Gavin had examined the onset of Ash's horde, eight long canoes raced out of the morning mist, paddles flashing.

Aneas stood in the bow of the lead canoe, his shields prepared. At his shoulder, Looks-at-Clouds wore no expression at all. Looks-at-Clouds had given control back to the dragon.

Master Smythe made no comment about the transfer.

Aneas was watching the shore. The great island rose away from the beach, tall slopes not quite steep enough to be called cliffs rising from a narrow shingle, a fortress built by nature. Gas-a-ho, the only one of them to have been to the island, had chosen the approach and the landing as the closest point to the sorcerer's place of power.

Deadlock crouched in the bow of the next canoe, an arrow on his bow. He had piloted them through the Mille Isles and out into the Inner Sea. Behind him, Black Heron, the Huran warrior, sang the paddle song quietly into the silent morning. Wisps of sea mist rose like a *kraken*'s arms around the boats.

The slopes of the mountain rose, covered thickly in old-growth trees, maple and beech, their leaves red and gold with autumn, a blaze of colour even before the sun was on them.

No birds sang.

The air seemed heavy and potent, and Aneas could feel the incredible well of *potentia* in the lake, above him, at the top of the mountain.

The paddles dipped and dipped, and the long canoes shot forward, covering the last twenty paces. The beach was sand and gravel; the bow shot up, the hull scraped on the sand, and Aneas was running on solid ground.

A keening scream sounded the moment his moccasined foot touched the beach. The scream came from everywhere and nowhere, as if the trees themselves were screaming.

Aneas went forward, Looks-at-Clouds at one shoulder and Nita Qwan at the other.

The slope rose, all but impassable.

Aneas grabbed a tree, leapt, and pulled on the next tree, and the others emulated him, climbing steadily. In ten paces, his breath came in gasps. He dropped his pack; looked left. All the rangers were dropping their packs. The Outwallers had left theirs in the boats.

The keening scream went on, shrill and terrible.

Aneas didn't allow himself to look up. He climbed, steadily, efficiently, aware of his companions, of the canoes emptying behind him, of the two Gallish ships entering the bay now that surprise was lost, their sails huge, the brilliant red cross of the lead ship like an invocation in the first true light of the sun.

An arrow *whickered* past him. He moved to the next tree. And looked up.

He was halfway up the wall of the mountain, and the trees about him were dying. He could feel their blight; see the moss hanging from their branches, much as he had seen on the tree in his memory palace; there was lichen on every trunk, and dozens of downed trees where a wild wind had flattened a whole row of forest giants.

He went over a downed tree and another arrow rattled past him. It had already struck branches, and was losing force, and it fell just to his left—a bogglin arrow.

Until then, Aneas had hoped that the island might be empty, stripped by Orley for his war in the mountains.

He stopped behind a downed tree thicker than he was tall, and sounded his horn. The sun was rising; the sky was a patchwork of blue and grey, and there was rain in the air, cold rain.

But the sun peeked over the horizon, its golden light catching the autumn leaves and the trees yet alive. He winded his horn again, and twenty horns sounded back in an arc to his right and left.

Away to his right, a tree exploded.

Instantly, Aneas raised a shield. So did other casters, so that the whole arc of the ranger's advance was mottled in transparent gold and green.

Two trees to the west, Deadlock crouched and loosed his crossbow, leaning out to loose well up the ridge. A gout of power struck back instantly, and the ranger fell, screaming, as acid burned into his left hand and arm.

Looks-at-Clouds rolled, hir long form folding like an acrobat's, and s/he rose by the wounded man and *removed* the acid.

But others were harder hit; to the east, a fine mist of something fell on a dozen unsuspecting Albans, and in a single breath, they died.

"Ware poison!" came a panicked call.

"Forward!" Aneas roared.

A heavy casting slammed into his shield. He was rocked back.

He had an idea. "Cover me?" he asked Gas-a-ho, and the shaman spun his endless flower-petal shields faster; a variety of workings impacted, but the depth and complexity of the moving shields baffled each attempt in turn.

"Strong," he grunted.

Aneas was *deep in his memory palace, working. It was a variation of a simple solution he'd used before, even in combat; he was stronger, and his access to ops was unprecedented, but the scale of this working was beyond anything he'd attempted.*

There it was. He wrote a sigil in the aethereal *air of his mind, focused on the letters of fire, and sang a snatch of Irkish poetry aloud, focusing two effects in one effort. In his mind, he saw the slope; he defined the limits of his effort.*

In the real he sounded "Halt" on his horn. One long blast while he held all his potency in his head. "Lie down!" he roared, his voice tearing at his vocal cords.

Gas-a-ho turned a precise, deadly working, a stream of black, on a single rose petal of his mind...

Aneas triggered his working.

Six hundred dead trees between Aneas and the ridge top all exploded together, all their moisture concentrated and then superheated in a hermetical sleight of hand. The sound was like six hundred lightning bolts striking the ground all together.

He used the power of his will to channel the splinters and flechettes of ruptured hardwood in one direction, up the ridge.

He put his horn to his lips, but when he winded it, he couldn't hear a thing. He felt the vibration of the instrument against his lips, but heard nothing.

He climbed over the dead forest giant in front of him and there before him was a blasted waste: sixty yards to the summit, and covered in a dense carpet of wood splinters and bark with more falling, a silent rain of leaves and dead wood. There was little cover; in one place, a sheet of rock had been exposed when the explosion ripped the thin layer of soil off and flung it up the ridge.

Aneas ignored the ringing in his ears and ran forward, his boots strangely noiseless.

Fifty paces to the top.

He had two shields up, and he was still going. At the corners of his vision, he could see other rangers rising from their concealment. He prayed they had all lain down.

Now he was in the middle of a line going up.

At the top of the ridge, something stood up. It was huge, and an unnatural jet-black, like a suit of black armour.

Then another appeared.

The first unleashed a bolt of black fire.

Aneas parried it and went forward another step.

Gas-a-ho lifted a stag antler and one of the black-armoured figures snapped back, knocked flat by the kick of an unseen stag.

Celia loosed an arrow and was struck by a bolt; her arm turned black, and then she *dissipated*. Nothing was left of her. Spores of black drifted in the light breeze.

Aneas pushed forward another step. It began to seem impossible; the hill was too steep and the enemy's *puissance* too great for mortals. A fifth of his rangers were gone, and they were still thirty paces from the top.

And he was pushing through a wave front—fear, doubt, terror. He could feel them, over the fear he already felt: the gnawing of doubt, the suggestion of self-loathing.

Gas-a-ho and one of the black figures were exchanging spells at an almost inhuman rate. The black figure's armoured hands gathered raw *potentia* and flung it without shaping, and the shaman shaped it in the air and threw it back like an endlessly flexible mirror of will.

Nita Qwan paused for a single beat of his heart and loosed his arrow without consciously aiming; the shaft of a lifetime, it struck the black-armoured figure under the left arm in mid-invocation, and stuck deep, the charmed stone head of the arrow chewing into the wooden flesh. Its rhythm was interrupted; two of Gas-a-ho's counterworkings struck home, and it tottered and fell backward out of sight.

The surviving rangers gave a thin war cry and dashed for the top.

A volley of bogglin arrows dropped one woman, and then the leaders were in the last few paces to the top, where a handful of bogglins stood around the three remaining armoured figures and a wight, its pale ivory armour laced in purple-white fire.

Ricar Lantorn loosed a heavy arrow into one of the black figures from just a few yards and took a bogglin arrow in his gut. He fell; Tessen came past him, and her bow flexed three times in as many paces as she shot away the screen of bogglins, and Lewen and Cigne passed her, the latter with her sword out. A black hand caught her sword blow, her sword shattered, and she fell with a choked scream, her right hand desiccated, the withered bones falling away from the stump as she screamed.

Sythenhag, the wyvern, flashed in over the trees and stooped on the nearest black-armoured figure. She was so fast that he never had a chance; her talons took him, pulled him into two pieces, and dropped them far out in the lake, exactly like an enormous osprey seizing and then rejecting a crayfish.

Two more wyverns crested the ridge and went after bogglins, taking them and eating them.

Aneas watched one for a moment, and saw the surface of the lake, the still, black waters disturbed only by Sythenhag's wingtips and the ripples of her kill, and the island rising from the near shore, separated by only a narrow strip of water.

He raised his hand and coated the nearest black figure in fire. His fire stuck in ugly gouts, and his will refused his opponent's counter, and he seized on the darkest aspect of his mother's dark art, took all the fear and hate engendered by Cigne's fate, and the black thing immolated in red fire.

It leapt into the lake.

Aneas sprayed the other one; it raised a shield of shimmering purple-black, and Looks-at-Clouds pointed and spoke a work aloud.

The sun seemed to dim.

A hole the size of a man's fist appeared right through the black-armoured form; for a fraction of a heartbeat, Aneas could see the sparkle of the lake through the thing.

The purple-black shield fell, and Aneas's tide of fire fell on it.

It burned. And it made no sound, because the blank helmet of its head had no mouth.

Irene cut Cigne's dying arm from her body at the elbow with one blow of her hangar. Gas-a-ho cauterized it without altering the tempo of his casting, and the last bogglin fell. The wight vanished behind a screen of mirror clouds.

"The island," spat Looks-at-Clouds.

There was a narrow causeway, perhaps wide enough for two men to run abreast.

The keening scream went on.

Looks-at-Clouds shouted something, mouth stretched wide, and ran for the causeway.

Aneas followed, and Lewen, and Tessen, and Irene, and Deadlock, wounded but still game, the acid burn livid on his dark face.

Nita Qwan ran to the edge of the water and released an arrow almost straight down into the water, and again. "Ware!" he mouthed as his third shaft went up into the air. Black Heron stood by him, killing bogglins in the water.

Aneas heard nothing, but he followed Nita Qwan's shaft with his eyes.

A flock of black moths came fluttering out of the dead trees of the island.

They had black velvet bodies the size of fat children.

But suddenly the air was *full* of arrows; sixty rangers had made it to the top of the ridge alive, and fell as the moths might be, they were high in the air and easy marks.

Looks-at-Clouds cast into the moths—a simple, deadly rain of *ops*, a spray that coated moths and arrows, too.

"Go!" Aneas yelled. "Go!" He shouted in silence; he could hear nothing.

He understood that the moths could not be harmed by normal weapons. He laid a carpet of fire across them. But the rain of *ops* coated the arrows in flight, and they went home.

Nita Qwan sprinted for the causeway.

Aneas was right with him, and the others close behind as the surviving moths closed on them.

Gas-a-ho, behind them at the crest of the ridge, unleashed a wind that slammed into the surviving moths. It blew Aneas flat on the damp stones of the causeway; Irene almost went into the lake. But the moths had no defence and no weight; one was spun out into the lake, and the other had its wings bent right back. It bounced on the island, slammed into a tree, and fluttered limply.

Aneas got to his feet. Irene was just beyond his reach; a moth settled on her and she screamed, her arms scrabbling against the proboscis.

Black Heron drew a black arrow from his deerskin quiver. The head was of amber flint painted red. He licked it. And then, fluid, he nocked, drew, and loosed.

The magic arrow punched into the velvet skin.

The moth seemed to collapse; its fluids leaked, as if boiled from the inside, and Irene was coated in a thin black syrup that smelled of turpentine.

One of the black-armoured figures was dragging itself from the lake. It bore the marks of arrow and fire, but it was still coming up the bank of the island, limping.

Aneas took his axe from his belt, and threw it.

It struck blade first, and bounced.

Aneas ran forward, committed, trusting his friends, as it turned to him and grew two swords. Aneas saw it happen; a sword emerged from each arm. Aneas raised his green shield and rolled, passing the thing on his left as his shield of green *ops* took a massive blow and vanished with a *pop*.

He came to his feet, turned, and drew his long sword.

With his left hand, he unleashed a gout of fire into the creature's visored face.

It cut at him.

He stepped off line and parried, and his sidestep saved his life as the black thing's sword went straight through his, cutting it in half.

"Jesus," Aneas said aloud into the silence.

He threw the stump of his sword at the thing's head and tried a lightning bolt. Neither had any effect.

"What the fuck are you?" he shouted. He could hear his voice dimly inside his skull.

Its purple-green sword cut down and he made a buckler of gold to cover his head, and then he was lying on his back. When the purple met the gold there was an explosion of force. Even his adversary had been driven back.

He rolled before the thing could gut him, breaking the strap on his shoulder bag and losing his quiver. He got to his feet with nothing but a curved knife more useful for skinning game than fighting monsters.

All Aneas could think was, *What the fuck is this thing?*

Then Looks-at-Clouds appeared behind it; there was a flicker, and it lay full length on the leaf mould. A massive kinetic blow.

But it rose again.

A pit opened between Aneas and the monster; a curious pit, as it was perfectly made, as if a geometric cube of earth had been removed...

Aneas understood. He threw a lash of white fire, a rope of thought. It caught on the thing's shields, but Aneas cared nothing for the shields. He pulled even as the thing tried to rise, force exerted in the real, even as the black thing flung out one arm and threw a gout of its purple-black fire. The glob struck Looks-at-Clouds and knocked hir down so hard that hir body bounced.

But Aneas had it. He pulled. The thing's arms rotated, and it fell backward, into the pit.

Looks-at-Clouds cast from the ground, rose to a knee as Aneas hurled simple gouts of *ops* at the thing. S/he stepped to the edge of the pit and unleashed a crescendo of workings straight down. The earth boiled. Aneas's face was burned as he scrambled away, and then he ran for the opening in the earth, where two great stones rested against each other like a tent of rock. The sense of urgency had not left him, and he was sure that this could only be done in one rush or not at all. Either they seized the well of power...or...

Farther along the shore were some squalid huts. There were bogglins—dozens of them—boiling out of the huts, one in the lead, two strides from Aneas, and something emerged like a shadow from the tent of stones—another wight.

Krek shot the lead bogglin. It was a long shot; the old bogglin was back by the edge of the causeway. But his arrow was true, and Aneas had another three heartbeats to ready himself.

Nita Qwan, thirty feet away, loosed the arrow on his bow and downed the next bogglin. Then he reached into his belt and drew his short sword and threw it in one motion, hilt first. It rotated in the air like a tomahawk, and Aneas reached and plucked it from the air by the hilt, using the momentum to cut left to right, high to low, through the third bogglin's attempt at a parry and then through all four hinges of its jaw. Tessen came up, her long Irkish sword plucking one off the edge of the pack; then she swept low, even as Lewen loosed and loosed again, a steady ripple of shafts rolling off his fingers, the range too short for the veteran irk to miss. Irene's crossbow coughed just behind the irk's shoulder and Aneas heard the ratchet clack as she cocked again; then he kicked one of the smaller creatures; it tried to seize his leg and he cut into it with his skinning knife and thrust with his sword.

Nita Qwan was coming closer; a step, an arrow, then another step.

The wight cast. The range was too close; Aneas could not cover the blow, and white fire struck his shoulder, annihilated his amulet, and his skinning knife fell to the ground. He stepped right and cast, a weak, one-word working, and snapped a rising true edge cut that rolled into a thrust with Nita Qwan's broad-bladed short sword in the same tempo.

The wight made a human mistake—the instant of decision as to which sword should cover the center, complicated by trying to shield itself against the hermetical attack. Aneas's thrust went into the joint where the shoulder chiton met the elastic neck; the wight stumbled, both swords cutting reflexively—Aneas passed to the left, his countertempo exact, and he severed the wight's right sword from the stalk of its armoured arm even as the second sword reached for him; the tip cut his leather coat and scored into his arm, but he was inside, his hand turning; the wight's chitonous arm tried to turn, lost the race, and his thrust went home into its face even as Black Heron's arrow went in under its second arm to the fletchings.

The bogglins broke. There were eight bodies on the ground, and the will of their lord was not on them; they turned almost as one and ran for the huts.

Nita Qwan ran past Aneas, an arrow on his painted bow. Irene got another wood-fletched bolt onto her latch and held it pinned with her thumb as she ran forward behind the Sossag.

Aneas made himself follow them. He was wounded; the wight had used up anything he had left.

The light inside the stone tent was odd: dark and light, red like fire, flickering. Aneas understood instantly that it was a vent; that this was a place where the *aethereal* and the real touched. It was terrifying, but he was already terrified.

Irene shot a bogglin at a range of perhaps five feet; the creature was trying to hide in the junction of two great stones and she was not feeling merciful. She latched her crossbow again, working the lever without thought. Her face was set; the network of black left by the moth's blood made her look like a *bain sidhe* from legend.

Aneas reached out. The *potentia* was right there, and unfettered; he drew on it, and made a shield for himself and his two immediate companions.

Nothing came at them.

The ruddy light shone like a glimpse of another reality, which indeed it was; the roof of the cavern glinted like the eyes of an insect, the reflection of thousands of crystals growing in an endless profusion, the points of light stretching away into infinity, lit from below.

Looks-at-Clouds came through the gateway into the fire-shot dark.

"Ah," s/he said. "Ah! Mine!"

There was a flash.

Master Smythe stood beside Looks-at-Clouds.

He bowed, a deep, courtly bow. "My dearest changeling," he said. "A thousand thanks for the loan of your beautiful body." His voice... Aneas was just beginning to hear again, and he sounded odd, distorted.

The changeling shaman wriggled, like a woman putting on a new dress for the first time. "Ahh," s/he said. "Such a pleasure having you inside me." S/he laughed. "The things I have *learned*."

Master Smythe's eyes flashed red. "And now," he said.

He saw Irene. Her crossbow was pointed at his temple. She was perhaps three feet away in the rich orange light, her face etched with black, her beautiful eyes huge.

"And now?" she said, her voice full of steel.

"I thought you trusted me?" Master Smythe asked.

"No," Irene said. "We told *you* to trust *us*."

Master Smythe raised his hands. "I mean you no harm," he said. "And by now, Ash knows I have his reserve of power. Things will become very complicated. You, of all people, need my help. You know what is in your head."

Aneas watched Irene.

"I know, thank you. And things are already very complicated," Irene said. "Looks-at-Clouds?"

The changeling nodded. "We have to trust him. He could kill us all and fly away if he chose. You can't keep a crossbow pointed at his head forever," s/he said.

"I know," Irene said with icy calm. "I'm considering simple murder. But I suppose I shall not." She raised her crossbow so that the bolt aimed at the ceiling.

"I do not like being threatened," Master Smythe said.

"I do not like being called a patricide," Irene nodded.

Master Smythe looked at her and nodded. "You, I understand," he said. "May I? While I have this marvelous advent of sheer *power*?"

He reached to touch her, and she flinched.

Aneas moved toward him, but he was too fast.

"There," said Master Smythe. He had a black egg in his hand. "Good-bye," he snarled, and tossed it into the inferno behind him.

Loomsack Mountain—Ash

Ash's breath of unreality swept along the stones of the shore and into the stream; Mogon's shields shriveled; wardens died at the very moment of salvation, and a Golden Bear, heavily pregnant; a dozen Morean knights who'd survived the fight with the cave trolls, twenty foresters running for safety, half a hundred Morean mountaineers caught by ill luck in close order...

Ash filled the morning air. Even with the loss of his tail, he was bigger than a ship, or a castle, and he blocked out the sun, his wings beat the air, the trailing wingtips black as night, lifting vortices of water off the river's surface, his head already across, his black, forked tongue like a banner of wickedness as he opened his mouth to breathe again where Tamsin, 1Exrech, and Gregario held the rear guard together. Every horse panicked; the wave front of his terror was such that men fell on their faces; Mogon herself simply stood in midstream, unable to act, her great shoulders hunched against the weight of his presence; Tamsin lost her working, her mind clouded.

Now! Ash exulted in the moment of his triumph.

And now? asked Lot, two hundred leagues to the north.

And his life line, his unending reserve of *potentia*, was cut. And in the next moment, one of his precious eggs was destroyed; a little bit of himself, dead.

In one moment, a tolerable risk became deadly peril. Ash rolled, so low to the ground that his wingtips ripped dead leaves from autumn trees, and turned his vast bulk upstream toward the west, where the looming dark of vast ash clouds rose still from the burning craters of the battlefield of N'gara. It took him time to turn; time, his foe.

Not an arrow rose to strike him.

Not a hermetical working leaped to wound him.

Loomsack Mountain—Lady Tamsin

Tamsin had a hand to her throat. She looked *old*, with creases in her face that Gregario had never seen before; her skin appeared tight over her bones, and her hair fluttered around her face.

"Why are we still alive?" she asked.

Gregario watched the immensity of the black-brown dragon sailing off into the west against the leaden sky. The size of the dragon drew the eye like the beauty of the dawn.

He was having to force his body to breathe.

"Sweet Christ," he said.

A hundred feet away, 1Exrech was faster to recover; a different blood chemistry and an immunity to some forms of fear powered him, and his cold, layered understanding leapt to the moment.

He directed his scent glands at 53Exrech, just a few paces away, her wing cases vibrating in agitation. In scent, he proclaimed:

Truth.

Justice.

Revelation of Falsehood.

End of Slavery.

She writhed, her legion almost at the tips of her enemy's spears, and then she inhaled. No countercommand reached her; no uttering of her master's mighty will.

She did not try to resist further. In a moment, her own scent glands echoed those of her former adversary, now her senior.

In their next inhalation, all the bogglins south of the Cohocton River changed sides.

High above, on Loomsack, both Tapio and Master Niko understood immediately.

"Now!" Tapio said.

Niko, the only allied magister who had not been directly in Ash's path, threw a ripple of simple energy strikes down the mountain against the relatively defenceless wardens and bogglins still pressing east toward the ford. Their own casters rose to the challenge, shielding many, but again, the precision of Niko's involvement allowed his castings to penetrate shields and then expand, a single strand of hermetical *ops* exploding into hundreds of deadly filaments.

"I must keep the rest for shields," he said.

The irk knights whose mounts were able to move leapt down the hill; the charge was pitiful compared to the might of their earlier attacks, but the creatures of the Wild at the foot of the mountain were rudderless, demoralized, and had just had windrows of death carved through their ranks, leaving only desperate islands of safety around their shamans. Hukas Helli alone held his people together in a great shield wall, but Tapio left them on his shield side and carved his way through easier prey, and his tired knights simply widened the road made by Master Niko and his choir of magisters, and the survivors of the allied right wing pushed tired muscle to the limit, running north, away from the river and the road, and following Tapio.

Niko and his choir were almost last, covered by Bill Redmede and a dozen Jacks, their bows useless, all their arrows spent, their swords and axes in their hands, but the sounds of fighting had died away. The sun was high; in the east, bells would be ringing the hour for ten. The bogglins were as exhausted as the Jacks; the enemy wardens stood in ranks, their crests deflated, and watched the last survivors of the allied rear guard pass through their lines with weary indifference. Nor did Niko unlimber the mighty working he had ready to his mind; once cast, he would have no further ability to shield them, but he was determined to sell himself dearly.

No challenge was offered, and the Battle of the Cohocton ended, not in glory, but in a stillness broken only by the shrill despair of the wounded and the fatigue of the survivors; a stillness deepened by the silence of the dead.

Then Bill Redmede had to drive his people as if he were master and they slaves; Tapio's knights all dismounted and led their poor, stumbling beasts; Niko was as pale as a corpse and Kwoqwethogan walked like an animal, his tongue hanging listlessly from his mouth. Niko tried to talk to him, feeling guilt, and shame, that he had so overtaxed an ally. He was worried, very worried, that the great warden mage's mind was damaged.

Bill Redmede made himself run to Tapio's side. "How far do we go?" he asked.

Tapio looked at his knights, walking through the daylight woods leading their great antlered elk. "Until one of the animalsss fallsss," he said.

"Holy Trinity," Redmede blasphemed. "What if I fall first?"

Tapio's face was set. "I leave you behind," he said.

South of the Cohocton, the allied army was in rout. The column that had crossed in the darkness had no idea that the dragon was gone; the wave front of his terror had been more than enough. Nor did the rear guard do much better; Mogon walked, hollow eyed, her feather cloak lost. Gavin had lost both his horses and all of his squires, and he walked beside her, his sabatons weeping water as they trudged over a trail churned to black soup by the flight of his army. Ahead went Tamsin, her powers so far spent that she spared nothing for the glamour of beauty with which she usually surrounded herself; Ser Gregario walked his horse and contemplated cutting away his greaves and sabatons and leaving them to rust.

But behind them, it was the bogglins' day. 1Exrech had not just proved victorious, but had tripled his numbers, and in the wake of the shattered allied army, the phalanx of free bogglins marched in close array, unbeaten, unbroken, and ready, if required, to save the army.

Gavin looked back at them. He was trying not to ask questions; Tapio lost, and Master Niko, and the flower of Alba's chivalry. It was a dark hour, despite the sun, but there was a host of bogglins, marching, their spear points glittering. There were certainly more of them than there had been the night before.

He was trying to get his head around that when Giannis Griatzas rode up with a riding horse by the reins.

"My lord earl," he said. "Your horse."

Gavin shook his head. "For Tamsin," he said.

She was too tired to even protest at his chivalry. She needed young Griatzas to help her into the saddle. Once there, she sobbed once, and her hands went to her face.

"Ah!" she said. "My love!"

Under her horse's hooves, flowers burst from the leaf mould; a carpet of Adnacrag wildflowers.

She whirled, as if startled, or under attack, but her face was alight. "He lives! They live!" she said.

Gavin's heart gave a great beat.

Chapter Nine

Harndon—Queen Desiderata of Alba

Far to the south, on the Albin River's wharves, a hundred river-boats and barges were loading under the direct eye of the queen and her officers, barricaded by a line of guardsmen.

Ser Gerald Random stood on the wharf, remonstrating with his queen.

"My lady, you are safer here," he said.

"With the plague?" she said. "Nay, Ser Gerald. There is no safety here. This is the last effort, the last throw. I am too puissant to cower here in my castle; indeed, such is my inclination that I would go if I were the least of my archers, with a bow in my hand."

Ser Gerald paused. "Then I can only wish that I were allowed to accompany you," he said bitterly.

"Hold my city," she said. "Keep my people alive so that they may enjoy victory."

"A victory so dear won that we will have nothing but the shell of a city and the husk of a nation," Random said. "There is hunger in the streets. And the plague is spreading again."

Prior Wishart came up, having overseen the loading of the last of the Order's chargers. "I leave you fifty knights," he said. "I cannot spare more. Even that is almost half of my Order."

The queen put her hand on Ser Gerald's arm. "I would say this to no one but you," she said in a low voice. "But it would be better to lose Harndon than to lose everything. You are the rear guard, sir knight. Hold here if you can."

Behind him, Master Pye called out as an immensely heavy bronze tube was swung up on a network of ropes.

Prior Wishart put his hand on his queen. "Madame," he said. "Even as you command your rear guard, I beg your leave to ride with my vanguard. We are few but we have remounts and I fear for Lissen Carak. I fear everything: betrayal, siege, battle, magic. Please let me go."

She gave him a queer look and returned the pressure on his arm. "Bide, my lord. I have a plan for you, and will take care of my fortress at Lissen Carak, too."

"Belay!" he roared. Two hundred men paused; a heavy hawser was tied off to a bollard. The old master leapt down onto the deck of the barge and eyed the bronze tube. "Cast her off!" he called. The men grunted; the tallow-greased blocks squealed as they took the immense weight. The oxhide and canvas cradle holding the tube seemed to groan, and then the whole contraption swung a finger's breadth, and then another. A nimble apprentice took a sharp knife and, at a nod from his master, cut a yarn, and the cradle came down a hand's width, and then another was cut, and another, and the cradle descended in short jerks, a finger or two at a time until the massive thing touched the barge's supports, and came to rest, pressing the big boat down in the water like a giant's hand, and the whole vessel groaned, and water came in at several seams.

The queen walked up beside Master Pye, where he stood in the bowels of the barge, watching his apprentices remove the cradle from the massive bronze tube. The tube was decorated from butt to mouth with handles shaped like dolphins and with a muzzle shaped like a dragon's roaring mouth. Around the breech were cast the words *Ultima Ratio Humanum.*

"How long, Pye?" she asked.

"Seven more," he said. "I'm sorry, Yer Grace. This cannot be hurried."

Her captain, Ranald Lachlan, spoke quietly to Rebecca, his wife. She nodded and approached the queen.

"Your Grace, the river convoy is already very large. Ser Ranald suggests that the advance guard take the tide and go." She looked down at Master Pye, who was watching the apprentices test the cradle for stress. "And begs you release the good prior."

The queen nodded. "My very thought, Lady Almspend. Ah! Lady Lachlan."

She went back to her officers. She paused to kiss her son's head, and then turned to the city officers. "My lords and ladies. I am determined that we will *all* march today. Tell me of the cost?"

Prior Wishart pointed at the barges. "There is a real risk of defeat in detail," he said. "Even as it is, we have to fear that our enemy will attempt to divide us, Ser Gavin north of the river and we south of it, and defeat us, first one and then another. Any division in our forces makes us weak."

"Weaker still if we arrive too late and find Lissen Carak fallen," she said. "Gentles all, I find this to be very like the fight of two years ago; indeed, it is almost as if the former contest were a rehearsal. But this time we are better prepared: better wagons, better training. Let us march." She looked at Becca Lochlan. "Where is the Count of the Borders?" she asked.

"Your Grace, he marched west two days ago," she said. "On the Market Road."

"Then he will be at Lissen Carak, or near enough," the queen said. "Surely his force will cover us."

Wishart shrugged. "Your Grace, anything we do has risk. It is all … fortune. And the will of God."

She nodded sharply. "I trust in the will of God," she said. "The advance guard will march immediately. All the wagons will go now, empty; I expect them to make Lorica tonight and sixth bridge tomorrow."

Her logistics plan was simple; but the details were complex, as details always were. She was sending the wagons overland, empty, so that they would be at seventh bridge when the riverboats came up and needed to be carried, with all the goods, past the cataracts. Beside the royal guard and the Order, she was out of crack troops; the chivalry was already in the north with Count Gareth and her brother, Prince Tancred. The militias had been summoned; now they had to assemble.

Some had only just arrived home from the last effort, and not since the summer of the great battle in the north, thirty and more years ago, could anyone remember the militia being summoned twice in a summer.

"We will have our most valuable assets strung out on the river and road, and no one to defend them," Ser Gerald said.

"So we will," she said. Her eyes flashed with her old vitality; her hair burned red-brown-gold in the sun, and she threw her head back. "*She either fears her fate too much, or her deserts are small, who dareth not put it to the touch, to win or lose it all,*" she said. "Go!"

One by one, her captains saluted. And then they sailed, rowed, rolled, or marched.

When they were all gone, she moved briskly to Prior Wishart. He bowed deeply; in some ways, with Gerald and Harmodius, he was her most loyal servant.

"I beg your pardon for making you wait," she said. "I share your fears. I have a letter for you, for the royal post houses. You will go like the wind."

Wishart bowed. "I still might have left an hour before," he grumbled.

She smiled. "Not with the potent magister I will send with you to the relief of our fortress," she said. "See that this valuable person arrives alive."

Less than an hour later, a hundred belted Knights of the Order, their squires, and two hundred great warhorses trotted through the gates of Harndon, their steel-clad hooves ringing on the cobbles. Men and women came out to cheer them in their black cloaks and scarlet surcoats.

A single cloaked figure rode in their midst; slighter than the knights, and unarmoured, but wrapped close in a great black cloak with the eight-pointed white cross.

As soon as they passed over First Bridge, the whole array began to ride faster.

Arles—The Red Knight

Gabriel stood on the battlements of Arles watching the roads: east, west, north, and south. Arles stood at the crossroads.

"The gates open in seven days," Michael said from behind him. "Or ten, or seventy. Christ." He clasped his hands and leaned on the parapet.

The plain below Arles was covered in tents and hasty shelters. The autumn air was cool; the smoke of hundreds of campfires rose into the air, and the carefully laid-out camps ran into the distance. Close into the walls, the camps were full, where the Milice of Arles and the phalanx of scarecrows, as Michael called them to their faces, survivors of the Necromancer's worms, drilled and lived. And there were the Scholae, their own horse lines and fires, their small hospital, and the mess tent of their officers, one of whom was now co-emperor.

But beyond, there were rows of empty tents awaiting Sauce's army; the company camp with a skeleton crew of veterans living well and sleeping too much; the camp prepared for the Nordikaans, with fifty new recruits who had swaggered in from the north and who had already proven that they could at least drink with heroic prowess; a camp for the *casa* and another for the guilds of Harndon and their regiment; then more shelters for the Venikans and the Beronese, and then, beyond, in all directions, miles of white linen tape delineating blocks of tents as yet not erected, and lines of fires as yet unstoked, for more soldiers. More and more, lines of white tape that extended as far as the eye could make out their tracery against the black earth.

"Bad Tom tomorrow?" Michael asked.

"Or day after. Every day he stays in the west, we save a day of shipping oats and straw. It will be close, even as it is. And we're leaving this place to starve unless Sauce brings them supplies…" Gabriel shrugged. "Never mind. She's done everything we asked and more; her chevauchee has netted another four hundred wagons and she's filled them with grain."

"And it is still close," Michael said.

"Oh yes," Gabriel answered.

Blanche emerged onto the narrow parapet walk, and behind her was Kaitlin and Syr George Comnena, now Caesar.

Michael watched the horizon. "And Sauce?" he asked.

Comnena settled into a merlon. He produced a flimsy. "Bird," he said. "Sauce is climbing the San Colombo. She says…" Comnena smiled. "A lot of things about oxen. She says five days."

Gabriel nodded.

"Perfect," he said.

Michael turned, so that the setting sun seemed to cast fire across his face. "We're on schedule. By God, Gabriel, I thought it was impossible. And if the astrologers are right, we only have six days. And we *are still on schedule*."

"New motto," Gabriel said. "We make the impossible seem merely really, really difficult."

Blanche laughed. "I'll have it put on the household banner."

"Food?" Gabriel asked her.

She produced a tablet. It was not, in fact, wax; the plain ebony wood held a smooth substance, like fired clay with a glaze, except that the glaze was hermetical. Mortirmir had made the tablets. There were six sets so far; all of them could communicate with each other, and they had an inexhaustible supply of invisible pages.

She flipped through those pages with one finger. "We're preparing to use fifty tons of food a day," she said.

"Fifty *tons*?" Kaitlin asked.

"With four hundred wagons, we can only carry four days' rations for the army," Blanche said quietly.

"Carry where?" asked Kaitlin.

Michael was still shaking his head. "Four hundred wagons..." he said. "And all pulled by horses and oxen who eat—"

Gabriel shrugged. "Don't worry," he said. "If we fuck up the numbers, we can eat the draught animals. Thanks, my dear."

Michael looked back at the setting sun and the plain. "So we have seven days, and a rising tide of soldiers. What do we do?"

"Do?" Gabriel said. "Do? We train like athletes. We practice until every man hates us." He turned to them, and his smile was broad. "We're not going to dick this away, my friends. We're going to do this beautifully. So we will train. For six days. And all our hermeticals are preparing a lovely set of surprises."

"And what do we do on the seventh day?" Blanche asked, and she was smiling before she finished, aware...

"On the seventh day we have a party," Gabriel said. "At least, I think there should be a party."

Morning. Cocks crowed in the town of Arles.

Gabriel lay in bed and looked at the glowing gold in his good hand.

He could hold it up in the darkness and see Blanche by it. It was brighter each day; noticeably brighter since his extravagant expenditures in battle.

"Oh God," he said, and then stopped at the edge of a blasphemy even he did not find funny.

Blanche stirred, frowned, and awoke. "Gabriel?" she asked.

He kissed her.

"My lord?" came a voice. It was Anne, opening the door to the bedroom.

Gabriel kissed his wife. She didn't respond the way he wanted, but put a hand on his chest and gave him the very gentlest shove.

He tried to insist, and she pushed hard.

"Oh," he said.

She shoved him hard, rolled over suddenly, and cursed. Then she threw up, spectacularly, all over the bedclothes.

Arles—Empress Blanche

"Pregnancy," Kaitlin said, shaking her head. "Honestly, women should stick to knitting and good books." She frowned.

Her husband smiled. "Surely we're good for something," he said.

Blanche looked pale. "Nothing comes to mind," she said. "Could I have some privacy, please? Doesn't the emperor need you for something?"

Michael sighed and went out into the solar. Master Julius's quill was flying; the emperor was being shaved. Pavalo Payam had on a magnificent scarlet silk khaftan and emerald green silk trousers tucked into yellow leather boots worked in gold; he looked as if he were the emperor, not Gabriel. The Mamluk was bent over a chart.

Michael pulled a wooden stool from against the wall as the Queen of Arles was announced. She was in men's clothes: green hose and a plain brown cote and a knight's belt. Her beautiful red-brown hair had been cut short.

"Your Highness," she said formally.

"Your Grace," the emperor said from his chair.

Clarissa broke from a somber look to a wide grin. "Say it again," she said. Everyone laughed. "I just love hearing it."

Michael walked to the fireplace, poured himself some rewarmed hippocras, and then walked to Master Julius's writing table. He took the stack of copied messages on the board labeled *Imperial* and, with them, settled into his hard chair. He drank off about half of his hippocras.

"Ready?" he asked the emperor.

"Go," Gabriel replied.

Albinkirk. Ser Shawn. Multiple reports of Odine activity west of Albinkirk. Observed Odine emergence in standing stones personally. Request Magister immediately.

Lissen Carak. Abbess Miriam. Multiple sightings of Odine-infected creatures in townships. Screening process in place. Choir to cast Al Rashidi counter tonight. Pray for us. Four thousand, two hundred and six laborers employed on field works; am concerned for their camp. Request military support.

Harndon. Desiderata in person. Advance guard under Ranald Lachlan on river for Albinkirk fastest route. Harmodius with Lachlan. Plague attacks in Harndon now sporadic. Will accompany rear guard in person.

Southford. Prince Tancred. Allied reserve army moving west . . .

Michael looked up. "Did we order that?"

"Nope," Gabriel said. "Gareth Montjoy has a mind of his own and no great love for me."

Michael looked down again . . . *moving west. South bank of Cohocton, looking to relieve Ser Gavin. Odine-controlled creatures in woods. Due caution employed . . .* Damn it? Is he wode? He could be supporting Miriam at Lissen Carak.

"The Odine are moving," Gabriel said. "So they think the gate's opening in six days, too." He laughed grimly. "You know, the Odine are awakening to a nearly empty landscape, so the last three years of war may have actually been for something."

"We can hope Miriam will burn them back tonight," Michael said.

Anne's razor lifted, and the emperor raised his head. "Think how fast the *rebel* responded," he said.

Morgon Mortirmir was cutting an apple on Master Julius's table, to the notary's considerable consternation. "The *rebel* was a mishmash," he said. "An amalgam. A multidisciplinary entity of men and Odine in rebellion against the *will*." He made a face. "Apple, anyone?"

"What are you saying, Morgon?" Michael asked. He seldom understood the young magister, who operated so deep in a web of his own perceptions that he spoke in mysteries.

"Ah, apologies," Morgon said, raising his head. "I mean that the *rebel* had…skills, and attributes, and even…capabilities that the *will* is unlikely to possess."

"Do you *know* that?" Michael asked.

Morgon smiled nastily. "I subsumed the last of the *rebel*," he said. "I can read its memories."

As was common when Morgon spoke, no one had an answer.

"Well," Gabriel said. "We'll just accept that, then."

Anne cut away at his sideburns and murmured something, gave him a hot towel, and he sat up, thanking her.

The Caesar, George Comnena, came in, bowed, was bowed to. Took a cup of hippocras, and leafed through Blanche's and Sukey's notes on logistics.

Michael went back to the messages. He read:

San Batiste. Giselle. Accepted reparations from Mitla and added them to rear guard. No further news on salamanders. On my way.

San Colombo. Alison. Four hundred fifty-one wagons intact and on the way. Advance guard at the top. Three days if weather holds. No news on salamanders.

"Nothing from Gavin?" the emperor asked.

"Nothing today, my lord," Michael answered.

"All of those except Sauce must be from yesterday, so we're two days behind with Gavin and he was facing a major engagement at the fords of the Cohocton," Gabriel said. "Time to assume he lost. Badly."

"Pretty much guaranteed," Michael said. "Tell me again why we let Harmodius and Desiderata go south?"

"Because we can't lose Harndon," Gabriel said. "And because the Queen of Alba isn't really subject to my commands."

Michael shook his head. "Don't you find it…ironic that the Sieur Du Corse is a more reliable ally than the Queen of Alba?"

"No," Gabriel said. "Not at all. I've beaten Du Corse twice, and Desiderata still thinks I'm her subject, not the other way around. I am married to her laundry maid, for example. We're lucky she responds to our messages. Listen, Michael. She is a sovereign queen. Despite which, she sees herself as the head of the alliance. For many reasons. I cannot give her orders, and despite that, she's taking the right actions. Let it go."

Michael nodded. "But if she and Harmodius were at Lissen Carak..."

"We'd all sleep better?" Gabriel said. "True enough. But we all have to plan for a world after the gates open and then close again. And there's one of the questions no one has asked... how long do the gates stay open? Regardless of it all... even if we win, we have to eat and trade and farm and continue to have lives. Or there is no point to winning. Harmodius has his own agenda, and so does Desiderata, and to be honest, so do Tom and Sauce and probably Cully and MacGilly here. Even Blanche..." he said as the door to the bedroom opened.

Master Julius rose. His report was interrupted by the emergence of the Queen of Alba's former laundry maid, who entered in a purple silk kirtle and a matching overgown of purple wool trimmed in squirrel. "My lord," she said.

Gabriel beamed at her.

"May I just say of my former mistress that she is absolutely loyal; she is, if anything, painfully aware of who kept her on her throne and saved her from the stake, and nothing short of death would keep her from the coming fight." Blanche found her voice shaking. She was still, in her heart, a loyal servant of the crown of Alba.

Michael rose and bowed. "I'm sorry, Your Highness," he said. "I..." He paused. "I am afraid," he admitted.

"We are all afraid," Gabriel said. "Revel in it; it is the bond that holds this alliance together. Master Julius?"

"Highness," the notary said. "I have a report from your astrologers."

"Go on," Gabriel said. Anne had his doublet; MacGilly had his hosen.

"Highness, they have repeated their experiments and they wish to report directly to you. But in brief..."

"Thank God," Michael said, *sotto voce*.

Master Julius glared. "...in brief, they are more certain of their date and time. They wish to discuss other ramifications."

"Yes," Gabriel said.

"When, my lord?" Julius asked.

"Now," Gabriel said.

Michael poured them both more hippocras.

"I'll be drunk as a lord," Gabriel muttered. "Which may be the best way to spend the next five days." He reached out to take the cup, a plain cup of red-brown earthenware.

Michael could not control his gasp of astonishment. "Holy Mary Mother of God," he spat.

Against the red-brown of the cup, the emperor's natural, human hand glowed like hot metal.

Every head turned.

Blanche stood. "Michael," she said firmly.

Gabriel was looking at his hand, too. "Damn," he said.

Then he looked at Michael. "Yes," he said.

"Oh my God," Michael said.

"Please don't call me that," Gabriel said.

There was nervous laughter. Payam frowned at the implied blasphemy while Clarissa laughed aloud. But the laughter was interrupted by Magister Bin Maymum and Magister al-Shirazi. Both of them looked fresh, well dressed. Surprised at all the laughter.

Bin Maymum unrolled a scroll dense with equations.

"Gentlemen, ladies." Gabriel took his hosen from MacGilly. "You'll note I still have to put these on one at a time."

There was further laughter, especially from the veterans.

As Anne and MacGilly began on the laces, he turned to face the scholars. "Please begin," he said.

"Highness," Bin Maymum began. "As you requested, we reperformed all of our observations from this point, and confirmed our timing." He looked at Blanche and bowed. "As Her Highness requested, we examined some of the errors we have observed, and we examined the errors in light of what we now know of gate locations." He nodded, and looked at his companion. "What follows is more in the line of a theory than an established fact."

Gabriel was getting a skin-tight scarlet doublet pulled over his torso. He had a variety of small wounds and his left shoulder still burned whenever he rotated the arm in his socket; he made a face as MacGilly tried too hard on the left sleeve.

"Stop!" he spat. "Not you, sir. MacGilly, I am not one of your fool sheep. Have a care."

The Hillman flushed.

Anne came over to the left side and deftly ran the tight sleeve up the arm without twingeing his shoulder. "Force is not always the answer," she said.

"Everything I do is wrong," the Hillman said bitterly. And froze.

Anne pointed. "Out," she said.

MacGilly looked horrified, humiliated; so upset that Gabriel felt for him. But Anne was right.

He began to lace his own doublet. "Give me your theory," he said. "You have two minutes."

"Highness, we think the gates will open in a sequence, at intervals, and not all at the same time. The sequence is not alterable, and is dependent on the constellation that dominates the particular gate." The Yahadut scholar tugged at one of his side locks and looked as nervous as MacGilly.

Gabriel stopped wriggling in the doublet. "Say that again," he said.

The Yahadut nodded. "There are at least seven gates, my lord, and you yourself have posited as many as fifteen."

Gabriel nodded and looked at Morgon, who had his hands steepled in front of him and his eyes closed. "Or twenty-two," Morgon said.

"Dame Julia's experiments were aimed at the only gate whose location she knew for sure," al-Shirazi said.

"Lissen Carak," Gabriel said with something like satisfaction.

"Yes, my lord. That is—"

"By God!" Gabriel said. "That is to say there's something like a three-day difference between Arles and Lissen Carak."

The eastern scholar bowed. "You have it."

"In our favour," Morgon said.

"How is it in our favour?" al-Shirazi asked.

Morgon's eyes were still closed. "It is not as if the opening of this gate leads us to Lissen Carak," he said, as if this was obvious.

"*Would you be lord of all the worlds?*" Blanche said quietly.

Gabriel closed his eyes and engaged that part of Al Rashidi's borrowed memory palace that showed him maps. Not really maps. More like pilgrim itineraries; lists of locations.

"Pavalo," he said. "You say you led the raid on the lost library..."

"Yes," Payam said.

"You saw these…maps. Charts. Itineraries." Gabriel didn't look at him.

"Yes. I saw them. I took pictures of them with my mind, and gave those pictures to my master." Payam's voice was rich and low, but somehow it contained a sense of a great fear, conquered.

"How old were they?" Gabriel asked.

"Very old," Payam said. "As old as the oldest things in the library."

Gabriel still didn't open his eyes. "When did the not-dead attack the library?" he asked.

"Before the *rebel* even existed," Morgon said. "Yes, Gabriel; I agree. This game has gone on a long time."

"Is there any way Ash can assume, or believe, or even guess we have these lists?" Gabriel said.

"It depends on whether we think that the *rebel* had allies," Morgon said.

"So much to fucking *know*," Gabriel said in frustration.

Blanche nodded. "Yes, my lord. But now you have three days, where before you had none." She smiled hesitantly.

George Comnena shrugged. "Very well, I'm the slow one. Why?"

Gabriel opened his eyes. "Here it is, George. The gates do not all interconnect. That is, you cannot go from each gate to any location. Imagine them as seaports, with a variety of seas beyond. It is easy to reach Galle from Liviapolis, and easy to reach Genua from Harndon. Yes?"

Michael blinked. "Damn," he said. "I thought we were going to—"

"Yes," Gabriel said. "I rather hoped we'd just march through and fight, too. But it doesn't work that way. Al Rashidi had the master lists; now Morgon and I have them."

Michael took a couple of breaths as the reality of it all hit him. "We're going to other worlds."

"We're taking the largest human army since Aetius won Chaluns to other worlds," Gabriel said.

The silence was absolute.

"And we will have three days to cross those worlds, locate the correct gate, win it from Ash's allies, and go through to face Ash," Gabriel said.

"Oh God," Michael said. But he smiled, because Gabriel was smiling. "But that's good?"

"Better than no days at all," Morgon said.

Michael rose. He looked at the star charts, understanding little of what he saw. "But," he said, "but... it takes a key, does it not? To open a gate?"

"You are wearing it," Gabriel said. "Or so we hope."

Blanche looked away. Clarissa sighed.

"So many hopes," the Queen of Arles said.

The Inner Sea—Aneas Muriens

Aneas and Master Smythe were the last awake. The dead were buried; the wounded tended as best as could be managed.

"When will Orley come?" Aneas asked. "I do not want to wait."

Master Smythe was smoking. "He must come immediately, or not at all," he said. "But either he comes in the next day, or Ash comes in person, and takes back the well; in which case, no power of ours can stop him."

Aneas nodded, and took the proffered pipe.

"Or he does not come. Once I have attuned the well to me, Ash cannot take it back without coming in person. Orley must strike soon. And thanks to the wyverns, we can watch his approach."

"He could come tonight," Aneas said. "We have not scouted him today."

"You grant him superhuman powers," Master Smythe said. "Our enemy could come tonight, in which case, I would stand here, half attuned, and probably die facing him in single combat. But in a day or so, I will have a limitless source of power, deeper and greater than my power in the circle of the Wyrm in the Green Hills, and even there, you will notice, our great enemy has never chosen to challenge me."

"There is a well?" Aneas asked, daring, in his fatigue, to question the dragon.

"Something like one. It is more a coincidence of aesthetics and other forces, but you may think of it as a well, if you wish." Master Smythe reached for the pipe. "Cover me for another day."

"I would stay longer than that for the chance of crossing swords with Kevin Orley." Aneas narrowed his eyes and they glittered in the near darkness.

Master Smythe smiled darkly. "Your people need rest. They have taken casualties; humans spend time mourning, in my experience. And are better for it."

"Dragons do not mourn?" Aneas asked.

"Dragons, in my experience, seldom have the fellow feeling that would create the necessary condition for mourning. Rejoicing is more usual." Master Smythe blew an excellent smoke ring at the moon.

"But you will not remain here?" Aneas said.

"I may," Master Smythe said after a long exhale. "I am still weak, and badly injured. This animation you are looking at is made of catch and clay; I cannot take the form of a dragon, I could no more fly than... than you. Indeed, I came within the changeling's whim of being unmade. If I did nothing but hold this place, I would still serve your need."

Irene stepped onto the moonlit beach. "Our need?" she asked. "Are we not your tools, Master Dragon?"

Master Smythe took the pipe and inhaled deeply. And then passed it to her. "I have tried my very best to treat you as allies," he said. "I fear you, but I do not hate you. Indeed, I rather fancy you."

"Me, in particular?" she asked.

Aneas looked back and forth between them. He felt a curious jealousy; he knew Irene well enough to know that this, from her, was flirtation.

The dragon laughed softly. "Perhaps from time to time," he admitted. "I have often admired the daughters of men."

"So often, that you have spread your fatal seed across all the Nova Terra," she said, when she'd handed the pipe to Aneas. She took a flask from her shoulder bag, pulled the cork with her teeth, and handed it to the dragon.

He sniffed and drank. "Mmm," he said. "Candied wine." He looked at the moon. "Yes, Irene," he said. "I confess. It has been my pleasure to give humans the weapons they need to survive."

"Your blood," she said.

He shrugged.

"Constantly nurtured, and reinforced, especially in the north country," Irene said.

Aneas was trying not to choke.

"And reaching its apogee in the Muriens family," she went on.

The dragon took another swig and handed Aneas the bottle. "Bravo," the dragon said.

"And your rivals never noticed," Irene said. "They missed your entire ploy, and you've had a thousand years to play the game of bloodlines and kings; Ash thought you were raising allies for a war, and instead you were breeding them like racehorses. A race of sorcerer soldiers. Or two or three."

"How *did* you fail to make yourself empress?" Master Smythe asked.

"I didn't fail," Irene said softly. "You succeeded. You succeeded so well that your finished tool is more dangerous than you are, yourself."

Aneas stood silently. He passed the wine to Irene, who drank a long pull.

And passed the bottle to Master Smythe.

"It goes so well with the pipe," he said apologetically. "Irene, even if I allow what you say...still, admit that my way has done men no harm and much good?"

She took the wine, drank some, and said, "Shouldn't this be empty by now?"

Smythe nodded. "Allow me my little ways," he said.

She smiled. "I do not think that Ghause Muriens would agree with you. She was harmed; used as a brood mare."

"My mother was no one's tool," Aneas said hotly.

"How many others have been harmed?" Irene went on.

"If I meant you harm, you would be harmed," the dragon said. "Sometimes people use their own will. Ghause was never my tool."

"You have manipulated us; treated us like horses in a stud farm," Aneas said suddenly. "Oh my God..."

Smythe looked at the distant stars. "You do it to each other," he said. "And I am much better at it. And Aneas, before you launch into a torrent of recriminations because the *patricide* here has uncovered my little plan, may I note that, without me, the gates would still be about to open, but Alba would have no more *talent* at its disposal than Etrusca or Galle? Mmm?" He breathed the pine-scented night. "The pipe is almost dead." The moonlight shone on his pale face and dark beard, and for a moment he looked demonic. "And yes, Irene, I find you attractive. Even your...brilliance." He bowed. "But I will not interfere further. Aneas, I will remain here until I am healed, or until the alliance is desperate. I beg you to protect me against our common foe while I am weak."

Aneas glanced at Irene. "What should we do?" he asked. He bottled up whatever he might have thought about the manipulation of his family as breeding stock for sorcery. The thought might have made his mother smile. Or spit.

Irene met Aneas's eye and for a moment they held eye contact. She looked away first. "Kill Orley," she said. "I will sleep better knowing he is dead." She looked back. "Can we defeat him?"

Aneas shrugged. "We destroyed a great many boats, and he must have pursued closely if he can attack soon. And Master Smythe insists that if he does not attack soon, he will have control of the well."

"So either he attacks soon, at nearly even odds, or never," Irene said, finishing the wine.

"Precisely," the dragon said.

"But we have almost no watch set," Irene said.

"A calculated risk," Aneas said. "Tessen and Lewen can stay awake."

"And if he comes, and we defeat him?" she asked.

Master Smythe nodded. "I am ever more hesitant to offer advice, this deep in the entanglement," he said. "But I'd say, when the danger is past, go south. And find ... Tapio." The dragon took a deep breath, as if he was smelling the air, and he looked south. "Tapio is about a hundred and fifty leagues from here, give or take a swamp. If you go south, you will find him."

Aneas blinked. He was falling asleep on his feet; his head had just nodded to his chest. "Ten days' travel?" he asked.

Smythe's smile was inhuman. "Perhaps not so much. Ask me in the light of day. You need sleep. Even I need sleep." He nodded. "Good night."

Irene kissed his cheek. "Good night, dragon," she said.

He laughed, but only when he was well up the beach.

"Oh," he said to the darkness, "what fools we mortals be."

Behind him, Irene hugged herself. The autumn air was chill.

Aneas looked at her. "You should ..."

"Go to bed?" she asked. She tilted her head to one side. "It is odd; three weeks ago, I bathed every day, sometimes twice, and I was very particular about every aspect of my person; fastidious. Cautious. And ruthless, because I thought that was what was required." She turned and glanced at the stars. "I have learned more from these weeks than from a mountain of scrolls and books. And despite that, this takes every iota of my courage."

She stepped up to him and he flinched; she put a hand behind his head and pressed her lips to his so hard that their teeth bumped.

Aneas was wide awake in an instant.

His heart hammered away in his chest.

Her mouth tasted of wine and cloves; the cloves told him she'd planned to kiss him, which seemed reassuring. And very like her.

He put a hand on her back as her tongue explored his mouth, and tried not to think.

She had no idea how to kiss. None whatsoever. She was clumsy as his first partner. And brave.

And a woman.

Aneas began to laugh. "No, silly!" he said.

"Oh," she fell away. "Oh. I'm sorry." Her eyes were bright. "I had to try."

He looked at her in the moonlight.

"I am a fool . . ." she began.

"Shut up," he said.

"No, it's alright. I thought perhaps—"

"Irene," Aneas said.

"I'm sorry," she said, stepping back.

"Are you," he might have said, "*so very intelligent that you are an utter fool?*" but he was wise enough not to need to ask. Instead, he put his mouth over hers, carefully. Her eyes widened. One of her legs rose off the ground and then went back.

She swayed.

"Oh!" she said, breaking free.

Aneas bowed. And grinned.

"Oh," she said again.

"Now, do we roll dice for Looks-at-Clouds?" Aneas asked.

Irene giggled. "No," she said. "Ohh," she said softly. She broke away. "Oh," she said again, and shook her head. "Shouldn't we be on watch?"

"I have stood some watches this way," Aneas said.

"Really?" Irene asked. She kissed him again. "No," she breathed. "I wouldn't notice a dragon landing. Oh, what a traitor the body is." She slipped away. "Watch. I am not going to lose a battle to Kevin Orley because I have discovered kissing."

Aneas laughed. "I have just discovered something greater than my hatred for him," he said. "But I will kill him."

Irene had slipped away, but she paused and looked back. "Not if I kill him first," she said. "Now we're on watch. Let's watch."

Aneas laughed to himself when she had gone to her post. He tasted her cloves in his mouth, and thought about Ricar Fitzalan. And being Duke of Thrake.

Redesdale—Ser Gavin Muriens

Redesdale was widely considered the western limit of Alba. *No king's writ past Redesdale* was a saying, and the words *west of Redesdale* were synonymous with *in the Wild*. Sometimes a wag would use *west of Redesdale* to describe someone who was not quite right, or an idea too mad to be considered seriously.

The wall ran through Redesdale. It was a curious place on the wall; the Rede was a small stream with rust-red water running out of the big iron deposits at Luckhead and down into the Cohocton, out of sight but very close to the north. The terrain west of the wall was rolling hills with ponds and marshes at their feet, and the Empress Livia's military road, built of layers of stone over a crushed stone foundation, headed west across the ridges on the south bank of the Cohocton, all the way west to Dykesdale, where Livia had lost a battle and a legion and the will to continue conquering the Nova Terra, almost two thousand years before.

The wall at Redesdale had intact towers every mile, which were sometimes garrisoned by the small town's militia, and a fortified, triple-turreted gatehouse. The gatehouse had been rebuilt twenty times on old foundations, and the great marble statue of the empress herself had been knocked down, re-erected, beheaded, and had the head replaced countless times by various monsters and administrations. Her cloak had been so damaged in the years of the past that the stubby remnants looked like wings, and locals called her *The Angel* or *Winged*

Livia. Courting couples came to touch her, and her feet, in military sandals of a lost age, were worn smooth. The iron portcullis of the central gate, a huge and very imposing piece of work, had thousands of locks of hair tied to it, so that it appeared furry in the weak autumn sunlight. Enterprising swains climbed to the top rungs to prove their love.

Behind the gates ran the wall road, about thirty paces east of the line of the wall; heavily built with rain gutters, mile markers, and decaying post houses. In times past there had been a great military bridge at Redesdale; the last bridge over the Cohocton. It had been broken in the time of the old king; the piers still stood. And on the other side, the road could be seen, running along inside the wall, and the wall itself still stood almost fifteen feet tall. In times of peace, it made an excellent sheep barrier.

The Earl of Westwall rode up at sunset with Ser Gregario and six hundred knights and men-at-arms at his heels. The rest of the army was strung out for ten miles behind him, and he had ridden ahead to get the gates open and to see if there was anything to be had out of the town, in the way of hot food or barracks space. His people were on their last legs; men shuffled along the road, barely lifting their feet, hollow eyed and slack jawed. In the day and a half since Ash descended from the dark heavens screaming his rage, the army had never stopped moving. Their commander kept them moving, terrified that the great dragon would come back and finish them while they were defenceless.

The towers were manned, and the gate; local Redesdale militia in russet red wool cotes over browned maille; hard men and women who lived on a frontier and saw more fighting than most militia, every year. They numbered in the mere hundreds, but their well-oiled gear and clean swords gave Gavin hope.

"Milett, my lord," said the grey-haired man at the gate in a nice Etruscan kettle helm. "I'm the capt'n, right eno; hight Ralph Milett. I ha'e six hundred good people; another thousand in my arriere ban, but they're mostly unarmed and good for digging; small folk, and tenant farmers, and new folk out from the east."

Milett said *east* as if it was a curse word.

Ser Gavin looked back out the gate. "I have more than ten thousand soldiers coming in, Captain. My people include wardens, bogglins, and irks. I expect my allies to receive every courtesy..."

"Not past this gate," said a man in a fine maille shirt.

There was grumbling.

The Green Earl backed his horse. "Listen up," he said. "I only have an army because the wardens and the bears and the bogglins and the irks fought like lions to keep us in the thing. My people have fought six times in three weeks. Any of you *farmers* have any idea what that means?"

"No need to insult us," Milett said. "There's good men here who ha'e faced the Wild. Good *men*."

"No fucking monster is passing my wall," said another man.

"Stow it, Rob Hewitt," the captain said.

"We'll all be kilt," the man said. Others nodded.

Gavin shook his head. "Listen, gentles. We are *allies*. We are fighting the enemy *together*."

"Monsters *are* the enemy," the first man said. "And who are you, any road?"

"I'm the Earl of Westwall," Gavin said. "And you?"

"I'm a free farmer, Rob Hewitt by name, and I take orders from no man. Monsters are the fuckin' enemy of man; allies o' Satan..." He looked around.

Gavin could see that he had some support.

Gavin leaned forward. "Well, Master Hewitt, I'm the queen's commander for the west, as well as your feudal lord."

"Feudal lord? I wipe my arse—"

"Stow it, Rob," said another.

"That's Jack talk," the captain said.

"Let him have his say," Gavin said. He dismounted, and his worried squire dismounted and took his horse.

"You come here, lording it, and I say, fuck off to yer castle and leave us be. We need none o' ye." Hewitt stood his ground, hands on hips. Men nodded.

Ser Gavin pursed his lips. "Master Hewitt, I have ten thousand men and monsters who've spent the last six weeks fighting so that you can farm."

"Dogswaddle," Hewitt said. "We protect our own. Don't need you."

"They will be coming down this road," Ser Gavin continued, "all night and into tomorrow and I expect you to feed them and help them build a camp..."

"Who's payin'?" Hewitt asked. "Not my food!" He laughed. "Show me yer gold."

The militia captain looked pained. "My lord," he began.

"Nah, we'll have no 'milord' here." Hewitt waved at the men who stood behind him. "Will we? No lords an' no monsters."

Gavin pushed forward. There was now quite a crowd of men in the three gates—militia, but also Albin knights and squires. Ser Gregario followed him, and a dozen others.

Hewitt stood his ground.

"I command you to let us pass," Gavin said formally.

"Sod off. There's another road north o' the river," Hewitt said. "An' no free farms to mess about."

"This is treason," Ser Gavin said in a reasonable voice.

Hewitt shrugged. "War an' plague is all the kingdom has ever brought us. You want to bring monsters in the gate? You're the fuckin' traitor. Everything we have here, we made. None of it is yours."

"Every knight who has died in the last year died for you, you fool. Every knight, every archer, every irk and bogglin who died fighting for the alliance died for you. And you did not make everything; you have an Etruscan helmet paid for by the king; a Harndoner made your sword; the wall was built by Livia, not by you. Your roads are maintained by the queen."

"Words," the man said. "Empty words."

More and more of the chivalry were packing into the gate.

No weapons had been drawn yet.

Gavin was now nose to nose with Hewitt.

"If I order my knights to take the gate," Gavin said, "you will die."

Hewitt drew his sword. "A lot of you will die..." Hewitt raised it, point first, and he put the point threateningly on Gavin's breastplate. "You first."

Gavin took his sword away. He grabbed the blade with his left hand and rotated the man's arm, stripping the weapon with his steel-gauntleted hand, and his right hand shot out, caught the other man's armoured shoulder, and threw him effortlessly to the ground.

Swords leapt from scabbards.

"This is not what I expected in the first chartered town of Alba," Gavin said. He had the farmer's sword at the prostrate man's throat. "Treasonous talk and ingratitude."

"They're just a faction," Captain Milett said. "I'm sorry, milord."

"Behind us on the road," Gavin said, "is an army of a million monsters, led by a dragon as big as your town. A *million*, Captain. When the morning comes, look west. See the columns of smoke rising there. The arch enemy raised volcanoes, mountains of fire, from the ground by magic. That is our foe. All free peoples stand together. The world teeters on a razor's edge." Gavin looked at the man at his feet. "I will not hesitate to put the entire population of your town to the sword to prevent defeat. Do you understand?"

The captain shook his head. "It don't ha'e to be this way—"

"Apparently it does. So let's understand each other, gentlemen. My people will take control of the gate. Then we will lay out the ground for a camp, and you will bring food. If we do not receive enough food, we will come and take it. I don't have the time to be nice, so I will kill anyone who gets in my way. And Captain, if you tolerate any more of this treason, you will become my enemy. I hold you responsible, personally, for your people. I will keep Master Hewitt, and these twenty men with him, as hostages." He turned to Gregario. "Take this man."

Ser Gregario nodded. "With pleasure," he said. "On your feet, traitor."

Alban and Brogat knights moved rapidly through the gate. It was clear that the militia contemplated resistance, but they thought too long about it, and there were armoured men-at-arms everywhere.

Gavin stared down the militia captain. "I had hoped to find friends here," he said sharply. "Do not make me treat you like a conquered populace. I need food for ten thousand men."

"Milord," the captain said. "No one will give their food willingly. Folk could starve come winter."

"This will be a hard winter for everyone," Gavin said. "Harder still if Ash wins."

"You'll eat well eno'," spat a disarmed militiaman. "Grow yer own food, ye fuckin' noble."

Gavin ignored him. "Food," he said. "About twenty tons of it."

"Twenty tons?" Milett paled.

"Five hundred head of cattle, and five tons of grain," Gavin said.

"You will beggar us!" Milett protested.

Gavin tried to keep his savage reaction at bay. He was too tired to shrug. So he looked back, where his two surviving squires and

Ser Gregario's household had a dozen militiamen who'd stood with Hewitt under guard. "Food," he snapped. "Now."

The army's baggage arrived next, and then the army itself. Despite the losses at the fords, the baggage had escaped; tents sprang up, and fires were lit from firewood provided by scared-looking yeomen with heavy wagons of their own. With the baggage came the militia of Brogat and Albin and the Morean spearmen; Thrakian veterans who had marched with Demetrios and were now doing their penance for former treason in the Army of the West. The guild bands of Lorica were in once-gaudy purple and gold, so faded from the long campaign that the hues almost matched the leaves on the trees.

Behind the Moreans came the Long Dam bears, now led by Stone Axe and Elder Flower. The bears were footsore and dull-eyed, although they gave great growls when they could smell the cooking from over the wall. A small huddle of locals watched them come in, and there were jeers.

Then came the wardens, led by Mogon.

No one jeered. The wardens projected fear, and the crowd simply melted away. Mogon accepted an armoured embrace from Ser Gavin and saw her people into two stone barns seized for that purpose.

The N'gara irks marched in, heads high, in their shining maille of bronze links, with Tamsin riding at their head, but there was no crowd to see or greet or curse. The irks went into tents; enough men had died to leave a surplus of them.

"Thirty days of retreating and we haven't lost a wagon," Gavin said bitterly.

Ser Gregario was out of his harness for the first time in weeks. He shrugged and swallowed more roast beef. "*Grumf*," he said around his fourth plate of food.

They were sitting in Ser Gavin's great green pavilion, lined in green wool and heated by braziers full of charcoal. "*Grumf?*" he asked.

Gregario wiped his mouth. "What I meant to say is, we haven't done so badly."

Gavin nodded. "I have lost almost half the army," he said.

Gregario gave a wry smile. "Looked at another way, you've preserved more than half the army," he said. He rolled more beef in good white bread and ate it. "My clothes are dry," he said. "What happens now?"

Gavin stretched out his booted legs. "We have to take a day," he said. "We only have Tamsin and some minor university types for hermetical defence, so we can't fight. We need to get under the defences of Lissen Carak as soon as we can."

Gregario nodded. "Over the bridge at Lissen Carak?" he asked.

"Yes," Gavin said.

Gregario nodded. "So we need to beat the enemy to the bridge," he said.

"Yes," Gavin said. "And we need to find Tapio. I was hoping to convince the militia to put boards over the piers at the river; the old bridge piers."

Gregario frowned. "That seems unlikely," he said.

Ser Gavin nodded agreement. "Give everyone a few hours of sleep and another meal, and we'll march," he said.

He was still yawning, but he took a pen case and began writing a dispatch. It occurred to him that he was almost thirty hours late in writing about the Battle of the Fords, and that there would no doubt be panic in some quarters.

He had a thought and woke Griatzas. "Sorry, lad," he said.

His Morean squire looked like an eyeless mole resisting the light. "Mmm?" he mumbled.

"I need you to find Lady Tamsin," he said. "And one of the imperial messenger officers. Quick as you can, and then you can go back to sleep."

If Tamsin had been asleep, she showed no sign, and if she was worried that her powers were all that stood between the army and extinction, she showed no sign of that, either.

"Gavin?" she asked in her low voice and she straightened from entering the pavilion's low door.

He rose and bowed. "I'm sorry to wake you, Your Grace," he said. "Can you magick a messenger bird to find Tapio?"

She considered only a moment. "Yes," she said.

Gavin nodded. "If you do this," he said, "Tapio will have a bird. And once he has one, he can start communicating with us. And with Alcaeus and Gabriel." Gavin was tapping his teeth with a quill.

Tamsin laughed. She reached out a motherly thumb and wiped ink and spit from the corner of his mouth. "You look like a child who has eaten too many berries," she said.

337

"Damn," Gavin said, looking at the ink, and then he subsided and allowed the Faery Queen to use her powers to remove it. "I'm glad I can still be funny," he said.

She smiled. "A little sleep and the world will be bright again," she said.

"Really?" Gavin asked.

She shrugged. "It is better to think so, is it not?" she asked. When the messenger arrived, a great black-and-white bird on her fist, Tamsin talked to the bird at length, and B.13 cocked her head to one side as if listening intently.

"Does she understand?" Gavin asked. "What does she say?"

"She says, 'More chicken,'" Tamsin answered. "That's mostly what they say, to tell the truth."

Grazias entered and bowed. "Captain Redmede to see you, my lord."

Gavin sat back.

Harald Redmede came in. He didn't bow. "The enemy has passed the fords," he said. "He is moving the whole host east. Some bogglins crossed the ford this morning and probed the rear guard." He smiled. "They found something they like; they're all with 1Exrech now."

Gavin sighed. "And the dragon himself?"

"Not a sign," Redmede said. "I'm the last, by the way. We're all inside the wall. I hear you had trouble with the locals?"

Gavin managed a smile. "Jacks," he said.

Redmede didn't smile. "When this is over," he said, "without the enemy looming over us…do you think there will be change?"

Gavin frowned. "What kind of change?" he asked.

"Justice," Redmede said. "Justice for the poor. An end to slavery."

"These men didn't want justice for the poor! They wanted to keep their grain and pretend that they didn't need the rest of the world." Gavin looked at Redmede. "You and I have more in common than either of us do with the likes of them."

The captain of the foresters nodded. "It's always funny," he said. "I have passed this frontier fifty times. The men in the towns will join my brother and be Jacks and fight you nobles, but the men here on the wall are the most like Jacks. But they won't call themselves Jacks."

Gavin sighed. "It just makes me tired," he said.

"Imagine how a man who works behind a plow all day every day for some other man must feel," Redmede said. "Listen, my lord. You are a good leader; men follow you right willingly. I say this to you, man to man. Even friend to friend. When this is over, do you think that all these men and women—the militia of Brogat and Albin, the town guards, and the guildsmen—do you think that after three years of fighting to free themselves from a tyrant, they'll just lie down? Do you think that my foresters will ever see the Jacks as enemies again? Things will change. You and your brother can lead it, or you can... be swept away. The militia here? Certes, they're foolish and pigheaded and hidebound. But what they say..."

Gavin leaned back. "Christ," he said, "I'm not working you hard enough if you have time for all this political blather."

"It's not blather, my lord," Redmede said. "We're not fighting Ash so we can go back to being serfs."

Gavin put his head in his hands. "Alright, Harald. Point taken. Can we go back to the war now?" He shook his head. "No. Go sleep. We have rested men on the wall and gate. But we'll march in the morning."

"One night o' sleep?" Redmede asked. "That's all? I could sleep the clock round."

"One night," Ser Gavin said. He paused. "Listen, I *do* hear you. We ain't Galles. And my brother... has plans. For real change."

Redmede the elder grinned. "Now that's a better tune. We ain't just fightin' here, my lord. We could be building something. Something new."

Gavin nodded wearily. "If we survive, aye."

After the forester was gone, he finished his dispatch, and sent it off by F.34.

F.34

F.34 rose into the rainy darkness of a September night on the Cohoc-ton, attuned to all the dangers of air, and flew east, skimming north of the river at times, passing abreast of an endless flood of bogglins sprawled carelessly in the mud and sand, asleep; passing above cave trolls and swamp trolls, wights and wardens. Just before dawn she sensed something larger flying to the north and she turned south, away from her goal, which burned before her like a beacon, and she saw the two wyverns in the first light of a cold, wet day and easily outdistanced them, untroubled by their alliance. F.34 was not trained to discriminate; she merely avoided potential danger, flying well south into the Albin and passing, by coincidence, over the great manor house of Weyland, where, in happier times, Lord Gregario had given great feasts and dispensed justice.

Passing over the Albin River, she turned north and followed it to the ford at South Ford, and she flew over the chapel that had been Amicia's where a surprising number of pilgrims had, even in those dark times, or perhaps because of them, virtually buried her altar in flowers and offerings.

She flew on, in the new day, and landed with a rush of wings on the waiting perch in the citadel's north tower, where a black-and-white-clad imperial messenger fed her a whole chicken and detached her tube. Her work was done, but the messenger took the tube down a floor, opened the flimsy, and copied it twice. The original went into a new tube, carried by I.31, who rose into the morning air, helped by a warm current, and raced east even as the sun rose to meet him. The first copy went to E.49, who made the shortest trip of his week, a one-hour flight to Lissen Carak, where his message was read immediately by Sister Miriam.

But F.34 flew on, wings beating, riding a thermal higher and higher into the air so that she climbed over the passes into the Green Hills and then, in late afternoon, a long, fast glide over the western plains of the Morea; Middleburg grew in the middle distance, and she passed directly over the fortress, one of her waypoints and often her destination, but today she had a mightier mission, and she flew on, tired now, but she was fortunate in her weather, and before the September sun fell into the ash clouds at her back, lighting the sky a livid orange, she glimpsed the sea, and stooped, a long, last dive into the waiting arms of a handler in the imperial messenger aviary in the stables of the imperial palace, Liviapolis. She was exhausted, and she'd lost weight; a handler weighed her and passed her to the rest cages, where birds who were not fit for immediate duty were kept.

The tube was taken from her leg by no mere messenger, but by Ser Alcaeus himself, the Regent of Morea. Alcaeus read the dispatch, and was seen to smile.

"Three copies. Ready a bird for Arles; the emperor will need this immediately," he said.

F.34 didn't care; she was already gorging on chicken.

But E.2 cared. She was a long-distance bird, one of the fastest; she was almost never sent on short trips, because of her powerful build and extreme stamina, and now she seemed to quiver with joy; the sense of urgency in her lord's voice was itself cause for joy, because she was going to fly!

The messenger officer brought her a pellet. She knew the pellet meant a mission; it looked like a solid gold bead, although the gold leaf was merely the conductive element for the hermeticist who set the parameters of the flight.

E.2 ate the pellet, and instantly understood. She nodded, bobbing up and down expectantly while her message was prepared.

The imperial messenger took her from her perch and stroked her black-and-white head. "You're eager as a child for Christmas, aren't you, my honey?" the messenger crooned.

"Who is that?" Alcaeus asked.

"E.2, my lord. One of the best." The messenger bowed.

"Such a smart bird," Alcaeus said in a crooning voice. "Will she be well enough, launching into full night?"

"All the star patterns are in her instructions," the messenger said. "She's probably better off at night than in broad daylight."

Alcaeus took the great bird on his thumb while the messenger affixed the tube and checked the seals.

"Ready," said the messenger.

Alcaeus nodded. "You are the heroes, my dears," he crooned to all the messenger birds waiting on half a hundred perches. "Without you, we wouldn't have a chance. Fly fast, my friend." He raised his fist, and E.2 leapt into the air.

She rose from the tower of the stable block to spiral up over Liviapolis, using the warmth of the city to rise against the cool of the air coming down from the mountains to the west, and then she started out over the sea. The sea was an endless pool of spilled ink, the moon just eight nights short of full, waxing, casting a path of light across the black water, and she went fast, her wings beating powerfully; she crossed over the islands, nine thousand feet in the air and with a powerful wind behind her; ignored a handful of lights on the islands where terrified fisher folk stayed high on their hills to avoid the monsters that dominated the deeps. No sea monster gave her the least concern, nine thousand feet in the air, and she raced on into morning, which found her well up a great river valley, passing over Lucrece in the grey light and then turning south and east, straight into the rising sun at two hundred miles an hour.

Before the cocks of morning had ceased crowing, she was eating chicken in the tower of Arles, undisturbed by the triumphant whoop of the Emperor of Man.

"You'll want to read this immediately," Anne said, waking her master. She wondered if she would ever sleep with her head on a man's shoulder; Blanche was curled against her husband in a way that made Anne smile, and yet a little sad.

Gabriel sat up. "Bad news?" he asked. He'd been ready for it for two days. Silence was very bad at this point. Lissen Carak fallen? Gavin dead?

All too possible. So much risk, so few certainties...

"Good news, Your Highness." Anne handed him a steaming cup of warm cider.

He sat up. Blanche raised her head. She was already turning green.

"Bucket is there," Anne said.

"God!" Gabriel crowed. "Oh God. Oh damn," he said, ripping his legs out of the entangling embrace of his linen sheets and leaping onto the cold floor. "Gavin is alive! He passed south of the Cohocton and he has the army, rallied, at Redesdale." He walked out into the solar in his nightshirt. MacGilly was ironing; Master Julius was smiling from ear to ear.

"Chart?" Gabriel asked.

Master Julius had the northern Brogat and the Albin maps open, and he had marked positions on Kronmir's master map in coloured pins.

Gabriel drank off his cider and took a pair of dividers from Master Julius, measured the distance, and pumped a fist in the air. "Damn!" he said again. "On the wall. That was—"

"Almost exactly a day ago," Master Julius said. In the town, the cocks were crowing for the dawn.

"There's more good news," the notary said, handing over a flimsy. "I haven't copied this yet."

It was from Aneas. "Master Smythe is not dead?" Gabriel said. "It's fucking Christmas, that's what it is." He embraced his surprised notary. "Christmas!" He walked to the window. The sun was rising in the east, and the day promised to be fine, and perhaps even warm. Below him, almost directly under the high tower of Arles, perhaps seven hundred feet below, a man the size of a pinprick was moving very slowly. The sound of his activity—rapid hammering—gave away what he was doing. He was driving in stakes.

"Four days," he said to the sky. "Julius, at noon today we start a full-time, armed watch on the gateways."

Master Julius made a note.

Three hours later, Gabriel was washed, shaved, and dressed in plain arming clothes. He went into the lowest levels of the great castle of Arles; down a ramp wide enough for the march of an army. At the base of the ramp stood an interior courtyard. A week before, it had been a hand's breadth deep in mouse shit and dust and spiders and dead beetles, but now the whole floor, the size of twenty ballrooms, shone in the blaze of a hundred mage lights. The floor had an elaborate pattern worked in mosaic: star fields and astrological signs, thousands of years old.

"Jesu Christe," Michael said, and crossed himself.

At the far end of the vast hall with a roof hundreds of feet over their heads, soaring like all the cathedrals in the world run together, stood a huge surface like the rose window of a great church, but dark, the panes of glass unlit. The portal stretched one hundred and twenty imperial feet from side to side; Mortirmir and Gabriel had just measured it. The portal had petals like an enormous flower; close examination showed each of them to contain scenes and words, like any religious stained glass, but in the darkness of the deep, even the mage lights could not illuminate the petal-shaped panels that spread like inky wings and arches away over their heads.

"Big enough for an army," Michael said in awe.

"Or a dragon," Gabriel said. "You know what we haven't thought of?" he asked.

"Everything?" Michael asked.

"Yes, that," Gabriel said. "But there must be some gates under the sea."

"Of course," Mortirmir said. "Why didn't I think of that? So there are more than twenty-two gates. We don't even know of the sea gates."

"What else don't we know?" Gabriel said. "A hundred and twenty feet wide, and sixty feet high at the center." The three of them stood and contemplated the darkling gate.

Gabriel put a hand on the central panel, where the stone tracery that supported all the glass came together in a gold medallion with a keyhole.

"Damn," he said. "It's cold."

Mortirmir reached out a hand and snatched it back. "Interesting," he said, and snapped his fingers.

The underhall was cast into utter darkness.

"Hey," Michael complained. And then he was silent.

Because, as his eyes adjusted to the unrelenting darkness, the darkness itself relented. A very, very faint radiance came through the great rose window.

"Oh damn," Michael said.

"It is starting," Gabriel said. "Assign troops, and casters, to guard it on a strict rota."

Michael wasn't looking at the gate. He was looking at the captain, whose skin emanated a glow slightly stronger than that given off by the gate.

"Don't even mention it," snapped Gabriel.

They stood in the barely lit darkness, watching the gate, which appeared like the sky at the very first hint of day.

"Have the astrologers given us an estimate of *how long* the gates stay open?" Gabriel asked.

Michael looked away, because he didn't want to look at the golden radiance of Gabriel's skin. "No," he said.

Mortirmir was still looking at the gate. "It's one thing to plan and scheme," he said quietly. "Another thing to see this. Gates to other hermetical realities. Think of it. Who built them? The power... unimaginable."

Gabriel frowned. "Really?" he asked.

Mortirmir tugged at his beard. "Well, perhaps not unimaginable. But incredible." He paused. "Harmodius has a theory that when we cast a summoning, we may actually be connecting to other realities. But this..."

"You like a challenge," Gabriel said. "Any idea of how they were made?"

"None," Mortirmir said. "I suppose that if you had a caster at either end in perfect cooperation, with staggering levels of power and near instant access to *potentia*..."

"When?" Gabriel asked.

Mortirmir shrugged. "I have been down here every day," he said. "What you see, the stained glass and the stone, is about a thousand years old. It is massively reenforced. And it was meant to be seen... from either side."

Gabriel started.

"I think that the gates remain open for quite a long time," Morgon said. "More than long enough that the light of another world lit this hall."

"I see," said Gabriel, who wasn't sure he saw. "And how old?"

Mortirmir shook his head, his dark hair just visible in the near-darkness.

"This hall," Gabriel said. "Can we have the lights back?"

Mortirmir snapped his fingers, and the room was flooded with light. Gabriel blinked, looking at the vast, high-ceilinged room.

"This hall was built as an entry point. It is defensible, but elegant." He looked at Michael.

Michael was looking at the floor. "These stones are huge," he said. "Perfectly fitted together."

Mortirmir bent down and looked at the floor. "Yes," he said. "This is very old stonework," he agreed. "Probably not human."

"Why?" Gabriel asked.

Mortirmir shrugged. "It is all theoretical," he said. "But I don't think humans have been here for more than five or six thousand years."

"How old do you think this is?" Michael asked. He'd found a corner in the stone; it was five paces by eight paces. Huge.

Mortirmir shook his head. "I cannot speculate," he said. "Too old for any hermetical resource to read."

"How old is that?" Gabriel asked. "I hadn't thought of using a detection." He looked at Mortirmir. "We're not going to try to hold the gate, are we?" he asked suddenly.

Mortirmir smiled wickedly. "Not if you take my advice."

Michael looked at the huge ramp. His smile was as wicked as Mortirmir's. "You mean, let them in?"

"And unleash hell," Mortirmir said. "The hall is subterranean, the blocks of titanic stone. I can cast anything here." He looked around, and his voice echoed off the stone walls despite the decorative baffles.

"Anythinganythinganythinghereanythinghere..."

He glanced at Gabriel. "I took a lore working and retooled it for distance *back*," he said. "I don't have enough confirmed data points to make my measurement exact—dates of buildings, artifacts..." He glanced at Michael. "I'd kill for something that I *knew* was twenty thousand years old."

"But?" Gabriel was leaning forward.

Mortirmir went and put a hand on the great basalt column that rose from the left side of the gate to the magnificent arches supporting the roof and the whole weight of the castle above. "I would be surprised if this was less than twenty thousand years old," Morgon said.

Conversationally, Michael said, "I am not as well educated as a magister, but I was nearly certain that the Bible told us the earth itself was about seven thousand years old."

"Foolishness," Mortirmir said. "The earth itself is incalculably old. I'm very interested in the matter; our astrologers have some incredible calculations..."

Gabriel shook his head. "This is interesting, Morgon. And yet, I fear, I must prepare for the future. The *immediate* future."

Mortirmir nodded slowly. "I worry that our ignorance of the past will be our undoing," he said. "Why are there gates? Who built them?" He looked around. "Killing our enemies seems so banal by comparison."

"Not to me," Gabriel said.

Gabriel rode out of the castle of Arles in armour with Michael and Cully and Morgon and his squire, and met Count Zac on the field of Arles, the great parade ground that he and Michael and Cully had paced off in person.

Zac gestured with his golden mace. His regiment, three hundred sabers, maneuvered from a column of fours to a line four horsemen deep, every man and woman wearing a scarlet khaftan, a dark fur hat, and deep soft boots. Under their khaftans they wore maille; every horse had a pair of heavy quivers; every rider had a long saber and a bucket of javelins.

And two spare horses.

The Vardariotes opened their ranks, and the emperor and his staff rode in among them. Kriax, the most famous of their warriors, saluted her emperor, unnaturally rigid. Mikal Dvor, the left squadron commander, saluted, and the two horsetail standards dipped. Gabriel rode slowly down all four ranks; looking at buckles, and bruises, horseflesh and arrows. He stopped before a very small man with a flat nose and high, slanted eyes.

"Arrows," he said.

Dvor had to translate. The man nodded, swung a leg over his horse, and dismounted. Then he pulled both quivers off; one economical movement, untying the laces that held the quivers in one pull, the way he would have to do if required to fight dismounted. He knelt, laying out the quivers; sixty arrows, points up, fletchings down. He began to draw them from the quivers. Anne Woodstock leaned forward, fascinated.

Gabriel flashed her a smile. "Let's take a closer look," he said, and dismounted. MacGilly, the page, sprang forward and took his horse, and then took Anne's, and Gabriel, armoured head to toe in his old harness, went down on one knee as the small easterner told of his arrows.

Mikal Dvor, a different kind of easterner, with high cheekbones and pale eyes, dismounted, slipping easily to the ground and nodding back over his shoulder at Count Zac, who looked pleased at the man chosen; *better him than almost any other man in the third rank...*

"He says here are forty arrows for men or horses. He says they have no soul, but they are fine arrows." Dvor held one up: a Liviapolis Arsenal manufactured arrow, with a cane shaft, a light steel head, diamond cross-section, armour piercing point, goosefeather fletch.

"No soul?" the emperor.

The small man spoke at length.

Dvor shrugged. "He is Klugthai, a nomad from so far to the east that it is as far from his homeland to mine as it is from mine to... Lucrece." He spread his hands and winked at Anne.

She flushed for no reason and was annoyed at herself.

Dvor waved at Klugthai. "He says when a warrior makes his own arrows, he gives them something of his soul. But he says he rides far, and eats the emperor's salt, and kills his enemies, and he admits that the emperor's sorcerers make arrows that kill." Dvor met the emperor's eyes. "I find him hard to understand, and I have ridden with him ten years."

"Show me the other arrows," the emperor commanded.

Klugthai held out a handful of arrows. "These five are for very long shots. He made them himself," Dvor translated. "These two are signal arrows; they shriek. Every rider must have one. It happens that he is one of my squadron's best men and has a spare."

Morgon took the arrow. He moved his hand over it. "Is louder better?" he asked.

Dvor repeated the question.

The little man grinned. "*Da,*" he said.

Morgon released the working and handed back the shaft. "It will be very loud," he said.

The small man bowed, clasping both hands and tapping them to his forehead.

"And these?" the emperor asked.

"One for killing horses. One for killing very big things; monsters."

"Just one?" the emperor asked.

Dvor shrugged. "Most of us shot away all our monster killers facing the Umroth, Your Grace."

"Got it," Michael said. He made a note on his wax tablet.

"And that's why you have inspections," the emperor said to his squire.

She nodded, fascinated by the row of arrows left.

"And that one?" she asked, greatly daring.

Dvor smiled at her. "It holds a line. For shooting a rope, or starting a trap."

"This one?" she asked.

The emperor looked at her.

Dvor smiled and the small easterner laughed. "Bird hunting. It is his own, for knocking down game. To eat."

She smiled.

Gabriel reached over and took the easterner's hand. "Tell him that I believe that of all the men who serve me, he has come the farthest, and I treasure his service," Gabriel said.

Dvor spoke. The easterner's heavily wrinkled face, windblown and bright-eyed, broke into a brilliant smile.

"Rose Leopard," he said to Anne, and she fumbled in her purse and produced one—the most valuable imperial coin, solid gold, worth five Leopards. The easterner took it and dropped it inside his khaftan and nodded his head.

All of them remounted. The emperor noted that the easterner retied his quivers *while he was mounting*.

Gabriel raised an eyebrow to Michael, who caught the direction of his attention. "The value of veterans isn't just that they understand war," Gabriel said aloud. "It is that they know how to do *everything*."

The Vardariotes were merely the first of the regiments of the *casa* to return from the campaign in Galle, and as the day wore on, the Nordikaans rode in, and then the guildsmen, and then Ser Thomas Lachlan himself leading the lances of the imperial bodyguard, as they had taken, somewhat mockingly, to styling themselves. Some wag had painted a small banner on silk, the black silhouette of a tusked Umroth with a red line through it *per pale* on an ivory ground.

The man under the Umroth banner was Ser Tobias, and he couldn't keep the grin off his face, and neither could Francis Atcourt or de Beause or any of the other household knights.

The emperor's inspection was detailed and personal, but it was clear that the men were ready; horses groomed, kit clean.

The emperor reined in by Kessin. "You've lost weight," he said.

"Vittles was poor, Cap'n," Kessin said with a smile. He was still a big, broad-shouldered man with a heavy gut, but his eyes no longer vanished when he grinned. He dismounted and produced fifty-two arrows, a long coil of rope, his section of a portable scaling ladder and a clean, rust-free shirt of maille and a brigantine, a steel bridle gauntlet, and a fine *storta*, a curved Etruscan saber. His hardened steel basinet was polished like a mirror and had a fine red and white silk turban woven around it in an intricate pattern.

Kessin saw the emperor looking at the turban. "Which Ser Pavalo showed us a better way o' windin' her," he said. "Cap'n. Sir. Highness."

The emperor walked around Kessin's horse, looked at the shoes, and then back at Bad Tom. "Are all the horses in this good shape?" he asked.

Tom nodded in satisfaction. "The Venikans gave us the best horses," he said. "And I bought some remounts from the Ifriquy'ans. And we just had almost a week on good grass wi' oats." He nodded. "Lookin' good, Kessin."

"He needs a bath," Gabriel said with a smile. "And some food. He's starving away to nothing."

"I am, that," Kessin said.

Gabriel gave him a Rose Leopard and rode over to Ser Tobias.

"Me?" Ser Tobias asked. He dismounted, and began to strip out of his harness, and his squire came forward to help him strip his kit. In a minute, it was laid out on the ground: armour, maille, cloak and eating kit, purse and sword and dagger, a small Ifriquy'an war hammer, and a heavy wool hood.

"You're the newest," the emperor said with a smile. "Who taught you to clean armour anyway?"

"You," Ser Tobias said. "And Jehan."

Gabriel swatted his former squire on the back. "Tom? Any other awkward sods I ought to examine?"

Tom shook his head. "Not a one."

"Ser Michael has your tent assignments. Gentlemen and ladies, the gate is waking up. We will be fighting in four days. Eat well and rest." He mounted up.

"Just like hisself." Kessin nodded to Cully.

Cully made a face.

"What?" Kessin hissed.

"He's worried," Cully said. "I never like it when Cap'n's worried."

Dawn.

There were two stakes in the ground; each stake was six feet tall, and they were planted on the field of Arles, exactly one hundred and twenty feet apart.

Bodies of archers were drawn up facing inward on either flank, their file leaders touching the marker stakes. The *casa* was drawn up facing the area between the stakes: forty knights wide. Behind each knight was a squire, and behind each squire, a fully armoured page.

And behind the pages, ten ranks of scarecrows with fifteen-foot pikes, formed so close together that there didn't seem to be room for men to breathe.

Cully and Tom Lachlan walked up and down; Cully had archers

loft blunt arrows and played with the angle of his supporting wings, and Tom Lachlan moved the *casa* and its supporting block of spearmen back and forth, back and forth. He formed it and unformed it, ordering every man to run for his life, sounding a whistle and ordering them back to the ranks. He did this over and over, for hours, until his knights hated him, sweating through their arming clothes and rusting their newly polished armour despite the chilly autumn morning.

Cully did the same with the archers: run, re-form, run, re-form.

"There's Sauce!" called Francis Atcourt, and every head turned.

The Army of Etrusca was marching onto the field of Arles. And there was the emperor, with a guard of Vardariotes around him, and six Nordikaans in constant attendance.

"I hope she gave the poor bastards a day to polish their kit," muttered Kessin.

"Eyes front," roared Bad Tom.

They broke and re-formed again, facing the gate.

"When do we go through the fuckin' thing?" muttered Atcourt.

"When we've stopped whatever is waitin'," Tom snapped. "Ever think o' that?"

Atcourt shook his head. "Tom, I'm a tired old man. And I know how to form on the marker."

Tom Lachlan didn't snap. Instead, he smiled. "Right ye are," he said. "One more time and we can go and see the company."

He blew his whistle. Then he leaned over to Cully. "Practice shootin' o'er our noggins, Cull. Imagine somethin' as big as a dragon."

Cully went back to drilling the archers.

The Army of Etrusca was preceded by almost six hundred wagons and carts, six traveling forges, a herd of remounts, and a second herd, a vast sea of beef. Dozens of Vardariotes in working clothes came up on their spare ponies and began to drive the cattle into fields and pens already marked, and Blanche could be seen, with her ladies and Master Julius, riding from pen to walled field, counting and marking, inspecting the food supply.

Behind the baggage and the wagons and the food and the remounts came the army; led by the company, hundreds and hundreds of archers; Iris and Elaran, northern irks, and Urk of Mogon, and Cat

Evil and Tippit, Jack Caves and Half Arse, sober and polished within a whisker of perfection. No Head grinned at Cully and he and Smoke saluted the emperor for their ranks and then arrayed the archers as Ser Danved led the men-at-arms onto the field. Ser Milus saluted with his lance and the Saint Catherine banner dipped, and Gabriel found that he had tears in his eyes.

"I feel as if I'm looking at my youth," he said. He hugged Sauce.

Behind him, quite spontaneously, the *casa* was mounting their horses and forming ranks, as if, after four hours of ruthless drill, they wanted nothing more than to stand on parade.

Tom Lachlan rode forward. He, too, embraced Sauce.

She grinned.

"I hear you won," Bad Tom said.

Her grin now split her face ear to ear. "That I did," she said.

The company was in a long column, formed by sections of sixteen—four knights, four squires, four archers, four pages—four wide by four deep.

Sauce raised her baton. "Company will form line from column by wheeling to the right by sections!" she screeched. "March!"

The whole column flowed, every section wheeling as little doors all together, to the right, and the column became a solid line, hundreds of men long, faced in armour, tipped in steel.

"Halt!" Sauce roared.

Silence.

Sauce drew her sword, held it up before her eyes, and flashed it down by her side.

Conte Simone's chivalry began to enter the field of Arles behind the company, riding to the left. Behind them came more troops, and more: crossbowmen, spearmen, Venikan marines.

But among the company, discipline was breaking down; men embraced their friends; wives threw themselves into the ranks; men and women from the company dismounted to embrace their comrades in the *casa*.

The emperor watched them, beaming, and when Sauce's face grew stormy, he put a hand on her shoulder.

"Let them have their day," he said. And with Michael and Bad Tom and Sauce at his back, he rode down the field to congratulate Conte

Simone, to shake his hand and inspect his knights before meeting all the other officers.

That night, a dent was made in the army's supplies of wine and ale, as the two armies renewed their acquaintance and told their stories; tales of the Patriarch's sorcery locked horns with stories of the Umroth; Long Paw regaled his old messmates with the story of the salamander, and had to tell it again for Gabriel, slightly worse for drink, and Morgon Mortirmir. The rear guard, under the Duchess of Venike, marched into a riot at twilight; they had marched all day to keep the timetable, and found not food but drink awaiting them.

Cattle were slaughtered and new fires built, and men and women went from fire to fire, talking and listening. Long Paw found himself standing with one arm around Cully and another around No Head, listening to Duke talk about loading a cannon in the face of a charging not-dead mastadon; Conte Simone sat on an armour basket with a horn cup of wine and listened to Philip de Beause talk about jousting. Sauce spent time with Count Zac, but then found that she wanted to wander and enjoy the moment of triumph, and he wanted to drink with Nordikaans, so she left him to it and walked about, wearing her old arming coat.

She was fairly drunk when she found Tom Lachlan standing alone, looking at the stars.

She thought of walking by, but by then he'd noticed her, and he turned, stumbled, and grinned.

They looked at each other like wary predators.

"I hear you killed an Umroth with a lance," she said.

"A'weel." Tom's grin widened. "Ya' ken, he was already dead."

Somehow, that seemed really funny, and the two of them roared together.

"An' ye warred down yon Patriarch," Tom said.

"He was eashy." Sauce made a face. "Easy." She frowned. "That'sh bullshit, really."

Tom nodded. "Oh aye," he admitted. "It's never easy, is it?"

"They just fuckin' die," Sauce said. "People die." She looked at people around a fire. "I didn't even like Kronmir. And he'sh dead."

Tom nodded.

"Don't fuckin' die, Tom," Sauce said.

"Nor you, lass," Tom Lachlan said. He kissed her, and she stumbled off. The evening was warm, and she shed her arming coat and headed back to one of the fires where wine was being served.

Sukey emerged from her wagon and put her arm through Tom's. "Somehow I always think you two will end together and I'll be left at the post," she said.

Tom looked after Sauce, and then down at Sukey. "Na," he said. "I don't e'en think o' her that way."

"Not e'en drunk?" Sukey asked.

Tom was just discovering that Sukey was wearing a kirtle with nothing under it.

"I'm nae that drunk," he said. He ran a hand up her bare leg to her bare thigh. He growled.

"I hoped not," Sukey purred.

Ser Michael spent the next day passing orders. He had meeting after meeting, most of them in the open on the vast parade field, while a dozen other officers conducted inspections, while armourers tinkered and arrowsmiths passed out sheaves of arrows and horses were fed and shoes repaired and every magister in the host put in a share of time magicking arrows. Michael drew up lists, and passed them: orders of march, subordinate appointments.

By the time the church bells were singing out the midday, there were thousands of men and women facing various problems at pairs of stakes one hundred and twenty feet apart. More than a hundred practitioners, led by Mortirmir and Petrarcha, stood in another field, casting and casting, working *potentia*, passing *ops*, sharing palaces in the *aethereal*. The whole army was treated to a spectacular display as they raised a set of layered shields powered as a choir, each shield like a snakeskin armour, composed of thousands, tens of thousands, of scales that interlocked, and moved, flowed, layered up, and thinned out at the will of the conductor.

The emperor moved from meeting to demonstration to drill, watching, coaching, joking. He watched the mamluks of the Sultan of Ifriqu'a ride into camp; he saluted them graciously.

"No one has done this in two thousand years," he said.

Tom Lachlan shook his head. "What do we ha'e? All told?"

Michael raised a tablet. "Fifty-six thousand, two hundred and seventeen," he said.

Tom stood in his stirrups. "And ye're takin' 'em all?" he asked.

"Every blessed one," Gabriel said.

"Ye're a loon," Tom said. "How many fights?"

The emperor shook his head. "No idea. We have to pass through at least three gates. I'm fairly confident it's three. It might be four. Or five. At least two fights."

"How do you figure?" Michael asked.

"The *rebel* and the *shadow* expect an ally to come through this gate," Gabriel said. "So there's someone on the other side right now."

"Aye," Tom said, brightening. "Who is it?"

"Little green cheese eaters," Gabriel snapped. "How do I know?"

"Ye generally pretend that ye know everything," Tom said. "I just like to see ye squirm."

"And the second?" Michael asked. "Is whoever Ash expects to find at Lissen Carak?"

Gabriel shrugged. "I don't know. Is Ash trying to conquer or defend?" He looked around. "But assuming that the *will* is concentrated there, and Ash is there, then they might have an ally waiting on the other side of the gate. Or one or both of them is leaving, bent on the conquest of other...places." He reined in, looking over the vast, flat field. As far as the eye could see, tens of thousands of men and women were eating, polishing, building, drilling, shooting, wrestling, cursing. The breeze raised little dust devils. The sun shone down, still fierce enough to burn Tom's nose.

"...or..." the emperor said. "Damn."

He turned Ataelus to face his staff. "It doesn't matter. Morgon and I have a plan for the first moments, when the gate starts to open." He shrugged. "And after that we play it by ear. This is as far as the plan ever made it, really. Fighting—a lot of it—and then, when we come through that tunnel, if we win, there will be another set of plans, for rebuilding. For feeding the Albin and the Brogat from Etrusca. And eventually, for preparing to face all this again in some hundreds or thousands of years."

Tom Lachaln nodded. "A'weel," he said. "I plan to get drunk

tonight, and perhaps chase Sukey around a tent if she doesn'a move too fast. That's as far as my plans go." He looked across the plain. "An' that's all your notion o' wha' waits for us?"

Gabriel nodded his head. "Yes."

Tom made a face. "A'wheel, then." He smiled.

Chapter Ten

The road to Lissen Carak—Ser Gavin Muriens

Ser Gavin marched his army, better rested and better fed than in days, into a day blessedly free from rain.

"Where is he?" Gavin asked Tamsin.

She shook her head, watching the skies. "It is like a miracle," she said. "I can say this much: Something took him away in the last fight. Something surprised him, or hurt him. My guess is that Master Niko hit him hard, but I would have thought I'd have felt that." She smiled. "I'm sorry, Gavin. I really don't know. I would like to see Tapio alive. I would like..." She shrugged.

"I'd like it all to be over," Gavin said. "I was tired of being second fiddle to my brother, and now I think I'd happily be a second fiddle for the rest of my life."

The sun rose, and the army marched east. Before the sun was halfway across the sky, Gavin's advance guard reported contact with the Count of the Borders and his prickers, northern horse, and by midafternoon, Gavin had the near infinite satisfaction of bowing to the Prince of Occitan and introducing the Queen of Faery, who sparkled with pleasure.

"You are far west of where I expected you," Gavin said to Count Gareth.

The Count of the Borders nodded. "Mayhap a foolish notion," he said. "But I wanted to be here to support you if you were close pursued."

"As far as I know, I've broken contact, and the enemy is moving along the north bank of the Cohocton," Gavin said.

"I put all my foot into the works at Lissen Carak and came on," Count Gareth said. "Ranald Lachlan and the queen's advance guard should be only two or three days behind me; we should arrive at Lissen Carak together."

"Pray God that the dragon can't break past your infantry," Gavin said, deeply worried. "How is your hermetical support?"

"Thin," Count Gareth admitted.

Gavin's eyebrows seemed to knit together.

The Wild—Bill Redmede

Well north of the river, the Jacks and the irks moved very slowly east, sometimes making less than ten miles a day. The country was broken; the western flanks of the Adnacrags in autumn, with beautiful stands of beech interspersed with vast marshes and alder brakes that ran for hundreds of paces. The irks moved easily, the men less so.

Bill Redmede leaned on his bow and looked at the endless golden leaves. "We're too far north," he said.

Tapio shrugged. "We have to be well to the north," he said. "We cannot afford even the chanssse of detecsssshion."

Redmede shook his head. "My people have mayhap five shafts a bow," he said. "I agree; we cannot fight. But this is mortal slow."

Kwoqwethogan was recovering. He raised his head. "I know these trees," he said. "I know that great burl there, by the stream." He pointed with a bronze talon, and Redmede could see an ancient maple with a burl the size of a farmer's table growing from the side.

"We call him the old god," Kwoqwethogan said. "We are not so far from roads the people travel. Over the next ridge is one of our trails. It runs to the Sononghelan; what you call the Black."

Redmede's heart flickered with hope. "A trail?"

"Broader than my shoulders and smooth as my tail," the warden replied.

Redmede sighed. "Damn."

The Cohocton—Ash

Ash's war of metaphysical logistics had reached its limits, and the loss of his well in the north demanded an instant counterattack. But for the first day, he had to be careful; he'd overspent his resources, and he was vulnerable, and the endless limitations of the *real* continued to cloud his plans.

He abandoned a grandiose plan to trap the remnants of the enemy army with a force of bogglins thrown across the Cohocton with sorcery; he gave up the notion of throwing bridges of ice or even stone at key positions. He had the *power*, but it would have a cost. Even as it was, he knew he'd lost a sizable number of bogglins; some to the enemy, and some simply wandering off to live their own lives or return to their nests.

He rose from the ground at dawn, beating at the air with his enormous wings, feeling the shifting world of the real. To the west, four long columns of ash rising into the already clouded heavens showed that four of the newly formed volcanoes were still spewing. The clouds of ash and effluvia so generated were already changing the quality of the light.

Far to the north, north of the Inner Sea, he had another army, but it was too far away to seize the Sorcerer's Isle. He had set that force to laying siege to Mogon's network of natural caves and fortifications, the heartland of the mighty northern wardens. But they had become bogged in an endless series of small skirmishes that demanded his near constant attention; and the albino warden, Lostenferch, his lieutenant, was skilled at the use of magic but not at the employment of archers, and was wasting Ash's time every day.

Ash dismissed the northern arm of his efforts. *Too little; they will be too late. They failed to distract Mogon even from the prize.*

In the east, he had Orley. Orley had too much of what Lostenferch lacked; Ash was tired of the thing that had been a man and his constant demands. Orley had a force that might or might not be strong enough to retake the Sorcerer's Isle. Ash was poor at self-examination, but he had to confess that the seizure had surprised him; the revelation that Lot was not only alive but newly empowered . . .

Ash raised his head. Orley could never stand against Lot.

And the time, the time, the time. Suddenly there was so little time.

I will have to go myself.

It may be a trap.

How has he done this, my enemy? How has he raised all these forces and disposed them all across all the paths?

They are all against me.

I must defeat them all.

But doubt was now nagging him; the doubt of embodiment, of entanglement. He could no longer see anything of the future; had trouble remembering the pitfalls he'd seen from the *aethereal*.

How did Lot escape me? Why are his slaves so loyal?

One part of his many compartmented selves was moving the main army along the north bank of the Cohocton while another directed foragers and a third prepared workings in the *aethereal*. Too many of his compartments were brooding; counting casualties, trying to understand how many foes there were, from too little information.

I will retake the well and kill Lot.

At some point I will face the will.

Then I will turn and take the gate.

But even that was a complicated future; the ally he'd made and the deal for control of the gate were both gone. He no longer knew what stood on the other side of the gate—friend, or foe.

One of his many busy, planning selves offered a suggestion—of plain treason.

Ally with Lot.

In the physical world, his whole frame shuddered with revulsion.

Never! he screamed.

But the idea was still there.

Arles—The Red Knight

Gabriel had ordered a grand review, but when he awoke the next morning to the sound of his wife retching in a basin, he had doubts. He wondered if it was a waste of time, and his waking thought was to cancel the damned thing. Everything seemed to accelerate toward the moment that the gates were open; everything seemed to be fluid.

Blanche finished her morning sickness and collapsed on the bed with a groan.

Master Nicodemus, with his usual perfect timing, appeared at the door with a cup of something that smelled like *happiness*; apples and cinnamon and peppermint and honey and lemons. The smell filled the inside of their closed bed hangings.

"Oh, you are wonderful," Blanche said, and Master Nicodemus closed the bed hangings and she drank. "Oh..." She sat up.

Gabriel smiled.

"It's not funny," she said. "Not even a little bit."

Gabriel did his best to keep his face smooth.

"I couldn't sleep," she said. "If it's tomorrow, then I will never lie beside you again. I don't want to be pregnant. I don't want to feel this bad. I don't want you to remember me throwing up into a basin."

Gabriel lay back and looked at her.

"It could be tomorrow," he said. "I think this is what I was meant to do, and everything has been preparing for this." He watched her a moment. "I don't have time to hold a grand review. I need to tell Julius to copy out orders and cancel it. It's a waste of time; vainglory."

"Unless it is an important moment for building unity and good morale," Blanche said. She obviously felt better; she polished off her morning drink with relish, put the cup outside the bed hangings, and rolled over toward him.

"I take your point," he said. "But fifty thousand men; it'll take four hours to get them on parade and four hours for them to file off. They could be..." He paused, because she moved closer.

"Shut up," she said.

A surprising amount of time later, she leaned over him, her hair all around him. "They want to see *you*," she said. "It's not vainglory. It's monarchy. Also, cancelling will start a lot of rumours. And it will keep everyone's mind off... tomorrow."

"I know what would keep *my* mind off tomorrow," Gabriel said. He lifted his real hand and ran the calloused palm lightly across one of her nipples.

"Why, kind sir, what *can* you mean?" she asked.

He had new arming clothes. They were scarlet, dyed with the bodies of a type of small beetle found only in the east. Beautifully cut, carefully and lightly padded, they fit him like a second skin.

But in the way of tailors, some of the lacing points were in the wrong places for his new golden armour, and the solar was suddenly full of men and women. The grand review was less than an hour away, and Gabriel stood in his shirt and braes, drinking fennel tea and being besotted with his wife while she and Kaitlin and Gropf and her new maid Beatrice sat working eyelets through layers of linen and scarlet wool and velvet.

Master Julius brought him a stack of messages. The room was emptier than usual; most of his officers were out on the field of Arles, moving troops. Michael came and stood reading over his shoulder.

Master Julius was grinning from ear to ear.

Michael and Gabriel whooped together. "Master Smythe is alive," the emperor said. "It is confirmed."

Blanche looked up. "The queen will be so pleased," she said.

Gabriel nodded. "MacGilly, fetch me Magister Mortirmir."

"Yes, Your Grace," MacGilly said, and he went out.

"I need more red silk twist," Blanche said.

Beatrice rose, but Kaitlin waved her off. "I'll go; I'm up," she said, and she pecked Michael and continued, looking in on her sleeping child and stopping at the window with a gasp. Then she came back with a bone thread winder full of scarlet silk thread.

"You must look out the window," she said.

Gabriel continued reading.

"Aneas took Lake-on-the-Mountain right under Orley's nose," he said exultantly. "Nice work, useless little brother." He nodded at Michael. "He was our mother's favourite after…" He paused. "Never mind. Ash will be weakened now, and distracted."

He read through another, and another, his expression changing. "I am…*concerned* about Lissen Carak," he said. "The Odine are moving and the royal army is not yet in place. Even Alcaeus is moving; he's taking the rest of the Morean reserves toward Middleburg as of yesterday."

"All the eggs in one basket," Michael said.

"What can the Odine accomplish without bodies?" Blanche asked.

Gabriel thought a moment. "I don't *know* anything," he said.

"You really need to look out of this window," Kaitlin said.

Gabriel walked to the window, a cup in his hand, and looked out over the plain of Arles.

There, laid before him like a child's collection of toy soldiers, was the army. The *army*. Almost fifty thousand men and women, a sizable proportion of them mounted; a vast wagon train, grain carts, water carts, knights, archers, light cavalry...

They filled the plain.

Michael came and stood by his shoulder. "The company had a good recruiting day," he said with a smile.

"Fifty thousand," Gabriel said. "Holy...Lord."

The Wild—Bill Redmede

Bill Redmede stood looking at the morning mist rising over an autumn valley filled with beaver swamp and scrubby spruce trees that appeared dark and gothic against the golden brilliance of the foliage on the ridges above.

"We are more than halfway to the Inner Sssea," Tapio said. "It isss very beautiful here. Thisss valley sssings to me. I wish for Tamsssin."

Redmede frowned. "I wish there was more here." He shook his head. "I haven't seen a deer in a day. Nor a track of deer or moose."

Langtree, one of the Golden Bears that had broken out with them, paused to distribute late-season blackberries. "We know this, *grr*, valley," he said. He had a very expressive face; his big eyes were a golden brown. "*Grrr.* Strange, *rrrr*, valley." He swung his linen bucket by the handle, a fearsome warrior turned into a bear drunk on berries.

"Strange how?" Tapio asked.

"*Mrrrm*," Langtree said. "Witch-bears come, *grr*? Come here, *rrr*? Test their powers and grow them, *mmmmrrrr*?"

Kwoqwethogan ate a handful of the berries. "These are *full* of green *potentia*," he said. He took a wooden cup carved from a maple burl and beautifully inlaid in gold and silver, and with a nod of permission from Langtree, he dipped a measure of berries and poured them into his beak.

"Ahh," he said. "Ahhh," he said again, as purple-blue fire played along his back. His red ridge crest engorged and rose atop his head. "Ha!" he exclaimed. "Damn. That cleared my head."

Langtree nodded. "Witch bears say the berries here grow all year."

Redmede handed his berries to the warden. "Be my guest," he said. "I don't fancy being turned into somethin' unnatural."

Tapio was still watching the mist. "I agree that isss odd. Where are the animalsss?"

Albinkirk—Shawn

The Grand Squire, now captain of Albinkirk, had withdrawn most of the population of the Albin north of the river into Albinkirk. His garrison was small; mostly recovering wounded from the great battle at Gilson's Hole, reinforced by a trickle of volunteers and replacements for the western alliance army; two dozen Occitan knights under a famous troubadour, Ser Uc Brunet; a company of Occitan crossbowmen, all borderers, released by the termination of Outwaller raiding in the west country of Occitan, and a trickle of Morean cavalrymen. All told, he had almost five hundred men and women fit for duty; a far larger and better garrison than his predecessor had. In addition, he had all the farmers of the region; this time, unlike their response to Thorn's incursion, they had come in immediately when ordered, and every man and strong woman had joined their militia company willingly.

Albinkirk was packed not just with men and women but with animals, because by Lord Shawn's order, every animal larger than a house cat had been brought inside the gates. Since the alarm at Mistress Heloise's manor house, the militia had been digging out the old moat and fosse; dozens, if not hundreds, of small garden plots were ruined to scrape the old brick clean and dig the ditch back to its original depth.

Shawn had two of Slythenhag's brood—young male wyverns with too much courage and poor language skills—but he sent them out rather than risk his knights or his archers, and they brought back frightful pictures of a countryside suddenly denuded of life, interspersed with views of a field full of various animals: deer, cattle, wolves... all standing together. The Grand Squire emptied his roosts sending out warnings: to the queen, to Lissen Carak, to the Count of the Borders.

Leaning on a merlon and watching her daughter like a hawk, Mistress Heloise shook her head at the orderliness of the castle courtyard beneath her feet. "It is almost as if the last time was a drill," she said. "Or a warning."

The Grand Squire was watching the ground toward Southford. "The queen's army should be passing the falls today," he said. He shook his head. "I hope they are ready for this."

N'pana—Ash

"Ah, my lord." Orley went down on one knee as the vast presence filled the sky and then settled on the beach. The ruins of N'pana had provided enough bark and boards for a hasty camp, and three more invaluable canoes, sunk in the shallow bay, had been recovered, but Orley was afraid, deep in his soul, and angry at that fear. He knew he had failed, when his boats were burned; he knew that his dark master was angry, and he feared Ash as he had never feared Thorn.

Ash had no sooner settled his vast bulk to the sandy beach than he transformed, his enormity gone. A single dark-haired man strode up the beach, a long cloak trailing off his shoulders like a pair of sooty wings, and he limped heavily. He bore no weapon, wore no jewel.

Orley's host stood silent, their tongues stilled with terror. Because the entire wave front of the dragon's terror preceded the tall, dark-haired man like the prow of a great ship.

"How many?" Ash asked. His feet didn't actually touch the sand. His boots were black, a deep black, like velvet or soot. His appearance had an artistic falsity to it; the breeze did not move his hair, nor did the sand stick to his clothing.

"My lord?" Orley asked.

"I ask you how many. How many what, you ask?" Ash's derision was like the cut of a sharp sword. "Perhaps I mean gems, or beautiful damsels." He paused, his face almost slack; thinking, working on something else. Then the life returned. "How can Lot stand to work in such a limited carcass?" His eyes met Orley's, and they were circles of fire, as red and bottomless as the molten rock that burned under the Lake-on-the-Mountain. "Orley. How many useful fighting…things…do you have?"

"Almost four thousand," Orley said proudly. "My lord."

Ash nodded. His face was expressionless. "That is better than I expected. Open yourself." He did not look away, and his eyes, lacking pupils, also lacked any semblance of humanity. "How did you permit Muriens to delay you?"

Orley stood silent.

"Answer me," Ash said. His voice was quiet, and yet it carried through all the ranks of antlered men, twisted wardens, irks, and bogglins. The Rukh shuffled and looked uncomfortable.

Orley moaned. "My lord?" he asked again. "I..."

"Yes?" Ash said. He hissed the last syllable.

"My sentries failed me! And he had overwhelming strength of arms and *ops*!"

"Really?" Ash's voice drawled contempt. "Your collection of *things* outnumbered him ten to one. Your powers are the equal of his; you have other sorcerers to call upon."

"My lord, I..." Orley's voice crawled with self-contempt and irrational anger.

"I hate men," Ash said loudly. "I hate their vanity, I hate their promiscuity, I hate their selfishness, their endless greed, their pettiness, and most of all, I *hate* their failure to pay attention to details. When I have extirpated man, this world will return to its *natural* order. And the details will be properly attended to. Kneel."

Orley stood silent under the lash of his master's anger.

"You failed, and in your failure you exposed *me* to defeat." Ash reached out suddenly and put a hand between Orley's mighty antlers and forced him to kneel with a twist of his hand. "Open yourself, Kevin Orley," he said.

Orley squirmed. "My lord, I..."

"Comply," Ash said.

Orley complied, and Ash flooded him.

Orley tried to scream.

Ash left almost nothing of Orley's personality, although he noted that there was little enough as it was—a poisonous mixture of hatreds and insecurities. He went through them ruthlessly, leaving only buttresses of *himself*.

Thorn should have done this, Ash thought. He restructured the writhing, silently shrieking mind's internal processes and massaged the surviving consciousness into *talent*, replacing most of the mental structures with one of his own, but even this activity was interrupted.

Something was happening in the south. He felt a dozen bogglins slip

366

his control, then a hundred, and the mind he set aside for higher thought
wondered if "he noticed even a bogglin's fall" was humourous.

Ash reached out a hand without turning his head and beckoned at the line of dark, antlered men.

"Come," he said. It was an excellent precaution anyway—to distribute his selves. Insurance against disaster.

Most of them fell on their faces, shrieking in terror, and the smell of their fear—musk, and urine and worse—filled the air. The terror was palpable, like a *miasma*; hundreds of bogglins fell beneath it.

Five of the antlered men made themselves go forward into the fear.

Ash gave them a lopsided grin. "But men are very, very brave," he said. "Really, it is your only talent."

He repeated the process with all five; he rearranged them and made them better, according to his lights, and he imprinted himself on their meat, leaving them very little *self* and a reimagined node that would function only to receive and transmit his will. Each received an entire imprint of *him*.

But he found there were aspects of Orley that pleased him—in spite of its debasement, or perhaps because of it—and he overwrote these aspects of Orley on them all.

He grinned with pleasure, and his grin caused the same terror as his grimmer face.

"Good," he said. "Now you are *all* Orley. A triumph, of sorts." He touched each of them. "No mortal weapon of steel or bronze will touch you, my children. You *are* my will."

"Yes," all six of them said instantly.

"It is almost like talking to a person," he said.

"Yes," they chorused.

He couldn't stifle a giggle. "I am God," he said, delighted. "I can make and I can destroy."

He touched another dozen cringing slaves and made their slavery more abject.

And more efficient.

All of this required an investment of power, as did the maintenance of his armies, the empowerment of his various shields, and the bonds of adamant that held his aquatic "allies" to his purpose.

And through the ties of will that bound him to every bogglin in his host, he felt the further stirrings of the *will*. The process was not unlike the way a cat might *feel* the edges of a tunnel with her whiskers. And Ash's reaction was as instinctive.

Even as the distant *will* began to seize his slaves, Ash drew himself up. He withdrew his will from Orley's monsters and turned to walk back down the beach.

In a forest clearing, a hundred leagues to the south, two Rukh, a cave troll, and a hundred bogglins were *conquered*. The process was as swift as lightning.

The battle was on.

Ash cursed.

Trees died.

He took on his true form and leapt into the air, flying south. Almost as an afterthought, he ordered Orley's horde to follow him. Lot had won this round; he could not retake the well and face the *will* at the same time. And the well was not vital.

Ally with Lot?

The will *was the true enemy.*

Or so he might say to Lot.

The Inner Sea—Aneas Muriens

On the shore of the Inner Sea, Aneas's rangers were ready. The two Gallish round ships waited like floating fortresses in the two coves, covering possible landing beaches; the rangers waited in concealment, under webs of defensive spells, their own and those cast by Master Smythe.

The sun rose and dispersed the mist on the great lake, and eyes searched the sun-dazzled water for the flash or oars or paddles.

Aneas fell asleep, and woke, ashamed. But no crisis had occurred, and he changed his position, adjusted the screen of orange leaves he'd woven to cover himself, and listened.

Master Smythe walked out of the cover of the forest and onto the gravel beach as if Aneas was not concealed in any way.

"Aneas," he said. "He is gone."

"Ash?" Aneas said.

"We should not say his name," Master Smythe said. "Entanglement has many effects. He is now utterly of this world, and so in this world his name will now draw his attention." He looked out over the water. "He has other problems than losing his well right now, so he is running off to fight the Odine, who are awakening on schedule. He cannot spare me his attention."

Smythe was smiling.

"And that's good?" Aneas asked.

Smythe nodded. "Orley is headed south to the great battle," he said. "I thought you would want to know."

Aneas stood up. "You want me to follow him?"

Smythe shrugged. "Don't *you* want to follow him?" he asked.

Aneas narrowed his eyes. Other rangers were rising from their concealment: Ricar Lantorn, already recovered; Looks-at-Clouds, Nita Qwan, Irene, Gas-a-ho. "Can't you see the future?" Aneas asked.

"No," Master Smythe said. "But I know a good deal about the past."

"But Irene says you planned all this," Aneas said.

"Irene gives me far too much credit," Master Smythe said. "But what I have done is done. My role is largely finished. I planned some of it. But other hands shaped the wax, and some of them even I cannot see."

"Is that just mumbo jumbo?" Irene asked.

Nita Qwan began the process of lighting a small stone pipe from his pouch.

"Ask Amicia, if you can find her," Master Smythe said. "There are now forces in contention that are to me as I am to you."

"And so you drop your tools?" Irene asked.

Master Smythe frowned. "I prefer to think that I allow my allies the free will to complete the task ahead as they see fit."

"Will you help us to pursue Orley?" Aneas asked.

Nita Qwan had his char cloth lit with flint and steel, and he drew deeply of the pipe, pulled the smoke over his eyes and head like a hood, and turned to face the four cardinal points.

"Oh yes," Smythe answered. "But fairness requires me to tell you that Orley is no longer Orley. Your enemy, the man who was Ota Qwan, is effectively dead, and more horribly than any revenge of yours or sentence of the Sossag Mothers would ever have arranged. He is now a living extension of our enemy, in a way that Thorn never was."

Aneas nodded. Nita Qwan handed him the pipe and he, too, drew deeply on it and turned to face the sun, and then the other three points.

"I was never charged to punish my brother," Nita Qwan said. "The mothers told me that he will only punish himself. But I am to kill him, as one would kill a beloved dog who suddenly foamed at the mouth and bit strangers." He touched the blue stone dagger at his waist.

"There is much wisdom in men and women," Master Smythe said. "But it pains me to say that in this war I have discovered that we dragons are just like you men in this one thing: that we project on you what we are ourselves, as you do on your pets." He took another pull and shrugged. "I have reconsidered. When I am a little more secure in my form, I will follow you to war. If this is the last battle, I risk nothing by being there; I will not long survive defeat by any of the contestants. Even here. And you are good companions." He shrugged. "But I think it will be aeons before I can fly, or take my natural form again. Or work *power* anywhere but near my sources." He shrugged. "Still, I have sufficiently become a man that I cannot really imagine waiting here to find out who won, either."

Arles—The Red Knight

Every foot soldier occupies approximately one pace, or three imperial feet, of frontage and depth in a military formation. A mounted soldier occupies almost two paces in width, and almost four paces in depth, because horses are so big.

So fifty thousand men, in a single rank, on foot, occupy fifty thousand paces, or almost twenty-five miles. Even formed four men deep, they would occupy a frontage of almost six miles, and if a sizable proportion of them were mounted, it would amount to almost ten miles.

Even formed in deep divisions, the ends of the line would never even see each other, and they would take hours to take up their formations.

When Gabriel, clad head to foot in cleaned and repaired armour of gilded steel, worn with gilt maille and scarlet arming clothes, mounted Ataelus, most of his officers had been awake for ten hours, chivying men and women and the occasional inhuman into ranks and files; checking girth straps, reacting to foolish suggestions, reminding, cajoling, and sometimes threatening. The fifty thousand men, women, and monsters of the imperial army had recently been five armies and no army. The Sieur Du Corse's Gallish forces shared a language and a great deal of ill-will with the newly reestablished Army of Arles; the

Etruscan states had various internal conflicts and histories, and almost everyone in every contingent shared a mixed feeling of dread and distrust for the "scarecrows," former slaves to the *rebel*. The distrust was almost as deep for the magnificent cavalry of the sultan.

The opportunities for bad feelings, slights, petty jealousies, and subtle insults were legion.

Among all these, the company stood out; professional, multinational, and even multispecies, the company had the habit of cooperation...and of victory. The company's officers were the glue that held the alliance together, and yet the experience of creating this grand review stretched them to their collective limits.

Ser Tobias sat on his charger with the imperial banner in his fist: a golden, double-headed eagle on a ground of crimson silk. Next to him was Ser Francis Atcourt with the *casa's* three lacs d'amours, and Toby could see Ser Michael, mounting his charger after a short conversation with the Duchess of Venike, and Ser Milus, who had command of the company. Ser Alison was far off to the right, commanding the Army of Etrusca.

Ser Thomas, head-to-toe black and gold, was already mounted on his stallion, as big as a monster. He was commanding the same troops that he had led east: the Vardariotes, the Nordikaans, the *casa*, and the Armourers' Guild. Under the Umroth banner, no longer a joke, they were the imperial guard with the addition of Comnena's Scholae— almost two thousand mounted soldiers, the elite of the army. They were drawn up already, along the road that led to the castle.

To Toby's left, the empress and the Queen of Arles were mounting. Both wore armour.

"How are we doing?" the emperor asked his chief of staff.

Ser Michael nodded. "Just a little late," he admitted.

Gabriel looked back. MacGilly had his helmet and lance; Anne Woodstock carried his war sword, unsheathed. She glanced over at Toby, and Toby caught her look.

She grinned.

He grinned back.

Most of the women and men in the courtyard were grinning.

"If I die," Gabriel said to Michael, and Toby felt like a lightning bolt had gone through him. "Are you ready to take command?" he finished.

Ser Michael looked for a moment at his wife, who was across the yard, getting up on a horse he felt was too big for her. "Yes," he said.

He shrugged. "I mean, probably not, but what the hell else have you trained me for, the last three years?"

"Exactly," Gabriel said, at his most smug.

Toby wondered if he was supposed to be hearing this.

Atcourt glanced at him.

Ser Michael sighed. "May I ask what I hope is a very intelligent question?" he said.

"Is this an apprentice imperial commander question?" Gabriel said.

"Yes." Michael looked back at Kaitlin, who was mounted and looking apprehensive. "Did you send armies to finish the Necromancer and defeat the Patriarch of Rhum just to train all these people to obey our officers?" he asked.

Gabriel returned a smug smile. "Mostly," he said. "Idle hands are the devil's tools."

"You mean, it was all an exercise?" Michael asked.

"Oh no," Gabriel said with his most annoying smile. But then he looked at Blanche, and his smile changed. "We had to finish the Necromancer. Far too dangerous, and anyway"—he was looking somewhere else, but then his attention snapped back to Michael—"to cement the alliance with the sultan if for no other reason. Did I tell you the Necromancer tried to surrender?"

Michael whistled. "No," he said.

"There were lots of good reasons to fight both campaigns," Gabriel said.

Michael realized that the emperor was not really talking to him. He was talking to Blanche. "We had to pin Mitla in place so that Venike didn't feel threatened, nor Berona. We needed all these allies, Michael, and they all have their own concerns. And Kronmir—" Here Gabriel looked away. He took a deep breath and released it in a sigh. "Kronmir had a theory that needed to be tested in the field. We needed northern Etrusca secure. We couldn't have the Patriarch threatening our lines of communication." He shrugged. "But yes, in part they were exercises."

"Remind me never to go to war against you," Michael said. He looked back. "Everyone's mounted up."

"Then let's go and see this army," Gabriel said.

The emperor led the way, alone, out of the gate.

Behind him, Blanche, wearing her crown, and armour, rode between the banners. But today, the emperor rode out alone.

Just outside the gate, Harald Derkensun roared an order. Hundreds of axes went to shoulders. Most of the Nordikaans were so tall that their heads came even with the eagle on the emperor's coat armour, even when the emperor, not a short man, was mounted on Ataelus, eighteen hands of black warhorse.

Derkensun raised his great axe straight in the air. *"Ave,"* he called in a voice as deep as Ocean.

IMPERATOR

... came the reply from thousands of throats.

The emperor struggled to hold his composure. It was hard not to show what he felt; difficult not to let the tears in his eyes flow over his face. Almost impossible for a man who remembered being a despised adolescent to accept the roar of such acclaim with equanimity.

The Nordikaans closed in around his horse and walked forward with him. There were more than two hundred of them; more than there had been before the disasters of the last three years.

Beyond the Nordikaans were the Scholae; beyond them, the Vardariotes; beyond them stood the *casa*, who bore at their head the ancient Phoenix of the *Athanatoi*, the immortals of Emperor Atreus. Gabriel hadn't seen the banner before, but he paused, and smiled, and looked back at Blanche, who beamed.

The emperor looked down at Derkensun. "Blanche embroidered that," the emperor said proudly.

Derkensun smiled. His mind was elsewhere. Battle was coming.

As he passed, each company saluted and fell into the column.

Last among the "guards" stood the gonners of the Harndon guilds, augmented by the Etruscans they'd recruited as well as detachments of Galles, Mamluks, and Venikans, all states who had claimed to need to have the new weapons immediately. Edmund wore light harness and commanded almost a thousand men, but still only the three falconets. Arles could cast bronze hand-gonnes, but no one in Antica Terra could cast a two-ton bronze tube on such short notice.

The gonners were still learning to march.

"Pitiful," Derkensun muttered.

"They'll have lots of practice in the next few days," the emperor said.

"They make the guard look shabby," Derkensun said.

Gabriel looked back over his guard; thousands of men in brilliant red and green and gold, steel bright, silk-turbaned, moving in unison. "Oh, we don't look so bad," the emperor said.

From the end of the ridge on which the citadel of Arles sat, the whole of the army was laid out, lining both sides of the road for almost four miles, facing inward. On the right, Du Corse's Galles; on the left, the scarecrows. Gabriel led the guard down the plain at the center, and the guard marched eight abreast, thirty ranks at a time, led by a phalanx of flags.

The scarecrows were thin, and their eyes burned, and many of them were one-eyed like the king of the old gods, but they'd all come up with undyed white wool cotes, many of them donated by the women of the town, and every one of them bore the phoenix badge in red wool on their left breast over the heart. There were more than ten thousand of them, the Duchess of Venike had refused the regency of Etrusca to command them, and every man and woman had survived the experience of hosting a worm.

Across the road stood Du Corse's levies, the Arriere Ban of Galle. He, too, had armed his foot with very long spears, fronted with halberds and war hammers for crushing the larger monsters, and he had four big blocks of arbalesters and a big company of heavy brigans in good armour; the very men who had so oppressed the burghers of Harndon not a year before were now imperial infantry. Gabriel detected no flaw, no irony in their cheering; less than a year before, he'd ambushed that very company on the road south of Lorica. And captured Du Corse, who now sat on a magnificent charger with the silver crown of the Regent of Galle on his helmet.

The regent saluted the emperor gravely and Gabriel returned the salute, turned, and raised his sword to the Duchess of Venike, who also returned his salute.

After the scarecrows came the Mamluks; on the other side of the road, the Galles gave way to the company. Ser Pavalo sat easily on the parade's finest horse, his Fell Sword in his hand, facing Ser Milus across sixty paces of sunny dust.

Gabriel turned and made a motion to Bad Tom, four horse-lengths behind him, and Bad Tom's bronze lungs roared the order to halt.

As near as could be managed, the company's Saint Catherine banner was in the center of the whole army.

Gabriel rode his horse in a tight circle, looking at them all, and then he beckoned to Mortirmir, who, bored, had his feet up on the cantle of his saddle and was reading.

"A mighty tome of magik?" he asked, *sotto voce*.

"No," Morgon said. "Here?"

"Yes," the emperor said.

Mortirmir's fingers grew with a pale fire, and then he nodded.

Gabriel sat up straight.

FRIENDS

Even the emperor himself was startled by the sound, and Atealus laid his ears back and twitched.

Tippit mimed putting his hands over his ears and No Head slapped him on the helmeted head.

Gabriel took a breath. He felt foolish; felt that he should never have done this at all.

Every eye he could see was on him. And Blanche was probably right.

Friends! he said again. It was better this time.

For a moment he could not remember a thing he had intended to say. And then it was all there, like the hermetical workings in his memory palace; hung on neat pegs. Because...

Tomorrow, barring accident, we will begin the greatest adventure that any army since Livia's Legions has undertaken. We will go to another world. In fact, my friends, we will go to three other worlds before we return to our own. We have a map. We have food, and water, the best equipment, and for many of us, months or years of training and planning. This is not a desperate gamble. This is the culmination of a careful strategy. We do not have to die to the last man. We only expect everyone to do their duty, and we will triumph, and our children and their children will have peace.

You have survived the claw of the monster and the silence of the Darkness, the wing of the wyvern and the breath of the dragon. Many of you bear the marks of the weapons of the Wild and the weapons of Man.

Whatever awaits us across the gates will not be worse than what you have already faced, because your ancestors and your adversaries here are the survivors of other wars for those same gates. We have a level of hermetical support that our ancestors would have envied. We have the best weapons our world can supply.

Conquering fear is what everyone in this army has in common.

We have all done it, and tomorrow we will do it again. And in conquering fear, we will win.

Then, quite spontaneously, he smiled.

And all the loot will be divided equally, by the divisional commanders, he said.

Now there was laughter.

Cully roared "Now ye'r bloody talking!" so loudly he hurt his voice.

And when we are done, you will go HOME.

Men cheered, although some members of the company looked uncomfortable.

Gabriel waved to Morgon, afraid that if he even cleared his throat, the noise would resonate. Mortirmir bowed in the saddle, his feet now in the stirrups, and turned his horse, but the magister was stopped by Bad Tom.

Three cheers for the emperor! Tom's voice rolled over the fields so loudly that it raised dust devils.

It had all been arranged, Gabriel saw, because the Nordikaans had the right of leading any cheer for the emperor, and there was Derkensun by Tom Lachlan's stirrup.

He raised his axe.

Ave!

IMPERATOR

Ave!

IMPERATOR

Ave!

IMPERATOR

And then Gabriel, deafened and reeling from the waves of emotion not unlike the wave front of a wyvern or a mighty dragon, turned his horse, waved his sword, and began to ride along the cheering ranks. The Nordikaans grinned; the company roared; the Mamluk kettle drummers played crescendo after crescendo.

Beyond the company were the Etruscans; Sauce stood in her stirrups to cheer, and by her side was the famous Conte Simone; behind them stood ranks of Venikan marines, and Beronese knights and crossbowmen, and Padovans, Vrescians, and a handful of Venikan nobles, as well as contingents of mounted rangers and Venikan light horse, and a thousand professional soldiers of Mitla led by the new duke's bastard brother: hostage and contribution in one man.

Across the road stood the chivalry of Arelat and a party of volunteers from farther east; heavily armoured in elaborate, fluted harnesses and speaking yet another language, they were the chivalry of the many princes of the Almain, an almost mythical place with a high reputation for chivalry and for beer. There were almost five hundred of them, despite their own lands being invaded by the eastern Wild, serving under Ser Calvin von Ewald and Ser Parcival, and they had brought a party of easterners to reinforce the Vardariotes.

And beyond them, filling the rest of the parade, were wagons and drovers; more than a thousand high-sided military wagons, all of them already loaded; grain, spare wheels, sheaves of arrows, more than a dozen mobile forges, bar iron stock, thread, wool, beeswax, candles, bandages, hats, sword blades, and all the sinews of war; beyond the wagoners stood the corps of drovers, six hundred armed men and women who would drive thousands of head of beef across the gates.

"Incredible," Gabriel muttered. He saluted them all, Alemains, Arelats, and wagoners, and rode to the very end and embraced Sukey, who stood on the box of a wagon that had its own flag.

Adrian Goldsmith sketched it all.

There was no pay parade. Tippit called it; they were all standing in ranks, relaxed, or as relaxed as they could be with Ser Milus four paces away and watching the emperor recede toward the distant wagons.

"Going to take for-fuckin'-ever to unfuck this," Tippit said with a professional's disgust for amateurs.

"Oh aye," admitted No Head, who was already worried about an engineering problem that the captain had given him.

"No Head, how long will it take for fifty thousand men to file off to the right and left and march back to camp?" Tippit asked.

No Head stared at the cloudless afternoon sky a moment. "Four hours, give or take," he said.

Smoke looked back at them from his exalted place as master archer of the whites. "Hey, No Head, if you have your thinkin' cap on ... you know those stakes we've been practicing at?"

"The gates," No Head said wearily.

Smoke nodded. "So how long will it take fifty thousand o' us, wi'out animals an' wagons, to pass the gates?"

No Head nodded. He looked after the distant emperor, as if the man might hear him from almost a mile away.

"Call it twenty hours," No Head said.

"Fuck," Tippit said. "Gates open when?"

Smoke looked around. No one was supposed to know.

Long Sam shrugged. "Sometime after five, I hear."

"Aye, just when they ring matins, or so I hear," agreed Simkin.

"*Ave Maria*. Does every one of ye know the timetable?" No Head looked disgusted.

Tippit looked at the sun. "Let me measure this for ye, then, lads. The gates, if they open at all, will spread their wings for us at matins. That means Cap'n will call it an early night. An' we won't get off this parade for another hour, at best."

"Fuck," Smoke muttered, seeing where this was going.

"We're goin' ta' get fed a big meal, 'cause the company always gets steak before we fight…" Tippit continued.

"Fuck," Smoke ventured again.

"And then the cap'n, or Bad Tom or Sauce, will stroll by an' order us to our blankets, fer our own good," Tippit said with relish. "'Cause if'n the gates open at matins, Tom Lachlan will want us booted and spurred before the cathedral strikes three."

"Fuck," said Smoke. "Right y'are. Dammit."

"No pay parade," Tippit said with disgust. "We'll have to fight our way through somethin' 'orrible, just to get paid."

Mark my words. Smoke started. They all looked around.

"Damn him," Long Sam muttered.

"Jesu, Sam, ye had to know that Wilful was too fuckin' mean to stay dead." Robin Hasty shrugged. "No disrespect intended," he added, crossing himself.

Snot raised a hand in his tentative manner. "No Head?" he asked.

No Head rolled his eyes. "I ain't a bleedin' oracle," he muttered.

"I got a question about loot, No Head." Snot's voice was a little whiny at the best of times.

"Loot?" No Head asked.

Men and women who'd ignored the rest of the exchange glanced at them. Oak Pew paused and stepped out of her spot. "Loot?" she asked.

"How much loot d'ye think a whole *world* might ha', No Head?" Snot asked.

People held their breath. The silence was absolute; almost hermetical. No Head calculated.

The silence lengthened.

Finally the short archer shook his head. "No idea," he said. "I don' ha'e any basis for calculation. But whate'er it is..." He grinned. "Whate'er it is, you can expect that we won' get as much o' it as we deserve."

The last night was an odd one. No one in the emperor's confidence could doubt that the gates were going to open; there was light coming through the gate as bright as a new dawn, and all the magnificent stained glass burned with colour before the sun set in midafternoon.

They all knew what was ahead of them, or rather, they all shared a legion of doubts about what awaited them.

The emperor stunned his household by attending evensong in the castle chapel. The priest kept looking at the emperor as if expecting him to sprout wings—or perhaps horns. As soon as he had been served dinner, he ordered everyone in the household to bed. Toby appeared as if by magic and led Queen Clarissa's servants in clearing.

The emperor looked at his former squire and raised an eyebrow.

Toby flushed. "I thought I'd make sure that we were served by the castle," Toby said. "So the rest of the *casa* could go to bed. Master Nicodemus agreed."

"Bless you," Gabriel said. He glanced at Ser Michael, who was wolfing down little rolls of beef.

Toby saw the tables cleared and the boards pulled and stacked. The emperor took his lady by the hand, and she, attended by her new maid, rose, accepted bows, and went up the tightly twisting steps to their apartments.

The Queen of Arles sat alone. She was in a plain brown gown and wore a knight's belt as her only jewelry. She sat with her chin on her hand, looking out the great double window that dominated the upper hall.

Toby was the only other person there by happenstance. His purpose had been to find Anne, but he'd been too successful in organizing dinner, and she'd already gone up to help the emperor with his clothes and weapons. Toby knew how much needed to be done to prepare the man for dawn.

Toby was afraid. He was afraid to go up the stairs and help Anne; afraid that this would be too much of an admission. Afraid she didn't want him, as a man and as a squire.

He found the queen's eye on him.

"Wine, Your Grace?" he offered.

She smiled. "You are a knight now, are you not?" she said in her curiously accented Alban.

"Yes, Your Grace," he said, and when she held out a silver goblet, he filled it.

"So you will ride with them tomorrow," she said.

"Yes, Your Grace," Toby answered.

She smiled. When Clarissa de Sartres smiled, she was quite beautiful; the transformation was breathtaking. "I envy you," she said. "Many of my knights are going. I am not going. I will sit here and be queen."

Toby had no idea whether there had been acrimony about the queen remaining behind. He didn't know what to say. So he said nothing.

She looked at him, and drank some wine. "Do you think you will triumph, Ser Tobias?" she asked.

Toby nodded. "Yes," he said.

She rolled the goblet along the edge of the chair arm. "Why?" she asked. "Why so confident?"

Toby shrugged.

"Because of him?" she asked.

Toby felt trapped, but after a moment, he said, "I've been with him for some years, Your Grace. He doesn't... lose."

She nodded. "I want to be there," she said. "A moment will come; the moment of victory. I do not want to be a girl and sit at home. I want my barons to remember that I was there."

Toby was far out of his depth. But in that moment, he knew he would go up the stairs; Anne's rejection, on the cosmic stage, was a small thing, a risk he could and should take, compared to the unfairness of being left behind.

"Maybe you should just come," Toby blurted out.

Clarissa frowned. "That is not the path of duty," she said. "All my life I have done what I have been ordered to do. Because, for the most part, the world would collapse if rulers did not do their duty." She looked out the window. "I went to the Gallish court because my father ordered me to," she said softly. "And I stayed home when my father went out to face the Wild."

She shook her head. "I am unfair to you, young sir. These are not your troubles."

Toby nodded. "Well," he said. "I am a great one for duty, Your Grace. I ha'e been a servant, a page, and a squire; I generally do as I'm told." He shrugged. "If you was to go along o' us, and die . . ." He met her eye. "What would happen? Here?"

"My family line would end," she admitted. "There would be trouble. Political trouble."

"And if you don't go?" Toby asked. He didn't know why he was doing this.

"Ser knight, if we both survive this, I think perhaps you should return to my court and take a place as one of my counselors." She put her wine aside, and Toby knew what she had decided.

Toby paused, ready to walk up the steps. But daring was coursing through him; perhaps it was her flattering words, or his intention of confessing his love to Anne. Either way, he nodded. "Listen, Your Grace," he said. "Philipe de Beause needs an armed page. You can handle a lance?"

The Queen of Arles smiled again. "Oh yes," she said.

Toby bowed. "If you choose this path, I can see to it . . ."

"Say no more," she said. "Perhaps I will see you in the morning."

Toby sprang up the steps with the energy he'd have used in a storming action. He reached the top and the door to the outer solar was open; he walked boldly in, to find Master Julius copying rapidly with both of his clerks and one of the imperial messengers helping him. Through two open doors he could see the empress being undressed by her lady. The emperor had his back to the door and was reading a message. There was a fire in the grate, and darkness was falling across the world.

Anne appeared at the inner door with a doublet across her left arm and the emperor's war sword in her right hand. When she saw Toby, her face lit up. His heart beat very fast.

"I'll do the sword," he said, sitting on one of the benches at the second writing table. He drew the sword; it was spotless, but Toby took a rag and some oil and touched it up, checking the edge . . .

"Is that you, Toby?" called the emperor.

"Yes, Your Grace," Toby said. Sharp in the last ten inches toward the point; sharp enough to shave with. But the rest . . .

"Shouldn't you be rolled in a blanket with a sweet friend, Toby?" the emperor asked. "Since you are not, fetch the Megas Dukas, please?"

Toby ducked out, ran down the tightly curving stairs and up the opposite set to Ser Michael's room.

"Cap'n wants you," Toby called past Lord Robin, who was laying out armour.

Michael appeared, fully clothed, with a baby on his shoulder. "Lead on," he said.

His child was spitting up onto his silk-velvet doublet. Toby ran down the steps and heard Ser Michael following, and then up, noting that the Queen of Arles was gone.

Morgon Mortirmir was right behind them.

The emperor was waiting with wine he'd poured himself.

"I'm sorry, gentlemen," he said. "I won't keep you. A last adjustment," he said apologetically. "I will open the gate myself."

"It's a foolish risk," Mortirmir said.

"Morgon," the emperor said, his voice flat, "can we remember which of us is emperor?" He looked around. Blanche was in a shift, standing in the bedroom door with her lady's face peeping over her shoulder. MacGilly was laying out the emperor's arming clothes; Anne was already laying out a cold breakfast.

"I am the strongest," Mortirmir said.

"When Father Arnaud died, I swore that I would not risk another life if I could do the thing myself. I will do this, gentlemen." To Toby, it had the sound of an old argument.

Mortirmir shrugged. "If you fall—"

"Then I don't have to worry about the next part. Sorry to interrupt your evenings. Go to bed." The emperor bowed.

The Megas Dukas and the Magister Magi both bowed.

An armourer appeared at the door. He was very nervous, and Toby poured him a cup of cider, warm from the shoe on the hearth, and tried to calm him.

"I am to fit the empress!" he said.

Anne slipped into the bedroom and emerged with the empress, who was clearly not wearing anything under a linen shift, which added magnificently to the armourer's confusion.

"Your ... sabatons ... were too tight? Highness."

Blanche smiled. "So they were, sir."

She sat; Beatrice laced on her arming shoes. The armourer stepped forward and put the sabatons on. His hands were shaking.

Toby glanced at Anne and found that she was looking at him.

An eternity passed, and both of them were still in gaze-lock. Toby realized that someone had said his name.

The empress was smiling. "Toby?" she asked.

"Your Grace?"

"Get the poor man a cup of wine," she said.

Toby fetched wine, and helped the armourer away from the empress's feet. Blanche was trying not to laugh.

"Just a matter of a small change," the armourer said. "The rivets have to be just so loose. So happy..."

Blanche rose. The man stuttered and managed a very sketchy bow.

"They are perfect," the empress said. "I could dance in them." She began to execute the steps of an Etruscan court dance that she and Beatrice did every morning, her steel-clad feet winking in the candle-light. Her sabatons were edged in gold.

"I have never seen anything so beautiful," the armour said. "Oh! I said that out loud."

He turned bright red; so red that Toby was afraid he might do him-self a mischief, and he guided the man to a table and put wine in his hand. The empress grinned at her lady and then indicated the steel shoes, and Beatrice had them off in a flash.

"You'll start a new fashion," young Beatrice said. "We'll all have to have armour." She giggled. But she wiped the fingerprints from the steel with her very practical apron, and set the sabatons down with the rest of the harness laid out on the solar's carpet by the fire.

The armourer watched Toby examine the sword.

"May I touch it?" he asked.

Toby held it out, and the man simply put a finger on the hilt, and grinned. "Ah," he said in Galle. "What a night! I touched the empress, and the emperor's sword." He rose and walked out.

Toby followed him as far as the storeroom on the corridor, where he fetched a strop and a bowl. While Anne and Beatrice tidied away the last few things, he took some paste of wax and pumice and touched up the sharp blade of the war sword.

He put the sword back into the scabbard, heard Anne laugh with Bea-trice, saw Master Nicodemus come through with linens over his arm, and worked the sword a few times—half draw, return, half draw, return.

Just right.

The emperor leaned out of the bedroom. "Go to bed, friends," he said.

"Almost there," Anne said. Toby smiled. It was exactly what he had always said. He placed the emperor's sword in the upright rack near the fireplace. Next to the sword stand was a towel rack, which now held a spotless, newly made arming shirt and braes several sizes smaller than the emperor's.

Master Nicodemus smiled. "Thanks, Toby," he said. "I think we're ready. Anne?"

Anne nodded, her arms full of dirty clothes.

Beatrice curtsied.

"I will wake you all," Nicodemus said.

He swept out, as regal in his way as the emperor.

Anne dropped the dirty clothes in a hamper by the solar door and tried not to listen to the sound of talking from the bedroom.

Toby gathered up his polishing and sharpening and carried the refuse down the hall to the storeroom. He put the wax back, and wished he had water...

Anne came in with a candle. She rose on her toes to fetch another candle from a high shelf. Then she turned, and put her lips on Toby's. "Don't go anywhere," she commanded. She went out. Master Julius came by, yawning; Toby pretended to be fussing with something in the tiny storeroom.

I'm not fooling anyone, Toby thought. *She loves me!* he also thought simultaneously.

Anne came back. He heard her footsteps, and they seemed to last an eternity of joy; the anticipation warred with a nameless fear...

She came in with the stub of a candle, and closed the storeroom door. It wasn't much larger than a wardrobe. She looked up at Toby, and he leaned down and kissed her. It was clumsy, went on longer than they'd expected, and there was some dripped wax and then they broke apart.

"This is not the love nest of my dreams," Anne whispered.

Somehow, that seemed very funny indeed.

"If we knock down a shelf in here..." Toby said. His hip was resting against all the spare oil lamps.

They both giggled.

"Why did you marry me?" Blanche asked. She was lying on their bed, and her hands were on her stomach. There was a little hardening, as if she'd grown new muscles there. She didn't really show yet; but her kirtles didn't quite lace up, and her breasts were tender.

"Because I love you?" Gabriel said. He was looking out the window at the night.

"I have good legs," she said. "Or so I'm told." She sighed. "I'm a laundress. I'm an imposter. That poor armourer; he treated me as if I was the Blessed Virgin herself, and not some woman, a woman who farts and laughs and…" She paused. "I'm not a great warrior like Sauce, and I'm not a great magistrix like Tancreda. I come from no great family. My mother was the mistress of some great noble or other." She shook her head. "Sometimes I look at you… today, during the review. And I think… that it is like pretending you are married to God."

Gabriel turned from the window. His face was odd in the play of the candlelight; the shadows distorted him, and he looked fiendish. "You do have good legs," he said. He ran a hand down one.

She sighed. And slapped at his hand.

He shook his head. "My sweet, we are all imposters."

Their eyes met.

"One of the reasons I married you was that you are the companion I wanted for this night." He looked at her. She blushed but he went on, "I am taking a risk. Tonight, it seems insane. Jesus, why did I make this choice?" He shivered, and instantly her arms were around him.

"I pretend. I pretend I'm brave, and I pretend I'm in command, and I pretend that I have a magnificent plan, and half the time I'm making it up as I go, and I'm scared out of my wits and I am juggling eternities." He gave a great shudder and subsided. "I have killed an awful lot of my friends and I'm still not sure what the prize is, and in the morning…" He turned and wormed an arm out of her embrace, and he kissed her. "Listen. I'm not an astrologer. But more than a year ago, I imagined…" He frowned. "Perhaps this is too much. I imagined that if we made it this far; and I didn't even know yet how far this would be. If we made it this far…" He took a deep breath.

She kissed him. It wasn't companionable after the first few heartbeats. It was erotic.

"When I pulled you into my saddle," he whispered, "I knew you could… survive… anything I threw at you."

His skin was glowing like sun-lit metal. His metal hand was dark.

She sat up and shrugged her nightshirt over her head.

"Shouldn't we be asleep?" he asked. His hands were at variance with his words.

"No," she said.

Seven hours later, his skin was glowing enough that there was a rumble of comment in the *casa*, who stood, weapons unsheathed, at the very top of the ramp down into the great underhall.

The underhall was not dark. It was lit in a brilliant rainbow of colours, as if the sun shone directly in the great half-rose window. And on the window, the Emperor Aetius marched across window after window, making laws, ordering the execution of the former emperor's family, winning the great battle of Chaluns, living out his life as a monk.

The emperor himself wore his armour of gilded steel. He had his *ghiavarina* in his hand, and his helmet on his head.

Ariosto, in the hall above, gave a raucous scream.

"You're sure?" Mortirmir asked.

Gabriel looked at him and gave an easy smile.

Cully stepped out of the ranks. "Cap'n?" he asked.

"Cully?"

"I'd like to stand wi' ye, if you don't mind." Cully shrugged.

Bad Tom gave a fractional nod.

Gabriel nodded back. "Thanks, Cully."

The two of them walked down into the sun-drenched room. It was warm. The flood of colour was supernatural.

"Cap'n?" Cully asked.

"Yes?" Gabriel asked. He was trying to rein in his impatience to get it done.

"Look there," Cully said. He was pointing at the central figure of Aetius.

Gabriel shrugged. "Beautiful," he said in a meaningless way. He walked forward toward the central panel, and the keyhole, and Cully could see his hands were shaking.

Cully took his great bow off his shoulder and checked the string, and then drew a single heavy arrow from his belt and put it on the string.

"Good luck, Cap'n," he said.

Gabriel looked back. He looked up, at the waiting troops, and then he looked at the gate.

The light grew, if anything, brighter.

There was a sound, like a bell ringing, a perfect note, like silver or crystal. The sound seemed to fill the underhall.

Morgon raised his shields. So did Petrarcha and Tancreda and twenty other magisters.

Gabriel *went inside his palace, where the simulacrum of his tutor stood on her pedestal.*

"Ave, Prudentia," Gabriel said.

"Ave," she answered. "You stand on the threshold." She smiled, her white marble lips arching. "I hear the music of the spheres."

He nodded. He had prepared everything he could, the way he had for his tutor's examinations; shields hung, ready to use, and spears of light, clouds of darkness, balls of fire, a sword he'd designed himself, and some subtle, complicated stuff he'd decoded from Al Rashidi's fading mind.

He took a single shield of pure green and a living buckler of gold; perhaps the densest protective spell he'd ever cast.

"Ready?" he asked.

Prudentia smiled. "For this, you were born," she said.

He started. "What? You can't know that!"

Prudentia smiled. "Ask me no questions, and I'll tell you no lies."

"Damn it, Pru! This is not the time!" he said, but inside he felt as if a dam had burst.

Would you be lord of all the worlds?

The golden target burned like a sun on his left fist, yet being hermetical, it didn't interfere with his grip on his *ghiavarina*.

He put the golden key he'd stolen from Miriam into the gate.

Lines of white fire ran from the corners to the center.

"The gate is live," said Bin Maymum.

As the fire ran over the gate, Gabriel could see that, unlike Lissen Carak, with ten settings, this gate had only two.

He took a deep breath.

He turned the key to the second setting.

The tracery of stone and glass vanished, and a hot wind blew into his face.

Sand whispered against the edge of his green shield.

For a long heartbeat, Gabriel stood alone in the light of an alien dawn. Behind him lay the underhall of the Castle of Arles.

Ahead of him lay a road made of stone, running on a stone causeway above a desert. The road ran right to the mouth of the cave; he could see. Looking around, he seemed to be standing in what appeared to be the mouth of another cave.

His heart felt as if it might burst.

He took a step forward, even though that had not been the plan.

His green shield vanished. He stood, unprotected except by his golden buckler, in the intense heat of a desert summer day, just after dawn, and a ribbon of road ran away toward a lonely mountain rising at the very edge of the heat shimmer.

He took a breath.

It was so hot that the air seemed to burn his lungs, and he was already sweating.

"Jesu," Cully said beside him. "You are taking us to fuckin' hell."

Part II
Entanglement

"Fight, get beat, rise, and fight again."

Chapter Eleven

The Inner Sea—Aneas Muriens

Aneas landed his canoe on the south shore of the Inner Sea, and the peaks of the Adnacrags stretched away to the east like a wall. The shore of the great lake was ablaze with autumn leaves, and the sun was already high in a peerless blue sky.

"Once more into the woods," Irene said.

Aneas made himself smile at her, although he was finding her advances increasingly distasteful and he was almost sure that Master Smythe was attempting to put a *geas* on the two of them.

Behind her, eight more great canoes landed his rangers, and the two round ships began to disgorge men-at-arms and crossbowmen.

Aneas scouted the immediate landing area and found Krek, the bogglin, and Lewen standing among the beech trees.

"All clear," Lewen said in his odd lisp. "I have been away south, almost to the first river—*Liliwithen*."

"*Gardunsag*," spat the bogglin. Its four mandibles clashed together—laughter.

Lewen rolled his blue-black eyes. "Please," he said. "The mere sound of your distorted tongue makes my shoulders itch."

He showed his fangs, and the bogglin clacked away with pleasure.

"Gentlemen," Aneas said in almost exactly his brother's tone.

Lewen rose from his crouch and even the mighty irk favoured his thighs. "A long day and a long night," he said. "I smelt the taint of Orley and his kind by *Liliwithen*. They are ahead of us. Two days to the fortress for them; three for us."

Aneas looked into the silent woods. "I am tired already," he admitted.

Lewen nodded. "And I."

Aneas trudged back to the beach, where all of them were getting their packs on their backs, and the Galles were looking warily at the trees.

"Seventy leagues," he said. "We will go as quickly as we can, by paths that are mostly safe. But we must be aware that we might have to fight at any time."

Gas-a-ho waved a pipe. "I will know if Orley is even close. Our... host... gave me a sign."

Aneas wished the news cheered him, but he felt more fatigue than anything; the pursuit, the hunt, held no joy for him.

He looked around him, and mostly what he saw was how many of his people weren't there anymore, their places filled by strangers.

He took a deep breath, and tried to make himself focus on the scent of the trees and the taste of the sun.

"We will alternate running and walking," he said. "Twenty leagues is a long day. Twenty-five is even longer. Come!"

He sounded his horn, and all the rangers who had horns raised them and made a deep music, and then they were trotting through the trees.

The Cohocton—Ash

Ash passed south like a murder of crows writ large, and animals quailed beneath his wings.

From his vast altitude, he could see the earth almost as far as the great river in the west. His army moved along the valley of the Cohocton, a column of darkness like the march of an army of ants seen from the top of a house, and the three mounds in the west that still spat ash and molten rock were filling the sky in a way that boded freezing winters and enormous hardship, an unexpected and delightful consequence of his meteors.

But in the *aethereal*, his race's oldest foe was stirring, and more than stirring. It was *becoming*. Ash knew the signs, having in some ways deliberately weakened the old workings that kept the Odine trapped in the gate.

But it is too early, and too strong. I need it docile.

Ash gathered power as he flew, and he left lines of dead and desiccated trees in his wake. He had discovered—or rediscovered—that the *black* was almost always the easiest power to seize.

He raised his various protections and descended...

The first bolt raised against him was almost his undoing.

In the aethereal, *the thing in the gate was like an infinite web of organic mush linked by trails of slime. Its presence threatened to overwhelm him, and its coercive powers rose to choke him, but the massive bolt of raw power it tossed at him blew aside his more careful protections and challenged him as neither Kerak nor Tamsin nor Nikos had challenged him. The fire exploded along his senses and he roared his rage in the* aethereal *and the real.*

The house in which Phillippa had grown to womanhood was destroyed in a single outpouring of dragon fire. Ash's unmaking fire roared across the roof and left black earth behind, and continued into the field of standing stones. But the *thing* there withstood him effortlessly, a canopy of pearlescent grey shedding his breath of unmaking as if water ran off an upturned bowl.

Ash turned, looking for a threat in the real or the *aethereal*; he cast a heavy attack and was rebuffed, *and he began to doubt he could break the thing's shield; a genuine peer. And with that doubt, other doubts crept in immediately; his grip on the sea monsters was weakening, and the flow of bogglins from the west had slowed to a trickle, and he'd lost track of the enemy's main army; his changing of the antlered men into copies of his mind began to seem a little foolish, and his failure to retake the well like some form of self-delusion, and suddenly all his plans were laid bare, insufficiently realized, and he himself had failed on details, and he began to wonder...*

And then his overmind felt the trap, and he lashed out, breaking the coercion with a hammer of his contempt.

Lissen Carak

On the walls of Lissen Carak, Miriam watched the duel the way a child watches fireflies in the back garden. The sky was dark, but the pulses of light, red, blue, violet, and white, came at an accelerating tempo. The rolling sound of thunder came, each boom a few seconds after its corresponding flash of light.

"Half a day's travel to the east," Miriam said to Sister Anne.

Beneath their feet, the infantry of the royal army, most of them northern militia, stood guard in the long trenches and reinforced earthworks that a small army of northern peasants were still refining. Darkness was falling, and Miriam wished that the workers would retreat into the safety of the inner defences, but she could not cover all of them.

Worse, her two attempts at the *dragon working* had failed, either because the massive spell was too complex for her, or because the newly empowered Odine were too strong for her magicks. She knew that there were worms in the woods; already, she knew that workers had been lost.

A long series of flashes. Most of her people were on the walls, watching.

"The choir should be ready," she said aloud.

The roll of thunder: *crash, crash, crashcrash, crashcrashcrash CRASH.* Silence.

And then another brilliant display.

In the aethereal, Miriam could see the wispy magnificence of the new power; the dense web of what she assumed was the Odine, and the malevolent green pyre of vanity that called itself Ash. They were hammering at each other, throwing enough power to level a town with every gout of sorcery.

"Oh, Abbess! They will destroy each other!" Sister Anne said.

The most powerful of the novices echoed her.

Miriam watched them, like dark gods, showering each other with the very essence of the universe, and she began to raise her citadel's shields.

"I pray it will be so," she said. "But truly, my sisters, my heart tells me that the victor will have the power of the sum of them both."

After almost an hour, the light show ceased suddenly, and the night was dark, although no bird song or night noise returned to the air. Miriam sent word to the militia to beg them to keep a good watch.

Theodora, the messenger, a novice from the west, came and knelt before her mistress in the hall. "Lady, the captain of North Albin says that his people keep very good watch. And that he only takes orders from his feudal superiors, and not from old women in holy orders."

In the morning, from the height of the abbey's walls, her garrison could see the flicker of movement across the Cohocton and miles to the west, or thought that they could. And at the northernmost end of the new earthen fortifications, out toward Abbington, a work party was massacred by daemons—a sudden onset, and the only survivor was the first man to run. The abbess paced her walls all morning, because she had almost four miles of fortifications to man and less than three thousand infantrymen to man them. She sent an imperial messenger to the Count of the Borders to request that he march to her. She heard reports of a second attack south of Abbington, this time by bogglins.

Michael Rannulfson, her captain, joined her on the walls. He had white in his beard and he'd seen a life of war.

"Can we retake the section we lost?" she asked, pointing north into the magnificent autumn foliage of the wooded valley that came down from the high Adnacrags. The earthworks lay along the valley like a ribbon dropped on a carpet; a narrow wall of earth and timber, and a wider area of abattis and tree stumps to leave the militia a field of fire, all punctuated with small square forts outthrust from the walls to cover bad ground or take advantage of hills. Four miles of it, and now they'd lost a section.

He made a face. "I wouldn't try," he said. "We're like too little butter on too much toast as it is, lady. Let the Count of the Borders retake the lost section when they come." He shrugged. "I'm more for collecting yer taxes at fairs, my lady. I'm not a great captain."

"Would you try and retake it?" she asked. "If I let you take all our garrison?"

"My lady," he said. "I will do whate'er you order me to do. But let me tell ye as a soldier, that as long as you and yer ladies hold the . . . the air, so to speak, the hermeticals, my fifty lads can hold these walls against the legions o' hell. But when ye send us out into the woods, you are naked to any assault—ladders, engines, towers."

She snorted. "So you say me nay, in your very polite way."

He shrugged. "Order me," he said.

She shook her head.

An hour later, a second bastion was stormed, this time by irks. A whole company of the South Brogat militia shot wildly and ran, leaving a half a mile of newly built walls in the hands of the enemy.

Rannulfson went out and looked at the situation for himself, on horseback, and he rode back up the long ramp. His hoardings were long since mounted, and so were the machines that he'd built to copy those the company had used years before; he was confident in his elderly but very capable garrison.

But as soon as he dismounted in the courtyard, he shook his head.

"Their captain's a duffer and no mistake; he's no experience. He won't budge, and to be honest, my lady, he has no knights, and not enough armoured folk to mount a credible attack. His people are out for the second time this year. Their leaders are all off in the west. They're in a parrilous way, my lady. An' they could no more retake those walls than a crowd of yer novices." Rannulfson frowned. "In point o' fact, the novices would be a good deal more likely to succeed."

"Can you drive them back with the engines?" she asked.

He shrugged. "I can at least trouble them," he said, and gave the orders, and a dozen nuns worked on the first loads of stone, enhancing them.

They burst with satisfying concussions, well up the valley toward the remains of Abbington. But an hour later, there was an organized attack along the wall right below the abbey. All four towers loosed buckets of gravel from their massive trebuchets, and the militia held, but one of the novices reported that there were already bogglins inside the defences, moving along the valley.

Miriam had a messenger from the Green Earl in her hand, and she nodded.

"Lord Gavin will drive them out in a few hours. His whole army, with that of the Count of the Borders, is just over the next ridge. We need to be ready to open the gate on the bridge." She looked at Sister Anne.

Anne nodded. "Give me the key, my lady. I'll see it done."

Rannulfson sent six of his best men with the Prioress of Abbington, as Sister Anne was more formally known. The loss of Abbington's priory had not yet been made official within the Order. And Anne was, after Miriam, the most potent worker of *ops* in the choir.

Sister Anne rode down the long ramp, even as workmen were taking down the stone bridges that eased wagon access to the great fortress and the garrison women were heating vats of oil. In the chapel, the choir was practicing both music and their defence.

"I miss Amicia," Miriam told the air.

They should have been ready for this.

A little after the bells rang for nonnes, there was a flash *in the* aethereal *that gave Miriam a heartbeat of warning, and the defences of Lissen Carak sprang erect.*

The flash had been a deception. The real attack went in farther south.

The great fortified bridge that linked the south bank to the north, the vital link...

...exploded in a torrent of red fire.

In the real, the detonation was apocalyptic. The central tower and all four central spans vanished, and a vast cloud of steam rose to hide the wreckage. Massive stones began to fall to earth, some crushing hapless militia, some plunging into the already chaotic maelstrom of the river. Sister Anne was killed instantly, as were her knights.

Lissen Carak—Ash

Ash sighed with pleasure.

Attack! he ordered.

A mile away, at the top of the great ridge that dominated the valley of the Cohocton on the south bank, Ser Gavin watched his link with the fortress vanish in a single, cataclysmic detonation whose echoes rumbled along the Adnacrags for many heartbeats.

Gavin closed his eyes in disbelief.

"I thought that they had massive magical protections?" he asked Tamsin.

She shook her head. "They did," she said. "We need to run."

Lissen Carak

Immediately after the assault in the *aethereal* came the first real assault in the real. A wave of bogglins threw themselves at the entrenchments, and died; and a second. By the third assault, the garrisons of the little redoubts were aware that they were islanders in a rising tide of enemies, and most of them panicked; they were not professional soldiers, and there were not twenty knights among the whole host, and they were outnumbered by many hundreds to one.

Rannulfson stood on the tall north tower and tried to use his engines to best effect, hammering the wave front of the bogglins, isolating a huge company of irks off to the west, loosing rocks to cover a garrison as it attempted to cut its way free of the monsters surrounding it. It was the redoubt facing the castle gate and the village at its foot; indeed, the upcast of its ditch had been along the same line where the company had dug an entrenchment years before.

The garrison was almost two hundred men and women; Albans from the south Cohocton, local men, and Rannulfson's garrison knew them. They concentrated their machines to support that one redoubt as the others fell, most of them surrendering to irks or renegade men when offered their own survival.

The company of North Brogat burst out their own east-facing gate, charged through a few hundred surprised bogglins, and made it to the foot of the long path that ran up the flank of the abbey's ridge.

Every machine in the fortress loosed stone to cover their flight, or attack, depending on the point of view. The trebuchet arms bent and flexed like giants throwing rocks, and Rannulfson opened the sallie-porte in person and counted them as they came in: one hundred and sixty men and women. A few had kept their weapons; many had thrown them down in order to move faster on the Abbey Ridge slopes.

Almost two thousand militia and workers surrendered to the overwhelming force of the assault. They were stripped of weapons by their ravening foes, and the wilder western bogglins ate a few as the rest were prodded along a gauntlet of irks and trolls and bogglins. But even terror passes; they were taken out of the heart of the horde and made to walk east, pricked by the irks' spears, or reinvigorated by the shining beaks of the daemons.

Most of them moved in blank-eyed fatigue. Very few of them had any spirit left to fight when the worms came for them.

Ash chuckled as he donated fresh foot soldiers to his new ally. His alliance was cemented in a trade of powers, and his path was set.

He knew perfectly well that the *will* was seeking to mislead him. Alliance was nothing but a contest of liars at the best of times. But he would use the *will* to clear the armies of man from the gate. It was not his chosen form of absolute dominance, but the *will* was too strong to face.

He felt it seize the puny wills of the damned. He nodded. It was creating an army of puppets and Ash was happy to let it do so.

He placed ten bridges of ice over the Cohocton and unleashed his tide of bogglins onto the south bank, even as the boldest of his horde attempted to scale the ridge on which the great abbey sat. They were exterminated, of course.

He had chosen the worms over Lot. But Lot didn't need to know that, and neither did other people.

He opened a version of himself and reached out, across the river, across the *aethereal*, to the leader of the enemy: the ancient Queen of Faery.

"Come, my lady," he crooned in the aethereal. *"Now is the time for enmity to fade and alliance to change. Men have failed. Help me win the gate, and I will provide a vast reward."*

Tamsin hesitated, and then fled.

He let her go. If he could turn her; the armies of men would be chaff, or better, fodder for his new allies. Suddenly the Queen of Faery was a valuable prize indeed.

He was close. Very close. He could feel it, and he knew what his next step had to be.

North of the Cohocton—Bill Redmede

Guided by bears, Tapio's little army crept east along a chain of meadows. They were almost forty leagues north of the Cohocton; the stags looked better, and so did the men, and irks; three nights of sleep, three days of eating the fruits and meats of the Wild, and they were swinging along.

Tapio paused to let Bill Redmede cross a beaver dam.

"Sometimes I think we should just run off into the woods and never come out," Redemede said.

"Me, too," Tapio said.

The bears seemed to know every wrinkle in the ground, and the third night they brought in two dozen more bears in heavy maille with great steel axes clutched in their all-too-human hands. The tall white bear who led the newcomers inclined his head to Tapio.

"Hail, King of the Woods," he said.

"Hail, mighty bear," Tapio said. "Who are you, sssir?"

The bear nodded. "I am Blizzard," he said. "I fought for Thorn, not once, but many times." He looked at his bears; they were well provided with weapons and other spoils of war. "But I think this time I will side with you. Thorn is gone; this thing that remains is no friend of bears."

Stone Axe and Elder Flower both nodded to the newcomer. "There is no fighting among bears, except in evil times," Elder Flower said. She sighed. "These are evil times, but perhaps not so evil. Blizzard will stand with us. That opens the Baglash, the hidden valley down the lakes."

Blizzard growled. There followed an explosion of growls and mews, punctuated by something like coughing.

Tapio, in fact, understood the language of the bears perfectly well, but he allowed them to disagree among themselves. The Baglash was the very heart of the Bear Holds in the Adnacrags. Neither man nor irk had trespassed; not even the Earl of Westwall's patrols had ever penetrated into the Baglash.

Finally Blizzard nodded. "Very...*rrrrr*...well; in for an, *rrrrr*, ant's nest, in for a...*hmmmgrrrg*...honey tree, as my mother used to say. We will take you down, *grrrg*, our lakes, and to the Fishing Tree."

The big white bear was as good as his word, and the men and irks feasted on honey and muskrat meat as they moved east on smooth trails. Then Tapio and Redmede pressed them hard, and Magister Nikos ate his honey, cast his wards, and rode with them, conversing with the other magisters. Blizzard proved a worthy companion, although his views on the sanctity of the Wild were fierce.

"I am no, *ggrrrr*, friend of, *hararg*, men," Blizzard said. "I would have *none* in the, *grrrr*, in the, *hmmm*, woods and waters of my home. Indeed, *hrack!*, magister, I hate you all; even you, *hrarg!*, who speak so well, and who, I think, loveth truth. You are, *grrrr*, like a stain on the earth; you take and take and take, aye, *hrack!*, and never give. Your only code, *hrrm*, as a people, *hrrrm*, is greed."

"But you will guide us to Lissen Carak," Nikos said. The bears would allow no campfires in their holding, but insisted that the men and irks and stags and horses press close at night for warmth. So speaking to the white bear was like speaking to a shadow; his fur was a pale blob on the other side of the sleeping circle.

"*Hrrmmm!*" muttered the white bear. "*Garg.* Better men than dragons and worms." He chuckled. "We've tried, *grrrr*, we've tried them both."

Nikos leaned forward. "You have seen the gates open before? You remember?"

The great eyes opened and closed, but it was Elder Flower who answered. "We, *grrr*, remember," she said.

Outside Lissen Carak—Ser Gavin Muriens

Ser Gavin watched the escalade of the carefully planned entrenchments with something like death in his heart, and despair threatened to overwhelm him.

The Count of Borders was devastated. "It is all my fault," he said.

Ser Gavin was tempted, basely tempted, to agree. *You came west to show you could, and left them to die. If you had filled those entrenchments with knights and held the sword in your own fist, this would not be happening.*

But he didn't. "There's no time for blame," Gavin said. "We have an army; we have to move back east to the fords, at the very least. In the very worst case, we join hands with the queen's army and come back on the north bank to relieve the fortress."

"Christ, if it even holds," the count muttered. "I beg you to take command, Ser Gavin. I am unworthy." The count tore his surcoat from his body and threw it to the ground beneath his horse's hooves, and tears flowed from his eyes. Across the river, a crowd of workers were being herded along by their daemonic captors.

Gavin narrowed his eyes impatiently at the dramatic gesture. "No," he said. "I will not accept your resignation! You will stay, and we will command together. Damn it, my lord, I've cocked up every day. No one will take *my* job."

The Count of the Borders froze.

"I mean it. I cannot spare you, my lord." Gavin was watching the disaster, but he was also watching the sky. "We need to ride for the fords. Thank God that Wishart reopened the old road. Tamsin?"

"Gavin?" she asked, mimicking him.

"Can you keep us alive?" he asked.

She shrugged. "Ask me tonight," she said. "The dragon is trying to seduce me."

"Sweet Christ," Gavin said, a bolt of terror gliding up his spine.

Tamsin spat on the ground. "As if I would betray my mate, even if I would abandon you. Ash loves no one and knows not love. Let him stew." She frowned. "But if he comes for me…I cannot stop him for long."

Gavin thought a moment. "We cannot retreat forever," he said. "What about the nuns?"

"They are puissant," Tamsin said. "But for them we would long since have been conquered. Pray that the dragon keeps his yellow eye on them, and not on us."

Hounded by bogglins and worse, the remnants of the Alliance Army of the West moved along the road that ran south of the Cohocton. Gavin paused as they passed over the Little Nemen; just there, he'd faced a *behemoth*, and just there, he'd tried to kill his damned, arrogant brother, who'd returned from the dead with an army of mercenaries to save them.

Damn him.

Gavin might have chuckled, if he'd been less afraid. As it was, he wished his brother would reappear with his sell-swords and save the world, because Gavin had run out of tricks.

All day he watched the sky.

All day his unrested army ran, walked, trudged, and slunk east as the trenches they had expected to occupy were taken and the defenders massacred or enslaved within earshot.

Sometime after nonnes, the stroke fell on them, but not from the air. Instead, a series of bridges appeared across the Cohocton, most of them well behind his rear guard, but two just even with his bogglins and 1Exrech.

The enemy began to cross the Cohocton.

Gavin knew immediately that he had to fight, but he was low on arrows and fodder and almost everything that made an army an army, and the level of disorganization in his beaten army was greater than even he had expected, so that when he tried to find Lord Gregario, he found only Redmede and his foresters.

"Knights rode off and left us," Redmede said bitterly.

"We have bogglins coming right up against the rear guard," Gavin said.

Redmede sighed. "Alright," he said, and laid an ambush among the bones of the dead from the last battle on the banks of the Nessen. Gavin could see the bleaching bones of the *behemoth*.

"Six shafts a man," John Hand said.

"I *know*," Harald Redmede replied.

Half an hour later, Gavin found Gregario, with almost two hundred knights who were resting their horses, and he led them back in time to save Redmede's foresters, who were locked in a desperate struggle on the stream's bank, trying to hold while 1Exrech and 53Exrech extricated their legions.

The air smelled curiously musky as they retreated over a stream choked with dead things and beginning to overflow its banks into the tangle of Alders that marked the spring flood lines.

Gregario wrinkled his nose. "What the *fuck* is that?" he asked. He was looking at a series of deep nicks in his long sword and wondering if he'd ever see a sword cutler again.

"That's the smell of 1Exrech, recruiting," Gavin said. Indeed, if anything, the two bogglin legions, despite a day's fighting, looked *stronger*. In a day of disaster, it was the only ray of light.

Except that Ash hadn't attacked, and they were, mostly, still alive.

Gregario nodded, and forced a smile. He rode forward, thrust his rough-edged sword home in the scabbard at his hip, and leaned down to thank 1Exrech, whose white armour was stained and mottled from three weeks of fighting.

The wight raised his elongated head and the mandible opened in a hiss of praise. "*Your warriorssss...are...very...ssstrong...*" said the wight.

Gregario nodded as the haunting, sibilant voice rose.

"Allies," Gregario said.

And late in the day, the Count of Borders caught the easternmost host of bogglins crossing an abandoned farm, and he led his knights, who were, despite everything, rested, well fed, and on fresh horses, in a crushing charge that stopped the flow of enemies cold and rolled them back to the edge of the trees. A hastenoch was killed, and a dozen *adversariae*. He lost twenty armoured knights, but the little victory cheered them all, and the army tottered into the camp that the merchant convoys usually used on their last night before making the fair at Lissen Carak to find that they were linking up with the northernmost of Desiderata's logistics, and there was sausage and fresh apples for every woman and man, and fodder for horses.

"I feel like I'm living in my own nightmare," Gavin muttered to Tamsin. "Not far from here, I woke up to find I was covered in scales." He took a bite of sausage.

Tamsin smiled. "A miracle," she said.

"A curse," Gavin said.

"A miracle," Tamsin said. "As great a miracle as Ash not falling on us today. I could not have saved you. Why did he withhold his talons?"

Gavin couldn't answer her, because he was already asleep, sitting in his harness, on the bare ground, with a sausage in his hand.

Albinkirk—The Prior of Harndon

The sun was setting, as red as wrath, amid the dark columns of soot in the far west, beyond the foothills of the Adnacrags, when three hundred horses crossed the Cohocton at the fords, their riders swimming the navigable parts despite the freezing water and the risk in armour. They met a body of not-dead on the Albinkirk road and crushed them, and rode on, the sounds of the hooves like the thunder of a distant storm that rolled from the fords all the way to the gates of Albinkirk.

The Prior of Harndon was still mounted, wet, stiff from cold, and hoping for clean borrowed clothes when the Grand Squire ran to meet him at the gate of the citadel.

"Thank God you are here," Lord Shawn said.

Prior Wishart shook his head. "All we need is feed for our horses and dry clothes," he said. "We need to ride on." But as if conceding the point, he slid from his saddle.

"Ride on?" Lord Shawn put a hand to his chest. "Damn it, the woods are full of worms. Nothing can move between here and Lissen Carak. The not-dead have closed the road."

"Despite which inconvenience, we will be going on," the prior said.

Squires and pages were running about, linkboys illuminated the citadel's courtyard, and the chargers were being taken into the stables or dried right there, despite the cold air.

"You cannot chance it in the dark," Shawn said.

There were almost a hundred Order knights, and another fifty squires. They dismounted like automatons.

The Grand Squire frowned. "Damn it, Ser John. Your people are exhausted."

"If we don't ride tonight," Wishart shot back, "we can't even make the attempt until tomorrow at sunset. Do you have news of the armies?"

"I'll get you the latest," he said. Then Ser Shawn pushed Wishart into the hall, where a big cup of hot soup was put in his big fist—vegetable soup, full of beans. He drank it off the way a yeoman might quaff a foaming cup of ale. Ser Shawn ignored the slight figure by the prior to fetch him another cup of soup with his own hands, and then he checked on the men in the yard, but the preparations had been thorough, and men were being fed as efficiently as the horses.

He summoned his own squire and sent him for the day's messages. "Prior? There's little enough news. The earl and the count have linked up in the west, but our enemy presses them hard."

A black-and-white-clad messenger came in with a messenger bird on his wrist. He was as white as the right half of his tabard. "My lord," he said to Shawn.

Shawn took the new message. He closed his eyes and then opened them again. "Damn," he said carefully.

The prior raised an eyebrow, and the Grand Squire handed him the flimsy.

"The enemy stormed the entrenchments at Lissen Carak," Ser Shawn said slowly. "All our work..."

Wishart seemed to sag. "So now the place is under siege."

"You won't get in without an army," Shawn said. "I'm sorry, Prior. But we need you here."

The Prior of Harndon could be seen to be praying.

Harndon—Queen Desiderata of Alba

Night over Harndon.

The lights burned in the queen's apartments in the great tower of the castle. The garrison was down to the sick and the wounded; everyone else had marched with Ser Ranald.

Gerald Random sat at a desk by the foot of the throne. The figure of the queen sat above him, her chin in her fist, a picture of annoyance. She wore the usual brown velvet, and her hair seemed to glow with a life of its own, as if magicked.

"I wanted to go," she said. And turned her head away. "I'm useless here. Everyone will forget me!"

Random was looking through a stack of documents, each one representing a task more difficult than the last: wills in probate from plague victims, the wholesale replacement of the Galle-tainted Council of the Realm and many of the aldermen; a list of attainted families.

Somewhere, in the passages beyond the hall, there was a sound that made him raise his head. Ser Gerald looked, squinted, and asked one of the new maids to light the torches.

She went to the brazier and Ser Gerald heard the unmistakable sound of steel on steel.

"Guard!" he roared. Two of the royal guardsmen responded, coming from their alcove to the right, both of them with pole arms.

The first sprouted a cloth yard shaft in his chest. He dropped his halberd and fell to his knees, and his face worked as he sought to say something, but his wits were already going. He took another arrow anyway.

Then they were coming in at two doors: hooded men in white, with bows, and some with swords and bucklers, the swords already dirty and dull with death.

Ser Gerald drew his arming sword. He had a buckler on his belt, a fine one of steel and leather, and he put it on his fist as he hobbled to put himself between the dirty white figures and the throne.

The bigger of the royal guardsmen cut one of the Jacks almost in half with a swing of his halberd, took an arrow in the side, and cut again.

Random cut an arrow out of the air and then pushed forward on his wooden foot, anxious to close before they feathered him.

There were only seven of them now; long odds, but winnable. Random had seen worse.

The woman on the throne was screaming.

His target chose to shoot, and missed him, ten feet away; a big oaf in a filthy straw hat, with a wide fool's grin. Random cut his bow hand on the rising stroke from his right side, and then, as the man cringed away, killed him with a thrust to the neck, *imbracatto*, and went for the next man, who was entangled with the other guardsman; Random stabbed him in the back—too hard—and lost his sword in the wound as the man fell, tearing the hilt from his hand and making him stumble.

"Death to the queen!" shouted the tallest man. He loosed a shaft.

Random got the dying man's sword. It wasn't as good as his own but it was in his hand, and he used his buckler to cover a blow from his left side because he couldn't move his feet fast enough to make the correct parry.

There were more of the dirty white cotes coming into the throne room, and the woman on the throne was already full of arrows. She hadn't even tried to protect herself, and the glorious hair faded away with the glamour that supported it.

Random backed, and backed; avoided tripping over a corpse, and managed to sever a wrist with a rising cut. He was headed for the small door at his back—the door to the cells. He knew it all too well.

They crowded around him like amateurs, instead of shooting him down; he took a cut across his buckler arm, and as the man left himself overextended, broke the arm with the pretty steel buckler and then killed him, a blow through the bridge of his nose while he was stunned, and then Random had his back to the door and took a wound through his body, a thrust, in and out, and something was running over his abdomen. And the damned door was locked, and Random was pretty sure that his wife would never see him alive again.

"Death to the queen!" shouted a woman's voice. "Where is the child?"

There were more shouts, but Random had, despite the wound in his guts, landed another heavy blow, cutting between a man's buckler and his sword, opening him from breastbone to groin so that intestines glistened. The man fell back into his mates, and in that instant Random threw a little thrust and it went home—a little sloppy because he was probably dying—but still neat enough, grating over the man's breastbone and up into his throat.

He tried to feel behind himself again for the door latch, thrust out, made two heavy cuts to clear a space, and took another wound, this one really bad, in the back, because he had no armour. He tried to turn and found that instead he was falling.

Oh well.

He realized that he must be on the ground, and for a moment he panicked, because they would eat him. But then he realized that they were merely men; he wasn't at Lissen Carak.

"God save the queen," he said quite clearly.

"Find the child!" shouted the tall man. "Now!"

There were footsteps, and the tall man was over him. Random could feel him; could all but feel his anger.

Random didn't really care, as he was slipping into the darkness. *God save the queen*, he thought. His lips formed the words.

"Do you know who I am, Master Random?" the man asked.

Random didn't care enough to answer. *God save the queen.*

"I'm Nat Tyler, Master Random. I'm the King o' the Jacks, and I've just killed your precious queen, and now I'll…"

He stopped talking, because Ser Random's eyes had just developed the glassy stare of the dead, and the knight could not hear him anymore.

Lessa was searching the apartments upstairs. There were a handful of servants, and she and the other Jacks killed them as they went; two of the men laughed, hunting a screaming girl room by room, until they found her behind the hangings. Then they each shot her.

In the last room there was a cradle, but the cradle was empty, and Lessa swore.

She turned from the empty cradle to find Kit Crowbeard in the doorway with a sword in his hand. He wore armour, and looked considerably younger.

His sword was dripping with blood.

He nodded to her, as if they were meeting in a tavern. "Good evening," he said.

"The babe!" she said. "He's not here."

Crowbeard nodded, glanced over his shoulder at the rooms beyond, and back at her. "No matter," he said. "We have the castle."

"No matter?" she spat. "Nits make lice. They all have to die."

Crowbeard nodded, as if thinking about what she was saying.

"You promised!" she said. "All of them."

He stepped closer, a slight smile on his lips, as if he might kiss her.

She sighed. "Really," she began.

Crowbeard shrugged, and thrust her through the throat.

Lessa grabbed at the blade, shock warring with pain.

He put an arm around the back of her head like a lover and lowered her carefully to the floor.

"Sorry, my dear," Crowbeard said. "I liked you, but there's been a change of plan."

He was a meticulous man, and he regretted having to do the deed; he withdrew the sword without catching it on the vertebrae of her neck, and stepped clear of the falling body to avoid getting blood on his armour. Then he cleaned the sword on her dirty white cote. He really had liked her, but he also thought that anyone who trusted the Earl of Towbray was too stupid to live.

He walked back out of the royal apartments, leaving the other dead, servants and Jacks, artistically draped over one another. He collected his three best men, the men who had performed the bloody artistry, and went back to the great hall, where the Earl of Towbray sat on the bloody throne from which he'd just thrown the corpse.

Two of Crowbeard's men had Tyler.

"You fucking traitor," Tyler said. "You..."

Towbray smiled. "I am a traitor many times over," he said. "Why on earth would you choose to trust me? But I must say, your people did a fine job. Quite the massacre. You've left me very few murders to commit." He smiled at Crowbeard. "Ah, Kit. I have no further need of Master Tyler."

Crowbeard walked over. Tyler spat at him, and pulled, very hard, at the men who held him, but they not only had strong hands, they had armour and steel gauntlets.

"Ash will have you all! I will be avenged!" Tyler roared.

Towbray raised both eyebrows, as if appalled at what he heard.

"Ash sends you his regards," Towbray said. "He's finished with you now."

Crowbeard ran the old Jack through, just under the jaw.

"Lay him by Ser Gerald," Towbray said. "Ser Gerald will have died a hero's death, attempting to protect the queen. I think he'll have a statue, don't you, Kit? Alas, just before we could come and restore order." Towbray smiled. "And now, I am king."

"Your Grace, I regret to say that the boy is not here." Crowbeard was so used to giving his master bad news that he just said it.

Towbray shrugged. "Gone with the army?" he asked. "Inconvenient."

"Depends who has him," Crowbeard said. He was looking at the dead woman on the floor, and he didn't like what he saw.

Lissen Carak

Darkness before dawn.

The time when old men die, and when sentinels fall asleep, and when the world changes while no one is looking. Somewhere, out in the curtain of stars that was the embodiment of the infinite music of all the spheres of creation, a star moved, aligning with another star; the dance continued, the endless motes of life and light floating in the endless darkness.

By whatever mechanism the spheres drove, the gates began to open across the worlds.

Close, in metaphysical terms, to Lissen Carak, the *will* awoke to the movement of the gates. It had waited with infinite impatience as its billions of constituent beings yearned to be reunited with sisters and brothers and cousins across the million spheres; waited, and then, in a twinkle of a star, they were *right there*.

The *will* reached across the gap of stars as the gates aligned, and rattled the gate, but it was *locked*.

The *will* had had an aeon to plan its next moves. It attacked the lock.

Miriam awoke to Novice Maria Magdalena shaking her.

"Madam, madam, the gate!" the girl was shrieking.

Miriam shot to her feet, her nightgown flapping. "Gabriel said five twenty," she said.

The bells were ringing four.

"Choir!" she sang, in the real and the *aethereal*.

One hundred and thirty-nine nuns and novices leapt from their beds, put their feet into sheepskin shoes, and ran for the chapel, leaving prie-dieux and psalters and paternosters, hairbrushes and combs and mirrors and beds and bolsters behind them.

Every one of them knew this was the hour, and like soldiers, they were ready.

Mostly ready.

On the floor of the chapel, two middle-aged women were already singing, working their way through the end of the early matins. Despite the air of crisis outside the chapel, inside it was dark and calm, lit by a single vigil candle, which reflected just a little from gilt and gold and polished silver and brass; a hint of beauty like a brief sight of a veiled woman's face.

Sister Katheryn, a slight, birdlike figure, was already at her place; their lead voice in the right-hand choir. By ancient tradition, the abbey had two choirs—for special feasts they sang together—and a dozen Alban composers vied to write them masses. Most days, only one choir sang, in a strict rota.

This morning, both choirs were coming in, and Sister Elisabeth stepped up to the *bema* of the left choir, her face rapt in concentration. Sister Elisabeth was tall, broad shouldered, her long fingers caressing the jeweled cross at her throat while her lips moved through the last invocation of the morning prayer with Sister Katheryn across the aisle.

Miriam went to her place. She peered into the *aethereal* and saw the mist gathering around the gate, and indeed, she looked through her mirror at the face of the gate itself.

There was light behind it.

And pressure. The pressure was building. So far, the wards handled it easily, but a curious amount of *ops* was being drained, even with the improvements that Sister Amicia had built into the systems.

She raised a hand and pointed at Sister Elisabeth.

Sister Elisabeth took the time to finish the Holy Office. She sang the *Ave Maria*, and Sister Katheryn's voice soared with her. Many other sisters, just coming in, took up the well-known words, and Miriam channeled the power, effortlessly, into the wards.

The pressure against them suddenly exploded.

In a heartbeat, half of her stored reserves were squandered in the wards; almost as much *ops* as Thorn had managed to drain away in the whole of his siege.

Miriam was not an easy woman to frighten. She pursed her lips and raised a small black wand, tipped in gold.

"*Kyrie*," she said.

Ninety-two voices began to rise in the triumphant opening. Other women ran, *ran*, dropping whatever last-moment need had delayed them. The clear, high voices rose; steady, powerful, beautiful.

They *sang in the* aethereal, *and now they were a choir of a hundred powers, and their pitch and melody, harmony and tempo were thought, and worship, and spirit, and their power was vast, and their adversary was stopped in its tracks, unable to scale the sheer ice of their perfection.*

But the adversary had millions of voices. And what they lacked in precision and harmony, they made up for in unity and purpose and they were loud, in the aethereal. *Their noise peaked, but through them, like a knife cutting an old curtain, the choir of Lissen Carak sang, and the two leaders found the center of the adversary's sound and used it as a bass on which to build their soprano, and their voices soared, and the adversary's music was merely part of their music, and for one timeless aeon, the whole of the adversary's power was channeled into the wards of the ancient gate.*

Miriam did not laugh, or smile, in triumph. Instead, she pointed in the real at the left choir, and Sister Elisabeth fell silent.

To the right-hand choir, she said, "*Gloria*."

The battle for the gates had begun. It could end only one way—in defeat—unless a miracle occurred.

Sunrise was still an hour away, although the sky was beginning to show light.

Gavin, Earl of Westwall, was at Southford. He'd driven his vanguard all night; he'd refused them sleep and food, and he'd all but beat some of them with whips to keep them moving. And now, in the first pale, desperate light of day, his hardened militia and his Morean mountaineers splashed through the ford, too tired to worry about the cold, and began to form on the far bank.

They formed a hollow square, and Tamsin began to *work* to protect them against the Odine. But the worms were still. When terrified Moreans came across a huddle of them, they were as unmoving as stones, or pinecones, which they more resembled when seen in the real.

The sky was pink in the east when Count Gareth's knights began to splash across the ford.

Greatly daring, a Morean corporal took a shovel from the chapel at the ford and used it to gather a few dozen of the worms, which were lying about in terrible plenty in the nearby stand of maple trees. His mates had a fire, and some sausage. He took the shovel full of worms, and threw them into the fire.

They burned. But then all the other worms began to awake.

The Albin River—Harmodius

For five days, while the boats full of gonnes and grain and soldiers moved at what seemed to him a snail's pace up the Albin River, he'd sat in the stern of the first boat, his hermetical sense watching the sky while the rest of his intellect unpacked, sorted, and put to rest the subsumed power of Richard Plangere; royal magister, lover of the king's mistress; traitor, Thorn. In the process he had learned a surprising number of festering secrets that had driven his former master to despair. Most of them were no longer even pertinent to the world in which they lived; secrets about the court, about sex, about illegitimate birth, and murder, and the process by which a kingdom is governed. Harmodius was able to watch his former master's disillusionment, his crisis of faith, his change. His fall, as a poet would describe it. Yet there were other stories to be told from his fall; and in five days of reliving a great many of Richard Plangere's memories, the silent Harmodius found that he liked the cautious, thoughtful Thorn a great deal more than he liked the socially grasping, upstart Plangere; and he learned so much about Ash that he began to question whether he had ever understood anything before.

In fact, he thought he might understand Ash.

And on the last day, the day when Master Pye set his ambush and all the boatmen hid in the great cave, Harmodius had a long time to wait for Ash; time to think.

Time to think that he had subsumed Askepiles and Thorn. And thus, held within him the total knowledge of two servants of Ash.

"Indeed," he said aloud. "Now I might be said to *be* Thorn."

He smiled. He had no fellow feeling for Askepiles at all. But for Thorn…

Lissen Carak

Abbess Miriam felt the tipping point when her adversary began to lose control of its choir. It was as if it had been ambushed in the real; a pinprick, a tiny scream, and suddenly the enemy will was slipping away, elusive and alien, into the endless darkness.

She looked up. "Ladies," she said in the real.

Both of her choirs were there, every woman present. Even the women who would ordinarily be in the hospital; even Sister Helen, who was one hundred years old.

She smiled. "That was not the battle," she said. "That was the morning alarm. Our enemy is as great as ten cathedrals and outnumbers us the way the stars outnumber the earth. Remember your parts; remember prayer and faith. Remember that what we do here is not for ourselves, but for everyone who lives here. Sister Elisabeth, you will watch while the right choir takes communion. Then the right choir will have the watch. Carry on."

Women rose and stretched. Most prayed. A few brushed their hair.

Novice Isabella turned to Novice Stefana and said, "This is going to suck."

Stefana failed to stifle a giggle.

"Ladies," said Sister Elisabeth. She raised an eyebrow.

The left choir began the *Credo*.

"What is our plan?" Harald Redmede asked the Green Earl. Redmede had a horse now; food was suddenly plentiful, and the army was moving into a camp, a fortified camp, at least with a heavy abattis of felled trees built by the Albinkirk garrison.

They were joined by Lord Gregario, and Duchess Mogon, and then, after some desultory talk and a lot of sausage chewing, by the Grand Squire and the Prior of Harndon and Syr Christos.

Gavin grinned and shook hands with the Morean knight. "Does this mean..."

Christos nodded. "Syr Alcaeus is half a day away, south of the inn and marching hard. And I passed Donald Dhu on the road with almost a thousand Hillmen."

"We cannot defeat Ash with men," Gregario said.

Gavin glanced at his imperial messenger. "The royal army is at the falls of the Albin this morning," he said. "Harmodius is with them." He spread his hands.

"Now you're talking," Gregario said.

Gavin made himself smile. "We're just in time, gentlemen. The first attack on the gate took place an hour ago, in our time. The abbess now has to hold Lissen Carak from within and without. We need to lift some of the pressure off her."

Every man and woman present frowned, except Mogon.

"I agree," Mogon said. "I have not seen an opening, but I know what happens. All the armies converge, and fight whatever emerges."

"We need a lot more sorcerers!" Lord Gregario said. "We can't stand another day of being pounded by Ash. And the worms!"

Tamsin nodded. "I would wish we were a day later," she admitted. "I cannot face Ash alone. Even with Miriam and all her choir providing me with power. I am not the channeler that Kerak was. I am not the scientist that Lord Nikos was. My powers lie in other directions."

"The good news," Gavin insisted, "is that Ash sent a sizable force after us yesterday, irks, bogglins, and other creatures, and we've just left them behind on the south bank." Gavin scratched his unshaven jaw. "My sense is that we need to put in an attack, a serious attack, and distract Ash."

The prior nodded. "If you could get me and my knights into the abbey, I think we could guarantee its defence for a long time. And hand Ash a defeat."

The slim, hooded figure with him nodded.

Tamsin looked at the slim figure, and knew who she was seeing. An idea came to her.

Gregario shrugged. "I will fight where I'm told, but this seems… chancy. To me."

Gavin looked around.

Mogon squinted her eyes and clacked her beak. "We are at a point where all the chances are long," she said. "We have survived the retreat. Now I wish to get my beak into Ash." She looked at Tamsin. "Is there anything you can do?"

The Queen of Faery smiled. Her eyes sparkled. "It is, as you say, a long chance," she said. "But I have played fairly for long enough. Now I will play unfairly."

Tamsin appeared in the aethereal *as a female irk, but clothed in smoke and fire; and the smoke was incense, and the fire was a very different kind of heat.*

"Ash," she said.

Ash was with her immediately.

"What prize do you offer me, Ash?" she asked.

Ash regarded her. And despite layers of minds and protections, he saw what he saw, in glimpses, and he was more than satisfied. "What do you want?"

"Freedom for my people, and the safety of my hold, forever," she said. "What else would I want?"

Ash remade himself as a handsome, dark-haired man with a limp. "Power," he said. "All of you mortals want it. I have it."

She smiled, and her fangs were well hidden, and her lips parted slightly; lips lusher and redder than any human woman's. "Power?" she asked. "For what do I need power, Ash?"

"Power to work your will on the world," he said.

"Alas, my will is only that of an old irk woman," she said. A billow of incense showed a long arm, naked to a shoulder, and Ash stirred.

"If you are old, then I am ancient," Ash said. "Surely there is something you want."

Tamsin was already dancing away from him across the plane of the aethereal.

"Perhaps," she said with an enigmatic smile.

Ash shook, and suddenly she was looking at a single, baleful eye.

"Let me tell you what I want," Ash said. "I want you to leave all the little men to me. And my friends."

"Perhaps," Tamsin said. "To tell you the truth, Lord Ash, I am not at all sure you will be the victor in this contest." She turned, and the smoke turned with her, weaving tendrils. An ankle showed, and then a thigh.

"Of course I will be victor!" Ash roared.

"Not the will?" Tamsin asked. "Even now, the will attacks the gate. If it wins the gate, what will it give you?"

"I can master it. It is weak in the real; a mistake I have made too often. This time, I am the stronger in the real."

"Even now, a mighty army builds against you; it will be led by Harmodius and Desiderata." Tamsin's voice was laced with concern.

"You are a great fool if you think that bitch can resist me," Ash spat.

"But . . . she has, has she not?" Tamsin said.

"She is already dead," Ash said with enormous satisfaction.

"Really?" Tamsin asked. "I think you are deceived."

She allowed the dragon a glimpse of her apparently unguarded thought.

"At the falls?" Ash reacted. "That deceptive bitch."

He vanished.

Tamsin gathered her smoke about her. "And not the only one," she said aloud to the aethereal. She passed a signal to Harmodius, and she paused to examine the edifice that the Odine was building; she sent a message to Miriam, and then she betook herself into the real.

The falls were two hundred feet high, with a cave at the base and a magnificent cataract of water that could really be seen only from the bottom.

They were barely visible from the new roadbed, although their thunderous roar drowned out almost all sound, even fifty paces distant.

Harmodius received the signal he dreaded, and expected, from Tamsin, in the *aethereal*, and *he reviewed his preparations; most especially, his wall of golden bricks and his new tools taken from his efforts to unpick what he had subsumed from Thorn.*

He notified Ser Ranald with a single flash of light.

He raised a layered simulacrum of Desiderata. He twinned a tiny portion of his own talent into his illusion and built there a pale shadow of his own golden wall, creating an animated statue with an apparent will. It frightened him a little, to be able to create something so very nearly alive, and he wondered, for a moment, if he could actually create something alive, and what the ramifications of that would be.

He saw Ash coming. The dragon made no effort to hide himself in the aethereal, *and Harmodius sneered at him.*

He launched a veritable barrage of attacks across the entire spectrum available to his talent. None of them were illusions. And all of them intercepted the giant dragon fifty miles from his goal, in the real.

The lightstorm struck the dragon as he climbed for a better view of the landscape around the falls, and he had no warning.

What he had, however, was aeons of age and experience, and his defences went to work, absorbing, channeling, deflecting, mirroring. A tiny fraction of the intense gout of power thrown at him at such an incredible range leaked through, but what fell off his defences exploded ancient rock, blew the top clear of a tall hill, leveled thousands of acres of forest, and started a huge fire.

What penetrated caused him pain.

He launched a retaliatory barrage.

Ranald's men were scrambling for cover long before the dragon struck; the whole advance guard packed into the cave under the falls, workmen, sailors, rowers, and soldiers packed like mackerel in a barrel.

The boats were, for the most part, already up the rails and ready to launch. Their cargo lay on the sand of the riverbank, all except one, which was assembled with its carriage. Master Pye stood by that one, and it was a monster with a mouth like a dragon, twenty-six feet long.

The dragon's response came in, titanic and ill aimed, and it struck in an ellipse roughly a mile long, raining fire into the woods and waters.

Harmodius did not await it. He removed himself, leaving his simulacrum of Desiderata alone.

Ash rushed on, scattering massive emanations the way a child might throw a tantrum, screaming, as it rushed down the stairs. Trees burned, or withered and died, and waters boiled.

Harmodius flitted to a new position, a mile or more north of the falls, and launched a new battery of hermetical devices.

Ash stopped them all. He turned, and breathed, laying utter waste to a section of riverbank.

Harmodius was already gone, passing through the *aethereal* to yet another place, this one carefully chosen with Master Pye's help.

The dragon turned, eager to close with his elusive foe, and passed over Harmodius, his great wings cupping air so that for a moment he hovered...

Harmodius loosed nothing, but withdrew his entire array behind the wall of gold that Desiderata had taught him, and Ash's arsenal, even his breath of unmaking, crashed on Harmodius.

The old magister was weakened. But he was still there,

Two hundred paces distant, Master Pye touched fire to his magnificent bronze tube. The powder ignited, and burned; instant, to the mind of a man, and a long, slow burn to the mind of the dragon, except that Ash was absorbed elsewhere with layer upon layer of other considerations; hatred and fear of Desiderata, perhaps lust for Tamsin, fear for the Odine, and within them layers of demands, of orders and commands and an edifice of control, and over all, the need to defend himself and kill Harmodius. His wings fluttered and he hovered...

The vast gonne fired.

A fifty-pound stone ball, touched with magicks, the surface of the iron covered in runes, sliced through Ash's shields.

For a beast the size of a great ship, the ball was less than the prick of a pin.

But the pain was immense.

Again.

It was late morning before the *will* came again, and this time, the attack was swift and vast, and in the first moments, a novice panicked and died, her nose spewing blood, frightening another, and she, too, fell.

But the other sisters of the left choir sang on. Miriam had not left her place; now she raised her baton and pointed at Sister Katheryn, and the right choir stood in a rustle of long gowns and habits and a gentle clatter of beads.

"*Sanctus*," said the Abbess.

The music built immediately; the women's voices building, one, two, three sections, and then the sopranos rising over all, and the web was established, to the *Dominus Deus* and the refrain.

More and more voices.

Dominus Deus!

More, and more voices. Miriam added her own voice for the first time; in the real, an unimpressive alto; in the *aethereal* a mighty stroke of power.

Hosanna in excelsis!

And now all her voices were committed, and yet it seemed to her that more voices were there than should have been; she felt, for a moment, as if she could hear Anne, dead two days, and even Helewise, murdered so long ago...

In nomine Patris...

"Ash is attacking Harmodius and the *will* has thrown itself on the gate," Tamsin she said. "You must try now."

Gavin closed his eyes. "It's broad daylight," he said.

"Nonetheless," she said.

He looked around. He'd moved a mile north of the ford, to the low ridge, more a fold in the earth, that looked out over the valleys that ran like fingers into the Adnacrags; there was the West Kanata, and there, the Lily Burn.

Just for the moment he held the initiative, and he had the north road through the farms along the river, which ran west to Lissen Carak, ten miles distant.

As best he could see, there was a major force to his north, and slightly east; centered, he was told, on Mistress Helewise's manor house; thousands of not-dead and a veritable mountain of worms, and beyond that, tens of thousands of bogglins who had come through the woods from Lissen Carak in the night.

And there was another force of them in the low ground beyond the Lily Burn. A huge force that no one dared scout, but Tamsin guessed it was many times larger than his own.

And a third force right along the Cohocton.

And a fourth force on the south bank.

And a fifth force covering the siege of Lissen Carak.

Gavin grinned in the near assurance of having, for once, done something right. His adversary, like an impossibly rich man, was squandering his fortune on a dozen projects; Gavin, like a miser, had gathered all of his in one place.

Oh, my brother. How I wish you were here to help me decide this.

What if this is our only throw of the dice?
Where the fuck are you?
To Lord Gregario, he gave a wave. "Go with God," he said.
Gregario nodded. "We're really doing this?"
"Right now," Gavin said.

Chapter Twelve

Irks and wardens had set a trap on the road—a carefully sited ambush in deep old woods. But they were westerners who had not faced the Alban chivalry before, and both horns of the ambush were smashed by knights charging through the woods, moving almost as silently as hunters so that the ambushers had only a few heartbeats to see the glint of metal before the avalanche of steel and horseflesh fell on them.

Lord Weyland rode down one side of the road, and the Grand Squire down the other, and they cleared the woods for hundreds of paces.

Down the road, uncontested, rode the silent Knights of the Order, cloaked in black, a great golden and green shield rising over them, and behind them came Donald Dhu, tall as a monster himself, grim, in black maille, with a great axe over his shoulder, and behind him came all the men of the Wyrm of Erch. And with them were the survivors of the royal foresters, while north of the woods, in echelon, were the two bristling phalanxes of 1Exrech and 53Exrech.

Then came the militia, already formed in long lines, interspersed today with wedges of the Count of the Border's knights. Tamsin rode with Lord Gareth, the count, and he shook his head ruefully at their thinness on the ground.

Lord Gareth's Northern Prickers were out to the right, moving over ground heavily infested with worms. He got a regular stream of reports, but at a high cost, as horses and men were taken.

He sent messengers forward to the Earl of Westwall, but none were coming back.

Harmodius could not withstand Ash's full power. His resistance had a cost, and doubt began to creep in; he knew that Ash had not been fully manifest when he attacked Desiderata in Harndon, and even as he doubted, a wash of black began to seep through his golden bricks...

He made his move. He had the working ready to hand, and he went... *elsewhere.*

Ash turned over the falls, located his true target, and threw his will upon her. And had the immense satisfaction of watching the gold melt away, until he realized that this puny thing was not even a woman.

His fury was beyond rage. He had been deceived; tricked by Tamsin and misled by Desiderata; his loathing of their kind peaked in a kind of insane malevolence that leveled forests and hills and laid waste to the countryside for a mile as he flew back toward Albinkirk.

Master Pye took his hands from his ears, and blinked many times against the scene burned onto his retinas.

Then he ran lightly, for such an old man, down the steps carved by the falls.

"Would be a funny time to slip an' fall," he said aloud. He went all the way to the base of the falls, where the rich green grass was now burned to ash, and rocks themselves were scorched.

He poked his head in through the edge of the falls.

"He's gone," Master Pye called.

Ser Ranald pushed through the falls and ran for the steps.

Harmodius surfaced in the real long enough to throw a powerful attack, and then *left.*

Ash, lost to rage, turned and followed him. Again.

North of Lissen Carak, the white bear's scouts froze, far out across an autumn marsh, and the white bear's paws shot up, and every man, every irk, and every warden froze, or went to ground.

"My paws, my claws, they, *grrr*, see something." He was as still as a furry statue; Tapio was already down behind a clump of alder, his great white stag flat in the marsh grass. Bill Redmede nodded. He pointed with his left hand; drawing the white bear's attention to a line of alder clumps and the mouth of the stream.

Redmede could not read a bear's expression, but he knew careful consideration when he saw it.

"We're quiet," he said.

"Humans are all, *grak*, loud," Blizzard said. One great shoulder rolled up in a shrug. "Go."

Redmede waved back at Stern Rachel and Long Peter, and they put arrows to bowstrings and began to slip into the high grass of the marsh, their dirty white cotes almost invisible against the pale gold of the dead grass.

They led the way, moving like wraiths, and then there were more men and women crossing the marsh, and then Redmede went himself, slipping back along the column to gain the best ground, and then moving quickly, his head low.

They moved fast, even when being silent—out across the marsh, over the stream at a beaver dam without a single splash, and then into the Alder brake on the other side and up the ridge. Now with the marsh between them and the irks and bears, they went east into the sun. Redmede spread his arms, palms down; his Jacks began to move into a skirmish line, pairs sticking together closely, moving from tree to tree as they entered the open highlands with the bigger beeches. Autumn had killed the hobblebush; hardly a stick cracked as they went, soft-footed, up the ridge.

Then Grey Cat stood, suddenly, erect. The Outwaller gave a call. Redmede raised his horn; he didn't know what the Cat was doing, but the Outwaller was half mad and all daredevil, and…

The Outwaller call was answered, or echoed. *Eeeeeeaaaaauuuuuuu.*

Suddenly the woods to Redmede's left exploded in Outwaller calls, and there were painted figures rising from the leaves, and stepping out from behind trees, and close in to Redmede a man in red and black paint rose *out* of a hollow tree.

But Redmede's initial impression that they were all Outwallers was mistaken; many were, but there were dozens, hundreds of them; he saw the white of his own cotes and the dreaded green of royal foresters and Outwaller paint.

But the man in the red and black paint had dark skin, and a blue stone dagger slung at his hip, and Bill Redmede knew him. He knew them all; he certainly knew old Wart, who was already slapping Stern Rachel's back.

He was surprised at how much young Aneas looked like his brothers. Though the man had deep lines on his face, as if his youth had been erased.

Bill Redmede wasn't much for bowing, or authority, but he managed to incline his head in a polite manner.

Aneas Muriens returned the gesture.

Nita Qwan was enjoying the rare embrace of the Faery Knight. Tapio rarely displayed emotion to the children of men, but today, at the edge of battle, a century of rangers and a handful of Outwallers seemed like a gift from his gods of fortune.

Blizzard looked as if he might have to allow himself to be provoked by the accession of so many strangers in his innermost holding, but Lily, who had followed the rangers through a hundred leagues of forest, would not hear of it.

"There is no, *rrr*, owning!" she insisted. "It is this, *mmmm*, owning, that makes men so greedy. Let us not bear, *grrrrk*, its taint!"

Blizzard watched them crossing his marsh; now almost a thousand nonbears. It had just started to snow, a light dusting of snow falling thickly enough to obscure the head of the column.

He shook his great white head. "They will come here, *rerak!* With their ploughs and their swords. I have heard, *rrrgrrr*. They say they will beat swords into, *grrrrr*, ploughshares. I say, *arrrr*, to a bear, *rrrr*, one form of conquest for another!"

Lily shrugged. "They are dangerous, Blizzard. Their smell makes me, *grrrrr*, deep in my throat. They killed my mother." She touched her snout to his. "They are, *geerrrak*, dangerous allies. But if we, *mmmm*, hide in our, *rrrr*, woods and try to, *rrrr*, fight the world, we will be warming, *arrrr*, floors across the world, our, *grrrr!* hides for rugs."

"They killed your, *grrrr*, mother, young one? And you, *arrrrr*, you walk the woods with them?" The older bear nuzzled her.

She grunted, turning away from his advances. "I, *grrrr*, end the war! Not revenge, and not, *mmm*, a mating with you, old bear." She laughed a bear laugh at his surprise, and she put a paw on him. "Listen. *Grrr!* Some men killed my mother. *Grrr!* Other men let me go. The world is not simple. Let us help these human love us. *Arrrrgrrr?*"

Blizzard swiped a paw at her. "So much, *grrr*, talk, from one so, *grrr*, young," he said. And when she loped away, he said, "And, *rrrr*, beautiful," and ran a hirsute thumb over the razor-sharp blade of his great axe.

The Army of the Alliance cut west, into the setting sun and the darkening sky. Now, almost three full weeks since the battle of N'gara, the whole sky seemed to mourn the fall of the Irkish citadel and the ruin of their hopes. The setting sun made the western sky into a blazing quilt of reds and oranges and long trails of brilliant whites, like dangling threads, and under all a pall of dark orange like a looming storm. It would, under ordinary conditions, have been a terrifying sky.

Most of the men and women of the alliance were used to it.

To the north of the road, in the closed fields bordered by hedges of the Albinkirk out-towns, companies of bills and bows, or heavily shielded crossbowmen guarded by armoured men with heavy spears, stood their ground against a sudden flood of bogglins and worse. A whole company of Jarsay militia were caught moving by a sudden charge of imps and annihilated in a spray of blood and flesh, and the greyhound-sized monsters fed on the corpses and then on each other in a frenzy of bone and blood as hideous as anything a storyteller could imagine of some distant hell. But in most of the fields, the stone walls and low hedges helped the militia make their stands, and where they failed, a sudden charge by armoured knights could stem the tide or at least buy the militia time to retire.

Most of the fighting to the north was a development of commitments from Lord Gareth's second line; he was cautious, and fed only as many of his infantry into the fields as were absolutely needed to cover the flank of the advance on the road to Lissen Carak.

When the sun had begun to go down the sky in the west, there were three mighty pulses of light in the west. Just after, Gavin rode back from the edge of the Lillywindle Woods and looked out over the battlefield to the north.

"We're overextended," Montjoy said.

As they watched a horde of enemies roll down the distant Kanata Ridge and across the north road, they were joined by Ser Alcaeus. He dismounted and changed to a big stallion, a warhorse, even as he greeted them.

With him were a hundred knights of Liviapolis. Behind him, on the Morea road, could be seen a dense column of men and baggage wagons. Ser Christos was in among the phalanx of the men of Thrake, dismounted, greeting men he knew, men who'd survived the last three weeks in the west, and more.

"We're too overextended," Montjoy said again.

"Give us another hour," Ser Gavin said. "The woods are a nightmare."

Montjoy slammed his visor up. It kept falling over his face; the catch had broken in the fighting. "My lord earl; I am struggling to hold Woodhull. Livingston Hall is virtually under siege. The tide is rising, my lord."

Alcaeus looked blank. "Woodhull?" he asked. "Living-stone?"

Gavin waved a hand. "Livingston Hall is just north of here; look, there, through the trees at the base of the hill. A castle."

Montjoy shook his head. "A fortified hall at best."

"It can hold off an army," Gavin said. "Woodhull; see the steeple of the church? North. Farther." He pointed beyond the creek at the foot of the ridge, almost a mile distant. The red light glinted on men and steel.

Gavin then waved his hand at the Lissen Carak road, running not-quite-straight from the southern edge to vanish in the woods to the west. Halfway from the Albin Ridge to the woods' edge, there was a fine stone church and a small walled town. "Penrith," he said. "Right now, it's being held by royal foresters and some Moreans and all our wardens and bears, under the duchess. She's keeping the road open for us." He looked at the imperial troops coming up behind them, and at the distant edge of the woods to the west, where his knights had vanished. "We don't need to hold all the ground," he said. "Hold the towns, and we'll retake the ground between at will. So far, there's nothing out there that can stop a charging knight."

"So far," Gareth Montjoy muttered.

Harmodius was almost done; almost out of both *ops* and options. He'd been clever; he'd been magnificent; he'd been subtle.

Now he was just tired. It was time for his last trick.

When Ash eventuated, very close, Harmodius held his shields and took the whole brunt of the dragon's wrath, the light dusting of snow vaporized, the hills beneath him melting to slag.

He took the last of his enemy's effort and followed it back, as quick as an angler taking a trout on a wild stream. Except that instead of reeling in his great fish, he was reeled in; his consciousness snapped back along the line of his enemy's casting. It was Thorn's working; the irony was not lost on his former pupil.

And like that, he was aboard. That was how Harmodius thought of it, in the fastness of his own essence; he was a lone pirate, boarding a vast ship.

The halls of the dark temple that was the mind of Ash went on for infinity, and the walls were written in an endless script, an alien hand that confused and frustrated thought even from a glance.

It was not like taking the mind of Askepiles, with its wheels and levers. Whatever he had expected, it was not this: the endless corridors of madness. He had expected to confront his great enemy for one last fight; instead, he was alone with uncountable internalized truths and overwritten falsehoods and a vista of stony darkness and abandonment.

Harmodius drew a Fell Sword from within himself. His right hand burst into life; light shone, where only darkness had ruled for aeons.

Harmodius took the sword and slashed it along the tiny lines of script that seemed to ebb and flow in three or more dimensions on the wall. The spot was not carefully chosen; Harmodius was aware that at any moment, out in the real, his borrowed body might be killed; if not by some hammerlike blow of ops, then by superheated steam or molten rock.

His sword went through the wall like a sharp knife slices the belly of a fish; slowly at first; then deeper, then gliding easily, almost without friction.

Once he had it deep, he began to walk along the apparently infinite corridor, dragging the Fell Sword through the entrails of Ash's thought.

He couldn't help himself. He began to laugh.

He allowed some of Thorn to surface, to see what they were doing, and Thorn laughed, too.

And then they began to vandalize Ash's subconscious.

Ash had lost his enemy; and he turned away in the air above the dark hills, his great eyes searching the path of steaming ruin left by his breath, but he could see no sign. His adversary might have translated again; or might be dead.

Ash was confused, because there at the end, his adversary's casting had more and more resembled that of his acolyte, Thorn, whose passing Ash regretted the way an old woman might regret a lost love, with unrealistic half-memories of splendour.

But even while the part of him devoted to immediate combat turned and searched, his consciousness had other demands on it, and he passed one more time along the line of hills, breathing unquenchable fire into the dark and snowy woods and rising on a wave of heat to look north, to the walls of Albinkirk.

His great armies were in disarray, but his plans were maturing. The armies of men were contesting the areas around the gate. His slaves needed orders. The *will* was utterly distracted, its full attention on forcing the gate.

Best of all, Orley and his little army were entering the field from the north; inconsequential in their numbers, but Ash had prepared five commanders for this very moment, and he reached out through the *aethereal* and filled them with purpose, examining, analyzing, passing information and command to each.

Every one had a chosen bodyguard of antlered knights. Each of them could run all day and all night, at the speed of a horse.

Ash sent one south, to his army of bogglins on the south side of the river. He sent another south and east, to lead the attack on Penrith, the obvious key to the army of men. A third he sent to crack the walls of Albinkirk. Orley himself he sent to attack Lissen Carak in the real; a necessary component to Ash's end game. The last of them, neither the least nor the greatest, Ash sent to the head of his legion of black trolls; the stone trolls of the highest mountains. To go to them, and stand silent.

Because Ash had learned that reserves were the key to battle. And although he couldn't foresee a need for such a mighty reserve today, he knew that victory today only meant that there would be other days and other foes among the million spheres.

But his plan was working; his slaves were holding together, and he had what he needed to destroy the surprisingly potent alliance and then clear the Odine off the gate. His "allies." The moment the *will* showed weakness, he meant to finish it. He didn't need them to win; he just needed them gone.

He missed Thorn; the closest thing to a confident he'd ever had. He wanted to gloat. There was no one with whom to gloat. Still, as the dark air rushed under his wings, he burned with maleficent glory.

"I will make war on heaven," Ash told the destruction beneath his wings. "I will change everything."

The bells atop the abbey at Lissen Carak were just ringing for four o'clock when Ser Gavin entered the woods that grew, deep and dark, on either bank of the Lily Burn. There were corpses in the road, and he paused, looking down at a shaman of the *adversariae*, dead with a black lance through her, surrounded by her bodyguard.

Ser Gavin paused, flipped up his visor, and drank from his canteen.

Grazias, his squire, took the canteen and drank some himself. Other men-at-arms, most of them northerners from the Albinkirk garrison, drank in turn. They were watching the woods. Nothing happened, but they all knew that the alliance battle lines were porous and fluid and they could meet enemies at any moment.

"Warhorses," Gavin said. He slipped down from his favourite riding horse and mounted Bess, his great roan. She grunted.

He liked Bess, but he wasn't sure she'd survive the hour. She'd been waiting for him in Albinkirk, and she had a blanket of double maille and a magnificent caparison with his arms, green and gold, emblazoned, so that she was brighter than his banner, which Grazias had.

He smiled. He'd always enjoyed being a popinjay bragging with the brilliance of his accoutrements, just like his brother. And his father.

Grazias offered him a pair of gauntleted hands to get up on Bess, but he leapt—his boyhood trick—caught the war saddle's pommel between his hands, and scissored his legs over the high back and into the depths of the saddle.

Bess grunted, and then let out a fart. Her breath steamed in the cold air.

Gavin rode back along the little column; about two hundred knights and armoured squires. He made a joke, slapped a back, and exchanged a hand clasp.

"Gentlemen!" he said. "This is why we are knights. So that on a cold autumn day, when all is dark, someone does the fighting. Today is the day. We can win this. Fear no evil. Fear no magistery. Kill whatever passes beneath the hooves of your horse, and we will, God willing, have the victory."

Men cheered.

They didn't know him. He'd lost all his own knights and men-at-arms in the fighting in the west; when he used his own household as the reserve, time after time.

They didn't need to know that. Because they were about to be the fire brigade again. Tamsin said something was wrong, on the Lily Burn.

"Let's go," Ser Gavin called, and the column, now mounted on war-horses, went forward, their harness jingling. A little snow began to fall and the light was fading, developing a silvery shimmer.

They rode forward a half a mile without meeting any opposition, and then they hit a mob of bogglins, right on the road, and Gavin snatched his war hammer off his pommel and beat a couple of them to death, cracking their skulls, while Bess made a liquid ruin of another dozen under her hooves.

They had been feeding on a Knight of the Order and his horse, and there was another, and then another.

"Look sharp!" Gavin called.

His column trotted along.

He began to see movement in the woods to his right, and then to his left.

He ordered his rear to move up, and two dozen knights led by Ser Galahad d'Acon moved out into the woods and there was fighting immediately, but the big horses moved easily through the dead foliage and open trees, and bogglins died.

Even with his visor closed, Gavin could hear the fighting. It was all along the line of the stream; he knew these woods and he knew the sounds. And the presence of bogglins in the woods meant that the enemy was leaking around both ends of the alliance line. He had to guess; it was getting dark; this was their only chance.

It was all risk.

He slapped his visor up. "Galahad!" he roared in his father's voice.

"My lord?" D'Acon called, from fifty paces away. All the knights halted.

"Take half and go north until you are free of enemies; cross the creek and then fall on their line. Watch your flanks."

It was a huge, terrible responsibility for a royal messenger who'd been a knight for two weeks and was just twenty-two years old.

D'Acon put his fist to his visor. "Consider it done," he said.

Ser Gavin left his visor open, passing forward along the road. A gust of snow swept in; they came to a gentle bend in the road, and there it was.

The enemy was holding the bridge. The new stone bridge, four men wide, a high arch over the ink-black waters. It was called *The Warden's Bridge* because Gabriel had killed a daemon there.

Now there were a great many dead knights. Indeed, Gavin's heart almost broke; a third of the Order lay there, and twenty more knights, some dead, some terribly maimed, and their horses screamed and kicked, impeding any further attempts to force the bridge. The Knights of the Order had erected a shield of shimmering gold-green; even as he watched, a great gout of *ops* slammed into it.

There was *something* on the bridge.

"Prior Wishart is wounded," Ser Ricar Orcsbane reported. The young, usually silent knight was also wounded. "My lord, we cannot defeat this thing. Weapons will not bite on its hide, or armour; its weapons cut our steel like paper."

"Cave trolls," Grazias said, unnecessarily, at his shoulder.

Even as he watched, a Knight of the Order rode forward. His warhorse, despite massive armour and a heavy rider, leapt over the tangle of bodies that choked the bridge, and the horse's steel-shod hooves struck sparks from the stones that looked like fire in the falling darkness, and the knight's lance lined up with the great antlered thing's chest, and struck home, and the antlered demon was rocked back…

…but the lance shattered, and the dark thing struck back with an axe, killing the knight's horse in a single blow. The knight was thrown against the bridge. He didn't rise.

"Where is Ser Gregario?" Gavin snapped. He'd left Lord Weyland in charge when he'd ridden back to look over the battlefield only an hour ago.

"Attempting to turn the position from the north," Orcsbane said.

Another Knight of the Order saluted, made the sign of the cross, and charged. His horse sailed over the tangle of dead and dying and his lance, either perfectly managed or lucky, struck the antlered man in the forehead, between the sprouting antlers that stood out roughly parallel to the ground, two long black spikes. The thing had a dark coat, like matted sheepskin, and fire came from its mouth, and the lance knocked it flat, and the Knights of the Order on the road gave a great cheer.

It rose, muscles rippling, as the knight swept past and threw its axe, casually, and the axe split the knight's head all the way to the root of his neck and he slumped forward and his body burst into flame, a dark, smoking flame that immolated corpse and horse, and his fine stallion shrieked in terror as he burned.

The thing on the bridge turned, faster than a man could turn, caught the handle of his axe, and pulled it from the corpse-torch and brandished it, and all along the streamside, the bogglins and daemons and irks cheered. There were thousands of them.

Gavin rode to the Prior of Harnden as yet another young knight launched his charge.

"We must retreat," Gavin said. "This is foolishness."

The prior looked up. He lay against a tree with his right arm gone from the elbow.

"No," the prior said. "I'm sorry, but I *must* get into the abbey tonight. Everything depends on it."

Gavin shrugged. "We can't lose the rest of your knights." He looked over his shoulder.

Another young knight was cut down.

"Stop it!" Gavin roared.

The slim figure in the black cloak who was working on the prior's wound moved a hand.

"Ser Gavin," she said. "Hard Hand. We must win through to the abbey or we will lose everything."

"My lord," Grazias said. "My lord. The dragon."

Gavin turned, looking back along the forest road toward Albinkirk. The trees were mostly bare of foliage, and through them he saw a looming black shape, and then the bright sparkle of the dragon's fire.

Judging from the position of the thing, it was setting fire to Penrith.

The loss of Penrith would collapse his center.

Gavin looked around—at the prior, at the tall woman by the prior, at Grazias and at his own knights and at young Orcsbane.

"Right," he said. He bowed to the woman, and saluted the prior.

"Grazias," he said. "Give me the other sword."

"Other sword?" Grazias said. But he put his hand on it—the great black sword of Ser Hartmut.

He held the scabbard, and Gavin reached out and drew the sword.

"Time to fight fire with fire," he said.

He wheeled Bess on her back hooves, so that the great mare spun like a top, and he put her head at the bridge. But he didn't charge. Instead, he trotted up to the bridge, covered by the Order's shield, and the shaman on the far bank launched a forked attack that was wasted on the golden leaves of the defence.

Gavin came to the tangle of dead knights and let Bess pick her way around it.

He reined in at the base of the bridge.

The antlered man came and stood at the very crest of the bridge. He...very emphatically he, with a parody of manhood between his heavily muscled legs, raised his great steel axe and shouted. His shout was echoed by irks and bogglins and by the wyverns who had begun to circle overhead like huge carrion crows.

Gavin saluted with his sword, and it burst into flame.

"Do you think your puny magic can harm me, mortal? I am a Son of Ash! I am immortal! Your day is over, and my master will make a new earth."

Gavin listened, but his attention was not on the monster's words, but on the sounds from the north: the ring of steel, and the round of horses, and a trumpet playing a particular set of notes.

"Did Ash promise that you would be immortal?" Gavin asked. His right hand reached out and gave Bess's neck an affectionate pat. The black, fiery sword spat and crackled. It felt like a feather in his hand; beautifully balanced, but more than that. He was more than a little afraid of it, but at this moment, it was his hope of victory.

"Ready, my sweet?" he asked his horse. The trumpet sounded again. Darkness was falling.

He just touched his spurs to Bess's flanks and she leaped forward up the bridge.

Gavin leaned forward a little, against the slope of the bridge, sword held, blade down, on his left side, where the monster couldn't see it. His horse was passing the thing on his right.

Its axe swept up.

Gavin cut *up*. The thing's head was as far from the ground as his own, and his rising cut met the axe at the haft as it descended.

Hartmut's sword cut through the haft like a true sword through a twig. He wasn't at a gallop so in the same tempo his sword cut back down the same line, the simplest of re-attacks.

The horned man twisted, sweeping up the haft and slamming it into Gavin's right side under his arm; the blow rocked Gavin, the force was terrible...

… but not as terrible as the force of a mounted lance. His armour held; he shrugged off the blow and turned Bess, even in the tight confines of the bridge.

One long, spiked antler fell to the bridge with the sound of breaking crystal.

"Immortal?" Gavin asked. His sword licked out, faster than thought, fastidious as a house cat.

The other antler fell.

The denuded monster roared with anger and cut at Gavin with his staff.

Bess danced.

Gavin cut the monster's staff at his hand. Fingers sprayed like blood and the shaft fell to the bridge. Bess planted one steel-shod hoof on the thing's chest, and then another, *one, two*, like the punches of a veteran boxer. Her hooves did the thing no damage, but her blows knocked it back. It stumbled, and the Knight of the Order who'd been thrown against the bridge put the butt of his broken lance between its legs as it struggled for balance, and it fell, back, over the wall at the edge of the bridge.

The knights roared.

Gavin pointed the sword over the bridge and Bess blew into a canter, the leap of a jousting horse; Gavin took a long moment to recover his seat, and then the daemon shaman was headless, slumping to the ground, and Bess was trampling bogglins.

Gregario's trumpet was closer.

The Order's knights began to come over the bridge; there were perhaps fifty left, or fewer, and behind them his reserve, the knights of Albinkirk.

Gavin burst through the back of the enemy and turned Bess in a shallow curve, filled with the spirit of combat, wanting to laugh and shout with joy, wanting to go sleep, wanting never to have to do such a thing again, and as he turned, he saw the dark thing coming up out of the streambed.

Gavin blinked. "Fuck," he muttered.

He saw the thing unhorse a knight with his fist, point at a second, and there was a burst of pus-yellow fire and a scream.

Gavin put spurs to Bess, who did not deserve any such.

His adversary let loose a torrent of sorcery, and knights and men-at-arms died in every direction—twenty, thirty in a heartbeat.

Bess went forward as if galloping through molasses.

Gavin rose in his stirrups and put the burning sword between him and the thing.

It loosed its bolt down the line at him.

Orley, if the armour of flesh and bone on Ash's auxiliary consciousness could still be called Orley, drew on his master's enormous power and began to throw his bolts against the vast, puissant shields of force that covered the whole of the abbey ridge and the towering fortress itself. Behind him stood a dozen of his own kind and twenty stone trolls lent him by the reserve; a host of bogglins who darkened the earth; and another thousand of the western daemons who, despite their dismay at the cold weather, were eager to fight their way into the warm caves beneath the fortress, their ancient and traditional hold.

They slammed weapons into shields.

Orley raised his arms and threw another impossible wall of power into the ancient wards.

Miriam was aware that she was losing. The loss was gradual; it might take the *will* aeons to break her, but its massive powers raged against her choir, her wards, and the impossibly ancient powers of the gates like a massive flood facing a very ancient dam. The water rose slowly, interspersed with sudden surges; the weight increased by degrees, on many levels, so that even as the allegory of the flood might be one reality, in another, Miriam's very sanity was challenged; her identity, her sense of self, her faith, her gender, her confidence, her love. All undermined; all sabotaged.

No abbess was chosen for anything but this; that she knew herself, and had that kind of spirit that cannot easily be broken. Miriam's identity was always a little malleable; her faith was open to doubt every day, her gender had never been the center of her being, her confidence had always rested in her faith in others, her sanity was always a matter for her private mind.

But her love for her people and all people she'd even known was like adamant.

And her choir was very, very good.

By the time that darkness was falling across the snowy fields at the base of the ridge, she had fought all day, resting her choir the way Ser Shawn was resting knights, but now the battle was approaching the inevitable climax and she was being forced, like a tiring swordsman, to resort to her last tricks.

She pointed at Sister Elisabeth, and the left choir, on note and on tempo, joined the *Ave Maria*.

Now she had both choirs in. Now there would be no rest until the end.

Miriam knew that the end was coming. She could see it; like a checkmate in chess, the inevitability inescapable. But she could postpone it as long as possible, in hopes of a miracle.

Gabriel, where art thou?

She dismissed Gabriel, and any dreams of glory, and focused on prolonging her own agony.

Beneath Ash's mighty wings, chaos reigned. He stooped, ignoring a hail of darts and arrows, and breathed again on the ruins of Penrith, and the steeple of the church fell, the stone cross crashing to earth, and the flame of his breath burned among the foresters. Harald Redmede died there, and John Hand, and a generation of Alba's best woodsmen. And then another of the antlered men led the bogglins forward, and crashed through the handful of men still able to face them, taking a few to eat alive and destroying the rest, scattering fire and lightning.

Ash's magnificent wings beat, and he stretched out his neck in glee. The army of men was broken; his slaves poured through the ruins of Penrith like the waters of the sea through a broken dyke.

Command of the Alliance Army had devolved to Alcaeus. Lord Montjoy had taken his knights and charged into the maelstrom behind Penrith. He'd said he was going to try to stem the tide, but he left Alcaeus with the impression he hoped to die well before the collapse became general.

Alcaeus smiled a bitter smile. It was a very Alban attitude. But Alcaeus was not Alban; he was Morean; he had seen many bitter defeats, and many hollow victories, and his people resisted the impulse to glorious self-destruction. Moreans endured. They were patient.

He watched for as long as it might take a priest to say a hurried communion prayer. He watched the dragon breathe fire into the ruins of Penrith; he saw the knights strike home, rocking the enemy back; then he saw them slow, unable to face the heat of the burning town, as the enemy began to leak in around them.

The dragon passed along them, and again his fire lashed men; hundreds died.

But then the dragon turned suddenly, his long, terrible neck curling north and west, and the titanic wings beat, and the vision of hell passed suddenly west, wings beating so hard that the wind raised a curtain of snow.

Alcaeus watched the dragon depart with narrowed eyes.

He looked down at his people: five thousand Morean veterans, the very last of Livia's ancient legions, armoured in long shirts of maille and armed with heavy spears and round shields. Some had fought all the way to N'gara and back; others had guarded Liviapolis until a few days before.

A man grinned at him. "Lead us, Alcaeus," he said.

And Syr Christos nodded. "We can save this," he said.

Alcaeus pointed at the very center. "Christos, go. All the way down the hill, and restore the center. I will go to the right..." He was looking at the base of the ridge, where 1Exrech and his legions still held. "I will go to the right and attempt to...do..." He smiled. "Something. Damn it, Christos. I'll try and do something."

"And so will I," Christos said. He saluted. "For the emperor."

"Wherever the hell he is," Alcaeus said.

Ser Gavin Muriens

The bolt struck Gavin's flaming sword, or perhaps he parried with it; the bolt was split into two, and each went into the ground, churned to mud by the blood and intestinal fluids of a thousand dead sentient creatures and a hundred horses' hooves, and he leaned forward, pressing Bess to do her best, and she responded, her stride opening.

The antlerless demon slammed a fist into Bess's armoured head; he crumpled the great spike, and her great strength was no match for its malevolence. Gavin went back over his crupper like he was practicing in the tiltyard.

He hit hard; the ground here was almost frozen, and he had a flare

438

of pain in his shoulder, and then he was up, moving, and the realization that he had lost Hartmut's sword was almost perfectly twinned with the sight of it pinned neatly under the demon's outstretched foot.

But it was an ungainly position for a monster with legs so long.

"Now," the thing said. "Now I will eat your soul...."

It was bigger than he was, but not immeasurably bigger, and its posture was ridiculous, and Gavin used the whole spiked peak of his bassinet on its abundant testicles as it pounded a fist into his armoured back, but it was toppling, its weight overextended, and Gavin, despite the crunching of his ribs from the blow, stumbled back and got his hand on the hilt of Hartmut's sword, and it burst into flame.

He cut at the nearest part, a flailing near-human hand, already missing a few black talons, and he severed it, and black blood began to come in great gouts, as if being pumped out by a strong boy at a summer well.

It pointed the bleeding stump at him and he was showered in its terrible blood, but he cut again, this time blind, but still a good cut, a simple *fendente* that caught something. Gavin stumbled back, threw up his visor, and saw it clutching its face.

"Noooo!" it said. "Noo! I am powerful! I am indestructible! I am immortal!"

Despite the burning of his skin, and despite a mote of pity in his heart, Gavin stepped in close and swung the sword right to left, a simple, snapping blow.

Its head fell clear of its body.

Ash felt the death like a blow. He already felt giddy; his memory was being attacked by a wave of unaccustomed memories and doubts, and yet a sort of bubble of success was rising in his dark heart as his slaves rolled forward in the last light, sweeping all before them.

And then...

One of his creations was injured. It should not have been possible; it represented a flaw in his foresight, as he realized that he'd left undone things that he ought to have done, which was of a piece with all the revelations in his innermost mind; why was he suddenly recalling a terrible betrayal an aeon old?

His creature died at the hands of a mere man.

The humiliation was immense. He felt revealed as a failure; he felt...

He paused, and wondered if he was being attacked by the *will*.

He could find no trace of such an attack, but the fire of self-doubt was burning strong, and he had to wonder...

And something was happening at the gate.

It occurred to Ash, too slowly, that he was being played. That the *will* had *used* him to distract the men from the main effort. That his own captain, Orley, was directly serving the *will*.

Ash paused in indecision, looking down over his victory. He could sense Tamsin, over on the ridge, trying to keep him off by misdirection; the seductive witch was next. And he could feel something else, beyond the ridge; something strange and powerful. And again, where his creature had just been cut down, there was another he couldn't identify. Very powerful. Burning like a fire.

In that moment, he identified her, and he screamed with rage and frustration.

Chapter Thirteen

Orcsbane had his orders, and he did not hesitate, despite the trenches filled with enemies and the way the enemy lines crawled with monsters.

He led forty knights and a dozen surviving squires across the trench lines, half of them empty, and cut through the fringe of bogglins that formed at the edge of the second rampart. They appeared and vanished under the hooves of his destrier and they were through, galloping over the shovel-smoothed ground.

A gout of fire blew over them, but their shared shield held.

There was another, and then three forked snakes of purple lightning that scored their hermetical shield and killed a warhorse, leaving the knight to fight, die, and be eaten alone in the falling darkness, because Ser Ricar had his orders and he was not going to fail.

His horse's hooves began to ring on stone, and he was in the rubble of the abbey's little town, and then his steed was running up the paved road to the great gates three hundred feet above him. Arrows flew, darts were hurled, but Ash's legions were hesitant, their master's intent muddled, and Orcsbane's band rode on.

A sudden wave of sorcery rose against them at the very edge of the walls—an obliterating mass of power of all colours and intents, unleashed by a horned figure close on the slope as they went past in a shower of hoof sparks.

The sortie gate opened. A single crossbowman emerged and loosed a massive arbalest bolt downslope as Orcsbane pulled savagely as his charger's bit, pulling the horse back on its haunches.

"Go! Go!" Orcsbane roared.

The slim woman in the black cloak rode directly through the low gate without dismounting, as if into the maw of a monster.

There were daemons coming up the slope, and a cave troll. Lightning played over them, and Orcsbane parried it. Fire fell past them—mundane fire, mere flaming oil, but the burning oil splashed the huge Saurians and the cave trolls generously.

"In!" Orcsbane roared.

Men passed him: a squire, leading two horses, another knight. Then another.

He kept the shield up; he could feel something downslope preparing...

He threw his lance. He couldn't think of anything else to do, and he needed to interrupt the caster; his lance flew, struck the antlered figure a sideways blow, and the thing turned.

It was *another* antlered man, and at the sight of him, Orcsbane prepared to sell himself dearly.

In the middle of the burning hell of Penrith, the Duchess Mogon stood with her household, unbeaten, under a shield that glowed emerald in the fire. Her knights were surrounded by the dead. To her left stood the bears—unbowed, dirty, and terrifying to their foes. To her right stood the royal foresters who had survived the dragon's fire. Mogon was pleased with them; for mere men, they were brave,

But she could feel the black presence coming. She thought perhaps that she was too tired to make him pay; she didn't even know if it was Ash in person. She only knew that it was the end; that the battle was lost. Her people had given everything for a cause that was now done. To her left, everything was gone; the lines of militia across the fields were swept away, the knights who had charged to the rescue driven back or eaten.

In front of her, Teskanotokex swung back his stone axe and killed another one. Or three.

She nodded.

"You are my brothers and sisters, as much as my nestlings," she said. "When we fall, may we go together to the swamps of the hereafter."

They bellowed with more spirit than she had herself. She stood straighter; wished she had her feather cloak to die in.

She leaked a little raw *potentia* into her people, and then took some herself, like a cake of opium. Her eyes glittered and her crest stood erect again.

Good.

She raised both arms. "Come and face me!" she roared at the darkness.

And the darkness came.

It was big—as big as she—and it had the shape of a man, but like the caricature of a man, or a terrible, humorless joke about a man; the muscles oversized, the penis huge and erect, the antlers contorted, the face savage. It was the figure of a man carved by a sculptor who hated men.

To the great Duchess of the West, it was not a figure of terror. It was more like a clown.

"Mine," she called to her knights.

All around her in the rubble, they stepped back.

She raised her great sword-axe and felt the sharper-than-razor flints along the edge of the massive wood core.

It raised a huge axe. "I am the Son of Ash and no steel or bronze weapon will touch me!" he roared.

Mogon licked her beak in derision.

"I am Mogon *Texetererch*. I am Duchess of the West, and in my caves no cold can come, and my reach is long. My sister Musquogan was duchess before me, and before her my mother, back and back to a time before your master was an evil egg." Her sword-axe carved a line of fire in the air. "My *shen* is of stone. Your life is mine."

"I am not mortal!" roared the beast-man.

"Dream of hell, Son of Ash," she said.

Then he threw *ops*.

She parried, tossing his ball of unformed power off into his own legions of imps with contempt.

"Is this a duel of powers?" she asked. "Or can Ash not face me blow for blow?"

Suddenly she unleashed her true power; the lash of her wave front of terror struck him, and in that moment, his spark of humanity failed him, and he was *afraid*. Terror lashed him, and he quailed, flinching away from her majesty.

And into his moment of failure she struck, once, and her stone axe burst open his chest, cutting down, smashing ribs and severing muscle and tendon and intestine. It was the culminating blow of all her years of training and combat. It was almost spiritually pure; she delivered it without thought, her mind blank, and he raised no defence, and he fell with a single despairing spasm, his face lost its fixed look of rage, and his spirit vanished.

She raised both arms slowly, taunting the cowering bogglins and the enemy *Qwethnethogs*.

"That is who *I* am," she roared into the darkness.

Hawissa Swynford had survived the day in Penrith. She had helped the other foresters hold the edge of the town for hours, loosing her shafts until her back and arms ached and her quiver was empty. Then she had fought with her sword, and when that broke, with a bogglin's spear.

When the dragon came, she was terrified, but only in a vague, distant way, because she'd experienced so much terror by then that the horror was a dull ache in her head. Luck and nothing more had left her with a blistered face and no worse. Half her regiment had died and she stabbed another bogglin and tried to find time to breathe.

Swynford was an old hand, a northerner with ten years of service. When Hand and Redmede burned, she found herself the senior officer of the survivors; or at least, no one else seemed inclined to give an order.

She might have stood and died in apathy, but for seeing the Duchess Mogon drop the "Son of Ash" like a butcher might kill a pig. The sight filled her with something: spirit, vitality, and maybe hope.

"Arrows," she spat at Collingford, one of the best of the old foresters she had left. "We need a thousand shafts."

"If wishes were buttercakes," he said tiredly.

"Go try," she ordered. "Get back to the ridge. Find...the Green Earl. Or the Faery Lady. Someone high up who knows where the baggage is. Tell them we ain't dead. We're fightin'. We need shafts. Do it."

He saluted her. Which seemed funny enough that they both laughed.

In the air west of the battle, Ash shuddered as if from a great blow. If he had had a god to curse, he would have. The risk of creating these pawns was that their deaths were a blow. Two in one day was a terrible loss. He staggered, and lost altitude.

But in the *aethereal* the true battle was raging, and there Ash *saw and thought that he understood. There, the two legions of the* will *faced the two choirs from within and without, even as his creature Orley smashed gouts of power into the hermetical fabric of the shields that sustained the abbey against his attacks in the real. It was like a child throwing water at a castle, but the castle was no longer built of rock, but of ice, and the water was slowly melting the walls. Orley was drawing freely on his master's power, reveling in the impression that it was he, and not Ash himself, who was the greatest warlock in the world.*

The castle shuddered again, and again.

The will *paused.*

For a moment, there was a sort of silence, and the Benedictus *of the choir rose slowly; the soprano voices began to rise above the strong alto; the altos began to add their* Glorias *to the hymn of praise...*

The will *struck. It struck with a single note, a note of discord that roared with the unison of a single will, and it cut through the* aethereal *empathy of both choirs, and a dozen women fell dead, their blood boiling in their veins, or frozen solid.*

The choirs faltered.

But the older sisters did not falter, and voices carried on, against the slighting note.

Outside, a massive fountain of raw ops *plastered itself against the shields by the north tower, and Miriam had to divert some of her choir's reserve to support the wards...*

She could no longer keep all the structures in her head...

It was too complex, too awful, and she had held them together as long as she could, losing a little here, a little there, and watching her own terrified dissimulation from a distance; a memory lost, a hope destroyed, as the will *took her one tower of intellect at a time.*

In the end, all she could do was pray.

Miriam slumped, blood pouring from her nose and mouth, and for a moment the choir leaders held the weight of the failing structures. And then *something*, something of an enormity that dwarfed even Ash, lifted a single note.

Far away, an unimaginable distance away, the other half of the *will* paused, and knew fear.

And in that moment a knight ran down the aisle of the choir, his sword drawn, and behind him, a figure in a long black cloak that flew behind her as she ran, all out, lungs bursting for air, for Miriam's podium.

All the universe balanced on the edge of a single step, and the woman reached out and scooped Miriam's wand from her lifeless hand. Her hood fell away and Desiderata stood in Miriam's place, and the wall of her mind was like a mirror of gold.

"*Magnificat*," she said.

And in that moment, the *will* failed. The half of the *will* close by seemed to scream, the single note of attack turned to disharmony of despair in a moment, and the choirs of the abbey, beaten a moment before, began to rally as Desiderata's mind and voice protected them.

Ash saw the abbey's shields flicker, the wards down, and he unleashed the lightning sword of his thought, not through Orley, but direct from one stretching talon, and the whole north tower blew off its foundations and fell in ruin across the slope of the ridge, crushing a thousand creatures, men and bogglins, trolls and daemons and irks. The chapel shuddered, and the stained glass of the great rose window shattered, and glass fell across the whole floor.

But the woman in the abbess's chair was unbowed. Her clear voice rose, and Ash could not stop it. The *will* slid off her mind like a child attempting to climb a wall of glass, and the dragon's assault did not move her. And the choir began to join her, a voice at a time; some trembling, some strong.

Ash was raining fire on the abbey, and the walls were falling, turned to rubble, but the chapel stood, and Desiderata stood, and then the gate, which had slid open the width of despair, slammed home again with the strength of hope, and the wards, empowered, sprang back.

Far off in the valley of the Cohocton, beyond the Lily Burn, Ash's great assault had stopped. On a field littered with dead knights and broken crossbows, the men of Thrake stood their ground, and then, in the darkness, their foes backlit by the wreck of Penrith, they locked their shields and began to press forward, step by step, hampered by the dead—a line of dead bogglins like the storm wrack left by a typhoon—step by step, and so great was the press of their enemies that even the hymn to the Virgin sung by five thousand Moreans could not overcome the weight of it, and they, too, stalled.

Then the city regiments charged, the *Tagmata* who had trained so unwillingly with the sell-sword who was now emperor, and then, into the balance, 1Exrech led the "free" bogglins, who had held the lower slopes of the ridge all day and now pressed home a slight advantage, and somewhere in the flame-lit hell of Penrith, the "Son of Ash" died, humiliated by the duchess, and the enemy line began to fail.

It was no victory. The enemy, disciplined or undisciplined, simply flinched back in the darkness, and no man, no irk, no bogglin, sought to follow them beyond the firelight of the burning town. But Mogon was not dead; her circle of knights was rescued, against all hope, and as the snow began to fall, Alcaeus came up from the victorious right and Gavin approached from the left. There was Tamsin, her emerald gown tinged with soot; she had bags under her eyes and lines on her face like an old woman, and the small choir that followed her all looked aged beyond their years.

With her was the Patriarch of Liviapolis. Alcaeus fell to his knees in the snow, and Gavin thought it politic to join him.

He shook his head. "No, none of that," he said. "I have come to do what I can, against the direct command of centuries of tradition."

"Since noon, he has kept us in the battle," Tamsin said. "Never have I felt so much love for any Christian." She smiled, and her fangs showed.

"Nor I for any faery," the Patriarch said.

Ser Gavin waved for drink, and Grazias, who had survived the day, and who bid fair to be the best squire Gavin had ever had, produced a flask of Candian wine and began to hand it around, so that in ten sips of liquor, the Queen of Faery, the Earl of the North Wall, the Patriarch of Liviapolis, and the Duchess Mogon drank with Alcaeus and 1Exrech and Lord Gregario and Ser Shawn and Donald Dhu.

The last swig Ser Gavin handed to his squire.

"Here," he said. "Finish this."

Grazias looked around the firelit circle, and took the bottle. He bowed, and drained it.

"Kneel," Gavin said. He knighted the young man in one blow to the shoulder, and turned to face them.

"We haven't won," he said. "In fact, we probably can't do that again. I'm still unclear why Ash so spectacularly failed to capitalize on his advantages."

447

"We haven't lost yet," Alcaeus said. "And Ser Ranald is beginning to unload at Southford."

Ser Shawn nodded. "Albinkirk proper is under attack," he said.

"Where the hell is the emperor?" Gregario asked. "He said he'd be here two days ago."

Tamsin's eyelashes fluttered.

"I wish I'd seen you drop the daemon," Shawn was saying to the duchess.

"I'll dance it for you, man," she said.

Over fifteen miles away, there was a titanic explosion. The earth rumbled, and there was a spray of light into the air, so that for a moment, every man and woman and *Qwethnethog* cast a dark shadow on the new-fallen snow.

Tamsin stood up straight. "Desiderata is in Lissen Carak," she said. "She is facing Ash." She narrowed her eyes. And then closed them. "The *will* is failing."

The distant lightning played on the abbey like a storm in the mountains. They watched it, mere spectators.

"So," Gregario said. "Tomorrow?"

Ser Gavin shrugged. "Today worked because we had a ton of luck and a very simple plan," he said. "And we lost ten battles' worth of people. Can we even fight again tomorrow?"

Alcaeus shrugged. "My people only fought in the last hour, and they were victorious," he said. "Even now, a man is saying he had a vision of the Virgin."

"My people are mostly dead," Mogon said. "I pray that the Sossag have been loyal, and my eggs and nests are safe, or we are done as a people."

Gregario frowned. "My knights are exhausted. I've lost a third of my horses."

Exrech nodded. His voiceless voice clicked. "Wine excellent. Fight tomorrow." His mandibles opened halfway, a fairly horrible sight that allowed those standing near him to see straight down the hairs of his outer throat to his first stomach.

The wight belched. He clacked his mandibles. "Every hour, the scent of truth brings me recruits. Tomorrow, I will have twice what I had today. Ash is not strong. We, together, are strong."

Gavin looked around at all of them. "That is it exactly, damn it." He laughed. "The one thing we seem to be good at is staying together."

"Say rather, the one thing at which we have excelled is distracting Ash," Tamsin said. "Nothing I could have planned, no wile or deception, could have been as effective as our chaotic probes." She shrugged. "I have almost nothing left. But if that was our last day..." She managed a smile.

"Where is Tapio?" Gavin asked.

"Close," she said with a smile. "Close enough that I hope to see him, ere the end."

"The end?" Gavin asked. "I don't think so."

They all looked at him.

Gavin shrugged. "You don't know my brother," he said. "If he says he's coming, he's coming. If he has to march through hell to reach us, he will. If he has to war down Satan, he will."

Gregario laughed. "Damn, I love your faith. I just wish he'd get on with it." He looked around. "Anyone have more wine?"

And Tamsin nodded. "I have no faith, man, except in my Tapio. If Gabriel does not come now, we can only make a song."

For more than an hour, Desiderata held the gate and the wards with the survivors of the two choirs, and one by one, when the walls were clear, she added the deep bass and tenor voices of the Order's knights to her choir, in the real and in the *aethereal*, and the mixed choir was stronger than the two choirs had been together. And ever she held the *will*, and ever her wall of gold stopped Ash, and when he came close, she forced him to see himself reflected in her, and he flinched.

But the struggle was unequal, the addition of twenty male voices could not change the inexorable mathematics of power, and as the time for vespers approached, Desiderata began to endure the same tendrils of doubt, except that she was facing the whole of Ash in addition to the *will*. *The* will *became strident; the stridency rose to a desperate pitch, and Desiderata began to feel a thread of hope among the warp of fear; the* will *was no longer as united, and voices were leaving its discordant note, and she felt a weakening in it.*

And then it rose like a suffocating fog, and all Desiderata could do was to say, in the real:

Sing!

And every man and woman in the chapel, cut with glass, wounded by sword and claw or unhurt and merely exhausted, raised their voices

449

in praise as best they could. And the *will* rose like a tidal wave threatening to engulf the world, but its desperation and dissolution were inherent in the force of its last throw.

Something was happening.

In the *aethereal, just the other side of the gate, it lost its note. The discord became silence…*

Then, in a moment, it was gone.

The choir, without it, actually stumbled a moment before one voice rose over all the rest, a novice whose pure note towered and led, and then, voice by voice, the others rejoined.

And in the *aethereal*, a mighty power rattled the gate. It shook Desiderata for a moment; at the instant of victory, there was a new foe.

Chapter Fourteen

The gates—the company and Gabriel

There was no opposition. Tom Lachlan led the *casa* forward the moment the emperor passed the gate, and before Cully had taken a second breath, the *casa* emerged in fighting formation: knights in front, dismounted, with squires at their shoulders, holding the same spear, and archers in the intervals between lances.

They came through the gate, all together, as they had practiced, because there were so many things they had worried about; they were in superdense order, sixty men wide. Bad Tom was in the center.

The wind burned at them. The sun was rising, so rapidly that they could see it move.

"Tar's tits," Tom said. "It *is* hell."

Gabriel was at the edge of the cave, looking down at the desert floor below the road. Dust swirled, and the sand moved as if it were alive.

"Halt the advance. I want to scout," Gabriel snapped. His voice sounded odd.

Cully went back through the gate. And reappeared.

Gabriel allowed himself to smile. "They work," he said. "Both ways. By God, friends, we may yet be in business."

The green banda was passed to the front; this contingency had also been envisioned, and the greens filed off and came through mounted, and were followed by a dozen Vardariotes under Kriax, who saluted.

They cursed, too.

Gabriel took Kriax to the edge of the cave. He pointed at the swirling sand.

A vicious mouth emerged and vanished.

The wind blew, dust moved, sand slipped...

Legs. A hundred insectile legs, each as long as a tall man's.

"Green magic doesn't work here," Gabriel said. "And the sand is *full* of those things. Stay on the road." He turned to Daniel Favour. "The road may be trapped. My chart says we only have to go sixteen miles; those are old imperial miles. I am guessing that takes us to the mountain. It may be defended, and I'm not sure what the hell we do next. But we don't have time for caution."

Favour gave a wry smile. His hands were shaking.

Kriax just shrugged. "I should have died a hundred times," she said. "Maybe today?" She shrugged again.

Tom Lachlan looked at Gabriel. "I want to go me'sel."

"No," Gabriel said.

"Ye'r jus' like yersel!" Bad Tom said.

Gabriel was looking past him. "Go back through, tell everyone to water up. Tell them there's no battle, and that we need to go like blazes. Tell them what we know: no green magic, hot as hell, sixteen miles."

"Don't forget the fuckin' centipedes," Cully said. "I fuckin' hate centipedes. And that's when they're smaller 'an my finger. Not bigger 'an my fuckin' head."

"What do they eat?" Gabriel asked the red-hot air.

"Each other?" Bad Tom opined. "Kill one, Cully."

Gabriel paused to remonstrate, but Cully suited action to word. The next time one of the things showed a set of segments, Cully put a livery arrow at the joint.

The whole creature spasmed, and for a single heartbeat, it was clear in the sand; the incredible, hideous length of it and the legs... kicking...

A dozen other centipedes converged on it, their furry armoured bodies obscenely fat, their hundreds of legs working in sand. In the feeding frenzy that followed, one monster, gorging on a section of carcass that bled what appeared to be thick milk, clawed its way up the wall of the ridge or hillside from which the cave emerged.

Sixty livery arrows struck it. It fell away into the sand, and another horde of the things devoured it.

"Sweet Jesus," muttered Michael.

The feeding swirls were dangerous; they forced the centipedes close to the walls, and seemed to remind them they could climb.

Gabriel tossed a small fireball out into the sand, well out.

The burst was very satisfying.

Like the tide turning, the insectile creatures turned away into the sand. This time, the feeding coruscations could be seen five hundred paces away as a temporary writhing hill was formed, the creatures warring for the choicest bits, rearing their great bulk.

The emperor shook his head.

"Yon's dis*gusting*," Bad Tom said. "I seldom seen somethin' I didn't reckon on fightin'." Yuck."

The emperor just stood there in the furnace heat, shaking his head. "Let's get out of here," he said.

He went back through to the cool underhall, and Tom Lachlan brought the whole *casa* back through. Although there was no "through." The gate was real. There was no distinct feeling of passage, although the hot wind was warming the hall.

Gabriel went to the golden plate that now stood at waist level above the floor, inserted the key, and turned it.

The coloured window sprang back.

Gabriel nodded. The hall was packed.

"Water up!" he roared. "You have half an hour."

Blanche was there. She looked at him, eyes wide.

"It's real," he said. A smile was threatening his face. "Damn, Blanche, it's real."

He and Michael narrowed the order of march, leaving the edge files plenty of room, and ordered more water brought forward.

Beyond the gate—The Red Knight

The scouts cantered forward, the horses restless and skittish with the wind and sand. Daniel Favour watched the road ahead; from time to time, he swept the roiling sea of sand to his left and the sand flat to his right, which went all the way out to the horizon of tall, jagged peaks capped, it appeared, in snow. The crawlies were horrible enough, and yet, in ten minutes of riding, they'd faded into the background of his thoughts. He tried to concentrate despite the hellish heat.

They rode almost half an hour, and Favour's mare began to flag, and he reined in.

"Water up, and switch horses," he said. "Wha'hae! Daud! Watch the sand."

One of the Vardariotes walked over to the edge of the road and began to relieve himself. Suddenly he stumbled back, spraying urine.

Kriax was there, her strung bow in her hand, and Daud the Red. Both shot immediately, even as Favour moved to his latchet, which hung from his saddle.

The crawlie came right up the embankment of the road and half a dozen legs showed, as well as its coarse hairs and the jaws...

Kriax got off a veritable string of arrows. They seem to go so close together that the head of one touched the fletchings of the last, and she hit it with every arrow, but none seemed to penetrate very far.

Daud loosed, and saw a full-weight war bow arrow shatter on the thing's foreparts even as a pair of wicked mandibles the size of a child's legs reached for its victim.

Old in war, Favour looked back. Sure enough, there was another crawlie coming up the left side of the road. "Even files!" he roared. "Left side!"

The sound of pottery shattering as someone dropped their canteen. A horse bolted.

Chaos.

Arrows.

Favour ran across the smooth, even stones and spanned his latchet at the same time. He ran up the road, widening the gap, working on a theory. He stepped to the edge of the road...

There were ten of the things *right beneath his feet.*

"Jesus," he spat. Paused, aimed, and shot—back, at the monster going for Kriax. In the side, between the segments, as he'd seen Cully do.

His bolt sank past the wood fletchings, opening a hole that spouted white ichor like a fountain.

Instantly, another crawlie attacked the wounded one. It was pulled down off the road, and eaten as fast as Favour could stumble back from the edge and span his crossbow for another bolt, ratcheting the slide with all the power of fear.

The scouts knew their business; every man and woman knew exactly how the kill had been made, and they spread out along the road, enveloping their immediate attackers in a crossfire. A dozen crawlies were hit, and suddenly there were exploding mounds of carnivorous nightmares...

"Mount!" roared Favour. "Go, go, go!"

He got up on his remount and shot, put the ring of the latchet over his pommel, and turned his horse. Most of his people were up, but Daud had been caught too far from his horse and his remount had bolted and was already being pulled over the edge by a crawlie, screaming in shrill horse terror...

Favour cantered forward, put down a hand, and swung Daud into his saddle as if they practiced such things every day...

...which they did.

"Liked that horse," shouted Daud.

Kriax was up and moving, and the near-side mound of feeding frenzy began to collapse onto the road; six of the things were falling, rolling, their hundreds of limbs unnatural and horrible, their mouths questing...

They were nowhere near as fast as men on horses.

The scouts cantered clear. "Holy fuck," Kriax spat. She was deathly pale, and her hands shook. "Holy fuck," she said again.

Favour looked over his command and back toward the crawlies. Most of them had already left the road. He had no idea why, but he wasn't going to waste time on it.

"We could go back," Wha'hae said. His voice had no tone; no whine. He was in shock. "We *should* go back."

"We're not going back," Favour said. "We're scouts, friends. We scout."

Then he dismounted, giving his remount to Daud, and putting a casual hand on his shoulder, but the glazed look was already leaving the hill man's eyes.

Daud was praying, his eyes closed.

"We didn't lose anyone," Favour continued. "Now let's get this done."

He stepped up onto the stirrup of his mare.

Kriax turned to the man who'd gone to the edge to relieve himself. "Pee on the fucking road next time," she said.

The easterner looked bad. Daud rode to him and looked him over. "You hurt, brother?" he asked.

The man couldn't talk. He was grey with terror; his cheeks looked splotchy.

Daud put a hand on the man's shoulder and the easterner flinched.

"Let's ride," Favour said.

Now they clumped up near the center of the road. Favour tried not to look over the edge. The lone mountain that seemed to be the destination grew closer, and closer, and—

"Holy fuck," Kriax said, reining in so hard that her big steppe pony slid on the smooth surface.

There was a cut across the road.

It was forty paces wide and the edges were jagged.

Against his own will, Favour made himself go to the edge and look down.

"Fuck," he said.

The whole space was full of crawlies. He could see them as they surfaced—legs, a flash of the red sun on a carapace...

His hands were shaking as he backed away from the edge.

Kriax looked at him.

He walked to her and put a hand on her horse's bridle. "Any thoughts?" he asked quietly. His people were skittish; everything was wrong, the colour of the air, the smell, the incredible heat; the crawlies, the huge red sun like a malevolent eye. It was all alien, and the scouts, who specialized in alien, were spooked.

Kriax was *not* looking over the edge; Kriax, who was, short of Bad Tom, the most insanely brave person Favour knew. "Holy fuck," she said for perhaps the fifteenth time. "We go back and get a sorcerer," she said.

Favour tugged at his short beard. "Costs the cap'n two hours," he said.

Kriax shrugged.

Favour wished he were a scout and not a corporal. But he'd been briefed and she hadn't. He knew that time was everything. "I want to try something," he said.

She shrugged. "Sure," she said, with an easterner fatalism that told him what she thought.

"I want you and Daud and... Short Tooth. You are the best archers. Pop a crawlie... way out. Like Cully did. Like the cap'n did with sorcery." He gestured vaguely.

Kriax's eyes were blank. "Sure," she said. "And then what?"

"I try and get across the gap. On foot." He shrugged. "We send Wha'hae back with two of your troopers to fetch help, but I go across and keep going." He paused. "No Head will need to know exactly how wide it is."

Kriax looked around. "Yes," she said. "Yes, it is a good plan. Stupid and good. I will go with you."

Favour was tempted to say something brave, but instead he smiled and said, "Good."

They moved forward with the plan before Favour could have second thoughts, or really, fiftieth thoughts. Half a dozen arrows flew, and then another flight, and a third; well out in the sandy plain, the maelstroms started.

And the gap began to empty. The crawlies left like fish swimming upriver; Favour saw that they even had fishlike tails.

"Three down," Kriax said.

"Ragnar," muttered an easterner. "Look at that."

Favour spared a glance to see that there was a towering pile of crawlies, all going for...

"We got two, right together," the easterner said proudly.

Favour shook his head.

Kriax was already crawling down the broken embankment.

Favour followed. Wha'hae and two of the Vardariotes were mounted, their horses head-up and ears back.

He had trouble breathing. He'd sweated through his jupon in the terrible heat, and it was *worse* down on the plain. And the sand was soft; too soft. As soon as his foot touched it...

Kriax *screamed*.

She was sinking into the sand.

Favour didn't hesitate. He powered forward, one foot and then another; he felt the slight sinking, the unnatural softness.

He threw himself full length on the sand and caught her hand.

"Oh god oh god ohgodohgodohgod," she said.

He pulled and nothing happened.

He saw movement at the corner of his eye.

"Crawlies!" came the shout from above him.

He pulled at her, a surge of power from raw fear, and he shouted.

Something caught his feet and pulled.

Favour fought the urge to scream and turned his head, his face full of sand, and there was Daud the Red, pulling his feet. There was a surge, and shout, and Kriax came free of the sand. A shower of arrows fell somewhere off to his right.

Favour got to his feet.

Daud had Kriax.

Favour snapped up his latchet and began to run. He didn't look to the right or left, and he ran soft footed and very fast. Men were shouting; a woman's voice, and someone close to him shouted, "*Fuck fuck fuck fuck fuck fuck…*"

It was his own voice.

A crawlie erupted from the sand, just to his right, and he raised the latchet one handed and popped a bolt and *ran* without missing a stride.

His eyes were on the rocks; the collapsed stone structure of the ancient causeway. He leapt onto the first one, got his feet under him, and leapt to the second, and the third, and then with one surge from his thighs he was up, his hands grabbing the iron-hot edge of the road, and he swung his legs like an acrobat, and got one knee up, and for a moment, just a moment, he paused, unable to do more.

Something rustled below him, a clicking, slithering noise.

In one panicked explosion he got his shoulders up and he was over, rolling on the road, scrambling back.

The crawlie came up, the mandibles searching for him. He could see its eye patches and smell the horrific acid exhalation from its pink-purple gullet, and he was on his back, his hands and feet going like some reversed crab.

He rolled, his latchet still in his left hand, and drew his short sword as he got to one knee, and his cut went into the mandibles almost at the root, and he cut one free even as he covered the other with the steel bow of his latchet.

The thing gave an odd, pitiful mewling cry and slipped away, and Favour stumbled back and saw that the thing's carapace was studded with arrows, a hundred fletchings protruding from it, and a flood of love, of companionship and fellowship, filled him.

His people had his back. The whole other side of the cut was lined with scouts. An arrow whistled past his head; he ducked.

The crawlie fell away.

Daniel Favour took four or five deep breaths, and then saluted with his sword across the gap, and the scouts roared back.

Then he sheathed his sword. It took him four tries. He stepped back to the edge. The usual feeding pile was already as high as the road surface but evilly silent, the grotesque fishtail of one of the crawlies spasming in death...

"Fifty-four running paces," he shouted.

He latched the crossbow and put a bolt on the stock, turned, and began to lope down the road toward the mountain.

Wha'hae appeared at the gate and Gabriel opened it. There were three scouts and Gabriel immediately knew there was trouble; all three men were badly shaken, like men who had endured real pain.

"There's a gap, Cap'n," Wha'hae said. He was a big man with a big head and a wiry mustache, and fear sat ill on him. "Crawlies came at us over the road."

"Losses?" Gabriel asked. "No Head!" he roared back in the cavernous hall behind him.

"We only lost one horse. Fuckers came at us—'orrible." Wha'hae shrugged. "If'n they see movement, maybe."

Mortirmir was pulling on gloves. "I'll go," he said. "They are flesh and whatever. I'll handle it."

Gabriel thought for a moment, balancing the squandering of *ops* against lives and time.

"Go," he said. "No Head?" In fact, he desperately wanted to go himself. The delay was ripping him apart. He needed to *do something*.

The man appeared.

"Dan says the gap is fifty-four paces wide. He were running like a deer; bra'est thin' I e'er seen."

"What?" Gabriel asked.

"We shot some o' the fuckers and then—you know? They eat each t'other?"

"Yes," Gabriel said, making a face.

"Favour and Kriax ran for it. Kriax went in some hole. Or it's quick sand. I wasn't…" Wha-Hae paused. "Any road, Favour made it across and counted. Fifty-four."

"Kriax?" Gabriel asked.

"Daud the Red pulled her out o' the sand. Bra'est thing I e'er saw." Wha'hae was calming, but he wasn't fully in control of his words.

No Head thought a moment, then went back and started roaring orders at Sukey, who was still at the top of the ramp.

"I'll need two wagons and the rest o' the greens," No Head said over his shoulder. "And my pick o' men."

Long Paw appeared.

"Ser Robert?" the emperor nodded at Long Paw. "Your command. There's a gap in the causeway. Report when you have a bridge or it is untenable. Magister Mortirmir is *under your command*." Gabriel looked at the young mage, his eyes slightly narrowed.

"Yes, sir," Mortirmir muttered.

"Wha'hae—how far?" he asked.

"An hour's fast ride. Call it eight miles," Wha'hae answered.

"Paw, as soon as you know it can be bridged, I want a report. And then another messenger so I can start an hour before you complete. We do not want the army strung out on that causeway and then halted, waiting, with the local flora and fauna coming at them."

"Christ almighty," Wha'hae said.

Gabriel turned to Michael. "New march order?"

Long Paw ran to his horse; No Head already had Sukey and Blanche and a set of tablets. He was running through supplies, and he was simultaneously naming off men or women with carpenter or siege engine skills. They came out of the ranks, most of them archers, and brought their horses.

In less than ten minutes, the green banda rode out, with two heavy wagons between them—one loaded with lumber—and Morgon Mortirmir riding just ahead of the wagons.

"I want to go myself," Michael muttered.

No Head paused as Gabriel opened the gate. *Casa* knights led by Philipe de Beause moved out into the cavern and made sure the ramp and road were clear.

"Fifty paces is a long bridge, Cap'n," No Head said. "If I can't patch it, I'd have to use all our stored lumber and all our pontoons. And it'll take…"

Gabriel was watching as Bad Tom gave the all-clear sign. "How long?"

"Three days," No Head said.

"We don't have three days," Gabriel said.

No Head saluted, rare for him. "I'll see it done," he said.

"We have to do this just right," Gabriel said. "It's going to be like one of those logic problems with so many logs and so many salmon sandwiches. Michael, you and I are going to stay here, in the rear with the gear, and make decisions."

"I'd rather fight monsters," Michael said.

"Me, too," said the emperor.

Daniel Favour jogged through the overpowering heat, stopped and drank off his canteen, and ran on. The mountain was close now; maybe a mile. He could see a gate, or an opening.

He tried not to think.

About half a mile from the mountain, he came to another gap, but this one was only partial. Something like the fist of a malevolent god had slammed into the causeway and broken away about two thirds; for several hundred paces the road was just wide enough for a man on horseback.

Favour didn't stop or think. He ran on, his pace increasing. He didn't look down; like a tightrope walker, he kept his eyes on the approach to the gate and kept going. Nothing struck him; perhaps he was too small, or too fast, perhaps there was nothing below him. He knew if he looked down and saw crawlie legs, he'd lose it.

He kept running, his lungs on fire, his legs weakening. He tried to think of a prayer, but nothing came; he tried to think of home, and nothing came.

And it all took a long time.

But he crossed the broken patch, and then, almost instantly, he was in the mouth of the gate. There was a ramp up, worn almost as smooth as glass. It seemed to exhale age; a vague smell, like old books and graveyard.

Favour looked into the mouth of the arch.

Well? What'd you come here for, if not to go in? he asked himself.

"Come on, scout," he said aloud. "Scout."

He made himself go into the mouth. There was writing on the walls, and here and there the sparkle of a black jewel, perfectly polished like an insect's eye.

Ten paces in, it was as dark as pitch. He paused, much against his will, and his imagination supplied it all: spiders and webs and unseen hands and nameless horrors waiting just beyond the last light, things older than man...

He stopped and breathed, his hands on his thighs.

His eyes began to adjust to the darkness.

The cavern was huge. It rose above him like ten cathedrals, and there were carvings and perhaps even a hint of colour. And deeper in, there was a kind of light, like the glow of fungus in the night of an Adnacrag forest; the kind of glow you best see out of the corner of your eye.

Favour managed a prayer. Then he started forward, his terror only slightly overbalanced by his sense of duty.

Step by step he pushed himself forward.

The fungus glow grew brighter. Not very much brighter, but it developed a shape and a sense of distance, and he took ten more laboured steps, wondering if he was walking into a dragon's mouth. His sweat was cold; undigested food roiled in his gut.

Ten more steps. The silence was older than humankind, the hall higher than history, the darkness around him deeper than sin.

He had a temptation to scream, or sing. But he was a scout; he moved quietly and stayed to the left-hand wall, latchet up, the point of his bolt and his eyes moving together, discipline overcoming fear.

Or perhaps simply cohabiting with fear.

Ten more steps.

His heart began to beat very fast. Very, very fast.

There was... *something* there.

It was like a curtain of starlight. He had trouble judging the distance, but in the center was a small pillar, like a giant's tooth. Like...

Like...

He almost bumped into it.

It stood waist high off the glass-smooth floor, and it held a flat plaque. Beyond it was the curtain of night sky without stars—the deep blue-black of the abyss.

He put his hand on the plaque and felt the keyhole.

"Son of a bitch," he said.

He turned and was immediately shocked at how far he'd come into the cavern. The mouth now burned like a furnace in the distance, like a white-hot eye.

He turned and started back, moving as quickly as he dared.

Long Paw rode up to the gap and shook hands with Kriax. She was already mounted.

"Bad?" he asked.

She shrugged.

No Head rode up and looked at the gap, and then the others were halting, forming ranks, and dismounting. The men-at-arms immediately turned outward, watching the edge of the causeway. Every archer put a shaft to his bow and another five in his belt.

"Fucking hot," someone said.

The wagons rolled up, the horses rolling their eyes in fright.

"Water the horses," Long Paw ordered.

Mortirmir dismounted and walked to the edge. "Ser Robert?" he asked.

Long Paw had to struggle to recognize himself as "Ser Robert."

"Yo?" he called out.

"With your permission," Mortirmir asked. "I will empty this area of these...things."

Long Paw made a face. He had just seen his first crawlie. "Do I need to know how?"

Mortirmir raised both eyebrows and then shook his head. "No," he said.

Long Paw looked back at No Head. "Can you bridge it?" he asked.

No Head looked at the gap. "No," he said. "With Morgon's help, I can make a ramp down and ramp up the other side."

"Then we need to hold the crawlies off for...twenty hours," Long Paw said.

No Head was looking down at the sand. "If'n I told you what to move, could you move the big rocks?" he asked.

Mortirmir was briefly reminded of the day he'd put up the weather-proof roof on the great amphitheater in Liviapolis. "Yes," he said.

No Head gestured. "Clear these disgusting bugs away and I'll look at the sand. Mayhap there's foundation left under it. Otherwise I'll need ten days and a forest o' trees to cross this."

"What about Mag's ice bridge?" Long Paw asked.

Mortirmir shook his head. "Ice melts," he said, as if to an idiot.

Long Paw frowned. "Right. Magister, roll the bugs back and let's see what No Head can improvise."

Mortirmir walked away without a word. He stood alone for a long time, like a statue, and then he nodded once.

"Erue me circumdantibus me," he said.

There was a little disturbance deep in the sand between the outflung edges of the gap, and then a little ripple like the disturbance of a pebble thrown into still water ran outward into the sandy plain on either hand. The wave front ran, and ran, until it was out of sight.

Mortirmir dusted his hands like a man who had done a job of work.

Far out on the plain, there was an explosion of mandibles and legs, a feeding frenzy of titanic proportions. Dozens, if not hundreds, of hills of struggling, vicious monsters surfaced, tearing at each other, but they were almost a thousand paces away. Nonetheless, they raised a curtain of sand.

Men crossed themselves.

Mortirmir took a pebble from a pouch at his belt and tossed it on the sand. He raised an eyebrow.

"Nothing down there is alive," he said. He shrugged. "Well, to be honest, I suppose something more powerful than me might be alive. Or something whose whole notion of life is outside my perception." He shrugged again.

"You fuckin' *fill* me with confidence, magister," No Head said. But he climbed down the ruin of the embankment and walked out onto the sand.

Nothing happened.

Far out, so far that it was almost imperceptible, a mountain of squirming crawlies broke the horizon above the dust clouds.

"God, that's gross," spat an archer.

No Head was down in the gap, and he walked along, slamming a spear butt into the sand. Kriax called out to him and he found the spot into which she had fallen. He marked the edge with an orange flag. Then he walked along the edges, planting more flags, little pieces of painted canvas often used to mark maximum ranges for the archers. He poked under the sand and found a huge block of stone, poked again, and leapt in the air.

"Dead bug," he said. "Disgustin'."

Morgon nodded absently. "Oh yes," he said. "I will have killed quite a few."

No Head came back up the side while most of the green banda stood and sweated and watched the distant struggles for dead crawlie flesh expand and expand, but still well beyond the reach of an arrow.

"How much juice ha'e you got?" No Head asked Mortirmir.

"More than you can imagine," Mortirmir said.

No Head rolled his eyes. "Right. Under the left side, the foundation inintact. I need ye to pick up them big rocks; I've marked 'em all in blue. And set 'em neatly, all touching, on the foundation. Y'll need to clear yon dead bug an' all that sand."

Mortirmir nodded. He waved a hand.

The dead bug rose, all two tons of it, and was flung like a round from a trebuchet off into the maelstrom.

Archers made approving noises. There was a patter of applause, and Mortirmir flushed with pleasure.

"Really, that was nothing…" he began, and then caught himself.

Mortirmir moved his hand like a scoop, and sand was moved; inaccurately at first, but in minutes, the line of the old foundation and the damage to the center of it were cleared like digs of an ancient ruin.

No Head coached the magister, grinning at his facility.

"Master Mortirmir, when this is over, you and I will build some beautiful things together."

Mortirmir paused, one hand in the air, as if seeing No Head for the first time. "I'd like that," he said. "I'm tired of blowing things up. The hermetical is for more than war."

No Head nodded. "We're going to make a palace," he said. "Like no world anywhere has ever seen."

Long Paw called out two women known to have fast horses and sent them for the column and the emperor.

"Tell him it'll only be single file here," he said.

As soon as there was a single line of massive blocks cleared and laid, Long Paw ordered his column forward. They left the wagons with No Head, and his carpenters, who were already working on a hand rail and a small, portable engine tower.

Kriax nodded to Long Paw. "We want to go ahead," she said. "We want to get to Favour."

Long Paw nodded. "Got water? Good. Lead the way."

Kriax's Vardariotes rode across the line of blocks and up the other side and went forward. The rest of the scouts followed; Wha'hae gave Long Paw a somewhat ironic salute, and then Long Paw himself was crossing. Behind him came the men-at-arms, squires, and archers of the greens, leaving half a dozen lances to cover the work.

"What if they need more?" Kriax asked Long Paw.

He grinned. "Mortirmir's worth more than an army," he said.

The scouts cantered off with spare horses trailing after them.

Four hours later, Mortirmir was standing by the pedestal and the plaque of the second gate with the emperor. Tancreda was manning one causeway point, Magister Petrarcha another, and a dozen lesser magisters were shuttling the troops along the road.

A great many crawlies were dead.

"Fifteen hours to pass the defiles," Michael said. "If all goes well, no one oversets a wagon..."

"No Head has the second patch in," Ser Milus reported. "Sukey says she can cross with wagons."

"Nowhere to camp and no water," the emperor said crisply. "We *have to go through*." He paused and looked at his staff. "But if there's an army waiting on the other side, we are fucked. I admit it; this isn't a contingency I could plan for. I thought... damn it, I thought we'd fight at the gate."

"Now we're strung out on a hostile causeway with terrible temperatures and no water." Michael frowned. "We could call everyone back and scout all the gates..."

"If I had worlds enough, and time," the emperor said. "Only we have no time. We have two thousand men here and enough magistery to level a city. I say we open the gate and hope for some luck."

"Or God's will," Father Antonio said. He'd brought up a message from Sauce, and stayed to see a gate.

Gabriel smiled. "You know, Father, at the moment I would be delighted to accept God's will." He looked around.

Tom Lachlan tapped a thumbnail on his teeth.

Father Antonio raised an eyebrow at Mortirmir. "Why no green magic?" he asked.

Mortirmir shrugged. "Master Harmodius has a theory," he began, and paused of his own will. "Never mind. I really do not know, but I will guess that there is a tie between a world, and its native ... *potentia*. I will speculate that there is another native magik here, and that with time and effort, we could find it."

Father Antonio nodded.

"Just do it," Tom Lachlan said to Gabriel. "We're playin' fer keeps. No room fer caution."

"You would say that," Michael said.

"Aye," Tom admitted. "I would."

"Right. Gate formation," Gabriel ordered.

The *casa* came up to the gate. Spears glittered in the cold darkness and armour took on a strange colouration, as if the men and women in the mirror-bright armour were ghosts, spirits of themselves.

Armoured squires leaned into their knights.

Armed pages stepped up. Behind Philip de Beause, a thin, graceful page in fine armour leaned her slight weight against the back of his squire.

"Note that the gates are the same width," Morgon said.

"Shield up," Gabriel ordered. He looked back at Cully. "What did you want to ask me, back at the last gate?" he asked.

Cully was looking at his arrow. "You saw the stained glass? O' old Aetius the saint?"

"Of course," Gabriel said. He was watching men fidget, and wondering why de Beause's page didn't know her place in the line and had such good armour, and calculating the hours lost, and thinking of Blanche, and ...

"Only, Cap'n, his face were brown in all the panels until the battle, eh?"

"Yes, Cully," Gabriel said. He wondered where his archer was going with this, but Cully had earned the right to rattle nervously.

"Right you are. No, listen, I'm going a twisty road, Cap'n. Here's the point. In the panel of the battle, his face were golden yellow. Eh?"

Gabriel's breath paused. "You're sure?" he asked.

"Thought you'd want to know," Cully said a little smugly.

Mark my words.

Gabriel started, his hair standing up on the back of his neck. He looked back, calmed himself, took three breaths for concentration, and went *into his palace.*

He raised his own shield of gold; he placed the golden buckler on his arm. He paused and winked at Prudentia.

"For this, you were born," she said again.

"I wish you'd stop saying that," he said.

Mortirmir's shield covered the entire phalanx of the *casa.* Behind, the Duchess of Venike had her scarecrows on their feet, their long spears shining in the starlight. They almost filled the great cavern, and they were packed very closely.

Gabriel waited a full minute; so long that Ser Michael thought the emperor might have changed his mind.

"I need a piss," muttered Cully, and people laughed.

"Ready?" Gabriel shouted, and his voice, attenuated by the hermetical shields, echoed off the ceiling far overhead.

He took the answering growl for assent.

The plaque had eight settings and four lines. He consulted the itinerary in Al Rashidi's memory for the twentieth time and turned the key from the bottom of the cross to the top.

The curtain fell away instantly.

Gabriel's heart beat so fast he wondered if he could die of it.

There *were* stars. They had been hidden by the working of the gate, but now they seemed to fill the sky; millions of stars of brighter than normal intensity. A night sky, and a mighty comet burned across it in splendour.

A smell of vegetation and something else, like cinnamon. Maybe like basil. Cool. Pleasant.

The emperor stood that way for perhaps three heartbeats before the Nordikaans surged forward to surround him, and then the whole line of the *casa* stepped forward ten paces.

They were on a hillside in starlight, surrounded by ferns that smelled like cinnamon and stood higher than a mounted man. The gate behind them was two great pylons of what appeared to be ivory—seamless, beautiful, and the colour of an old moon.

There were sounds: a call, and then another, and a creaking, like a cricket from home, but higher pitched, and another droning noise.

The *casa* crushed the ferns flat despite their size and marched on, forming a hollow square as practiced, filling in from the gate. The hill was high and bald except for the ferns; at the foot of the round hill was a stream, deep and wide, bridged with a high span of the same seamless ivory as the pylons.

The square grew until there were fully three thousand forming its sides.

Gabriel stood in the middle of the square, drinking in the night air.

"How far to the next gate?" Bad Tom asked.

"Twenty-four imperial miles," the emperor said.

"Ain't we lucky it's not four thousand," Tom said with a laugh.

Gabriel's glare was lost in starlight.

Michael rode up with Toby at his side. "Camp here?"

"As soon as Morgon certifies the water," the emperor said. "Gentlemen, have you ever imagined what we *could* face? Poisonous air? No air at all?"

"God between us and evil," muttered Michael. "But yes, I've thought of it."

"Good," Gabriel said. "We have to think of everything. All the time."

Mortirmir was in full armour. He didn't even look uncomfortable. In the starlight, he looked like a young god. "Absurd," he snapped. "Illogical. If the atmosphere were poisonous, no one would ever have come here. People *did* come here, or we wouldn't have a map. QED."

"That's you, told." Derkensun laughed and Michael winced.

A pair of wagons came through into the square, and Michael rode off to pass the word to No Head for a camp.

"I don't see na' firewood," Tom said.

"We can burn the wagons we empty of supplies," Gabriel said.

Tom nodded. "Ye ha'e a muckle answer for ae. For me, I want a good fight. An' I miss Sauce. I miss…why can't we all be together?" he asked.

Gabriel backed Ataelus until he was almost nose to nose with the big man. "Because if I fuck up, everyone in front will die," he said. "And someone has to be ready to carry on. Right now, that's Sauce."

"Oh," said Tom. Just for once, he was at a loss for words.

"Move the scarecrows forward," Gabriel said. "And get Ariosto."

"Have you noticed how little the stars move?" Mortirmir asked Bad Tom.

The big man raised an eyebrow. "I canna' say that I ha'e," he admitted.

Mortirmir was watching the sky. "The gates must all open at different times," he posited slowly. "Astronomical times? Hermetical times? Thomas, I didn't even *look* into the *aethereal* in the last place. Well, a peek perhaps. But these are different *worlds*."

Bad Tom smiled. "Aye, so I'm told."

Mortirmir wasn't really listening, but then, he seldom did. "Dan Favour looked at the gate, what, seven hours ago? And it was night here. And it still is, and no sign of dawn."

Gabriel emerged from his candlelit red pavilion in his flying harness. There were tents going up as far as the eye could see. But those were tents for officers and artificers and cooks. The men, no matter what their social rank, were sleeping on the ground, which was soft, a little spongy, and smelled spicy, but seemed wholesome enough in the odd light.

"Ye'r goin' flyin' in the dark," Tom Lachlan said. "On a fewkin' alien world in the middle o' hell, and it mayhap full o' de'ils, and ye'r goin' to ha'e a wee flyabout."

"Yes," Gabriel said. He grinned.

"Ye'r a loon," Tom said affectionately. "I wish I had a beastie like yourn. We'd go and find trouble."

Gabriel laughed hard; so hard he had to lean against a surprised magister magus. "Tom, we're marching through hell. We're *in trouble.* We don't have to find it."

Bad Tom laughed in turn. "God's truth," he said.

"Michael's going to sleep. Tom, you're in command." Gabriel slapped the hill man's hand. Tom grinned.

"Ah, a'wheel," he said. "I'll do me best."

Gabriel got up on Ariosto, already tired from a day in the saddle. He knew that somewhere two worlds behind, it was just coming on for late evening. But in his head, it was the middle of the night.

Love you, boss!

Love you, too, brother.

Smells funny. Feels odd. Air feels odd.

Give me half an hour…

No! Let's fly!

Ariosto leapt into the air. The hillside was just steep enough to give him an easy lift, and he was away on a rising air current and his pinions were almost invisible in the bright starlight, an iridescent wink and he rippled his control feathers.

Up, Gabriel ordered. *I want to see.*

They went up.

When it was cold, the way the air suddenly grew cold at home at a certain height, Gabriel prepped and cast the opening frames of Al Rashidi's working against the Odine. It worked to illuminate the enemy; Gabriel cast it as a separate working, to see what might be seen. It was sluggish; difficult to cast, as if he'd only just learned it, or lacked the *ops*, which he did not.

Either it failed, or it found no target.

Then he did what Mortirmir had taught him—he looked for silent talents by looking for movements in the currents of *potentia*.

It was his first look into the world's *aethereal* and Gabriel was startled by the emptiness, the lack of colour.

There was a rich brown outside his iron gate. He opened the gate cautiously and looked, but the brown was below him, and nearly uniform. Of gold potentia *there was very little.*

Gabriel surfaced in the alien real. Ariosto had climbed while he cast; now he could see nothing but the stars above and a few campfires at his feet, very far down, like candle lights.

He took Ariosto down.

Careful, boss. I don't even know…

Gabriel leveled them out somewhere around a thousand feet. He could see the difference between water and woods and what appeared to be open fields. He could see the river below their camp, and the bridge that seemed to be of bone or ivory.

Lower.

He dropped down until he could see the road going over the bridge and then he followed it away from camp. It was clear for a minute or so, and then it vanished to reappear as a wide trail or cart track.

Lower.

Any lower and we might as well walk, Ariosto complained. But he dropped down another hundred feet and they glided silently over the track, lost it in a patch of high ferns, and they were in open country— a hill, as high as the one on which their camp was built, and then another stream and another ivory bridge.

Was there a very faint smudge of colour off to the right?

He continued, following the track; it passed over three little streams and then climbed up onto a causeway, and suddenly there was a road, exactly like the road through the crawlies, smooth, well built.

Gabriel took Ariosto down almost to the road surface and swept along the road, and then up, up, climbing hard.

This air is heavy.

Gabriel had no idea what his mount meant, but the lack of *potentia* concerned him. They rose high enough that Gabriel was sure he was looking at dawn; a very, very faint smudge of rose off in the endless starlight.

He could also see the end of the road; another pair of ivory pylons like huge Umroth tusks rising out of the…

He could see bright light, and something…

He turned. The gate was open.

It was open.

He banked, his attention suddenly everywhere, trying to find an enemy. He flew a little farther and watched the gate collapse sideways until it didn't seem to exist, confirming his observation that the gates had only two "real" dimensions.

He cast a very small working with enormous effort, allowing himself the ability to see heat. The gate burned like a sun, and he could not look at it; it reflected passively on huge ferns…and he saw that the gate was empty, but nothing had come through; or rather, nothing he could see had.

He turned Ariosto again.

Nothing there, boss, his mount said. *Nothing to eat anyway. Now, off to the right there's something. A herd.*

Where? Gabriel thought.

There. Ariosto turned slightly. *What are those?*

They looked like deer, or horses, in the uncertain vision of warmth. They were somehow reassuring. And they were more than a mile off the road.

Not for us, Gabriel said.

He turned and Ariosto beat his wings strongly, and they were coasting along the track again. The causeway was already gone.

Something tried to destroy the road, Gabriel thought.

Full dawn; the longest, slowest dawn any of them had ever experienced.

Gabriel rose from his camp bed and left Blanche asleep. He took a proffered cup of *quaveh* from Nicodemus, pulled the bed hangings closed, and stretched.

"Isn't it odd that we're here, at the end of all things, marching through hell to save our world, and we all just go to sleep?" he said. "Like it's the end of another day on the farm?"

Nicodemus smiled inscrutably. "Yes, Your Highness."

"I'll bet you say that to all the boys," Gabriel said.

Nicodemus refilled his cup. "No, Your Highness."

Gabriel sighed.

"I have a stack of messages for you. And Ser Robert has had the green banda out all night. He begs leave to report in person."

Gabriel nodded. "Ser Robert first," he said.

Long Paw stepped in to find the emperor naked, washing himself. MacGilly and Woodstock were laying out arming clothes.

"Morning, sir," Long Paw said. *Highness* was a silly title, and Long Paw couldn't stomach it. Most of the old company men couldn't, so they didn't.

Gabriel grinned. "I'm still alive and the camp wasn't attacked, so I guess we're alright?" he asked.

Long Paw held out a clod of what appeared to be mossy earth.

"We own the ground," he said. "We've patrolled right up to the gate. It's open, alright. But…" He shrugged. "It's the salamanders. They're on the other side."

Gabriel was washing under his arms. He stopped moving a moment as he absorbed the words.

"Ah," he said.

"I looked right through, Captain. They're there, camped. Looks cold. No guards. I shit you not." He shrugged. "I'll wager they're getting ready to come through."

Gabriel's eyes grew hard.

"It's fifteen miles or a little less," Long Paw continued. "We could stop 'em dead at the gate."

"No," the emperor snapped. "Towel." The last comment was directed at MacGilly.

He looked back at Long Paw. "No, we want them to come through. To clear the gate. We need to beat them and then move through. Not get locked in a long contest of attrition on a narrow frontage. How many?"

Long Paw shrugged. "No idea. Honestly, Captain, I peeked through and ran like hell."

"Good," Gabriel said. "Shirt."

MacGilly handed him a shirt.

Gabriel looked back at Long Paw. "Nicely done, Paw. Any idea how many troops we have this morning?"

"All the *casa*, of course. All the scarecrows. Du Corse is having breakfast outside; his people are just coming through." Long Paw yawned. "Christ, what a day."

Gabriel got his braes on, one leg at a time. "And the start of another. Get some sleep," he said.

"Count Zac has the pickets now," Long Paw said. He gave a vague salute and wandered out.

Mortirmir came in. He handed Gabriel a stack of messages.

"Read that," he said.

Gabriel read and his eyes closed. "Damn," he said.

Blanche was just rising. She poked her head out the curtains, alerted by his tone. "What is it, love?"

Gabriel was trying to breathe. "Ash won the race to Lissen Carak somehow. He stormed all our nice entrenchments and he already holds the town. And..." He shook his head. "All the workers." He looked at Blanche. "All the workers are...*taken*. By the *will*. Which means that Ash is allied with the *will*. The only worse news would be that Ash had taken the gate. Miriam is dead." He was shaken.

Blanche swung her legs over the edge of the curtained bed and walked to her husband and kissed him. "Shit washes off," she said softly. "Whatever Ash breaks, we can make right."

Mortirmir smiled at Blanche. "Exactly. Your words to God's ear, my lady. We will build such wonderful things."

"The dragon spell didn't work on the *will*," Gabriel said.

Mortirmir shook his head. "May I speculate?"

Gabriel showed a little of his old humour. "Could I stop you?" he asked.

Emperors have to be resilient.

Mortirmir ignored him. "This war; for the gates. For...whatever they are fighting for..." He waved his hands. "It's gone on forever. For a very long time. Someone built this web of hermetical gates; Derkensun calls it a *Sky Road*, which I like. Inaccurate, but yet, accurate. And the *Sky Road* was meant to unite all the hermetical races. But instead, it is the conduit of war. They are all..." He looked out the door. "They are like fencing opponents who know each other very, very well. They have responses and deceptions, but they know each other's styles. You taught me this, Gabriel."

Gabriel was reading the other messages. It amused him, even in a moment of maximum crisis, that he was getting a message from Alcaeus, who was marching the last of the imperial army over the Green Hills, via a messenger bird who had flown to Arles, and then an imperial messenger who had ridden a horse across hell, to his camp on a world his people were calling Arden.

"Yes," Gabriel said.

"The dragon spell, as we call it, is far too complex; it rests on endless sloppy base works; it is really a compilation of hundreds of subworkings, and they don't even join up properly, and to me..."

"Is this going somewhere?" Gabriel asked, reading more bad news. "Get Ser Michael," he said to MacGilly.

"Yes!" Mortirmir said, frustrated. "We're going to change all that. We don't have to learn the great workings by rote with subhermeticals created by wardens and irks who don't think like us. We can strip it all away and write new workings. But it is because no one is writing new workings that they can learn these responses and deploy them."

Gabriel looked up. "Right. I got that last part. But right now, I'm about to fight an alien army on alien soil and I'm apparently already two days late to save the world." He paused. "But if you are right," he said, and looked into Mortirmir's slightly mad eyes. "If you are right, Morgon, then we really are the monsters, and the dragons are right to fear us."

Morgon laughed. "Of curse they're right. Why do you think I used Al Rashidi's huge working?"

"Because we knew it would work?" Gabriel tried.

"No," Morgon said smugly. "Because I'm saving the real stuff for the real fight."

The adolescent master magister was practically hopping with excitement.

"How's your *ops* right now?" Gabriel asked. Michael came in wearing his arming coat over a nightshirt.

"Terrible," Morgon admitted. "There's no *potentia* here. It's all been used up."

"Used?" Gabriel asked. "Morgon, you are beginning to sound every bit as confusing as Master Smythe. Michael, we're fighting. Today. Army of salamanders, we think—superfast, hot to the touch, good weapons skills."

Michael *smiled*. "So one of Kronmir's predications was accurate."

Gabriel waved a hand as Anne put his jupon on the other arm. "I don't care about the plans of our adversaries just now, no matter how pure an intellectual problem. I care about our plan. We're suddenly behind schedule. We have to fight for the next gate, and we need to move. We have very little magick. This will be a straight-up fight..."

"It's not *that* bad," Mortirmir said.

"Salamanders have some serious *talent*," the emperor said. "Shields first."

Michael already had his tablet in his hand. "Order of march?" he asked.

Gabriel went to Long Paw's sketch of the road and terrain. "I saw this hill last night. This is where we'll fight. It will be more like an encounter than an ambush; it'll take us hours to get there."

"We could fight closer?"

"It's a nasty mess of ground," Gabriel said. "After this hill, it's grassy downs, or whatever passes for grass here—the little low ferny things. Cavalry country. We want to use our knights, is my thought."

Michael nodded. He was copying the hasty sketched map onto his slate.

"*Casa*, Du Corse, scarecrows?" he said. "And ask Sauce to send Conte Simone through first?"

"No," Gabriel said. "Get Payam and his Mamluks if it can be done."

Michael smiled. "Five *thousand* heavy horse."

"With bows," Gabriel said. "Suit the punishment to the crime."

The odd, long dawn continued, and the *casa* marched through rose-coloured light, emerging from a forest of heavy ferns, or fern-like plants, to a rolling plain of basil-scented "grass" that looked like dill and had occasional stands of the plant that looked like fennel and smelled like cinnamon rising from it.

Francis Atcourt waited with Count Zac and told the lead lances where to wheel off; Zac looked heavy lidded and angry, like a cat rubbed the wrong way, and Bad Tom chose *not* to mock him. The *casa* began to move to the right, through the odd, thick grass and up the dominating hill. Mortirmir was already at the top with the emperor and the staff; the imperial standard fluttered in the fitful breeze. Two hundred Nordikaans were lying in the grass, asleep.

The emperor was going over the battlefield with George Comnena, the Caesar. A field forge, using wood transported from Arles, was cheerfully lit behind the emperor's standard, and three Harndoner armourers were refitting Lord Michael's troublesome front fauld; Edmund was making rivets from wire, the anvil singing under his hammer; Duke was shaping. Marcy, one of the apprentices, was being taught how to make *quaveh* in a small copper pot, the Ifriquy'an way that the emperor and his officers preferred, thick with honey, by Anne Woodstock, who was already fully armoured.

The emperor was being armed in his flying harness by MacGilly and a new page, Hamwise, a very young man indeed, someone's younger son. Toby stood eating an apple and coaching them both.

The emperor continued. "No, George. If they do not want to fight, we let them pass."

Woodstock appeared with a tray of small horn cups of *quaveh* and offered them around. Morgon Mortirmir took his and sipped at it, made a face redolent with pleasure, and drank the rest off in a shot.

"I think your highness is wrong," the Caesar said. He drank his *quaveh*. "I think that—"

Gabriel raised an eyebrow. "Go on," he said.

"What if they take our gate?" Comnena said. "Why risk it?"

"We're on a tight timetable, and I'm sure that Clarissa and her rather excellent choir of modest sorcerers can hold the gate, much less the constable and his garrison, who are all professionals." Gabriel was watching the green banda and the Vardariotes moving farther out on the plain, their positions only occasionally betrayed by a flash of metal.

Comnena took his cup, looked around at the other members of the inner circle, and shrugged. "It seems like a risk," he said carefully.

"It's all a risk. Very well, I hear you; but we have no time for this."

"Half the garrison of Arles is hiding among the Alemain knights," Comnena said. "And the Queen of Arles is standing about sixty feet away. I'm sorry. No one else dared tell you."

Gabriel Muriens let fly a string of profanities. He turned and looked back at the lances of the *casa*. He needed no guide now to spot the slim figure in the excellent armour. He saw Clarissa de Sartres standing by Philip de Beause and he set his jaw.

Then he looked back, under his brows, at Comnena. He laughed. "I guess I really am emperor," he said. "People are hiding things from me."

Bad Tom drank off his *quaveh*. "E'ery loon wi' armour wants to be here, wi' us, doing the great deed." He grinned. "Ye canna' blame 'em."

Gabriel shook his head. "Doesn't anyone want to die in bed? Fine. Fine. Anne, send a tumbler of *quaveh* to the Queen of Arles with my compliments and tell her that she is too tall to be a page, and if she has that much armour, she may as well serve as a knight. But my will remains; if we can avoid this fight through either maneuver or negotiation, we will avoid it."

Mortirmir was kneeling now. He was cutting at the odd grass with his eating knife.

Everyone was used to him, and they ignored him. He looked disconcerted for a moment and then he wandered forward to where the archers of the *casa* were digging in the springy turf, throwing an upcast while sweating pages placed stakes that the baggage wagons had carried all the way from Arles.

Comnena shook his head. "We could ambush them," he said.

"Told him that me'sel," Tom said.

The emperor bowed coldly to the Queen of Arles, who approached with her face burning red like the long-rising sun.

"Morally, ambushing an alien army on an alien world without prior warning would be the equivalent of jumping a stranger in an alley, killing him, and taking his purse." He looked around.

"Aye," Tom Lachlan said. "And?"

Michael was still being fitted by the armourers, but he guffawed. "When did we get such tender consciences?" he asked.

"Conscience has been growing on me," Gabriel snapped at Michael. "I blame all of you. The pretence of being a mighty and beneficent emperor perhaps."

Before the tension could escalate, Long Paw rode up on a tired pony, made a courtly reverence to his emperor, and swept his arm over the plain. "We have it all," he said. "They are already marching on the road. They have a handful of scouts out; a dozen on the road, fifty either side."

"Tell us about fighting salamanders," the emperor commanded.

"Hot to the touch, incredibly tough, but no better armoured than a person, and the *one* we fought had no metal armour. Very, very fast. As fast as me, or faster." Long Paw spoke with the unconscious arrogance of a master swordsman. He was so fast that there were good men and women who didn't practice with him.

"Hermeticals?" Michael asked. Duke was kneeling by him, punching new holes in a new leather tab.

"Our sample of one salamander had a single, powerful bolt, bright red, not like anything I've seen; he threw it repeatedly." Long Paw spread his hands apologetically. "No real idea about shields. Must have had some. Where's Brown?"

Gabriel fingered his beard. "With Sauce," he said. "They're on the causeway right now."

"The Regent of Galle is just entering the field," Long Paw said. "Ser Pavalo has passed the gate and is urging his Mamluks forward." He looked around, unfazed by the eminence of his audience. "The biggest thing is that they grow things back. They *regenerate*."

Gabriel nodded. "Very fast, hard to kill, no metal armour, and when you put one down, you have to finish it. Tell all the troops. Put the scarecrows right here on top of the ridge. They'll be the anvil."

"I thought we weren't fighting?" Michael asked, a little mockingly.

"Send for a herald," Gabriel said.

In moments, an imperial messenger appeared.

The emperor exchanged bows. "There is an army of salamanders moving on this road," Gabriel said. "I wish to negotiate with them."

Gabriel wrote out a message, and handed it to the messenger. She bowed, mounted a borrowed horse, took a long white lance with a green and white pennon, and rode off, unarmed.

"That's courage," Gabriel said.

"She's a loon," Tom agreed. "Won' you feel a louse when they kill her an' eat her?"

"Yes," Gabriel said. "My, everyone is so fucking helpful this morning."

Gabriel allowed himself a long sigh of relief when the tiny cloud of road dust was revealed in the rosy half-light to be his herald, returning. She was flushed; her robes blew behind her like wings.

She leapt from her horse with a flare and bowed on one knee, and Adrian Goldsmith's charcoal moved rapidly, sketching her, sketching her restless mount.

"Your Grace, it took us time to find...a language." She met the emperor's eye. "They know Low Archaic but refuse to speak it. They called it the 'slave's tongue.'"

Gabriel raised an eyebrow. Then he shook his head.

"Regardless," he said, "you have performed a great deed."

She flushed again, this time with pleasure. "Majesty, I fully admit I was terrified. But they were very courteous. The old tradition of the green and white banner; they have a creature bearing the same."

Gabriel's face twisted in a parody of a smile. "So we will meet, and negotiate?"

The messenger shook her head. "No, sir. They are deploying to fight you. Their council evinced amazement that you have moved so fast, and pleasure that they will have an engagement so early in what they referred to as 'the contest' in the language of the *adversariae*." She bowed her head. "Majesty, in truth, I could scarcely follow what they said. They all speak at once; I was introduced to a council but I could not tell the councillors from foot soldiers. They are of all sizes, from taller than Lord Lachlan to smaller than Squire Woodstock. I was offered neither insult nor attack, but those to whom I was introduced seemed to know all about men. She paused. "When we had settled on language, Sire, they asked me if I was worm meat or slave."

Gabriel looked at Michael. "Get Mortirmir," he said.

Comnena grinned. "He's making mud pies with the archers," he said, and sent one of his gentlemen to fetch the magister.

"And?" Gabriel asked.

"When they discovered that I was man, they insisted that I should become a slave for my own good. But they offered me no violence." She bowed.

Sukey pushed forward. She was in a man's leather jerkin and heavy silk hose, and nothing about her looked masculine. She had a heavy hangar on her hip, borne on a belt of gold links, and she stood with one hand on a hip when she paused and caught the emperor's eye.

"Sukey?" he said.

"Cap'n?" she said. "This thin fodder kills horses. Don't let anyone eat it. Lila Crowberry thinks the smoke is bad, too; we have a line of cook fires behind the ridge and now we're digging the fire pits deeper. And the soil is very thin..."

Gabriel cursed. After months of discussing the need for people to eat, of reinforcing to everyone how dangerous the alien worlds might be, nonetheless, the tendency of every horse, mule, donkey, and bullock to put its head down and munch anything it found...

"How many have we lost?" he asked.

"Fifty? A hundred?" She shrugged. "Cavalry need to know to keep their mounts from eating."

Tom Lachlan walked off toward the horse lines, as did every squire and page within earshot.

Mortirmir approached. "Tell me about your fire pits," he said to Sukey. She shrugged. "It's all rock under five inches of soil."

"Rock?" the magister asked.

She frowned. "Well, not all rock. More like old crap; roof tiles..."

"We are in the midst of a great city," Mortirmir said. "It covered all this; in fact, the whole great hill on which we stand is a pile of rubble five hundred feet high or higher. The ground here is flat. That ridge over there"—here he pointed across the low valley—"that ridge was another huge town, or palace complex or massive temple."

"Jesu Christe," muttered Ser Michael.

"What happened?" Sukey asked.

Mortirmir shrugged. "I don't know. It would take generations to dig all this out."

481

In the two hours that had passed, Du Corse had come up and deployed all his Gallish levies to the left of the round-topped ridge. When he was done, he rode to the emperor and now stood with him, and most of the household knights who were part of the unspoken inner circle, as well as most of the mages.

Mortirmir had dug several holes in the turf, and stood with the astrologers. They were talking animatedly; Mortirmir could be felt to be loaning them *ops*.

He came over. "We'll be fighting almost without access to the *aethereal*," he said to the staff.

The emperor nodded, watching the enemy. They were moving over the next line of hills; most of their right wing was still hidden along the road in the heavier ferns and a series of small ridges like fingers playing out from an arm, which was what the far ridge had looked like from the air, even in the oddly lit darkness.

Their force clearly *had* a center, right, and left; its organization was not so alien. Opposite him, the center was cresting the ridge; a heavy block that occupied a little more space than his own, with the *casa* and the scarecrows included. They had banner poles displaying pennons, and iridescent flashes, and in one case, the whole skeleton of what a scout assured them was an irk.

To their right, there was a column; it was wedge tipped, and well organized, and even as he watched, it extended to his right, outflanking the *casa*.

He pointed.

Bad Tom was already mounted. "I'll refuse a little and invite 'em in," he said.

"Best hope Long Paw can read our minds," the emperor said.

Du Corse was also mounting.

"Just tell your lads to hold. They're coming at us in a standard, ancient formation; there are the loins, there are the horns. See it? Their left is in disorder; no idea why, but if it was on better ground, it would look just like their right, with a wedge tip and an extended order to allow a long envelopment." Gabriel was pointing with a white baton that Woodstock had handed him. "See it?"

Du Corse looked smug. "Of course," he said.

"If we can stop their first charge, we have them," Gabriel said. "Or that's how I see it." He looked wistfully at his messenger. "Seems wasteful. But I strongly recommend, gentlemen, that you use your knights, mounted, to break up that charge so that it is easier on your infantry. You have heard Ser Robert Cavel's views on the salamanders. And we won't have much in the way of *ops*." He shrugged.

He noted Edmund standing off to the side, clearly eager to speak.

"Edmund," he asked.

"Sir. We could fire on them; they are in range." Edmund bowed.

"Be my guest," Gabriel said. "Try and break up the point of the rightmost wedge." He looked at Comnena. "If the gonnes have a little luck, I want you to roll forward and use your bows; trade distance for time. Remember they are almost as fast as horses; treat them like cavalry."

Comnena smiled. "Ave, Imperator," he said, and bowed.

"If we go over their wounded, behead them," he said, his voice grim. "Needs must when the devil drives."

Ser Michael frowned.

Gabriel went behind the smoking field forge, where Ataelus had just had a new nail put into a horseshoe, and where Ariosto waited. The griffon looked ill; his feathers were not as shiny, as iridescent, as Gabriel was used to, and his purple-pink tongue was partway out of his mouth, and he crouched low, his lion parts like the back of a great cat lying in the low ferns.

Are you hot, my friend?

No potentia *to breathe, boss. I hate this place. Let's go home.*

I'm afraid we need to fight these salamanders first, my dear.

The griffon stretched, his black, razor-sharp talons digging into the loam.

I will do my best. I worry . . .

Gabriel ran a hand over the soft feathers of his head and then gave Ariosto a good scratch along the spine and where the feathers met the fur. He gave the griffon a little of his own stored *ops*.

Immediately the griffon's head came up. *Ahh.*

You rest, my dear. I will do this on horseback.

Hate to let you down, boss. But I'd hate to fall out of the sky more . . .

Gabriel walked back to Anne Woodstock. "Fighting harness, and Ataelus, please. And very quickly."

Mortirmir came up. "Have you been in the *aethereal* here?" he asked.

Gabriel nodded, watching the enemy. "Yes. Thin, patchy, and not at all like home."

"There's no colour to the *potentia*. No green. Very little gold." Mortimir shrugged. "We will only have the *ops* we have stored."

"The enemy will be in the same situation," Gabriel said with a confidence he did not really feel.

Mortimir was watching the central block of the enemy. "Most of their strong casters are right there," he said. "But all of them, every little monster, can cast. This is a hermetical race, like the dragons." He shrugged. "I worry that they know the terrain better. The hermetical terrain."

Gabriel nodded.

"There's one colour here that's very strong," Mortimir said.

Gabriel frowned.

Woodstock had issued orders to her little staff; Hamwise now came back with a basket of golden armour, and Cully came up with another. Cully laid out his cloak and they began to put the armour on it. MacGilly took the flying helmet and the fitted *corazina* and replaced them with the golden breast and back.

The center of the enemy army was coming on boldly, flowing over the ground like a wave in a heavy sea. The flanks, or horns, were hanging back.

"What's that?" Gabriel asked Mortimir.

"Black," Mortimir said.

Gabriel felt a little bile in the back of his throat.

Mortimir shrugged. "Power is power," he said.

Gabriel made a face as his leg harnesses went on. "That's not what we know of the black," he said.

Mortimir shrugged. "I'll be with the *casa*," he said. He sketched a bow and wandered toward his warhorse.

Off to his right, Edmund's falcons spoke; *crack, crack, bang.*

The smell of rotten eggs moved through their position on a fitful breeze.

A dozen red lightnings rose from the enemy's left flank. Mortimir turned them with a minimum of *ops*.

Then there was a blink, as if the universe had paused.

Mortimir's hands shot up.

Gabriel found himself lying on his back. Anne Woodstock was lying across him, and MacGilly was kneeling on the ground, holding his head.

Gabriel got a knee under himself and got to his feet. Mortirmir helped Woodstock off him.

There was a long gash running across the center of the battlefield, burned black; the edges glowed red, and there were fires even in the green, green ferns. Thick, choking smoke rose.

All along the emperor's ridge, men were getting to their feet.

Morgon was still standing with his hands spread. "I could use some help," he muttered.

Gabriel went *into his palace, feeling the odd, dry air of the local* aethereal. *Viewed from here, Mortirmir was standing on a plain with a huge shield over his head, holding back a titanic working like a wave coming to overwhelm them all. He spent his store of* ops *like water, reinforcing Mortirmir and then rolling a gossamer shield back over them, over the whole of the army. And then, like two woodsmen rolling a log off their shoulders, the two of them let the enemy working roll on, past their barriers, over them to crash down into the low ground behind the ridge, just clear of the rapidly forming wagon park.*

Gabriel looked behind, and there was a line of fire two miles long.

Mortirmir was already striking back. Each of his hands was a weapon, and fireballs flew; ten of them, and then, almost instantly, another ten. And another.

The gonnes fired again. This time Gabriel was watching; the balls struck right among the snakelike monsters at the point of the left horn and ploughed deep furrows in their formation.

Mortirmir was shaking his head. "They have a lot more *ops* than we do," he said. "They just tried to drain us."

The center of the enemy formation was coming on almost as fast as a galloping horse. Their right, opposite Du Corse, was just getting loose from the tangle of ferns and creepers around the road.

Du Corse's infantry had been closest to the misplaced detonation of the enemy working, and the ranks of halberdiers and crossbowmen were shuffling, their banners moving. They were uneasy, and Gabriel was worried.

Right opposite him...

A forest of red-pink lightning bolts reached for his pikemen.

He swatted them to earth with a sweeping parry of *ops* and managed to turn three of them back on the salamanders. The bolt moved with near instantaneous speed, and his return was too fast to cover, or too unexpected, and it burst two hundred paces away and there was consternation in the rapidly advancing enemy wave; the wave developed a flaw, and an eddy.

The Duchess of Venike, in excellent armour, stepped out of the ranks of the scarecrows. "They're coming on like rabid dogs!" she roared. "Do not flinch!"

Morgon's fireballs had moved with the deliberate pace of lofted arrows; Gabriel knew that the first wave of them had been low-energy illusions, and their opponents were undeceived, but curiously incompetent at turning the second wave, fielding only four of ten. The rest burst and added to the pall of thick, sticky smoke that had the scent of burning bitumen and charred nutmeg. But the fireballs didn't seem to have had much effect beyond the evil smoke.

"Virtually immune to fire," Mortirmir said. "Damn."

Down in the low ground between the ridges, Comnena's Scholae rolled forward against the disordered far-left of the enemy, opposite and even outflanking the *casa* on Gabriel's right.

Red lightning emptied a dozen saddles, and then the first flight of arrows went in, and the second, the Scholae loosing by caracole. The salamanders were caught at a stand, and disorganized. Individuals launched themselves as a harassing cavalry; a man was pulled from his horse and killed, but in several places the mounts themselves trampled the monsters.

A trumpet sounded, and the Scholae wheeled away and shot again.

In the center, the enemy halted perhaps two hundred paces from the scarecrows, well below them on the hillside.

"You have already died, and you have already been in hell," the duchess shouted. "There is *nothing* you can fear."

Gabriel found a great deal to fear. The salamanders took their casualties and closed up. They had shields, and spears or swords, and they waved them in the odd pink light. A low moaning rolled from the left of their line to the right, perfectly timed, a wave of unseelie sound.

Men and women crossed themselves.

Gabriel had time to note that many of the salamanders had white or grey armour of some kind, despite the reports.

A creature stood forth from the enemy center with a great white shell. It raised the shell and blew a raucous call, and a thousand red bolts emerged from the enemy center, a near-perfect volley intended to overwhelm their shields, and it did. Mortirmir's great shield went down, torn to ribbons, and Gabriel's smaller shield had a hole the size of a knight's pavilion torn in it.

At least two hundred scarecrows died in that single torrent of sorcery.

The phalanx didn't flinch. One-eyed men and women stepped forward into the gaps left by the messily charred dead. File leaders called, "Lock up, lock up," and their pike heads remained steady.

The raucous horn sounded again.

Gabriel poured his horded *potentia* into his shields; the gossamer projection of the first encounter stiffened into a new working, as if a carpet of protection were being woven in real time. But this time he worked *with* Mortirmir, and with both astrologers and every other caster along the ridge top.

The volley was, again, beautifully coordinated.

The shields held, for the most part. But Gabriel was spending his stored *ops* with both hands, and the rate of consumption was shocking, especially as he couldn't convert *potentia* to replace his used *ops*.

Comnena's Scholae loosed another flight of arrows and cantered back, exposing the right of the *casa*. But there were hundreds of dead or dying salamanders, and the gonnes fired again; again they used round shot, and this time, the salamanders could be seen to flinch, visibly, at the casualties...

...and Comnena's cavalry were back like flies on a corpse, riding in close and loosing arrows.

Gabriel heard his own voice give the order, "Advance the *casa*."

He himself was just having his arm harnesses put on his arms. And he was *in his palace, casting*.

The whole mass of the enemy center came forward at a signal, their order almost perfect, with a haunting cheer like the call of an owl.

Morgon threw a dozen bolts of white fire and two gouts of oddly prismatic lightning. The lightning went through unturned, and seemed to grow and spread in one patch, and to have almost no effect in the other.

Suddenly Mortirmir was *in his palace.*

Layer like this. Like this...like leaves on trees. There, there, brothers, Mortirmir ordered. *All with me. There! there...They have much more* ops *than we have. Gabriel! We cannot continue this exchange! You must win in the real!*

In the real, a new shield rose from the ground in front of the center, like a sparkling forest of faery trees.

The salamanders halted less than a hundred paces away. The creature with the great opaline conch strode out and blew.

A thousand bolts of fire struck the glittering forest.

A hundred scarecrows fell. Widows stepped forward over dead husbands; a man stepped past his dead wife, her head split with red fire; a child raised his pike so that the butt spike would not trail in the charred remnants of his father.

"Close up!" came the call, like a battle cry, and they closed forward.

Giselle turned to Gabriel. "We should charge them," she said. "If the monsters are flesh and blood, we are better going into them than awaiting them."

Gabriel's left arm harness was being laced. "*Ghiavarina,*" he said. "Helmet. Yes, Giselle. We take one more volley and go." *In the* aethereal*, he said to all the casters in the link: We will go forward into them. Be ready. This is not the end.*

"Derkensun!" he called.

"Nordikaans!" roared Harald Derkensun. The Nordikaans had been lying down, a few paces back from the scarecrows. Now they rose and, like the killers they were, shed their magnificent cloaks, dropping them onto the ground like discarded trash. A few swung their axes; most laughed, a few took a long pull from a canteen, and they went forward to gather around their emperor.

Gabriel turned to Francis Atcourt. "I will go with the Nordikaans," he said. "Wait until we stop the enemy charge, or we break into their line, or we're desperate, and then charge them."

Farther down the line, Bad Tom was directing the archers. The whole of the *casa* advanced down the slope in echelon, led by the gonners.

"Ready," Woodstock said, slapping his pauldron lightly. MacGilly lowered the helmet over his head and Hamwise did the chin strap, even as the next volley of red bolts crashed into them.

The glittering forest was stripped of leaves.

Mortirmir shook his head. "We are running out of ops," he said. "I can't take another volley. I'm sorry."

Nordikaans were down, burned like roast meat, along with dozens of scarecrows. The boy, Hamwise, was standing, staring at the man dead right next to him.

"*Ghiavarina*," snapped Gabriel.

The boy put the spear across his hands, and he took it. Anne slapped his visor down and stepped in behind him with her own sword, shoulder to shoulder with the Duchess of Venike on one side and Harald Derkensun on his right.

The enemy was forty paces away.

The monster with the magnificent shell stepped forward and raised the shell.

"Cully?" Gabriel said.

Cully leaned past his captain, his bow pointed at the sky as his great shoulder muscles took the strain, and then descending, his back contorted, and he released like a harper strumming a magical harp, and Cully's arrow took the conch blower high, just above the breastplate of white he wore. He stumbled, and then folded forward over the heavy arrow.

A few red bolts came up the hill.

The scarecrows' trumpeter blew, and the *casa*'s, and they went forward in echelon, the *casa* slightly advanced. The archers of the *casa* were now loosing continuously, and Edmund's gonners halted and fired a volley only twenty paces out from the enemy's skeleton standard.

But Gabriel saw none of that. As a blizzard of uncoordinated red lightnings shot up the hill at him, he moved out with the scarecrows, and the hill added enormously to their impetus as they rolled down the hill.

The horn blower in front of the enemy tried to get to his feet and Cully feathered him again.

Ten paces from the line of the enemy, Gabriel realized that their armour was made of marble. It didn't matter a damn, except to add to the exotic and terrifying nature of the alien enemy.

He wanted to run forward, to charge, to use the whole power of the hill, to free his legs and get it over with, and even while he thought a torrent of thoughts, he was trying to keep his part of the hermetical shield steady, as there was a constant trickle of red lightning attacks.

Five paces out he lost the ability to hold his hermetical working against the torrents of fear and the immanence of combat. The salamander opposite him had flat black eyes and red-brown skin and raised a bone flute...

Too far from his hermetical palace, Gabriel used the *ghiavarina* to parry the bolt. But at point blank, hundreds of scarecrows died in the last, hurried burst of red fire, despite shields and a clear lack of coordination among their enemies. Those struck fell, incinerated.

Another rank of pikes came down, filling the space.

Gabriel's *ghiavarina* came down, and his first opponent fell away, cut in half at the shoulders, his juices black and brown and hot as melted pitch.

The pikes struck home—ten to fifteen ranks, five pike heads in every square foot of space to their front—so that the salamanders foolish enough to stand and attempt to block the pike heads were hit as if by steel sparks blown by a human fire. Hundreds of the monsters were skewered, and their superior speed was utterly negated by lack of space; smaller of stature than men, and downhill, they gave ground, and then suddenly, being mortal, they broke; Gabriel was just cutting up from *dente di ciangare*, cutting his opponent's stone axe, its haft, its marble breastplate, and its head with one mighty and unstoppable *sottano*; he looked to the left through the narrow slit in his visor and the scarecrows were moving forward at an even walking pace.

He ran to Giselle's side. "Halt!" he called.

She frowned. "Why?"

"Halt and get back to the ridge top," he shouted into her face, then he ran along the front to where the Nordikaans had already closed up. Their axes had decimated the salamanders.

Francis Atcourt flashed past the Nordikaans to the right, leading the knights of the *casa*, and they crashed into the fleeing salamanders a hundred paces farther downslope. Tom Lachlan had already halted the archers and gonners. Their right flank was absolutely hanging in air, with half the enemy left wing well behind them, but themselves badly threatened by the Scholae. Still, they began to fling their red fire into the hand gonners, who wheeled as if on parade and poured fire back into them.

"I hate this," Bad Tom roared. "I want to kill something."

"Kill their wounded," Ser Michael snapped. He beheaded a salamander on the ground; the creature had taken a pike wound and it was visibly closing.

"Back up the hill," Gabriel shouted in his face, so their spittle flecked each other's faces. He couldn't remember opening his visor; but he had to get this done.

"No!" Tom bellowed. "Pursue!"

"OBEY," Gabriel roared like a wounded bear. He cracked his voice, but Tom flinched.

He turned to Woodstock, at his shoulder. "Ataelus," he shouted.

Hamwise ran.

"Where's MacGilly?" he asked.

Woodstock shrugged. "Dead," she said, her voice flat. "My lord."

It was all taking far too long. Women and men paused to behead a salamander, to drink water, to stare blankly. The scarecrows had taken heavy casualties in their front ranks, where the leaders and trained soldiers were, and many of the rest of them were rail-thin peasants with ten days of training.

Gabriel closed his eyes for a moment. He could not bear to watch.

Giselle's voice rose over the battlefield. "Back! Back, *mes enfants*! We are not done yet."

Gabriel opened his eyes, and the scarecrows had turned about and began to labour up the hill. The *casa* flowed, with better parade ground order, except that the hand gonners disintegrated into huddles of men and began to run back where Edmund stood with a banner waving.

Gabriel saw the boy coming with his warhorse and ran to meet them, his sabatons tearing at the turf, his mind searching the near-empty *aethereal* for attacks. He was almost drained; he dreaded a big working like the one with which the enemy had begun the combat.

One foot in a steel stirrup, a sense of foreboding, of a stitch dropped, or impending peril. Ataelus grunted happily as his weight came on; he turned the horse, sparing a smile for his youngest page and then cantering away to the high ground to the left, and looking...

It *was* a trap, and he'd read it correctly—either too late, or just in time. The enemy center was running, but all together; and the flanks were turning inward to catch his center and eat it.

But the scarecrows were pulling his head from the noose. Their order was far from perfect, but they were getting up the hill faster than the jaws of the enemy flanks could close on them.

Off to his left, a whole separate battle had been fought. The Sieur Du Corse's banner was gone, the crossbowmen had held, but there were huge gaps in the Gallish line....

It shouldn't matter immediately; the crossbowmen and the halberdiers had held.

With heavy losses. They'd been driven back two hundred paces, or more, exposing the flanks of the hill. It was possible they hadn't held; it was possible his adversaries had accomplished exactly what they had wanted and were being cautious.

Gabriel took a heartbeat to admire the skill of his adversaries.

He turned his horse and rode back across the face of the hill to where Bad Tom had the *casa* in line with the scarecrows. Gabriel rode along their front, saluting them with his heavy spear, and they began to call out, cheering.

The enemy center had stopped running and was re-forming. Francis Atcourt came up the hill; it looked as if he had not lost a man or a woman, and his knights were still in formation.

But the whole face of the hill was covered in dead salamanders.

"They are very good," Gabriel said, matter of fact, to Tom. "They expected to break us with the red fire; but the rout of the center was a second intention, like a deep deception in a sword fight."

"Oh aye," Bad Tom said, disgusted. "We could just fuckin' fight them. Get into 'em and keep killin'."

"I'm guessing that when they decide that they failed to outflank the hill or break our center, we'll have some very serious fighting indeed," Gabriel said. "Where is Zac? Where is Ser Pavalo?"

Lachlan shrugged. "So we just hold?"

Off to the right, Comnena was *still* inflicting terrible damage on his adversaries, and their supply of whatever powered the red fire seemed to have dwindled, or perhaps been expended in the center.

But in the center, the skeleton banner went up, and terrible low moaning sounds came from the rallied enemy, and a working rolled at them like a wind.

Gabriel gave what he had, saving only his reserve; he gave with a dozen mages and he saw Mortirmir fling a gout of ops into the maelstrom, trying to steady the forest of light against a gale of chaos...

All along the crest of the hill, men and women died. Flarch died with a dozen household archers; Sidenhir, an irk, far from her home and trees, fell by him as the malevolent wind licked under Morgon's fluttering fractal leaves of light. Ser Giovanni Gentile fell dead with his horse, and Lord Robin, Michael's squire, and Angelo di Laternum lay in the ferny grass, screaming their lungs out as a deadly stuff poured in on them. The whole line at the top of the hill shook as if the wind blew against them.

Then, like the stoop of a falcon and as swift, the Vardariotes appeared from *behind* the salamander's left wing. The change was sudden: One moment, the enemy left outflanked the embattled *casa*'s right, kept in check only by the relentless, courageous pressure of the Scholae. And then, in the next, the enemy left began to melt, and like lions breaking into a cattle pen, the Scholae reacted immediately, charging with drawn sabers against the enemy as they ran. This time the Scholae were merciless, and so, too, were the Vardariotes; as the foe ran, they were ridden down by flashing hooves and sabers.

"Here they come," Giselle said from the left. And sure enough, re-formed and flanking the hill, the enemy center and right attacked, their order good, their speed like charging cavalry.

Gabriel ran to the wreck of the *casa*'s wedge, casting what healing he could with his empty purse of *ops*. He and a young Alban woman he didn't know saved Lord Robin's pierced lungs, but had to leave the young man lying where he had fallen.

The knights steadied their horses. To his right, the archers waved; men he'd known five years were drifting back.

"Cully! Get them shooting!" he called.

Cully ran across the open ground. Three red bolts reached for him from the enemy center, just a hundred paces away.

"Nock!" he roared. His voice was something to fear; he sounded like the angry father of every archer's youth.

Oak Pew barked. "Nock!"

The ranks stiffened. Short Nose was embarrassed to find that he'd taken two steps back; he pressed forward while Oak Pew glared. He got a shaft on his string, too, and so did the irk Elaran, who looked like he'd had a whiff of the necromancy; his old eyes glittered and his fingers seemed weak, but he got the jaws of his horn nock around the meat of the string.

"Draw!" Cully roared. "And, LOOSE!"

The heavy shafts fell away downslope into the salamanders, who were now very close indeed.

Gabriel rose from Lord Robin's side, watched as the Alban girl pushed *ops* into Angelo di Laternum, and looked at the scarecrows, who stood as stolid as cattle despite their losses.

He rose to his feet, looking farther left. He could feel something wrong, or more wrong; a feeling, a lack of sound.

Hamwise still stood holding Ataelus, keeping his head up; the big horse wanted to eat the soft green stuff.

Gabriel remounted, his joints already protesting.

He was sure now that the crisis would come on the left. He looked at Mortirmir; the young master magister looked as if he'd been kicked, but he was working; Gabriel could tell he had *ops* left.

"Morgon," he said. "Come with me."

He rode along the back of the scarecrows. There was a flood of power, cries, and grunts. More scarecrows died.

They shuffled. Viewed from the back, it was as if a breeze stirred their upright pikes.

Michael followed him, and Clarissa, of all people; and Mortirmir, and Anne. Cully had stayed to command the archers. Gabriel wished he had the company, wished he'd had a different order of march, wished he had Harmodius or just Tancreda and Petrarcha, away with the rear guard. He wished a thousand things.

He blinked. More scarecrows died. The enemy seemed to have an inexhaustible supply of *ops*. And all along the flank of the hill, salamanders were rising to their feet and dragging themselves into the ranks of their great blocks. They were *regenerating*.

And they were rolling forward like the sea. Gabriel had to assume that they, too, had people marching up from the rear; their right flanks were being reinforced and seemed as big as the whole army he'd faced an hour ago. Or had it been ten minutes ago?

Michael looked ashen.

"Zac or Pavalo," Gabriel said to his apprentice.

Michael looked back. "They are *flaying* us with magic!" he shouted at Mortirmir.

Gabriel took Michael's shoulder. "It's not his *fault*!" he said.

Michael looked at the emperor. "He's always so cocksure," he spat.

"Like other people I know," Gabriel said gently. "Save it for the salamanders, Michael."

Mortirmir looked as if he'd been struck, but he turned his head away. Gabriel saw the moment that the young man passed into his palace, and wondered if he had the *ops* left to act.

The new tide of monsters rolled up to the Galles, and a single flash showed that the enemy had a volley of fire left in them. Some crossbowmen shot back, but the Galles lost the exchange and did not await the onset; they were losing one man in five. They shuffled back, and the enemy right swung like a door as the Galles fled.

"Michael?" Gabriel said. "Tell Tom to charge. Right now."

Michael waved a fist and dashed away.

"Clarissa," Gabriel said. "Duchess of Venike. Charge, keep going." He waved, she saluted, but he was already beckoning Mortirmir.

He rode along the back of the scarecrows, whose flank was now wide open. "Morgon!" he called. The magister's face was slack, and his eyes were unfocused, but he turned his warhorse and followed.

From the hilltop he could see the dust on the road to his left rear; his heart beat faster. And he could see Du Corse's banner waving again; *behind* the enemy right.

"On me!" he called to the Nordikaans.

Despite the weight of ankle-length maille and heavy axes, they sprinted along with him like hunting hounds, and he led them left, left, ever farther left, around the scarecrows waiting to die. Five hundred long paces to get clear of them. A race.

The salamanders had launched their third-order attack; their right and center were closing like a vise on the salamanders. Fires raged all along the front; in many cases the enemy came forward through fire, the flames licking around them.

He pointed down the hill at the rising tide of unbeaten salamanders coming into the left flank of his phalanx. "Stop them, Harald," he said. About eight thousand salamanders.

About two hundred Nordikaans.

"Ave, Imperator!" Derkensun responded. He raised his axe.

"Cover the flanks of the Nordikaans for as long as you can," Gabriel said to his magister.

Mortirmir's face sharpened. His eyes focused.

"Hmm," Mortirmir replied. He stood in his stirrups. A cruel smile danced across his face. "Let's try this, shall we?"

His working came; *Gabriel glanced at the mixture of* ops, *the gold and black. Black.*

"Needs must when the devil drives," Mortirmir said bitterly, and unleashed his working.

It was not fire.

It was ice, and a thousand salamanders screamed in agony as they were desiccated and frozen in a single, horrible emanation. It was an ugly magic, cruel and deadly.

The salamander line shuddered and in some cases halted, fifty paces from the flank of the scarecrows.

Mortirmir's cruel smile intensified into the full satisfaction of a man who was wrecking havoc.

"*Encore*," he said.

It happened again. The desiccations were explosive this time. The enemy moaned in fear...and rage...and came on.

Gabriel considered forbidding him to cast it again.

And he judged himself for it, cursed, and rode on, down the hill, after the Galles. They were not cowards; they had been overmatched, and they were not running, but milling helplessly, bereft of most of their leaders. Du Corse had stripped them of local squires and knights to build up his own chivalry, and now townsmen and musicians and peasants and butchers tried to find it in themselves to form a line in the face of the red fire and the deadly spears of the alien foe.

Gabriel had hoarded a little *ops* to use as a shield, but now, instead, he used Morgon's sound enhancement, *reaching into himself; draining everything; and even here, on an alien world, he drew a little and little more from the golden chain that still pulsed with life, trailing away into the thin* aethereal *and full of hope...*

Men of Galle! I need you now!

He rode along the edge of their mass, waving a sword he hadn't realized that he'd drawn. Off to his left the knights were pouring in; clearly they'd gone through the enemy line and ridden too far, like knights all over the world except the military orders. But now Du Corse was lashing them with his voice, and they struck along the edge of the salamander line, their hooves leaving a trail of black blood, and then began to form with the crossbowmen.

Du Corse swung himself off his mount and knelt, an actor on the stage of chivalry, and Gabriel leaned down and gave him a mock buffet on one shoulder, and then the former sell-sword was up, bellowing for his knights to dismount. The crossbowmen and halberdiers shuffled forward and formed well with a wall of trained muscle and steel between them and the foe; the Gallish line was suddenly formidable.

The scarecrows were invisible, over the shoulder of the great hill; but the Nordikaans and Mortirmir were still there.

"We must go forward!" Gabriel shouted, his visor up. He waved his sword.

Du Corse's banner was up; it began to advance, and the Galles flowed forward.

Men began to sing. They were singing *Te Deum*; the red fire lashed out, and the voices went on, and the Galles would not flinch. Harald Derkensun fell, his head cut away by a stone axe.

Morgon Mortirmir went sword to pole hammer with a salamander banner bearer. He waited for his adversary; crossed the heavy blow, left to right, using his lighter weapon to guide the heavier, off line, rotated his hips, and his left hand reached out, a heavy, unnecessary blow; the turning motion he'd been taught, but as soon as his fingers caught the creature, its water was ripped from it, and it fell lightly, its horrified black eyes the last to lose expression at its awful death, but Mortirmir had already passed forward to his next victim.

He could hear the *Te Deum*.

But the black fire flooded him, and he didn't want to stop. It was a joy like sexual release; greater, even, than creation, greater than...

Tancreda appeared in his palace.

"Stop!" she screamed.

For the time a mortally wounded being has to scream one last time, the battle balanced on the edge of a Fell Sword.

But that sword was in the hands of Pavalo Payam, and he pointed its gently curving blade across the last low ridge of the fingers and into the flank and rear of the salamander army.

Time had crawled while he marched; while he expanded his

magnificently trained horsemen from a thin column to their battle line, while they passed unnoticed through a dozen gullies and a forest for ferns. It had all taken too long.

But now, like the release of healing, they had arrived, and the whole battle was laid out to his right; the scarecrows plunged deep into the enemy ranks like a dagger; the *casa*, the victorious Vardariotes and Scholae on the right wing; the left, where a tide of mixed militia and Gallish knights tried to force the enemy off the flank of the scarecrows. Red fire fell on the army of men, and they died. But they died with their faces to the enemy, and those who survived went forward. The salamanders were held in place like bugs on a pin.

The Fell Sword descended, cutting only air, but six thousand Mamluks rode forward, sabers on shoulders, lines well dressed, flowing organically around stands of fern trees or piles of stone.

The earth began to shake.

Gabriel was near the spot where the line of Galles met up with the line of Nordikaans. Except that, even in his closed helmet, from the back of Ataelus he could see that the two didn't meet; that the Nordikaans were a shield-gang, a hundred or fewer in a circle of axes and swords, and that the enemy had begun to turn the flank of the Galles, expertly flowing through the failure of his own line.

A salamander shot him with a red bolt.

His armour turned it, and he cut, his sword shattering on the thing's stone helmet, and Ataelus punched twice, once with each foot, and the thing's stone armour cracked and it fell, and Ataelus trampled it.

He threw the hilt, and took his steel mace off his pommel. Ataelus reared; there was a flash of red fire, and he was falling, falling…

He hit hard, and they were on him, and he'd lost the mace. Ataelus thrashed, but luck, or fate, had thrown him clear, and he got his left leg under him, free of the saddle and the stirrups and he got his metal hand up and triggered the working he kept there; the hand went dead, but every salamander around him fell, blind; several went down and never rose, and he stepped back to raise Ataelus, but the horse was spasming, and then there were dozens of the dark red things and he put his dead hand into every incoming blow, as if the magnificent work of a master craftsman were a cheap iron buckler. He covered and punched with his dagger, covered and punched; grappled close against a tall monster with a sucker mouth and turned the thing to the right, holding him into the way of his brother's bolt of red lighting, throwing the broken corpse into a third, and then the dagger, hot now to the touch; he left it in a bulging-eyed face, kicked with his pointed sabatons, and struck with his gauntleted fists—one, two. He was taller and stronger than any of them; he overrotated arms, and felt the alien musculature tear under his hands, dislocated shoulders, and slammed the dead hand into another, and another, and they pressed closer...

Ataelus was his undoing. Ataelus the loyal, who, dying, dragged himself by three scraping hooves to his master; Ataelus, whose teeth continued to rip salamanders from their feet, until a dozen of the red-brown things carved him with axes, and Gabriel fell backward over the stallion's outthrust neck.

He'd already used his reserve. He had nothing, even to save himself.

Luckily, he had Anne Woodstock.

Her blade was everywhere for five beats of his heart, and he got one foot on Ataelus's head and pushed himself away; got the other foot under and turned his own weary body over, so that he was on his hands and knees and a great blow struck him in the back, and he went flat on his face. His left hand was dead; his right was not strong enough for the duty, and he rose a few inches and fell.

He never saw the ten more human heartbeats during which Woodstock covered him and dealt death.

He only knew that he took a breath, and then another, and then another, and in between them, he was not dead. The terror was impenetrable; facedown and unable to see or rise. He had no *ops*. He considered adventuring the black *potentia*, but his own panic was too strong for such an endeavour.

He tried to pray, and nothing came.

Perhaps he screamed into his visor.

Perhaps not.

The earth was shaking. Even through terror and fatalism and fatigue and sorrow, he felt the earth shake.

Something fell over him.

"Stay down!" Anne screamed. That made it through; almost, in the place he was, it made him laugh.

As if I have a choice.

And then the line of Mamluks burst over them like water bursting a dam in springtime, and the earthquake was all around him, and then past, like rain on a sparing day, sweeping along the plain. It was almost silent, and then he could hear the singing—very faintly, the Gallish *Te Deum*.

"Oh God, my lord, he's…dead…" Woodstock said.

Gabriel lay still for another eternal moment, unable to speak or rise.

And then he admitted that he was not dead. And that he had to complete his task, or die trying.

He flexed his right hand.

"He's alive!" called a man in Gallish.

They got him up; embarrassed as, aside from abrasions and a deep bruise, he was uninjured. But so was Woodstock, and she flushed at his praise and the praise of others: Tom Lachlan, Ser Michael, Sukey…

Hamwise and Cully got his harness off; it was scorched, and the gilding was ruined, but it had kept him alive. There was a terrible mark in the back plate; a stone axe had bitten deep, but it hadn't touched his spine. He had a bruise; when he pissed, blood came out, but it wasn't the first time.

Sukey put a cup of hippocras into his hand. There was still fighting on the next ridge; the scarecrows were passing over the field in a huge long line, killing the wounded. Sukey had a field chair.

The *casa* knights and the Nordikaans began to gather around him.

Francis Atcourt threw his arms around his emperor. "God!" he all but sobbed. "If you are going to die, take us with you."

Then both of them turned to the unusual site of the emperor's squire with her mouth firmly planted on the mouth of Ser Tobias.

Gabriel raised an eyebrow and began to feel alive.

Michael shook his head. "I'm sorry, Gabriel," he said. "I'm so fucking sorry. I stayed with the *casa*."

Gabriel managed a smile. He was coming out of it; he'd been… somewhere else. "We were fine," he quipped. "Weren't we, Anne?"

She surfaced from the longest armoured kiss anyone had seen and flashed a smile.

"Where's Morgon?" Gabriel asked.

Sukey pointed.

The young master magister stood with his head down, in the midst of his desiccated enemies.

He wasn't moving.

Gabriel looked at Michael. "Finish it," he said. "Did Long Paw..."

"He's holding the gate," Michael said. "Pavalo is cutting through to him." He nodded to the far ridge. "If they surrender, do we accept?"

"Fuck, yes," Gabriel said, exasperated. He was looking over a battlefield with at least ten thousand dead. "Christ, Michael, why *would we not accept their surrender?*"

Michael quailed. "I'm sorry. Of course we will."

Gabriel took a deep breath. "Finish this and march for the gate. We have another battle to fight."

Michael nodded.

Gabriel walked toward Mortirmir.

Michael began to issue orders. The imperial messenger joined him, and the whole command staff moved away, headed for where a great square of salamanders had formed on the far ridge.

Gabriel walked up to the younger man, put a hand on his shoulder, and went to the *gate of his palace.*

It was shut, a lofty barrier of spiky iron.

Gabriel had no ops *with which to play. So he knocked.*

"Morgon Mortirmir," he called.

He called three times.

"Damn it," he called. "I'm your emperor, and perhaps your only friend."

The gate opened. It didn't creak. It didn't make any noise.

Gabriel walked in, and found himself instantly in a paneled room with a fire in the grate. Mortirmir sat in spotless black velvet. He held a skull on his lap, and in it was the imprisoned soul of Harald Derkensun.

"He was my friend," Mortirmir said. "And now he's dead. But I will bring him back." He looked at Gabriel. "I know you'll try to stop me. But you can't. I can do this. I have the power."

Gabriel sighed, and noted that his right hand burned a bright gold. An almost unbearably bright gold, and he lit Mortirmir's palace like a lamp. As he did, a number of realizations struck him, all together.

"I have the power to stop you," Gabriel said. "Let him go, Morgon."

"It's my fault!" Mortirmir said. "You all think it's my fault, and it is! But I told you there wasn't enough potentia! *And you fought anyway!"*

Gabriel sighed. "It's really all my *fault," he said. "I brought you all here.*

On a short timeline, with no choices but to conquer or die. Morgon, I need you. Let Harald go. He's in a limbo of undeath. We are not the Odine. We are not the dragons."

"We could be," Mortirmir said. His voice was at the hermetical edge of sounding…sly. "We could be anything. I think you cannot face the reality of war, Gabriel. War kills. We will kill to win. The means do not matter. Do they?"

Gabriel was looking at the burning, hermetical gold of his hand in the darkness of Mortirmir's mind.

"I think the colours are a distraction," Morgon insisted. "Power is power."

"I think you are being turned," Gabriel said. "I think that you have been tempted to evil. So have I. And I have fallen, many times. So I know all about climbing back out, Morgon. Evil is a choice. So is good. I think the powers have colours to teach us something; the way poison berries are bright red."

Morgon's avatar set its jaw.

"Be a knight," Gabriel said. "Think of all the times you failed; at the pell, at the quintain…"

"…in class," Mortirmir admitted.

"Failure is not all that painful," Gabriel said. "And I have discovered I learn nothing unless I admit that I have failed. I have met swordsmen who delude themselves into believing themselves great; I have met housewives who delude themselves into believing that their houses are clean and their cooking good."

"I could bring him back," Morgon said. "I have the power. You have no idea how much power I have, Gabriel."

Gabriel chose not to say, I just watched you murder two thousand sentient beings.

Instead, he shrugged. "I know you have great power," he said.

"You could not stop me," Mortirmir said.

"I am stopping you right now," Gabriel said. He rose to his feet, and the gold fell off him like rain. "I am not commanding an army right now. Michael is doing that. I am sitting with you. Can I tell you something, Morgon? I have about two days. Then I'm dead. I almost died today. In fact, at the rate I'm turning to gold, I might not even last until we pass the last gate. You may have to face Ash without me, Morgon. And I carry the weight of responsibility. Every death. Every fight, every wrong decision, every battlefield error, every horse dead of poison grass. I even get to enjoy *the adulation of the people I lead to die. If ever there was a poison pill... a black power, it is that. Listen to me, Morgon. Let Harald go. Let them all go. Let it all go. Admit your failure..."*

"I did it for you!" Mortirmir said.

Gabriel shook his head. "Yes, and no. I don't know if we'd have held the hilltop without you. But by God, Morgon Mortirmir, we will not defeat Ash without you, and I could lose you right here. And you did it, at least in part, because you wanted to do it. To see how powerful you really are."

"I am like a god," Mortirmir said.

"Not even a little bit," Gabriel said. He reached down and plucked the grim black skull from Mortirmir's hands.

Mortirmir didn't move.

"May I?" Gabriel asked.

Mortirmir was weeping. "I want to do it," he said.

"Good," Gabriel said.

He stood silently while Mortirmir released the soul.

He awoke to the feeling of Blanche's shoulder against his chest. His pavilion was dark. He listened to her breathe for a long time.

He rose in darkness, when Master Nicodemus woke him. Blanche was already awake and gone, and Hamwise appeared and began to dress him. He glowed like a lantern, and his new page made no comment.

"Think what we're going to save in candle wax," the emperor said.

His page made no comment.

Blanche came in. She smiled when she saw him; he treasured that.

"Anne said you were awake," she said. "Ser Robert held the gate. The Council of Three Hundred has agreed to capitulate. Michael has made a great many decisions with me and George... I hope—"

Gabriel waved a hand. "Good," he said. "Kiss me, Blanche."

She came and kissed him.

His page, embarrassed, turned away.

His hands roved over her back.

And then he sighed. "Let's go."

"Snow and ice," Long Paw said. "And... irks. Slaves. I saw 'em."

Ser Vizirt, the highest-ranking irk in the army, sat with Long Paw. He shook his head, his face deadly serious.

"We have no legend to cover this..." he said.

Gabriel looked at Morgon. The young man was silent. He sat holding the hand of his wife, Tancreda. She shook her head.

But then he raised his head. "This whole world was a giant city," he said. "And now they are all dead." He looked at Gabriel. Then he looked at Bin Maymum. "How long will the gates remain open?" he asked.

Bin Maymum looked at his companion and they both made a nearly identical face.

Bin Maymum rose, bowed, and scratched his head. "A hundred years?" he asked.

Every man and woman at the table gasped.

Mortirmir nodded slowly.

Gabriel felt his heart sink within him. "Oh God," he said.

Mortirmir looked at his emperor and nodded. "So the waves come, on and on, fighting for the gates. Someone built the gates because they thought all the sentient races would live in harmony—"

"Or maybe some bastard just liked fightin'," Tom Lachlan said. "Tar's tits, friends. We can hold all the gates if'n we must."

Blanche said, "There'll be nothing left of our civilization. No art, no song, no dance. Only war."

Gabriel sat back. "Let's take this one crisis at a time, shall we?" he asked.

Mortirmir steepled his fingers against his lips, looked over them, and nodded. "Ser Robert, these *were* the same creatures that you fought in Etrusca?"

"The same," Long Paw said.

Morgon looked away. "So," he said. "These were the *rebel*'s allies; and the soldiers of *shadow*."

"And now we hold a gate to one of their spheres," Long Paw said. "That's my understanding, Cap'n."

Gabriel shook his head. "Too complicated. Our goal is the same. These two gates should be quite close..."

"Aye." Michael nodded. "It's waiting for us. I'm sorry, Gabriel. I ordered the march to commence. I reversed the order of march; that's the only reason we're still sitting here. You said you would do it at the last gate. The *casa* is exhausted. So are the Galles and the scarecrows."

"Well done," Gabriel said. "Company?"

"In front, with Milus and Sauce and the Etruscans." Michael smiled his wry smile.

"The salamanders just opened their gates?" Gabriel asked.

Michael shrugged. "They *surrendered*. They are in what I can only describe as a state of shock. The messenger here tells us that they do not have a king, but a council; that their council is the leading three hundred creatures of their entire…*Imperium*. And that we seem to have captured them entire."

"There's always someone cockier than you are yourself," Gabriel said. He sat up. "Tell me about the irk slaves."

"You went and had a battle without me," Sauce said. She smiled. "Look at that."

There was a valley between enormous mountains; they rose into the snow and vanished into the grey clouds, and high above them there were roads, and snow-covered roofs, and fur-bundled irks came down to the roadside to stare at them; but anytime a knight looked at them, they would cast their eyes down like bashful maidens, or… slaves.

The irks with the company and the *casa* were traumatized. The abject, craven behaviour frightened them, and they were even more angered by the failure of any of the irks to respond to any spoken words in *their* language, which sounded like song to humans. *Tangwaeri* was virtually unknown among men.

None of the slaves spoke a word of it.

At least, not at first.

There were eddies of irks, but there were few salamanders about; those they saw were in thickly curtained palanquins, heated with coal stoves and borne by twenty irks. But around midday, as they passed the two huge cairns in the center of the valley, some ancient demarcation or graves perhaps, an ancient Irkish woman came down the mountain, brought on the shoulders of a dozen young Irkish men. And she spoke no words to Elaran, but she wept when he spoke to her, wept and clutched his hand. He dismounted by her on the snow-swept road as the army marched by, and he sang to her a little song that sounded very sad to Sauce.

Syr Vizirt, another irk, could not stop himself from weeping.

Gabriel watched. "What does he sing?"

"Once there was a great queen, and she had done evil, and she was barred from ever returning to her home. She laments, and she wonders if, in truth, only her own sense of wickedness keeps her from her home." Vizirt shrugged. "It is nothing, told like that, man. In our tongue, it is the song of exile."

The old irk was weeping uncontrollably, great racking sobs.

"Ask her how old she is," Mortirmir said.

"You seem like yourself again," Gabriel said.

Morgon looked at him, and their eyes locked a moment. "Isn't it terrible?" Morgon asked. "How quickly the feeling of failure wanders off?"

Blanche laughed. "No," she said. "If it didn't, we'd never dare do anything."

Mortirmir smiled at her. "Now, there's a truth," he said.

"Just like childbirth, then," muttered Kaitlin.

Sauce leaned forward; she put a hand on Syr Vizirt's shoulder, and he smiled at her through his own tears, and then he spoke in a low voice, and the irk answered, and the messenger translated, because the words were in a language none of the rest of them spoke.

"Nine hundred years," she said to the emperor. "As best she remembers."

"Was she born here?" Gabriel asked gently, and the chain of translation passed his words along.

"Her parents were brought here." The messenger frowned. "Are they from ... home?"

Morgon looked at Gabriel and then at his wife, and shrugged.

"We don't know," he said for all of them.

"We don't know anything," Gabriel said. "March on."

"Makes me feel like I should cut a Christmas tree," Tippit said.

"You ha'e wood between yer ears," muttered Smoke.

"Nah," No Head said. They had a small fire; they had volunteered to watch the next gate while the army got a hot meal and marched in the snow. "Nah. We've looked at they crawlies, and we fought the salamanders. And this is just bleedin' snow."

"So far, it's all a lot like fewkin' hell," muttered Half Arse.

"Don' you worry, mate," Smoke said. "It'll get worse before it gets better."

"Mark my words," they all said in unison.

Sauce took direct command of the green banda, allowing Long Paw to get some sleep. She waited, her warhorse blowing steam like smoke from its great slit nostrils.

Gabriel was looking at the gold plate on the pedestal. It wasn't actually gold; it was golden stone, or glass—very hard, and very beautiful in the purity of its form.

"It has five settings," Gabriel said in a low voice. "But Al Rashidi said four."

Sauce shuddered.

Perhaps the most disconcerting thing about the plaque was that it had been defaced. There was a flaw, like a hammer stroke, across the face of it, and one of the stations, sometimes, but not always, marked by a cabuchoned jewel, was black, the stone ripped away.

Gabriel turned and looked back down the cave; another vast cave quickly filling with battle-ready troops. The company was already drawn up across the gate. But the gate was dark, and the light coming from it was barely perceptible.

"Bring me the translation team, and a representative of the *Quazitsh*," Gabriel said. He was tired; the weight of fatigue was there, behind his eyes and in his hips and shoulders. And he was entering the very stuff of his nightmares—that Al Rashidi's map of the gates was inaccurate.

The messenger, whom Blanche had coaxed into revealing her name was Maria, appeared, leading Brown and Lucca and three salamanders as tall as Brown.

The messenger took a knee. Gabriel drew his sword. "Stay kneeling," he said. Before she could resist, he had knighted her; Sauce provided a pair of spurs.

"The duty of a messenger is to speak accurately and be selfless," she said, her head high. "I was taught to strive that no one would even remember I was there."

"Then you have failed," Gabriel said. "I know you are Maria Dariush of Thrake; I know what your language scores at the Academy were. And I know that you are incredibly brave." He smiled. "The war we are fighting cannot be won with weapons, but it can be won with information. If anyone ever writes a history of this war, an honourable historian will say that E.34 won us Arles; a mere messenger bird whose heart and skill got through the Darkness when we knew nothing. I take hope from that. And from you."

Other knights gave her a belt, and a collar; she was virtually bedecked in gold, and the three tall *Quazitsh* watched without comprehension. The middle one, who wore a torque of jade, bowed and spoke carefully in the stentorian tones of *Qwethnethog*, the language of Mogon and many creatures of the Wild.

"He asks if I am made a king. He understands that men like to be kings, even though they are naturally slaves." She smiled hesitantly. "He doesn't mean an insult. He's not in that modality and his head inclination is polite. He has no experience of men as…anything but beasts of burden."

"Fascinating," said Tancreda.

"Later, you may explain chivalry to him. Right now, please tell him you have been rewarded for courage and intelligence and careful study."

Ser Maria turned a delicate rose-pink, and a great many men among the company felt their hearts race to look at her, tall and slim and dark, her skin like old mahogany, her cheekbones like razors.

Maria spoke briefly, her eyes elsewhere.

The *Quazitsh* all made odd bows, twitching their prominent tail stumps and moving their hips.

She turned even pinker. "They honour me as well."

Gabriel nodded. "Since we're all getting along," he drawled, "perhaps our…hosts…could explain the state of this plaque, and the nature of the gate."

Tancreda's eyes were so bright, they might have started fires in the snow. "Ask them…" she interrupted. "Sire, I need to know. I think I understand…"

Gabriel's temptation to snap at her, to slap her down, was enormous. *I just want to get this over with.*

He made himself refocus. "Speak, Tancreda," he said.

She bowed, conscious of her error. Mortirmir was looking away, amused and embarrassed.

I'm so glad there's someone who can interrupt Mortirmir the way he interrupts me, Gabriel thought.

"Ask them what they call the two gates," Tancreda said.

Maria spoke.

All three salamanders answered—one at length, and then the torque wearer, more briefly.

Maria shrugged. "We came through the Gate of Danger, and we will leave through the Gate of Dragons," she said. "There is an inference…"

"Yes?" asked Tancreda, her eagerness causing her to step past the emperor.

"That all…inbound traffic…" Maria turned and asked a question in *Qwethnethog*.

"All inbound traffic enters through that gate, and all outbound goes through this one," Tancreda said triumphantly. "Listen; it's not luck these gates are so close…"

Gabriel had passed through irritation and annoyance to amusement, but now his attention was fixed. "Brilliant," he said to Tancreda.

Mortirmir looked at his wife with something very like adoration. "I didn't think of that," he said.

"I did," Tancreda snapped. "So any army coming through—"

"Comes in behind us," Gabriel said.

The *Quazitsh* were all talking, their lightly taloned hands flashing at increasing speeds.

"Gate of Dragons?" Sauce spat.

"Once, long ago, dragons came *through* this gate. They say it should not be possible. But it happened. They fought a great battle with *Odine*. No one here remembers it." Maria shrugged. "He says it was a *Qwethnethog* legend; that the *Quazitsh* took this place from the *Qwethnethog* so long ago that the weather has changed. He's telling me some legend. I cannot understand one word in three."

Gabriel's mind raced. But after a moment, he shrugged. "We know nothing," he said. "We have a plan, and we will stay with it. Ask him why one of the jewels is broken."

Animated conversation.

"He is trying to tell me another legend. Sire, this is like someone asking me to explain the Bible." She looked frustrated.

"Try," Gabriel said.

"He describes the leftmost setting as the least of places, a tiny outpost of his people. Not worth our time." She was keeping her face serene, but he caught her meaning.

"His home perhaps?" Gabriel asked.

"He is very anxious to dissuade us from going there," she said.

Gabriel nodded, looking at the three creatures and trying to read them.

"The next is a barren world, wasted by the wars," Maria said.

"A whole world, wasted?" Sauce asked.

There was animated chatter from the smallest *Quazitsh*, the one covered in white tattoos or perhaps paint, narrow, angular strokes that looked to Gabriel like writing.

"They ask: How can we not know that most of the spheres are destroyed or ravaged by war?" Maria kept her tone neutral.

"By the blood of Christ," Sauce muttered.

"And the next?" Gabriel was adamant.

"A very rich place, held sometimes by the...now he wants to tell me it is undefended, almost easy to take and hold, with thousands of slaves. Or millions. I'm sorry, Sire; the words are the same." Maria didn't take her eyes off the three.

"Millions of slaves, and easy to take..." Gabriel smiled. "I'm sure they are telling the truth."

"I am not," said the translator.

"We have some notes, too, my lord," said Lucca, who was standing by.

"And this place?" Gabriel asked, pointing to the red jewel closest to the black hole.

Agitation, obvious hesitation, and then an outburst.

Maria listened for a long time. Horses fidgeted; men went out into the snow and relieved themselves. Sukey began to issue food.

"The *Odine* took it." She looked at the tattooed creature. It looked miserable.

"And this?" Gabriel pointed to the blackened hole, or socket.

Silence.

Finally, the tattooed salamander spoke. The one in the jade torque interrupted him, and bared his fangs. The exchange grew heated, in what sounded to the better-trained ears present like two or even three different languages, and at one point, Brown pushed between the two.

Lucca glanced at Sauce, got a nod, and bowed to the emperor. "Lord, I don't have the language to follow; but I know how to run the *Question*. Send the bastard in the torque away."

"They have factions?" Gabriel asked.

Maria shook her head. "I cannot even hazard a guess," she admitted.

Gabriel motioned to Ser Daniel and a dozen green men-at-arms. "Take this gentleman to the warm springs and let him bathe," he said.

The torque wearer drew himself, or herself, up to fullest extent and spat a long speech in heavy syllables. And then was marched away.

"He says that we are fools, slaves playing at masters; that he now understands that we do not even know what we are doing; that he will not aid us or speak again, and he wishes he had ordered this other one killed, but he is a priest and not really a person." Maria shrugged. "I think that's what he said. Honestly, my lord, I am out of my depth."

"I think you are the hero of this piece," Gabriel said warmly. "Now ask our friend here again."

"Through that gate used to be a *Qwethnethog* world. There was a war, after which sorcerers and priests closed the gate forever." She took a deep breath. "She says, that way lies the *Qwethnethog* empire. Or it did. I have no reference for time, my lord. She refers each time to cycles and I cannot guess how long these cycles are."

"Ask where the *Quazitsh* empire is located," Gabriel said.

Silence.

He nodded.

So did Brown. "They ain't fools," Brown said.

"So," Gabriel said to sum up. "Leftmost green jewel is probably the root into their heartland."

"Gates open different times," Mortirmir said. "They might have come through one, or two, or five."

"Why is she helping us at all?" Tancreda asked Maria.

"She thinks we might be allies. She doesn't seem to have the . . . prejudice . . . of the war leader, about our being slaves. Permission to speculate wildly?"

"Of course," Gabriel said, looking at the jewels.

Maria's shoulders hunched; her hesitancy was in every inch of her spine, but she pushed on. "Everyone makes war on everyone," she said, "and the war between *Quazitsh* and *Qwethnethog* is very old; but they, at least, ally against dragons and *Odine*. Who, I may add, they refer to as *Odine*."

Gabriel pulled at his beard. "This is incredibly fascinating," he said. "But of no use whatsoever. "Gate one, *Quazitsh*. Gate two, unknown. Gate three, something we probably don't want to find, since it was where our host wants to send us. Gate four, a world wasted by the Odine. Gate five, destroyed." He shrugged. "I'm going to assume that Al Rashidi's source only thought of this as having four gates. And that he counted from left to right."

"Widdershins?" Sauce asked.

"Ifriqu'an," Pavalo put in. "Yes."

Gabriel nodded, and then inserted his key and turned it once.

The gate grew, if anything, darker.

"Ready?" he yelled, and a trumpet sounded: the two-minute warning. A falconet was brought up, the company closed ranks; women finished a sausage and dropped the rest into a purse; men thumbed the edge of a handy dagger and adjusted a sword belt. Arrows went to bows.

Morgon Mortirmir raised a shield of pure golden *ops*. "You expect the gate to be contested?"

"I expect every gate to be contested," Gabriel said.

Mortirmir nodded.

Gabriel flexed his left hand. This world, despite its snow, was rich in *potentia*.

He turned the key, a soft click.

The gate opened.

A powerful, warm smell of seawater permeated the cave.

A narrow path of sand extended off into the light of *four* great moons. Black water lapped the ridge of sand from both sides. Traces of embankment and road could just be made out.

"Nowhere for an ambush to wait for us," said Tancreda.

"Under the water?" spat Sauce. "By the Virgin. All our armour will rust. Alright, my children, on me. Let's go!"

Sauce led her banda out into the darkness. They went forward at a trot, the horses a little spooked by the water but clearly delighted by the warmth.

"What are we doing with the *Quazitsh*?" Michael asked.

"We're taking them with us," Gabriel said.

Maria bowed. "The priestess wants to take...me. To her home. To negotiate."

Gabriel nodded. He was watching the green banda press forward.

"I'll think about it," he said. "Atcourt!"

Ser Francis appeared at his side.

"We can't afford to wait. I'm going with Sauce. Six lances, your choice, now." He waved at Woodstock. "Ataelus. Oh God, he's dead."

Gabriel stood there a long moment, considering how many people were dead, and how he missed a horse, and then he shook it off. "Get me...a good horse."

Woodstock brought him a big bay stallion, who was instantly interested in one of the sultan's mares. But he was a genial fellow for a warhorse, and Gabriel mounted. Then he reconsidered, dismounted, and sent for Ariosto.

"Never mind, Francis," he said. "I'm tired."

He walked through the gate. Mortirmir and Tancreda were already there.

"It's remarkable," Mortirmir said.

"*Aethereal?*" Gabriel asked.

"Capable. Not robust," Morgon said. "We are really very lucky at home."

"Shouldn't it be the same everywhere?" Gabriel asked, and then he gasped.

Tancreda nodded.

"Oh my...God," Gabriel said.

There were stars. The constellations were alien, of course.

But almost directly overhead...

...there was a patch of pure black. It was...

...huge.

And empty.

He went into his *palace and found the dominant colour outside the iron gate of his mind to be blue. There was the omnipresent black, there was gold, and there was some green as well.*

"The water is full of life," Mortirmir said. "There is something in there with talent. In the water."

Gabriel thought of the beaked *kraken*. Of the Eeeague. The whales, the serpents....

He shook his head. "I thought there were seven worlds," he said. "And then I thought there might be twenty-five."

"There are hundreds," Mortirmir said.

"Thousands," Tancreda said.

"Again, no water, no food, and no place to camp," Gabriel said.

Ariosto appeared with a burst of warmth and affection, and Gabriel went back through the gate to get armed.

"We're jamming up," Sukey said without preamble. "I'm through most of the food and most of the horse fodder."

"Tell me some good news," Gabriel said.

Sukey shrugged. "Bad Tom loves me?" she said, more a question than an answer.

"One more gate after this one," Gabriel said. "We could be fighting at Lissen Carak in four hours."

Sukey blinked.

But I don't like this gate, and I don't like those moons and the black hole in the sky. This is wrong. I can feel it.

He led Ariosto through the gate.

"Mortirmir?" he asked.

"Gabriel, something fell in the water. I'm... listening to it. My advice... is not to disturb it..."

Gabriel tried not to admit to himself that he was afraid to fly out over the black water alone. The surf was rising; the night was dark despite the moons.

Gabriel mounted, and Ariosto didn't wait; he ran forward along the causeway and leapt into a sea-scented breeze and they were away in a wind of kelp and lobster, and his great wings worked, up and down, the pinions of his wingtips brushing the surface of the water, and wherever they brushed, some sort of life bubbled up.

Gabriel looked down. There were whorls of phosphorescence like pinwheels in the dark water, and they had both light and depth; at first, his eyes were fooled and he thought them reflections, but the more he looked...

... the patterns troubled him, and he raised his eyes to confront the blackness beyond the stars.

This place is wrong, Ariosto said.

Wet and wrong, Gabriel said.

At least I am strong here. You burn bright gold, brother. What is this? A disease? Or a power?

I don't know. What was that?

In the real, a tentacle erupted from the water, slashed through the air, and struck back into the water with an explosion of spray.

Gabriel turned them back over the ruins of the embankment, which shone like a ribbon of white in the multiple moonlights. His heart was racing and he felt a mindless fear creeping over him.

He passed over the vanguard, and Sauce. They were racing along the shingle, and he thought maybe Sauce waved, and then she was gone, falling away behind, and he looked forward past Ariosto's head and now he could see the next gate; a horned head, or a minaret, in bone white, stained with seawater the colour of a rotting tooth.

They banked, and then turned back as Ariosto sought the easiest air currents. Gabriel, taught by wyverns, looked up and back, right into the moons, but if there was an air creature, he wasn't seeing or sensing it.

Hooooooom hoooooooooooooooooooooom.

Gabriel sat back. The sound, if it was really a sound, had come through the *aethereal.*

Gabriel dropped into *his palace despite his racing heart. But he hesitated with one hand on his first shield.*

Prudentia was dead and cold. He'd drained her when he was fighting the salamanders and never recharged her. Now he took the shield hanging on her outstretched arm and considered....

Hooooooooooooooooooooooooooooooooooooooooooooooooooooom.

"*It is looking for us," Morgon said. He was sitting in an armchair with a harpoon in his hand.*

"*With* ops," *Gabriel said.*

"*Yes," said Morgon. "It is casting huge gobs of* ops *into the* aethereal *to see if any comes back."*

Gabriel snapped into the real to find the rotten tooth of the gate filling his vision, and Ariosto braking, his great wings fluttering and then cupping the moist air, and they were descending.

Another cave, the griffon said. *And not a sheep in sight.*

Can we get through the opening? Gabriel asked.

Ooooh, Ariosto said.

Gabriel's guts squirmed, he rammed himself back in his saddle and gave a strangled scream, and then they were in near complete darkness and he dared a working, throwing light. There was a red glow far off, like a forge fire burning.

They were under an ivory dome four hundred feet high and big enough to cover the central square of Liviapolis. Ariosto banked; the walls sped past, and...

Did you cast? It's coming. Morgon was insistent.

Call Sauce and tell her to turn back. Gabriel realized that Morgon had no more control of Sauce than he did himself.

He could see the plaque, glowing gold in the light, shining like a star, and he could see the gate at the far base of the dome, a low arch, this one lit bright red. The light was like the angry sunlight of a red sunset.

Out. We have to help Sauce.

Got it, boss.

The passage out was as mad as the passage in; Ariosto folded his wings and dropped through the tall gate, and even though the gate was a hundred paces wide, it seemed to reach for them like a leering mouth, and then they were out in the warm, moist darkness with the sea, the moons, and the lurking feeling of fear.

He was over the greens instantly. They were moving quickly, looking over their right shoulders.

Lower, Gabriel said, readying one of Morgon's javelins from the bucket by his hip.

He came out of the darkness and Sauce's head turned.

"Ride for it!" he roared. They were closer to the new gate than the old one, and he gestured and was past.

The column of soldiers opened out to a gallop as he climbed, heading out over the sea and into the darkness. All the phosphorescent patches were together now, a galaxy of constellations dancing together, a thousand paces off the causeway. Something was down there, and it was close.

He turned over the wheeling patches of sickly green brilliance. To his left, Sauce seemed to race over the moonlit sea, and the moon dazzled on her armour as if she was, personally, the tip of a moonlit spear.

The water began to move.

Don't try and face it, Morgon said.

This from you?

It's the size of a dragon, or larger, in the aethereal.

Right. Gabriel did not drop the charged javelin. He turned away, out over the sea. The thing was rising; it was the size of Harndon. Or so it seemed in the unseelie moonlight.

As fast as you can, he said.

Like you needed to tell me, brother.

Gabriel felt the shift in speed, the force of the wind against his body, and he crouched. They went on . . .

Why are we going this way? Ariosto asked.

So that it doesn't look at Sauce, Gabriel said. *Farther.*

Their speed was formidable; even in leather and fur and armour, Gabriel's sense of their passage was deep and cold. He could no longer see either of the gate towers in the real, and both of them were hundreds of paces high, and white.

Hungry, Ariosto said.

Oh dear, Gabriel thought. *We need to turn.*

Sure. Where are we going now? Hungry.

Gabriel thought through the fatigue and the vague fear and the growing panic. It was dark; the moons were in the wrong place, and the phosphorescence was everywhere; there were patches like eyes as far as he could see, a dazzle of them under the darkness where there were no stars, like false reflections, like . . .

Where to, boss?

In the real, it was all one seamless image—flat water speckled with phosphorescent images as far as his eyes could see.

They banked.

Morgon?

Silence.

Fear. Palpable, choking, rising to meet him. Alone, lost, with a tiring griffon under him and the weight of the alliance on his shoulders and no room to make an error.

Oh God, if there is a God, this would be a good time.

They turned. The phosphorescence dazzled his eyes with its dim and endless magnificence.

MORGON, he all but shouted in the *aethereal.*

Gabriel.

I need a beacon. Gabriel tried to keep calm, keep hold of his memory palace, keep a grip on the great monster between his legs. And reality.

Wait one.

Gabriel couldn't decide whether to turn in place or continue on what he thought was the right course. His disorientation was so great that he almost slipped from the high-backed saddle, and Ariosto side-slipped under him.

Steady, boss. I'm really hungry. Can I go down now?

Just a second.

Gabriel. Beacon in the count of ten. There will be three flashes in the real.

Morgon began to count down.

Gabriel leaned back, looking. Desperate.

Number one.

Gabriel saw...

Nothing.

Number two.

"Damn it. Damn it. Damn it." Gabriel was looking in every direction, his head moving in near panic, his body leaning forward.

Got it, boss.

Number three.

Gabriel's relief surpassed any other emotion he could remember. The fire-orange flash was a pinprick, miles away, but he saw it. Ariosto was lining up on it.

Close, he said.

You worry too much, Ariosto said.

A moment later he could see the causeway, and his heartbeat began to slow.

It's the thing in the water, Ariosto said. *I can feel it. The things. There are hundreds of them.*

Gabriel pointed them at the gate. *Straight through*, he said.

They passed through the outer gate for the third time and Gabriel's sense of dread fell away to mere fear as they passed the ivory portal.

The green banda were drawn up by the fiery gate, and Ariosto cupped his wings, sparkling in the firelit air, and skimmed the floor, which appeared to be a dazzling mosaic. Gabriel tried to remember what the other floors had been.

He dismounted, wondering how many times he could be terrified in a single day.

"What the *fuck* is out there?" Sauce asked him.

He shook his head. "Big, ancient creatures who live in the darkness," he said. "Let's not disturb them."

"I hate it here," Sauce said quietly.

"They don't like us, either," Gabriel said. He was looking at the gate plaque. It was quite simple: a single jewel. The jewel was a milky white, like a moonstone.

"It is the wrong gate," Gabriel said. He took a deep breath.

"Wrong?" Sauce snapped. "It's wrong? More wrong than fucking ancient sea monsters in a world of black water with no fucking sun?"

"Yes," Gabriel said.

"How can you tell?" Sauce asked.

"There should be three jewels," Gabriel said.

Sauce shrugged. "Let's see it," she said.

Gabriel looked at her.

She met his eye. "I heard the briefings, Gabriel. This was always a wild hunt. We're committed. But at this point, Al Rashidi could be wrong. You could be wrong. Everything is already wrong. Open the gate again. What's the worst that happens?"

Gabriel smiled. There was something about Sauce that made him feel...calm. Maybe because, when he was ready to slit his wrists all those years ago, she'd been there. Maybe...

Maybe...

He grinned. "An ancient god from beyond the stars emerges and eats our souls," he said.

Sauce shrugged. "Sure. That could happen." She shrugged again. "What if this *is* the right gate? We could lose hours..."

He turned the key.

The gate opened.

Chapter Fifteen

There was no causeway.

A red, red sun lit a world of ash. The ash was pale grey and almost completely uniform and stretched away to a red horizon, and everything was tinted with that red except the next gate portal, a few miles of heat distortion away across the plain of ash.

No ancient god awaited them.

But there were bones. Charred bones.

As far as the eye could see, resting on the fine grey ash, there were bones.

In the foreground, nearest the gate, was a dragon. Part of its skeleton was buried in the fine grey ash, but the vast skull was obvious, and one whole wing that trailed away to the right until it vanished out of sight, perfectly polished to a gleaming white by the windblown ash.

Gabriel raised a shield and stepped through. He was wary of using power for a variety of reasons, but precautions seemed necessary.

Sauce came at his shoulder, and Daniel Favour and Wha'hae, too. They walked out onto the plain, and the ash resolved itself into an endless sand of powdered bone.

A wind stirred the ash and it rose, choking them. The scouts pulled up scarves. Gabriel closed his flying helmet.

The wind rushed past them like a charge of cavalry.

It subsided.

Under the bones of the dragon were other bones.

"I might as well check the next gate," Gabriel said.

Sauce shook her head. "These places are all horrible," she said slowly. "Had God no mercy? Look at them." She bent, and lifted the skull of a *Quazitsh*. A freak of the wind exposed a vein of them, as if a regiment had all died here. They were so tangled together that they might have died in a vast embrace—hundreds, or thousands, of salamanders...

Gabriel put an arm around Sauce. "We're lost," he said. "I have to see. I have to check everything. It's all a nightmare, Sauce. But it was never going to be easy."

She smiled. "We don't do easy, do we, Cap'n?" She leaned forward and kissed his cheek. "Don't die. You're glowing like a lamp."

He was, too. He passed back, took Ariosto, fed him some *potentia*, and they were in the air.

Really tired, boss.

Five miles.

Sure. But I bet you want to go back, too.

Gabriel was looking down at another dragon. And another.

He flew along, too stunned to think. They passed a fourth dragon. And a fifth.

And by the fifth dragon he saw something amid the ash. They weren't very high; he was saving Ariosto as best he could.

But he had no time, and he was filled with a different foreboding.

The skeletons of the dragons were...

He was struggling to think of what could kill six dragons.

Seven.

They descended toward the second portal. It, too, was the bone white of most of the other gates, but it was different, at a distance, less shapely, the dome lower.

Closer, and it became clear...

...that the dome had been destroyed.

Gabriel landed and entered to confirm what he suspected. His heart was too tired to race. He felt almost nothing.

The pedestal was blackened, and the jewels, all three of them, were gone, leaving sockets like wounds or abscesses. *We can't get out*, he thought, and then he realized that, if Tancreda was correct, his only hope was that the gate behind him was still open. He thought he'd left it open, and he had left the key in it.

It was an irrational fear. He knew he'd left it open. But he all but fled the broken chamber.

The moment he mounted Ariosto, the monster's love calmed him.

He took some breaths. The red sun was terrible.

"Let's get out of here," he said.

On it, boss.

They flew back. Gabriel tried not to look down at the line of skeletons, but it was like a boil, and he kept worrying it, looking down, feeling the dread and the sense of skewed scale, and looking down again.

He saw the glare, the wink of light on something metal, by the great skeleton of the dragon, and he could not resist.

I want to see that.

Ariosto coughed. *Very hungry, boss. We might have to walk, and I don't really want to walk on all this dead stuff.*

Gabriel hesitated.

Oh, fine, Ariosto said.

He landed. *Water?*

Gabriel handed over his canteen after taking a single pull. He held it until the eagle beak grabbed it, tilted it back, and the purple tongue moved, and then the canteen was crushed.

Oops. Better than nothing, though.

Gabriel walked across the ash, his flying boots leaving clear tracks. The dragon's skull was huge, like a building.

But under it were the skulls of men.

He knew what he was looking for a moment after the skulls registered, and he reached in among the skulls and the bones. It was a single ornament: bigger than the head of a man, and hollow, made of pure gold.

An eagle, wings back, holding lightning bolts in each talon.

He held it a moment, and then put it gently back near the bony hands of his fellow men.

I will never know.

He got back on Ariosto.

Can you get us back?

Sure, boss, Ariosto said. *But don't we still need to get back past the sea monsters?*

One thing at a time, Gabriel said.

*

They landed at the gate, and Sauce was there, and a dozen greens, prowling through the bones and making a pile of finds. There was more evidence of men: an ivory-hilted dagger, a gold medallion, an ivory shield boss, the ivory warped and mangled by time, grey with age and ash.

And a comb. The comb was magnificent, solid gold, with the figures of a soldier or knight on horseback fighting a footman, each figure as perfectly realized as a statue. Wha'hae handed it to Gabriel; he held it for a while.

"She must ha'e been something, eh, Cap'n?" Wha'hae said.

"What do you want for it?" Sauce asked.

Wha'hae looked at it a moment. "Fifty leopards," he said. "Gold." He smiled. "An' that's for a friend."

Sauce laughed, but she snapped it out of his hands and put it in her long black hair.

"Like it were made for ye," Wha'hae said.

Gabriel looked at her a moment. "I'm not sure I'd recommend wearing ornaments until a magister..." He shook his head.

She grinned her crooked grin. "My brain's too tough to get fried by some sorcerous claptrap, and I'm wearing a fortune in Magister Petrarcha's amulets, and a few by the Mighty Mortirmir hisself. I'll be fine."

Daud the Red produced a small silver mirror. Sauce preened a little.

Gabriel laughed. He drank some of Wha'hae's water and laughed again.

"We're surrounded by horror and you lot are busy looting," he said.

Wha'hae shrugged. "And?" he asked. "There's a fortune out there, Cap'n. I say we bring the whole company here and *comb* through it for days..."

"I say we get our arses back past the sea monsters and march on," Gabriel said. He smiled.

The greens hastily pocketed their finds.

"Who were they, Cap'n?" asked an archer.

Gabriel shook his head.

Sauce appeared by him, the gold comb magnificent in her hair.

"Isn't that going to hurt under a helmet?" he asked.

She shrugged. "When did you last eat?" she asked.

Gabriel tried to think.

She handed him a whole sausage and an apple and a chunk of cheese. "The boys and girls are happy finding a fortune in old crap," she said. "Eat this and rest."

Gabriel ate while walking across the mosaic floor to the watch post at the outer gate. There, the smell of the sea was omnipresent, and the men-at-arms and archers were alert.

"Somethin' unnatural came up at the edge o' the water," the lead man-at-arms said. Green banda men-at-arms were not all knights; many had come up the hard way, former royal foresters or Jacks.

"I don't know you," Gabriel said, embarrassed.

"Jeff Kearny," the man said. He was short, broad, and red bearded. "This here is Tom Wilsit. You know Short Tooth and Long Tail, eh? Sir?"

Gabriel looked out into the oddly lit night. The patch of pure darkness had the same effect as an hour before.

"Don' look at it," muttered Short Tooth. "Seriously, Cap'n. That's fucked up."

"No shit," Gabriel said. "And then what happened?" he said to Kearny.

"It moved back," Kearny said. "We did nowt, like Sauce said."

"Never piss off somethin' ye cannae' kill," said Short Tooth. "Long Paw's rule number two o' scoutin.'"

Gabriel finished his apple and lobbed the core out into the endless night. "Rule number one?" he asked.

"Scoutin' an' fightin' are two different jobs," Kearny said.

"He's full o' crap like yon," Short Tooth said.

Gabriel nodded, suddenly feeling much better.

"We're going to cross in groups of three lances," he said when he'd walked back to Sauce. "I'll go first with whomever you choose. You'll come last. I'll pause at the midpoint in the causeway, in case—"

Sauce leaned up and gave him a sudden kiss. "You are so full of shit," she said. "You go. All the way to Mortirmir. If'n you want to cover us, send *him* to the midpoint. Not you, Mister Emperor. Not now."

He thought about it.

"Just once, do as I say," Sauce said.

Gabriel made a face. "Sure," he said.

She laughed. "Things must be desperate."

The first three lances included Wha'hae, and they went out at a trot. Gabriel mounted Ariosto and they launched into the wet air.

So hungry, the griffon said. *Love Sauce, too?*

Gabriel's breath caught. But there was no lying to a griffon. *Love Sauce*, he admitted.

The griffon seemed to chuckle, and something like a rippling purr passed along its trunk and spread to the wings.

By then they were high enough to make out the first three spots of phosphorescence. They were farther away—two or three thousand paces. Gabriel watched the second party of lances depart. And the third.

On the far side of the causeway, a great lidless eye of pale green began to drift in.

Gabriel turned Ariosto. *Sorry*, he thought. *I need you to fly about ten more minutes.*

Ouch, Ariosto said.

Gabriel turned again, coasting *back* along the causeway. He flashed over the fourth trio of lances, spooking Kearny's horse, and he turned Ariosto and they went in through the gate as if it was not a magnificent flying achievement.

Gabriel didn't augment his voice; he was trying to use no *ops* whatsoever. But he used his lungs, which were powerful.

"Everyone. Right. Now!" he called, and pointed with his spear at the outer gate.

They all saw him. And Sauce understood immediately.

He turned Ariosto, or Ariosto turned him, and they were out in the moist dark, the griffon's wings beating strongly in the eerie moonlight. Another phosphorescent patch was creeping in.

The fear was palpable, like the onrush of a dragon or twenty wyverns.

Gabriel rolled Ariosto at about the midpoint of the causeway and took him down over the water in a long dive away from the causeway. *Three minutes.*

Doing it, the griffon seemed to pant in the *aethereal*.

Gabriel plunged *into his palace and began casting, working new* ops *from purest gold and pushing a quantity of this sphere's dark blue into it, raw. The result was crude and it leaked raw* potentia. *Gabriel hung the bag from one of his javelins...*

In the real, he turned again, now over a black patch of empty water between the two nearest whorls of phosphorescence.

Here goes nothing. Literally.

He dropped the javelin into the fathomless water and turned.

Gate! he called.

Which one? Ariosto asked.

You think that's funny? Gabriel thought as the griffon put on a burst of speed in three great wingbeats that pressed him back into his high-backed saddle.

Yes, the griffon said, just as the water behind and below began to boil like a pot on a campfire far too long, huge bubbles rising.

Both of the spiral clusters began to drift rapidly toward the boiling sea.

Hoooooooooooooooooooooooooooooooooooooooooooooooooooooooooooooom

A third came in from farther out at sea. From altitude, the whorls and whirls and globs of phosphorescence out there, out to the far horizon, began to move in, drifting on some invisible tide.

Oh yes, Gabriel thought. Ariosto was labouring, the wings jerky with fatigue, his noble head down, drooping…

The last horse was past the midpoint on the causeway. They were racing, galloping through the moonlight. The sea had risen, and the horses were raising spray as they cantered along the beach.

A huge dome, wrinkled, black, slick with seawater and crusted with some nameless parasite, began to rise from the sea. The size of it baffled the eye and the human sense of distance. Veins of glowing ice green ran across it. It rose slowly, and with it, the nameless dread increased…

Gabriel fed his mount some of his *ops*. He was burning gold, and he knew how dangerous it was now for him to cast almost anything.

What would happen if I achieved apotheosis here? he wondered, even as he passed over Sauce and Ariosto's wings gave a shiver.

Love you, Gabriel said.

I bet you say that to all the monsters, Ariosto said. But the wings shot back and cupped the kelp-reeking air and then the lion legs were on the sand, running.

Gabriel was thrown right over the pommel of his saddle even as Ariosto rolled over his folded wings.

Gabriel lay in a hand's depth of warm salt water, staring up at the darkness as the water filled his helmet.

Tancreda stood over him. He wriggled his toes; his neck hurt.

"Damn," he said aloud.

Hungry! Ariosto wailed.

"Get through the gate! Get clear!" Gabriel roared, coming to his senses. He was soaking wet. "Go, go!"

A dozen greens poured across the last sand spit. Mortirmir was casting; Gabriel could tell from his posture. So was Petrarcha.

"Go!" Gabriel screamed at the company archers who stood across the gate. "Milus! Form ranks *on the other side of the gate.*"

Ser Milus turned immediately, gesturing. The Company Saint Catherine retired; the line of lances went back with it.

More scouts were coming down the end of the causeway. The water was rising.

"They know we're here," Morgon said. "And they hate us."

Gabriel grabbed Mortirmir by the shoulder. "Run. Don't walk. Run."

He put an arm around Petrarcha, even as he could feel the malevolent will working out in the water... working... magnified...

Sauce was galloping. She had someone riding double; she was last, and alone.

Behind him, Anne Woodstock got Ariosto through the ranks of the company and through the gate.

Sauce had a long way to go still. She'd stopped for someone.

Gabriel *went into his palace and slammed the iron gate shut, just to be sure. Then he reached down through memory and practice to the Umroth, and their passive shield. He took it out, examined it, and rolled it off as an effort of will powered entirely from within himself; from the same source that made his skin glow gold. He didn't need to understand it completely; he knew enough, now.*

It was like working with emotion instead of power, and he wove a shield of hope. And he built a wave front of hope; the antithesis of the hate of the sea creatures.

It was as if everything he'd ever learned, from Prudentia, from Harmodius, from his mother, from the Patriarch, from Al Rashidi and Mortirmir, all came together in a single expression of his innermost will.

There was no casting.

There was only being.

In the real, the sea rose until Sauce was galloping through water up to her charger's fetlocks. And the deep dweller rising from the water was exposed; vast, bloated, and it threw a fell wave of pale green light...

The light struck something invisible, like the prow of a ship, and passed along either side of the causeway to break against the island of rock that contained the gate; and the stone began to crack.

Sauce, with Daud clinging to her, burst past Gabriel who began to walk backwards, carefully. The green light was everywhere; not the green of home, but a watery green, pale, and eager to drink his essence.

His hope met its desire to destroy, and defeated it.

He took another step backward, and another, and another.

"Gate!" called Mortirmir.

A hand seized his hand and placed it on the key in the plaque.

He turned it.

The gate closed in silence.

He let go his nonworking and stood breathing, feeling *superb*.

Mortirmir leaned around him. "That was spectacular," he said.

"I liked it," Gabriel admitted. "Ready the company. Two minutes. All magisters, on me."

"You need rest," Sukey said.

"We are out of time. Is everyone fed?" he asked.

Sukey nodded, on the edge of anger. "Fed, and horses foddered. I'm out; unless we send back to Arles or start looting these poor irks, we're done." She shook her head. "Of course, I have forty useless wagons of loot and Umroth ivory..."

"Not useless," Gabriel said. "Well done, Sukey. I hope everyone had a nap." He looked around; there was Michael, his great sword in his hand; there was Tom Lachlan, already dismounted, with the lances of the *casa* dismounted right behind the white banda; there was No Head, and Francis Atcourt; Sauce, directing Conte Simone's knights. The vast hall was packed with soldiers; maybe twenty thousand men and women, a few irks, and a single bogglin.

He walked back, pressing through packed and armoured people. He was dripping as he walked, but he wasn't cold. The people were warming, even this vast place.

He found Blanche. "Wish me luck," he said. "If this one isn't it..." He shrugged, "Then I don't know where we are."

She kissed him. "Go," she said. She smiled. "You look like a fantastical beast, my love."

He smiled. His feeling of joy remained, and he squelched back across the hall, and men called out to him, and he paused to kiss Oak Pew on the cheek.

He got back to the pedestal, and he nodded to Mortirmir. "May I borrow your voice?" he asked.

"Of course," Mortirmir said. He snapped his fingers.

Soldiers.

We have marched and we have fought. Now, I hope, we will find what we seek.

If our guess is correct, this will be a fight. You need to be ready. You have drilled for this. Follow the drill and we will win quickly and with a minimum of fuss.

Ready?

There was a roar. And then three giant cheers, a flood of sound echoing from the high ceiling, three roars that shook the mountain.

Gabriel stood very straight. "Ready?" he called to the red banda, first at the gate.

"Get on wi' ye," shouted an archer. Men laughed.

Ready? he asked in the aethereal.

They all answered him; Mortirmir, Tancreda, Petrarcha, and a dozen lesser lights.

He turned the key four places.

And pressed down on the jewel.

Instantly he felt the will *fighting him for control of the gate, and his heart soared with victory.*

Got them! he yelled.

Mortirmir appeared inside his palace, and then Petrarcha in long, blue velvet robes, and Tancreda in the habit of a Liviapolitan nun, and as they entered they took his aethereal *hands. The other casters, mostly Morean and Alban university students, pushed* potentia *into the link.*

The will *pressed against the gate.*

Gabriel pushed back.

Mortirmir laughed. "Anytime," he said.

If the struggle for the gate was like arm wrestling with hermetical will, Gabriel did the equivalent of rotating his adversary's hand and wrist. He slammed his opponent's arm down on the metaphorical table.

The gate opened.

It was open for exactly as long as it might take a faery to blink her eye.

Mortirmir displaced a small, round egg of pure gold through the gate.

The gate shut.

Three. Two. One. They all counted down together.

Gabriel reached for the gate again.

No resistance.

He flicked it open, and the sun of a bright day fell across the line of the red banda.

They were looking out across a rocky down slope; volcanic, the earth red brown, the stone grey and black in contrast, with clumps of grass and a marvelous yellow sunlight. It was warm.

The air was full of dust, so full of dust that nothing of the landscape was visible beyond a few spear's lengths.

The ground outside the gate was thick with the corpses of bogglins. They were messily dead, their juices splattered across the ground in front of the gate.

"Go," Gabriel said.

The red banda marched through the gate. They marched forward two hundred paces, flowing around an ancient altar and two downed basalt columns and a huge volcanic rock and halting with both flanks resting on dry streambeds.

The white banda went through the gate and wheeled to the left by sections of lances. The *casa* came through on horseback, at the double, and formed to the right, and by then, the first wave of enemy had appeared out of the dust and died.

Mortirmir had passed the gate. He took a moment while Tancreda and Petrarcha raised immense shields in the *ops* rich air to draw the baselard from his hip and slit open the carcass of a bogglin.

Gabriel looked down at the mass of the thing's pink-grey innards.

"Not bogglins," Mortirmir said. "And look."

Gabriel knew what he would see. And it caused his heart to swell with joy; it meant they were on track, it meant he was right...

A worm. An Odine possessor worm in an alien bogglin-thing.

"We did it," Morgon said, and for once his adolescent superiority was utterly punctured, and joy covered him, and he threw his arms around Gabriel, who pounded his back.

Tom Lachlan looked down from his great black horse as if the two were idiots.

"Ye'r wode!" he said.

Gabriel thought he might cry, the relief was so great. So painful.

"Ye can tell 'em. Are we fucked?" asked Tom.

"No," Gabriel said. "No, Tom. We're fine. There's nothing left now but the fighting."

Tom's face broke in his broad grin. "Ah, laddy. Now yer fewkin' talkin…" He looked up. "Watch yer pennons!" he roared. "Keep your dress!"

He rode off, and the army continued to pour through the gate even as the archers of the red banda engaged a charge of imps, the small greyhound-sized monsters quick and deadly and very vulnerable to plunging shafts in this open ground.

Gabriel mounted the big bay. "Do you have a name?" he muttered. "I'll call you John."

John pricked his ears.

The attacks coming at the face of his square were uncoordinated, the creatures clearly Odine-animated. Gabriel watched the army unfold; there was confusion early on when the *casa* wheeled up into line as the Venikan marines came up on their flank; almost a half-century of Venikans died, caught moving by a flood of imps and a tide of sorcery, before Peterarcha stepped forward and countered it. Conte Simone was surprised by another assault coming from *behind* the gate, because it had a two dimensional quality that was evident only to the hermeticists; but the Etruscan knights were all fully armoured, from toe to groin to helm, and the imps found them almost invulnerable, and even a man pulled down by their horrible strength was cut free without loss.

Despite the setbacks, it was not a battle, or if it was a battle, it was one of near constant movement. The army fed through the gate, and the army advanced, filling in from the flanks, scouting the ground fifty paces ahead. It called for constant management; a bad decision could result in fifty people lost, or *taken* but the company stepped forward, stepped forward again, shaking off the counter attacks and occupying the ground and the magisters began to shift from defensive to offensive and the rate of movement increased.

Gabriel began to feel like a spectator. He rode back and forth along his line, making corrections, but he avoided the *aethereal*. He was on the edge, and he knew it; and he was damned if he was going to God before his task was finished.

But when the immediate ground of the gate was clear, his staff pulled themselves out of their combat roles; Michael was back at his side, and Tom Lachlan, and Sauce, and Milus.

Michael looked at the imperial standard flapping over their heads in Toby's fist.

"Like old times," he said to Sauce.

She gave him a grin. Her face seemed lit from within with the ferocity of her joy, and that look was reflected in every archer, every man-at-arms, every marine and every waggoner. The golden emperor raised his sword and pointed; Adrian Goldsmith sketched rapidly with charcoal in his book, and Francis Atcourt prayed.

The line moved forward.

Gabriel rode up a little hill that resembled a protruding tooth. "We're behind them, and our surprise is complete. Have you found the target, Mortirmir?" he asked.

"Target?" Sauce said.

Michael shrugged. "Long story. We figured the last gate had to be held by Odine, ready to back Ash. Or the *will*. Or both. Had to be, really."

Andromeche Sarrissa, one of the Morean students, was with the banner. She said, shyly, "We're looking for the Odine Will, my lady."

Sauce nodded. But her eyes were on her Etruscan infantry; their line was starting to trail off into the increasingly low ground to the right. "We sound really cocky," she said. She smiled. "Tell his nibs to keep me up-to-date on what to kill." She turned and rode off to the right, already shouting orders.

Now, for the first time in a long time, the whole of the company was displayed together; almost a thousand lances, with two hundred more in the *casa*. Carts appeared from the gate, and bags of livery arrows were delivered by pages through the dust, bags of twenty-four heavy arrows held by leather spacers. Other pages appeared with water. Wounded men were dragged to the rear, inside the box that continued to form out of the gate, but the front of the army vomited arrows that fell like a wicked sleet, and the enemy died.

Three hours into the action, Gabriel could see the sea off to the right, beyond a marsh; a glorious expanse of seamless blue.

"Found it," Mortirmir said.

Instantly, all the magisters' faces fell, like puppets with their strings cut, but that was only all of them turning inward.

Gabriel joined them, cautious about his expenditure.

They all joined hands, and he stood aloof; Tancreda provided a lead, and they powered shields they'd woven and laid aside, the new, fractal shields of interwoven scales and leaves.

A titanic bolt of purple-white lightning struck their shield.

There was leakage, and in the center, six lances of the red banda died; Ser Richard Smith; Kessin the archer, and Lowper, and twenty other men and women who'd marched across four worlds and fought their way from Lissen Carak to Arles were turned to ash.

Five paces away, Urk of Mogon drew a heavy clothyard shaft to his four cheeks and released into the clump of irks who seemed rudderless and stood in the open. By him, Heron drew, grunted, and loosed. The smell of cooked flesh floated over and Urk's mouth cracked open to expose his sensory organs to the wonderful smell of cooked human flesh. It was all unconscious; he was drawing his next shaft from his belt, listening for Smoke's orders.

Forty paces away, Edmund cursed. "Heave!" he roared. His voice cracked, but the wheel came free from between two huge chunks of volcanic rock and the falconet rolled forward again. There were twenty men on each drag rope, every one of them with a hand gonne slung over their shoulder, and a dozen smaller gonnes on platforms were moving forward on donkeys; a last-minute innovation by Sukey.

But there had been no time to employ the slow falconets; he had his third set of crews on the drag ropes and his fourth set ready, but the gonnes moved more slowly than the rate of advance.

There was a purple-white flash that illuminated a faery forest of golden light hundreds of feet in the air. A concussion rolled back over the panting men. The sound rolled like thunder.

Tom Lachlan raised his long sword. "We only get home by going forward," he roared. "Follow me!"

The *casa* went forward into the fire.

Out on the right, the Vardariotes joined the line, which was now more than a mile long and seemed to outflank any resistance.

Count Zac didn't need direction or orders. He could *feel* the vacuum in front of him, and he moved his command more rapidly, and Comnena linked on him, and they began to pass the main line.

Edmund's gonnes fell farther and farther behind as the *casa* accelerated away. And began to turn like a door on the hinge of the Nordikaans, swinging inward.

Two thousand paces to the left, Simone raised his visor just in time to see the five hundred-fold forked purple lightning strike the center. But like Count Zac, he could feel the *absence* of the enemy, and he pushed his knights to mount; their stumbling advance became much more fluid; and the Venikan light horse suddenly had Sauce at their head and they were outpacing him, spreading through the thorny brakes and probing out to the left of the road.

The third pulse of purple-white burst on the center. It was followed by a massive surge of bogglins, or whatever they were; they had long spears and they came in dense clumps. This time, it was all coordinated, and on the flanks of the central phalanx there appeared two massive blocks of *Grecklins* (Snot coined the term for them between one shaft and the next) who had crossbows.

The company archers shot them away.

The lightning didn't even scorch the ground.

The company went forward. The Saint Catherine streamed in the breeze; and by it, a sable banner with three lacs d'amours and the red banner, a massive golden lion on scarlet silk.

Gabriel was under the red banner now. He'd raised his new passive shield over the center of the center; it seemed to him the only contribution he could make.

"How are we doing?" Michael asked. "To me, it looks like we're winning."

"We're winning so handily that I'm saving myself for the real fight," Gabriel said. He looked to the right; where he could see Robin Carter and Gadgee and Scrant all drawing their bows together, and beyond them, a hundred men and women he knew by name; thousands; there was Oak Pew, calling orders, and there, far off on the plain, the brilliant sun shone on the red coats of the Vardariotes as they turned inward and there was Zac, and the Scholae drew their sabers and they shone like the spears of the phalanx of angels in heaven.

The magisters cantered up.

The phalanx of enemy spear-creatures was melting under the shafts of the company, but they stood, stolid, stubborn, waiting. Their unshielded crossbowmen were gone; already lying in long rows in the volcanic dirt, like sea wrack washed up after a storm.

Edmund's gonnes appeared, and with the surviving Nordikaans

covering them, they ran forward, the heavy bronze tubes bouncing up and down as forty strong men and women hauled them by ropes, another dozen carrying the trails of the long carriages.

The enemy *will* rose and cast, and Gabriel's passive shield of *hope* and *joy* swatted it to earth. Gabriel didn't even realize that his wave front was as wide as the front of the whole red banda; that as he went forward, it went forward, like a great power of the Wild.

Edmund's sweating apprentices dropped the trail on *Blanche*, the first falconet. Cat Turell, eyes squinting through the dust, traversed the tube until the mouth was squarely in the center of the spear-things phalanx.

Another apprentice came forward with a wooden plug bound with twine; inside were one hundred and forty four iron balls. It went into the dragon's mouth.

Morgon Mortirmir spread his arms.

"Everyone ready?" he said. He raised both eyebrows and favoured his wife with a look.

She blew him a kiss.

The Ifriquy'an kid whirled the porte-fire through the air as if he'd been doing it all his life and put it to the touch hole of the falconet.

Twenty four iron balls blew through a corner of the enemy phalanx, passing diagonally through the dense-packed things.

A shrill shrieking erupted.

Kaitlin, gonne two, fired.

Clarissa, gonne three, fired.

Morgon cast. In the real, he and Petrarcha and Tancreda were momentarily outlined in light, and then an uncountable number of lines of fire arced away into the heavens. They burst, all together, in tens of thousands of lines of angry red that raced earthward, arcing and turning at impossible angles like lightning on a dark day.

All this in the time a congregation might say "Amen."

They struck all together silently.

Gabriel motioned with his sword. "Forward," he said. He nodded to Payam, whose Mamluks were now filling the field behind the company. The Ifriquy'an waved. The Mamluks were deploying from column into line at a canter.

"What is happening?" he asked.

Michael turned his horse. "The Odine have formed up a great army to invade," he said. "We're pulling it to pieces. Just as we planned. Morgon is now pounding their wormy masters."

"Il Conte Simone is now turning their flank," Payam motioned with his Fell Sword. "Perhaps I should join him?"

Gabriel shook his head. "There's no flank to turn," he said. "This is not a formed host. The *will*... that is, this *will*... They weren't ready. *It* isn't ready." He shook his head. "It is what I dreamed." He turned to Michael. "Go see what the left is doing. Pavalo, on my word, I want you to exchange lines with the *casa*. In a little while, we will face the Odine."

Payam nodded. "Allah hath a thousand hands to chastise," he said with a smile. "And we have brought a few thousand more." He smiled broadly. "We have faced the Odine a few times."

Gabriel went back to watching the company.

The enemy phalanx stood its ground in the center, and died. Too late they attempted to charge, but their cohesion was failing them, and the gaps torn in them by gonnes and shafts were too great to heal.

Gabriel followed them forward, his body burning gold so that now, in bright sunlight, he gave off light. He paused to watch No Head cutting up another corpse. One of the not-bogglins.

"Need Mortirmir to be sure," No Head said. "Looks to me like this beastie's been bred to host the worm."

Gabriel frowned.

The company went forward over the last of the phalanx, and there was a moment of vicious hand to hand, a cloud of dust, and the line buckled, knotted, and moved on, righting itself. The flanks were still pressing in.

The company had taken losses. There were fifty men and women down; knots of magisters tried to save those *taken* by worms even as they tried to fight their mates.

Gabriel winced that it had become routine to his people.

The banners pressed forward, and the fighting slackened. Ser Milus began to consider ordering his people to mount, but he rode over to Gabriel.

"Boys and girls are tired," he said. "And what do you think o' that?" he asked, pointing at a dust cloud at the gate.

"I'm putting the company into reserve," Gabriel said. He waved to one of the imperial messengers and snapped orders.

Michael rode along the left of the army, watching the Etruscans form from their columns and then link their lines, the whole as they began a great turning action toward the now visible gate pylons, a little more than a mile away. Sauce gave orders as effortlessly as Gabriel.

"You are having too much fun," Michael said.

"Yep," she answered. "I thought I wanted to be a knight. Turns out I wanted to be a great captain."

He had nothing to add, so he watched.

A messenger cantered up. "Lord Michael?" she asked. "The emperor asks for the *casa* to take the center of the line. And for you to attend him."

Michael looked left, along the line; then he turned and rode toward the center. The whole of the imperial army was moving forward, the wings closing as they had practiced, the center pressing ahead slowly. Michael rode to Bad Tom.

"Gabriel wants us in the center," Michael said.

"Aye," Tom said. "Already heard. Watch this."

Even as Michael watched, the *casa* began to mount the horses brought forward by pages and servants, and suddenly they were four lines of mounted men and women, their armour glittering in the brilliant sun.

Behind them the Mamluks came forward, closer and closer.

The *casa* began to file off from the left of sections. As they filed off, mounted, they passed to the left of sixty-man sections of Mamluks, who passed through them, moving forward, so that in the twinkling of an eye, the *casa* was in the second line.

Payam saluted with his long, curved sword. "Odine," he said. "I can smell them."

"This is it," Michael said.

Tom nodded, as did Payam.

The center halted.

The wings continued to move in, overcoming knots of resistance.

The Beronese chivalry charged, annihilated a mob of not-bogglins, and rallied.

Tom Lachlan appeared in the command circle.

Mortirmir was on horseback, his feet out of his stirrups, his hands at his sides. He looked terrible, but the *ops* rolled off him in waves.

And then, very suddenly, his eyes opened, and he looked directly at Gabriel.

"There it is," he said. "The *will*."

Far off, almost at the edge of the gate, something was rising.

A mile is a long way. Across a battlefield, few things register at the range of an imperial mile; people are like a stain of colour, blocks of men big enough to take kingdoms are smaller than fleas. A fleet of ships can vanish in the haze, a mile away. A dragon looks like a bird, a mile away.

Something like a living mountain began to shamble erect. A mile away, it was *huge*.

His voice matter of fact, Mortirmir said, "That is it."

"It's in the gate," Gabriel said.

"I think we've failed to put the facts together correctly," Mortirmir said. "I'm willing to wager that it is *stuck in the gate*. Where the dragons trapped it, a thousand years ago."

Gabriel was watching it in horrified fascination. "But..." He paused. "No. I see it. Its head is in Mistress Helewise's back garden and this is the arse end."

Michael smiled. So did Tom Lachlan, and Zac, and a dozen other men and women around the emperor.

"It's trying to take control of the gate," Mortirmir said.

Gabriel smiled. "And it hasn't yet!"

"QED," said Mortirmir. "Lissen Carak is still fighting."

Gabriel's bay turned in a circle as he looked around at his officers.

"Damn it," he said with as smile. "We can win this, my friends."

Michael glanced at Tom.

"Ye sound as if ye didn'ae believe it, your own sel'?" Tom asked. He laughed.

The horrendous compendium of worms writhed a mile away.

"Mortirmir?" Gabriel asked.

"My rede would be to press it hard in the real, as we did the Umroth.

When it responds, I'll…" Morgon shrugged. "I'll hope to do better than last time."

"Same massive wave of coercion?" Gabriel said.

Mortirmir shook his head. "The *will* is to the *rebel* as ten is to one," he said. "But the *will* has never been a man, nor understands hermetical science."

Gabriel nodded. "Form the choir. Get me Edmund Chevins."

An hour later, and the army was halted in a rough semicircle facing the writhing titan at a range of roughly a thousand paces.

"It does appear pinned in place," Mortirmir said. They had survived a probe of coercion; the *casa*, having experienced the mass despair before, stood their ground, gritted their teeth, and tried not to think.

Gabriel did the same as he witnessed, again, his abject failure on every front.

The gonnes rolled forward.

"Can you hit it?" Gabriel asked Edmund Chevins.

He bowed. "My lord, I expect we'll hit it with every shot. It is… very…large."

"Then what happens?" Ser Michael asked. He was dismounted. Every one of the emperor's *comitatus* was dismounted with their lances behind them, and the fractal forest of white faery leaves was already before them, hiding the worst horrors of their enemy.

"Then we teach it a basic law of war," Gabriel said.

Michael turned. "God, I love it when you claim there are laws. What law of war?"

"You can't hold ground with magic," the emperor said. "You can kill things, but you can't take ground, or hold it. See that tower of worms? That's not a monster. That's an absence of effective infantry."

Michael looked at the thing. It had no great fangs, no glowing eyes, no face of any kind. No thousands of legs, no body hairs.

Merely billions of worms writhing together.

"Jesus, I hope you're right," Michael said.

"I hate it when you call me Jesus," Gabriel said with his old, blasphemous smile. "Gonner?"

Edmund bowed.

Gabriel took his *ghiavarina* in hand and walked to the very center of the *casa*, and shoved into the front, with Anne against his back and Cully ready to loose, down the open file. He had ten monster killers in the ground beside him. Every *casa* archer did.

Edmund walked to the right, to his gonnes. He and Duke slapped hands, and then Edmund crouched over his trail, had a peek, and muttered, "Here goes nothing."

His porte-fire went down, and he slipped sideways, out of the way of the recoiling wheel.

Five hundred and twenty-one paces away, the first iron ball smashed into the Odine. It passed all the way through the thing, crushing individual worms, and exploded out the far side in a gout of semireal worm paste.

The second gonne fired; Duke's body nimbly avoided the wheel as it passed him, and Edmund's loader was already putting a wet sheepskin sponge down the smoking tube. Giron le Courtois, a Galle, was just putting his porte-fire down.

The third gonne slammed out.

Sulphur powder smoke drifted over Gabriel's position.

The Odine raised a massive shield in the real.

"Here we go," said Mortirmir.

"Gonne one," Edmund said.

Bam.

In the *aethereal, a short, vicious war was played out in which the coercion tried to control Edmund; Mortirmir tried to open a hole in the shield, and both failed.*

"Gonne two," Duke called. Edmund was retching; he felt *defiled.*

Bam.

The wave of coercion played about the casa; *Tom Lachlan had doubts, and Cully relived something he'd done, once, to Sauce. Michael heard his captain remind him of his many shortcomings. Oak Pew drank herself to death. Urk of Mogon missed with every arrow and Mogon stripped him of her scent.*

The iron ball ripped through a perfectly timed hole in the worms' casting and a gout of superheated white mush erupted on the thing's far side.

It went for *Mortirmir in the* aethereal, *and the whole choir covered him, but he choked in his own inadequacy, and* fire raged along the edge of the fractal shield and it collapsed, leaving another, golden shield in its place.

"Tom," Gabriel said. "We are going to have to do this on foot. The old-fashioned way."

"Now y'er fewkin' tellin' me a story I want to hear," Tom said. "*Prepare to advance!*"

The new trumpeter played, and a dozen horns took up the sound.

The *casa* began to walk forward.

Fifty paces to the rear of the *casa*, Ser Milus squinted and then shrugged.

Sauce appeared at his shoulder. "You goin' forward?" she asked.

The *casa*'s shields crackled and a huge hole appeared. Hand gonners died. Horses shied in the Vardariotes. The Nordikaans were down to only a few, under Thorval Armring, now Spatharios, and he went forward as if he had two hundred axe-brothers with him and not sixty.

"No orders," Milus said with a shrug.

"I'm ordering it," Sauce said. "Forward."

The gonnes fired again; bam *bam bam*.

The *casa* was already two hundred paces away when the company rumbled forward.

"This is gonna suck," Tippit muttered. He looked up at the vast *puissance* of the worm.

"Always does," Smoke agreed.

Mortirmir was *deep in his palace. He was waiting for the waves of emanation off the enemy, and then working to cancel them, not with blunt defences like shields, but at their roots.*

He was learning the hermetical language of the Odine. It was very like the language of the rebel, *and yet different. Rigorous. Pure. Undiluted.*

A little naive.

He could feel it planning, preparing, building power.

He tried sabotaging a thought, and failed; it ignored him.

He lost the initiative and spent a great deal of his choir's ops on defence. He wasn't altogether successful and lost almost a hundred people, and the will *pounced. It knew the code by which mere humans lived, and it assaulted Mortirmir with a wave of revulsion and self-loathing based on his failure, his love of his fellow men, his betrayal of their hopes.*

The Odine was as mistaken as the man had been. Mortirmir was not very interested in people. He protected them because by doing so he could win, but he could sustain losses and still win, and the coercive attack washed over him. And in it he found information. He changed his own message; he fine-tuned the choir's shields and exchanged, at the speed of thought, some ideas with his wife and with Magister Petrarcha.

The gonnes fired in the real. They were working; the will *feared them. Even though their immediate effects were infinitesimal, Gabriel had correctly assessed that the* will *must view the world in very long aeons. The* will *could not afford a siege of its* puissance *by gonnes.*

The will *shielded itself. But the kinetic force of the gonnes was huge, and required a massive manipulation of* potentia *and thus a huge display of information in the* aethereal, *and Mortirmir watched, manipulated, and unleashed.*

He failed, and the balls were stopped on the magnificent shield that towered over the thing.

It struck back.

In the real, the *will*'s counterstrike fell like a sheet of lightning two hundred paces long, and it burned through the *casa*'s shields in a dozen places. Comnena fell at the head of the Scholae, burned down one side of his body and saved only by one of Mortirmir's finest amulets, and behind him, a hundred gentlemen of Liviapolis were burned to death in an instant.

Count Zac died as the air in his lungs ignited. Forty Vardariotes died with him, and the white lightning played over into the hand gonners, killing a dozen Venikans and an Ifriquy'an.

The *casa* went forward into the fire.

The company followed. Out on the flanks, men and women began to edge forward because courage is infectious and because there were no orders not to. Sauce was now at the head of the company; Conte Simone was not a man to wait while others did the fighting, and the duchess, on the far flank, walking easily at the head of her scarecrows, thirsted for vengeance against this very monster, the personifier of her fears, the epicenter of her nightmares.

The scarecrows went forward.

But in the center, the *casa* covered ground; they were less than five hundred paces from the great worm of worms now, and they began to pick up speed because they were afraid, and they all, collectively, wanted to get it over with.

The gonnes fired again.

The *will* responded, concentrating its efforts directly at the gonnes.

But this was the attack that the choir had anticipated, and now it struck shield after shield, knocking one down only to meet another. The gonnes had been a trap; Mortirmir had expected the *will* to attack them first.

Now Mortirmir had the initiative, and not a single gonner was killed.

Mortirmir recast shields, along with a dazzling array of attacks: balls of spectacular fire, bolts of lightning in various colours, a driven wind of colours from beyond the human spectrum of perception, through the rainbow and beyond again.

The *will* stopped them.

In the real, the world beyond the shields was a rolling cacophony of noise and light.

Anything you could do to distract it would be appreciated, Mortirmir said inside Gabriel's palace.

People were down. There were gaps in the *casa*; the Scholae had stopped advancing altogether. The Vardariotes were unable to continue forward and began, despite Kriax's entreaties, to run. Edmund's hand gonners were wavering, unable to see beyond the ends of their weapons.

But...

Even as Gabriel prepared himself in his palace, the Saint Catherine came forward, the company dividing along the middle to pass on either side of the *casa*. They were less than a hundred paces from the maelstrom of chaos.

Gabriel, despite his fears, prepared to cast. He *went into his palace and saluted Prudentia.*

"You are very close now," she said quietly.

"My friends are dying," he said.

"Yes," she said.

He pointed to three simple sigils.

"Allow me," she said. "You really should not power anything just now."

Gabriel stepped back out of the line in the real and augmented his voice.

Archers! he called.

Knights! Forward!

Then he pushed past Woodstock and went forward into the storm. He could not see that the Etruscans and the scarecrows were also pushing forward. He couldn't see that Cully was loosing heavy arrows behind him, aiming high at a conglomerate of terror that towered over them. He couldn't see Tom Lachlan or Michael or Sauce or Francis Atcourt or any of the rest of the men and women he'd led for years.

But he knew they were there.

And together, they went forward.

The shield of the Odine was like a wall of soft clay—clinging, cloying, sickening, an assault on every sense. But soft.

The *ghiavarina* cut it like butter, and Gabriel was momentarily reminded of fighting his mother's curse of black felt, except that every stroke of the weapon took his deeper and opened a hole.

And then he could see the mountain of worms on the other side, a thousand thousand ravening mouths. He set himself and cut, even as the first worms began to turn on him. Two paces to his right, Bad Tom's sword burst through in a spray of fire and even in the hell of the Odine's maw, Gabriel heard, "Lachlan for Aa!"

Then he was cutting. It was like exercise; like cutting at air, except that the worms themselves had the same consistency as the shield, and they fled him and Lachlan, the wall of mouths and glistening grey bodies writhing away.

Lachlan, as casually as if he were fighting in a tournament, spared two blows to widen the rift in the shield.

Gabriel cut to his left, opening the tear wider.

Mortirmir couldn't handle the ferocity of the attacks.

But he didn't have to. He wasn't alone, and Tancreda spun her web faster than a hermetical spider while Magister Petrarcha wove a fabric of deceit and reconciliation. A Morean magister dropped, exhausted, and was killed; the choir faltered, and the shields flickered. Women died, and men. Irks died.

But...

The choir held. The will was distracted; swords were eating at its base in the real, and its shield of flexible adamantine had become porous. It began to change its priorities, and orders flowed through the aethereal as its millions of component beings demanded, ordered, shouted, received...

Mortirmir found what he sought; and in the haze of communications that the Odine used to master themselves, he and his choir deciphered. Analyzed.

Prepared.

If the duel had been with swords, then all the attacks, all the lightning, all the fireballs, all the swords would have been an attack in an outside line.

A feint.

Mortirmir gathered every shred of power remaining to his choir.

His chessboard was empty. His wall of diagrams was complete. He didn't even have time to savour the moment at which he was either triumphant or annihilated.

He cast. A single pulse, a single ray of light. Or perhaps a single musical note. Or perhaps a single colour. A texture. An emotion.

He cast it on what he had perceived as the moment in the spectrum wherein the Odine's components communicated, and he sustained it. . . .

In the real, the worm of worms began to collapse like an undermined tower in a siege; slowly at first, like a wounded man subsiding, and then . . .

. . . then the worms were everywhere, writhing like larvae, mouths pulsing. Swords took a few; arrows snapped through the air and nipped others, but the effect was like that of a single gardener attacking a forest. And the knights and men-at-arms were buried in the collapse, the grotesque unmaking of the Odine into its components, but the components themselves were still deadly.

Gabriel felt the *dissolution* and knew, too, that the moment had come.

He went into the *palace.*

"Don't!" Pru said.

He spun, pointing. Spun again, and siphoned the gold of his own burning will into his working. Complex, layered, with limitations and stops and buffers he'd learned and mastered until he raised one arm.

In the real he said, *"Fiat Lux."*

There was a flash. Thunder rolled, and Gabriel still stood in the worlds of the real, shining with unshadowed gold.

From his outstretched hand to the pylons of the gate, and beyond, the earth was clear except for a fine grey dust that lingered, and the sun lit it in brilliant shafts.

Outside the circle of his choice, millions of the worms writhed in the sunlight and could offer no hermetical response.

The gate was clear. The golden pedestal stood where he had expected it to be. Gabriel walked forward, the metal sabatons on his feet crunching against the tiny fragments of desiccated worms as he walked.

Tom Lachlan was beside him, and Sauce. The company was in chaos; intermixed, knights and men-at-arms, archers and pages spread over hundreds of paces of ground, most of them ferociously stomping, cutting, or kicking.

Lachlan looked angry.

Gabriel managed a smile.

"Don't worry, Tom," he said. "There's still an army of bogglins. And the dragon."

"Oh aye," Bad Tom said. "Fuck." He shuddered. "I hate worms."

Gabriel laughed. It was a good laugh. He hadn't ever imagined that Tom Lachlan hated anything.

He was still chuckling when he got to the pedestal, and found the key inside his breastplate. He had to drop his gauntlets to fumble it out. His hands were shaking so badly that he had to pause and breathe. His knees were weak; his heart pounded.

All for this, he thought. *Please, God, let me have been right. Please. I will not brag or be smug or claim I figured it all out. Just let me be right.*

It was the most complex gate yet: six stops on the plaque, and none closed.

But only one of them could be the right one. The green jewel, on the far left; the one already burning, because, of course, the *will* had been trying to *force* its way through.

He turned the key.

His shaking hand reached out to press the gem.

It would not push.

Please. Please. Damn it.

Nothing.

An exhausted Mortirmir appeared in his memory palace, standing beside Pru. And there was Tancreda and Petrarcha and the rest of the surviving choir.

"It is locked from the other side," Mortirmir said carefully. "Miriam must have been holding it against the will all this time."

Gabriel felt a rush of frustration almost as intense as physical pain.

He put his right hand, physical flesh, on the jewel. *Hello?* he called into the void.

And Desiderata replied, *Gabriel!*

Chapter Sixteen

Gabriel felt Desiderata's response and he almost burst into tears, so great was the relief, the sheer joy.

And the overwhelming feel of triumph.

Under his fingers, the jewel moved.

With a click, the key turned.

By now, Bad Tom had a rough line across the gate: knights and squires, pages and archers, mostly *casa*; some company; and a handful of mamluks and Etruscan knights and a pair of Gallish knights. The collapse and defeat of the *will* on their side of the gate had led to some chaotic local fighting, and no group who had entered the fight had emerged unscathed.

"Tom!" Gabriel roared. "The second it's open, we'll be fighting the other half."

"I am..." Mortirmir groaned. "Gabriel. I'm exhausted."

Petrarcha appeared on a mule. "I am not. I am ready."

The gate was opening.

"Woodstock," Gabriel called. "Bring me Ariosto."

Ash felt the movement of the gate, and knew in his black heart that victory was in his taloned grasp at last.

He was using his superior mobility and his new commanders to rebuild his line and prepare for the last act; the loss of two of his puppets had disinclined him to take a direct role in the end-of-day fighting, but even as the winter clouds rolled in, he used the last of the visibility to identify the pitiful weaknesses of the alliance lines; their grip on the ridge above the road was tight, but in the open ground between Penrith and the woods, their forces were spread so thinly that *any* attack would break them. To the east, his lieutenant threw assault after assault at the outwalls of Albinkirk. And Orley had pushed daemons right up the slope of the abbey, and now had cave trolls burrowing into the rubble of the collapsed north tower.

Ash's eye swept the field; at Lissen Carak he saw Ser Ricar Orcsbane sword to stone club with a cave troll, and to the south and east, he saw the bears who had fought all day alongside the Duchess Mogon, now slipping away to the west. This confirmed Ash's thought that his enemy's army must break up now; their alliance must be tattered, the internal stresses too great to sustain losses.

Yet something in his head was not right; his connections to his out-consciousness seemed frayed, and full of disorder, and he kept thinking of Thorn...

Why had he discarded Thorn?

And then the gate began to move. There was a sort of choked scream *in the* aethereal *and his ally began to shout, to give orders; there was a sudden frenzy of Odine chittering in the* aethereal, *near and far off to the north.*

Now the gate would open, and his "allies" would come through, and it would be complete, and infinitely more powerful. He would be threatened. Or defeated. By the Odine.

But of course, he had planned for this, and the Odine had served their purpose.

Ash had known this moment would come. He had made his preparations; so much simpler, because war in the aethereal *was in many ways more natural and cleaner than war in the real.*

Ash leapt across the nonspace of the aethereal, *and sank his hermetical fangs deep into the Odine's* aethereal *throat.*

His betrayal was immediate, the surprise complete. The Odine, the one holding the gate, seemed distracted, even as he sucked its life away; its distant sister, the will *north of the Inland Sea, shrieked in rage and swore revenge.*

Ash bore down, even as the Odine under his assault began to crumple. Its collapse was ridiculously quick, and he wondered if he had misjudged its power in the first days.

The gate swung fully open in the timeless time of the aethereal.

Chapter Seventeen

Tom Lachlan sprang through the gate with the whole line at his back, and with Petrarcha pouring *ops* into the *casa*'s great golden shield as they advanced, and a firework of potent sorceries rolled off the old scholar as he went forward just behind Cully, his head up and his hands opening and closing like a puppet master working marionettes. It was dark, and there was snow in the air, and Tom had somehow expected to arrive in the cellars below the abbey; instead, he was fighting between two great bloodstained pylons of yellow-white, his sword flickering effortlessly through crowds of unmotivated not-dead.

On the other side of the gate, where it was warmer and the sun shone, Ser Michael was rebuilding the army in a parade ground voice. The gate gapped, with a vision of snow-laced darkness, just as, a hundred paces away, Tom Lachlan's fight was illuminated strangely by the sunlit day pouring through the gate behind him, lighting the falling snow in a most unnatural way.

The *will* collapsed, its constituents struggling for supremacy. Thousands of worms and larvae fled, on the ground, virtually vanishing into the falling snow.

Petrarcha cast a rolling fire that cleared the ground of both snow and *Odine*, at least closer in.

In the aethereal, *Ash reached out and began to subsume the power of the massed wills of the Odine. He needed the power, to replace all that he had used and squandered, but the subsumation of the scattered wills of the Odine was not like taking a single defeated entity, and it took time.*

Blue Berry of the Long Dam Clan had fought all day, and her fur was clotted with blood and other fluids, and her gold was dimmed to a dingy brown, and she had a bad wound all down her left side, the slash of a cave troll's stone axe. But she and her clan had stood their ground with the duchess and held her flank until the very end.

And the men had come, and freed them from the trap.

It was all very well for men to offer them food, and she ate well, but as the darkness deepened, she wanted trees over her head, and to be away from the open sky and the falling snow, which made her, and all her kin, sleepy. Together they loped west, their axes on their backs, into the debatable ground between Penrith and the woods. There were men there, where the ancient road rose up four feet above the fields on either side; and Blue Berry could see other men landing from boats to the south, and more snow coming into the east. But she craved the safety of the woods, and she and her clan went into the open trees at the edge, where in better times men kept pigs and all the undergrowth was clear; and when she was under the branches of the huge old maples, she relaxed.

But she kept going, moving carefully, because the woods were not clear of enemies and the fields to the east were now beginning to fill with bogglins and worse. Blue Berry led her bears north, avoiding combat; looking for a huddle of fallen trees or a little cave to spend the night.

After an hour of steady moving, she found a fire, and a little cautious exploration showed that there were men at the fire. Blue Berry had little trust in men, but much experience, and she liked the look of the two caves the men had found.

She motioned with a paw and her warriors went flat in the snow. Then she approached carefully, until she was challenged by a sentry, a young knight with a heavy crossbow cradled in his freezing-cold arms under a heavy cloak.

"Halt!" the young human cried. "Identify yourself."

She gave a growl. "I am Blue Berry of the Long Dam Clan," she said. "I have fought all year alongside men."

"Galahad!" roared the boy.

Before the ice on her paws between her long toes could harden uncomfortably, another man came. He bowed to her, and she thought she might recognize him.

"I knew Flint," he said. "I am Ser Galahad d'Acon."

"Ah, the gallant Galahad," purred Blue Berry. "I come to share, *grrrr*, your caves."

Gabriel nodded. "Come and join us."

The crowd of fighters who had cleared the gate were tired, and Bad Tom pulled them back; he had not lost a one, but he was troubled by the worms and the snow.

Ser Michael replaced them with the scarecrows. The whole phalanx came through the gate very quickly and formed a hollow square, covering the opening of the gate.

The snow squall ended. Moonlight fell on snow; to the west, a long line of clouds marched in, presaging worse weather, but for the moment, there were stars.

The Duchess of Venike shrugged into a fur-lined khaftan held by her servants. Edmund Chevin's hand gonners were filing through the gate and gazing around in astonishment, and then Ser Michael was there with her, and Sauce.

"It is *fucking* cold," muttered Sauce. "Hello, honey," she said, kissing the duchess.

Michael bowed.

Sauce stepped back, snapping orders, as the Venikan marines began to move through the gate, followed by her other Etruscan infantry.

"The emperor will come through in person in a few minutes," Michael said. "We'll eat and sleep in shifts—back there. It's too damned cold here." He was already shivering.

The duchess nodded. "How long?" she asked.

"Two hours," Michael said. "Tom Lachlan says to watch for worms and not-dead."

The duchess nodded. "Can I take some ground?" she asked. "There's a house over there, and farm fields, and a hill..."

"We need someone who's been here before," Michael said. He shivered again.

And then the emperor was there; he came through the gate on foot, and Anne Woodstock was leading Ariosto, who was beaming at her.

"I've been here before," Gabriel said. "This is Lady Helewise's back garden; what a lot of blood. You can tell Tom's been here, can't you? Giselle, there's a ridge just there, to the west. Take it and clear all the ground from there to here. Sauce? I'm going for a fly. Don't lose the gate. And someone stay awake; I'll want a drink when I come back." He grinned. "We did it!"

He swung up into the high-backed saddle. He was grinning ear to ear, and Sauce found that she was grinning, too.

"We did it," she shouted at him.

"We certainly did," he said, and then the griffon leapt into the freezing air.

Outside Lissen Carak—Gavin Muriens

It was colder atop the ridge than down in the valley, but the view was better. Gavin was very cold, and he had no one to blame for it but himself; his cloak was somewhere with the camp, away down by Southford.

But there was a line of huge fires along the top of the hill, as much to rally the army as to warm it, and he had a stool, and he sat with his back to one fire and his face to the battlefield. Now that the snow squall had passed, he could see Penrith, still burning, in the distance; closer in, he could see the smoking ruins of Woodhull to the northwest, now full of bogglins, and the church steeple of Saint Mary's almost due north, at Ambles Inn. He could not find the inn itself. At the foot of his ridge, directly to the north, lay Livingston Hall, which had been the scene of brutal fighting since late afternoon; even now, another clutch of daemons attempted to storm it in darkness.

The Prince of Occitan was there in person. It would hold, or all the world would fall.

And behind him were the suburbs and walls of Albinkirk, and the enemy had made two attempts on it since darkness. So the enemy held a huge semicircle, from Penrith to almost Southford. Gavin was surprised, and pleased, to find that the enemy's army was almost countable; he reckoned it not in numbers but in frontage. Today they'd stretched Ash's forces over almost fifteen miles, and in that kind of fighting, good armour and good training had repeatedly overcome ferocity and predation.

But now they were being pushed into shorter lines. Tomorrow, Ash would come with his terrible fire, and Gavin would have no response.

"What I want to do," the Green Earl said, "is attack."

"Attack?" Gregario asked. "Aren't we a little thin on the ground?"

"It worked today," Gavin said. "Listen, if 1Exrech turns around and faces the other way, he'll be looking out toward the walls of Albinkirk. He could cut the enemy off; force Ash into a fight under the walls."

"Where our folk are protected from most of his sorcery," Gregario said.

Mogon nodded. "How do you people deal with this cold?" she said slowly. "I should have stayed in the burning town and spent the night killing bogglins. Freezing to death seems a poor way to go."

A cup of steaming apple cider was put in Gavin's hand.

Lady Tamsin was smiling like a girl at Christmas. She grinned at him, her fangs showing.

"You look better," Gavin said.

"Wait," she said.

He drank the cider. "Anyone want to comment on my attack?"

"It's an excellent idea," a voice said.

Gavin knew that voice. He rose, cold forgotten, and whirled into a steel-clad embrace.

"You bastard!" Gavin said, pounding his brother's back.

"Probably," Gabriel said.

At Lady Helewise's manor house, the duchess and Sauce had a brief discussion, and then the scarecrows formed with crossbowmen on either flank and crunched off across the snow, headed north. Almost immediately they came across irks and bogglins, also moving. Sauce threw in some of Conte Simone's knights, and the thing was done; the bogglins fled, and even the irks ran, panicked, scarce believing what had suddenly come at them out of the snow.

They fled away north, into the eaves of the great wood along the Lily Burn, and there they rallied, for they were a great host all by themselves, and there they prepared to counterattack.

But Galahad's sentries were alert, and his camp turned out, unaware of how close they were to the center of events. The fugitives tried to overrun the men and bears by sheer numbers. The fighting along the northern Lily Burn became general in the frozen dark.

Tapio and Blizzard and Aneas gave up trying to get into Lessen Carak before they really made an attempt; the enemy were so thick in the lines that Tapio allowed Blizzard to lead them east, to the Lilywindle, and before darkness they were at the new bridge at North Ford, which marked the uttermost northern limit of the world of men, and the southernmost border of the Wild, at least in these parts.

"There used to be a trail along the banks of the Lily Burn," Blizzard said.

Now Nita Qwan stepped forward. "I was here three years ago," he said. "If I do not lose my way in the snow, I know where there's a trail just the other side of the bridge." He shook his head ruefully. "I feel I have come full circle," he said.

Tapio shook his head. "But why?" he asked.

Magister Nikos pointed. "Because the greatest battle of our lifetimes, even yours, my prince, is being fought right *there*." He pointed south and east. "Desiderata is holding Lissen Carak. The real fight will be in the fields below Albin Ridge."

"I want Orley," Aneas said.

"I want victory," Tapio said. "I want thisss to end. I want Tamsssin in my arms." He grinned, and his fangs showed. "I want to kill Asssh."

They started south, moving single file along the path of the Lily Burn in the moonlight. Aneas was tired, but he had now been tired for so long that he couldn't really remember any other way to be; Irene cradled her crossbow in the moonlight. Her heart was hammering, wondering, as she was wont to, whether she really loved this or had made herself love it; and ahead of them, Tapio rode on his great elk, singing quietly to himself of his lady Tamsin.

When they had gone a mile, there was a sharp snow squall, and Tapio felt something like a blow in the *aethereal*. He motioned, and all his people dismounted and lay with their mounts in the new snow; but the feeling passed, and Tapio wanted, with all his heart, to go into the *aethereal* and find Tamsin, and see what he could see. But this force, even this small force of men and irks and bears, might yet have a role to play, and he kept them quiet and secret, forbidding his knights access even to the simplest of warming spells.

But he paused and listened to the *aethereal* as often as he could, and then, while he was listening, he heard not the tinkle of his beloved's magical bells, but the sharper sounds of dying creatures and weapons striking shields. It was close, but not close; almost due east.

There was no one to ask but his own knights, and their eagerness told him what he wanted to know, so he turned, looking south for a moment. The Flow, the largest pool on the Lily Burn, lay just south of him, covering his flank. He turned east into open spruce trees, a veritable cathedral of magnificent straight trunks stripped by generations of foresters of their dead lower branches, rows and rows, with little underbrush and only a dusting of snow.

His knights began to spread out in an open line, and behind him, Aneas brought on the Galles and the rangers, and Blizzard brought the bears, silent and purposeful in the sudden snowfall. The mounted Galles, only a handful, pressed forward and joined Tapio's knights, and the two dozen of them made more noise than all the irks, but there was no foe to contest the woods, and they began to cross their second thousand paces since they had left the trail, a long line that glittered in the pale moonlight like steel-clad ghosts crossing the snow under the ancient trees, the breath of the horses and elk like the smoke of a hundred dragons, the starlight on the golden fur of the bears and their sharp axes.

And then he could see the enemy: hundreds of irks in a shield wall, and a wash of bogglins and other creatures. They were calling to each other, and there was a golden helmet gleaming in the moonlight.

For a heartbeat, Tapio's eyes had a feral beauty, and his features transformed in the moonlight, and his elk seemed to grow, and every spike on the great animal's magnificent rack began to glitter with its sharpness.

Tapio reined in with nothing but his mind and the weight of his body, and his elk reared, pawing the air, and all along the line of Faery Knights, they raised their silver and ivory oliphants, and the cold night air was filled with the hunting horns of Faery, and the irks facing the scarecrows were suddenly filled with fear.

Almost five miles away, Gabriel was just embracing his brother on the top of the Albin Ridge when he heard the low, eldritch music. He looked off into the darkness a long time.

"Penrith is no longer the axis of our lines," he said. "Tapio has entered the field."

And Tamsin began to cry, for joy.

Gabriel looked at her. "Stop that, or I'll be doing it in a minute," he said.

"I've never seen you grin like that," Gavin said.

Gabriel embraced him again. "We did it!" Gabriel said.

Gavin was still trying to adjust to this. "Christ. We almost lost everything yesterday. We…I…"

Gabriel was walking around the fire, shaking hands, and embracing Tamsin, and in the background, Ariosto was slurping down the entrails of a sheep, his beak raised to the heavens.

Tastes like home, he sent.

And then the reality of it struck Gavin. And then he threw his arms around his brother again, and said "God damn it, Gabriel, I thought you weren't coming. I thought…I thought this was one of your stupid schemes; that we'd have to hold it ourselves."

Gabriel nodded. "Good," he said. "You almost did have to. And God helps those who help themselves." He put his hands together, and his grin was almost demonic. "Now let's put it all together," he said. "I intend to win this in the real, with as few casualties as can be managed. But first…"

Tamsin was quivering, and Gabriel put a hand on her arm.

"You want to find him in the *aethereal*?" he asked.

"Yes," she answered. "But we cannot reveal our position to Ash…"

Gabriel nodded. "That's over now," he said. "Who else do you have here? The Patriarch?"

"Yes," she said.

The emperor went to the Patriarch and knelt in the snow and kissed his ring. Then he rose and took their hands, and he reached *into the aethereal, and he took the hand of Queen Desiderata, and Magister Petrarcha, of Tancreda and Mortirmir, of Master Grammarian Nikos and of Kwoqwethogan. There were dozens of others; there was the entirety of the choir of the abbey; there was the new Archbishop of Lorica on the floor of his cathedral in Albinkirk, and there was Tapio. And there was Desiderata.*

And Gabriel held them all in his mind, and he threw open the gate outside his memory palace, and he said, ASH.

In the cold darkness, Ash was watching victory and the taste was remarkable—like food after aeons of hunger. His enemies thought the day was over; he was preparing to show them how many of his slaves could fight in the dark. If he traded twenty for one . . .

ASH

In that moment, Ash felt the full weight of his error. It was as if he had been blind, and suddenly was able to see.

What he could see was the power of the choir facing him, which he had only ever known as a divided set of individuals, and the leader of the choir burned a solid gold in the aethereal, and Ash quailed.

"Lot? Is that you?" he asked.

And Gabriel laughed. "Ash. I have crossed seven worlds and won the gates. Your cause is lost. Surrender to our mercy."

Ash looked at them, from one to another. He was looking for weakness; for division; for hatred or contempt or any flaw. But when he looked at them, he saw nothing but the walls of golden bricks that Desiderata had taught them, and they showed him his lone image reflected back twenty, thirty times.

"Surrender?" He laughed. He was silent a long time, and then he spoke carefully, as if considering them all. "You are nothing. In a generation you will done, and nothing will be left of you but the wind. The gates will be open for years, and I will be here waiting for your alliance to collapse. The irks will fight the men, and the men will hunt the bears, and the Outwallers will rise to old grievances, and I will be here to make sure you all drown in your own blood for daring to impede me."

And Gabriel said, "All that may be. All that you say is my greatest fear, so I thank you for threatening it; men's memories are helped by such terrible words. But today, I have a great army; the greatest army that any being has assembled here since the Empress Livia passed the gates. And I have a choir of magisters who are your match. And I say to you: Dragon, surrender, or we will end you. I offer no other choice; no condition, no bargain, no truce. Surrender to our mercy, and allow us into your mind. Or we will make an end of you."

"I cannot die. At best, you will force me into the immaterium." The dragon's voice betrayed his fear.

In a pocket of the real, the word *mind* keyed something. Gabriel had an odd sensation, so that he looked around, as if he'd heard a hail, or a call for help, or a woman's scream.

He went back into the *aethereal. He made his avatar's face take on a lazy smile. "Are you sure?" he asked. "If I were you, I would wonder how this all came to be. How I came, as a being that can transcend reality, to have lost a war so thoroughly to a mob of mortal rag pickers." Gabriel nodded. "Perhaps you are losing your mind," he said.*

(Again, the word mind. *Again, a call; this time he felt it in the* aethereal, *a sort of substrate under the voice of the dragon.)*

"I am the lord of this world," Ash said. "I will do with it as I please, and no mortal hand will keep me from the least of my desires. And I have subsumed the Odine, and you have no idea of my power. I could break this world and kill you all."

Desiderata laughed. "You dream dark dreams," she said. "You can no more break this world than I can."

"I spit on your pitiful offer of surrender," Ash said.

Gabriel nodded. "I knew you would," he said.

(He knew that note now. It was Harmodius. The instinct to aid him was stronger than revulsion or fear, and he extended a tendril of his thought...

The non-moment seemed to stretch into an eternity of possibilities. The aethereal *was, at best, a chaotic place full of paradox and ambiguity and immeasurable essence; now, Gabriel, standing on a hill in the real, was simultaneously on the featureless plane with his allies, and sitting in the firelit sitting room of his own memory palace, where there was now a tall, fit young man in hunting clothes. And he was also inside the mind of the dragon, Ash, and also outside it, looking at it from the point of view of Desiderata, and he was also aware of another presence, a strong light at the edge of his vision.*

Harmodius laughed, clearly shaken. "Well. I'm here." In one instant, all his nightmare experience in the mind of the dragon was laid bare.

Gabriel bowed. "You are in his mind?"

"We are," Harmodius said. "Ah. Thanks for the rest." He stretched. "Do not trust Lot. That's my last word to you."

"Who is we?" Gabriel asked into the timelessness.

"I am the lion," Harmodius said. "And my former mentor is now the Thorn."

And then he was gone.

Gabriel, who did not fully understand, sighed in the timelessness and returned to the immediate reality of the aethereal.)

"Who are you?" Ash asked.

"I am your nemesis," Gabriel said. Even in the aethereal, his voice was resonant with grim humour. "That is all I am. Surrender, Ash."

"I will destroy you," Ash said.

"You are already defeated," Gabriel said. "You were done in the moment the gates opened. I offer you the preservation of your self, and the ability, perhaps, to wait out the aeons of our supremacy and perhaps effect your own restoration. I offer this freely, because I offer mercy, in hopes that you might change."

Ash laughed. "This is hubris, personified. You, an insect, offer me, a god, your mercy?"

Gabriel nodded. "We, the allied insects, offer you our mercy."

"I still spit on it," Ash said.

"Good," said Gabriel. "You are better dead. And tomorrow we will defeat you utterly. Once more! Spare the thousands who will die tomorrow. Surrender to our mercy."

"They are insects, as you are an insect. Why would I spare them? It is the way of the worlds, that the insects serve the will of the mighty." Ash laughed.

Gabriel nodded. "Then tomorrow, you will be killed and eaten by insects," he said. "So be it."

In his sitting room, there was Desiderata, and there was Gabriel.

"Harmodius is Ash's mind," Gabriel said. "Do you think he has another body stored somewhere?"

"No. If Askepiles's body was destroyed yesterday, he has nowhere to go," Desiderata said sadly. "He has nowhere else to go."

"I thought of offering him sanctuary," Gabriel said. "He did not seem to want it, and he is a puissant ally, placed where he is. And I may very shortly be nowhere myself." Gabriel thought he ought to be appalled, but actually, he found the old wizard's placement a comfort.

"It is clear to me that you are at the very edge of transformation," Desiderata said. "I... don't know what to say."

"Imagine what I think," Gabriel said with an aethereal smile.

Desiderata met his smile. "To me, it is fitting. Perhaps God has a sense of humour."

They both laughed. But then Gabriel spoke bitterly.

"I'd like people to stop saying that it is fitting," Gabriel spat. "I would happily live a long time, raise a lot of babies, and indulge in a host of the sins of the flesh. I am no saint; I lack any of Amicia's qualities. I am a killer. Why is this happening to me?"

"Ask a priest," Desiderata said. "That it is happening is beyond doubt. I would be sorry for you, but in this space it seems I ought to be sorrier for Blanche. What will she do? I cannot imagine."

"I have made arrangements for her," Gabriel snapped. And then, relenting, "She will be a very powerful woman," Gabriel said. "Enough of my personal life. Are you ready?"

"I have the well and the choir," Desiderata said. "With the knights around me in the real, Lissen Carak is invincible."

"The last few days have made me doubt that anything is invincible," Gabriel said. "Very well. Go with God, as they say."

And Desiderata came and kissed him, in the aethereal. *"My, my," she said.*

Gabriel laughed.

Ash's rage shot into the *aethereal* and into the sky above the ruins of the inn.

A forest of shields snapped into place over the alliance, showing their army in an arc from Helewise's manor house, to Penrith, to the Albin Ridge and across to Albinkirk; green and gold and sometimes deep blue or red. There was a sudden cheer from the soldiers; men and women, freezing in the snow, saw the solid shields and knew that there had been a profound change in the battle.

"What now?" Gavin asked.

"Now we rest. And move troops. And in the morning, we go in and get him." Gabriel nodded.

"What are you not telling me?" Gavin asked.

"Quite a bit, Gavin. But none of it matters." Gabriel glanced at his hand to make sure that Morgon's protections were holding, but the hand appeared merely human and so did his face, when he looked at his distorted reflection in his light steel vambrace.

"Won't he attack in the dark?" Gavin asked.

Gabriel shrugged. "He can. But now we have the hermetical edge. He'll be better off in the morning."

"How can you be so sure?" asked Gavin, with something of his old, brotherly annoyance.

Gabriel was looking north. "Do you remember my sword master's definition of a battle?"

Gavin nodded. "When two commanders both think they can win, and only one of them is right," he said.

Gabriel nodded. "He couldn't break you yesterday," the emperor said. "And now you have forty thousand more men, and Mortirmir, and me." Gabriel glanced at his brother in the firelight, and raised an eyebrow. "It'll be hard, and bloody. Ash will want to be sure we pay dearly for it. But this time tomorrow, we'll be done."

Gavin thought his brother sounded sad.

Then he came over. "Listen, Gavin," he said. "You performed...a miracle. You kept it together. I can't believe how many men you got here. You *might have held Ash by yourselves*." Gabriel smiled. "Don't be jealous that I came and stole your victory. I know who the architect of it was."

Gavin nodded. Then he grinned.

"We did it, didn't we?" he said. "The plan."

"The plan. Even Aneas did his bit," Gabriel said. "It should make a good song."

When he was gone, Gavin realized that his brother had, as usual, avoided answering his question. *What are you not telling me?*

Just before dawn, the snow started again. It came in from the west: big flakes, full of ash from the volcanoes, or so some of the old weather women said. Edmund Chevin had marched his hand gonners through the light snow, right along the edge of the Lily Burn woods; their cavalry escort had to fight twice, but the hand gonners had moved on, unimpeded. Well before the first tendrils of dawn, they'd passed behind the ruins of Penrith, and Edmund and his vanguard had shifted the stones of the church steeple, collapsed across the road, so that there was enough of a lane to roll their three falconets through the gap.

And then they marched in the moonlight along the black ribbon of the ancient road toward Albinkirk. Half a mile on, they found hundreds of workmen unloading boats. Edmund heard the voice he was seeking, and he ran past the long line of wheeled tubes to Master Pye, who was directing the swaying up of a great gonne barrel on a heavy oak tripod with a set of pulleys, by torchlight. The tube went up about five feet, and then the gonne's carriage, a two-wheeled contraption, was pushed by boys too young to be on a battlefield; they grunted, and shouted, and the carriage rolled up over two chocks to stop precisely where Master Pye wanted it; but then he measured, quickly; and then the great tube was lowered by men on the ropes, inch by inch, as Master Pye embraced the young man who had once been the lowliest of his apprentices and was now one of the emperor's war captains.

The gonne's cast-bronze trunnions dropped into the grooves made for them in the carriage.

Two boys leapt up and put the trunnion guards across the trunnions and hammered home iron keys, and the lethal monster, the muzzle cast like a raging dragon, was rolled away into the darkness and snow.

"Thirty-seven," Master Pye said. "I could only complete thirty-seven of the fifty that were commissioned." He shrugged. "Mold problems, for the most part, and a certain hesitancy by my brother-in-law to supply the arsenic for my bronze." He shrugged. "But what was really interesting was how easy it was to change the casting point of the molten bronze by adding—"

"Master?" Edmund had never interrupted his master before, but the world, he was told, hung in the balance. "Master, I'm very interested in how the gonnes were cast, but I have brought you a thousand men and women."

"A thousand men? Are they intelligent? Are they strong?" Pye smiled.

"Yes," Edmund said.

"For the shop?" Master Pye asked, and his smile was knowing.

"For the war, master. To serve the gonnes. I trained them; that is, Duke and Tom and I trained them. Just as we said we would." Edmund bowed, and waved his arm at his gonners, who stood in three ranks on the road.

Master Pye walked over and looked at them.

He looked back at Edmund.

"Master Swynford made the paper," he said. "And from it we folded cartridges. Master Donne's shop made the powder from the chemicals Master Gower found for us. Mistress Benn made the ironwork. Master Landry cast the gonnes. Six hundred out-of-work weavers and furriers helped make the carriages." He shook his head. "It is the largest project I have ever undertaken, on the shortest notice, and I have learned so much…" He was looking over the men and women who stood in the ranks; all in neat black wool cotes and caps, with hose striped; some plain, and some fantastically adorned. The magnificent hose had become a sign of the gonners, a brag, a complement to the sober and powder-stained jackets.

"But you have made the people," he said. He walked up to a woman, a tall, pretty woman with pouting lips and two heavy gold earrings. "Miss?"

"Master," she said with a heavy Etruscan accent.

Pye nodded and switched to Low Archaic. "If I were to ask you what weight of powder would throw a six-pound iron ball five hundred paces?" he asked.

She bowed, her unease visible even in moonlight. "Master, I can't say." She looked anxious. "Master, I would have to know many things: the length of the barrel, the quality of the *poudre*. And with a strange gonne…" She shrugged. "I would start with one half a bag, just to see how she throws."

"Are they all this good?" Pye asked his former apprentice.

Edmund grinned at the tall woman. "No, Master. Sabina is especially talented. A wonderful cook, an excellent gonner. They are not all so good."

Pye bowed to the woman. "You may come to my yard anytime, mademoiselle," he said.

She flushed, and bowed her head in pleasure, and Pye walked along the ranks, making his odd, technical small talk with a number of the gonners; he embraced Duke and Tom.

Then he stopped, looking at the three falconets now dwarfed by the mighty cannons and the sakers and demi-cannon. "You brought them all the way?" he asked, amazed.

Duke couldn't resist. "Master, last night we shot them on another world."

"And before that, another world yet," said Tom.

Master Pye shook his head. "Well," he said. "Well, well." He was grinning. "What artifice and the hand of man can do, we've done. Now you must take them into action."

Edmund hesitated. "Me?" he asked.

Pye frowned. "Of course you," he said. "You are now the master. I have fired one of these—the great cannon. Once. You have made all these men and women, and you have commanded them in battle. This is your art, your craft. Please take command."

Edmund looked around, unable to speak. Finally he said, "But, Master Pye…"

But his master was already walking away, shouting orders about unloading the prepared cartridges.

Edmund shrugged. He glanced at Duke, who winked.

"Right," Edmund said. "Now we need forty crews. Tom, get the weights of the gonnes and tell off the crews."

"Saint Barbara!" muttered Tom. "Do we have forty gonne captains?" he asked.

Edmund nodded. "I'm sure we do," he said. "And if we don't now, we have until dawn to practice."

Hawissa Swynford was wakened from her cloak between two warm mates by the off-going watch—Bill Stouffy.

"Fucking creepy," Stouffy said. "Snowin'." He shrugged. "Come on, Hawi. Yer turn. I wanna' get some shut-eye."

Swynford wanted more sleep more than anything in the world. She had been so warm.

She got up. They were in a shed—a furrier's shed for storing furs—and the roof had somehow survived sorcery and dragon fire. She got her feet under her and groaned a fair amount, but she felt better than she had in days, and better still when Sarah Goody put a steaming cup of chicken soup in her hand.

She drank the hot soup, scalding her tongue, chewing on the chicken bits automatically. Her sword was ruined; she had a dagger…

Stouffy was already deep in the piles of furs and cloaks. "Arrers," he said. "Bales o' they. Stacked on the north side o' the shed. Nighty-night."

Swynford went out into the icy darkness, where the snow was now coming down steadily, and found the arrows, in neat bags with spacers, all stacked against the back wall under the overhang. She took a sack, opened the end, and withdrew one. It had the Royal Armoury mark on the head, over the broken circle of Master Pye.

She kissed it. And dropped the whole bag into her open quiver.

Then she buckled on her heavy belt and pulled her cloak over her kit and ducked into the snow.

Collingford was waiting for her, and they checked their sentries: half a dozen cold and tired men and women staring out at the snow.

Then they went north along the edge of the town. There were still fires burning, and the snow was mostly ice melt here; terrible on the feet.

"Should be milice here," she said. She moved carefully, and Collingford spanned his crossbow. It wasn't a war bow, which he had across his back, but a light arbalest; the sort of thing a fine lady might use to shoot birds. Collingford liked it because he could carry it cocked and ready.

Swynford wished she had one. The darkness was *wrong* and the snow only made it worse. She moved carefully, her feet freezing in the icy water, the fires flickering like a vision of hell through the snow.

She saw a shadow of movement, and she froze and put a shaft on her bowstring, the horn nock gripping the waxed string. "Halt!" she called.

"Halt!" the shadow spat back.

There was a noise; a sound of steel scraping on rock.

"Advance and be recognized!" shouted Swynford.

The figure emerged from the snow like a conjuror's trick: a tall man in good armour.

Swynford knew him immediately: Gareth Montjoy, the Count of the Borders. She sank to one knee.

He stepped forward, and there was a heavy dagger in his fist, and his face was utterly blank, and one eye was gone. He moved swiftly, but Collingford was faster, and he put his light shaft in the earl's other eye. Then he stepped forward, his heavy forester's cutlass in his hand, and in one fear-fueled swing, he beheaded the stumbling, blind thing and saw the worm emerge from dead earl's neck.

Swynford was running on training alone; she drew the short mallet from her belt, the one she used for pounding stakes, and smashed the count's neck repeatedly until the worm was worm paste.

Then she whimpered a little.

Then she hugged Collingford. "Thanks," she said.

"Think nothing of it," he said. "Fuck."

"Fuck," she agreed, and took the dead count's beautiful arming sword. She started to walk away, trembling in every limb, but even in the grip of terror, she was a veteran; she went back to the messy corpse and took the belt and scabbard, too.

Collingford was already sounding the alarm on his horn.

Dawn was almost in the sky, to the emperor, a thousand feet in the icy air. He could see the first flush of colour away to the east, but there was an hour or more before it would reach the ground. The Odine were contained—the surprise had failed, if it had even been an attempt, and not the kick of a corpse—and his preparations were made.

It was all done.

Tomorrow? Ariosto asked.

Today, brother, Gabriel replied.

Whatever, Ariosto said. *I will achieve my full growth today.*

I thought you were bigger, Gabriel said.

Ariosto laughed.

They landed by the gate, and Jon Gang took Ariosto with Hamwise, and there were half a dozen fat Alban sheep waiting with fully justified terror, bleating their last.

Do you ever consider that in the universe of sheep, you are the ultimate villain? Gabriel asked.

No, Ariosto said. *Should I?*

Absolutely not, Gabriel said.

He dismounted, and walked wearily through the gate, waving at the sentries and the murmured "good nights" of his people.

His great red pavilion was set up just inside the gate. It was instantly warm; a pleasant night, and he walked into the pavilion to find every evidence that there had been a fine party. Tom Lachlan was asleep, his head down on the table, snoring, with Sukey sprawled in the next chair; Anne Woodstock lay with her head in Toby's lap on the carpet; and Michael lay asleep with Kaitlin's head on his shoulder and their daughter between them. Master Nicodemus was asleep; Mortirmir was asleep with Tancreda by him, an untouched cup of wine in her hand; Francis Atcourt was stretched full length on the far side of the table from Toby; de Beause appeared awake at first, but he had fallen asleep in his armour.

Gabriel looked around at all of them, and his first thought of annoyance was replaced with a simple warmth. He wanted to cry. It was an absurd feeling.

And then Blanche was there. "I stayed awake," she said softly. "I hoped you would come back."

"You are a wise maiden," he said.

"There is, in fact, still oil in my lamp," she said.

"Is that a double entendre?" he asked.

"Did you want me to help you with your armour?" she asked. "Or just walk off and leave you to your fate?"

And a few quiet moments later, he had a hand on her belly and was listening to his son or daughter move.

"You should sleep," she said.

He shook his head. "I don't want to sleep," he said. "I want this cup taken from me. I want time to stop."

She kissed him. "At least, if we cannot make time stand still," she said, "we can make him *run*."

He laughed. "I love you," he said.

She laughed with sadness, because weeping would waste time.

Sunset. The long, pleasant sunset of the last world; a world cleared of predators by the Odine. Through the gate, Gabriel could just see snow falling from the open doors of his red pavilion. Today the emperor's pavilion was almost empty, and he stood in the vast red space while Jon Gang and Hamwise and Woodstock put him in his newly polished golden armour. His officers came through and there was little talk—an embrace or a handshake, and not much more. Ser Michael came in and took a whetstone and sharpened his dagger.

Morgon Mortirmir came in and stood watching them. "I finished *felling* the weapons," he said. "It's done. All the *casa*. Most of the company. Really, all of them, but some of them wanted daggers as well as spears, and I'm not—"

"Morgon," Gabriel said.

The young magister flushed.

"We've defeated the *shadow*, the *will*, and the *rebel*," he said. "We'll win."

Mortirmir nodded. His hands were shaking.

Gabriel went and took them.

Mortirmir suddenly embraced his captain. "You are so close," he murmured.

"I know," Gabriel said.

"Don't cast. You can never cast again. You must not..."

Gabriel's smile was distinctly unsaintly. "We'll see," he said.

"I should touch up your...disguise," Mortirmir said.

"Save it," Gabriel said. "In a few minutes, I will cut it free."

"You will burn like a torch," Mortirmir said.

Gabriel nodded. "Yep," he said.

In the end, he shook hands with his squire and his pages.

"Kneel, Anne," he said. He knighted her, with Ser Michael standing close by, and Sauce just coming into the pavilion.

She couldn't stop herself from crying, and she was mortified, which made the emperor smile.

Then he stepped out into the sunset of this world and knighted a dozen more young men and women.

Lucca appeared with a pile of messages; Ser Michael started through them and gave a cough.

"Tell me," Gabriel said.

"Towbray has stormed the palace in Harndon," he said. "Lady Mary was left as a surrogate for the queen. It appears he killed her." He looked stunned. "My fucking father," he spat. "Christ, I feel unclean."

"Michael, do not, I pray, take this personally. *Michael!*" Gabriel snapped as if the younger man were still his squire.

His first squire stiffened.

"I need you. Here. In command. Forget your father. He is nothing. *This* is the battle of our time." Gabriel waved at the gate. "Fetch me Bad Tom, please."

"Yes, Your Grace," Michael said. He went out to the tent, his face set.

"Lucca," Gabriel said. "I need a favour."

"Anything, my lord."

"Go to Harndon and kill the Earl of Towbray. Don't even make it look like an accident. And Lucca, if he ever asks you, tell Michael that I ordered it." Gabriel smiled.

"Now, or after the battle?" Lucca asked.

"After will be fine, but do it," Gabriel said.

"Ser Maria, my lord," said Ser Anne Woodstock.

Gabriel spent a minute on his gauntlets, and then looked at his gold bascinet and sniffed the lining, which was very clean.

Anne showed him his sword. He touched it, making sure that it was sharp at the tip and dull where he liked to grab it when he was half-swording. He noted that it now bore a small Gothic letter *M* under Master Pye's maker's mark.

"Highness," Ser Maria said, and made a full reverence. "Master Brown and Master Lucca and I have been made an offer."

Master Brown, as unremarkable as ever, bowed. "My lord," he said. "The salamanders have invited us to their home."

Gabriel nodded. "Remarkable," he said.

"I think so," said Ser Maria.

"I have given Master Lucca a little task to accomplish first," the emperor said with his most annoying smile. "I think both of you might accompany him. But then, yes, I think you should go with my writ and seal. Master Julius?"

"I'm writing," he said. "Ambassador?"

"Perfect," Gabriel said as Tom Lachlan entered and kissed Blanche. "Tar's tits, Gabriel. You look like a fewkin' angel." Behind Tom, Sukey came in with a tablet in her hand, and she and Blanche kissed and then began to copy.

"That's me," Gabriel said. "Kneel, Ser Thomas. Sukey? Come. Kneel."

Thomas Lachlan did not kneel easily; it took an effort of will, but he managed it, his great blue-black armoured knee crashing down. Sukey knelt with bony grace at his side.

Gabriel took his great sword of war, which was naked on the table. "Thomas Lachlan, I hereby vest you with the title of Earl of the North Wall, and the lands adjoining that wall and formerly owned by the Orleys, as well as the Imperial Barony of Birdeswald. And Sukey, I vest you in your own right as Imperial Count of Osawa. I recommend that you two get married and solidify all this feudal magnificence before I change my mind." He grinned, and Sukey rose and gave him an almost unsisterly kiss, and then so did Bad Tom.

"Couldn't that ha'e waited?" Tom asked.

"No," Gabriel said. "I will leave my house in order, and my debts paid." He blew a kiss to Blanche, who made herself smile.

They walked out into the fading sunlight of an alien world.

"What the hell did he mean by that?" Tom asked.

Blanche finally burst into tears.

Full dawn. To the west, heavy black clouds, like thunderheads, and behind them a leaden sky. To the east, a bright sunrise, and the red ball of the sun sitting on the Green Hills.

The emperor stood on the Albin Ridge with the Earl of Westwall and his officers. All the ground from the distant slopes of the Kanata ridge to the ruins of the Ambles Inn and the shattered steeple of Saint Mary's was full of the enemy—a dense carpet of monsters.

The first attacks had been made at dawn, against the garrison of Livingston Manor. The cave trolls had discovered that Ser Ranald and the royal guard had moved in during the night, and they had the direct support of the entire choir of magistery up the hill behind them five hundred paces.

As the sun rose, and Gabriel flew slowly and carefully at very low altitudes along the line of the Lily Burn to the Cohocton and around to Ser Gavin's position, a massive sorcerous assault shattered the outwalls of Albinkirk and discovered a nest of workings and a labyrinth of pre-dug defensive trenches behind the walls, and legions of bogglins flung themselves into the assault. Prince Tancred of Occitan and the new Captain of Albinkirk stood with almost a thousand knights and most of the militia who'd survived the day before and stopped the bogglins in the breach.

In the west, the man who'd once been Ota Qwan and more lately been Kevin Orley led his own horde over the smoking ruins of Hawks Head and Kentmere and across the fields, pushing back a skirmish line of rangers and militia archers and then advancing into the woods that lined all seven miles of the Lily Burn's length. Orley and his master expected the Lily Burn to be unoccupied or thinly defended.

As the sun rose over the Green Hills, Orley's first attack on the Lily Burn woods was stopped dead by Mogon. The fighting spread from the center, just south of the Flow, but as the enemy spread, they found ambush after ambush, and the icy waters were in flood and difficult to cross.

But Ash and his lieutenants had learned a great deal about war in the real. And so a second captain led all the *schiltrons* of irks, and *tlachs* of daemons west, into the low hills around Lady Helewise's manor house, clever enough to know that their enemies coming through the gate would be trapped between the two pincers and destroyed, or neutralized.

But all of those were merely pinning attacks. None was Ash's great effort.

Ash unleashed that as the sun rose.

Gabriel pointed out over the fields of Woodhull. "He'll attack right here," he said. "Right down between the ridge and Penrith, and break our army into two pieces."

Gavin was smiling, and so were the rest of the men and women on the hilltop.

"He'll attack in the real to draw us out," Gabriel continued. "And

571

then, when we contain his attack, he'll turn to the *aethereal*." He smiled like a beatific saint.

"And we will stop him," said the Patriarch.

"Holiness, we will more than stop him. We will leave him no choice but to come at us in person. On our ground, in a place of our choosing, on a day of our choosing." Gabriel smiled his most damning superior smile.

The Patriarch narrowed his eyes. "How are you so sure?" he asked.

Gabriel laughed. "I'm not. I'm telling you what I'd like to happen." He shrugged. "But the pinning attacks are happening, and we're in it. And there..." He smiled again. "There they are."

Out in the fields south of Woodhull, there came a seeping stain of dark colours, tinged with the rose pink of the snowy dawn.

Gabriel pointed with his baton and continued his commentary. "Front is about a mile wide," he said. "Three thousand creature front. Fifty deep? A hundred?" He nodded, and behind him, Anne Bateman made a note and accepted a message from a black-and-white bird. By now she knew her friend Ser Gerald was dead; everyone knew that Harndon was in the hands of the traitor. But the messengers were still flying; the garrisons were all still linked.

In the fields below them, on the line of the road to Lissen Carak, there stood the imperial veterans; all the Thrakian spearmen, leaning on their spears, and beside them, the tagmatic cavalry, all dismounted; the other Moreans were off to the west, covering their flank along the Lily Burn, but all of the Albin militia had been put under Ser Alcaeus's command as well, and he had most of the available infantry; almost sixteen thousand men and women on a one-mile front, stiffened by wedges of knights who waited behind the embankment of the ancient road.

"I don't know if this is really their main effort," Gabriel said to his magisters. "But I'm pretty sure that if we break it, he'll have to come."

Edmund was chewing a sausage when the trumpets sounded. There was cavalry moving off to the west, in the fields beyond the ruins of Penrith. He had to assume they were friendly, although there was a steady combat sound from the line of the Lily Burn beyond them.

"They all know to cover their ears?" Duke asked for the third time.

"They know," Tom said.

The phalanxes of Thrakians covered the front of the gonnes. There were forty gonnes, almost hub to hub, along the line of the raised road. Pioneers had built up dirt and snow platforms behind the great gonnes, the six cannon in the center of the line, so that they had room to recoil fully without rolling off the road.

The crews were standing about; a few played dice or cards. Some jumped up and down, or blew on their hands.

The dark stain spread across the distant fields by the tiny and now extinct hamlet of Woodhull. The stain covered the whole front of open ground while, behind them, more and more creatures seemed to move west, aimed at the place marked on Edmund's map as *Helewise's Manor*.

Duke looked at him, a nervous smile on his face. "Here they come."

Edmund was finishing his sausage. Since the Umroth, he was less impressed with monsters. He watched them for a while. They had great booming drums, audible already, and they were coming right at him.

"To your gonnes," he called between his cupped hands. Forty gonnes covered almost a quarter mile of frontage. Each gonne had a stack of shot for the right tube, and bags of appropriate grape shot. Each gonne had a single round marked with the letter *M* created by the infamous Mortirmir.

Edmund's mind was much given to calculation, and he wondered how fast a bogglin walked. *Four miles an hour? So they'll be here, one way or another, in fifteen minutes. In range in seven minutes. Point blank in fourteen minutes. One minute in the beaten zone of the grapeshot; time for most of the gonnes to fire twice; a few to fire three times. Say one hundred and twenty rounds of grape, with twenty-four pellets in each. Roughly twenty-five hundred iron balls, five to the pound. But some much more.*

Edmund shrugged at the uselessness of calculation. *Now in range in six minutes*, he thought.

The pressure on the Lily Burn increased with every minute, and now there were forty thousand creatures trying to cross. When they hesitated, Orley reached out and took power from his master and forced them into the icy black water, where they drowned, and the creatures behind them followed them in, and they died, too.

Aneas watched them come in waves, but he left the arrow on his bow unshot.

"Wait," he called. "Wait until they stop drowning. Don't waste your arrows."

Nothing could make it alive across the Flow, and the enemy's main effort channeled toward the southern ford until Orley flung in his cave trolls and took it.

Then Tapio charged out of the woods. He had, not just his own knights, but hundreds of bears, and irks on foot, and wardens; his name had attracted some of the finest warriors of the Wild, and their wedges burst into the cave trolls and knocked them down in the shallow water and drowned them in the wretched cold mud, or pounded them to splinters with their steel-clad hooves, or simply burst their chests asunder with their lances. A hundred bears died, but the trolls were destroyed or forced back across the river.

Then barghasts came, and wyverns. But the power that mastered them had not troubled itself to coordinate closely, and the weary bears under Blizzard and their kin under Lily stood their ground, clan by clan.

Then it was Bill Redemede's hour, and the hour of the Jacks. Where the bears and irks could only endure the torment of their aerial foes, the archers could clear the air in a single volley. Even in heavy snow, the massed archery of the rangers and the Jacks flayed the barghasts, who had no armour. Wyverns dropped wing loads of gravel and did damage, but the archers made them pay, made it too dangerous for them, and many dropped their stones into the mere or farther north in the Flow and did no harm beyond smashing the ice.

The woodlands veterans took cover in the trees, right at the edge—two bows behind each, so that every ranger was covered. And for an hour they disputed the fords below the Flow, and the banks of the Lily Burn against five times their number.

The line was restored.

In the south, at the bridge, there were daemons on both sides, and Mogon taunted her enemies, but they could not respond, so heavy was the *compulsion* on them, and they came on. Mogon was sickened of slaughter, and hated killing her own, but her spells were in vain. She reached into the *aethereal and begged for aid.*

She had expected the Red Knight, but she found young Mortirmir.

"I need sorcerous aid," she said.

Mortirmir heard her out.

"We are trying to stretch Ash as thin as we can," Mortirmir said.

"These are my people," the duchess spat.

Mortirmir nodded, "On the way," he said crisply.

A surge of almost incredible power ran through Mogon.

She raised her axe and the power of the choir behind her crushed the net of workings that covered the other Qwethnethogs.

Orley, or Ash, or some other potency struck back, directly at her.

Shields covered her; shields she had never made. She stood a moment, surprised that she was not dead, and struck back. And again. Not with power, but with nuance. Not with lies, but with truth.

The hordes assaulted Albinkirk for the third time that day. Already Ser Shawn could barely stand, and the Prince of Occitan was pale when he opened his visor, and there was blood leaking down his right cuisse. But his squire brought wine, and he and the other Occitan knights sang as the assault came forward.

But this one was different. This time, tongues of fire leapt from the enemy—fifty of them or more—and they smashed into the protections and wards of the ancient town.

And took them down.

The new Bishop of Lorica lay bleeding on the floor of his cathedral of Albinkirk.

Then the men defending the breeches began to die. The fire fell on them, and rolled forward, and the bogglins came in right behind it.

Prince Tancred died there with his household knights, fighting to the last in a shield wall. Ser Shawn was pushed back and back again, and each time he rallied the militia and the chivalry and struck back, until he found that he was standing at the base of the town wall itself.

And that was the second hour of battle.

In the center of a battle that spread over ten miles of front, time was elastic.

Six minutes can be very quick, or very slow. Time to give a wonderful pre-battle speech and drink a little wine, or to pray, or to just stare off into space.

Edmund did all of those things. People cheered his speech, based on the emperor's: victory, a little loot, all the best things.

Very little came to him when he prayed.

In the end, he stood watching the distant monsters as they came closer to his little line of red flags, and he wondered about it all. The work, and the killing.

All the gonnes were long since loaded. Every gonner was in his place. The porte-fires burned in the still air; forty threads of smoke wound into the freezing air, tiny tendrils that marked each gonne.

Far out on the fields, a little under a thousand paces away, a line of bogglins passed the red flags.

Edmund didn't think he had to give an order. All the captains were watching the flags. Every type of gonne had a different range.

The waiting lasted so long that Edmund wondered if they really were waiting for his word.

And then the captain of one of the great cannons put her porte-fire down.

The gonne roared.

Nine hundred and seventy paces downrange, the ball slapped through two bogglins, shattered the mandibles of a third, disemboweled the fourth and fifth, and then fell toward earth, removing double-jointed legs on its way. It skipped on the frozen ground and ploughed through two more creatures, took off three or four legs, and then skipped again and began to roll, removing limbs. The ball weighed thirty-six pounds, and it left a furrow of death and dismemberment and pitiful sound behind it as it rolled and rolled through the packed creatures. They had no way to stop it except with their bodies.

Even as it killed, the next cannon fired, and then the next.

Gabriel saw the flashes and then heard the thunder as the great gonnes fired along the road. The damage they wreaked was like the attack of wyverns, visible from a mile.

As if summoned by his thoughts, wyverns rose from behind the vale of the Lily Burn and began to converge on something. Sythenhag's brood rose into the air from the Lily Burn bridge, followed by three more Adnacrag clans. Yet, as if by agreement, the wheeling predators didn't meet; instead, each attacked the other's infantry.

Gabriel sighed.

The firing of the gonne line had become general.

From the left end of the enemy horde in the center, a flash of violet light. One of the falconets was hit; twenty men and women died by fire.

Gabriel raised his baton.

Now, he said in the *aethereal*.

Across the battlefield, from the Lily Burn to Albinkirk, the alliance magisters dropped their cloaks and cast. From Gabriel's vantage, great bubbles of translucent light, like glass Christmas ornaments, sprang up all along the line; mostly gold in various hues, but one red, where the Patriarch cast his own strange style, and many green, especially on the Lily Burn.

The gonnes were firing steadily now, a constant rumble and roar. Their firing lit the main battle with an arcane glow from within, pulses of light like fireflies.

At the ford below the Flow, Orley grew impatient. He summoned his surviving trolls and the best of his daemons; he called his wyverns and his hastenoch. And as they closed at the ford, already choked with dead, with the steel-tipped shafts of his enemies falling like snow, he unleashed his borrowed powers, cutting a swathe through the bears and Tapio's ancient irks. Tapio slashed back, as did Aneas, and Gas-a-ho and Looks-at-Clouds and a dozen other, lesser shamans.

Looks-at-Clouds began to unleash clouds of terror amid the waiting monsters, frightening them into fighting each other.

Into the chaos and death, the cold and icy mud, Orley led his monsters.

Aneas, casting, went to meet him. He had layers of protections, and he used the golden buckler on his arm to cover anything that leaked through his shields, and then he threw everything he could think of: deception, manipulations of nature, a bolt of lightning conjured from the approaching storm front.

Orley parried them or ignored them. He was on the banks of the stream, and then his cloven feet were in the inky water.

Their shields met in a shower of sparks. Irene shot over his shoulder, and her shaft bounced off Orley's hide, the shaft of the bolt shattering, and then Orley's axe swung, and Aneas leaped clear.

Aneas threw his last major offensive preparation—three bolts of white levin—as he slipped under the antlered monster's guard, so that his fingers were all but touching Orley's breast.

The Son of Ash was not even singed.

Aneas rolled; not fast enough, and he took a wound. He took his pipe tomahawk from his belt as he came to his feet and threw...

And hit. The blow staggered his enemy, but then Orley had his balance. He cut back as if balance was nothing to him.

Aneas twisted, caught it on his golden buckler.

Blizzard came up, axe back.

Nita Qwan shot at Orley from very close by; the flint-headed arrow pounded home in Orley's flesh, but had no immediate effect, although there was a trickle of very red blood.

Blizzard struck, rocking the dark captain. But Orley turned and smashed a fist into the bear's jaw, breaking it and knocking the bear into the mud.

Aneas had two wounds: one in his thigh, and a heavy cut in his left arm that showed fat and muscle whenever there was a pause in the blood flow. But he was damned if he was letting Blizzard die, and he stepped close, short sword in his hand, turned his enemy's axe, and cut into his calf. The blow was clean, and well powered, and it bounced off Orley's flesh as if Orley were made of oak. Then Aneas moved off line, to his strong side, covered by the buckler of light, but the blood was flowing from his arm, too fast, and he was scared, and the axe cut back; he was off balance, and the axe severed his buckler arm above his hand and his blood fountained. He raised his spurting arm and splashed blood across his enemy's face.

He cast then, covering the wound, but he had no buckler, and he could only stumble back on his increasingly weak legs. Irene shot again, from his right, and bought him a breath. Blizzard tried to rise on a broken leg and failed.

Gas-a-ho tossed a handful of smoke, and the smoke gathered around Orley like a swarm of bees and went for his eyes, but Orley's lance of fire licked out, catching Gas-a-ho virtually undefended. The shaman dropped.

Looks-at-Clouds was coming from farther downstream, a line of lightning connecting hir to Orley, and hir shield of intertwined vines of green and gold fell between Orley and his prey.

Orley batted hir shield aside and raised his axe.

Irene was spanning her crossbow. She couldn't tear her eyes away as the malevolent thing's axe went back.

Nothing could save him.

The axe fell like a bolt from the darkness, and Aneas's head parted from his shoulders and his blood soaked the ice at the edge of the stream, and Orley roared, still trying to wipe his enemy's blood from his eyes.

Gabriel felt his brother fall out of the choir, and Gas-a-ho, too. And on the other flank, he felt the weight of the assault on Albinkirk.

Gavin looked at him.

"It's a race now," Gabriel said. "Whether they can collapse our flanks, or we can eat their center. A contest of wills." He blinked. "Aneas is dead."

"Jesus," Gavin said.

"Steady," said the emperor.

At his feet, the vast and terrible legions flowed over the fields of Albinkirk, and the workings of a century of dark sorceries played over the gilt and green and red baubles of the alliance shields.

The gonnes roared on, ripping the dark cloth of the enemy and leaving eddies and ripples of death and blood. Irks older than the oldest maples were struck dead by a weapon that flew so fast as to seem like hermeticism or sorcery, except that it left no trace in the *aethereal* and no enemy could raise a shield fast enough to respond.

The wave front of the bogglins came to the irrigation ditch, once a tiny stream, that ran across the fields north of the road. It was lined in dark grasses and sunk five feet below the level of the fields, and it was invisible to those who did not know it was there.

The bogglins began to fill it with corpses.

They keened in despair, and the gonnes ripped away their lives.

But Ash had prepared for this. Trolls came forward from the reserve and threw bridges across, slabs of slate, and the irks and bogglins flooded forward.

"Grape!" called Edmund. His first command.

Ultima Ratio was a great gonne. She took a thirty-pound load of half-pound iron balls and, in addition, a six-pound load of lead balls, ten to the pound. Her gonne captain saw her loaded with love, and then depressed the muzzle so that the load of grape would strike just at the leading edge of the now charging mass of bogglins.

Ultima Ratio fired. Less than a third of a second later, sixty half-pound balls struck, all together, spread about eight inches each from the other over an ellipse fifteen feet long and seven feet wide. Everything in that ellipse died, and then everything behind it to a depth of forty feet, and then the balls began to bounce off the hard ground.

Off to the left, Duke, captaining his favorite gonne, put his sights on a cave troll three hundred paces away and slapped his porte-fire down.

The cave troll dropped like a sack of wheat, its torso penetrated in the front and exploded out the back from the pressure, spraying the stone troll behind him with a lethal hail of shattered stone.

Another discharge from the second cannon, and a dozen more cave trolls became sticky gravel.

In front of him, the *Taxiarchoi* were ordering their spearmen to stand up. They took their great round shields on their shoulders and began to lock up, eight deep, so close that an imp could not run through their legs.

The enemy was one hundred paces away.

The gonnes were four feet above them, and their sound was deafening.

The firing roared on, and on, and the enemy, driven by the will of their dark master, ran forward into the hail of shot. They died, and died; they fell over the entrails of their mates and they crawled through the mud of their own juices in the deep soil, and they slipped in the snow, but every heartbeat brought them closer to the unflinching line of the Morean spears.

The spears came down, all together and the wall of spear points faced the oncoming warbands.

Ash's attack was spread across the fields of Penrith; his slaves, the subjects of his will, filled almost a square mile with desperate, terrible creatures. The gonnes had killed a little fewer than one in twenty of them.

But they had no formation, and the rips and tears inflicted by the great iron balls were irreparable; the creatures who survived the bombardment were more interested in closing with their enemies than in any formation.

And then the choir of alliance magisters began to cast.

From the glowing bubbles emerged streams of light; cascades of stars; balls of lightning. They targeted anything that had previously targeted them, and their calculations were remorseless; in the *aethereal* the daemons and irks and wights who could harness *ops* were identified, coded, and passed as targets to the dozen casters who specialized in this.

The center of the Morean line began to cheer first. They saw as the whole ink-black shield covering their foes burst, lashed with lightning, and collapsed, so that a web of fire fell into the center of the enemy and there was a terrible popping sound and the screams of the wounded and maimed floated in the cold air.

Then the Brogat Milice, off toward Penrith, who'd stood a whole day of attacks with little or no hermetical cover and then stood their ground all night against *not-dead*, began to roar their approval as a curtain of rose-gold closed over them, and a cyclone of raw *ops* burst over their enemies.

The fastest bogglins were dying on the spears of the Thrakians.

For the rest, their shields and covers and protections and wards were being stripped away, their casters butchered.

And off to the left of Penrith, the earth began to shake.

There was almost a mile of open ground to the east of Penrith. There had been almost no fighting there; Ash's great effort had almost ignored it. Farther east, Mogon and her people struggled to hold the bridge over Lily Burn.

Battles have strategies, and times, and places. Mogon had won hers. Orley would force the line of the Lily Burn, but it was too late.

Because in that mile gap waited Pavalo Payam and five thousand Mamluks, and Lord Gregario and all the chivalry of Alba who could be mustered, and Du Corse and all the knights of Galle. All told, there were twelve thousand armoured men and women, behind four great standards.

The Mamluks had all dismounted at sunrise, laid their prayer rugs on the snow, knelt, and prayed. And then they stood by their horses while the Christian priests moved along the lines of knights, and the knights and squires took their communion in their mouths and prayed.

And when Edmund's gonnes were belching grape, they all mounted, so that it might have appeared that a ripple of light almost a mile long was flickering in the fields of snow.

Payam's men, the best horsemen and the best drilled, had the hardest task, the outside of the wheel, the wheel of a line a mile long. It took them long minutes while the gonnes fired, while Thrakians died, and trolls, and irks and bogglins and men and women died, and then they were in place, swinging like a great door against Ash's mighty center.

Payam raised his golden lance.

The Mamluks gave a great shout.

The Galles answered it.

A single trumpet sounded, and the whole line began to rumble forward into the flank of Ash's attack.

Gavin turned to speak to his brother, and found that he was gone.

So was Ariosto.

"So this is the battle," he said to no one in particular. On the hill, unengaged in all the carnage, there stood 1Exrech's legions, and some Albin militia, who were delighted by their role as spectators, and a hundred knights kept as his last reserve: Ser Ricar and the royal household.

Gavin walked over to 1Exrech, his sabatons gathering snow. To the west, the storm line was sweeping over Lissen Carak. A wind was picking up.

"Let's attack their center," Gavin said.

"Concur," 1Exrech said. He made the mandible sign of pleasure.

The spear bogglins lowered their spears.

"We will cover you," Gavin said. He waved at the knights. Ser Ricar slapped his visor down, and the household knights gave a cheer.

"Good," said the wight.

Gavin was shocked at how many of them there were. And they kept coming, marching over the hill. He was leaving Albinkirk to its fate. But for once he agreed with his brother. This was the battle.

This was their last throw.

Well to the north, safe from harm, Ash circled the highest peaks.

His slave sorcerers were being smashed flat.

It was time to exert himself.

Because if you want something done right, you must do it yourself, Ash said inside one of his many minds.

Things were dark and muddled in there, and for the first time, he began to really wonder why.

It took a moment's attention. He was flying south, and the last of the Adnacrags was passing under his wings. The storm front would have an effect; it was huge, swollen with the dark dust of the western volcanoes by a delicious irony that he savoured even as he sent a ghost of himself dashing through all the corridors of his mind...

Harmodius. He is here, and he has hurt me.

And so has Thorn...

Just south of Helewise's manor house there were fields full of stubble, the wheat already harvested and gleaned, and beyond them a hill, the tallest hill for a mile or so, which gave the manor its name: Middle Hill.

The Duchess of Venike had rolled the scarecrows up the hill in the darkness, after finishing the force they found to the north, and then she'd cleared the hill with her marines. Sauce had fed her troops as the morning began to brighten, and she held a frontage almost a mile wide, centered on Middle Hill. On her left, Conte Simone and his Beronese waited under the eaves of the forest with the Almain cavaliers and the other men and women from far off in the north of the Antica Terra. The hill was held by the scarecrows, who were, this morning, living proof that the army's arsenal and logistics continued to function, as, while they stood in their ranks, wagons pulled in behind them and the front ranks began to don maille collars and breast plates made in Vrescia and Venike and now finally arriving.

Behind them, around the gate, the company waited. Most of them were lying in ranks, on their packs, asleep, with their military cloaks over them against the snow. The *casa* waited with the company, and the officers of both gathered in knots, and then, against direct orders from Gabriel, began to drift up the hill to have a view.

Because Middle Hill stood like a tower on a flat plain, and the view was wonderful and terrible, horrific and awesome.

Bad Tom stomped up the long hill, already out of sorts because he'd discovered that his emperor was away, aloft on his flying beast, and not with his household, where Tom Lachlan wanted him.

Ser Alison trudged up the hill, eager to fight.

Ser Michael trudged up the hill, dejected to find that on the day for which he had helped prepare for so many years, his was such an inglorious role. And trying to ignore that he was secretly delighted to be safe, with Kaitlin safe, and their child safe, on the other side of the gate. And angry at his father's treason, and saddened by it, too.

And then the three of them crested the hill.

Round hills can have several crests; a sort of dividing line at the top is what most people think of as the crest, the top. But to a soldier, the most important crest is the point from which you can see down the far slope; see, shoot, inflict death. Often from the very top, you cannot see more than a few yards, and then some far-off point. But from the military crest, you can see everything.

The scarecrows had just staved off an uncoordinated attack. They stood, as solid as a wall of steel, and the ground between them and the military crest was littered with dead irks. Many were alive; some screamed out the last of their near immortality; an irk woman in beautiful maille lay curled around her mortal wound, weeping.

Giselle, the duchess, walked over as the company's officer cadre crossed the back of her position.

"Good morning," she said cheerfully. In her hands was a short, heavy spear with Mortirmir's mark on the beautiful blade. "We just had a little *entertainment*."

Tom Lachlan was looking down into the beautiful eyes of the dying irk. Then he knelt, cradled her head, and cut her throat with his eating knife, which he kept razor sharp.

In a moment, the look of pain faded from her eyes.

"I may yet be sick o' war," he said harshly.

Sauce was walking forward, picking her way among the dead, who lay thick in front of the pikes. "Oh yes, you're a big softie, you are," she muttered. She used the needle-sharp butt of her own fighting spear to finish any wounded she passed; she was fastidious about it, but her face registered nothing but the annoyance of a woman who had to clean her spear later.

Michael followed them. He didn't even really see the carpet of dead. His eyes were on the battlefield.

All the ground from Middle Hill to the Albin Ridge, almost three miles distant, was covered in battle. Most of it was full of Ash's great assault; far to the south, the long line of magnificent, glowing hermetical shields glowed and shifted and sparkled in the red, red sun, and up on the Albin Ridge, there was a towering ward of green that glowed as if it was alive and crackled with lightning like a spring storm.

And almost at his feet, the massed cavalry of the alliance had just started their charge.

"Fewkin' hell," said Tom Lachlan. "He left us out. I want to be *there*!"

Michael looked over the battle he had helped plan. "He wanted us here," he said.

Sauce shook her head. "Sweet Saviour of man," she said, and touched the cross on her breastplate. "Payam is going to break their center."

Indeed, the alliance cavalry, by good fortune and careful planning, was attacking into a maelstrom of disorganization and hermetical failure; the dark shields were falling all across the three miles of the enemy front, and lashes of fire and ice and lightning and earth and pulses of superheated air wreaked catastrophe among Ash's creatures. And into this struck the heavy cavalry of seven nations on a front almost a mile wide.

"I want to be *there*," Tom Lachlan said wistfully.

Michael nodded. "We're not done, Tom," he said.

And behind them, the wall of the storm front had passed Lissen Carak, where the garrison stood, fighting utter exhaustion; where Desiderata stood, looking fifty years old, in her chapel, and defied Ash yet again.

"Break! Why will you not break!" screamed Ash.

"You trained me too well," Desiderata replied.

And by the gate, No Head shook his head. He was smoking with his mates.

"Greatest battle in the history o' the world," No Head said. "And we're in fucking reserve. I can't even see what's goin' on."

Tippit frowned. "Ha'e you lost yer noggin?" he asked. "Biggest battle in the fuckin' history of the fuckin' world, and we ain't in it. An' we get paid, any road. So shut yer gob. No one likes to fight."

"Tom Lachlan does," muttered Smoke.

"True. No one likes to fight 'cept Bad Tom and Sauce." The pipe was passed. A flask of wine was going around, exceptional wine. Cully had brought it, and everyone knew it was the captain's.

"It ain't right," No Head insisted. "We fought *all* the battles. We faced all the fuckin' foes. This is the end. Win or lose, and I say win."

"Do ye now?" Tippit asked, knocking the pipe out casually on the wood of his bow. "Sure we ain't here to stop a rout?"

"I can't see, but I ha'e ears. Cavalry is charging. Deed is done. Haven't launched a shaft." No Head shrugged.

Smoke shook his head. "You know what Wilful would say if he was here?"

"Pass the fuckin' pipe? Don't hog the wine?" Tippit said.

Smoke waved over the hill. "Nope. He'd say the most powerful warlock in seven worlds spent all his spare power on magicking our steel. An' not for nothin'. He'd say, it's not over until it's over. He'd say, we're being saved to face the fuckin' dragon."

That brought a moment of silence.

"*Mark my words*," they all said together, but no one laughed.

To all things, and all plans, there comes a day and a time, and a moment. Some never come to fruition; some plans eventuate in forms that are barely comprehensible to their designers, or bear fruit long after the initiator is cold clay.

But to the lucky few that see great plans bloom under their own eyes, there is sometimes a moment when all is laid bare; when success is there to be grasped, and for the very most fortunate, there is a moment to savour the eternal moment of victory.

And so it was given to Gabriel Muriens, high in the air over Lissen Carak. Below him, the storm, and beyond it, the success of the arms of the alliance. And Ash rushed into the maelstrom of defeat, in his last error, desperate to restore the balance of a battle already fatally lost.

And indeed, to Gabriel, in that moment, came the knowledge of victory; that even if Ash achieved the destruction of every knight, every Mamluk, every militiaman and Thrakian spearman and free bogglin on the field, he would never take the gates. His day was done.

Ash had failed. And now he intended to take them all with him into failure, and that had to be prevented.

Gabriel reached *into his memory palace, and motioned to Prudentia.* "Banish the little working," he said.

"It is time," she said. She smiled.

In the real, Mortirmir's disguise vanished, and Gabriel's golden flesh burned like the fire of the sun.

Gabriel took as long as a man might pray the *paternoster* to savour his victory.

And then Ariosto took them across the line of the snow, and all the high thoughts fled as Gabriel rode a wild beast through the very edge of the storm.

To Michael and the rest of them on Middle Hill, it was as if night was falling again, the storm front was so dark, and onto the fields of battle, coming from the north and flying very low, came the monstrous presence; the wave front of terror, the real presence of Ash, hundreds of paces long, his head alone the size of a tower, his neck, thin at a distance, still as thick as the height of three men; his body as long as a ship, or even two ships.

And his terror had no allies; his own slaves ran, and so did many Mamluks and belted knights. Pavalo Payam stood his ground, and the horse under him, but many horses lost their wits and bolted for the woods, and even the Thrakian veterans of twenty battlefields knelt and hid their heads from the Black Drake in the sky.

To Gavin, the Black Drake looked so vast that it seemed impossible. He did not lower his head; even as the bogglins in front of 1Exrech's bogglins gave way, and the free bogglins fell on their faces in the snow churned to slush, and all hope fled, Gavin watched the dragon. He was afraid, but he had been afraid ever since he had lost a fight with a Gallish knight in an inn yard, and his humility was finally greater than his pride.

And so he saw a golden spark against the black wall of the oncoming snowstorm. The light was like a meteor, and it burned like a little sun.

Even at this distance, it resolved into a golden griffon, and on the back of the griffon was a knight all in gold and red. For a moment he hung like a sigil of chivalry in the dark air over the battlefield, and then the griffon stooped on its dark prey, and the wild screech of its war cry carried over the battlefield.

On the Lily Burn, Irene shot her last bolt and stood with her back to one great maple and her cheek to another. Orley still raged among the brave Gallish knights and the rangers and Outwallers and bears who tried to hold the ford; a dozen Golden Bears lay dead, and his antlered men were crossing the mucky water on the corpses of their own dead, and behind them the whole host of Lissen Carak's former besiegers clamoured to follow.

Irene thought, *Not all stories end happily.* She wanted to cry.

But she didn't. Despite the end of all her hopes, she was a creature of duty, and despair was a waste of time. Instead, she dropped her now-useless latchet and drew the short, heavy sword that Ricar Lantorn had given her.

Lantorn himself put a hand on her shoulder. "No blade touches yon," he said. "Don't waste yersel'."

And there, suddenly, was Looks-at-Clouds. "Do not die, Irene, merely because he died," s/he said. "Let us end this Orley instead."

Looks-at-Clouds cast, and cast again, throwing fire and ice into Orley's creatures. S/he tripped and baffled, rose and dashed, and bought the rangers another breath, and another.

And finally, s/he caught Orley's attention. The huge dark stag-man rose on his hind feet, fire flickering from his human hands, and behind him, a new, dark wind whipped snow at Looks-at-Clouds and into the face of the rangers as the storm broke on them.

Orley stepped into the edge of the woods, hands weaving blue fire, and he borrowed more of his master's power. But he was still blinded by Aneas's blood and Gas-a-ho's viscous smoke.

Redmede put a clothyard shaft into the black torso just above where a man's heart would be. His shaft stuck, and Orley shuddered, but he came on, and Redmede turned and ran deeper into the wood.

Almost blind, Orley blundered after him...

Nita Qwan dropped on him from a tree. The Outwaller fell, and got his legs on the massive shoulders, staggering Orley. He took the blue knife from his sash and slammed it into his brother's neck with all his might, and the blade snapped against Orley's *potency*.

Orley staggered back, slamming Nita Qwan into the trunk of a tree. Ribs broke.

Fast as the wrestler he was, Nita Qwan threw his prisoner tie over his brother's head. The rope had been woven by his wife, of her own hair; he'd used it to climb walls, to hang laundry, to drag a dead deer.

Now he used it as a garrote.

He slipped his legs off Ota Qwan's shoulders, if there was indeed any of Ota Qwan left, and he dropped, holding the rope. And then despite the massive pain in his sides and lungs, he kicked out, spinning, so that the rope tightened inexorably.

Orley, or Ota Qwan, or the Son of Ash, slammed him into another tree. But now other hands were on his; Irene had leapt and caught the strangling rope, and Looks-at-Clouds was raining something on the dark captain's front, and Redmede hacked at him with his sword, and Lily, the bear, pounded the sorcerer's body with her talons, and he staggered, and staggered, and Nita Qwan hung on. Around them, the rangers surged forward, covering the fight; to the left, Tapio's knights flung their exhausted mounts forward, and the Fairy Knight himself put his lance in Orley's chest. It did not kill Orley, but slowed him.

And then Nita Qwan began to say the prayer; the prayer that Outwallers said for an animal they killed for need.

Go swiftly, brother. I need your skin, I need your meat, I need your bones. I will waste nothing of you. And we will remember you at the fire, in the food and in the clothes and in the flute we play. Go swiftly, brother.

Orley did not go swiftly. To Irene, the torment seemed eternal; she was dashed from tree to tree; her nose broken explosively, and her skin ripped and then her arms finally broken, and she fell like a broken doll in the blood-soaked mud.

She lost consciousness.

But she had protected Nita Qwan with her body, and he hung on for a few more beats of Orley's heart, and Tapio and Looks-at-Clouds poured their workings into the damaged creature until Orley sagged. And sat, suddenly, tearing at the cord around his neck, and then the storm burst over them, even as Orley died.

Gabriel emerged from the wings of the storm above Ash by a little too much, and behind him, on his right side.

Ash shuddered.

Ariosto needed no urging.

He only said, *This was great fun, boss. Thanks for all the sheep.*

And he dropped like a stone from a trebuchet, his great golden wings afire in the last of the sunlight, straight onto the back of the Black Drake. And Gabriel threw a great working, a simple burst of light, one of the very first workings he'd ever learned, but thrown on a titanic scale.

The immense dragon began to turn, writhing in three dimensions, the head reaching, reaching back on the sinuous neck...

Gabriel threw all his not inconsiderable *ops* in a blast of white fire that was not equal to breaking Ash's invulnerable wards, but where the fire met Ash's breath, chaos reigned, and men saw stars and deep blackness.

Gabriel had never expected to strike Ash with mere *puissance*. It was merely another feint in a long line of feints. But he'd blown a hole in the wards and Ariosto screamed through it, talons reaching, reaching...

Gabriel felt a pull, almost as if a hand was reaching to take him from his saddle, and he exerted his will. *Not yet, into the dark.*

The head snapped away with supernatural speed, the vulnerable eyes the size of a man just beyond the griffon's reaching talons...

The huge Wyrm rolled to evade the griffon's claws.

Another feint.

Ariosto turned on a wingtip, *inside* the circuit of the neck, *away* from the head. The head was coming around; Ash was in mid-exhalation and the backflow of his malevolence burned the very air, but Ariosto turned and turned, and the golden wings gave one great beat, the griffon lifted its talons and its hind feet so that it was flying along the great black body, inches above the surface of Ash's back, down the drake's right side as it rose, curling, like the hull of a black ship.

And Gabriel leaned out like a boy using a lance to strike pegs on the ground. He had the *ghiavarina* in both hands; Ariosto knew the game, and it was far too late in the game to worry about a fall. He leaned out; Ash turned, and the great wing of the black dragon reached back, cupping the cold air and exposing the wing root, where the massive bones and muscles that powered a creature that could not possibly exist met and knitted; a wing root that was itself only the height of a man or so, and into that wing root went the *ghiavarina*; a single stroke, the blade, *made for this exact purpose*, cutting deeper, and deeper, and deeper...

His left hand seemed to immolate, and a huge pulse of power traveled through the *ghiavarina*...

Gabriel smiled, even as his burning gold skin seemed to float away. It was excruciating and joyful. He could hear singing; he could imagine Amicia's voice, or Miriam's...

...and Ash's head continued to come back, the infinitely flexible neck allowing his head to turn all the way back along the body even as the huge red eyes registered their peril...

In the same beat, the wing root burst asunder, and the breath of extinction crossed the man and his mount, and they were gone.

Blanche was not supposed to ride into the snowy fields of Alba. She was with Gabriel's last reserve, and she had the key to the gate.

But she couldn't stop herself. When she was fully armed by Beatrice, who made it clear that she had never, in all her life as a maid, expected to have to buckle armour, Blanche walked out of the empty pavilion of red silk, past the round table that was clear and clean. By Gabriel's old folding campaign chair there was a silver cup lying on the tent's carpeted floor; Anne had missed it in the rush to get armed, and Blanche stooped, her breastplate butting into her swelling stomach, and picked it up.

Pregnant and wearing armour, Blanche thought.

And behind that thought came legions of other, darker thoughts. They marched like invincible armies at her uppermost mind, and she refused to receive them. Instead, she checked the hang of her unfamiliar sword belt and walked out onto the springy turf of an alien world, where Jon Gang stood with her fine Ifriquy'an charger, who was milk white from tail to nose. Gang gave her a leg up.

She felt like an imposter. She was a laundress. She was certainly no knight.

Gang was wearing a light half-armour. He chuckled. "Cap'n said you'd be riding," the man said.

Blanche felt herself flush. But Gang's words gave her heart, and she took the reins. She had been riding for a year; she was competent enough, although she couldn't imagine riding and fighting, too. Her gauntlets restricted her wrist movements. Everything felt odd.

Her baby kicked.

I am a fool, she thought, and then she rode through the gates and into her own world. She had time to savour the odd violet light of the moment that the portal was crossed, and to feel the disassociation as she entered into Alba, and the baby squirmed and kicked so that for a moment she bent double as if she'd been kicked in the gut.

"Hello in there," she said calmly. "That's enough o' that."

Jon Gang looked at her.

"The baby," she said. Her small unborn son or daughter had just crossed all the worlds...

She had a flash of vision, and she retched.

She'd never had a waking dream quite so vivid, and it disturbed her, made her doubt things, so that she looked back through the gate and wondered what...

She took a deep breath and steadied herself, as she always did. She thought for a moment of the laundry in the palace in Harndon. She wondered where the queen was, and whether her sheets were ironed.

"The *casa* is over here," Press said. "Top of the ridge."

They began to ride up slowly. As she passed through the archers, who were lying on their backs or sitting, men and women pointed, and then they began to cheer.

"The empress!" Oak Pew shouted, and they were all coming to their feet.

Off to the west, a wall of black seemed to carry all of the ill-omen that the world could provide. Tall, slate-coloured clouds pregnant with snow rolled toward them, a blanket of cloud and snow that gradually cut off the sun and seemed to cover the world beyond Lissen Carak in a whirl of darkness.

Blanche turned and looked up into the clouds.

The wave front of Ash's terror rolled down the plain of Albinkirk, but it passed her by; and as she rode up the last of the hill, the company's archers were closing up and forming their lines, and the lines were coming up the hill behind her like waves crashing on a beach.

Sauce was shouting at Michael, and Michael was ignoring her.

She crested the hill, and there was the dragon. It might have shocked the breath from her, but her vision at the gate had taken away her capacity for shock, and she viewed a dragon hundreds of paces long with the calm of despair. The dragon was black; black as night; black as velvet hanging in a dark closet. The dragon breathed, and men died; or were simply unmade; Ash's breath was a chaos of destruction, at the edges of his breath, a blue fire burned, but in the very heart of the black flame there was no light, and where it passed, the earth itself had scars and the men and horses were *gone*.

And Blanche thought, *This is his enemy.*

Behind her, the archers were cheering. They could not see the dragon, for the steep summit of the hill; but their cheers were no longer for the empress and her white horse, and she turned her head away from the pale sky and the black dragon, to the dark sky.

And against the dark sky, a golden knight burned like a second sun.

Her heart came into her mouth. Her pulse seemed to resound in the base of her throat, and her cuirass was like an iron band constricting her breathing.

"It's the empress," someone said, but she could not take her eyes off him. He burned like a comet, and he was above and behind the vast black wings, and then Ariosto stooped like an eagle carved in gold, and there was an incredible flash of light, and Blanche could not see. She wanted to turn her head away.

But she did not cry out. Instead, she reached into the *aethereal* and prayed.

Ser Michael watched the golden knight merge with the black Wyrm.

"Oh!" shouted Sauce. "Oh, oh! Get him!"

Tom Lachlan slammed an armoured fist into his palm. "Damn him," he spat.

Michael didn't want to watch, but he did. He watched, and all the rest of them watched. The gold and black merged, and then there was a massive flash of light; men and women and bogglins and irks across the battlefield blinked and stumbled, and then there was a massive concussion wave, and the dragon was falling, its neck seeming to trail behind it, one huge wing falling away and both wing and dragon spouting rivers of black ichor onto the snow below.

Of the golden knight there was no sign.

The earth shook as if an earthquake had hit; Lady Helewise's chimney collapsed; barns fell across the fields, and fire-damaged walls fell.

The black Wyrm fell across thousands of men and other creatures, and they died.

But the dragon was not dead, and it raised its maimed head and breathed again, shattering the ranks of the surviving Mamluks. It began to roll itself over, to breathe into the waiting lines of Moreans.

Gavin watched the dragon fall. 1Exrech was making scent; bogglins were shaking snow out of their wing cases and getting to their feet.

By Gavin's side, Tamsin said, "The emperor is gone."

"He's dead?" Gavin asked.

Tamsin put a hand on him. "Yes, man."

Gavin drew the Fell Sword that had been Hartmut's and spurred his charger toward the dread Wyrm, who lay across the field before him.

Gabriel had always intended to bring the dragon down.

And finally Michael blinked away his tears and turned to his friends. "Now we go and finish it," he said.

Sauce nodded, her face grim.

Tom's eyes narrowed. "Yes," he said, and that was all.

But all of their eyes went to Blanche; slim and white and gold. By chance, or fate, she had ridden in among them and was by the banner. Her face forbade any comment, any show of grief, any condolence.

"Finish it," said the empress.

The Duchess of Venike stood back from their grim grief and instead led her scarecrows down the hill, to the left, to complete the encirclement. The dragon had fallen half a mile from the base of the hill; the duchess needed no orders to know what happened next.

Michael and Tom and Sauce had a long walk down the hill through the snow. Long, and yet very quick; and already the trumpeter was calling the company to their feet, and to their horses. Everyone was awake, thanks to Blanche; Oak Pew had already rolled out of her cloak, folded it, and had it stowed behind her saddle before Bad Tom was fully in sight. They were just behind the brow of the hill.

A slim, dark man walked slowly out of the gate behind them, bearing in his hands a heavy spear. He walked uphill, toward the trio of officers.

Closer to, Ser Michael saw that it was Master Smythe.

Smythe bowed. And handed Michael a *ghiavarina*.

"I am almost without power now," he said. "But this much I can do."

"Is it ... his *ghiavarina*?" Michael asked.

Master Smythe shrugged. "Yes and no, as always," he said.

"He is dead, then?" Blanche asked, her voice cold.

Master Smythe nodded. "He is gone, and he will not return as mortal man," the dragon said.

And then Michael was mounting his warhorse, and grief and betrayal and death fell away from him.

He rode to the side of Conte Simone, and pointed across the field at the great reserve of stone trolls standing like rocks. "Would you open the ball, my lord?" he asked.

"Hah!" Conte Simone said. He threw his sword in the air and caught it. "It will be my delight!"

The knights of the north and east raised their lances and gave a cheer, and the earth began to shake.

Michael trotted back to the wedge of banners at the front of the company and Blanche, sitting like a white fury in their midst.

He looked left and saw Oak Pew and Cully and Tippit and Francis Atcourt, and looked right and saw Toby and Bad Tom and Sauce and Mortirmir and Tancreda. Around him were all the men and women who had marched and fought, and perhaps beyond them, the ones who had died and never left the ranks.

"Let's go kill the fucking dragon," Michael said.

There was no cheer. They were silent as they went forward.

They climbed the hill in a single body; knights in front, then armed squires, then pages, then archers. All told, they were almost five hundred lances; two thousand men and women, and a smattering of irks, and a single bogglin.

They crested the hill from which they had watched the duel with the dragon, and the battle lay before them. The snow was falling; the wind was ripping over their shoulders and driving the snow, and they, like their fallen captain, came on the wings of the storm and it drove them in its fury.

There was half a mile of snowy battlefield between them and their prey; a field still crowded with foes. But on that day, they faced nothing; no fallen man nor irk nor daemon nor bogglin would stand, and many creatures quailed and slipped away, or ran. Because like many creatures of the Wild, the company now exerted a wave front of fear.

The wind howled. The snow fell. The company marched on, their banners streaming in the wind so that the banner bearers could scarcely hold them, and Blanche's golden hair burst from her cap and snapped behind her as if she were a living banner.

The company rode across the great field as if riding to a pay parade.

About five hundred paces from the fallen dragon, Mortirmir raised his arms, and a huge ward sprang into being, red and white and green like the banners of the company.

Ash rolled, and breathed. And his breath was black, and it sublimated acres of snow, and struck Mortirmir's impudent wards like a blacksmith's hammer, and the wind howled, the wall of steam rose...

...and from the curtain of steam and snow emerged the line, unbroken, untouched, five hundred lances long; each banda covered in its own opalescent shell, as if Mortirmir, unsatisfied, was still touching up the exact colour and transparency of his wards and covers.

Ash breathed again. The ground between his claws was already black, and would not grow a crop for five generations.

Mortirmir's wards held. They were far more than his own; as Ash focused the whole of his terminal will on the company, so Mortirmir had the support of the whole of the choir of the alliance. But he was the conductor, and he played his part with a dark delight. He might have begun throwing *ops* from the hilltop.

But he had no intention of denying his friends their part.

One hundred paces from the vast beast, now on its forelegs and dragging itself along, the entire company and the *casa* dismounted. Pages came forward and took horses who were as calm as they might have been in a pasture, because the casters had them covered.

The horses were not terrified.

The four ranks closed forward as if they did this every day, because, in fact, they did.

And the old officers clustered in the center, by the banners; Michael in the lead, and Tom and Sauce at his shoulders, and behind them, Atcourt and de Beause and Milus and all the others.

And then they went forward into the dragon's fire.

Gavin galloped across the wasted land and into the snowstorm. His horse seemed to float beneath him. Once the mighty stallion stumbled, and he never knew why, and then he could see the black shape, the sinuous neck, the claws and the wing dragging across the fields.

Gavin could see the dragon breathe and breathe again, then over its back he saw the very tops of three great shields of *puissance* and he laughed.

Then he set his shield and put spurs to his borrowed horse.

When the company's Fell Spears were twenty paces from the black wall of the dragon's looming, scaly hide, Mortirmir let go. *The Patriarch, the Queen of Faery, the Lady of Alba, the choir of Lissen Carak, the will of Looks-at-Clouds, and even the least novice among the choir.*

And Morgon did not push it all into a single bolt. Instead, he divided the power among his choir, so that the vise of their combined vengeance closed on Ash from every direction.

The black Drake's will held.

But in the drgaon's head, the soul of Harmodius and the revenge of

Thorn unleashed a last assault. And then, in that very moment, the spears began to cut through his wards in the real. Only then, at the bitter, bitter end, did Ash begin to see how deeply the insects loathed him; even as he tried to roll and crush them, he knew that his wards were down, and the tide of fire was rising against him, and this was his end...

In the end, it was Tom Lachlan, and Sauce, and Michael and Gavin.

They cut through the wards as if exercising in a castle yard; the *ghiavarina* burned like blue lightning, and the black shield parted, and Michael was facing the wall of scales and dark flesh of the dragon's neck.

He passed into a back-weighted garde, and struck. Michael's *ghiavarina* was the first weapon to bite the flesh of the dragon. His slash went four feet deep into its neck; a neck many times that thick.

Then Sauce's beautiful sword from Firensi flashed in.

Hartmut's sword burned in Gavin's fist.

But it was Tom Lachlan, Bad Tom, who feared nothing, who shouldered into the grim wounds and cut deeper. He pushed past Michael, and entered into the dragon's black flesh; the burning ichor fell on him, and he cut with the blade he'd taken from another dragon, and he roared "Lachlan for Aa!" with each cut.

And Sauce, for once, followed his lead; her cuts were neat, precise, and chunks of the dragon's neck fell at her feet, and Gavin was by her, and Michael pushed in with them, opening the hole like a sailor flensing a whale. Michael's spear burrowed into the dragon's side, as a stream of magicked arrows rolled from Cully's fingers, and even in a wind like a hurricane and a wall of snow the great bows loosed and spat, and the shafts, arcane and deadly, plunged deep into the flailing thing's hide.

Perhaps it was Urk of Mogon who first struck one of the great red eyes. Or perhaps it was Tippit or No Head or Long Paw. But by the time that Tom Lachlan was swinging his sword like a woman splitting wood, by the time that Michael was black with ichor, his hands burned raw even under the weight of twenty amulets, by the time that Philip de Beause was shoulders deep in the very flesh of the dragon, and Gavin was almost drowning in black blood, it was blind, and it had ceased to cast. Gouts of fire and *ops* struck it; the last tatters of its defences fell away, never to recover, and it was naked to its enemies, and now they were without mercy.

The whole line of the company pressed forward into the black shield.

A vast rainbow of light began to rise from the valley of the Lilly Burn, and float like a child's dream of a cloud across the battlefield. Thousands of faeries; perhaps millions of them. Their fury of colours and lights swirled amid the storm.

Blanche was walking with the banners, and Francis Atcourt clearly wanted to go forward, to strike a blow, and she drew her own sword. She looked over her shoulder, and there was another figure in armour pushing at her shoulder, and she went forward again, into the black shield. Arrows flew over her, and she didn't have a helmet, and she was empty of fear, terror, joy, or even the lust for revenge.

"Keep pushing!" said the shrill voice behind her.

Blanche glanced back and saw Clarissa, the Queen of Arles, flushed, and with her shoulder in Blanche's back.

Blanche had a sword in her hand. She went forward with the line. No one tried to stop her, and when the black shields parted, she went forward with the banners, and her lithe sword, marked deeply with Mortirmir's *M*, slashed a strip off the black hide with eight hundred other swords.

And deep in the cave of black flesh, Tom Lachlan roared "Lachlan for Aa!" again, and struck, and more black flesh rolled away; Sauce cut up, *sottano* and the *ghiavarina*, almost a live thing, cut high, *mezzano* as if slicing a curtain, and another panel of flesh fell away, and there was white bone.

The spine.

Bad Tom paused, faced with the reality of the thing.

A grin covered his face.

"HECTOR! I AVENGE THEE!" he roared, and cut into the bone of the dragon's spine.

And then they were covered in faeries; the tide of colour descending on the dying dragon, leaching his black and taking him for their own.

When the fortress of his mortal immanence was no longer practicable, Ash fled to the high *aethereal*, to wait another hundred aeons, grow new allies, and...

He was not alone. Even as the hideous faeries stripped his essence like hermetical heyaenas on a carcass, he was naked on the endless plain, and he was not alone.

There in the aethereal *stood an infinite tide of figures of gold, more than an army of bogglins; and each of them imbued with the shining gold of transcendence, rank upon rank, like a phalanx of angels. Some he knew; most he knew not; and at their head, the golden figure of a knight. His nemesis the Red Knight, at the head of the phalanx; men and women, irks and wardens, rank on rank his victims and his enemies and all the others; men and wardens, women and irks blazing like suns.*

And on the glass-covered floor of the chapel of the abbey of Lissen Carak, Desiderata raised her hands and said, *"Te Deum."*

Epilogue

Christmas Eve

Adrian Goldsmith was the last man to leave the scaffolding. He was an odd young man, a study in contrasts, like so many of his generation; he wore the somber, plain clothes of a workingman, and yet on his hips was a knight's belt, and on his collar was the wheel badge of the company.

Below him, in the nave of the great hall of the new palace of Liviapolis, the dowager empress, great with child, sat on a chair specially made for her to watch the progress on the vast fresco. Goldsmith waved, and she smiled, and her knight, Galahad d'Acon, waved, too.

It took Adrian a long time to get down; No Head's scaffolding was itself a miracle of design, and he had included ladders and platforms enough for a siege, or so it seemed to the artist-knight as he climbed down.

He bowed to the dowager empress when his feet were on solid marble. "Majesty. I wanted you to see what it would look like."

Mortirmir accepted a nod from No Head and raised his arms, flooding the upper portions of the palace with light. But he did more than add light; working from Goldsmith's drawings, he added touches of colour that would be there in the final work; he gilded pieces of armour, and added a deep black to the dragon.

The Porphyrogenetrix, Irene, caught her breath. "Oh my God," she said simply.

By her side, Gavin Muriens burst into a grin. "He'd like that," Gavin said.

"When Adrian is done," Mortirmir said in his most pedantic voice, "I'll add a level of enhancement, and then make the whole ceiling an artifact; with its own hermetical lighting and protections..."

"Thank you, Morgon," Blanche said. She was still lying back, looking at the wonder of the depiction above her. "Are we all there?" she asked. "I mean..."

Goldsmith laughed. "I've done seven hundred portraits," he said. "1Exrech is the only baron I have yet to do; I'm going west when the thaw comes. I got Duchess Mogon this morning, and Looks-at-Clouds."

Blanche looked at the hermetical sketch. "We have been asked if this work is not...too frivolous for such a brutal winter," she said. "But we say, no man would cancel Christmas Day because he had a bad harvest. Let us remember our hour of triumph, even as we roll up our sleeves to work. What matters is not Gabriel and his...death." She paused, and commanded herself. "What is important is that we, together, triumphed."

"That is what I am painting," Goldsmith said.

Irene glanced at Gavin.

He was trying not to cry.

The next day, Christmas Day, as part of Christmas Mass, Tom Lachlan and Sukey were married in the great hall of the palace of Liviapolis. Sukey had insisted that they be married amid the rebuilding and the repairs. And Sukey generally got her way.

The bride was given away by the new Earl of Towbray, who had only just been invested with his new lands and title by the Queen of Alba. His father had died suddenly, in an accident, while hunting. The queen stood by Earl Michael on this occasion, Kaitlin being a step behind. And Tom Lachlan, whose family was dead, was supported by Ser Alison Audley, known to almost everyone as Sauce, who was now also the Marquesa of Albin; and by her stood Donald Dhu, for the Hills.

The vast hall was packed; every man and woman who could get a ticket was there; the front rows had most of the nobility of the Nova Terra and a surprising number of nobles of the Antica Terra, too. The gates remained open; the soldiers of the empire kept the road clear;

grain from Etrusca was feeding the farmers of Alba in the worst winter anyone could remember. The snow fell, and fell; the cold deepened. But the grain rolled through four worlds, and the farmers of Alba had other allies; allies who left a bag of nuts by a cottage door, or a basket of dried berries on a front step.

Regardless, at the wedding, everyone wore their best and tried to forget the snow, the press of business, the alliances, the betrayals, and the dead, and the succession crisis of the empire. Because some stories end, and other stories begin; and even as it is foolish to forget the past, so it is foolish to cling to it.

The Patriarch of Liviapolis said the blessing; Tom and Sukey exchanged a kiss that had Tippit bellowing "Get a room" in his old accustomed way. The company cheered the new earl and his lady, and then three thousand men and women, bogglins, irks, and wardens sat to feast. The dowager empress gave the toast; the Queen of Alba cried, and the two sat together, laughing and weeping by turns, as women who have endured much often do.

And when the feasting was drawing to a close, the Empress Blanche rose and led her people out into the great square, which the Nordikaans had sweated to clear of snow, and there ten thousand of her people joined all the revelers in forming circles, circles within circles, and the music began to play, and all across Alba, all across the Nova Terra and the Antica Terra and even across other worlds, there was dancing to celebrate the new sun, to shore up the wards that hold the dark at bay, and that promise tomorrow.

And then, when Blanche's baby stirred in her, and her breath came in gasps, and it seemed that everyone might have reached an exhaustion of everything that made a party great, there fell a silence across the square. And from the west, from the gates of the city, there came the sounds of bells, thousands of bells, or perhaps millions, and in rode the knighthood of Faery and their ladies, hundreds of irks on great stags and forest horses, and there was Tapio on a magnificent white hart, and there Tamsin, like a flower in the midst of winter.

And the Faery Knight rode to the center of the square, and his great stag reared, and people roared their approval.

He bowed to the dowager empress, and to the Queen of Alba.

"I beg leave to ssspeak," he said.

The dowager waved that he might.

"I am the Lord of Faery," he said. "And on thisss night when all the worldsss are open, and all magicksss true, isss there by chance sssome knight here presssent with a vow, who will run a courssse with me for the love of hisss lady?"

Because when some stories end, others begin.

Characters and Names

Ablemont
    Friend and confidante of the King of Galle. Architect of the Gallish plan to take Alba, and betrayer of Arles as well. Uncle to Clarissa de Sartres.

Acon, Ser Galahad, d'
    Also referred to as D'Acon. One of Queen Desiderata's most loyal knights, a royal messenger (not an imperial messenger) and a rising star in Alba. Hopelessly in love with the Empress Blanche.

Adam, Ser Eustace l'Isle d'
    A knight of Galle, friend of De Vrailly.

Aetius
    Warlord and Emperor of Man in the very distant past.

Alamain Borders, the
    The mountains and woods at the eastern edge of the "Antica Terra" (the lands commonly held to fall under the control of "man"). The limit of the conquests of Livia and Aetius. In fact, the Steppes run from the Alamain Borders to the Empire of Qin and are full of nomads of every culture, including irks.

Alcaeus, Syr
    Gentleman of the Morean Empire, as well as one of the Red Knight's most trusted lieutenants.

Almspend, Rebecca
    Also known as Becca, Lady Almspend, Rebecca Lachlan, or Lady Lachlan. The

	queen's confidante and friend. When necessary, also the Chancellor of the Realm and the Head of Military Logistics. Lover and eventual partner of Ranald Lachlan.
al-Raisouli, Salim	The greatest of the Ifriquy'an magisters after the death of Al Rashidi.
Al Rashidi	The greatest magister alive; one of the creators of "the plan." Friend and teacher of Harmodius, and the founding intellect behind the great plot to win the gates. His full name is Abū l-Walīd Muḥammad bin 'Aḥmad bin Rušd.
al-Shirazi, Magister Qatb al-Din	An astrologer and philosopher from the far eastern kingdom of Safir.
Amicia, Sister	Formerly the Red Knight's love; a sister of the Order of Saint Thomas, and a living saint.
Angelo di Laternum, Ser	A knight of the company.
Anne, Sister	The Prioress of Abbington, second in command of the Order of Saint Thomas's nuns.
Antonio, Father	One of the company's chaplains.
Archbishop of Lorica, the	Lorica was the first diocese of Alba recognized by the Patriarch of Liviapolis, and the Archbishop of Lorica, not the Bishop of Harndon, is the religious head of the Alban church.
Ariosto	Gift of Ghause Muriens, the Red Knight's difficult mother, and enamored of both Blanche and Amicia, the griffon is perhaps the most powerful of the Red Knight's allies. Likes sheep.
Armring, Thorval	Nordikaan axe bearer.
Arnaud, Father	Former chaplain and knight of the company, a priest-knight of Saint Thomas.
Ash	The great dragon, the enemy.
Askepiles	The now dead (although his body is occupied by Harmodius) magister of Thrake.
Ataelus	The Red Knight's black warhorse.

Atcourt, Francis	Friend of the Red Knight, an old, experienced knight who wants to live to retire.
Aubrichecourt, d'	A knight of Galle, friend of both De Vrailly and of Clarissa de Sartres and the Sieur du Corse.
Baillie, John le	Retired mercenary in Abbington, and baillie for the Order of Saint Thomas. Then knight of the company and eventually corporal before dying in the fighting in Thrake in *The Fell Sword*. Lover of Mag the Sorceress.
Barbara, Saint	Patroness of gonners and explosions.
Bateman, Mistress Anne	Lady Anne—one of the richest and most powerful people in Harndon.
Beatrice, Donna	The Empress Blanche's "lady maid."
Beause, Philip de	Veteran knight and master jouster of the company, whose magical resistance to death is now drained.
Benn, Mistress Aphra	Master ironworker, a leader of the crafts in Harndon, as well as an amateur poet and playwright; close friend of Rebecca Almspend, whose lover she may or may not have been at other times.
Bent	A veteran archer of the company.
Berengar, Ser	A veteran knight of the company, best friend of Ser Danved. Silent and cheerful.
Berrydrunk	A Golden Bear warrior.
Bess	Partner of Bill Redmede, a veteran Jack on her own, now pregnant.
Bicci, Lucius di	*See* Patriarch of Rhum, the.
Bin Maymum, Magister Yusuf	Yahudat philosopher and astrologer.
Black Drake	Another name for Ash.
Black Heron	A veteran Outwaller (Sossag) war leader and hunter, serving as a ranger with Aneas. Not to be confused with Heron, a Huran, serving with the company in the Antica Terra.
Blessed Virgin	The Virgin Mary from Christian mythos.

Blizzard, King of the Woods	A powerful albino Golden Bear Clan leader from the central Adnacrags.
Blue Berry	A young bear of growing power.
Born, Grand Seigneur Estaban du	A lord of Occitan.
Brewes, Ser George	Veteran knight of the company, formerly no friend of the Red Knight and now a senior leader.
Broadarrow, Ser Balin	Prior of Harndon. Second in command of the Knights of Saint Thomas.
Brown	An assassin.
Brunet, Ser Uc	An Occitan knight.
C.2	An imperial messenger bird. The birds are all known by a letter-number designation.
Carlos	A company archer and sometimes the company trumpeter.
Carter, Robin	A company archer. Also a great friend in real life, and the reviewer @ParmenionBooks.
Cat Evil	An Outwaller and a Jack officer. A master woodsman.
Caves, Jack	A Jack.
Cheney, Edmund	Also referred to as Chevins, Edmund and Allen. A journeyman Bladesmith and captain of the Harndoner militia.
Christos, Syr	A Morean knight, former captain of the army of Demetrius, now reconciled to the new emperor. Went sword to sword with Bad Tom and lived to tell of it.
Cigne	An Occitan ranger.
Clothyard, John	A royal forester officer.
Comnena, Syr George	The Caesar. Friend of Morgon Mortirmir and the Red Knight, from an ancient imperial family. He will become the next emperor should the Red Knight fall.
Comyne, Hamish	One of the Red Knight's household pages.
Constantine III	Son of the former king and Queen Desiderata; King of Alba. Currently in diapers.

Corner, Matteo	Captain of the Venikan marines. Venike has a vast fleet and her marines are the toughest and most flexible troops in the old world.
Corse, Sieur Du	Formerly one of the Red Knight's enemies. Now Regent of Galle.
Coucy, Haegert	Squire of Albinkirk.
Courtois, Giron le	A legendary knight.
Crabbe, Old Mother	A survivor in Lady Helewise's manor house.
Crayford, Ser John	Formerly captain of Albinkirk and lover of Lady Helewise. A great knight.
Crom, Abby	A woman of the company.
Crowbeard, Ser Kit	Captain of the Earl of Trowbrey's knights.
Cully	The Captain's archer.
Cynthia	A ranger from northern Albin.
D.13	An imperial messenger bird. Imperial messengers are roughly the size of a golden eagle and are black on one half of their bodies and white on the other half.
Dar as Salaam	A great city in Ifriquy'a and also the name usually given to the sultanate that stretches all the way along the north coast of that continent and that held most of Hatti as well (since lost to armies of the Wild). The inveterate foe of the Necromancer and usual ally of Venike despite their religious differences. The people of Dar and parts of Occitan and Iberia do not follow Christianity and are pious followers of "Submission to God," or Islam.
Dabbaj, King Rostan	The easternmost King of Man; King or Shah of the Safir.
Daispainsay, Ser Edward	Lord of Bain. A loyal officer of the Queen of Alba.
Daniel, Ser	A leader of the green, or scout, banda of the company; also called Daniel Favor.
Danved, Ser	Veteran knight of the company, a man who makes loud jokes, a master of the poleaxe.

Dariush of Thrake, Maria	Mother of Alcaeus, sometime mistress of emperors and a master of the game of power.
Daud the Red	Master scout for the company, green banda.
Davide, Father	Chaplain of the company and a friend of Sauce.
Deadlock	Veteran ranger of the Adnacrags, also an explorer. Will probably get his own stories in time.
Demetrios	Former Duke of Thrake and son of Antiginos, who tried to make himself emperor. Killed by the Red Knight.
Derkensun, Harald	Sword bearer (Spatharios) and captain of the Nordikaans. Friend of Morgon Mortirmir.
Desiderata	The Queen of Alba.
Dhu, Donald	Rival and friend of Tom Lachlan.
Diodora, Master Elena	A Morean paper-maker living in Harndon.
Doge Mikal Loredan	Husband of the Duchess Giselle, lord of Venike, friend of the Sultan of Dar.
Donne, Master	A master alchemist of Harndon.
Duke	Journeyman of Harndon, former street rat and now officer of the militia and a gonner.
Dvor, Mikal	Officer of the Vardariotes from the very farthest east of the Antica Terra Steppes. Well, almost. Klugthai has come from even farther. The Steppes are vast; yet another battleground between the Wild and man, separating the Empire of Qin from the Alamain Borders.
E.2	An imperial messenger bird.
E.34	The most famous imperial messenger bird, the "Savior of Arles."
E.49	An imperial messenger bird.
Elaran	Irk and archer of the company.
Elder Flower	A Golden Bear.
Elisabeth, Sister	A sister in the Order of Saint Thomas.
Eu, Guillaume, Count of	De Vrailly's right hand, his cousin and friend. A great knight, and a modest man undeceived by Ash.

Ewald, Ser Calvin von	Captain of the Alamain knights who go with the Great Crusade through the gates.
F.34	An imperial messenger bird.
53Exrech	Former chieftain of Ash's bogglins.
Fitzalan, Ricar	Veteran ranger and Aneas Muriens's lover.
Fitzroy, Ser Ricar	Bastard son of the "Old King" and captain of the royal household.
Flarch	Veteran archer of the company.
Flint	A Golden Bear so powerful that he is viewed as a "Power of the Wild."
Françoise, Father	A chaplain of the company.
Gadgee	Veteran archer of the company and veteran complainer.
Gang, Jon	A page in the emperor's household.
Gardunsag	A wyvern.
Gareth	Ser Gavin's warhorse.
Garter, Quill	An Outwaller ranger.
Garth No Toes	A veteran Jack with no toes.
Gas-a-ho	An Outwaller sachem and philosopher.
Gentile, Ser Giovanni	A knight of the company.
Gilchrist	A Hillman, and senior ranger in the green banda of the company.
Giselle, Duchess	The Duchess of Venike, wife of the Doge, Mikal.
Gold, Empress Blanche	The Empress of Man; former laundress, lover of the Red Knight.
Goldsmith, Adrian	Artist and veteran mercenary.
Goody, Sarah	Woman of the company.
Gower, Master	Master craftsman of Harndon.
Gregario, Ser, Lord Weyland	A great knight and senior officer of the Alban Army of the North; commander of the knights of the alliance.
Grey Cat	Outwaller scout and sometime archer of the company.
Griatzas, Giannis	Ser Gavin's Morean squire.
Gropf	Archer of the company and former master tailor. No one knows how he lost his business.

Guisarme, Ser Tancred	High constable of Galle.
Half Arse	An archer of the company.
Hamwise	A page of the company.
Hand, John	An officer of the royal foresters.
Harmodius, Magister	Now in the body of Askepiles. Probably the greatest living human magister.
Hartmut, Ser	The Black Knight.
Hasty, Robin	An archer.
Helen, Sister	A sister of the Order of Saint Thomas.
Helewise de Roen, Mistress	Also sometimes called Mistress Heloise. Lady of the Middle Hill manor, lover of Ser John Creyford. A survivor who leads a party of other survivors to reestablish her farm in the North Albin. Mother of Phillippa. Her back garden holds a terrible surprise.
Helli, Hukas	An irk who serves Ash as a volunteer.
Heron	An Outwaller ranger serving in the company as an archer.
Hewitt, Rob	An archer of the company.
Hoek, Conte de	The Count of Hoek. Ruler of the land of fens and marshes north of Galle, where wool is felted and knights are plentiful.
Hoek, Jamie Le	Former squire of Ser John Creyford, a brave young man for whom war is not the sole purpose of life.
I.31	An imperial messenger bird.
Irene of Liviapolis, Princess	Porphyrogenetrix, Heir of the Empire and former empress, now just nineteen years old. Probably killed her father.
Iris	An irk archer of the company.
Isabella, Novice	Member of the choir of Lissen Carak.
Jane, Lady	The old king's mistress.
Jehan, Ser	A veteran mercenary, one of the Red Knight's early instructors in the art of war. Dead since the events of *The Red Knight*, but still remembered.
Julia, Dame	A famous, perhaps mythological, astrologer from two or three centuries ago, who

predicted the opening of the gates and the times and some of the places. A founding member of the conspiracy of mages that created "the plan."

Julius, Master — Notary of the company and functioning Chancellor of the Empire. A very quiet, competent man.

Katheryn, Sister — Mistress and leader of the left choir of Lissen Carack, where the design of the ancient chapel allows two choirs to sing together, comparable to Saint Mark's in Venice.

Kearny, Jeff — Knight and lance-leader of the green banda of the company.

Kerak, Lord — A Saurian (or warden or adversarious) magister, of enormous powerful. A "Lord of the Wild."

Kessin — An archer of the company.

Klugthai — A Vardariote, the easternmost man in the company, and the only one who has seen the Empire of Qin, although no one thinks to ask him about it.

Kriax — Woman officer of the Vardariotes, one of the best warriors in the army.

Kronmir, Jules — The master assassin who narrowly misses killing the Red Knight and ends up running his intelligence service.

Kwoqwethogan — A Saurian mage, brother (egg brother, not gland brother) to the Duchess Mogon.

Lachlan, Hector — Bad Tom's cousin, or perhaps brother; a hero of the men of the Green Hills and the Drover. The clan chief of the Lachlans, and a vassal of the Wyrm of Erch. Bad Tom has sworn to avenge his death on Ash.

Lachlan, Ranald — Master of the royal household. Cousin of both Hector and Bad Tom; a fearsome axe fighter and lover of Lady Rebecca.

Lachlan, Ser Thomas — Also known as Bad Tom, or the Drover. Primus Pilus of the company, friend of the Red

	Knight, and eventually Earl of Northwall, lover of Sukey. Well, and a few others, not to be named here. Afraid of nothing, but not altogether fond of worms.
Landry, Master	A master bronze caster and bell maker in Harndon.
Langtree	A Golden Bear, apprentice shaman, and warrior.
Lantorn, Ricar	Archer of the company, brother of Kaitlin, and bodyguard of Princess Irene.
Leary, Donald	Apprentice of Harndon and gonner in the militia.
LeFleur, Ser Shawn	The Grand Squire. Friend of Ser Gregario, formerly senior squire of the king, now Captain of Albinkirk.
Lessa, Mary Magdalene	An aristocratic young woman, Alban, and now a Jack.
Lewen	An irk ranger.
Lilly	A Golden Bear, companion of Berrydrunk.
Livia, Empress	The original conqueror, of almost unimaginable antiquity, who, according to legend, led the first armies of man to the world and founded the empire. Liviapolis was named after her, and she won many victories and built the wall. The irks claim she lost the battle of Dykesdale.
Long Paw	Also known as Ser Robert Caffelo. A former archer, now knight of the green banda of the company. The best swordsman of the company.
Long Peter	A ranger.
Long Sam	An archer of the company.
Long Tail	A veteran archer of the company.
Looks-at-Clouds	An ungendered or perhaps "all-gendered" individual (pronouns: *s/he*, *hir*). A powerful magister, a shaman of the Huran, although s/he hirself is thought to be from the far west.

Author's note: These books were written before the author was fully conversant with the current conventions for gender neutral pronouns and the initial "created" pronouns *s/he* and *hir* were kept for consistency.

Second note: The Western Outwallers have a whole empire west of Occitan, which was originally going to be part of the books. Their capital is at Cahokia, and Looks-at-Clouds is a *mico* (noble) of that empire.

Lorenzo Tucchi, Captain	Ranger officer of the Venikan ranger regiment. Venike has a corps of rangers who guard the great woods of Dalma in the east so that Venike can harvest the old trees to build her ships.
Lostenferch	An albino warden, or adversarious, or daemon; Ash's "White Captain" in the northern war against Mogon. Lostenferch's egg was culled as defective but his mother defied Mogon, hatched the egg, and raised it to maturity. Lostenferch hates Mogon and intendeds to displace her entire lineage with his own. So many stories still to tell!
Lot	Master Smythe's "dragon name."
Lowper	An archer of the company.
Lucca, Master Fernando	Kronmir's assistant and lieutenant.
M'bub Ali	A spy and warrior of the Sultan of Dar as Salaam.
MacGilly, Jock	A Hillman serving in the imperial household.
Macgitchie, Magdalene	Also known as Mag the Seamstress, Old Mag, or Mag. A former military camp follower and goodwife, small holder in Abbington, and one of the greatest latent talents of the era, Mag was the lover of John le Baillie, a knight of the company, the head woman of the company, and a self-taught sorceress powerful enough to face Ash. Mag

	is probably the daughter of Master Smythe and the once-famous witch Ninnie Macgitchie. Mag's daughter is Sukey (Susan) Macgitchie.
Marche, Charles de la	A Gallish sea captain, who served under Ser Hartmut and was martyred by him for refusing to accept the massacre of Outwallers. Brother of Oliver de la Marche.
Marche, Oliver de la	A Gallish merchant and sea captain with wide-ranging experience with sea monsters.
Maria Magdalena, Novice	Novice in the Order of Saint Thomas.
Maria, Ser	An imperial messenger. The messenger corps incorporates not just the birds but also their handlers, who serve as heralds, ambassadors, and occasionally, assassins.
Mary, Lady, Hard Heart	Daughter of Count Gareth and lover of Ser Gavin, as well as one of the queen's closest friends, exiled by the Galles but now returned to court.
Mary, Sister	One of the choir of Lissen Carak.
Matteos, Ser	A knight of the company.
Maymum, Magister Bin	A powerful magister and astrologer from Iberia, a Yahudat theologian and rabbi. Yahudat is the third major religion in the world of the Red Knight, a highly intellectual monotheism with complexities that form social conventions comparable to medieval Judaism.
Michael, Archangel	Also known as Saint Michael, Holy Saint Michael, Saint Michael the Commander of Paradise, and Taxiarchos. In the Christian mythos, he is the captain of the hosts of angels, the commander of the phalanx of God.
Milett, Ralph	Captain of the Redesdale militia of northern Albin.

Milus, Ser	Commander of the white banda of the company, originally the company standard bearer and sometime captain of Liviapolis. The company has three colors—red, white, and green—and three banda—the red and white, which form the main body, and the green, or scouting, banda. Each banda has at least a hundred lances and sometimes more; the company grows with success and is always recruiting. A lance is composed of a knight or senior unknighted man- or woman-at-arms, an armored squire, a half-armored page, and an archer.
Miriam, Abbess	Also known as Sister Miriam, the abbess. The head of the great fortress abbey of Lissen Carak. Of common birth, she rose to lead based purely on hermetical and administrative brilliance. A woman of great faith and uncommon sense.
Mitla, Duke of	The ruler of the great city-state of Mitla, one of the most powerful and richest states in Antica Terra.
Mogon *Texetererch*	Duchess of the West. An ancient Saurian, and a great power of the Wild, with hermetical skills and legendary fame as a warrior and politician, and bearer of the sword-axe "Stonekiller," an artifact of the wars with the *Rhank* before the humans came.
Monteverdi, Alessio	Musician and trumpeter for the company.
Montjoy, Gareth	Count of the Borders, father of Lady Mary, commander of the Western Army of Alba, and faithful knight of the queen.
Monts, John de	A royal forester.
Mortirmir, Ser Morgon	A young prodigy of hermeticism. Mortirmir's intellect brought him to the notice of the great Academy in Liviapolis; his power appeared late, and was only fully harnessed when

	Harmodius seized his body and reordered his memory palace, a crime according to some. Technically, a knight of the company.
Motte, de la	Galle and Alban ranger. One of the founders of the Outwaller and Gallish town of Kebec, but that's another story...
Muiscant, Eufemmie	Initiate squire of the Order of Saint Thomas; on her way to be the first female Knight of the Order.
Muriens, Ghause	Mother of the Red Knight, Duchess of Westwall, sister of the former king and plotter extraordinaire as well as one of the great powers of the Wild *and* a master magister. A very powerful woman indeed.
Muriens, Ser Gabriel	Also known as the Red Knight, the Red Duke of Thrake, the Emperor of Man, the emperor. Son of Ghause and her brother the king, brother of Gavin, lover of Blanche. Intended to be the Dark Prince of the Wild by his mother, he rebelled and became the Red Knight.
Muriens, Ser Gavin	Earl of Westwall, the Green Earl. The Red Knight's brother, also known as Hard Hands and the Green Knight, a captain of the alliance, one of the most feared knights in Alba, and lover of Lady Mary. Sometimes called Ser Gawain.
Musquogan	A powerful Saurian lord.
Necromancer, the	An amalgam of "taken" personalities and rebel Odine, sometimes called the Rebel, an ancient voice of dissent in the hive mind.
Nicodemus, Master	The steward of the imperial household, a Morean.
Nikos, Master	Master grammarian of the Imperial Academy. A Morean mage of great and precise skill, with less direct power than some but more precise control than any. Even Ash. That's the importance of grammar...

No Head	An archer of the company and self-taught military engineer. A common-born man with a genius for design, the author of the fortifications at Gilson's Hole, and also the architect of the new imperial palace.
Oak Pew	An archer of the company, formerly a great lady of Galle and somewhat given to drink. Her name on the roster is Sarah de Charny, and a few friends call her Sally.
1Exrech	Bogglin chieftain, sometimes known as a wight; a faithful member of the alliance and perhaps the only bogglin ever to achieve the rank of "Power of the Wild."
Orcsbane, Ser Ricar	A junior knight of the Order of Saint Thomas, sometimes, but not always, silent. A friend of Pavalo Payam.
Orley, Kevin	Also known as Ota Qwan, the Black Captain, and by a variety of other fell names. The last survivor of the House of Orley, destroyed by the Muriens family in a feud.
Parcival, Ser	One of the captains of the Alamain knights from the eastern edge of Galle who joined the emperor's crusade. Like the Empire of Cahokia, the Alamain Borders were originally an important part of the story, the land of a thousand princes and a thousand castles.
Parmenio, Captain	A Venikan merchant, sea captain, and adventurer. In no way related to the archer Robin Carter.
Patriarch of Liviapolis, the	The Christian polity is split between the Patriarch of Rhum, who controls, for the most part, the Antica Terra, at least for religious matters, and the Patriarch of Liviapolis, who claims universal control of the church but is recognized only in the empire and Alba and sometimes in Occitan. The principal difference is that the Patriarchate

of Liviapolis practices in High Archaic and approves of the use of hermeticism, and the Patriarchate of Rhum practices in Low Archaic and has no toleration for any form of magic.

Patriarch of Rhum, the Lucius di Bicci, the most senior religious leader of the Antica Terra.

Payam, Ser Pavalo Also known as Ser Payamides. A Mamluk of the Sultan of Dar, friend of the Red Knight, admirer of the Empress Blanche, and commander of the armies of Dar; bearer of the last known Fell Sword from the First Making. Pavalo has known Harmodius since boyhood; was the military slave, servant, and friend of Al Rashidi; and led the expedition that brought back the information about the gates that allowed the creation of "the plan."

Pearl, Master A craft master of Harndon.

Petite Moulin A page and later a squire of the company.

Petrarcha, Magister The most powerful mage of the Antica Terra, a friend of both Harmodius and Al Rashidi; an architect of "the plan."

Plangere, Richard Also known as Thorn. Once the court mage of Alba; rival, with the king, for the favors of the king's mistress; a brilliant, driven man who rose to high office by sheer talent and then turned to the Wild, betraying the cause of humanity—or perhaps realizing that humanity needed to be stopped to preserve balance. He is dead and subsumed inside Harmodius, yet perhaps not entirely gone...

Porte, Pierre La Knight marshal of the Kingdom of Arles, captain of Arles (fortress) and hero of the siege, and a loyal supporter of Queen Clarissa.

Prudentia The Red Knight's tutor in the *ars magika*, murdered by the Red Knight's mother,

Ghause, and now a statue inside the emperor's memory palace. Dead? More than dead? It's hard to know, in the *aethereal*.

Pye, Master
A master craftsman of Harndon, whose craft work is so good that many of his creations seem to be magical; lately interested in large-scale bronze casting.

Qin
Another mostly human empire far across the world, of legendary wealth and power. There was originally an entire plotline in Qin, and maybe someday I'll write the Qin version of the opening of the gates.

Qwan, Nita
Once the Ifriquy'an Salim, then the slave Peter, and finally the Outwaller war leader Nita Qwan. A survivor, a fine warrior, and an excellent cook.

Qwan, Ota
See Orley, Kevin.

Rafik, Ali-Mohamed el
The exiled Mamluk of Dar, now in service to the Patriarch of Rhum as a mercenary.

Random, Ser Gerald
One of the richest of the Harndoner merchants. Ser Gerald's rise to great wealth and political power has been tied to daring guesses and a heavy investment in Morea and the fur trade. In effect, he has invested in the Red Knight and the company. Knighted for bravery at the first siege of Lissen Carak.

Rannulfson, Michael
A veteran mercenary, the commander of the paid military garrison at Lissen Carak.

Red Squirrel
An Outwaller ranger.

Redmede, Harald
Commander of the royal foresters, brother of Bill Redmede the Jack.

Redmede, William, Bill
Lover of Bess and the leader of the Jacks, a movement of escaped serfs and angry yeomen to overthrow the established order and eliminate ideas of aristocracy and vassalage. The Jacks began the Great War allied with Thorn, but the movement has become

	tangled in ideals and has split. Redmede leads the faction that believes the evil of Ash is greater than the evil of feudalism. For now.
Rhun	A dragon. The apparently taken or "not-dead" dragon in service to, or part of, the rebel Odine group called the Necromancer.
Rinir, Syr	A knight of faery. Despite massive differences between irk culture and human culture, the concept of knighthood seems comprehensible by both groups.
Roen, Phillippa de	Also known as Pippa, Prickly Pippa, or the queen of the field workers. Daughter of Helewise, a flirtatious young woman with a good head on her shoulders and too much experience of being a refugee and a poor relation.
Rohan, Guillaume, Sieur de	Courtier and knight of Galle, a royal favorite, a gossip, and a schemer.
Rose Drew	Phillippa de Roen's best friend.
Sabina di Berona	Friend of Lady Sophia di Castelbarco, cook, and gunner, commander of the bronze gonne "Lord of Light."
Sam	An out-of-work farm laborer who has joined Tyler's faction of the Jacks.
Sarrissa, Andromeche	Morean student of the Academy; one of Master Nikos's more promising talents.
Sartres, Lady Clarissa de	The acting Duchess of Arles, Queen of Arles, and quite possibly Queen of Galle. The De Sartres family, which included the Sieur d'Ablemont, the King of Galle's favorite and adviser, were the hereditary rulers of the Kingdom of Arles before Ablemont and the King of Galle seized it and forced Clarissa's father to accept demotion to a subordinate duchy. The King of Galle attempted to seize Arles Castle in a later coup and failed, largely because of the Red Knight and his

fledgling company's actions, but that's another story...

Lady Clarissa was sent to Galle as a sort of hostage for her father's good behavior, and when her father died fighting the Wild and she narrowly escaped sexual harassment at court, she found herself commanding a desperate defense of her home. The Necromancer laid siege to Arles for months, without success, and Lady Clarissa's defence of the city probably saved the world. She deserves her own novel.

Sauce	Also known as Ser Alison Audley, captain of the grande alliance, Marquesa of Albin. Sauce was born to a poor family and sold as a sex worker when she was eleven. She worked in brothels in Harndon and in Liviapolis until she was fourteen, when she killed a customer and escaped with the aid of the brothel's bouncer, a former mercenary named Cully, who thought he was in retirement, and a young, broken man who had not yet begun to call himself the Red Knight...but that's another story. Sauce, along with Tom Lachlan, is a pillar of the company, a brilliant fighter, and a dashing knight.
Scrant	An archer of the company.
Short Tooth	An archer of the company.
Sidenhir	An irk archer of the company.
Simkin	An archer of the company.
Simone, Conte of Berona	A benevolent tyrant of the De La Scala family, il Conte Simone is one of the most feared knights of the Antica Terra. Friend of Sauce, admirer of Blanche, and captain of the Crusade.
Skas-a-gao	A Sossag shaman and member of the Council of Dorling.

Slythenhag	An ancient and venerable wyvern brood mother, Slythenhag has served many lords of the Wild and is perfectly willing to serve the Red Knight as long as her brood is protected and enhanced.
Smoke	A master archer of the company.
Smythe, Master	The dragon Lot.
Snot	An archer of the company.
Sophia di Castelbarco	Lady of Ser Maurizio, the most beautiful woman in il Conte Simone's brilliant court. Friend of Sabina di Berona.
Srylot, Syr	A faery knight.
Stare, Gwillam	A veteran Jack.
Stark, Captain George	An officer of the Albin militia.
Stefana, Novice	A junior member of the choir of Lissen Carak.
Stern Rachel	A veteran Jack.
Stone Axe	War chief of the Long Dam Clan bears.
Stouffy, Bill	Veteran of the royal foresters.
Sukey	Also known as Susan Macgitchie or Dama Souga, Imperial Countess of Osawa. Commands the company's logistics effort; she is sometimes referred to as "head woman," but by autumn, her duties encompass the whole imperial war effort. Lover of Tom Lachlan, daughter of Mag the Sorceress, granddaughter of Master Smythe.
Swynford, Hawissa	An officer of the royal foresters.
Swynford, Master	A master craftsman of Harndon.
Sym	Also known as Low Sym. A street brat, would-be rapist, and general ne'er-do-well junior archer of the company, typical of the bad men and women who end up as mercenaries. Died heroically and was eaten by bogglins. "Evil is a choice" is the theme of these books, and Sym was the first target of those words.

Tamsin, Queen	Also known as Lady Tamsin, Faery Queen, Lady of Faeries, or the Lady of Illusions. A Great Power of the Wild, Tamsin is among the oldest of the powers and can remember past ages and wars for the gates. Apparently an irk, although some believe that she, like Lot, is actually a dragon. Lover of Tapio, the Faery Knight.
Tancred of Occitan, Prince	Also known as Tancred Poictiers. Poet, warrior, minstrel, and prince. Again, a hero in his own right who deserves his own story.
Tancreda, Magistera	Another of the incredible crop of talented young magisters produced by the university; in this case, of imperial descent, Tancreda, a serious intellectual, throws aside her plans for a convent to be the lover and partner of Morgon Mortirmir.
Tapio	The Faery Knight. One of the oldest and most powerful irks, and generally accorded the rank of "king" of the irks, although most irks are far too independent to have a king. Sometimes an ally of men and sometimes an enemy. A true protector of the Wild.
Tar, Lady	Probably a dragon. And then again, perhaps something even more powerful. In the north of Alba and the Hills, often confused or conflated with the Virgin Mary.
Tas-a-gao	Old Sossag hunter and veteran ranger.
Teskanotokex	A young warden, kin of Mogon and in her warband.
Tessen	An irk ranger.
Theodora	A brave novice of the Order of Saint Thomas.
Thomas, Saint	One of the military legates of the legions of Livia. According to legend, after years of leading the war against the irks, he learned the irk language and went west as an ambassador to make peace with the Wild, learned

to practice green magic, and achieved some sort of apotheosis.

Ticondonaga	A massive and ancient fortress on the wall, built by Livia and improved by successive generations of legates and lords, currently the hold of the Muriens family, the lords of the western wall and most of the north and the Adnacrags.
Tippit, Tip	Master archer of the company.
Tobias, Ser, Toby	First a page and then a squire of the Red Knight, Toby started as a street urchin in Harndon and may yet end up as a great captain.
Towbray, Earl of	Richard de Burgh. The most powerful non-royal lord in Alba, De Burgh holds most of the great estates in Jarsay, the southern, richest half of the kingdom, and the Burgh estates in the heartland run almost from the gates of Harndon to the border of Occitan. Through his grandmother, Towbray has a claim on the throne.
Towbray, Kaitlin de	Kaitlin de Burgh. Wife of Michael de Burgh, daughter-in-law of the Earl of Towbray, eventually the Duchess of Towbray. Kaitlin herself is a Lantorn of Abbington and Kentmere, a family best known for near-criminal behavior and laziness; curiously, Kaitlin and her brother Ricar seem immune to the family curse. Likable, and also a former laundress, like the empress. It's been a good year for laundresses.
Towbray, Ser Michael de	Ser Michael de Burgh. Son of the great Earl of Towbray, Michael ran away from his pampered life as a very young man to learn to be a "real" knight alongside veteran mercenaries. He very quickly ended up in the company and became the Red Knight's squire, and Kaitlin Lantorn's husband. One

of the "initiates" of "the plan" and also one of the best knights, the Red Knight made him his military heir.

Turell, Cat — An apprentice of Harndon and gonner in the Harndoner militia.

Tyler, Nat — Leader of a faction of the Jacks that favors the violent extermination of the aristocracy and alliance with Ash, or any other power that will help overthrow the hated aristos. He killed the king. One of the best archers in the world.

Urk of Mogon — A bogglin of the wild Adnacrag mounds, a master archer of the company. Formerly served Thorn but was scent-marked by Duchess Mogon as a member of her own clan, a high honor, unheard of for a mere bogglin.

Vizirt, Syr — An irk knight.

Vrailly, Jean de — The self-styled "best knight in the world." A great knight, misled by Ash in the guise of an angel.

Wart — A veteran Jack and ranger.

Waster, Dick — Former archer of the company, and now Ser Milus's squire.

Wha'hae — A veteran scout and ranger, member of the green banda of the company.

Wilful Murder — Dead, but somehow still present in the company, Willful Murder was an evil, lecherous, and dangerous master archer whose pronouncements were rarely correct while he was alive, even when he was sober. But as the company seems to gather some sort of supernatural power of the Wild to itself, it seems to have been focused on his legacy and memory.

Wilsit, Tom — Scout of the green banda.

Wimarc, Lord Roger — A lord of Jarsay in his own right, Wimarc volunteered as a squire with the Order of

Saint Thomas to escape abuse at home, and is now a knight of the company. Almost silent.

Wishart, Grand Prior John	John Wishart was born to a powerful Jarsay family heavily intermarried with the Gallish nobility. He was the third son, and his father placed him with the Order, which he has risen to command. A great knight, a modest hermeticist, and a good leader, he is adored by his men and women.
Woodstock, Squire Anne	The Red Knight's third squire, Anne Woodstock is from a knightly family in the Brogat, and is used to hard work.
Ydrik, Syr	Captain of the Faery Knight's bodyguard of irk knights.
Zachariah (Zakje) Ulk	Also known as Count Zac. Commander of the Imperial Vardariotes, one of the four elite regiments of the empire. The four are, in order of precedence: the Nordikaans, the Vardariotes, the Scholae, and the Athanatoi, who are also called the "company." Sometimes Sauce's lover. From Moska, far east of Galle and even the Alamain Border.

Cold Iron

Enjoy *The Fall of Dragons*?
Read on for a sneak peek of Miles Cameron's
brand new series . . .

Prologue

I t was late in the day when Syr Xenias di Brusias was ready to leave Volta. Almost everything that could go wrong had done so, and he was rushed and was prone, even after the life he'd led, to forget things, so he made himself stand by his fine riding horse in his two-stall city stable and review everything.

He still had not decided what to do by the time he mounted. He set himself in motion, mostly to avoid thinking too much.

His mare was delighted to be ridden; she'd been cooped up for as long as he had himself, and as soon as she was out in the street behind his house she was ready to trot, or more.

He kept her gait down because it was very important that he not be stopped. He was a little over-dressed for a common way-farer, in tall black boots all the way to his thighs and a black half cloak and matching black hat full of black plumes, but he liked fine things and he lacked the time to change.

He was riding out of a maelstrom, and he needed to stay on the leading edge.

He could hear screams from the north, where the Ducal Palace was. He patted the sword at his hip with his bridle hand then he turned his horse at the first cross street; away from the palace of towering brick on the hillside, and down towards the river, the bridges, and the street of steel workers where he had a commission to collect.

It struck him that if he collected the commission then he had made his choice; he would never be able to come back to Volta.

It also struck him that a violent political revolution could cover a great many dark deeds. There were already looters on the streets; two men passed him carrying a coffer, and neither looked up or caught his eye. The sound of breaking glass was almost as prevalent as the sound of screaming from the north.

He heard gonnes firing, and the snap of crossbows, and a sulphur reek floated past him and made his mare shy. There was the acrid reek of magic, too.

He let the mare trot, and her hooves struck sparks from the paving stones; Volta was one of the richest cities in the west, and it had fully paved streets and running water from the two great aqueducts, which was still nothing compared to the wonders of his home. The City.

Megara. Which he was about to help destroy.

Or not. He still couldn't decide.

The mare stopped abruptly. There was a corpse in the street, and the sound of steel crossing steel, and he tugged at her reins and turned along an alley that ran across the back of the shops and emerged on the next broad, empty street, with tall houses tiled in red rising high enough to block the sun.

He looked right and left, but the street was empty. From long practice, his eyes rose, looking at rooflines and balconies above him, but nothing moved, and he gave the horse her head. They flew along the street, past the corner of violence, and down to the riverside, where he reined in and turned the mare into Steel Street, where the armourers were. He knew the shop well; Arnson and Egg, the two families on the gold-lettered sign, had made fine *gonnes* since the principle had first been developed far to the east.

He had a moment of doubt; the street seemed deserted.

But he saw a light burning, and smoke from the chimney, so

he dismounted, tethered his horse to a hitching post and moved his dagger back along his belt from habit. Then he pounded at the door despite the darkening eve and the sounds of violence in the high town.

He heard footsteps.

'You came!' said young Arnson.

He pushed in beside the young man. 'I came for my *fusil*.'

The lad smiled. 'It is done.' He pointed at a leather case on the front bar. 'Pater is gone; he says it will be bad here. I'm to keep the doors locked and only eat food in the house.'

'Very wise,' the man said. He paused to admire the case; the fine steel buckles made by hand and blued, and expert leather work.

Then he took out the weapon.

'You made this?' he asked.

The young man grinned. 'I did, too. Pater helped with the lock; I'm not that dab with springs, yet. And I hired the leatherwork.' The boy was so pleased with himself that the man almost laughed.

He permitted himself a smile instead. 'And the compartment?'

'Just as you asked.,' the young man said. 'Not in the weapon, neither.' He showed his visitor the cunning compartment built for keeping a secret.

'Superb,' the man in the black cloak said, and slammed his dagger into the young man's temple, killing him instantly. The blade emerged from the other temple with admirable precision, and the man in the black cloak supported the corpse all the way to the floor, stepping away from the flow of blood. Then he filled the secret compartment with his deadly secret, wearing gloves; one tiny jewel skittered away across the table and he tracked it down, picked it up with coal tongs from the fireplace, and put it in his belt purse. Then he threw his gloves, fine, black gloves, in the fire, where they sparkled as if impregnated with gunpowder. He left, satisfied, leaving the shop door wide open to the looters already moving along the street like roaches.

But then he paused. The decision was made; there was no point in being sloppy or sentimental now. He took the tiny jewel from his purse, using his handkerchief; covered his horse's head with his cloak, and tossed it back through the open door. It was so tiny he didn't even hear it hit the floor.

He led his horse away. Only after he counted one hundred paces did he trigger the jewel's power.

The house behind him seemed to swell a moment. Then fire, white fire, blew from every window, the glass and horn panes exploding outward, the shutters immolating, the doors blowing off their hinges. It sounded like a crack of thunder, followed by a rushing of wind, and then the fire began to catch the other old houses in the row, even as the first house collapsed inward in a roar of sparks and a burst of thick black smoke.

He mounted his mare, who didn't like the smell of blood on him or the sound or smell of smoke, and he used some of his *power* to cast an *occulta*. It didn't make him invisible; it merely compelled most people to look elsewhere.

He drew a second pair of gloves from his belt and tried not to acknowledge that he'd always intended this.

The killing.

The secret.

The compartment.

The fire.

The massacre to come.

He had a little difficulty at the bridge; angry, unpaid mercenaries were holding the near end, and they wanted money and no amount of magical compulsion was going to fool them. So he paid, handing over one hundred gold sequins – almost five years wages for a prosperous craftsman – as if it was his entire purse. They wanted to open his case, the case with the secret and the little *fusil*, and he prepared to fight them, but they lost interest.

There were more unpaid sell-swords in the streets of the lower town, and they were killing. He had to wonder if the Duke was dead; and if he was, if the plan was still valid.

He considered changing sides.

Again.

To his enormous relief, there was no one on the Lonika Gate. He rode through un-challenged, and he was tempted to let the mare gallop; he needed to put time and distance between himself and Volta. The weight of his secret was tremendous; he flinched from it, trying to occupy his mind so that he would not think too carefully of what he was doing or what it would mean. He knew this would end his relationship with his wife.

Myra, his mistress, wouldn't care. She might even prefer him alone. She wouldn't even understand.

But he understood all too well what it would mean.

All too well.

People were fleeing the violence; he passed a long line of carts in the winter fields. He rode aside at a barn, dismounted, and took off all his jewelry and his dagger belt, and put it all in his leather case; sell-swords might search the case, but at least his rings wouldn't give him away. He put his beautiful black doublet in the case as well and pulled on a smock. It was not as cold here as it would be in the mountains, towards the barbaric Arnaut lands, but it was cold enough, and refugees trudged past him carrying beds and bedding, blankets and furniture.

Lonika was five days away; Megara three or four more days beyond. He could arrive exactly on schedule, if he was fast. Dark Night. The night the ignorant feared. The perfect night, or so the Servant said. That was not his problem. Delivering was his problem.

He had to make the Inn of Fosse in two days; he'd managed as much on other occasions.

There were soldiers ahead, stripping a wagonload of a poor merchant family as a mother cowered with her children and a man held his split scalp together, five men in rusting armour threw the family's worldly goods into the mud, rooting for coins. Ten years of falling grain prices and increasingly violent weather had already stripped the countryside of coin and brought out the worst in people.

This was going to be worse.

He rode down a farm lane and well around the soldiers, and emerged on the turnpike into near darkness.

It was a major risk to travel in the dark. But he could see a farmhouse on fire off to the west, and it seemed to him that the whole world had come apart, which gave him comfort for what he was choosing to do. The world might end, but it would be far away and he'd be very well paid. Rich, even. And he'd have Myra. And other entertainments.

He left Volta on fire behind him and rode through the night.

By morning he was just twenty leagues from the Inn of Fosse; he knew the road and the hills, and he was wary, because the Arnauts, although they hadn't made trouble in a generation, were a race of degenerate cattle thieves and sell-swords.

He climbed into the snow-clad hills, his horse tired and hungry, and he was watching the trees either side of the road. But when the road curved sharply into an ancient gully, he had no sight line, and the unpaid mercenaries had chosen their spot perfectly; they had a tree across the road, and he had no warning to turn aside or prepare a working, and he had to halt.

He loosened his sword in the scabbard and reached to unbuckle his *fusil.*

He never saw the crossbow bolt that hit him in the chest. It took him ugly hours to die.